THE GURSKY FAMILY TREE

GIDEON = SOPHIE KATANSKY
(1773-1828)   (1780-1827)

EPHRAIM = SARAH LUCHINSKY
(1817-1910)   (1820-1880)

AARON = FANNY
(1841–1931)   (1850-1932)

(1)   (2)   (3)

LIBBY MINTZBERG = BERNARD   MORRIE = IDA
(b. 1909)   (1898-1973)   (b. 1901)   (b. 1913)

SOLOMON = CLARA
(1899-1934)   (1912-1949)

LIONEL   NATHAN   ANITA   BARNEY   CHARNA
(b. 1929)   (b. 1931)   (b. 1933)   (b. 1930)   (1935-1963)

NIALIE = HENRY   LUCY
(b. 1936)   (1929-1974)   (b. 1932)

ISAAC
(b. 1961)

Gideon begat Ephraim
Ephraim begat Aaron
Aaron begat Bernard, Solomon & Morrie
Bernard begat Lionel, Anita & Nathan
Solomon begat Henry & Lucy
Morrie begat Barney & Charna
Henry begat Isaac

PENGUIN BOOKS

Solomon Gursky Was Here

Mordecai Richler's novels include *The Apprenticeship of Duddy Kravitz*, *Cocksure*, *St. Urbain's Horseman* and *Joshua Then and Now*. He has also written the children's books, *Jacob Two-Two Meets the Hooded Fang* and *Jacob Two-Two and the Dinosaur*. His essay collections include *Hunting Tigers Under Glass*, *Home Sweet Home*, and most recently, *Broadsides*. Rooted in London for 20 years, he returned to Canada with his wife and five children in 1972 and now divides his time between Montreal and a cottage in Quebec's Eastern Townships.

Also by Mordecai Richler

NOVELS
The Acrobats
A Choice of Enemies
Son of a Smaller Hero
The Apprenticeship of Duddy Kravitz
The Incomparable Atuk
Cocksure
St. Urbain's Horseman
Joshua Then and Now

STORIES
The Street

ESSAYS
Hunting Tigers Under Glass
Shovelling Trouble
Home Sweet Home

CHILDREN'S BOOKS
Jacob Two-Two Meets the Hooded Fang
Jacob Two-Two and the Dinosaur

ANTHOLOGIES
The Best of Modern Humour

For Florence

"Gerald Murphy got it wrong — living twice, maybe three times, is the best revenge."
Solomon Gursky in conversation with Tim Callaghan.

"Cyril once observed that the only reason for writing was to create a masterpiece. But if you haven't got it in you to make a great work of art there is another option — you can become one."
Sir Hyman Kaplansky,
as quoted in *The Diaries of Lady Dorothy Ogilvie-Hunt*.

SOLOMON GURSKY WAS HERE

ONE

ONE

◆

One morning — during the record cold spell of 1851 — a big menacing black bird, the likes of which had never been seen before, soared over the crude mill town of Magog, swooping low again and again. Luther Hollis brought down the bird with his Springfield. Then the men saw a team of twelve yapping dogs emerging out of the wind and swirling snows of the frozen Lake Memphremagog. The dogs were pulling a long, heavily laden sled at the stern of which stood Ephraim Gursky, a small fierce hooded man cracking a whip. Ephraim pulled close to the shore and began to trudge up and down, searching the skies, an inhuman call, some sort of sad clacking noise, at once abandoned yet charged with hope, coming from the back of his throat.

In spite of the tree-cracking cold a number of curious gathered on the shore. They had come not so much to greet Ephraim as to establish whether or not he was an apparition. Ephraim was wearing what appeared to be sealskins and, on closer inspection, a clerical collar as well. Four fringes hung from the borders of his outermost skin, each fringe made up of twelve silken strands. Frost clung to his eyelids and nostrils. One cheek had been bitten black by the wind. His inky black beard was snarled with icicles. "Crawling with white snakes," one of them would say too late, remembering that day. But the eyes were hot, hot and piercing. "I say," he asked, "what happened to my raven?"

"Hollis shot it dead."

Ebenezer Watson kicked the runners of the long sled. "Hey, what are these dang things made of?" Certainly it wasn't the usual.

"Char."

"What's that?"

"Fish."

Ephraim stooped to slip his dogs free of their traces.

"Where are you from?"

"The north, my good fellow."

"Where . . . north?"

"Far," he said.

It was forty below on the lake and blowing. The men, knocking their throbbing feet together, their cheeks flaring crimson with cold, turned their backs to the wind. They retired to the warmth of Crosby's Hotel, to which a first-class livery was attached. A sign posted in the window read:

WM. CROSBY'S HOTEL
The undersigned, thankful for past favours
bestowed upon this
LONG-ESTABLISHED HOTEL
is determined to conduct this establishment in a
manner that will meet the approbation of the public,
and therefore begs a continuance of Public Patronage.
REFRESHMENTS SERVED AT ANY HOUR
OF DAY OR NIGHT
Wm. Crosby
Proprietor

Ebenezer Watson took a coal-oil lamp to the window and cleared a patch of frost to keep watch.

"What did he mean *his* raven?"

Ephraim was throwing slabs of bear meat to his leaping dogs, settling them down, and starting to clear snow from a circle of ice with a board, flattening it to his satisfaction. Then he took to stacking goods from his sled on to the ice he had cleared. Animal skins. Pots and pans. A Primus stove. A soapstone bowl or *koodlik*. A harpoon. Books.

"See that?"

"What?"

"Crazy bastard's brought reading books with him."

They watched him pull a rod and what appeared to be a broadsword free of the sled ropes. Then he slipped into his snowshoes and scrambled up the sloping shore, jumping up and down there, plunging his rod into the snow like one of their wives testing a cake in the oven with a straw from a broom. Finally finding the texture of snow he wanted Ephraim began to carve out large blocks with his sword and carry them back to his flattened circle. He built an igloo with a low entry tunnel facing south. He banked the walls with snow, tended to the seams, and cut more blocks for a windbreak. Then just before he got down on his hands and knees, disappearing inside, he banged a wooden sign into the snow and ice.

CHURCH OF THE MILLENARIANS
Founder
Brother Ephraim

The men turned up early the next morning, fully expecting to find Ephraim dead. Frozen stiff. Instead they discovered him squatting over a hole in the ice, taking a perch, setting the eye in the hook, taking another, starting over again. He threw some of the perch to his dogs, some he stacked on the ice, and now and then he nimbly skinned one, filleted it, and gulped it down raw. He also harpooned two landlocked salmon and a sturgeon. But it was something else that troubled the men. Clearly Ephraim had already found the yard in the woods where the deer wintered, walled in by some seven feet of snow into a trap of their own making. A buck hung on a pine pole lodged in the ice. Obviously it had just been dressed. The dogs, their snouts smeared with blood, were tearing into the still-steaming lungs and intestines that had been tossed to them.

"You shouldn'ta told him I kilt his bird," Luther Hollis said.

"You scared?"

"The hell I am, Mister Man. I figger he's only passing through."

"Ask him."

"You ask him."

It continued overcast, the fugitive sun no more than a milky stain in a wash of grey sky. The men stopped counting the cracking trees or bursting pipes or exploding bottles. The temperature sank to fifty below. The men checked out Ephraim the next morning and he was still there, and the morning after and he was still there. The fourth morning the men had something else on their minds. Luther Hollis had been found hanging from a rafter in his sawmill. Dead by his own hand, apparently. He hadn't been robbed, but neither had he left a note. It was baffling. Then, even as the men were deliberating, Crosby's boy came running up to them. "I talked to him," he said.

"Wipe your nose."

But they were impressed.

"He told me he was something called a Four by Two. What's that?"

Nobody knew.

"He invited me inside, eh, and it's really cosy, and I got to see some of the stuff he has in there."

"Like what?"

"Like he has a book by Shakespeare and cutlery in sterling silver with crests of some kind on them and a blanket made of the skin of white wolves and a drawing in an oak frame of a ship with three masts called *Erebus*."

The Reverend Columbus Green knew Greek. "Erebus," he said, "is the name of the place of darkness, between Earth and Hades."

The cold broke, the wind gathered force, and it began to snow so thick that a man, leaning into the wind, squinting, still couldn't see more than two feet ahead of him. Overnight the drifting snow buried roads and railway tracks. The blizzard blew for three days and then the sun rose in a blue sky so hard it seemed to be bolted into place. On Friday the men who had waited things out in Crosby's Hotel found that the only exit was through a second-floor window.

Ephraim was still in place. But now there were three more

igloos on the lake, many more yelping dogs, and what Ebenezer Watson described as dark little slanty-eyed men and women everywhere, unloading things. Ebenezer, and some of the others, maintained a watch from the window in Crosby's Hotel. When the first evening star appeared they saw the little dark men, beating on skin drums, parading their women before them to the entry tunnel of Ephraim's igloo. Ephraim appeared, wearing a black silk top hat and fringed white shawl with vertical black stripes. Then the little men stepped forward one by one, thrusting their women before them, extolling their merits in an animated manner. Oblivious of the cold, a young woman raised her sealskin parka and jiggled her bare breasts.

"Well, I'll be damned."

"Whatever them Millenarians is it's sure as shit a lot more fun than what we got."

Finally Ephraim pointed at one, nodded at another, and they quickly scrambled into his igloo. The men, beating on their drums, led the remaining women back to their igloos, punching and kicking them. An hour later they were back, all of them, and one after another they crawled into Ephraim's igloo. There was a good deal of hollering and singing and clapping and what sounded like dancing. The Reverend Columbus Green, who had been urgently sent for, bundled up and listened by the shore, not going too close or staying too long, a Bible held to his breast. Then he reported to the men waiting in Crosby's Hotel. "I think they are singing in the language of the Lord in there," he said.

"Don't sound like English to me."

"Hebrew."

"That's just bullshit," Ebenezer Watson said, affronted.

Pressed, the Reverend Columbus Green allowed that he wasn't absolutely sure. The wind had distorted things and it had been a long time since he had studied Hebrew in the seminary.

"What's the Church of the Millenarians?" Ebenezer asked.

"I'm afraid I've never heard of it."

"Figgers."

The next evening the little brown men and women were

gone, but before they left they had erected a sizeable sailcloth tent on the ice. There was something else. White robes were being aired on lines supported by pine poles, maybe thirty of them exploding like crackers each time they were slapped by the wind. The men in Crosby's Hotel drank several rounds and then descended in a body to Ephraim's igloo on the frozen lake.

"What are them sheets for?"

"Them aren't sheets, my good fellow. Them are ascension robes to be worn for the ascent into heaven. Those among you who can read raise your hands."

Six of them raised their hands, but Dunlap was only bragging.

"Wait here."

Ephraim was gobbled up by his entry tunnel then emerged a moment later to distribute pamphlets: *Evidence from the Scriptures of the Second Coming of Christ in the Eastern Townships about the year 1851.*

"It is more difficult," Ephraim told them, his eyes hot, "for a rich son of a bitch to enter heaven than to piss through the eye of a needle. Do not comfort yourselves, my good fellows, thinking hell is an abstraction. It's a real place just waiting on sinners like you. If you have ever seen a hog on a spit, its flesh crackling and sizzling, squirting fat, well that's how hot it is in hell's coolest regions. The first meeting is tomorrow night at seven in the tent. Bring your womenfolk and your children. I have come to save you."

TWO

◆

1983 it was. Autumn. The season of the sodden partridges, drunk from pecking at fallen, fermented crab apples. One of them wakened Moses Berger with a start, slamming into his bedroom window and sliding to the grass. Responding to the brotherly call of another dipso in trouble, Moses yanked on his trousers and hurried outside. He had turned fifty-two a few months earlier and was not yet troubled by a paunch. It wasn't that he exercised but rather that he ate so sparingly. He was not, as he had once hoped, even unconventionally handsome. A reticent man of medium height with receding brown hair running to grey and large, slightly protuberant brown eyes, their pouches purply. His nose bulbous, his lips thick. But even now some women seemed to find what he sadly acknowledged as his physical ugliness oddly compelling. Not so much attractive as a case to answer.

The partridge hadn't broken its neck. It was merely stunned. Flapping its wings it flew off, barely clearing the woodpile, undoubtedly pledging to avoid fermented crab apples forever.

Some hope.

His own head far from clear, Moses retreated to his cabin high in the woods overlooking Lake Memphremagog and reheated what remained of last night's coffee, lacing it with a shot of Greysac's cognac, now yet another Gursky brand name.

The Gurskys.

Ephraim begat Aaron.

Aaron begat Bernard, Solomon, and Morrie, who then begat children of their own.

Morning rituals. Moses conceded yet again that his wasting life had been drained of potential years ago thanks to his obsession with the Gurskys. Even so, it could still be retrieved from insignificance, providing he managed, between bouts of fermented crab apples, to complete his biography of Solomon Gursky. Yes, but even in the unlikely event he ever got to finish that unending story, the book could never be published unless he was willing to be carted off in a straitjacket, declared mentally unbalanced.

Slipping on his reading glasses, scanning the faded charts and maps tacked to his wall, Moses had to allow that were he an objective observer he would be the first to endorse such a judgement. The one living-room wall free of ceiling-to-floor bookcases was dominated by an enormous map of Canada, *circa* 10,000 B.C., when most of the country had still been buried under the Cordilleran and Laurentide Ice Sheets. Alongside there was a smaller 1970 government surveyor's map of the Northwest Territories, Ephraim Gursky's journey out traced in red ink. Moses's Arctic books were stacked here, there, and everywhere, most of them annotated again and again: Franklin, M'Clure, Richardson, Back, Mackenzie, M'Clintock and the rest, but that was not what concerned him right now.

Right now Moses was determined to find his missing salmon fly, a Silver Doctor, which he had misplaced somewhere or other. He knew that he shouldn't waste his morning searching for it. Certainly he had no need of it until next summer. All the same, he turned to his work table, speculating that it might be buried among his papers there. His work table, made up of an oak door laid on two steel filing cabinets, was strewn with pages from Solomon Gursky's journals, tapes made by his brother Bernard, clippings, file cards and notes. Dipping into the mess, he retrieved his copy of *The Newgate Calendar*

Improved, Being INTERESTING MEMOIRS *of* NOTO-RIOUS CHARACTERS *who have been convicted of offences* AGAINST THE LAWS OF ENGLAND. He opened it, pretending he didn't know that beginning on page 78 he would discover an account of the early years of Solomon Gursky's grandfather.

EPHRAIM GURSKY

Several times convicted — Sentenced once to Coldbath Fields, once to Newgate — And finally on October 19, 1835, transported to Van Diemen's Land.

Moses, who could recite the rest of the calendar entry by heart, poured himself another coffee, enriched by just a squirt of cognac.

Greysac's cognac. Gursky cognac.

Drifting into the bedroom, he raised his glass to the portrait of his father that hung on the wall. L.B. Berger in profile, pondering the mysteries of the cosmos, enduring its weight. Moses turned away, but in his mind's eye, L.B. confronted him at the kitchen table once again. "I've got news for you," he said. "I didn't make you a drunk. I deserved better."

If not for his father taking him to that Gursky birthday party when he had been only eleven years old, Moses might never have become enthralled with Solomon. The legendary Solomon. His bane, his spur. Instead he might have enjoyed a life of his own. A wife. Children. An honourable career. No, the booze would have got to him in any event.

Once, enduring the first of his many confinements in the clinic in New Hampshire, there to dry out, Moses had foolishly submitted to prying questions.

"You talk about your father with such rage, even . . ."

"Contempt?"

". . . but when you tell stories of your childhood you make it sound enviable. How did you feel in those days?"

"Cherished."

"Yesterday you mentioned there were quarrels."

"Oh yes, over the validity of Nachum Schneiderman's 'Reply to the Grand Inquisitor'. Or the Stalin-Hitler Pact. Or the question Malraux posed to the Communist Writers' Congress, namely, 'And what about the man who is run over by a streetcar?' "

"Well?"

"In a perfect socialist transport system, the answer goes, there will be no accidents."

Those, those were the days before Bernard Gursky had summoned Moses's father — L.B. Berger, the noted Montreal poet and short-story writer — with a mighty hand and an outstretched arm. The Bergers had not yet been lifted into tree-lined Outremont, but were still rooted in that cold-water flat on Jeanne Mance Street. A flat that rocked day and night with the unscheduled comings and goings of loopy, loquacious Russian Jews. Yiddish poets, essayists, playwrights, journalists, actors and actresses. Artists, the lot. Washed on to the shores of a cold country that was as indifferent to them as they were to it. Except, of course, for L.B., who was sustained by larger ambitions and had already seen his poetry published in English-language little magazines in Montreal and Toronto, as well as once in *Poetry Chicago*. L.B. was the sun around which the others spun at a sometimes dizzying speed. Sleep-walking through the day, they grudgingly rendered unto Canada what was Canada's, earning their keep as minor Zionist functionaries, bookkeepers to the needle trade, insurance collectors for the Pru, synagogue secretaries, beneficial loan society officials or, as in the case of L.B., as a parochial school teacher, badgered by pushy parents. But at night they wakened to their real life of the soul. They elbowed for places at the great L.B.'s table in Horn's Cafeteria on Pine Avenue or, more often, at the dining-room table with the crocheted tablecloth in the cold-water flat on Jeanne Mance. There they consumed gallons of coffee or lemon tea with tray after tray of cinnamon buns, honey cake or *kichelach*, all prepared by L.B.'s wife.

Except for his mother, Moses remembered, the women were glamorous beyond compare. They wore big floppy hats pricked by peacock plumes, and flowing black capes, never mind the patches. They favoured ivory cigarette holders. Zipora Schneiderman, Shayndel Kronitz and, above all, Gitel Kugelmass, Moses's first unrequited love. The voluptuous

Gitel, who usually wore an ostrich boa or a fox biting its own tail, missing either clumps of feather or fur. Chiffons, silks. The celebrated *Roite Gitel*, who had led the millinery workers out against Fancy Finery. Perfumed and powdered she was, her eyes kohled, her lips scarlet, her hands heavy with antique rings. Occasionally she sipped apricot brandy in a sticky shot glass to warm her *kishkas* in winter. Moses, anticipating her every need — emptying her ashtray — fetching her coffee — was rewarded from time to time with a perfume-laden hug or a pinch of his cheek.

Except for his mother, the women, who had never heard of inequality, poured oil onto the flames of every dispute ignited by the men, arguing along with them far into the night about the show trials that had been held in a faraway city as cold as their own, pitching into quarrels over the merits of Osip Mandelstam, Dali, Malraux, Eisenstein, Soutine, Mendele Moykner Sforim, Joyce, Trotsky, Buñuel, Chagall, and Abraham Reisen, who had written:

> Future generations,
> Brothers still to come,
> Don't you dare
> Be scornful of our songs.
> Songs about the weak,
> Songs of the exhausted
> In a poor generation,
> Before the world's decline.

Shloime Bishinsky, a latecomer to the group, was an interesting case. Slight, droopy, seemingly the most mild of men, he was a fur dyer cursed with catarrh, a hazard of his trade. When Poland was about to be partitioned, he was caught in Bialystok, in the Russian zone. More politically informed aunts and cousins fled to the other zone. They knew, say what you like, that the Germans were a civilized people. But Shloime's family, too late for the last train out, failed to escape to Auschwitz. Instead they were transported to Siberia, a journey of two weeks. From there, Shloime slipped into the Middle Kingdom and then Harbin, in the puppet state of

Manchuko, where once grand White Russian ladies now stripped in cabarets. Eventually he reached Japan itself, sailing as a stoker from Yokohama to Vancouver.

"What was it like in Siberia?" Moses once asked.

"Like Canada," Shloime Bishinsky said, shrugging, "what else?"

For them Canada was not yet a country but the next-door place. They were still this side of Jordan, in the land of Moab, the political quarterlies as well as the Yiddish newspapers they devoured coming out of New York.

Friday nights the men read each other their poems or stories in thundering voices, moving the group to outcries of approval or disdain. Quarrels ensued. Men, who deferred to *goyishe* bank tellers, addressing them as "sir", who bowed their heads to the health inspector, on the boil over a clunky rhyme, a slipshod thought, a phrase like a splinter under a fingernail, slamming their fists against the table, rattling the teacups. Insulted ladies fleeing to the toilet, tears flying from them. Each poem, every story or essay, generating a morning-after of hand-delivered letters that provoked even thicker envelopes filled with rebuttal.

In principle the group endorsed racial brotherhood, burning both ends of the candle, an end to private property and all religious hocus-pocus, free love, et cetera. But in practice they feared or scorned gentiles, seldom touched anything but apricot brandy, dreamed of owning their own duplex, paid Kronitz fifty cents a week for insurance policies from the Pru, and were constant husbands and loving parents. Mind you, eavesdropping from behind his bedroom door, an enthralled Moses learned that some hanky-panky was not unknown. Take, for instance, what became celebrated as the Kronitz-Kugelmass scandal. One morning Myer Kugelmass, fishing through his wife's handbag for a streetcar ticket, blundered on a red-hot billet-doux from Simcha Kronitz, peppered with obviously filthy phrases in French, and invoking celebrated lovers from Héloïse and Abelard to Emma Goldman and Alexander Berkman. A triumphant Gitel Kugelmass, her illicit *affaire de coeur* revealed, packed her balalaika and her musical compositions and fled to a boarding house in Ste.-Agathe, dragging a terrified Simcha Kronitz with her. Myer Kugelmass, abandoned by his wife, betrayed by his best friend, wept at L.B.'s dining-room table. "Who will I play chess with now that Simcha has dishonoured me?"

A messenger was dispatched to Ste.-Agathe with a stinging letter to *die Roite Gitel* from L.B., quoting Milton, Lenin, Rilke, and of course L.B. himself, and the couples were soon reconciled, if only for the children's sake.

The children, the children.

The children were everything. Friday nights they were brought along to L.B.'s flat, free to play run-sheep-run in the lane, stuff themselves in the kitchen, and finally flop four to a bed if necessary. They were hugged and kissed and pinched and squeezed and all they were obliged to do in return was to demonstrate, to cries of astonishment, the different ways in which they were bound to dazzle the world. Pudgy Misha Bloomgarten, who would later go into plate-glass windows, had only to scrape out a simple exercise on his violin for the names of Stern and Menuhin to be invoked. Giggly Rifka Schneiderman, who would marry into Kaplan's Knit-to-Fit, had merely to stand up and sing "The Cloakworkers' Union Is a No-Good Union", her voice piercing, for the dining room to rock with applause. Sammy Birenbaum, the future television oracle, had only to recite Sacco's speech to the court for it to be recalled that Leslie Howard, the quintessential Englishman, was actually a nice Jewish boy, mind you Hungarian. But it was Moses (after all, does the apple fall far from the tree?) who was recognized as the prodigy. L.B. flushing with pleasure, his mother summoned out of the kitchen, he would be called upon to deliver a socialist critique of *The Count of Monte Cristo* or *Treasure Island*, or whatever it was he had read that week, or to recite a poem of his own, its debt to Tristan Tzara duly noted.

> Pens need ink,
> Leaky boats sink.

Moses clung to his father, constantly searching for new ways to earn his love. L.B., he noticed, often delayed his morning departure to the dreaded parochial school, blowing on his pince-nez, wiping the lenses with his handkerchief, as he stood by the front window waiting for the postman to pass. If there was no mail L.B. grunted, something in him welcoming the injustice of it, and hurried into his coat.

"Maybe tomorrow," his wife would say.

"Maybe, maybe." Then he would peer into his lunch bag, saying, "You know, Bessie, I'm getting tired of chopped egg. Tuna. Sardines. It's coming out of my ears."

Or another day, the postman passing by their flat again, she would say, "It's a good sign. They must be considering it very, very carefully."

One ten-below-zero morning, hoping to shave ten minutes off his father's anxiety time, Moses quit the flat early and lay in wait for the postman at the corner.

"Any mail for my father, sir?"

A large brown envelope. Moses, exhilarated, raced all the way home, waving the envelope at his father who stood watch by the window. "Mail for you!" he cried. "Mail for you!"

L.B., his eyes bulging with rage, snatched the envelope from him, glanced at it, and ripped it apart, scattering the pieces on the floor. "Don't you ever meddle in my affairs again, you little fool," he shouted, fleeing the flat.

"What did I do, Maw?"

But she was already on her hands and knees, gathering the pieces together. He kept carbons, Bessie knew that, but these, *Gottenyu*, were the originals.

L.B. went to Moses that evening, removing his pince-nez and rubbing his nose, a bad sign. "I don't know what got into me this morning," he said, and he leaned over and allowed Moses to kiss his cheek. Then L.B. declined supper, retired to his bedroom, and pulled the blinds.

A baffled Moses appealed to his mother. "That envelope was addressed to him in his own handwriting. I don't get it."

"Sh, Moishe, L.B. is trying to sleep."

It would begin with a slight tic of discomfort in the back of his neck, a little nausea, and within an hour it would swell into a hectic pulse, blood pounding through every vein in his head. A towel filled with chopped ice clamped to his forehead, L.B. would lie in the dark, staring at the ceiling, moaning. *One day a floodtide of blood, surging into my head, seeking passage, will blow off the top. I will die drenched in fountains of my own blood.* Then, on the third day, bloated, his bowels plugged, he would shuffle to the toilet and sit there for an hour, maybe more. Afterward he would stagger back into bed, fall into a deep sleep and wake whole, even chirpy, the next morning, demanding his favourite breakfast: scrambled eggs with lox, potatoes fried with onions, bagels lathered with cream cheese.

Moses adored accompanying L.B. on his rounds. After sufficient funds had been raised by the group, he went with him to Schneiderman's Spartacus Press on St. Paul Street, present at the creation. Sorting out pages of L.B.'s first collection of poems. Pages of *The Burning Bush* as they peeled hot off a flat-bed press that usually — much to Nachum Schneiderman's embarrassment — churned out nothing more socially significant than letterheads, business cards, wedding invitations, and advertising circulars. Commercial *chazerai*. Schneiderman treating Moses to a Gurd's ginger ale and a May West, saying, "When he wins the Nobel Prize I'll say I knew him when . . ."

Mrs. Schneiderman arriving with a thermos of coffee and her own apple strudel covered with a linen napkin, saying, "If this were Paris or London or even Warsaw in the old days your father would be covered with honours instead of struggling to earn a living."

The money hadn't found L.B., not yet, but neither was he really struggling any more. L.B.'s wife had decreed his teaching job soul-destroying, obliging him to resign, and she had gone back to work, bending over a sewing machine at Teen Togs. L.B., free at last, slept late most mornings and roamed the streets in the afternoons, usually stopping at Horn's for a coffee and a Danish, nobody coming to his table if he had his notebook open, his Parker 51 poised. Back home he wrote deep into the night.

"Sh, Moishe, L.B.'s working."

Poems, stories, and fiery editorials for the *Canadian Jewish Herald* on the plight of the Jews in Europe. Some nights he would be invited to read from his work at modern synagogues in Outremont, Moses tagging after through the snow, lugging a satchel full of signed copies of *The Burning Bush*. When his father mounted the podium, Moses would take up a position in the back of the hall, applauding wildly, torn between rising anger and concern, as it became obvious that once again there would be only eighteen or twenty-three poetry-lovers in attendance, though folding chairs had been provided for a hundred. Most nights Moses was lucky to peddle four or five copies of *The Burning Bush*, but once he actually succeeded in unloading twelve for three dollars each. No matter how few he sold he always managed to inflate the number by three, nine dollars having been slipped to him by his mother before they left for the synagogue. Sometimes L.B. would crack sour jokes on the way home. "Maybe next time we should fill the satchel with neckties or novelty items." More often, inconsolable, he cursed the Philistines. "This is a raw land, an empty space, and your poor father is a soul in exile here. *Auctor ignotus*, that's me."

The breakthrough came for L.B. in 1941. Ryerson Press, in Toronto, brought out their own edition of *The Burning Bush* in their Ethnic Poets of Canada series, with an introduction by Professor Oliver Carson: "Montreal's Eloquent Israelite". There was a stunning review by Rabbi Melvin Steinmetz, B.A., in the University of Alberta's *Alumni News*, which was immediately enshrined in one of the scrapbooks kept by Bessie.

Not long afterward fame found L.B., fame of a sort, although not the kind he yearned for. His impassioned guest editorials about the plight of the European Jews, published in the *Canadian Jewish Herald*, led to invitations for him to lecture, not only in Montreal but also in Toronto and Winnipeg. He was, without a doubt, an inspired orator. All that banked anger, those glowing coals of resentment, fanned into flame by his long cherished feelings of being a man wronged, winning him the praise of his dreams so long as he directed the fire at the enemies of the Jews. L.B., thick around the middle now, his greying hair allowed to grow even longer, thumbs hooked into his waistcoat pockets, rocking on his heels, red in the face as he inveighed against the obloquy of the gentiles in phrases that released howls of recognition from his audiences. Audiences that no longer numbered eighteen or twenty-three but that turned up in the hot hundreds, squabbling over folding chairs, sitting on the floor, standing three deep in the back; L.B.

gathering in their outrage, orchestrating it, and then letting fly. Understandably he began to strut a little. He acquired a broadbrimmed felt hat, a cape, a foulard. On the road he now refused to sleep on pissy old mattresses in the rabbi's spare bedroom but demanded a room in the most stylish hotel. Back in Montreal, where invitations to dine with the affluent began to proliferate, he would assure Bessie that she wouldn't enjoy dinner with materialists like the Bernsteins, starting with the outside fork. He would endure it alone.

L.B. continued to write. Ryerson's edition of *The Burning Bush* was followed by poems and stories and literary pensées in *Canadian Forum, Northern Review, Fiddlehead*, and other little magazines. Ryerson brought out a second volume of his poems, *Psalms of the Tundra*, followed by a first collection of stories, *Tales of the Diaspora*. He was interviewed by the Montreal *Gazette*. Herman Yalofsky invited him to sit for his portrait. L.B. in profile pondering the mysteries of the cosmos, enduring its weight. The fingertips of one spidery hand supporting his wrinkled forehead, the other hand holding his Parker 51.

L.B. now began to wander further afield, making forays into gentile bohemia, tippytoe at first, but soon *con brio* as he found himself, much to his astonishment, welcomed as an exotic, a garlicky pirate, living proof of the ethnic riches that went into weaving the Canadian cultural tapestry. Soon he was at ease at their soirées, collecting compliments from young ladies who, although educated in Switzerland, now wore Russian peasant blouses and drank beer out of bottles and talked dirty. He became a proficient punster. He found that he was adept at flirting, especially with Marion Peterson (such a trim waist, such nice firm breasts) who trailed a sweet scent of roses. Just a tasteful *goyishe* hint, mind you, not drenched in it like Gitel Kugelmass. Marion sculpted. "Your head," she said, cupping it, cool fingers running through his hair.

"What's wrong with it?" he asked, alarmed.

"You have an Old Testament head."

Traipsing home through the snow, his scalp was still tingly. Bessie, as usual, had left the hall light on for him. She sat in a worn robe at the kitchen table, trimming her corns with a knife. The following evening L.B. refused the stuffed derma, a favourite of his, that she had prepared for him. "Didn't you have a movement this morning?" she asked.

"It's too fattening."

L.B. became a regular at evenings in the apartments of dedicated McGill professors who also wrote poetry, swore by the *New Statesman*, and toiled long hours to save Canada through socialism. They proved a bizarre lot, these gentiles, their intelligentsia. They had not been nourished on Dostoyevsky, Tolstoi, the Zohar, Balzac, Pushkin, Goncharov, the Baal Shem Tov. Among them it was G.B.S., the Webbs, H.G. Wells, board-and-brick bookcases red with Gollancz's Left Book Club editions, *New Yorker* cartoons pasted on the walls of what they called the loo and, above all, the Bloomsbury bunch. Catty, clever people, L.B. thought. Writers who luxuriated on private incomes and knew the best years for claret. But when he brought back news of the *goyim* out there to his acolytes who still gathered round the dining-room table with the crocheted tablecloth on Friday nights, he made it sound like a world of wonders. L.B. now eschewed chopped liver on rye with lemon tea and, instead, nibbled Camembert and sipped Tio Pepe.

Then came the summons from Sinai. L.B. was invited to an audience at Mr. Bernard's opulent redoubt cut high into the Montreal mountainside, and he descended from those heights, his head spinning, pledged to unheard-of abundance, an annual retainer of ten thousand dollars to serve as speech writer and cultural adviser to the legendary liquor baron.

"And this," Mr. Bernard had said, leading him into a long room with empty oak shelves running from ceiling to floor, "will be my library. Furnish it with the best. I want first editions. The finest morocco bindings. You have a blank cheque, L.B."

Then Libby was heard from. "But nothing second-hand."

"I beg your pardon, Mrs. Gursky?"

"Germs. That's all I need. We have three children, God bless them."

L.B., once he had acquiesced to the deal, grasped that he had a lot of fancy footwork to perform. For, as far as his acolytes were concerned, the sly, rambunctious reformed bootlegger, worth untold millions now, was still a *grobber*, a hooligan who rained shame on Jews cut from a finer cloth. Saddened by the seduction of their mentor, they were as yet unable to rebuke their cherished L.B. to his face. Except for Schneiderman, who beat his fist against the table and cried out, "Ask him why he betrayed his brother."

"What?"

"Solomon."

Moses, clearing cups from the table, heard for the first time the name that would become both quest and curse to him.

Solomon. Solomon Gursky.

"There are many versions of that story," L.B. protested.

"His own brother I'm telling you."

"Didn't Jacob slip one over on Esau and isn't he still one of our fathers?"

"To the Jesuits you would be a real credit, L.B."

"Artists have always had to dance a jig for their patrons. Mozart, Rousseau. Mahler, that bastard, actually converted. Me, all I have agreed to do is to write speeches for Mr. Bernard about the plight of our brethren in Europe. Coming from me, it's noise. From Mr. Bernard *they* will prick up their ears. Gates will open, if only a crack. In this country big money talks."

"To you maybe," Schneiderman said, "but not to me."

"So, *chaverim*, does anybody else want to put in his two cents?"

Nobody.

"Me, it breaks my heart to have my sweet Bessie go off to Teen Togs every morning. I have a son to educate. Am I not entitled, after all these years of serving my muse, to put some bread on the table?"

Uncertain of themselves, with so much to lose, the group seemed about to forgive, to make amends. L.B. sensed that. Then Shloime Bishinsky, who seldom said a word, surprised everybody by speaking out. "That Mr. Bernard is rich beyond anybody's dreams, that he is powerful, is not to be denied. The bootlegging was clever—not such a sin—and many who condemn him do it out of envy. Jay Gould and J.P. Morgan or Rockefeller were worse bandits. What I'm trying to say, forgive me, is that such princes in America are entitled to their mansions, a Rolls-Royce, chinchilla coats, yachts, young cuties out of burlesque shows. But a poet they should never be able to afford. It has to do with what? Human dignity. The dead. The sanctity of the word. I'm explaining it badly. But the man I took you for, L.B., you are not. Forgive me, Bessie, but I can't come here any more. Goodbye."

Only a trickle of the regulars came to read stories and poems the following Friday night and a month later there were none.

"If those dreamers stop coming here to feed their fat faces and read me their *dreck* once a week, it's fine with me. I require solitude for my work."

The little tic of discomfort started in the back of his neck, the nausea came, and L.B., his pulse hectic, retired to his bed for three days.

"Sh, Moishe, L.B. isn't well."

Venturing out among the gentiles, anticipating disapprobation of another kind (they stick together, never mind the class struggle), he was surprised to discover they were impressed. One of the girls, a Morgan, said her aunt had once had a thingee with Solomon Gursky. "He made her a cherry wood table. She still has it."

L.B. would stand at the back of the hall listening to Mr. Bernard, watching him rake in acclaim for a poet's unacknowledged eloquence. Edgar Bergen and Charlie McCarthy that's us, L.B. thought. It stung. But there were compensations. The Bergers moved out of their cold-water flat on Jeanne Mance into a detached house with a garden and ornamental shrubs on a tree-lined street in Outremont, Mr. Bernard guaranteeing the mortgage. There was a proper study for L.B. with an oak desk and a leather armchair and a samovar and Herman Yalofsky's portrait of him mounted on an easel. L.B. in profile pondering the mysteries of the cosmos, enduring its weight.

THREE

◆

One afternoon in 1942 L.B. told Moses that they were invited to the Bernard Gursky mansion. Moses was ordered to have his hair cut and he was dressed in a new suit and shoes. L.B. explained, "It's a thirteenth birthday party for the eldest son, Lionel, and Mr. Bernard said that you would be welcome. You are expected to play with the two younger ones, Anita and Nathan. Say it."

"Anita and Nathan."

"When you are presented to Mrs. Gursky you will thank her for inviting you to the party. She has a horror of germs. Polio, typhoid, scarlet fever. So if you have to go to the toilet you ask me and I'll show you where there is one for the guests."

"*You mean even you,*" Moses asked, his cheeks hot, "*aren't allowed to use their toilet?*"

"You and that temper of yours. I don't know where you get it."

The three Gursky brothers had built neighbouring fieldstone mansions on the Montreal mountainside. Mr. Bernard had three children. Mr. Morrie had two, Barney and Charna. And following Solomon's death his widow lingered on in her husband's mansion with her two children, Henry and Lucy. All of the Gursky children, secure behind the tall stone walls of the estate, had been munificently provided for. Once through the wrought-iron gates, an awestruck Moses, totally unprepared by his father, was confronted with undreamed-of splendour.

There was an enormous swimming pool. A heated, multi-level tree house, designed by an architect and furnished by an interior decorator. A miniature railway. A hockey rink, the boards thickly padded. A corner candy store with a real soda fountain tended by a black man who laughed at everything. There was a musical merry-go-round (this actually rented for the party) and a bicycle track running along the perimeter. The railway, the corner candy store, the rink and bicycle track had all been built shortly after the kidnapping of the Lindbergh baby. At the same time the chauffeurs entrusted with all the little Gurskys (except for Henry and Lucy), driving them to their private schools, had taken to carrying arms.

Some twenty children, most of them as petrified as Moses, had been invited to Lionel's birthday party and they stood in line to congratulate him.

"And what's your name?" Lionel asked.

"Moses Berger."

"Oh yeah, your father works for us."

The party was enlivened by clowns who rode around the grounds in a little circus jalopy. The jalopy, given to backfiring explosively, had an outsize klaxon that played the opening bars of Beethoven's Fifth Symphony (which, in Morse code, also stood for "V for Victory" at the time). There were strolling accordion players and saucy French-Canadian fiddlers dressed like the *voyageurs* of old. There were jugglers. A torch singer, appearing at the Tic-Toc, dropped by to sing "Somewhere Over the Rainbow". Four middle-aged midgets dressed like six-year-olds sang "The Lollipop Kids". A magician was flown in from New York. An Indian from the Caughnawaga reservation, appropriately costumed, performed a war dance and then presented Lionel with a tribal headdress, pronouncing him a chief. Mrs. Gursky immediately removed the headdress and warned Lionel that he had to have a shampoo before going to bed. Then there was a birthday cake, large as a truck tire, the marzipan icing cleverly done up like a *Time* magazine cover, featuring Lionel Gursky, Boy of the Year.

Moses followed the arrows to the basement GUEST FACILITIES, just in time to collide with a flustered Barney Gursky emerging from the bathroom.

Afterward Moses wandered past the pool to the far side of the estate where he came upon two children seated on a swing. The boy seemed to be his own age. The girl, possibly a few years younger, was sucking her thumb. Popping it free, she said, "Why don't you go back to the party where you came from?"

Henry introduced himself and his sister, Lucy.

"My name's Moses Berger."

Lucy shrugged, as if to say so what, slid off the swing and sauntered back to the fieldstone mansion.

"What school are you at?" Moses asked.

"I don't g-g-go," Henry said. "I'm not allowed."

"But everybody has to go to school."

"I have a t-t-teacher who comes here. Miss Bradshaw. She's f-f-from England."

Not to be outdone, Moses said, "My father's L.B. Berger. You know, the poet. What does your father do?"

"My f-f-father's dead. Would you like to see my room?"

"Sure."

Just as Henry jumped off the swing a lady with tangled hair, black streaked with grey, shuffled out of the French doors of the fieldstone mansion. She was barefoot, wearing no more than a baby-blue nightgown, supported on one side by a stout lady in a starchy white uniform and, on the other, by a young man in a white jacket.

"Who's that?" Moses asked.

"My m-m-mother isn't well."

Then to Moses's surprise, Henry took his hand and held it tightly, leading him into the house.

The living room, the largest Moses had ever seen, was crammed with paintings lit from above, many of them in heavy gold frames. Moses recognized one of them as a Matisse and another as a Braque. He knew as much because his *Folkshule* teacher, Miss Levy, used the Book-of-the-Month Club News as a teaching aid and in those days the covers featured work by famous artists. But what caught his eye was a clearly outlined blank space on the wallpaper. Obviously a big picture had once hung there. Dangling wires from a lighting fixture were still in place.

Months later Henry told him that the blank space had once been filled by a portrait of a beautiful young lady. When you looked at it closely you saw that one of her eyes was blue and the other brown. Either the painter had been drunk when he was working on the picture or he was crazy to begin with. Lucy had a theory of her own. "I think the lady wouldn't pay him for the picture, so he got even by painting her eyes in different colours." Anyway, shortly after their father's death the picture had been stolen. Everybody had a good laugh at what real dummies the crooks were. They left behind a Matisse, a Braque, and a Léger, among others, and made off with nothing more than a worthless picture by a local artist.

Enormous teddy bears filled every corner of Henry's huge bedroom. The bed was unmade and Moses could just make out the outlines of a rubber sheet under the linen one. Then he saw the antique lead soldiers arrayed in ranks on the floor. British grenadiers on one side, French dragoons on the other.

"How old are you?" Moses asked.

"Th-th-thirteen."

"And you still play with toy soldiers?"

"You don't have to if you don't want to."

Actually Moses wanted to, and the two of them settled on the floor, Moses behind the French dragoons.

"They lost," Henry said, offering him the grenadiers instead.

"What?"

"W-W-Waterloo."

As the battle developed, incredibly detailed field pieces being brought into play, Moses really began to enjoy himself. Then, suddenly, he leaped to his feet. "Jeez. I'd better get back. My father will be worried."

"You're my prisoner now," Henry said, racing to the bedroom door, blocking it with his outstretched arms.

"Aw, come on. Don't be such a jerk."

Henry, biting back tears, let his arms collapse. "Will you come and p-p-p-play with me again?"

"Offer to pay him," Lucy said, standing in the doorway. She smiled. Her fist curling over her mouth, her cheeks hollow from the strain of sucking.

"I'll come again."

Moses ran all the way back to the party, arriving in time to stumble on its closing ceremony. All the kids were gathered in a circle close to the gates, their beaming parents waiting to drive them home. One of their number, a plump redhead called Harvey Schwartz, wearing a ruffled blouse and magenta velvet trousers, skipped forward and presented a bouquet of red roses to Mrs. Gursky. "This is for our gracious hostess," he said, kissing a stooping Mrs. Gursky on the cheek, "who was kind enough to invite us here for a day we will remember forever and ever."

"You're an angel," Mrs. Gursky said, wiping her cheek with a Kleenex.

"We wish the birthday boy continued good health and success in all his future endeavours," Harvey continued. "And now, three cheers for Lionel Gursky!"

As everybody but Barney Gursky joined in for three rousing cheers, Harvey Schwartz's mother descended on Mrs. Gursky. "Harvey's the rank-one boy at the Talmud Torah. He's already skipped a grade. I hope he can come again."

Moses spotted L.B. pacing up and down, obviously in a rage. "Where in the hell were you?" he asked, as a smiling Mr. Bernard joined them.

"Over there. With Henry and Lucy."

L.B., appalled, looked imploringly at Mr. Bernard. "I'm sorry," he said.

"Don't worry. How would he know."

"What's wrong with their mother?"

"Damn it," L.B. said.

But Mr. Bernard was chuckling. He pointed a stubby finger at his forehead and twirled it like a screwdriver. "She's as cuckoo as a fruit cake," he said.

An agitated Mrs. Gursky joined them, propelling little Harvey Schwartz before her. "Tell him," she said.

"I'm sorry, Mr. Bernard, but somebody has written bad words about Lionel on the wall of the guests' toilet."

"What are you talking about?"

Strolling down from the heights Moses told L.B. that Henry had invited him back to play again.

"Absolutely out of the question. He's Solomon's kid."

"So?"

"It's very complicated. Family history. Old quarrels. We don't want to get involved in that."

"Why?"

"When you're older I'll explain."

"How much older?"

"Will you stop now please. I've had enough for one day."

They continued down the steep twisting mountainside road in silence.

"Solomon was a *bulvon*," L.B. said. "A dreadful man. He came to one of my readings once and he was the first with his hand up in the question period. 'Can the poet tell me,' he asked, 'whether or not he uses a rhyming dictionary?' I should have socked him one."

"Yeah," Moses said, and trying to picture it he giggled and then took his father's hand. "Let's go to Horn's for a coffee."

"I can't today. In fact I've got to leave you here."

"Where are you going?"

L.B. sighed, exasperated. "If you really must know I'm late for a sitting with a sculptor."

"Hey, that's great! What's his name?"

L.B. flushed. "Questions questions questions. Don't you ever stop? Somebody I met at a party. Good enough for you?"

FOUR

$\blacklozenge$

When L.B.'s poem celebrating Mr. Bernard's twentieth wedding anniversary in 1950 was published in *Jewish Outlook*, it enraged Moses. A committed socialist himself now, he lashed out at his father for having betrayed his old adoring comrades to become an apologist for the Gurskys, one of Mr. Bernard's lapdogs.

"Calm down. Lower your voice, please. It just so happens," L.B. protested, "that Mr. Bernard did more for our refugees and the State of Israel than any of those *nebbishes*."

But Moses would have none of it, going on to accuse his father of having become a *nimmukwallah*, somebody who had eaten the king's salt. They quarrelled, Moses pronouncing L.B. pretentious for keeping carbon copies of all his correspondence. L.B. replied, "I want you to know that the first edition of *The Burning Bush*, the Spartacus Press folio, now sells for ten dollars, if you are lucky enough to find one. It's classified as 'Rare Canadian Judaica'. A real collector's item."

Seething, Moses fled the flat on the tree-lined street in Outremont and turned to Sam Birenbaum for solace. He phoned him from a downtown bar. "Meet me for a drink," he said.

"Well . . ."

"Oh, come on, Molly will be glad to have you out of the apartment for once."

Sam, who had once enchanted L.B.'s group by reciting Sacco's speech to the court, had been the first of the children to disappoint them. An ironic turn of events, because no sooner did Sam become a teenager than he was the one the group came to depend on for one thing or another. Oh my God, one of the women would sob over the phone to Birenbaum's Best Fruit, send Sam over right away, all the lights have gone out. Or the toilet's blocked. Or the kitchen sink faucet is going drip drip drip all night. Or no heat is coming through the radiators. Or my sister-in-law's car won't start.

So Sam would hurry over to replace the burnt-out fuses or pump something unspeakable out of a toilet or change a washer or bleed the radiators or fill dry battery cells with distilled water or whatever. And then, though they were grateful, sometimes effusively so, he sensed each time that he was somehow diminished in their eyes for being proficient in such plebeian matters.

L.B. had not approved when Sam and Moses became inseparable in high school, always picking on Sam when he came to the house. "Could that be a book you are reading, Sam, or do my eyes deceive me?"

"It's a magazine. *Black Mask.*"

"Trash."

Then Sam and Moses were at McGill together. Sam, some three years older than Moses, was editor of the *McGill Daily* until he dropped out in his final year and took a job on the *Gazette*, because his girlfriend was pregnant. Molly, who had wanted him to continue with his studies, enabling him eventually to tackle serious writing even while he taught, had offered to have an abortion. Sam wouldn't hear of it. Ever since he and Molly had started dating in high school, he had feared she would find somebody more intelligent and less rolypoly than he was, but now she had to marry him. Moses recalled the day an exuberant Sam had broken the news. "Molly Sirkin my wife. Imagine."

They went to the Chicken Coop for lunch to celebrate.

"Don't look now," Sam said, "but there's Harvey Schwartz, who never met a rich man he didn't like."

Harvey came over to introduce his fiancée, Miss Rebecca Rosen, who was wearing a gardenia corsage. "We're just coming from Mr. Bernard's," Harvey said, letting it drop that he was going to join McTavish Distillers as soon as he graduated. "I consider it a great personal challenge."

"I want to ask you a question of an intimate nature," Moses said. "When you are visiting Mr. Bernard's mansion and you have to piss which toilet do you get to use?"

"Let's go, buttercup," Becky said. "They're just being silly."

And now Sam, not yet twenty-three, was the father of a two-year-old boy vulnerable to earache, measles, diaper rash, kidnappers, child molesters, crib death, and only Sam could guess how much more.

The two friends met at the Café André. Moses told Sam about his quarrel with L.B. and inveighed against the Gurskys, the new Jewish royalty in America, America. "From the Rambam to the rum-runner. We've come a long way, don't you think?"

"I thought you were friendly with the Gurskys."

"Only with Henry."

They drifted over to Rockhead's Paradise, where Sam immediately phoned home. "Don't look at me like that. I always like her to know exactly where I am, just in case . . ."

"Just in case what?"

"Okay, okay. Now I've got something to tell you, but this is strictly between us. I submitted some of my stuff to *The New York Times*. They've invited me down for an interview, but even if they offer me a job I'm not going to take it."

"Why not?"

"Molly wants to go back to work next year. Her mother could take care of Philip during the day and I could quit the *Gazette* and try my hand at some real writing."

Hours later Sam, driving his father's car, managed it back to the Berger house in Outremont without incident. Moses had considerable difficulty with the front-door key. Sinking to his knees, the better to concentrate on threading the key through the slot, he began to giggle foolishly. "Sh," he cautioned himself, "L.B.'s sleeping."

"Dreaming of unstinting praise," Sam said.

"... Pulitzers ..."

"... Nobels ..."

"Statues raised in his honour."

"His hair, for Christ's sake. Beethoven."

"Knock it off."

They sat down together on the porch steps and Moses started in on the Gurskys again. "I'm told the real bastard was Solomon, who died in the thirties."

"Molly will be waiting up for me."

"Can you arrange for me to go through the Solomon Gursky file at the *Gazette*?"

"Why are you so interested?"

"Remember Shloime Bishinsky?"

"Of course I do. What about him?"

No answer.

"You want to shove it to L.B., right, comrade?"

"Can you arrange for me to go through the Solomon Gursky file or not?"

"Yeah, sure."

But the file had been stolen. The large manilla envelope in the library was empty. And when Moses dragged out the old newspapers that dealt with the trial, he discovered that somebody had cut out the relevant stories with a razor blade.

He was hooked.

FIVE

◆

Late one winter afternoon in 1908 Solomon Gursky tumbled
out of school into the thickly falling snow in Fort McEwen,
Saskatchewan, to find his grandfather waiting on the stern of
his long sled. Solomon was a mere nine-year-old at the time.
Ephraim, whom the Indians called Mender-of-Bones, was
ninety-one and running short of time. He was rooted in a
tarpaper shack out on the reservation, living with a young
woman called Lena. A team of ten yapping dogs was
harnessed to the sled. Ephraim, his eyes hot, stank of rum. His
cheek was bruised and his lower lip was swollen.

"What happened?" Solomon asked.

"Not to worry. I slipped and fell on the ice."

Ephraim tucked his grandson under the buffalo robes, laid
his rifle within reach, and cracked his whip high, urging on the
dogs.

"What about Bernie and Morrie?" Solomon asked.

"They're not coming with us."

George Two Axe was waiting for them, pacing up and down
in the failing light of the platform behind his general store. He
hastily loaded large quantities of pemmican, sugar, bacon,
tea, and rum on to the sled. "Go now," he pleaded.

But Ephraim wouldn't be hurried. "George, I want you to

send somebody to my son's house to tell him that the lad is spending the night with the Davidsons."

"*You can't take the kid.*"

"Steady on, George."

"Anything happens to you out there he hasn't got a chance."

"I'll write to you from Montana."

"I don't want to know where you're heading for."

"I trust you," Ephraim said. His eyes glittering with menace, he thrust a wad of bills at George Two Axe. "Make him a proper pine coffin and the rest is for the family."

"You are crazy in the head, old man."

Instead of turning right at the railroad tracks, Ephraim took a left fork on the trail leading out to the prairie.

"I thought we were going to Montana."

"We're heading north."

"Where?"

"Far."

"Are you drunk again, *zeyda*?"

Ephraim laughed and sang him one of his sailor songs:

> And when we get to London docks,
> There we'll see the cunt in flocks!
> One to another they will say,
> O, welcome Jack with three years' pay!
> For he is homeward bound,
> For he is homeward bound!

They travelled all through the night, Solomon snug under the buffalo robes. Ephraim didn't waken his grandson until he had already built their first igloo, warmed by a stone lamp. Then he asked Solomon to help him sort out their things. "But mind how you go," he said.

Surprisingly, among the supplies that had to be unloaded, there were a number of books, including a Latin grammar. "Right after breakfast," Ephraim said, "we're going to start in on some verbs."

"Miss Kindrachuk says Latin is a dead language."

"That school of yours is no bloody good."

"I don't have to stay here with you. I'm going home."

Ephraim tossed snowshoes and his compass at him. "Then you're going to need these, my good fellow. Oh, and no matter how tired you get don't lie down out there or you could freeze to death."

Outside, an indignant Solomon wandered in a sea of swirling snow. He was back within the hour, his teeth chattering. "The Mounties came to our school yesterday," he said, testing.

"Have a cup of char. I'll make bacon."

"They came to get André Clear Sky. There was a big fight on the reservation."

Ephraim undid a canvas bag and laid out fresh clothes for Solomon. "This," he said, indicating a parka with a hood attached, "is an *attigik*. And these," he added, holding up wide pants, reaching only to the knee, "are called *qarliiq*." Both garments, he explained, were made of caribou hide and were to be worn with the skin side against the body. There were also two pairs of stockings, the inner pair to be worn with the animal hair inside, the outer pair the other way round; and a pair of caribou-hide boots.

"Where are we going?" Solomon asked.

"To the Polar Sea."

George Two Axe was right. He *is* crazy in the head.

"Now you eat your bacon and then we'll get some kip."

"How long will we be gone?"

"If you are such a baby and want to go home that badly, take the dogs before I wake and beat it."

Ephraim propped his rifle beside the sleeping platform and drifted off, his mouth agape, the igloo resounding with his snores. Solomon briefly considered knocking him out with the rifle butt and making his escape, but he doubted that he could manage the dogs, and he didn't want to go out into the cold again. Tomorrow maybe.

"You still here?" Ephraim asked, wakening. He didn't seem pleased.

"So what?"

"Maybe you were worried about how I would manage without the dogs."

"I've never seen the Polar Sea."

Ephraim brightened. He actually smiled. They travelled

through the night again, conjugating Latin verbs, Ephraim taunting him, "Now I'm stuck with you, and I don't even know that I brought along enough food for two."

The next evening on the trail Ephraim said, "Why don't I keep warm under the buffalo robes tonight and you run the dogs for a change?"

"What if I took the wrong direction?"

"You see that big diamond there, low in the sky, well you just keep heading right for it."

After the first week they no longer travelled by night. Neither did Ephraim bother to destroy all evidence of their igloo before they broke camp. He taught Solomon how to harness the dogs, looping the shortest traces through those of the laziest ones stationed closest to the whip. Before chopping their food with an axe, Ephraim made a point of overturning the sled, securing it as tightly as possible to the slavering dogs so that they couldn't run off with it in their excitement. Then he hurled the meat at the pack, laughing as the strongest ones, a couple of them with their ears already torn, lunged at the biggest chunks. "From now on," Ephraim said, "this is going to be your job."

Ephraim understood that the boy enjoyed handling the dogs, but he continued to watch him closely, annoyed by his churlish manner, the grudging way he undertook other chores and his Latin studies. He began to wonder if he had been wrong about him, just as he had been mistaken about so many other people over the wasting years. Then he discovered that Solomon had been surreptitiously filling the pages of one of his exercise books with a map of their progress, landmarks carefully drawn. He noted with even more satisfaction that each time he had apparently dozed off, Solomon would sneak out of the igloo, hatchet in hand, marking a tree in every one of their camps with a deep gash.

Their first real quarrel followed hard on a Latin lesson.

"You're eating while I'm asleep," Solomon said. "I can tell when I pack the supplies."

"Cheek."

"I think we should split the food in two right now and if you run out before we get there, well . . ."

"You don't even know how to hunt yet. At your age I was reading Virgil. Go harness the dogs."

"So that you can complain I did it wrong just like everything else?"

"Hop to it."

"You do it."

"I'm going back to sleep."

They lingered in the camp for three days, not speaking, until Solomon finally went out and harnessed the dogs. Ephraim followed after. Solomon had done it well and Ephraim intended to compliment him, warming things between them, but, old habits dying hard, he stifled the impulse. All he said was, "You managed not to bungle it for a change."

It took them many days of hard sledding to reach the shores of Great Slave Lake.

Elsewhere Tsu-Hsi, the Dowager Empress of China had died; Ephraim's old friend Geronimo was ailing and would soon expire as well; Einstein surfaced with the quantum theory of light; and the first Model-T rolled off an assembly line in Detroit. But on the shores of that glacial lake, Ephraim — not so much shrunken now as distilled to his very essence — squatted with his chosen grandson, man and boy warming themselves by their camp-fire under the shifting arch of the aurora. A raven was perched on Ephraim's shoulder. "One of the gods of the Crees," he said, "can converse with all kinds of birds and beasts in their own language, but I can only make myself understood to the bird that failed Noah."

Ephraim stood up and pissed and threw the dogs some jackfish. "Do you hear that in the hills?" he asked.

"Is it a wolf?"

"The Chipewyans, who will kill anything, just out of spite, even small birds in their nests, never harm the wolf, because they believe it to be an uncommon animal. Me, I'm no Chipewyan. Come," he said, offering his hand.

But Solomon, sliding free, wouldn't take it. He was longing to, but he couldn't.

"I'm going to show you something," Ephraim said.

Ephraim slid a long knife free of their sled and planted it

upright in the snow. He melted honey over the fire and coated the blade with it, the honey freezing immediately. "The wolf will come down later, start to lick the honey and slice his tongue to ribbons. Then the greedy fool will lick the blood off the blade until he bleeds to death. Do you understand?"

"Sure I do."

"No, you don't. I'm trying to warn you about Bernard," Ephraim said, glaring at him. "When the time comes, remember to spread honey on the knife." Muttering to himself, he heated a kettle of snow to make tea. "There's gold to be found here. We're sitting right on it." Then he reminisced about his boyhood in the coal mines in a manner that assumed Solomon had been right there with him in the pit, also chained to a sledge, sinking to all fours, mindful of scuttling rats as he dragged his load along to the gob. Remembering the pithead girls, Sally of County Clare. Cursing old enemies Solomon had never heard of, obviously put out when the boy failed to pepper the broth with invective of his own, instead looking baffled and just a little scared. "In Minsk," Ephraim said, "and then in Liverpool, your great-grandfather was a cantor and when he sang *Kol Nidre* no synagogue was large enough to seat all of his followers."

Long before they reached their destination, they rode into their first gale. Ephraim sat down on the sled, wrapped himself in skins, and said, "You'd better build us an igloo now."

"But I don't know how."

"Build it," Ephraim said, tossing him the long knife.

"You do it," Solomon said, kicking the knife away.

"I'm going to sleep."

Crazy old bastard, Solomon thought, but he retrieved the knife. Tears freezing against his cheeks, he began to cut snow blocks. When he was done, he shook his grandfather as hard as he dared, waking him. Once inside, Ephraim lit the *koodlik*. He sat Solomon on his lap warming the bright burning spots on his cheeks with the palms of his hands and then he tucked him in under the skins on the snow platform and sang him to sleep with one of his songs, not a profane song but one of the synagogue songs he had learned at his father's table.

Strong and Never Wrong is He,
Worthy of our Song is He,
Never failing,
All prevailing.

The boy safely asleep, Ephraim was able to gaze fondly at
him. Warming the back of his hands against his chosen
grandson's cheeks and then retreating to a corner to get
quietly drunk. *I'm ninety-one years old, but I'm not ready to die until I
see him face to face.*

Standing over his grandson in the igloo, wearing his black
silk top hat and *talith*, Ephraim, soaked in rum, spread hands
stiff with age and pronounced the blessing his father used to
say over him: "*Yeshimecha Elohim keEfrayim vechiMenasheh.*"

As far as Solomon was concerned Ephraim was unpredict-
able, cranky. A quirky companion. On the rare occasion
gentle, but for the most part impatient, charged with anger
and contradictions. One day he would be full of praise for the
Eskimo, an ingenious people, who had learned to survive on a
frozen desert, living off what the land had to offer, forging
implements and weapons out of animal bone and sinew. The
next day he would drunkenly denounce them. "Their notion
of how to cure a sick child is for the women to dance around the
kid singing *aya, aya, aya*. They have no written language and
the vocabulary of their spoken one is poverty stricken."

Before slicing frozen meat for breakfast, Ephraim would lick
the knife with his tongue, which immediately adhered to the
blade, and then he would wait for the heat of his body to warm
the knife sufficiently for blade and tongue to separate. If he
tried to cut with a cold knife, he explained, the blade would
rebound or maybe even break.

Each time they broke camp it was infuriatingly clear to
Solomon that rather more food had been consumed than they
could possibly have eaten together. Obviously, the selfish old
bastard was gorging himself in secret. He was most irascible
when unable to remember the names of old friends. He tended
to repeat stories spun from his jumbled memories. Even
wearing his reading glasses, a curse to him, he had trouble
making a sewing needle from a ptarmigan bone and had to

fling it away, a bad job. Five hours sleep was enough for him and on occasion he would shake Solomon awake early, claiming he had something urgent to tell him. "Never eat the liver of a polar bear. It drives men mad."

Ephraim, the first old man Solomon had ever looked at nude, was an astonishing sight. A wreck, a ruin. What remained of his teeth long and loose and the colour of mustard. His jaw receding. Those arms, surprisingly strong, although spindly, the muscles attenuated. His narrow chest a mat of frosty grey hair. His sunken belly slack. A red lump bulging like an apple out of one hip, pulling the flesh taut. "My very own pingo," he called it. A ruby tracery of veins disfiguring one leg. His disconcertingly large testicles hanging low in a wrinkled sac, his penis flopping out of a snowy nest. Old wounds and scars and purplish places where he had been sloppily sewn together. His back reamed with welts and knots and ridges.

"How did it get like that?" Solomon asked.

"I was a bad boy."

Some mornings Ephraim wakened frisky, eager to plunge farther into the tundra. On other mornings, complaining of aching bones, he lingered on the sleeping platform, comforting himself with rum. Drunk, he might mock Solomon, listing his inadequacies, or prowl up and down the igloo, unaware of his grandson, arguing with himself and the dead. "How was I to know she would hang herself?"

"Who?"

"Don't pry into my affairs."

He made considerable ceremony out of winding his cherished gold pocket watch before retiring each night, a watch that was inscribed:

From W.N. to E.G.
de bono et malo.

One night he shook Solomon awake, raging, "I'd like to see him face to face, like Moses at Sinai. Why not? Tell me why not?"

They ate arctic hare and ptarmigan. Ephraim taught him how to handle a rifle and hunt caribou, shaking his head when so many bullets were wasted. But once Solomon had brought down his first bull, shot through the heart, Ephraim astonished him with hugs and tickles and the two of them rolled over together in the snow again and again. Then Ephraim slit the caribou open, careful not to puncture the first stomach. He scooped out hot blood and drank it, and indicated that Solomon was to do the same. Back in the igloo, he cracked some bones and showed Solomon how to suck the marrow from them, then sliced chunks of fat out of the rump for both of them to munch. Afterward Solomon, overcome by nausea, fled the igloo.

A week later they camped on the shores of Point Lake and the Coppermine River. Ephraim told him that so far only five leaders of Israel had lived a hundred and twenty years: Moses, Hillel, Rabbi Yochanon ben Zakai, Rabbi Yehuda HaNassi and Rabbi Akiva. "I'm already ninety-one years old, but if you think I'm ready to die you're bonkers."

As they moved further along the Coppermine, Ephraim's mood seemed to sweeten. There were nights when the old man entertained his grandson with stories, the two of them lying together under the skins, the light dancing in their igloo, but other nights Ephraim drank too much rum.

"How would you find your way back if I died in my sleep?"

"Don't worry about me."

"Maybe you were a fool to come out here with me. I wouldn't even be good to eat. I'm just a bag of bones now."

Solomon withdrew from him under the skins. "I don't want to be teased any more, *zeyda*."

"I could be mistaken in you. Maybe I should have brought Bernard with me. Or Morrie." He grabbed Solomon and shook him. "Morrie could be the one to watch out for, you know. Damn. You don't understand anything."

"If you hate me so much, why did you bring me here?"

Startled, stung, Ephraim wanted to protest, he wished to tell him how much he loved him. But he choked on it. Something in him wouldn't allow it. "Why did Saul throw that javelin at David?"

Once they reached their destination, the shores of the

Polar Sea, the old man and the boy built an igloo together and hung their clothes out to dry on a line stretched over their *koodlik*; then Ephraim tucked his grandson between the skins spread on the sleeping platform. "It was the dying Orkneyman," he said, "the boatman I met in Newgate prison, who led me and now you to this shore."

Ephraim celebrated their safe arrival by drinking a bottle of rum and singing songs for Solomon. Synagogue songs. Then he told him a story. "Long, long ago not only the north, but most of the land was under ice, maybe a mile thick. When the ice melted there was a deluge and the waters swept over the lands of the Eskimos, the Loucheux, the Assiniboines and the Stony people. Many were drowned before Iktoomi took pity on them and decided that he must save some. Iktoomi saved one man and one woman, and one male and one female of each kind of animal. He built a large raft and they floated on it over the flood waters.

"On the seventh day Iktoomi told the beaver that he must try to dive right to the bottom and see if he could bring back a chunk of earth. O, that poor beaver, he dived and dived but he couldn't reach the bottom. So the next day Iktoomi sent a muskrat into the water to see if he could bring back a bit of mud. The brave muskrat dived very deep and they waited and waited. In the evening the dead body bobbed to the surface of the water near the raft. Iktoomi took it on board and found a little mound of mud in the muskrat's paw. He brought the rat back to life and took the little bit of mud and moulded it with his fingers and as he did that it grew and grew. Finally he put the mud over the side of the raft, and it went on growing into solid earth so that soon he could land the raft and all the animals. And the land still went on growing and growing from where he had moulded it.

"When all the animals were ashore and the land was still growing, he waited till it was out of sight and then he got hold of the wolf and told him to run round the earth and only to come back and tell him when the earth was big enough to hold all the people. Now the wolf took seven years in his voyage and in all that time he couldn't complete his tour of the world. He crept back home and fell exhausted at Iktoomi's feet. Iktoomi then asked the raven to go out and fly over the bit of the world that the wolf hadn't seen. Now the raven in those days was absolutely white, that's the way it was with him, and he flew off to do Iktoomi's bidding. Or so it seemed. But instead of flying as he was told to do, he got hungry, and seeing a corpse floating by, he swooped down and began to pick at it. Then he flew home again and when Iktoomi saw him he knew that he had been eating a dead body because his beak was full of blood. So he seized hold of the raven and said to him: 'Since you have such a dirty nature, you shall have a dirty colour.' Right then the raven was turned from white to black and that colour he remains to this day."

Ephraim slipped between the skins with Solomon, the two of them embracing to keep warm. In the morning he said, "We will wait here until my people find us and then you will no longer have to warm yourself in bed against a bag of bones."

"How will your people know we're here?"

"The first man made by the Great Being was a failure," Ephraim said, "he was imperfect, and therefore was cast aside and called *kub-la-na* or *kod-lu-na*, which means white man. Then the Great Being made a second try and the result was the perfect man, or *Inuit*, as the people call themselves. They will find us and they will hide me here until I die."

"You mean you aren't taking me home again?"

"You can have the dogs. The sled. One of the rifles and half of the ammunition. When my people come they will also load you down with seal meat."

"How will I find my way home?"

"I taught you what I know. How to read the stars and how to hunt. An Eskimo boy could do it."

"I'm not an Eskimo."

"I can get two of the people to lead you back as far as the tree line."

"I should have killed you while I had the chance."

Ephraim unstrapped a leather bag from the sled, dug into it, and extracted an ancient pistol. "Here," he said, tossing it to Solomon. "Go ahead."

HMS *Erebus* was engraved on the pistol butt.

SIX

◆

Moses, still searching for his salmon fly, had to acknowledge that he didn't need the Silver Doctor. He could buy another one next time he was on the Restigouche. But, on the other hand, if he continued to hunt for it for another hour — say, until eleven A.M. — it would be too late to start work. The day shot, he then might as well retreat to The Caboose to check out his mail and maybe hang in for a drink. Just one, mind you. So he lifted a large cardboard carton out of the hall closet and emptied it on the living-room floor. Out spilled a Hardy reel, his missing cigar cutter, a Regal fly-tying vice, years of correspondence with the Arctic Society, and his collection of notebooks, documents, and maps that dealt with the Franklin expedition.

Moses had been a member of the Arctic Society until his disgraceful behaviour at a meeting in 1969 had led to his being declared *persona non grata*.

The first item he retrieved from his Franklin papers was an interview, published in *The Yellowknifer*, with a granddaughter of Jock Roberts. Roberts had sailed into the Arctic in 1857 with Captain Francis Leopold M'Clintock. M'Clintock was seeking survivors of the lost Sir John Franklin expedition, a search that engaged the attention of the British Admiralty, the

President of the United States, the Czar of Russia and, above all, Lady Jane Franklin. A ballad, popular in London at the time, ran:

> In Baffin's Bay where the whale-fish blow,
> The fate of Franklin no man may know.
> The fate of Franklin no tongue can tell,
> Lord Franklin along with his sailors do dwell.

Poor Franklin.

In 1845, only days before he set sail for the Polar Seas in quest of the Northwest Passage, the fifty-nine-year-old veteran of the Battle of Trafalgar was stricken with a premonition of the icy grave that awaited him. While he was napping on a sofa, Lady Franklin, thinking to warm him, spread over his legs the British Ensign which she was embroidering. Franklin promptly leapt to his feet. "There's a flag thrown over me! Don't you know they lay the Union Jack over a corpse?"

A complement of 134 officers and men and two stout, three-masted vessels of the bomb-ketch type were put at Franklin's disposal. Both ships, rigged as barks, were fortified for their Arctic ordeal, their planking doubled, their bows and sterns bolstered to a thickness of eight feet. Crowds flocked to the dock when the *Erebus* and the *Terror* were scheduled to depart from the Thames. The officers were turned out smartly in tailcoats, round jackets, monkey jackets and greatcoats. For the voyage to circumnavigate the globe through the Northwest Passage they also took with them double-breasted waistcoats, stick-up collars, black silk neck handkerchiefs, and other fashionable items becoming to gentlemen at sea. Stout, jowly Franklin read his crew a sermon, taking the text from the seventeenth chapter of 1 Kings, wherein Elijah the Tishbite told how he hid himself by the brook Cherith, that was before Jordan, and how the ravens were commanded to feed him there, bringing him bread and flesh in the morning and again in the evening.

Among the supplies that had been loaded on to the ships were thousands of cans filled with preserved meat, soups, vegetables, flour, chocolate, tea, tobacco and, as proof against scurvy, lemon juice. Even so, some of the more fastidious members of the ships' company thought it prudent to look to their needs. One officer, for instance, took on board assorted bonbons especially ordered from Fortnum & Mason. And then on the dark night before they sailed out of Stromness Harbour, in the Orkneys, their last home port, there was the curious case of the assistant surgeon of the *Erebus* boarding with a cabin boy wearing a silk top hat, the two of them lugging sacks of personal provisions. Six coils of stuffed derma, four dozen kosher salamis, a keg of schmaltz herring and uncounted jars of chicken fat, their pockets bulging with garlic cloves. The assistant surgeon and the cabin boy were jabbering in some guttural tongue, which the third lieutenant, whose watch it was, took to be a German dialect. On inquiry, however, the cabin boy insisted it was a patois that he and the assistant surgeon had picked up on a voyage to the South Seas.

Concern for Franklin did not surface until 1847. The Admiralty sent out three relief expeditions, unavailingly. By 1850, fleets of ships were searching the Arctic. One of them found three graves marked by head-boards. They were the tombs of two sailors from the *Erebus* and one from the *Terror*. The three men had been buried in 1846.

The quest for Franklin continued. In 1854, John Rae, surveying the Boothia Peninsula, met with a band of Eskimos who told him that Franklin's party had starved to death after the loss of their ships, leaving accounts of their suffering in the mutilated corpses of some who had evidently furnished food for their unfortunate companions. Rae's story was published in the Toronto *Globe*.

The fact that a Christian would accept the word of the natives on such an insidious matter inflamed not only Lady Franklin, but also other Britons, among them Charles Dickens. The source of these stories, Dickens wrote, was a covetous, treacherous and cruel people, with a proven taste for blood and blubber. Members of the Franklin expedition represented the "flower of the trained English navy," and, therefore "it is in the highest degree improbable that such men would, or could, in any extremity of hunger, alleviate the pains of starvation by this horrible means."

Three years later Jock Roberts joined the continuing

search, sailing with M'Clintock on the *Fox*. In April 1859
M'Clintock reached King William Island, where he found a
lifeboat from the *Erebus* on the western shore, some sixty-five
miles from the last position of Franklin's ships. It lay partially
out of its cradle on a sledge and had neither oars nor paddle.
M'Clintock calculated the total weight of the sledge to be
1,400 pounds, a ridiculously heavy burden for sailors ridden
with scurvy and close to starvation. The only provisions in
sight were 40 pounds of tea, a quantity of chocolate, and a
small jar of animal fat, probably walrus, that surprisingly
enough tasted of chicken and burnt onions. For the rest, the
boat was laden with an amazing amount of dead weight.
Towels, scented soap, sponges, silver spoons and forks,
twenty-six pieces of plate with Sir John Franklin's crest, and
six books, all of them scriptural or devotional works. Two
skeletons lay in the boat, both of them without their skulls. The
skeleton in the bow, M'Clintock wrote, obviously considerate
of Lady Franklin's feelings, had been disturbed "by large and
powerful animals, probably wolves."

A born jackdaw, Jock Roberts had brought back mementos
from his long and arduous voyage with M'Clintock. A silk
handkerchief, two buttons from an officer's greatcoat, a
hair-comb and, most baffling, a black satin skullcap with
curious symbols embroidered on it both inside and out.
Clearly the skullcap was not standard Royal Navy issue and
was unlikely to have belonged to any member of the
expedition. So it was immediately assumed that it had been
left behind by native scavengers of the site and was probably
the property of a shaman. This, however, led to the intriguing
conjecture that, contrary to popular belief, there was at least
one wandering band of Eskimos sufficiently advanced to have
a rudimentary form of a written language. Then one day Jock
Roberts, hard-pressed for cash to support his drinking habit,
took the satin skullcap to the curator of the northern museum
in Edmonton, rambled on at length about its origins, and
speculated that such a rare Eskimo artifact was worth plenty.
The curator, who happened to be a doctor of divinity,
denounced Roberts as a lying drunkard. "Don't take us for
fools here," he said. "These so-called symbols embroidered

into the fabric are not Eskimo, but Hebrew. For your information the inscription on the outside says, 'Observe the Sabbath, to keep it Holy' and inside we have what I take to be the rightful owner's name. 'Yitzchak ben Eliezer'. I suggest that you return it to him immediately. Good day to you, sir."

That was not the end of it, however. For the skullcap, soon to be celebrated as "The Jock Roberts *Yarmulke*", was not the only Hebraic artifact to be found in the Arctic. Another was discovered by Waldo Logan of Boston, captain of the whaling barque *Determination*, who landed at Pelly Bay in 1869. Logan was met by a friendly band of Netsilik Eskimos. One of them, In-nook-poo-zhee-jook by name, claimed to have found a second lifeboat on King William Island with a large number of skeletons strewn about. Some of the bones had been severed with a saw and many of the skulls had been punctured the easier to suck out the brains. He had taken a book back with him from the site for his children to play with and it was the remnants of this book, later established to be a *siddur* or Hebrew prayer book, that Logan would bring out of the Arctic.

Logan, an observant man, noted that the parkas worn by this band of Netsiliks differed in one significant detail from the usual. Four fringes hung from the outermost skin of each one, the fringes made up of twelve silken strands. One of their number, Ugjuugalaaq, told him, "We were on King William Island to hunt seals when we met a small party of whites pulling a boat on a sledge. They all looked starved and cold. Except for the young man called Tulugaq, and his older friend, Doktuk, none of them wore furs."

Here, in *Life With The Esquimaux, A Narrative of an Arctic Quest in Search of Survivors of Sir John Franklin's Expedition*, Logan noted in parenthesis that *tulugaq* meant raven in Inuktituk.

"We camped together for four days and shared a seal with the whites. Tulugaq was short and strongly built with a black beard and was most concerned about Doktuk who seemed very sick."

Ugjuugalaaq was careful not to say anything about Tulugaq's struggle to the death with the officer who dressed like a woman or about the miracles wrought by him. Neither

did he mention the death of Doktuk, who was buried beneath
a wooden head-board that read:

> Sacred
> to the memory of
> Isaac Grant, MD
> assistant-surgeon
> HMS Erebus
> Died Nov. 12, 1847
> My God, my God, why hast thou
> forsaken me? why art thou so
> far from helping me, and from the
> words of my roaring?
> Psalm 22

A hundred years later academics were still squabbling over
the enigma of the Hebraic artifacts, ventilating their theories
in learned essays that appeared in *The Beaver, Canadian
Heritage*, and *The Journal of Arctic Studies*.

Professor Knowlton Hardy, president of the Arctic Society,
put forward his hypothesis at the meeting in the spring of 1969
that led to Moses's expulsion. The so-called Jock Roberts
Yarmulke, he said, was not a bona fide Franklin clue but a red
herring. Or, he added, looking directly at Moses, more
properly, perhaps, a schmaltz herring. It was inconceivable
that it had ever belonged to any member of the Franklin
expedition or even a native. Most likely it had been the
property of a Jew on board an American whaler.

"Possibly," Moses said, "the keeper of the ship's ledgers."
Then, improvising on a bellyful of Scotch, he advanced a
proposition of his own. One or more members of the Franklin
expedition had been of Jewish extraction and the artifacts had
been among their personal possessions.

"Fiddlesticks!" Hardy said.

Moses, acknowledging Hardy with a lopsided smile,
pointed out that more bizarre objects than a *yarmulke*, or a
siddur, had belonged to certain of the officers or crew. This was
proven by understandably unpublished but meticulously
itemized accounts (available to serious scholars at Admiralty
House) of articles found in searches of Beechey and

King William Islands. They included a filigreed black suspender belt, several pairs of frothy garters, some silk panties, three corsets, two female wigs, and four diaphanous petticoats.

"I don't have to sit here and listen to this drivel," Hardy shouted, slamming his fist against the table. The latter items, he protested, catalogued with such a typical drunken smirk by Berger — casting doubts on the sexual proclivities of brave officers and men — impugning the honour of the dead — were in fact absolutely innocent. They would have been the property of either Lieutenant Philip Norton or Purser John Hoare. Both of them had been to the Arctic with Parry, on the HMS *Hecla*, and had distinguished themselves on the boards of the Royal Arctic Theatre that had been set up in Winter Harbour in 1819. Norton had played a saucy young lady in a number of farces and harlequinades and Hoare's interpretation of Viola had earned him five curtain calls as well as the sobriquet Dolly. "As for Jews having signed on with Franklin," Hardy charged, "nonsense!"

"And why not?" Moses asked.

"Let me be direct with you, Berger. It is a well-known fact that Jews who immigrated to this great country in the nineteenth century did not risk the Arctic Circle, but tended to settle in cities where there was the most opportunity for trade and advancement."

Rising uncertainly to his feet, Moses drifted over to Hardy's place at the U-shaped table, picked up a jug of water, and attempted to empty it over his head. Hardy, leaping free, knocked it out of his hand.

In the summer of 1969 a scientific expedition was flown out to the Isaac Grant gravesite on King William Island. The expedition, led by Professor Hardy, included a forensic scientist and an anthropologist, as well as a support group of technicians armed with the latest in mobile X-ray equipment. They lifted the body of Isaac Grant, undisturbed for more than a century, out of its resting place and defrosted it. Grant had been buried in a narrow plank coffin. But his body, unlike the other three previously exhumed, was wrapped in a curious shroud. The anthropologist pronounced the shroud disconcertingly similar to the sort of shawl that had once been the everyday outer garment of ancient nomads and farmers in the Near East. The shroud or shawl was made of fine woven wool with occasional black bands, its corners pierced and reinforced to take knotted tassels or fringes. When photographs of the shawl, taken from every possible angle, were later distributed among Arctic buffs, Moses Berger pounced. He wrote to the Arctic Society, identifying the garment as a *talith*, the traditional prayer shawl common to the Ashkenazi Jews of Northern Europe.

Professor Hardy was outraged, Moses's letter seemed to confirm his outlandish theory that one or maybe even more members of the Franklin expedition had been Jewish. However, an examination of the startling documents buried with Grant belied that notion. There was, for instance, a letter from a vicar, addressed to the Reverend Isaac Grant, praising him for his diligent work on behalf of a mission to the savages of the Gold Coast, and beseeching other Christians to heed his plea for charitable contributions. Other documents and letters, tied with ribbon, were even more impressive. There was a letter, uncharacteristically effusive, commending Grant for his medical acumen, signed by Mr. Gladstone. Another letter, this one from Sir Charles Napier, celebrated his unequalled skills as a bone-setter, and thanked him for mending a leg that had been broken by a French musket ball. Other letters, signed by still more dignitaries, recommended Grant as a devout Christian and a surgeon blessed with unsurpassed talents. Confirming these panegyrics, Grant's medical degree, also buried with him, showed that he had graduated from the College of Surgeons in Edinburgh *summa cum laude* in 1838. Folded between two of the letters was an old theatre bill from Manchester, announcing:

JUST ARRIVED
Canadian North American
INDIANS!
Headed by Two Chiefs

Alongside Grant's corpse, secured to his trouser belt, was

what appeared to be a ceremonial Indian hatchet or tomahawk. On close examination the blade was seen to be impressed with the logo of its Birmingham manufacturer.

The deep scars on Grant's back proved that he had been flogged more than once, but Franklin was known to consider the practice abhorrent. Furthermore, such punishment seemed inconsistent with the sterling character described in the letters buried with the assistant-surgeon.

Finally, there was consternation.

A researcher who had the wit to write to the College of Surgeons in Edinburgh discovered they had no record of a student named Isaac Grant, never mind one who had graduated *summa cum laude*. The archives of the British Medical Registry had no intelligence of a surgeon with that name and a search at Somerset House yielded no Grant born on October 5, 1807.

Put plainly, except for the evidence of his corpse, it seemed that Isaac Grant, MD, had never existed.

SEVEN

◆

Sean Riley was the first person Moses Berger looked for whenever his research obliged him to pass through Yellow-knife, the capital of the Northwest Territories. Riley had gone right from Spitfires over Malta during World War II into three years of crop dusting in Kenya. Then, back in Canada, he had enrolled in a Trans-Canada Airlines school, emerging as a Viscount pilot in 1951, a tour of duty that ended in ignominy. One day, before setting out on a run from Montreal to Halifax, Riley read aloud to his passengers a head-office edict that cited the variegated role of a Cunard liner's captain and enjoined TCA pilots to be entertaining hosts as well as fliers of unrivalled skill. "I am now," he said, yanking a harmonica out of his pocket, "going to play 'Kisses Sweeter Than Wine' and will accept two more requests before taking off into the wild blue yonder."

Inevitably Riley, like so many free spirits or undischarged bankrupts, runaway husbands, unredeemed drunks and other drifters, retreated to North of Sixty, flying DC-3s, Cessnas and Otters out of Yellowknife. He became the favourite pilot of the NWT's Superior Court Justice, flying him over the barrens on the court circuit again and again. One night in 1969, drinking late with Moses in

The Trapline, Riley told him that he was flying the court party, as well as a few reporters, out on the circuit in the morning. Moses, who was bound for Tulugaqtitut, the settlement on the Beaufort Sea where Henry Gursky had been rooted for years, could hitch a ride with them.

The court party was comprised of the judge, a crown prosecutor, two defence lawyers, and a clerk. They were joined by three reporters, two of them from "the outside". The two men from the "outside" represented the Toronto *Globe and Mail* and the Vancouver *Sun*. The third reporter, a girl named Beatrice Wade, was a native of Yellowknife, then with the Edmonton *Journal*. A raven-haired beauty, with breasts too rudely full for such a trim figure and coal-black eyes that shone with too much appetite.

Riley, assembling the passengers on the runway, couldn't resist performing for the reporters from "the outside". "This old heap, held together with bobby pins and glue, is a DC-3, which some call the workhorse of the north, our own Model-T, but what more experienced northerners refer to as the widowmaker. Anybody want to take a picture of your intrepid flyboy before we take off?"

One of the reporters obliged.

"Now, hold on a minute, this may not be O'Hare or Kennedy, but safety is our first consideration. We've got to have this baby de-iced."

Riley gave Beatrice the nod. She promptly slipped two fingers into her mouth, whistled, and an Eskimo boy arrived on the trot, clearing the wings of snow with a kitchen broom.

Moses, who had hoped to sit next to Beatrice on the flight, was outmanoeuvred by Roy Burwash, the tall sallow Englishman from the Vancouver *Sun*, and had to settle for a seat across the aisle.

"Oh, Vancouver's all right," Burwash allowed, "but something of a cultural desert, and journalistic standards aren't what I was used to in London."

"Who did you work for on Fleet Street?" Moses asked.

"I have been published in *Lilliput* and *Woman's Own*."

"Who did you work for is what I asked."

"*The Daily Sketch*."

"And what do you miss most in Vancouver? The gas fire in your bed-sitter in Kentish Town, luncheon vouchers, or your weekly night out with the lads at Raymond's Revue Bar?"

Beatrice, seated by the window, leaned forward for a better look at Moses. "You're bad," she said.

Light snow began to fall as the DC-3 lowered into the first settlement on the court circuit. Moses, taking advantage of the stop, slipped away to seek out aged Eskimos who might remember tales told to them by their grandparents about the man with the hot eyes who had come on the ship with three masts. He also looked out for any Eskimo who had four fringes hanging from his parka, each fringe made up of twelve silken strands.

After lunch Riley took off in a partial whiteout, soon rose above it, and a couple of hours later found a hole in the clouds, plunged through it, and skittered to a stop just short of a signpost thrust into the ice.

WELCOME TO AKLAVIK
Pop. 729 Elevation 30 ft.
Never Say Die.

A party of bemused Eskimos greeted the DC-3. "You guys bring the mail?" one of them asked.

"We haven't got your bloody welfare cheques," Riley said. "We're the court party, come to fill your jail, and standing right over there, well that's the hanging judge."

The Canadian flag was planted in the snow outside the community hall even as the judge hurried into his robes. The first defendant was a surly, acne-ridden Dogrib sporting a Fu Manchu moustache, FUCK inked immediately above the knuckles of one hand and YOU on the other. Charged with breaking and entering he stood before the judge, swaying on his feet.

"Did you heave a rock through the window of the Mad Trapper's Café in order to gain access?" the judge asked.

"It was closed and I was hungry."

Moses sat next to Beatrice on the flight into Inuvik and that night they became lovers, Moses apologizing for his inadequacy. "Sorry. I'm afraid I've had too much to drink."

"How long have you known Henry Gursky?"

"Ever since I was a child. Why?"

"Are you also filthy rich?"

Unwilling to tell her about his legacy, he said, "I'm just a stop-gap teach filling in here and there until they find out about me."

"Find out what?"

"That I'm a drunk."

"Why?"

"Don't be ridiculous."

"But there has to be a reason."

"Why are you left-handed?"

"That's not a proper analogy."

"Isn't it?"

"Have you ever tried stopping?"

"Christ."

"Have you?"

"Regularly."

"What gets you started again?"

"Enduring other people mostly."

"Nosey ones like me?"

"Like that bloody Burwash."

"But he's no worse than you. Or didn't you also want to get me in the sack the minute you saw me on the plane?"

"That's not fair."

"I don't mean that I'm special. I mean that I was there, that's all, which is enough for most of you."

"Let's go to sleep."

"But we can't yet. We still haven't reached the apogee of the evening, you know, the point where you show me a picture of your wife and tell me what a terrific gal she is, and you don't know what got into you, maybe it was those northern lights, maybe it was the booze, but would I please not ever write or phone you at home, now there's a good girl."

"I'm not married."

"That's difficult to credit. I mean a guy like you. Such an obvious barrel of fun," she said, making him laugh for the first time.

"You're nice," he said.

"No hyperbole, please. My head will swell."

"Beautiful?"

"I'm thirty years old."

"Now you know that I'm not married," he said, "but surely a girl like you—"

"—as talented and intelligent as you—"

"—must have a boy friend?"

"The men around here are afraid of women, especially talky ones. They like huntin' and fishin' and watching 'Hockey Night in Canada' on TV and talking dirty about us in The Trapline," she said, reaching out for him.

"I'm afraid I've had too much to drink to be of any more use tonight."

"You're not sitting for an exam, Moses. Relax. Give it a try."

When he wakened in the morning, he found that she was already up, reading in bed. A paperback edition of *One Hundred Years of Solitude*. "Surprise, surprise," she said, "I'm not just a sensational lay."

The following spring the ebullient commissioner of the Northwest Territories convened his council, declared 1970 Centennial Year, and invited Queen Elizabeth, Prince Philip, Prince Charles and Princess Anne for the revels.

Beatrice, recently appointed to handle the commissioner's public relations, slipped into his office one afternoon and surreptitiously added Moses's name to the guest list for the royal banquet.

"Who's Berger?" the commissioner asked, going through the list the next morning.

"Why, the distinguished Arctic scholar," Beatrice said, simulating surprise.

Moses, who was lecturing at NYU at the time, his status shaky, flew in from New York a few days early, bringing everything Beatrice had forgotten in his apartment on her last visit, as well as a gift, a black silk negligee. Beatrice met him at the airport and they proceeded directly to her place. They were still in bed together when she made him promise that he would turn up sober for the banquet. So going about his rounds in Yellowknife the morning in question, Moses drank nothing but coffee. However, once he caught up with Sean Riley at noon in The Gold Range, he saw no harm in joining him for two and a juice, providing he sipped his beer slowly.

"Right now," Riley said, "I'm being pursued by a publisher in town for the banquet, one of your brethren out of Edmonton. A smiler born, awfully fancy, he sits down at your table and you're surrounded. He wants me to write a book about my thrilling adventures in the Land of the Midnight Sun."

True to his pledge, Moses turned up sober and properly attired in black tie for the royal banquet in the Elks Hall. Then he caught a glimpse of Professor Knowlton Hardy, surrounded by admirers, and hastened over to the bar for just one, a quick one, a double.

Before dinner the royal couple was entertained by a group of outstanding Inuit artists, flown in from remote settlements for the occasion. Professor Hardy rose to introduce the first poet. He explained that unimaginable hardship was the coin of the Inuit's daily existence, but, reflecting on the woof and warp of their lives, they made ecstasy the recurring theme of their anacreontic salute to the world. This remarkable people plucked odes of joy, *pace* Beethoven, out of the simplest blessings enshrining them in their own form of haiku. Then Oliver Girskee stood up and recited:

> Cold and mosquitoes
> These two pests
> Come never together. . .
> *Ayi, yai, ya.*

Following the traditional drum dancers, there was a demonstration, rare as it was lively, by the Keewatin and High Arctic champions of the mouth-pull, a contest wherein the two opponents hook their fingers into each other's mouths and pull away until one of them faints or admits defeat. Then Minni Altakarilatok and Timangiak Gor-ski, the justifiably celebrated Cape Dorset throat-singers, were heard from.

"The distinctive sounds of throat-singing," Professor Hardy

explained to the royal family and their entourage, "part of a time-honoured native tradition, are made by producing guttural nasal and breathing sounds, rather like dry gargling. The art cannot be described, but it can be likened to the sounds of great rivers . . . the gentle glide of the gull . . . the crumbling of the crisp white snow of the mighty gale of the Arctic."

Once the performers were done, Professor Hardy stood up to announce that the evening's artistic events, which had displayed the many-faceted face of Inuit culture to such advantage, were now over. Next a beaming Moses — terrifying Beatrice — rose to say a few unscheduled words. He expressed the hope that this prized part of the Canadian mosaic would never be contaminated by the introduction of mindless American television into the pristine northland, and sank back into his seat, acknowledging applause with a blissful smile and calling for another drink.

Then it was time to eat. Smoked Arctic char and cream of tomato soup followed by caribou steak. Vanessa Hotdog, who was serving Prince Philip, hesitated before removing his steak plate. "Darn it, Dook, hold on to your knife and fork, there's dessert coming."

For years the Eskimos of the Keewatin, the Central and High Arctic and Baffin regions, were known to Ottawa only by the numbers on the identification discs they wore around their necks. Then, in 1969, they were granted surnames. Many chose traditional Inuktituk names, say Angulalik or Pekoyak. More rambunctious spirits insisted on invented surnames such as Hotdog, Coozycreamer or Turf'n'Surf. One name that recurred among a roving band of natives out of King William Island was Gursky or variations thereof including Gor-ski, Girskee, Gur-ski and Goorsky.

Moses had found what he believed to be the first mention of the name Gursky, in this case spelled Gor-ski, in the diaries of Angus McGibbon, the Hudson's Bay Company chief factor of the Prince of Wales's Fort. The entry was dated May 29, 1849.

"The weather continues extremely cold. Severe frost again last night. Jos. Arnold has taken very ill with considerable pain across his body from his back to his breasts. The ignorant natives who are wintering with us have offered all manner of herbs and potions for a cure, but I will have none of it. Ordered some blood taken from Arnold, after which he found the pain somewhat easier.

"McNair and his party arrived before dinner from Pelly Bay by way of Chesterfield Inlet with the most astonishing tale, if true."

McNair's tale:

"A young white man who is unknown to the Compy. or opposition is living with a wandering band of Esquimaux in Pelly Bay and appears to be worshipped by them as a manner of faith-healer or shaman. He goes by the name of Ephrim Gor-ski, but possibly because of his dark complexion and piercing eyes the Esquimaux call him Tulugaq, which means raven in their lingo. McNair, hardly averse to claiming the reward, dared to conjecture that the young man might prove to be a survivor of the Franklin expedition but this vain hope was soon dashed. Gor-ski had no intelligence of either the *Terror* or *Erebus*. He claimed to be a runaway off an American whaler out of Sag Harbour, but was not in want of rescue. Gor-ski was obviously at ease with the Esquimaux in a snow house and when one of them brought in freshly killed seal he partook with them of the soup of hot blood and invited McNair and his party to share in that disgusting broth.

"McNair lingered for two days in camp, his curiosity aroused by this man who claimed to be an American yet spoke with a Cockney accent, and who lived as a native, but was proficient in Latin and had a Bible with him. On the eve of the second day McNair witnessed an odd ceremony. Gor-ski emerged out of the entry tunnel of his snow house wearing a silk top hat and a fringed white shawl with vertical black stripes: and then the native women did disport themselves before him.

"McNair: 'Eight of them exhibited some most curious dances and contortions, till at length their gestures became indecent and wanton in the highest degree, and we turned away from the display.'

"Of course McNair is a low, superficial creature, who lies more frequently than he speaks the truth and can take more than a glass of Grog. He fell into the habit of intemperance after he got into Disgrace in consequence of employing one of the Compy.'s Servants in cutting off the Ears of an Indian who had had an intrigue with his Woman, but which would not have been thought so much of had it been done by himself in the heat of passion or as a punishment for Horse Stealing. Quite possibly there is more bibulous fancy than truth to McNair's tale.

"Had Jos. Arnold bled again tonight, but he continues to complain of dizziness and a general weakness of the limbs. He is a born malingerer."

McNair's tale and its possible connection with Sir John Franklin's fate — not to mention the reward and glory waiting on the man who solved the riddle — must have worried McGibbon, for six weeks later he sent a party out to Pelly Bay to investigate. They found that the Esquimaux had long gone, and the white man with them, if he had ever existed. All that remained of their camp was seal bones, other animal scraps, a discarded ulu, a tent ring, and that celebrated soapstone carving that is still on display at Hudson's Bay House in Winnipeg. Another northern enigma. For while small soapstone carvings of seals, walruses, whales, and other mammals indigenous to the Arctic are far from uncommon, "The McGibbon Artifact", as it has become known, remains the only Eskimo carving of what was clearly meant to represent a kangaroo.

EIGHT

◆

Beatrice had never cared for his cabin in the woods. His Gurskyiana mausoleum. The first time he had driven her out there, she said, "But I come from the backwoods, Moses, and couldn't wait to get out. Why would you bring me here?"

1971 that was, shortly after he had been fired by NYU for "moral turpitude". They were living together in Montreal, Moses idle, Beatrice working for an ad agency, hating it. After work she joined him in one downtown bar or another, usually finding him already sodden, his grin silly.

"Weekends," he said, pouring himself a drink. "It's not that long a drive."

"I suppose."

They separated for the first time the following summer and ten days later Moses was back in the clinic in New Hampshire. Discharged in the autumn, he first had to endure the traditional farewell meeting in the doctor's office. "So tell me," the doctor said, glancing at the fat file on his desk, "it's 3:30 A.M., August 5, 1962. They break in and find Marilyn Monroe lying face down on the bed, bare shoulders exposed, the phone clutched in her right hand. Who was trying to reach her just before she died?"

"How would I know?"

"Clever clever. Now turn over your hands and let the nice doctor have a look."

His fingernails had driven deep cuts into the palms.

"Be well, old friend. Please stay well this time."

Moses immediately struck out for the 91. He drove through New Hampshire and Vermont to Quebec's Eastern Townships, crossing the border at Highwater. Wet slippery leaves lay scattered everywhere on the Quebec side, the bare trees already black and brittle. BIENVENUE. Even if the border had been unmarked Moses would have known that he was back in the Townships. Penury advertised. Suddenly the road was rippled and cracked and he had to swerve to avoid potholes. Rusting pickup trucks, bashed and abandoned, cannibalized years ago, lay in the tall grass and goldenrod here and there. Sinking barns rotted in the fields. Small mills, which had once manufactured bobbins — employing eight of the locals — chewing their fingers — were shuttered. In lieu of elegant little signs directing you toward the ivy-covered Inn on Crotched Mountain or the Horse and Hound, originally built as a farmhouse in 1880, there were roadside CANTINES with tarpaper roofs, proclaimed by a stake banged into the dirt, OPEN/OUVERT, and offering Hygrade hotdogs and limp greasy *pommes frites* made of frozen potatoes. There were no impeccably appointed watering holes, where the aging bartender, once Clean for Gene, would offer you a copy of *Mother Jones* with your drink. However, you could pull in at "Mad Dog" Vachon's and knock back a Molson, maybe stumbling on a three-week-old copy of *'Allo Police*. Or the Venus di Milo, where scantily clad pulpy waitresses out of Chicoutimi or Sept-Iles stripped and then sank to a bare stage to simulate masturbation, protected against splinters by a filthy flannel sheet.

Before turning off on the old logger's track to his cabin in the woods on the other side of Mansonville, Moses stopped at The Caboose, where he found Strawberry exactly as he had left him a month ago, brooding over a quart of Molson.

"It's good to see you, Straw."

"That's not what my wife said the last time I seen her. She said would I be wanting some of the same when I'm eighty. Not from you I ain't is what I told her. Besides I'm thinking of divorcing her for being so unsanitary. Every time I want to pee in the sink it's full of dirty dishes." He guffawed and slapped his knee. "You look like I feel."

"Have you been taking care of my cabin?"

"You only just got here, Mister Man, and you're starting to put the pressure on. Nobody's gonna break into your place because they know you got nothing there but all those damn books and maps and empty bottles and salmon flies that ain't no good here. Whatever you're drinking will be good enough for me."

"I'm not."

"Again?" Strawberry asked, amused.

If Canada had a soul (a doubtful proposition, Moses thought) then it wasn't to be found in Batoche or the Plains of Abraham or Fort Walsh or Charlottetown or Parliament Hill, but in The Caboose and thousands of bars like it that knit the country together from Peggy's Cove, Nova Scotia, to the far side of Vancouver Island. Signs over the ancient cash register reading NO CREDIT or TIP-PING ISN'T A CITY IN CHINA. A jar of rubbery pickled eggs floating in a murky brine, bags of Humpty Dumpty potato chips hanging on a spike. A moose head or a buck's antlers mounted on the wall, the tractor caps hanging from it advertising GULF or JOHN DEERE or O'KEEFE ALE. The rip in the felt of the pool table mended with black tape. Toilet doors labelled BRAVES and SQUAWS or POINTERS and SETTERS. A Hi-Lo Double-Up JOKER POKER machine in one corner, a juke box in another, and the greasy sign over the kitchen door behind the bar reading EMPLOYES ONLY BEYOND THIS POINT.

The Caboose had a notice board.

SURPRISE DART COMPITITION
FRIDAY NIGHT
TROPHY'S

The board listed a cottage for sale on Trouser Lake, last month's Slo-Ball League schedule and a HONDA MOTOR-CYCLE LIKE BRAN NEW FOR SALE.

The Caboose was a clapboard box mounted on cinder

blocks, more flies inside than out. Tractors and dump trucks
and pickups began to bounce into the parking lot around five
P.M., uniformly rust-eaten, dented badly here, taped together
there, often an old coat hanger twisted to hold a rattling or
leaky muffler in place. Once the men settled in they began to
mull over the day's events. Who had been found out by the
welfare office and who was the latest to be caught putting it to
Sneaker's wife, Suzy, and was it Hi-Test again who was
stealing those big outboards on the lake. Whether the new
barmaid at Chez Bobby was worth the cost of a dinner first or
if she was only trying it on because she had graduated from
high school in Ontario, she said. Where you could get the best
deal across the border on used tires for a grader and at the
bottom of which hill were the fucken provincial police lying in
wait right now.

The lot outside The Caboose, punctured with potholes,
overlooked a lush meadow lined with cedars. There were
picnic tables out there as well as an enormous barbecue, the
engine a salvage job done on an abandoned four-stroke lawn
mower. Sundays in summer the truculent and hungover
Rabbit would turn up at seven A.M. to begin roasting a pig or a
couple of shoulders of beef for the community dinner, all you
could eat for five bucks, proceeds to The Old Folks Home in
Rock Island. The Rabbit was once dismissed for pissing in the
fire. "People was looking and it puts them off their feed." He
was fired again for falling asleep in the grass after guzzling his
umpteenth Molson and failing to notice that the spit hadn't
been revolving properly for more than an hour. Then he beat
up an inspector from the *Commission de la Langue Française*
outside The Thirsty Boot on the 243. According to reports the
inspector had ordered The Thirsty Boot to take down their
sign and replace it with a French one. "Sure thing," the
Rabbit had said, kneeing the inspector in the groin, just to cut
him down to his own height before laying into him. "We're
gonna put up a pepper sign all right. Only it's gonna read 'De
Tirsty Boot'." After that he could do no wrong.

Behind The Caboose there was a gravel pit and a fished-out
pond and beyond that the mountains that had been lumbered
twice too often, the cherry and ash and butternut long gone.
Bunk, who also trapped during the winter, had a shack

somewhere up there. He took the odd fisher, some fox and racoons and beaver. The deer were everywhere.

Moses had stopped at The Caboose in the first place by accident. Late one afternoon six years earlier, having spent two days sifting through historical society files in Sherbrooke, searching for references to Brother Ephraim, he went out for a drive and got lost in the back roads. Desperate for a drink, he pulled in at The Caboose and considered not getting out of his Toyota because two men, Strawberry and Bunk, were fighting in the parking lot. Then he grasped that they were both so blind drunk that none of their punches were landing. Finally Strawberry reached back and put all he had into a roundhouse, sliding, collapsing in a mud puddle, and just lying there. A gleeful Bunk reeled over to his pickup, climbed in, the piglets in the back squealing as he gunned his motor, aiming himself at the prone Strawberry.

"Hey," Moses yelled, leaping out of his car, "what in the hell are you trying to do?"

"Run the fucker over."

"He'll bite a hole in your tires."

Bunk pondered. He scratched his jaw. "Good thinking," he said, reversing into a cedar, jolting the protesting piglets, then charging forward, swerving into the 243.

Moses helped Strawberry to his feet and led him back into The Caboose.

"Whatever you're drinking will be good enough for me, Mister Man."

Strawberry, blue-eyed, tall and stringy, all jutting angles, was missing two fingers, a souvenir of his days in the bobbin mill, and had no upper teeth. Moses drank with him and the others until two A.M. Then Strawberry, insisting that Moses was now too drunk to drive, settled him into his Ford pickup and took him to his house on the hill to spend the night on the sofa. No sooner had they staggered inside than Strawberry dug out his shotgun, rolled back out on to his rotting porch and fired a couple of rounds into the air.

"What are you shooting at?" Moses asked, startled.

"If I lived in some big-shot apartment building in the city like you probably do, Mister Man, all I'd have to do is drop my boots on the floor and the neighbours would know I was home safe. Here I fire my shotgun so's they know I'm back and they don't need to worry no more. I may be stupid, but I ain't crazy."

The next morning Strawberry's wife made them bacon and eggs and then they moved on to Chez Bobby, having agreed to have just one for the ditch before Moses proceeded to Montreal. Three hours passed before Strawberry suddenly leaped to his feet. "Shit," he said, "we got to get to Cowansville."

Strawberry, charged with drunken driving a month earlier, was due to appear in court that afternoon. First, however, he took Moses to The Snakepit, a bar around the corner from the courthouse, where Bunk, Sneaker, Rabbit, Legion Hall, and some of the others were already waiting. By the time Strawberry's supporters, Moses still among them, drifted into the courtroom, they were quarrelsome drunk. They waved and whistled and hollered imprecations at the first sight of Strawberry standing there, grinning.

"Order, order in the court," the judge called out.

"I'll have a hamburger," Strawberry said.

"I could give you ninety days for that."

"That's nothing."

"How about a hundred and twenty?"

Fortunately, Strawberry's lawyer intervened at this point. He was the judge's nephew and the local Liberal party bagman. Strawberry got off with a suspended sentence and everybody repaired to Gilmore's Corner to celebrate. They made three more pit stops before they ended up at The Beaver Lodge in Magog. "My great-grandaddy Ebenezer used to drink here," Strawberry told Moses, pointing out a sign over the bar that had been salvaged from the original hotel, destroyed by fire in 1912.

WM. CROSBY'S HOTEL
The undersigned, thankful for past favours
bestowed upon this
LONG-ESTABLISHED HOTEL
is determined to conduct this establishment in a
manner that will meet the approbation of the public,
and therefore begs a continuance of Public Patronage.

REFRESHMENTS SERVED AT ANY HOUR
OF DAY OR NIGHT
Wm. Crosby
Proprietor

The next afternoon Moses phoned Henry Gursky, in the Arctic, and borrowed enough money to buy the cabin high in the woods overlooking Lake Memphremagog.

Strawberry, Moses discovered, painted houses between drinks. He could also be driven to cut wood or plough snow. But, for the most part, he was content to hibernate through the winter on the fat of his welfare cheque. "Hey, I coulda been rich, a big landowner," Strawberry once said, "if not for what my crazy great-grandaddy done. Old Ebenezer Watson gave up the bottle for God, a big mistake, joining up with a bunch of religious nuts called the Millenarians. Eb lost just about everything, his life included. All that was left was some ninety acres of the old family farm. It went to Abner, my grandaddy."

Strawberry failed to turn up the next afternoon. Moses was seated alone when one of the rich cottagers stumbled into The Caboose. Clearly distressed, he held a slip of paper before him like a shield to guard against contagious diseases. "*Pardonnez moi,*" he said, "*mais je cherche —* "

"We speak English here," Bunk said.

"I'm looking for Mr. Strawberry Watson, the house painter. I was told he lived up on the hill, just past Maltby's Pond, but the only house I could see there is obviously abandoned. It's unpainted, the grass hasn't been cut, and the yard is full of rusting automobile parts."

"You found it, mister."

The day Moses drove in from the clinic in New Hampshire, Gord, who owned The Caboose, was tending bar. He wore a black T-shirt embossed with a multi-coloured dawn. A slogan was stencilled over it:

I'M FEELING SO HORNY
Even The Crack of Dawn Looks Good To Me.

After a hard Saturday night Gord's first wife, Madge, had died in a head-on collision on the 105, totalling their brand new Dodge pickup in the bargain, and ever since Gord wouldn't hear of buying another new truck. "I mean, shit, you drive it out of the dealer's lot and five minutes later it's already second-hand, ain't it? Like my new wife."

His new wife was the widow Hawkins. The courtship had been brief. One afternoon, only a couple of months after he had buried Madge, Gord got into a bad fight in The Thirsty Boot with Sneaker over his wife, Suzy. Actually Sneaker wasn't living with his wife at the time, but was shacked up with a hooker from the Venus di Milo in a trailer tucked into the woods off the 112. Still, he resented anybody else cutting his grass. Gord made the mistake of saying, "I don't know why you ever left her. As far as I'm concerned, she's still awful good fucking, eh?"

Gord, nursing a sore jaw and a couple of loose teeth, carried on to The Snakepit, Crystal Lake Inn, Chez Bobby, and the Brome Lake Hotel, stopping somewhere along the line to buy supplies at a *dépanneur*. Tins of baked beans and soups, a bag of frozen fries, some TV dinners, and a big bag of Fritos. He also bought a chicken and made straight for the widow Hawkins's cabin in South Bolton, kicking in the door at two A.M. "I'm tired of eatin' shit. So this here is a chicken," he said. "Got it at a *dépanneur*. You cook it good for my dinner tomorrow night and I'll fucken marry you. But if it's tough, forget it, eh?"

Gord liked to post items clipped from the *Gazette* on his notice board. Once it was the news that troopers in Vermont had arrested a man wanted for the serial murders of thirty-two women within the past five years.

"He sure as hell shouldn'ta done that," Strawberry said. "There ain't enough of them to go around as it is."

One of the men who frequented The Caboose ran a gravel pit, another owned a dairy farm, others picked up carpentry jobs here and there, and still more worked as caretakers or handymen for the rich cottagers on the lake. For most of them it was a matter of stitching twenty weeks of summer work together in order to qualify for unemployment insurance in the winter. Failing that they went on welfare, bolstering their take on the barter system. If Sneaker painted Gord's barn he came away with a side of beef. If Legion Hall retiled Mike's roof he could have the hay from the field across the road and sell it in Vermont for $2.50 a bundle. The men owned their own cottages, cut their own winter wood, and counted on shooting a deer in November. Some of the wives worked on the assembly line in the Clairol factory in Knowlton and others served as cleaning ladies for the cottagers on the lake. The wives, who usually gathered at their own tables in The Caboose, ran to fat, bulging out of tank tops and stretchy pink polyester slacks.

Moses usually avoided The Caboose on Friday night, Band Night, which brought out the noisy younger crowd, who were quickly herded into the basement, where—according to Strawberry—they smoked Hi-Test. "You know, whacky tobaccy." But he seldom failed to turn up for the Sunday night steak dinner because Gord's father, old Albert Crawley, was always there. Albert remembered Solomon Gursky from the days, during Prohibition, when he used to run convoys of the booze into Vermont through the old Leadville road. More than once, Albert said, the word out, the road bristling with customs men or hijackers, they had hidden the stuff in the old talc mine, which had been in the Gursky family since 1852. Other times they had unloaded the shipment at Hector Gagnon's farm, which straddled the border, packed it in saddlebags that were strapped to the backs of cattle, and drove the herd into Vermont at three A.M.

After Albert was badly wounded one night, taking it in the gut, Solomon set him up in a hotel in Abercorn, and weekends couples drove in from as far away as Boston and New York. W.C. Fields had slept there. So had Fanny Brice. Once Dutch Schultz, accompanied by Charles "the Bug" Workman, had come to look over the hotel, but Albert had sent for Solomon, who had hurried out from Montreal with some girls from the Normandy Roof Bar, smoothing everything out nicely. Then along came Repeal, rendering the hotel redundant, and it became necessary to burn it down for the insurance money.

Whenever Moses turned up at The Caboose after a long absence Gord would send somebody to fetch his father. He

would also, as he did the day Moses drove back from New
Hampshire, unlock a cabinet under the bar and fish out a
bottle of Glenlivet, which Albert and Moses, in a joke they
never tired of, would call Glen Levitt. This in remembrance of
the time Mr. Bernard, never a great speller, had ordered the
wrong labels for a shipment, endearing himself to Solomon
for once.

"Legion Hall has a pile of mail for you," Strawberry
said.

"Let the man enjoy his drink," Albert said.

"Hold the phone, he don't any more."

"Again?"

"Yeah."

Albert Crawley's head bobbed upright. He began to laugh
and cough at the same time, heaving, spilling tears and
phlegm. "If I could drink with Solomon Gursky just one more
time they could plant me happy tomorrow." Then his head
slumped forward and in his mind's eye Albert Crawley was out
there with Solomon again, standing in the dark of Hector
Gagnon's farm on this side of the border, waiting for the long
overdue blinking headlights from the other side, a perplexed
Solomon digging out his cherished gold pocket watch again,
the watch that had once belonged to his grandfather and was
engraved:

> From W.N. to E.G.
> *de bono et malo.*

Albert had held his cigarette lighter to Solomon's watch
and the instant it had flared the firing had started and
Solomon had pulled Albert down into the tall grass with him,
but too late.

"Pour me another one of them Glen Levitts, will you,
Moses?"

NINE

◆

Moses was wakened the next morning by a phone call from Gitel Kugelmass's daughter. Gitel had been arrested for shop-lifting at Holt Renfrew. Other ladies, Moses reflected, might be caught pilfering at Miracle Mart, even Eaton's, but for *die Roite Gitel* it had to be Montreal's classiest emporium. Moses agreed to drive into Montreal and take Gitel to lunch at the Ritz "for a talk," something he hadn't done for several years.

In her late seventies, somewhat shrunken but unbent, Gitel still favoured a big floppy hat, a fox collar more moth-eaten than ever, antique rings. But her startling makeup, more suitable to a harlequin, was applied with a tremulous hand now, an unsure eye. A nimbus of too-generously applied powder trailed after her. Cheeks burning bright with rouge suggested fever more readily than *femme fatale*.

"I realize," Moses said, "that you meant to pay for the perfume, you forgot, but please be careful in the future, Gitel, now that you have been charged once."

She thought it best not to correct him. Instead she said, "Isn't all property theft?"

"Yes, certainly, but there are still some unenlightened running dogs of capitalism about who see things differently."

They fell to reminiscing about the dining-room table with the crocheted tablecloth, L.B. reading one of his stories aloud.

"Were you too young to remember, Moishe, when Kronitz carried me off to the mountains to take his pleasure with me?"

Bits of green pasta adhered to her feathery moustache and clacky dentures.

"Too young to remember? Gitel, it broke my heart."

Kronitz had been carried off by cancer long since. Kugelmass, hopelessly dotty, was wasting in the Jewish Old People's Home. Gitel dabbed at her tears with a black lace handkerchief, an Ogilvy's price tag dangling from one of its corners. "Does anybody care about our stories now? Who will sing our songs, Moishe, or remember me when my breath was still sweet?" *Die Roite Gitel* fumbled in her handbag and brought out a sterling silver compact. "Birks," she said. "Now tell me how come a handsome boy like you, such a catch, isn't married yet with children?"

"Well, Gitel, if only I had been somewhat older and you just a little younger," he said, reaching out to squeeze her knee, frail as a chicken bone.

"Oh you're such a devil you. So why did you ever break up with Solomon Gursky's daughter? What's her name? Remind me."

"Lucy."

"Lucy. Of course. Everything she touches on Broadway turns to gold. If it's a hit, she's got a piece of it. And her dacha in Southampton, it was featured in *People*, you could die. She collects those paintings, you know the kind I mean, they look like blow-ups from comic books. Oy, what a world we live in today. Did you know that the Chinese now rent out railway crews and construction gangs to richer Asian countries? Fifty years after the Long March they're back in the coolie business."

"And *die Roite Gitel* reads *People*."

"Moishe, you could have been living on easy street."

"Like father, like son."

"Shame on you. I never blamed L.B. for writing those speeches for Mr. Bernard. As for the others, with the exception of Shloime Bishinsky and maybe Schneiderman, it was envy pure and simple. Those days. My God, my God. Before you were even a *bar mitzvah* boy, the Gurskys were mobsters as far as our group was concerned. Capitalism's ugliest face, as we used to say. Then when I led the girls out against Fancy Finery during that terrible heat wave you could die, certainly nobody could sleep, and there was *bupkes* left in our pathetic strike fund, guess what? Knock knock at my door. Who's there? Not the RCMP this time. Not the provincials again. But Solomon's man, your buddy Tim Callaghan with a satchel and in it there is twenty-five thousand dollars in hard cash and that isn't the best of it. Buses will pick up the strikers and their kids on Friday afternoon to take them to the mountains for a week. Everybody's invited. What are you talking about, I say? Even Solomon Gursky can't have a big enough house in the mountains for that bunch. They're going to Ste.-Adèle, Callaghan says, and there will be rooms for everybody. Tell them to bring bathing suits. Hey, hey there, I say, Ste.-Adèle's restricted, no Jews or dogs on the beach. Just make sure, Callaghan says, that everybody's gathered outside here by four o'clock.

"So when they finally put Solomon on trial I naturally had to get to see our benefactor up close. It wasn't easy. Listen, you'd think it was John Barrymore playing His Majesty's Theatre, or today say one of those rockers who dress like girls singing at the Forum, you had to line up for hours before the courtroom opened. Not only Jews waiting to get in, but *mafiosi* from the States. And big-shot *goyishe* lawyers there to take notes if one of their bosses' names is taken in vain. And all those debutantes of his, mooning over him. I didn't blame them one bit. If Solomon Gursky had curled his little finger at me, I would have quit the Party. Anything. But it wasn't me he had eyes for. It was obviously somebody who never turned up."

Yes, Moses thought, one eye brown, one eye blue.

"Every time the courtroom door opened he looked up from the table, but it was never whoever he was waiting for."

"Were you in court when the customs inspector testified?"

This country, Solomon had written in his journal, *has no tap root. Instead there's Bert Smith. The very essence.*

"Who?"

"Bert Smith."

"No. I was there the day of the fat Chinaman, you know the one who was supposed to have known plenty. Well let me tell you he waddled up to the witness stand and he couldn't even button his suit jacket over his belly, but then he stopped and looked at Solomon and Solomon smiled and said something to him in Chinese, and I've never seen anything so amazing in my life. By the time the fat Chinaman sat down in the box his suit seemed too large for him, he was swimming in it, and he couldn't remember a thing."

"I'll tell you what he said to him. '*Tiu na xinq*', which means 'Fuck your name'," Moses said, and then he asked Gitel if she would like a liqueur with her coffee.

"What about you?" she asked, fishing.

"I don't these days."

"Thank God for that much." She ordered a B & B. "And what are you living on now that you can afford to invite me to the Ritz for a flirt?"

"This and that."

"And what do you do out there, buried in that cabin in the woods?"

If he told her the truth her manner would change, she would begin to humour him, an unredeemed nut-case, obsessed with delusions about Solomon Gursky. Moses lit a cigar. "I go to A.A. meetings. I read. I watch hockey games on TV."

"*Oy*, Moishe, Moishe, we all had such hopes for you. What kind of life is that?"

"Enough personal questions for one day."

Gitel refused to let him put her in a taxi, saying, "You sit here and drink your coffee. I've got some shopping to do."

"Gitel, for Christ's sake!"

Outside, maybe a half hour later, Moses found her wandering down Sherbrooke Street, looking stricken. "It's my address," she said, tumbling into his arms. "I know I'm staying with my daughter, but sometimes I just can't remember . . ."

Moses drove Gitel home, out to the suburban barrens of Côte St. Luc, then he made right for the Eastern Townships Autoroute, peeling off at exit 106. Back in his cabin, he flicked on the TV and Sam Birenbaum's face filled the screen. Sam, who had fallen out with the network years ago, now pontificated on PBS.

My God, Moses thought, lighting a Monte Cristo, how many years was it since Sam had taken him to that lunch at Sardi's? Twenty-five at least. "I've got something absolutely ridiculous to tell you," Sam had said. "CBS wants to hire me for more than twice what I'm earning now and send me to London. But if I leave the *Times* I could freelance. Molly thinks it's time I got some real writing done."

"Ah ha."

"What are you ah-ha-ing me for? I hate TV and everybody associated with it. It's out of the question."

Moses flicked off the TV, poured himself a Perrier, and resolved once more to sort out the clutter in his cabin, starting tomorrow.

There was a shelf laden with material on Marilyn Monroe, including a photograph taken at Peter Lawford's beach house and Dr. Noguchi's autopsy report. The photograph, taken in July 1962, showed a group sipping cocktails at Lawford's poolside: Marilyn Monroe, President Kennedy, and several unidentified figures, among them an old man seated in a chair, a malacca cane held between his knees, his hands clasped over the handle, his chin resting on his hands. Dr. Noguchi's autopsy notes described Marilyn as a "36-year-old, well-developed, well-nourished Caucasian female weighing 117 pounds and measuring 65½ inches in height." He ascribed the cause of death to "acute barbiturate poisoning due to ingestion of overdose." Moses had attached a file card and a telegram to the report with a paper clip. The file card noted that the FBI had impounded the tapes of the phone numbers Marilyn had dialled on her last day. The telegram, sent to Moses from Madrid and of course unsigned, read: I KNOW WHAT YOU ARE THINKING BUT THE LAST PHONE CALL WAS NOT FROM ME. I TRUST THE WORK GOES WELL.

Moses's work table was strewn with xeroxed pages from Solomon's journals, tantalizing segments mailed to him when least expected from Moscow, Antibes, Saigon, Santa Barbara, Yellowknife, and Rio de Janeiro. The pages sent from Rio de Janeiro began with a description of the dragon's chair:

"The accused was obliged to sit in a chair, like one in a barber shop, to which he was tied with straps covered over with foam rubber, while other foam rubber strips covered his body; they tied his fingers with electric wires, and his toes also, and began administering a series of electric shocks; at the same time, another torturer with an electric stick gave him shocks between the legs and on the penis."

An earlier volume was introduced with lines from Milton's *Samson Agonistes*

> All mortals I excell'd, and great in hopes . . .
> Fearless of danger, like a petty god
> I walk'd about admir'd of all and dreaded
> On hostile ground, none daring my affront.

The margins of each page of the journals were crammed with notes and queries and cross-references in Moses's untidy scrawl. See Otto Braun, *A Comintern Agent in China, 1932–39*. Check Li Chuang on *Snowy Mountains and Marshy Grasslands*. Smedley and Snow contradict each other here. Consult Liu Po-cheng, *Recalling the Long March, Eyewitness Accounts*.

Solomon's Chinese journals luxuriated in detailed descriptions of barbarism. A Twenty-fifth Army scout, captured by the KMT, suffers the death of a thousand cuts. A weeping KMT spy is buried alive in the sand. A landlord's head is lopped off in Hadapu, his last words, *Tiu na xinq*. There were acid portraits of Braun, the womanizer; Manfred Stern, later celebrated as General Kleber in Spain; Steve Nelson and Earl Browder in Shanghai; Richard Sorge's arrival. There was also an unflattering sketch of a forty-year-old Mao, long before he took charge. Gaunt, eyes burning, suffering from malaria.

Other pages dealt with the crossing of the Great Grasslands, that treacherous plateau, eleven thousand feet high, between the watersheds of the Yellow and Yangtze Rivers. Late August 1935 that was, and the journey, which took six days and many lives, was undoubtedly the worst ordeal of the Long March. There were no signposts, no trails, no food, no yaks, no herdsmen. Solomon, who claimed that he was with the Fourth

Regiment of the First Army Corps, calculating that they were the first human beings in three thousand years to pass through the tall, sometimes poisonous grass.

Rain, sleet, hail, wind, fog, and frost. For the most part the men chewed raw unmilled wheat. It ripped their intestines, bloodied their bowels. Some died of dysentery, others of diarrhoea. The Tibetan muck, Solomon wrote, reminded him of Vimy Ridge. Men being sucked into the bog, disappearing. Unfortunately there were no fat corpse rats to roast. When they did find sufficient twigs for a fire, the men boiled leather belts and harnesses. The starving and feverish soldiers of the rear guard were driven to searching through the feces of fallen comrades for undigested grains of corn or wheat. Then, on the fifth day, Solomon's bunch was lost in fog and frost. What appeared to be a trail made by the advance guard led them to a ditch filled with stagnant water. Late the next morning, a fierce wind blew the fog away. Then a raven appeared out of nowhere, soaring and swooping, and the men followed it to the banks of the Hou River. On the far bank, where there was dry ground and some wood to be found, they built a camp-fire and roasted their few remaining grains of unmilled wheat.

Chang-feng Chen, Moses had scribbled in a margin, mentioned the raven. So did Hi Hsin, who wrote that just before the appearance of the big black bird Solomon had tramped up and down, searching the skies, some sort of sad clacking noise, an inhuman call, coming from the back of his throat.

TEN

◆

Bert Smith had been living in Montreal for ten years now, since 1963, renting a room with kitchen privileges from a Mrs. Jenkins. He was used to being laughed at. Striding back from the meeting in the church basement in his scout master's uniform, a scrawny seventy-year-old, his snaggle teeth still in place, he had to endure the oily Greeks nudging each other on their stoops, setting down their cans of Molson to belch. He was obliged to tolerate the whistles of French-Canadian factory girls with curlers in their hair. Street urchins with scraped knees were sent out to torment him, buzzing him on their skateboards. "Hey, sir, you want to 'be prepared', wear a safe."

Their ridicule, far from being humiliating, was fortifying. His crown of thorns. Rome was laid waste by the vandals and Canada, corrupt beyond salvation, would fall to the mongrels. The native-born young of the once True North, Strong and Free undone by jungle music, rampaging sex and the sloth licensed by a Judas state.

Case in point.

Last summer there had been two able-bodied men sharing the room next to his own in Mrs. Jenkins's house. Both white, both Christian. They slept in until noon, then caught the latest porn movie at The Pussycat, subsisting on welfare, leaving instructions for their cheques to be forwarded to Fort Lauderdale during the winter. One day an indignant Smith invited them into his room and showed them a faded photograph of his parents taken in front of their sod hut in Gloriana. His father pale and wasted, his mother, who couldn't have been more than twenty-five, looking more washed out than her calico dress. "Theirs was the indomitable spirit that tamed the wilderness," Smith said. "Look at Saskatoon now. Or Regina."

"I been there, Smitty, and they're so far behind the times there's still dinosaur shit on the sidewalks."

"Where would this country be today had it been left to your sort to pioneer the west?"

One of the men asked if he could borrow a ten spot until Monday.

"No way," Smith said.

Mrs. Jenkins, a good sort, was blessed with a lively sense of humour.

Question: What is a nigger carpenter's favourite tool?

Answer: A jigsaw.

He did not have to worry about Jews on the street that he lived on in lowest Westmount, just this side of the railroad tracks. The street of peeling rooming houses with rotting, lopsided porches was altogether too poor for that lot. Even so, there was no shortage of trash. Noisy Greek immigrants cultivating tomato plants in rock-hard back yards. Swarthy, fart-filled Italians. Forlorn French-Canadian factory girls spilling over $4.99 plastic chairs from Miracle Mart, yammering each to each. West Indians with that arrogant stride that made you want to belt them one. Polacks, Portuguese. "Happily," he once said to Mrs. Jenkins, "we will not live long enough to see Canada become a mongrelized country."

The concern, deeply felt, came naturally to Smith, an Anglo-Saxon westerner, born and bred.

Back in 1907, the legendary Canadian journalist John Dafoe wrote an article aimed at enticing American immigrants to the prairie, assuring them there was no chance of a mongrel race or civilization taking hold in western Canada.

Yes, there had been an influx of land-hungry foreigners, but most of them were of Teutonic and Scandinavian stock. The only alien race present in numbers in the west, the Slavs, were being rapidly Anglicized. Mind you, among more fastidious westerners there was also considerable concern about the quality of British immigrants. J.S. Woodsworth, who would become a saint in the Canadian socialist pantheon, a founder of the CCF party, worried in *Strangers Within Our Gates or Coming Canadians*, published in 1909, about the immigration of Dr. Barnardo's urchins with their inherited tendencies to evil. He liked to tell the story of how an English magistrate had chastised a young offender: "You have broken your mother's heart, you have brought down your father's grey hairs in sorrow to the grave. You are a disgrace to your country. Why don't you go to Canada?"

The British, Woodsworth protested, were dumping the effluvium of their slums on the prairie. A case in point, certainly, was Bert Smith's father, Archie. A child of Brixton's Cold Harbour Lane, apprenticed to a butcher at the age of twelve, he married Nancy, the dim daughter of a neighbouring greengrocer ten years later, and then in 1901 had the misfortune to attend a free lecture by the Reverend Ishmael Horn. Short of stature, this obviously worthy greybeard with the hot black eyes was a compelling figure, eloquent as well, extolling the virtues of Gloriana, his projected all-British colony in the Canadian west. To begin with, however, the Reverend Horn ridiculed the wretched circumstances under which his audience lived now. "Look at you," he said, "packed like sardines in stinking hovels, enduring the rich man's contumely, your bairns prey to pulmonary consumption and rickets." His voice soaring, he told them about the fertile land with the invigorating climate that awaited them; a land where they could sow wheat and grow apple and pear trees; a veritable parkland rich in game of all kinds; a land of sweet grass and sparkling streams and brooks filled with leaping trout. Two hundred acres of their own choosing were there for the asking, he said. A manner of homestead that only the toffs could afford on this blighted island.

So Archie and Nancy Smith joined the queue, filling out the necessary forms for the Reverend Horn's secretary, the fetching Miss Olivia Litton, whom some would later remark had reeked suspiciously of spirituous liquors at the time. They signed the forms and pledged to pay a deposit against passage money within the week.

Some months before, the Reverend Horn had been to see an official of the Canadian Immigration Department in Ottawa.

"Sir, I cannot tell you how it grieves me to see the pristine prairie, the fine British province of Saskatchewan, polluted by dirty, ignorant Slavs in their lice-ridden sheepskin coats, and by the mad followers of Prince Kropotkin and Count Leo Tolstoy, the latter a novelist who celebrates adultery. Why are we welcoming these peasants when stout British yeomen, men of valour who held the thin red line against the Dervishes at Omdurman and marched through the Transvaal with Kitchener, are crying out for land?"

The Reverend Horn promised to deliver four thousand skilled farmers, the flower of the sceptr'd isle, to the prairie at five dollars a head. In exchange he was granted an option on homesteads in twelve townships in Northern Saskatchewan, the wilderness where he was to establish the all-British colony of Gloriana. He was also provided with a Boer War troopship, the Dominion Line's *Excelsior*, at Liverpool dock. The *Excelsior*, later to be dubbed the *Excrement* by its discontented passengers, was originally built to accommodate seven hundred cavalrymen and their horses. But on March 10, 1902, some two thousand emigrants were caught in the scrimmage on the gangway, the first of the settlers bound for the promised land of Gloriana. Among them was a terrified Archie with Nancy bearing her budgerigar in a cage. There were scrofulous Cockneys, Welsh miners spitting coal dust, and navvies from the Gorbals already staggering drunk. There were women with howling babes in their arms and children scurrying here, there, and everywhere, out to steal anything that wasn't nailed down. There were parrots and canaries and yelping dogs and a pet goat that would be roasted long before they reached Halifax.

Standing on the dock, acknowledging cheers, the Reverend Horn called out, "We are bound for the land of milk and

honey," and then disappeared into his cabin, Miss Litton
following after.

The settlers were far out to sea, sliding in vomit, before they
grasped that there was no bread and that the potatoes were
rotten and the meat crawling with maggots and the walls of
the hold they were crammed into thick with manure, the
pitching deck awash with overflow from the bilges, rats
everywhere.

In two weeks at sea the Reverend Horn, secure in his cabin,
was seen below decks only twice. On the fourth day out a
miner had his arm broken in a drunken brawl and it was the
Reverend Horn who set the bone and fixed it with a splint. He
was seen again after another fight, this one with knives, come
to stitch the men's wounds. But a certain Mrs. Bishop swore
she had seen him striding up and down the bridge the night
of the gale, the puny *Excelsior* scaling twenty-foot waves before
plunging into a trough, sliding trunks smashing into walls,
splinters flying, the ship's fracturing surely imminent. Bare-
chested he was, drunken, howling into the lashing wind
and rain. "Face to face, I want to see you face to face just
once."

Finally they docked at Halifax and were promptly bundled
into a train for the endless journey to Saskatoon, from where
they were supposed to trek by ox-cart a hundred and fifty miles
to Gloriana. Saskatoon, a smudge on the prairie, had no
common or shade trees or hedgerows or high street or vicarage
or public house. Instead there were mosquitoes and mud, rude
shacks, two hotels, a general store, a grain elevator, and a
railroad station.

The Reverend Horn had promised them that all manner of
necessities would be waiting for them at the station: oxen and
wagons, tents, farming tools, seed bags, and provisions. They
saw little enough of that and beyond, not a knoll, not a tree,
but a flat empty land extending to the horizon. The women sat
down on their scattered belongings, kitbags eaten by salt
water, trunks split and leaking cutlery, and wept for the
warrens they had left behind. The men, armed with clubs and
knives, a few of them with shotguns, demanded an audience
with the Reverend Horn. And when he appeared, mounting

an ox-cart and calling for silence, they surged forward, jeering, shaking their fists. The Reverend Horn, unconcerned, paced up and down the ox-cart, searching the skies, some sort of sad clacking noise, an inhuman call, coming from the back of his throat. A raven flew out of the clouds, swooped, and lighted on his shoulder, which silenced the mob. The Reverend Horn, his eyes hot, reminded them of the ingratitude the children of Israel had shown Moses, their deliverer, rebelling against him. " 'Would to God we had died by the hand of the Lord in the land of Egypt, when we sat down by the flesh pots and when we did eat bread to the full; for ye have brought us forth into this wilderness, to kill this whole assembly with hunger.' " Then the reverend said, "If any of you are so fainthearted as to want to turn back after all you have endured, board the train. I will stand your return fare to England. But rest assured that those who stay with me are visionaries, the first of the millions who will settle these rich fertile plains. I cannot provide you with manna. But within the hour those among you who are bound with me for Gloriana will be served hot soup and freshly baked bread. There will also be a keg of rum to celebrate our safe passage over stormy seas. Then it's westward ho to Gloriana, my good fellows!"

The Smiths survived but one year in Gloriana, fighting grass fires in the heat of summer and the bitter cold in winter, their only commercial crop buffalo bones for which they were paid six dollars a ton.

Following their flight from the colony, the Smiths moved back to Saskatoon, a town prone to drought and grasshopper plagues and early frost, founded by a group of liquor-hating Methodists out of Ontario intent on establishing a settlement where temperance would be the unbroken rule. Then the Smiths retreated to an even smaller railroad town. Archie found employment in a butchershop, stuffing sausages for a Galician; and Nancy as a dishwasher in McGraw's Queen Victoria Hotel, until she discovered exactly what was going on there and fled, taking another job, this one as a waitress in Mrs. Kukulowicz's Regal Perogie House.

Bert, born in 1903, had a strict upbringing. When he wet his bed, his father clipped a clothespin to his penis, and Bert was soon cured of that habit. His mother, horrified to discover that he was left-handed, tied the offending arm behind his back at mealtimes until he learned to behave properly. If she caught him reading a cowboy novel or daydreaming on the sofa, she immediately set him to doing chores. "Every day, every hour," she reminded him on his twelfth birthday, "you are drawing closer to the grave and the final judgement. See to it that sloth is not numbered among the sins you must answer for."

Ordered to bathe once a week in a galvanized tub, Bert was instructed never to wash his face in the same water in which he had scrubbed his privates, but to do that in untainted water in the sink, a habit that survived into his seventies. Sheets stained during the night required him to lower his trousers and submit to a thrashing from his father.

Bert Smith's father refused to chip in with the barbershop layabouts, a bunch of get-rich-quickers, risking his meagre savings when land fever struck the town in 1910, prices soaring. He was proved right when the boom collapsed so suddenly in 1913. "What you want to learn," he told Bert again and again, "is never to take foolish risks, the devil's temptations, but to get your schooling right and to qualify for a desk job in government service, the pay regular, the position proof against hard times, a pension guaranteed."

When Smith and Mrs. Jenkins sat down to their Sugar Pops with milk in the morning, he often amused her by reading items aloud from the *Gazette*. At a time, for instance, when unemployment was running at twelve percent, he came across something interesting in E.J. Gordon's social column. " 'Pot O' Gold, a unique wine-and-cheese party will be held by the Montreal section of the National Council of Jewish Women on Wednesday, February 4, from six to eight P.M. in Victoria Hall, Westmount. A pot of $10,000 will be won by a lucky ticket holder who paid $100 for a chance to win. Ticket sales are limited to three hundred and fifty.' "

"Drat it," Mrs. Jenkins said, "I suppose we're too late to buy."

" ' "The idea originated with our co-president, Mrs. Ida Gursky," said publicity chairperson Mrs. Jewel Pinsky. "We thought that offering a car as a prize was quite simply too blah.

As a gimmick it has been used too often. Then Mrs. Gursky had an inspiration. Why not a bar of gold?" ' "

As soon as she read the funny page and her horoscope, Mrs. Jenkins passed the *Gazette* on to Smith, who retired to his room with it. There was no respite. No solace. Not even on the sports pages, where he read of a nigger, freaky tall, who was paid better than a million a year for dumping balls into a basket, and of another nigger, earning even more, because he could strike a ball with a stick one time out of three. The latter's manager said, "Elroy comes to play every day. He always gives 110 percent."

Once, watching a baseball game with Mrs. Jenkins, they saw Elroy come to bat. "Look at him," Mrs. Jenkins said, "he never steps up to the plate he doesn't fondle his crown jewels. Rocky Colavito came up to bat he used to cross himself. Those were the days, eh, Bert?"

Whenever he was invited to watch TV with Mrs. Jenkins, her hair done in sausage curls, she provided the Kool-Aid and he contributed the Hostess Twinkies. On occasion Smith found her distressingly coarse. Once, for instance, exploding with mirth at a "Laugh-In" outrage, she shot him a sidelong glance, decidedly coquettish, and asked, "Hey, do you know the definition of an Eskimo with a hard-on?"

"Certainly not."

"A frigid midget with a rigid digit. Whoops. Sorry. I know you don't enjoy the off-colour."

Another night she was watching "Wagon Train" with Smith when a young man came to the door and asked to see the room she had for rent. His hair was blond but his eyebrows were black and he was wearing an earring. So she sent him away. Then she came mincing back into the parlour, her wrists hanging limp, and asked, "Do you know why there won't be any homos left after the year 2000?"

No answer.

"Because they don't reproduce and they eat each other."

Smith groaned.

"Oh, come off it, Bert. I think that was very cute."

Trying to make amends the next morning she passed him, along with the *Gazette*, the only hardback book she had ever bought: Rod McKuen's *Listen to the Warm*. Smith didn't bother

with it, but he did look at the *Gazette*. Mr. Bernard was going
to be seventy-five. A huge banquet in his honour would
be held in the Ritz-Carlton Hotel. An indignant Smith
crumpled the newspaper, dropped it to the floor, and reached
for his bedside Bible.

> Wherefore do the wicked live, become old, yea, are
>   mighty in power?
> Their seed is established in their sight with them, and
>   their offspring before their eyes.
> Their houses are safe from fear, neither is the rod of
>   God upon them.

TWO

ONE

◆

1973 it was. Out there on the rim of the world, in Tulugaqtitut, hard by the shore of the Beaufort Sea, midnight had come and gone, the fierce summer sun still riding high in the sky. Henry Gursky set his book aside—*Pirke Aboth, Sayings of the Fathers*—to glance out of the window. *Unto thee, O Lord, do I lift up my soul.*

Obviously the Otter was going to be late again, but it would turn up eventually, unless the pilot out of Yellowknife had been diverted by an emergency call. Or he's drunk again, Henry thought. Tomorrow's flight wouldn't do, it would be too late. Henry sighed and reached out to stroke his son's sleek black hair. "*Aleph,*" he said.

"*Aleph.*"

"*Beth.*"

"Not now," Isaac pleaded, "it's time."

"Oh yes, sorry." Remembering, Henry reached out to flick the dial of his radio. Isaac's eyes shone with pleasure as the familiar sounds reverberated through the living room of the pre-fab.

A gale-force wind raging across the barrens. The distant howl of a wolf. Electronic music, something from another world. "Into every life some rain must fall," the narrator began solemnly. "In Captain Al Cohol's case, catastrophe cascades upon his great blond head in a steady downpour."

Henry clacked his tongue; he slapped his cheek, simulating fear. Isaac, burrowing more deeply into the sofa, tugged absently at the ritual fringes of his undershirt. Four fringes there were, each fringe comprised of twelve silken strands.

"Once the good-hearted defender of the people of Fish Fiord against the monstrous Raven Men, Captain Al Cohol had descended into the gutter, deposited there by the poisonous effects of booze. First a beer parlour brawl, then a night in jail, and now an interview with the welfare people in Inuvik."

Fading in, the welfare worker said, "Now then, let's fill in the necessary forms, shall we? Your name is?"

"Captain Al Cohol, Intergalactic 80321."

"Yes . . . and your last address?"

"737 Twelve Moon Avenue, province of Lutania, planet Barkelda."

Oy vey, Henry thought, giving his son a gleeful poke. Isaac responded with a giggle.

"Fine, just fine. Now then, your profession?"

"Intergalactic space commander, with degrees in antigravity science and ionic transmutation."

"That's a problem of course. We don't have much call for that kind of thing around Inuvik. Unfortunately a person can be too highly qualified. What happened to your clothes? Were you forced to sell them?"

"Sir, these are my clothes. This is the fashion of the day on Barkelda."

"Not all that practical in the north. You'll never get a job anywhere around here wearing yellow, red, and blue underwear. We've got to get you into something decent and warm. And your hair! Shoulder-length hair just isn't in in Inuvik."

"I haven't had a chance to cut it for centuries."

"You can have it now. Captain Al Cohol, you have been highly recommended to us by the RCMP who state that Nurse Alley has given you the highest character references. Here is fifty dollars. Go and buy warm, decent clothing and a respectable haircut."

"I can't do this. I've never accepted charity in my life."

"False pride. We're here to help you, if you are prepared to help yourself. But stay away from alcohol, captain."

"I promise you by all the galaxies! Thank you and goodbye."

Henry, hearing an engine, leaned forward to peer out of the window, but it wasn't the Otter. It was a charter, a DC-3. On the radio, a door opened and closed. Street noises were heard. The narrator faded in, saying, "Out in the cold, inclement streets of Inuvik, Captain Al Cohol's heart was still laden over the loss of the lovely Lois. Somehow he must regain his pride and prove himself worthy of the brave little nurse of the north. But meanwhile he has the nagging need for nutriment and a place to sleep for the night. He finds a transient centre where he can bunk down with the other lost souls like himself."

Henry glanced out of the window again, unavailingly, and the next thing he knew Captain Al Cohol had fallen in with the ruffians in the transient centre, joining them in a poker game.

"This is a friendly game, stranger, and to make it friendlier I got a treat for all of us, a jug of moose milk. You ever tasted moose milk?"

"Never, but it sounds nutritious. I haven't eaten in some time."

"Good. Let's pour a round before we deal a game."

Glug, glug, glug.

"Drink up, stranger."

The narrator intervened, alarmed. "DON'T DO IT, CAPTAIN AL COHOL! YOU'LL BE RIGHT BACK WHERE YOU STARTED — IN THE GUTTER AGAIN!"

Glug, glug, glug.

"The valiant wanderer from outer space may have stepped out of the frying pan into the fire. Keep your fingers crossed and wait 'til the next episode in the ordeals of Captain Al Cohol, the hapless nomad of the high north."

The episode was followed by the usual warning that alcohol

can make you a different man, and that once hooked on liquor it was a hard habit to break. Like God, Henry thought, surprised by his own irreverence.

"So if you can't help yourself, call on someone who can, Alcohol Education, Government of the Northwest Territories, NWT."

Henry switched off the radio but continued to sit by the window, searching the heavens from time to time, a Bible open on his lap.

> By the rivers of Babylon, there we sat down, yea, we wept, when we remembered Zion.
> We hanged our harps upon the willows in the midst thereof.
> For there they that carried us away captive required of us a song; and they that wasted us required of us mirth, saying, Sing us one of the songs of Zion.
> How shall we sing the Lord's song in a strange land?

It was past one A.M. when he saw a dot in the distance. Gradually it sprouted wings, it grew a tail, both with blinking red lights attached. Lowering, it bounced in the wind, the wings fluttering. The Otter finally circled the bay — swinging out — banking — seemingly consumed by the blazing sun before it was miraculously there again, sinking, settling into the freezing water, kicking up skirts of spray.

Henry Gursky slipped into his parka and mukluks and started for the dock, wheeling a porter's cart before him. Henry, in his early forties, was a sinewy man with an inky black beard and long dancing sidecurls; he was knobby, with a gleeful face. Solomon's face. A knitted *yarmulke* was fastened like a stopper to his thin black hair. He waved at the settlement children and the hunters who had already gathered in the bay, happy for a diversion. Two grey seals, freshly killed, lay gleaming on the rocks, their eyeballs torn out, the sockets bleeding, festooned with black flies already feasting there.

The pilot, new to North of Sixty, had heard enough gossip in The Gold Range Bar in Yellowknife to inquire after the settlement nurse. "Tell her I have a surprise for her," he said.

Henry greeted the pilot with a smile. "*Baroch ha'bo*," he called out.

Squinting, suspicious, the pilot demanded, "What's that mean?"

"Translated loosely it means 'blessed be the arrival.' "

"You must be Gursky."

"Indeed I am. Did you bring it?"

"You bet."

It was the familiar zinc half-trunk, battered, but the locks intact. When the oil drillers of Inuvik, largely southern flotsam, had begun to move marijuana and even more lethal stuff through the territory, an alert RCMP corporal, unfamiliar with Henry, had asked him, his manner correct but firm, to unlock the half-trunk right there. Henry had obliged and the corporal, probing the contents, peering quizzically at the bill of lading, had shaken his head, incredulous.

"I never expected to find a Jew in such rough country," the pilot said.

"We're an astonishing people. Dandelions, my father used to say. Dig us out here and riding the wind and the rain we take root there. Any mail for me?"

There was a copy of *Newsweek*, a pensive John Dean filling the cover; two back issues of *The Beaver*; a quarterly report from James McTavish Distillers Ltd. and a cheque for $2,114,626.17; a gun catalogue from Abercrombie & Fitch; a copy of *The Moshiach* (or Messiah) *Times* for Isaac; a letter from the Rebbe at 770 Eastern Parkway, Brooklyn; another letter from the Crédit-Suisse; a parcel of books from Hatchards, but not a word from his sister Lucy in London nor from Moses Berger.

The pilot watched Henry heave the half-truck on to the cart and trundle off, past the Co-op, toward the settlement, oblivious of the swarming mosquitoes. The settlement was comprised of fifty pre-fab cubes, known as 512s because they each measured 512 square feet. The 512s were laid out in neat rows, huddling tight to a fire station, a meeting hall and school, a nursing station, the Co-op, and the Sir Igloo Inn Café, which was run by the local bootlegger. There was also a Hudson's Bay trading post with living quarters for the factor, a taciturn young man called Ian Campbell. Campbell had been recruited to North of Sixty directly from Stornoway, on the Isle of Lewis. A wool-dyer's boy, he now found himself master of credit and provisions, a keeper of ledgers, with something like the powers of a thane over the hunters in the community. He avoided the school-teaching couple from Toronto, who pandered to the natives, and he was no more than polite to the sluttish nurse who swam through his dreams, making him thrash about in bed at night. On occasion loneliness drove him to playing chess with the unbelievably rich crazy Jew, but, for the most part, he favoured drinking with the grey pulpy denizens of the overheated DEW line station, some eight miles from the settlement.

In the winter you could distinguish Henry's pre-fab from the rest, as it was the only one without quarters of frozen caribou or seal ribs stacked on the roof. It was also larger than the other pre-fabs, made up of three 512s joined together. Henry kept dogs. He could afford to feed them. Twice a week a wagon passed and filled everybody's household tank with fresh drinking water that had been siphoned through a hole in the ice of a nearby lake. Once a day the honey wagon stopped at each pre-fab to pick up the Glad bags filled with human waste. These were dumped on the ice only three miles out to sea in spite of the hunters' complaints. The problem was that following spring breakup the bags floated free and many a seal brought in was covered in excrement, an inconvenience.

During the long dark winter there was a ploughed airstrip illuminated by lighted oil drums, but in summer only float planes serviced the settlement.

A Greek immigrant, the pilot had been told in Yellowknife about Henry. He had thought, understandably, that they were pulling his leg. He had been seated in the sour-smelling Gold Range, knocking back two and a juice with some of the other bush pilots and miners when a Yugoslav foreman from the Great Con had said, "He's been all the way to Boothia with a dog team and he knows King William like the palm of his hand."

"What's he looking for?" the Greek asked, soliciting laughter. "Oil?"

"Brethren of his who have strayed too far from the sun."

"I don't understand."

"You're not expected to."

The nurse was there. Thinner than he liked, older than he had been told. "I brought you something," he said.

"Yes," Agnes said, "they usually do," and she turned and walked away from him. If he followed, all right, if he didn't, all right. It wasn't in her hands.

Henry, approaching the Sir Igloo Inn Café, a corrugated hut, saw a tangle of kids cavorting in the dust. As he drew nearer one of the kids squirted free, black hair flying, and disappeared behind an aluminum shed. "Isaac!" Henry called after him, abandoning his cart to pursue his son. "Isaac!"

He found him hidden behind an oil drum, chewing greedily on a raw seal's eye, sucking the goodness out of it. "You mustn't," Henry chided him, tenderly wiping the blood off his chin with a handkerchief. "It's not kosher. It's unclean, *yingele. Trayf.*"

Isaac, giggly, his coal-black eyes bright, accepted an orange instead. "*Aleph,*" Henry said.

"*Aleph.*"

"*Beth.*"

"*Beth.*"

"And next?" Henry asked, pausing to pull his ear.

"*Gimel.*"

"Bravo," Henry exclaimed, pushing open the door to his pre-fab. "Nialie," he sang out, "it's here."

His wife, an uncommonly slender Netsilik out of Spence Bay, smiled broadly. "*Kayn anyhoreh,*" she said.

Together they lowered the zinc half-trunk to the floor, Henry unlocking it, taking only the bill of lading from the Nôtre Dame de Grace Kosher Meat Market, in Montreal, to the rolltop desk that had once belonged to his father. There were two bullet holes in it. "We've got a new pilot today. A Greek. Agnes came out to meet him."

"Then he will find something wrong with his engine and he will stay the night."

"That's enough, Nialie."

At three A.M. the lowering sun bobbed briefly on the world's rim. Henry, who had only ten minutes before it would start to climb again, stood and turned to the east wall, the one that faced Jerusalem, and began his evening prayers. *Unto thee, O Lord, do I lift up my soul.*

Henry's faith, conceived on the shores of another sea, nurtured in Babylon, burnished in Spain and the Pale of Settlement, seemingly provided for all contingencies save those of the Arctic adherent. So Henry, a resourceful man in some matters, usually improvised, his religious life governed not by the manic sun of the Beaufort Sea, but instead by a clock attuned to a saner schedule. A southern schedule.

Henry slept for six hours, waking the next morning, Friday, to find Nialie salting a brisket that had defrosted during the night. She allowed the blood to drain into the sink, even as her grandmother had learned to do it as a child during the season of Tulugaq who had come on the wooden ship with three masts. The sabbath chicken lay trussed in a pot, the braided bread was ready for the oven.

His morning prayers done, Henry shed his *talith*, folded it neatly, and removed his phylacteries. Immediately after breakfast he sat down at his desk to write a letter to Moses Berger.

> By the Grace of G-d,
> 15 Nissan, 5734
> Tulugaqtitut, NWT

Dear Moses,

Have you heard that since February photographs taken from a satellite have revealed fractures in the Tweedsmuir Glacier? My charts show the Tweedsmuir to be 44 miles long and 8 miles wide. Since February it has stepped up its pace as it marches across the Alsek River Valley. In fact the glacier, which has been creeping southeast at a rate of less than 2 ft. 3 in. a day, is now heaving forward about 13 feet daily. At peak periods last winter Tweedsmuir was moving an astonishing 288 ft. a day. I realize this sudden restlessness is not without precedent and could be an isolated, freakish matter. But I would be grateful if the next time you see Conway at the Institute you had a word with him and checked out the movement of the other glaciers. I am particularly interested in any changes in the habits of the Barnes Ice Cap where, all things considered, it might begin again.

Conway, as you know, has no time for loonies like me, but you might point out to him that in the last 15 years there has been a marked increase in precipitation on the Barnes Ice Cap, especially in winter.

Nialie sends hugs to you and Beatrice and so does Isaac. Isaac (somewhat late in the day, it's true) is making gratifying progress with his *aleph beth*. I would be grateful if you would write soon. We worry about you.

Love,
HENRY

The last time Henry had seen Moses was just after he had been fired by NYU. Henry, in New York to consult with the Rebbe at 770 Eastern Parkway, had gone to visit Moses in his apartment. A fetid basement hole on Ninth Avenue. Furniture you couldn't unload on the Salvation Army. Empty Scotch bottles everywhere. On the bathroom sink a bar of soap resting in slime with indentations made by the teeth marks of mice.

Four o'clock in the afternoon it was and Moses was still lying in bed, his face puffy and bruised, a purple bloom on his forehead. "What's today?" he asked.

"Wednesday."

Henry rented a car and drove Moses to the clinic in New Hampshire.

"He looks like he ran into a wall," the doctor said. "Who did he get into a fight with this time?"

"That's unfair. He was mugged. Look here, Moses has never been violent."

The doctor extracted a typed sheet from a file on his desk. "On a flight to New York a couple of years ago — unprovoked, according to eyewitnesses — he tried to punch out a couple of furriers and had to be forcibly restrained by crew members. Your friend is filled with bottled-up rage. Shake the bottle hard enough and the cork pops."

Moses's last letter to Henry had been bouncy, even joyous,

which was worrying, because in the past that had always been an alarm signal. He and Beatrice were living together again, this time in Ottawa. Moses, who was lecturing at Carleton, didn't dare disgrace himself again, but he seemed well aware of that.

> . . . and I haven't had a drink or even risked anything as intoxicating as *coq au vin* for six months, two weeks, three days and four hours. Bite your tongue, Henry, I may have been through that revolving clinic door for the last time.
>
> Beatrice is in Montreal this week, writing an ode-to-Canada introduction to the annual report for Clarkson, Wiggin, Delorme. It's a grind, but surprisingly well paid. She says Tom Clarkson (LCC, Bishop's, Harvard MBA) is an insufferable bore, but, hell, he's putting her up at El Ritzo. For all that she's lonely, so I just might surprise her and fly into Montreal one of these nights in time to take her to dinner. . . .

Henry hesitated before sealing his letter. Should he add a postscript about his cousin Lionel's perplexing visit? No, he wouldn't, because he was ashamed and had already been rebuked by Nialie for his meek behaviour. Mr. Milquetoast, that's me.

Lionel's visit would have been a trial at the best of times, but as his cousin came during *Aseret Yemai Tushuvah*, the Ten Days of Repentance, it was a *mitzvah* to be reconciled with a family member who had wronged you, even as it was written: "A person should be pliant as a reed and not hard like a cedar in granting forgiveness."

Lionel, his sister Anita, and his younger brother Nathan were the heirs apparent to McTavish Distillers Ltd., Jewel Investment Trust, Acorn Properties, Polar Energy, and the rest of the increasingly diversified Gursky empire. Lionel, Henry remembered, had been the boldest of the Gursky brood even as a child. Grabbing maids where he shouldn't. Propelling his bicycle into whatever new boys had been screened to play with him, knowing that their palpitating mothers wouldn't dare complain.

Henry hadn't heard from Lionel, who presided over the
New York office of McTavish Distillers, for a good ten years
when the distressing phone call came. Henry grasped that so
far as Lionel was concerned he was certifiable if push came to
shove, and maybe he was right. Retrieving an old quarterly
McTavish report from a bottom desk drawer, and skimming
through it before being confronted by Lionel, was enough to
confirm to Henry his own inadequacies. *Oy*, was he ever in for a
drubbing! Lionel, unlike him, was bound to be in tune with
the songs that money sang. Bank debentures, floating bond
rates, amortization of deferred charges, et cetera. All Greek to
Henry.

Lionel, flying into Yellowknife on one of the Gursky jets,
recalled his cousin Henry as a backward boy — no, just this
side of retarded — whom he used to tease because he was such a
bed-wetter. Henry had actually had to repeat the sixth grade.
Then, if memory served, there had been no high school for the
little prick, but instead an endless spill of grim deferential
tutors and shrinks and maybe a private school or two for rich
kids whose elevator didn't go to the top floor. Somewhere
along that troubled road Henry had found God and retreated
into a Brooklyn *yeshiva* where he no longer dared to even
change his toothpaste brand without the approval of his
mighty Oz, the Rebbe who ruled the funny-farm at 770. And
then — presto! — he had lit out for the Arctic, of all places,
where he took a stone-age bride, an Eskimo. Wait, wait. There
had been a newspaper story that had prompted Henry's flight
to the far north — something that Lionel's parents had worried
about in the kitchen, gabbing away in Yiddish. Lionel dimly
remembered bits and pieces. A newspaper item recounting
that, inexplicably, for the third time in a century, a remote
band of Eskimos was starving. The authorities were baffled
because at the time there was no shortage of blubber or
whatever it was they ate. The nutty natives simply refused
food. Even when government officials airlifted in all manner of
supplies they still wouldn't eat. Psychologists who were
hurried out to the scene hinted at dark tribal rites, the curse of
shamans, referring dumbfounded reporters to *Wandlungen und
Symbole der Libido*, *The Golden Bough*, *Totem and Taboo*. But all

the natives would allow was that it was forbidden, it was the Day of the . . . what? The Owl? The Eagle? Some shit like that. Nobody could understand the problem, and then Henry flew out and somehow or other set things right. Some of the Eskimos had died, but many were saved.

Henry flew into Yellowknife on a Ptarmigan Air Otter, taking Isaac with him so that he could have a first look at Sir John Franklin High School, which he would most likely have to attend once he had graduated from primary school in the settlement. Nialie was not disposed to accept the alternative, the Rebbe's *yeshiva* high school in Crown Heights. "The other boys wouldn't accept him as such a *shayner yid*. He would be picked on just because he's a different colour."

The enterprising commissioner of the Northwest Territories, anticipating possible investments, had led the delegation greeting Lionel at the airport. Lionel, grown bald and portly, resplendent in a beaver coat, a Giorgio Armani suit and sheepskin-lined boots, his eyes hidden behind tinted aviator glasses. The commissioner had ordained that the penthouse apartment in the nine-storey building, known locally as The Highrise, should be made available to Lionel, the bar thoughtfully stocked only with bottles blessed with the Gursky brand names. The penthouse, lavishly appointed by North of Sixty standards, had been built to accommodate Queen Elizabeth II and Prince Philip on their visit to the Northwest Territories in 1970. "I hope you'll be comfortable between the royal sheets," the commissioner said, his eyes twinkling.

"I'll require a board to go under my mattress. My back, you know."

"Right, right. Now I'm sure you'll be pleased to know that there are old natives here who still tell tales about your great-grandfather, tales handed down from one generation to another. Would you care to meet any of them, Mr. Gursky?"

"Tight schedule. Can I get back to you after I've met with my cousin?"

Lionel was annoyed that when Henry, that God-crazed fool, finally did turn up, he had brought his little half-breed son with him. But the boy, obviously as dim-witted as his father, settled unobtrusively into a corner with a comic book and the latest issue of *The Moshiach Times*. Page one delivered a Tzivot Hashem Report from a girl named Gila, rooted in Ashkelon. She wrote, "Our *madircha*, our counsellor in Tzivot Hashem, tells us that there are children like ourselves all over the world, all trying to do the same thing, to carry out the commands of our Commander-In-Chief, Hashem." The proper noun Hashem was followed by an asterisk that led to a footnote explaining, "*Hashem*: A name of G-d," as if Isaac didn't know as much.

Isaac seemed self-absorbed, indifferent, while the two men talked or, more accurately, Lionel pontificated and Henry listened.

"I think it's time we put our fathers' quarrels behind us, Henry, don't you?"

Nialie had made Henry promise. Don't fidget. Look him in the eye. Yes, he had assured her, but he had already lowered his eyes and begun to cross and uncross his legs.

"You're a character, Henry. You're really something else. Do you know you still haven't cashed your last dividend cheque?"

"I'll send it to the bank first thing tomorrow morning."

"That cheque was for three million, eight hundred thousand and some odd dollars. Have you any idea what you've already lost in interest?"

Having managed to put him on the defensive, Lionel now did his shrewd best to evoke the old days, reminding him of the games they had played together behind those tall sheltering walls. Then, tired of dribbling, he went for the basket. Mr. Bernard, he said, was now seventy-four years old, he no longer dipped both oars in the water, so it was sad but inevitable that control of James McTavish Distillers Ltd. would soon fall into Lionel's hands.

"What about Nathan?"

"Let's be serious. It's a humbling thought," Lionel went on to say, "but also a challenge. Remember what John Kennedy (another bootlegger's son, eh) said? The torch has been passed to another generation. I used to shmooze with Bobby. I know Teddy. Sinatra has been to our place in Southampton. You know who sang at my Lionel Jr.'s *bar mitzvah*? Diana Ross. Kissinger has to use the can there's one of the girls from Rowan and Martin being *shtupped* by the *schwartze*. Not Sammy Davis Jr., but the other one. The funny one. Rocky was at the *bar mitzvah*. So were Elaine and Swifty and Arnie Palmer. We golf together. About the distillery. There will be changes. Long overdue. Control *should* pass into my hands, but there's a kicker. What we have to remember is that this is a public company with an enviable cash-flow and shares that are presently under-valued, so there are lots of vultures circling out there. The family, assuming all of us vote our shares as a block (after all, we're *mishpoche*, no matter whose version of the old quarrel you accept) still only controls 21.7 percent of the company. According to the best advice available to me — and I'm talking Lehmann Brothers, I'm talking Goldman Sachs — we're vulnerable. Maybe even a sitting duck. Now put plainly, Henry, you have no real interest in the company. Why, you've never so much as attended a board meeting. That's not a reproach. We're all so damned proud of you. You're into things that really matter. God and eternity and shit like that. Henry, you're a saint. A fucking saint. I look up to you. But somebody's got to stay in New York and watch over the shop. It isn't carved in stone anywhere that a Getty will always run Getty Oil or a Ford Ford. You're lucky enough to have it you've got to watch over it day and night. Henry, in order to protect everybody's interest, including yours and Lucy's, I need the authority to vote both your shares. I brought along some proxy papers. You could have the Rebbe look them over. Or I tell you what. And I want you to know I didn't come here intending to make this offer. I could regret it tomorrow. My lawyers will think I'm crazy. *I am crazy! I'm willing to buy out all your shares at 25 percent above current market value.* What do you think?"

"Does your father know about this?"

"Henry, this grieves me, but Mr. Bernard ain't what he used to be. He drools. He falls asleep at board meetings. Or he sits there, sucking on one of those damn Popsicles, farting away, while decisions involving millions are being made. You think the word isn't out on the street? The word is out. He also gives in more frequently to that notorious temper of his. Important executives I took considerable pains to recruit are fired, lost to our competitors. Why? Because they're too tall. Appointments with merchant bankers aren't kept. It's the old Henry Ford syndrome all over again. He's stuck with his first hard-on. He'll make you a Model-T in any colour you want so long as it's black. Mr. Bernard won't allow us to drop old dark heavy Scotches, no longer popular, because he once had a hand in the blending. He knocks down any new light blend if it comes from what he calls my marketing pricks. He could destroy the empire he built, and destroy me, just like the senile Ford all but destroyed his son and empire. No, Mr. Bernard doesn't know I'm here. This is between you and me, Henry. Our secret. I have decided to trust you, that's right, and I want you to trust me. Twenty-five percent above market value. What do you say, Henry?"

Henry, his head aching, leaped up. "It's time for my evening prayers."

"Henry, you're an example to all of us. A really exceptional Jew. It's heart-warming."

"I'll say them in the kitchen. I won't be long."

So Lionel was left alone with the boy, which he found unsettling. "What's your favourite colour, son?" he asked, impatiently tapping his gold Cross pen against the table.

Isaac simply stared.

"Come on, everybody has a favourite colour."

"Red."

"How would you like your Uncle Lionel to send you a big red snowmobile?"

"Do you believe the *Moshiach* is coming?"

"The Messiah?"

Isaac nodded.

"Well, that's a big question, isn't it?"

"I do."

"Hey, that's very nice. I'll buy that."

"Why?"

"Because it speaks very well for your character and your future development as a caring person."

The boy continued to stare. "What's interest?" he asked.

"I beg your pardon?"

"You said my father lost a lot of money in interest by not cashing a cheque."

"You don't want to worry about that, son."

"If my father doesn't sell, will it all be mine one day?"

"McTavish?" Lionel asked, resisting an inexplicable urge to swat him one.

Isaac nodded.

"I'm afraid not, son."

Henry was back. He had brought Isaac along for insurance. Alone, he feared that he would agree to everything, sign anything, just to escape Lionel. But with Isaac there, a witness, bound to spill the beans to Nialie, he was safe. He didn't dare acquiesce. "There's my son to consider. How could I sell his inheritance?"

"Booze isn't exactly booming these days. We might even have to report a loss in the third quarter. If you sold, and took good advice, you could double your yield, maybe better. The boy would be bound to inherit more."

"Please, Lionel, I can't sell."

"Would you sell if you were approached by others?"

"No."

"What if your infallible Rebbe asked you to sell?"

"The Rebbe is not in the takeover business."

There was a knock at the door. Two men had come with boards that had been hammered together to slide under Lionel's mattress. "It's no longer necessary," Lionel said. "I have to leave within the hour."

"But what about the commissioner's dinner party? It's being held in your honour, Mr. Gursky."

"Please convey my sincere regrets, but I've just had an urgent phone call from my father. He wants me to leave for Montreal at once."

The men left and Henry, his eyes welling with tears, reached out and touched Lionel tentatively on the shoulder. In spite of everything, he was a cousin: he was entitled to know. "It's coming to an end," Henry said.

"*Family control?*"

"The world."

"Oh, that," Lionel said, relieved. "Good to see you again and thanks for the tip. Knowing you it has to be insider's information."

A flock of the Faithful, on the annual pilgrimage out of Grise Fiord, was camped on the edge of the settlement. It was that time of year. So now, at six P.M., as proscribed during the season of Tulugaq who had come on the wooden ship with three masts, the most pious among them gathered before the front door of Henry's pre-fab and waited, their heads bowed, until he came out to receive them. A disgruntled Nialie retreated to the bedroom with Isaac and promptly drew the curtains.

"Why can't I watch for once?" Isaac asked.

"Because I forbid it at your age."

Isaac parted the curtains defiantly and Nialie, though she was distressed, did not reproach him, but withdrew meekly from the room.

The men wore parkas trailing four fringes, each fringe made up of twelve strands. Beating on their skin drums, they paraded their traditional sabbath eve offerings before them. Some of the older women, plump and gap-toothed, were already drunk. Their cheeks rouged, their lipstick unevenly applied. Two of the younger ones wore imitation-leather miniskirts and red plastic boots with high heels, probably acquired in Inuvik or Frobisher Bay. Henry averted his eyes, he blushed, but listened gravely as one by one the men stepped forward, their manner deferential but their words explicit, calculated to inflame. Effusive in his gratitude, Henry nevertheless declined each offering. Then, signalling that the ceremony was over, he smiled and sang out, "Good *shabbos*."

The men gathered in their disappointed and scornful womenfolk and turned to troop back to their camp, beating mournfully on their drums.

"Some *shabbos*," one of the women said.

"It will be different when it is the younger one's time. He was peeking through the curtains."

Nialie blessed the candles at seven-thirty and the family sat down to their sabbath dinner. Henry regaling Isaac with tales of Moses — "No, no, not your Uncle Moses, but the original. Moses, our Father" — that great *angakok* of the Hebrews who could turn his rod into a serpent, bring forth water from a rock, and part the seas with a command. Only Moses, Henry explained, had seen God plain, as it is written: "And there arose not a prophet since in Israel like unto Moses, whom the Lord knew face to face."

Later, Henry lowered his son on to the bed he had built for him. The letters of the Hebrew alphabet had been painted into the headboard. It was cleverly done. A seal barked a "*shin.*" A "*resh*" was tied to a caribou's tail. A "*daled*" danced with a muskox. And out of the raven's beak there flew the deadly "*gimel*". The sign of the great one who had come on the wooden ship with three masts.

Nialie stood in the doorway, watching over them. Her husband, her son. Isaac was stealing again, shop-lifting at the Co-op and the Hudson's Bay trading post. She had found things that he had hidden. Two packs of Player's Mild cigarettes, a girlie magazine, a pocket knife, a gold Cross pen. She wanted to talk to Henry about it, but once more she procrastinated. He was so devoted to the boy. He had such faith in him. Nialie wished she could admonish the boy herself, but that was out of the question — impossible — as she was understandably fearful of Isaac's name-soul or *atiq*, who was Tulugaq, the name she had cried out immediately before giving birth to Isaac.

While Nialie did the dishes, Henry retired to his rocking chair with the latest copy of *Newsweek*. In the outside it was still Watergate above all. Eighteen and a half minutes of a Nixon tape had been mysteriously erased. A committee, chaired by a Senator Sam Ervin, was in daily session. The people were perturbed.

Overcome by restlessness, a sudden tug of unease he couldn't account for, Henry hurried into his parka, slipped outside, and headed for the camp of the Faithful. Mingling with them always calmed his spirits. He could do with that now. But when he got there, he was surprised to find the camp abandoned. They had gone without a word to him. It was odd, very odd. Old Pootoogook was sifting through the camp's detritus.

"What happened?" Henry asked.

"Somebody came. Somebody from Spence. He was very excited. They gathered their things together fast fast and they were gone," Pootoogook said, beating his arms to scare off the other scavengers, the swooping ravens.

Ravens, ravens everywhere.

Henry jogged all the way back to the nursing station. When

Agnes came to the door in her fading dressing gown he didn't even apologize for wakening her, which was certainly not like him. All he said was, "I must send a cable. It's urgent."

The Faithful had left a message scrawled in the snow:

WE WANT THE MOSHIACH NOW!

TWO

MOSES BERGER
CARLETON UNIVERSITY
OTTAWA ONT
  THE RAVENS ARE GATHERING. REPLY SOON-
EST. HENRY.

HENRY GURSKY
NURSING STATION
TULUGAQTITUT NWT
  MOSES BERGER NO LONGER EMPLOYED HERE.
WE HAVE FORWARDED YOUR TELEGRAM.
DAVIDSON. BURSAR. CARLETON UNIVERSITY.

HENRY GURSKY
NURSING STATION
TULUGAQTITUT NWT
  I'VE GOT PROBLEMS OF MY OWN RIGHT NOW.
REST, PERTURBED SPIRIT. MOSES.

MOSES BERGER
THE CABOOSE
MANSONVILLE QUE
    SOMEBODY MUST WARN MR. BERNARD. REPLY
SOONEST. HENRY.

HENRY GURSKY
NURSING STATION
TULUGAQTITUT NWT
    RABBI JANNAI ONCE SAID THE SECURITY OF
THE WICKED IS NOT IN OUR HANDS. BEST.
MOSES.

THREE

◆

Mr. Bernard, as was his habit, charged out of his chauffeured limousine at 7:50 A.M., cursing the driving rain, the unresolved problem of numerous vacancies in his latest Montreal shopping plaza, the high cost of French-Canadian unrest, the uncertainty of sterling, a spread of northern oil leases as barren as his daughter (though penetrated as often, God knows), and Lionel's foolish investment in a sinking TV series (all in the name of more pussy, no doubt). Lionel had phoned Mr. Bernard at home that very morning, catching him just as he came out of his shower. "How are you feeling this morning, Daddy?"

"Bad news. I didn't croak during the night. So it isn't yours yet."

"I'm returning your call."

"I've enjoyed bigger honours in my time."

"Aw, come on, Daddy."

"The Dow-Jones is down again. Everybody knows we're going to announce a loss this quarter, but my little cabbage patch has put on another two points. Tell me why?"

"Some raiders out there are buying in New York, Toronto, and London, but your guess is as good as mine."

"Mr. Bernard doesn't guess. He knows. I say it's a real impatient *putz*, namely you, warehousing shares and hiding behind the skirts of surrogates."

"Daddy, if you would only sign those trust papers, delegating me as CEO upon your retirement, I'd stop those speculators cold in their tracks."

"Whatever you're into I'm not shaking in my boots. But one thing I want to lay on the line, you whoremaster. You absolutely mustn't try to buy out Henry or Lucy. There are things you haven't been told. Family things. So I want your word. No finger-fucking with Solomon's crazy kids."

"Daddy, I swear on the heads of my children."

"From which marriage?"

"I —"

"I-I-I. And I suppose you expect me to believe that I-I-I doesn't know how many shares changed hands in Tokyo yesterday?"

"Did you say Tokyo?"

"Don't act innocent with me," Mr. Bernard said, hanging up.

Lionel immediately buzzed Miss Heffernan. "Get me Lubin on line one and get me Weintraub and put him on hold."

"Yes, sir."

"I thought you were in Montreal," Lubin said.

"I'm flying in this afternoon. Sol, have we been buying McTavish in Tokyo?"

"No."

"That's what I thought. I'm putting you on hold. Yes, Miss Heffernan?"

"I've got Mr. Weintraub on line three."

Lionel asked him about Tokyo.

"Not us."

Shit.

There was, they said, ice lodged in Mr. Bernard's heart, glacial ice, but he had come by it honestly. From Ephraim walking out. A ball of phlegm percolating in his throat, Mr. Bernard negotiated the slippery sidewalk with care, mindful of bones grown brittle with age. Then he swept through the doors of the Bernard Gursky Tower on Dorchester Boulevard, stumbling into unaccustomed darkness — gloom — when he was startled by a sudden and blinding explosion of light.

Oh, my God!

Automatically throwing up his arms to shield his face, Mr. Bernard fell to his knees. He subsided, moaning, to the marble floor, curling into the fetal position, fearing the mindless guns of Arab terrorists even as he had once ridden out the fury of Detroit's Purple Gang, hunkered down with the bats, two hundred feet below ground, in that freezing talc mine shaft in the Eastern Townships for three terrifying weeks, waiting for Solomon to arrange a truce.

Miss O'Brien, surveying the scene, turned to Harvey Schwartz, flicking him with that special look of hers. "Oh dear," she said with a certain asperity, "are you ever in for it now, Mr. Schwartz."

A rattled Harvey Schwartz raced toward Mr. Bernard, helping him to his feet, a shivering blinking Mr. Bernard, whom he nervously pointed at the banner that flowed from wall to wall in the lobby:

HAPPY BIRTHDAY, MR. BERNARD
SEVENTY-FIVE YEARS YOUNG TODAY!

The banner was revealed to Mr. Bernard just as one-hundred-odd office employees of James McTavish Distillers Ltd., his corporate creature, burst into "For He's a Jolly Good Fellow."

His eyes brimming with grateful tears, if only because his body remained unpunctured, Mr. Bernard scampered forward to accept a sterling silver tea service from a delegation of his employees. Applause, applause. Dabbing his eyes, surreptitiously hawking phlegm into his handkerchief — a surprisingly hot wad — Mr. Bernard extended his tiny spindly arms to offer his benediction. "God bless you. God bless each and every one of you."

Two office girls wheeled out a cake on a trolley — massive — shaped like a bottle of Canadian Jubilee, their most popular rye, and crowned with figures of Mr. Bernard and his wife, Libby.

"I don't deserve such love," Mr. Bernard protested. "You're wonderful, absolutely wonderful. Not my employees," he cooed, blowing wet kisses as he retreated to the elevator, "but my children, my family."

Only a bemused Miss O'Brien and Harvey Schwartz, carrying the tea service, rode with Mr. Bernard in the express elevator to the forty-first floor. "Everybody chipped in," Harvey said, beaming. "From vice-presidents to office boys."

"But some people didn't think it was such an inspired idea," Miss O'Brien said.

"Their idea, not mine. I was enormously touched on your behalf, Mr. Bernard."

Mr. Bernard began to clack his dentures. "I have to piss," he said. "I have to piss something terrible."

"But weren't you pleased?"

Cursing, Mr. Bernard backed into the elevator wall, gaining purchase before he charged forward to kick Harvey in the shin, sending the tea service flying.

"You little runt, I could have fractured my hip out there. Now pick up that stuff, I hope nothing's bent."

Mr. Bernard, a short man, no more than five foot four, bald except for a silvery fringe, had the body of a carp. The wet brown eyes protuberant, his cheeks scaly, bleeding red whenever he was in a temper. Darting into his office, he pinched his nose with two fingers, snot pinging into the Florentine tooled leather wastepaper basket. Then he pitched his homburg on to his Queen Anne walnut settee which was upholstered in velvet and had been built in Philadelphia for William Penn. Over the settee there hung a Jackson Pollock, one of his daughter's *fershtinkena* acquisitions. Mr. Bernard was fond of using the painting, which reminded him of curdled vomit, to jab petitioners or job applicants who were visiting his office for the first time. "You think it's good?" he enjoyed asking. "I mean, hoo boy, you're a Harvard MBA. Tell me. I'd value your considered opinion."

"It's first-rate, sir."

"There's nothing wrong with it? Take your time, sonny. Have a good look."

"Wrong? I think it's lyrical, sir."

Then, his eyes bright with rancour, he would pounce. "It's hanging upside down. Now what can I get you?" Mr. Harvard *Tuchus*-Face MBA.

Only Moses Berger, that drunk, had outmanoeuvred him. Of course that had been years ago, when Mr. Bernard had first discovered that Moses was poking his nose into Gursky family affairs, asking questions about Solomon.

"You don't think there's anything wrong with the painting?"

Moses had shrugged.

Shooting forward in his desk chair, Mr. Bernard had barked, "It's hanging upside down."

"How can you tell for sure?"

"Hey, you're some smart cookie," Mr. Bernard had replied, brightening. "Come work for me and I'll pay you double what you can get at some shitcan university."

"I'm not looking for a job, if that's why you sent for me."

"I sent for you because I don't care for strangers trying to dig up dirt about the Gurskys to feed anti-Semites, as if they're going hungry these days. But if any trouble-maker dares to cross my path I'll squash him like a bug."

His face hot, his mood vile, Mr. Bernard ate lunch in his private dining room with his brother Morrie.

Mr. Morrie, who never forgot a cleaning lady's name, a secretary's birthday, or the illness of a filing clerk's wife, was adored by just about everybody who worked for McTavish. He occasionally ate in the employee's canteen, refusing to allow anybody to fetch for him, but lining up with his tray like the rest. It was amazing, really amazing, that he and Mr. Bernard were brothers. One a saint, they said, the other a demon.

Nobody had seen Mr. Bernard speak to his brother for years. Ever since Mr. Morrie, prodded by his wife, had dared to go to Mr. Bernard's office to plead Barney's case.

"I appreciate that eventually it's got to be Lionel who sits in your chair," Mr. Morrie said.

"Don't count Nathan out yet."

"Or Nathan."

"What are you talking, Nathan? That boy's a washout. The things that come out of your mouth. Christ."

"But what harm would it do for Barney to be a vice-president?"

"I'm not putting a rat in place to scheme against my sons once I'm gone."

"He won't scheme. He means good."

"That boy was once bitten by a bug called ambition and now he's infected from head to toe."

"Bernie, I beg you on bended knees. He's my only son."

"You want more, make more. I did."

"I never even told him I signed those papers years ago."

"Listen, why don't you go back to your office and do a crossword. I could finish it in half the time it takes you. Or go pull your *petzel*, you'll only need two fingers for the job, I've seen it, and that should keep you busy until it's time to go home to that *yenta* you married like a damn fool."

"Bernie, please. What do I say to him?"

"Out of here before I lose my temper."

Also joining Mr. Bernard for lunch were the still-fetching Miss O'Brien, his secretary of twenty-five years, and Harvey Schwartz.

Freckled and pink and plump Harvey was, inordinately vain about his full head of curly ginger hair, even though Becky was fond of announcing at dinner parties that baldness was a sure sign of virility. A short man, but still some two compromising inches taller than Mr. Bernard, Harvey wore shoes especially made for him with paper-thin heels. Only forty-three years old, he also affected a septuagenarian's stoop, his knees slightly bent.

M. Delorme, the chef, offered steamed Dover sole and boiled new potatoes for lunch. Mr. Morrie, as was the rule, was served the smallest portion last. Somewhat taller than Mr. Bernard, a full five foot five, the Chippendale chair Mr. Morrie was obliged to sit on differed from the others at the table. Two inches had been shaved off the legs.

"Harvey," Mr. Bernard said, his manner menacingly sweet, "I'm sorry I kicked you in the elevator. I apologize."

"I know you didn't mean it, Mr. Bernard."

"Fetch me the *Wall Street Journal*," Mr. Bernard said, nudging Miss O'Brien under the table. "I left it on my desk."

No sooner did Harvey limp out of the dining room than Mr. Bernard fell on the salt shaker, trailing it over Harvey's fish again and again, shaking vigorously.

"Naughty, naughty, Mr. B."

"He's not allowed. He's worried about his heart. Watch."

Harvey returned with the *Journal*, and Mr. Bernard, all but bouncing with glee as he pretended to be absorbed in the market pages, watched him gag on the first bite. "Anything wrong?"

Harvey shook his head no, no, reaching for the Vichy water.

"How's *your* fish, Miss O?"

"Firm but tender."

"Eat, Harvey. Low fat. Brain food. Good for you. Eat every bite on your plate or M. Delorme will cry and you know what that does to his mascara."

After lunch, somewhat mollified but still restive, Mr. Bernard asked Miss O'Brien to bring him the logs for the Gursky jets. When he found the entry that he had foolishly hoped wouldn't be there, he turned pale. He began to curse. And Solomon stood before him again, his eyes diamond-hard. "Bernie," he had said, "you're a snake, but not a complete fool, so I want to make something clear to you before I go. If you or any of your wretched children ever try to diddle Henry or Lucy out of their shares I'll come back from the grave if necessary and you are finished. A dead man."

Shivering, sweaty, Mr. Bernard grabbed the nearest thing to hand, a Chinese jade paperweight, and pitched it against the door. Miss O'Brien came running. "Mr. B., if you want me, there *is* a button on your phone."

He snatched her hand and led her briskly into the billiards room. They shot a couple of games of snooker, Mr. Bernard sucking on a Popsicle between shots. Then, abruptly, he pulled Miss O'Brien to him, digging his head into her high firm bosom. "I don't believe in ghosts. Do you?"

"Ssssh," she said, unbuttoning, unsnapping, stroking his head as he nuzzled there, sucking.

Later, sinking into the chair behind his Chippendale mahogany desk with the cock-beaded drawers and carved gilt handles, a still apprehensive Mr. Bernard began to shuffle through a stack of birthday telegrams. They were from the prime minister, President Nixon, Golda, Kissinger, a brace of Rothschilds, merchant bankers of New York, London, and Paris, and other supplicants, creditors, and enemies. The shank of the afternoon, which passed uneventfully, only served to feed Mr. Bernard's anxieties. He rang for Harvey. "I want you to tell reception that if any thick letters come for me, you know, parcel size, they're to be opened by the *goy* downstairs, even if they are marked 'private and confidential.' Wait. Hold it. Especially if they are marked 'private and confidential.'"

In the evening there was a banquet in the ballroom of the Ritz-Carlton Hotel, suitably bedecked for the occasion with Canadian, Québecois (this, in the name of prudence) and Israeli flags. Red roses, flown in from Grasse, festooned every table. There were one-ounce bottles of perfume for the ladies, from a house recently acquired by Gursky, and slim gold cigarette lighters for the men, that were manufactured by yet another Gursky enterprise. Ice sculptures of Gursky-endowed university buildings and hospitals and museums and concert halls, set on side tables everywhere, testified to Mr. Bernard's largesse.

The centrepiece on each table was a papier-mâché doll of Mr. Bernard, wearing a glittering crown at a jaunty angle. King Bernard. The figure, mounted on a charger, held a lance, banners flowing from it. Each banner broadcast another accomplishment of Mr. Bernard: a directorship, a medal, an award, an honorary degree. Lionel Gursky announced, "If you will be kind enough to turn over your plates, you will find that one plate at each table has a crown stuck on its underside. Whoever has the crown has won the right to take home the figure of Mr. Bernard at their table."

Everybody, absolutely everybody, who counted in the monied, if not the larger, Jewish community was there. The ladies perfumed, their hair sculpted and lacquered, their eyes shadowed green or silvery, outsize rings riding their fingers; the ladies were breathlessly there, triumphantly there, glittering in gowns of écru silk *façonné* or shimmering cyclamen satin or purple chiffon, acquired and tactfully altered for them by the Holt Renfrew boutique. The men were harnessed in velvet dinner jackets, wine-coloured or midnight blue or murky green, buttoned punishingly tight; they wore ruffled shirts, edged in black, like condolence cards, ornate satin cummerbunds and twinkly buckled Gucci shoes.

Their antidote for ungrateful children — unwanted polyps — was plaques, plaques and more plaques, which they awarded one another at testimonial dinners once, sometimes twice a month in this very ballroom. At ease in the Ritz-Carlton they took turns declaring each other governors of universities in Haifa or Jerusalem or Man of the Year for State of Israel Bonds. Their worthiness certified by hiring an after-dinner speaker to flatter them for a ten-thousand-dollar fee, the speaker coming out of New York, New York; either a former secretary of state, a TV star whose series hadn't been renewed or a senator in need. But tonight wasn't make-believe. This was the real thing. This, after all, was Mr. Bernard, *their* Mr. Bernard no matter how large his international importance, and they were there to bask in his aura. A pleasure immeasurably sweetened by the knowledge that some people whom they could mention by name if they wanted to, some cherished friends they would be sure to phone tomorrow if only to establish that *they* had been there, some so-called *knackers* had been excluded, adjudged unsuitable.

Bliss.

So now they applauded, they cheered, they banged forks against wine glasses as tributes to the great man proliferated, and Mr. Bernard himself sat there inexplicably charged with unease, grinding his dentures.

The Israeli ambassador, delivered from Ottawa in a Gursky jet, presented Mr. Bernard with a Bible, encased in a cover of hammered gold, the flyleaf signed by Golda. There was a bronze plaque testifying that even more forests paid for by

Mr. Bernard had been planted in Israel. Zion, soon to be Gursky green from shore to shore. There was a medal from Bolivia, where Mr. Bernard had copper interests, but an OBE, ardently pursued for the occasion on Mr. Bernard's instructions, had been denied him, just as he had failed in the past to procure a seat in the senate.

One of Mr. Bernard's most cherished charities was remembered: The Hospital of Hope, which cared for children with terminal diseases.

An official of the Canadian Football League passed Mr. Bernard a ball, a memento of last year's Grey Cup game, that had been autographed by all the players on the winning team, and then one of the team's most celebrated players, a behemoth who peddled Crofter's Best in the off-season, wheeled a paraplegic child to the head table. Mr. Bernard, visibly moved, presented the ball to the boy as well as a cheque for five hundred thousand dollars. Three hundred guests leaped to their feet and cheered. The boy, his speech rehearsed for days, began to jerk and twist, spittle flying from him. He gulped and began again, unavailingly. As he started in on a third attempt to speak, Mr. Bernard cut him off with an avuncular smile. "Who needs another speech," he said. "It's what's in your heart that counts with me, little fellow." And *sotto voce*, he told the player, "Wheel him out of here, for Christ's sake. People are beginning to feel shitty."

And hungry too.

Once dinner was done, the lights were dimmed for the ultimate surprise, the specially commissioned birthday film. Mr. Bernard, increasingly tense, his lower lip trembling, yanked out a handkerchief to hide his tears. And in his mind's eye he saw Solomon jumping off that corral fence again, right into the flow of wild mustangs, only some of them green-broke. *Follow me, Bernie, and I'll buy you a beer.*

"Oh my sweetie-pie," Libby said, patting his hand, "I'm so glad you're enjoying yourself. The best is yet to come."

Ignoring her, Mr. Bernard turned on Lionel. "What were you doing in Yellowknife?" he demanded.

"Somebody has to check out the oil-lease properties from time to time, don't you think?"

"There are no discos in Yellowknife. You went there to see

Henry to try to buy his shares. Then you flew to London to try to sweet-talk Lucy out of hers."

"Vanessa and I took the jet to London to take in Wimbledon."

"It's too late to lie. I know now. I know sure as I'm sitting here what you've been up to," he said, and his cheeks bleeding red, he reached out to snatch Lionel's hand, thrusting it into his mouth and biting down on his fingers as hard as he could. Lionel, groaning, finally wrenched his throbbing hand free, tucking it under his armpit . . . and the lights were extinguished and the film began.

Jimmy Durante, one of Mr. Bernard's favourite entertainers, stood before a concert piano, raised a glass of champagne to the old man, a Gursky brand, and then settled down to croak and play "Happy Birthday, Mr. Bernard" followed by a medley of his most famous ditties.

The Schnozz's impudent image yielded to that of the Chief Rabbi of Israel, who stood before the Wailing Wall and pronounced a blessing in Hebrew. His voice was soon superimposed over a montage of selected Gursky history, beginning with a shot of the sod hut on the prairie (now a museum, a Gursky shrine), the sod hut where Mr. Bernard had been born, and then dissolving to a shot of the first distillery, the St. Jerome distillery, Mr. Bernard and Mr. Morrie posing in the foreground, only the merry bright-eyed figure of the other brother, Solomon Gursky, air-brushed out of the picture, as it was out of all the others.

Next Golda offered a tribute.

Then Harvey Schwartz's wife Becky was discovered in a golden kaftan seated at her Louis XIV *bureau-plat* of deal veneered with ebony and boulle marquetry. She turned to the audience, her smile demure, and began to read a tribute she had composed for the occasion, even as the camera tracked in on a prominently displayed copy of her book, a collection of columns about family life first published in the *Canadian Jewish Review: Hugs, Pain, and Chocolate Chip Cookies*.

Jan Peerce proposed a toast to Mr. Bernard and then sang "The Bluebird of Happiness."

Zero Mostel raised a laugh extolling the virtues of Gursky blends, even as he staggered about a stage feigning drunkenness, singing, "If I Were a Rich Man".

A harpist played the theme song from *Love Story* as Mr. Bernard and Libby were seen strolling hand-in-hand through the streets of Old Jerusalem. The famous star of many a biblical blockbuster sat in the garden of his Coldwater Canyon home and recited Mr. Bernard's favourite stanzas from Longfellow.

Then there was a slow dissolve to the wine-dark sea. The custom-built one-hundred-and-ten-foot-long Gursky yacht was seen cruising the Greek isles as a voice that sounded like Ben Cartwright's began to recite:

> The barge she sat in, like a burnish'd throne,
> Burn'd on the water. The poop was beaten gold;
> Purple the sails, and so perfumed that
> The winds were love-sick with them; the oars were
>   silver,
> Which to the tune of flutes kept stroke, and made
> The water which they beat to follow faster,
> As amorous of their strokes.

The camera eye tracked past a snoozing Mr. Bernard to reveal a sixty-five-year-old Libby, lounging on deck in a flower-print halter and pedal pushers, attended by black stewards in white linen jackets.

> . . . For her own person,
> It beggar'd all description. She did lie
> In her pavilion, cloth-of-gold tissues,
> O'erpicturing that Venus where we see
> The fancy outwork nature.

Laughing, her belly rocking with delight, Libby fed caviar with chopped onion and Coca-Cola to one grandchild, chopped liver on crackers to another.

    ... On each side her
    Stood pretty dimpled boys, like smiling Cupids,
    With divers-colour'd fans, whose wind did seem
    To glow the delicate cheeks which they did cool,
    And what they undid did.

The image of Libby cavorting with her grandchildren yielded to a longer shot of the yacht at sunset as another voice declaimed, "From William Shakespeare, the Bard of Avon."

Finally the children of a kibbutz in the Negev, photographed from a helicopter, stood in a pattern in the Bernard Gursky Park and spelled *l'chaim*, the apostrophe raising a bottle of Masada Blanc, a Gursky brand, to Mr. Bernard.

The film done, a spotlight illuminated Mr. Bernard, seemingly crushed by such acclaim, swimming in tears, a sodden handkerchief clenched between his dentures. Everybody was enormously moved, especially Libby, who now rose into the light to sing their song to him:

        Bei mir bist du schön,
        Please let me explain,
        Bei mir bist du schön
        Means that you're grand. . . .
        I could sing Bernie, Bernie,
        Even say "voonderbar."
        Each language only helps me tell you
        How grand you are. . . .

There wasn't, Libby would remember, a dry eye in the house, the rest of her song lost in applause, soaring applause as Mr. Bernard leaped to his feet, knocking back his chair, and fled the ballroom.

"He's just an old softie at heart, you know."

"Don't you just want to hug him?"

The truth was Mr. Bernard had to piss again, he had to piss something terrible, there was such a burning inside him, and when it came out it was, to his astonishment, red as Big Sur burgundy, another Gursky brand. A week later they began to cut and a tearful Kathleen O'Brien lighted the first of many candles at the Cathedral of Mary, Queen of the World. Mr. Morrie, responding to a summons, visited his brother at home for the first time in twenty years.

"So," Mr. Bernard said.

"So."

"Look at Barney now. I was right about him all along. I want you to admit it."

"I admit it."

"No resentments?"

"No."

"How's Ida?"

"She'd like to come to pay her respects."

"Tell her to bring Charna with her. I don't mind."

"Charna's dead."

"Oh shit, I forgot. Did I go to the funeral?"

"Yes."

"I'm glad."

"Bernie, I've got something to say, but please don't shout at me."

"Try me, you little prick."

"You must make provision for Miss O."

"A big brown envelope. It's in the office safe."

They cut and pared Mr. Bernard a week later, pronouncing him fit, but Mr. Bernard knew better. He sent for Harvey Schwartz. "I want my lawyers here at nine sharp tomorrow morning. All of them."

Later the same afternoon Mr. Bernard saw Miss O'Brien.

"I'm going to die, Miss O."

"Would you like me to do your weenie now?"

"I wouldn't say no."

FOUR

◆

Passing his parents' bedroom door, a few years after they had moved into Outremont, Moses stopped, arrested by their voices. His mother was telling L.B. about the intelligence tests at school. A new-fangled notion. Moses had scored so high that the school inspector had asked to meet the bright Jewish lad who was bound to discover the cure for cancer. L.B. sighed. "You don't know how devoutly I hope he will go into medicine. Or law maybe. Because if Moses is really determined to become a writer he is certain to be compared to me and suffer for it. Possibly I never should have had a child. It was indulgent of me."

His mother's answer was lost.

"Costly too, to be frank. I mean do you think I would be singing for my supper at that *parvenu*'s table if I didn't have a wife and child to support? I would be living in a garret in Montparnasse, serving nobody but my muse."

The dreaded self-addressed envelopes continued to rebound. From *Partisan Review, Horizon, The New Yorker.* Again and again somebody else, a detested rival, would win the Governor-General's Award for Literature.

One morning, three years after Moses had scored so high on the intelligence tests, he discovered his picture in the newspaper: the sixteen-year-old boy who had come first in the province in the high-school matriculation exams, winning a scholarship to McGill. L.B. reacted to the news with a low whistle. He removed his pince-nez, polishing the lenses with his handkerchief. "I see that you made ninety-seven in your French exam. Okay, I'm going to read you the opening paragraph of a French classic and I want you to identify it for me," he said, turning to a book concealed behind a magazine. " '*Madame Vauquer, née de Conflans, est une vieille femme qui, depuis quarante ans, tient à Paris une pension bourgeoise établie rue Neuve-Sainte-Geneviève, entre le quartier latin et le faubourg Saint-Marceau.*' "

All the same L.B. dropped into Horn's Cafeteria so that old cronies could congratulate him.

"The apple doesn't fall far from the tree, eh, L.B.?"

Four years after Shloime Bishinsky had denounced him in a high squeaky voice L.B. published a story in *Canadian Forum* about a pathetic little Jew, unattractive to women, who had bribed his way out of Siberia, across China, into Japan, and from there to Canada, only to be knocked down and killed by a streetcar on his first day in the next-door place to the promised land.

Once Moses had asked Shloime, "How did you manage to walk out of Siberia?"

"Looking over my shoulder," he replied, and then he tweaked Moses's nose, making a plum pop out of it. "What kind of boy is this? Sneezing fruit."

Sometimes, while one of the men was reading a long solemn essay aloud in the dining room, Shloime would gather the children together in the kitchen to entertain them as well as Moses's mother. He could pluck a silver dollar from behind your ear, swallow a lighted cigarette, or make Bessie Berger squeal by yanking a white mouse out of her apron pocket. He could tear a dollar bill to bits and then only had to close his fist on it to make it whole again. Shloime was also capable of dancing the *kazatchka* without spilling a drop from the glass of seltzer water balanced on his head. He could comb chocolate-covered raisins out of your hair or stick out his tongue, proving his mouth was empty, and then cough up enough nickels for everybody to buy an ice-cream cone.

Eventually Shloime set up in business for himself, taking a floor in a building on Mayor Street, prospering as a furrier to the carriage trade. He married one of Zelnicker's shrewish daughters, a social worker, and she bore him two sons, Menachim and Tovia.

Years later, flying to New York, Moses was unable to concentrate on his book because two men, across the aisle, were playing with pocket-size computer games, new at the time, that kept going ping ping ping. Both men carried clutch purses, the top three buttons of their silk shirts undone, revealing sparkly gold necklaces with *chai* medallions. Finally Moses couldn't take it any more. "I would be enormously grateful," he said, "if you put those toys away."

"Hey, aren't you Moses Berger?"

"Yes."

"That's what I thought. I'm Matthew Bishop and this is my yucky kid brother Tracy. Belle de Jour Furs. You want to buy your chick a wrap, I'll give you some deal."

"I don't understand."

"My father once told me he used to shmooze with you when you were just a kid."

"Bishop?"

"Shloime Bishinksy."

"Oh my God, how is he?"

"Hell, didn't you know? He left for the ultimate fur auction in the sky eight years ago. The big C. Wasn't he a card though, eh, Moe?"

1951 it was, and as soon as the news was confirmed at McGill, a jubilant Moses tiptoed into the kitchen, embraced his mother from behind, twirled her around and told her.

"Sh," she said, "L.B.'s working."

Moses burst into L.B.'s study, daring to disturb him. "Flash. We interrupt this program to announce that dashing debonair Moses Berger has just won a Rhodes scholarship."

L.B. carefully blotted the page he had been working on and then slowly screwed the top back on his Parker 51. "In my day," he said, "it would have been considered presumptuous for a Jewish boy to even put himself forward for such an honour."

"I'm going to apply to Balliol."

"D.H. Lawrence," L.B. said, "who managed to get by with no more distinguished a formal education than I had, once wrote that the King's College chapel reminded him of an overturned sow."

"King's is in Cambridge. Besides, I won't be attending chapel."

"This country has always been big enough for me. Mind you, I have published over there. *The New Statesman*. A letter about Ernest Bevin's anti-Semitic foreign policy that led to a dispute that went on for weeks. You could take my greetings to Kingsley Martin. He's the editor."

Eighteen months later Moses flew home. L.B. had suffered his first heart attack. Once more he had failed to win the Governor-General's award, his *Collected Poems* not making the grade.

"It would break their heart to give it to a Jew," Bessie said.

L.B. was in bed, propped up by pillows, writing on a pad. Pulpy, pale, his eyes wobbly with fear. "How long can you stay?" he asked.

"Ten days. Maybe two weeks."

"I like the short story you sent me. I think it showed promise."

"I've submitted it to *The New Yorker*."

L.B. laughed out loud. He wiped tears from the corners of his eyes with his knuckles. "What *chutzpah*. Such hubris. You have to learn to crawl before you can walk."

"If they don't want it, they'll send it back. No harm done."

"You should have rewritten the story with my help and tried it on one of the little magazines here. Had you the sense to consult me, an old hand in such matters, I also would have advised you to use a pseudonym. You don't want to be compared to L.B."

"Would you like me to read to you now?"

"I'd better sleep. Wait. I see your friend Sam Birenbaum interviews writers for *The New York Times* these days. I don't know how many times I fed that fatty here, but now that he's a bigshot reporter he can't even remember my phone number."

"Paw, I'm sure he's assigned to do those interviews. He doesn't pick and choose."

"And why would he want to interview me anyway? I don't come from the south and I'm not a pederast."

"Do you want me to speak to him?"

"Begging is beneath me. Besides, he's your friend. Do what you think best."

Things got worse once L.B. found out that Moses had given *The New Yorker* the house in Outremont as his return address.

"When they turn down your story I don't want you to be drunk for three days. I don't need it."

Moses hid his bottle of Scotch behind books in the library. He sucked peppermint Life Savers.

"Bring me the mail," his father demanded each morning. "All of it."

One night, after they had both gone to sleep, Moses sat up drinking in the library, going through *The Collected Poems of L.B. Berger*. So much anger, such feeling. He pitched red hot all right, but he didn't always find the plate. Many of the poems were clearly vitiated by sentimentality or self-pity. W.B. Yeats he was not. Gerard Manley Hopkins he was not. Yes, but did the poems have any merit? Moses, sliding in sweat, poured himself another three fingers of Scotch. He shirked from deciding, unable to accept such a responsibility. After all, he held a life in his hands. His father's life. All those years of dedication and frustrated ambition. The sacrifices, the humiliations. The neglect. Moses thrust the book aside. He preferred to remember his father and himself as they once were. Man and boy trudging through snow to synagogue halls, holding hands when they chanced on slippery patches.

Each morning that the postman failed to shove a big brown envelope from *The New Yorker* through the mail slot L.B.'s mood darkened. Everything Moses did seemed to irritate him. "You're not on death-watch duty here," he said. "You don't have to hang around day and night. Go look up some of your friends."

But if Moses didn't return in time for dinner he would say,

"Did you come here to comfort your father or to chase the kind of girls who hang around downtown bars?"

L.B. was no longer confined to his bed, but he was wasting, fragile. Told to shed twenty pounds, he had clearly dropped thirty, maybe more. His clothes hung badly on a suddenly scrawny frame. He no longer hurried about the house, a man with appointments to keep and deadlines to meet, but shuffled, his slippers flapping. He seemed to be out of breath a good deal of the day and inclined to wheeze in his sleep. A frightened Moses grasped that his father, that powerhouse of his childhood, pronouncing at the dining-room table with the crocheted tablecloth, was actually a short man with bad teeth, a bulbous nose, and weak eyes.

Moses took to drinking heavily, often staying out until the early hours of the morning and sleeping in late. His mother spoke to him in the kitchen. "You mustn't be a disappointment to L.B. It would break his heart his only son a drunkard."

"What about your heart?"

"If you're flying back on Thursday you'd better give me your socks and shirts tonight."

Bessie Berger née Finkelman came from an observant family. Her father had been a ritual slaughterer. When he died L.B. had gone grudgingly to the funeral. "Your grandfather," he told Moses, "was a very superstitious type. An apostle, if I dare use such a word, of the Ravaruska Rebbe. Your *zeyda*, the torturer of cattle, was buried with a twig in his hand by those crazies so that when the Messiah comes, blowing on his *shofar*, he can dig his way out to follow him to Jerusalem. Isn't that right, Bessie?"

L.B. never brought her flowers or took her to dinner or even told her that she looked nice. Now her hands were rough, angry red, the nails clipped short. Embarrassed by the tracery of protruding veins in her legs she wore surgical stockings even in the heat of summer.

"Maw," Moses asked, "do we own the house now or is it still heavily mortgaged?"

"Don't talk foolishness. Go read to him. He likes that."

The next morning, while a badly hungover Moses slept late, a big brown self-addressed envelope from *The New Yorker* shot through the front-door slot. L.B. heard the thud, recognized it, and immediately fetched the envelope and took it into his study, shutting the door behind him. He sunk into the chair behind his desk, overlooked by his own portrait: L.B. in profile, pondering the mysteries of the cosmos, enduring its weight. Well, he thought, it was to be expected. If his poetry wasn't classy enough for Mr. Harold know-nothing Ross, what chance had a first short story by a fumbling neophyte talent? L.B. addressed himself impatiently to opening his own mail first. There was a royalty statement from Ryerson Press with a cheque for $37.25 clipped to it, as well as a note from his editor. He regretted that there seemed to be no copies of *The Collected Poems* in stock at Ogilvy's, Classic's, or Burton's, but this was not the fault of the Ryerson sales force. Demand for poetry was small. Unfortunately there would be no second edition. A CBC radio producer, another obvious ignoramus, wrote that while he considered L.B.'s notion of dramatizing stories from *Tales of the Diaspora* for radio an interesting one, his colleagues did not share his enthusiasm. Would he try them again next season? T.S. Eliot, of Faber and Faber, his anti-Semitism a matter of record, thanked him for submitting a copy of *The Collected Poems*, but. . . . Infuriatingly, the letter was signed by a secretary in Mr. Eliot's absence.

Finally L.B. reached for the big brown envelope from *The New Yorker* and slit it with his leather-handled letter opener which was a gift, in lieu of a fee, for a reading he had given at the B'nai Jacob synagogue in Hamilton, Ontario. Then he retired to his bedroom, removing his pince-nez, rubbing his nose, the small tic of discomfort starting in the back of his neck. It was noon before he heard Moses stumbling about the kitchen and called out to him. "Bring your coffee into my bedroom and shut the door behind you."

Moses did as he was asked and L.B. took his hand and stroked it. "Moishele," he said, his eyes shiny with tears, "you think I don't know how it feels right here?" Withdrawing his hand, he pressed it to his skittering damaged heart. "My work hasn't always been in such demand. L.B. Berger wasn't born famous. I've also had rejections from editors who print crap, so long as it is written by their friends, but who couldn't tell Pushkin from Ogden Nash. I have also suffered the slings and arrows of outrageous fortune. Prizes going to hacks with the right connections when it was obvious I could write circles around them. You have to have a thick skin, my boy. You want to be an artist your motto has to be *nil desperandum*."

Then he handed Moses the envelope. It had already been slit open and Moses could just make out the printed rejection slip clipped to his manuscript.

"The next attack could be curtains for me," L.B. said, squeezing his hand again, "so let me tell you that I have always expected you to follow in my footsteps, but not to be intimidated by them. I have such hopes for you. I have always loved you beyond anybody, including your mother."

Moses swallowed hard, his stomach rising, bound to betray him he feared. Like father, like son.

"Now this is not to be interpreted as a complaint against a good woman. A loyal woman. A real *baleboosteh*. But, to be frank, she has never been a true soul-mate for me. What a man like me needed was refinement, intellectual companionship, like Chopin got from Georges Sand or Voltaire from the Marquise du Châtelet. Whatever gossip you hear after I'm gone, whatever letters future biographers turn up, I want you to understand. I was never unfaithful to your mother, not in my heart of hearts. But I had need of ladies from time to time who I could talk to as an equal. My soul cried out for it. Don't look at me like that. You're a grown man now. We should be able to talk. You think I feel guilty? The hell I do. My family always came first with me. Costing me plenty. You think I ever would have signed on with Mr. Bernard, that *behayma*, if it wasn't because I wanted to do right by your mother, but you above all? Do you have any idea how many hoops I've jumped through there? Furnishing that gangster with a library. Feeding that hooligan literary allusions for his speeches. He couldn't even pronounce the words. I had to coach him. A man who sits glued to the TV for the Ed Sullivan show. You have no idea what I have endured at his table so that your future welfare would not be sacrificed on the anvil of my art. He's coarse beyond belief, Moishe. Even a sailor would blush to hear him in full flight."

Moses, about to protest, was dismissed with an impatient wave of the hand.

"Don't start. I know what your big-shot reporter friend Birenbaum thinks. I heard him say it to you behind my back. 'Who does he think he is the way he dresses? His hair. Beethoven.' You buy a poet in this poor excuse for a country, it doesn't honour its literary giants, you want value for money. Long hair, a cape."

Moses fiddled absently with the flap of the large brown envelope on his lap.

"Hey, wipe your eyes please. Shed no tears for me. At least your father didn't have to feign a hunchback or carry a jester's stick with a bell attached to it. Moishe, I smell talent in you and I have a nose for it."

"You had absolutely no right to open my mail."

"And maybe you had a right to give *The New Yorker* this as your return address? Or are you so self-centred, Mr. Rhodes Scholar, that you didn't realize it was meant as a provocation?"

"What in the hell are you talking about?"

"Don't you dare look at me like that. I'm your father and it goes without saying I forgive you this childish business with *The New Yorker*. It mustn't upset you either because it was only natural. You know your Oedipus and so do I. I never published there — not that I ever wanted to — so you would, administering a slap in the face to old L.B. Okay, that *narishkeit* is over with and you know what? You're goddamn lucky. Had they accepted your story you would have gone on to write more formula fiction tailored to their commercial expectations. Moishe, you have escaped a trap. Now I want you to continue to attempt to write and when the time comes I will try your stories on editors who can be trusted. But let's get right down to work, eh? Because the next time you come home I could have shuffled off this mortal coil. You know something? I'm really glad we're having this talk. Letting our hearts speak out before it's too late. I haven't felt as close to you since you were a little boy. My page, I used to say. So say something."

Moses fled the room, his stomach heaving, sinking to his knees before the toilet bowl just in time. Then he dug out his bottle of Scotch from its hiding place. When he finally entered the kitchen he found that L.B., celebrating his escape from a migraine, was already into his favourite meal: scrambled eggs with lox, potatoes fried in onions, bagels lathered with cream cheese. "Sit down, my boy. Maw has made enough for both of us."

"Some *baleboosteh*, isn't she?"

"I thought the conversation we had in there was strictly *entre nous*."

Bessie, sniffing trouble, looked closely at her son. "What's wrong?" she asked.

"Our neophyte artist here has had his first rejection slip and he's taking it hard instead of appreciating how lucky he is."

"I would like to say something," Moses said.

L.B. shot out of his chair, snapping to attention.

"Not all neglected writers are unjustifiably neglected."

"How dare you speak to your father like that?"

"Here is a boy," L.B. said, "once my pride and joy, bright with promise, who cannot accept responsibility for his own failures, but would lay them on his father's white head. Well, I've got news for you. I didn't make you a drunk. I deserved better."

FIVE

◆

The night before the big brown envelope from *The New Yorker* shot through the mail slot Moses had been a guest at Anita Gursky's first wedding. Actually he hadn't been invited. He had been strolling aimlessly down Sherbrooke Street, hard by McGill, past the sullen grey limestone mansions built by the Scottish robber barons who had once ruled the country. Self-absorbed, he passed the former homes of shipping and rail and mining magnates who had flourished in a time, sublime for them, when there had been no income tax or anti-trust laws or succession duties. Sir Arthur Minton's old house, now a private club; the Clarkson home, converted into a fraternity house; Sir William Van Horne's former residence with its delightfully loopy greenhouse. And then he ran into Rifka Schneiderman, of all people. Rifka Schneiderman, who had used to belt out "The Cloakworkers' Union Is a No-Good Union" on the other side of the mountain, but a world away, in the dining room of the cold-water flat on Jeanne Mance Street. Rifka, to his astonishment, had grown into a fetching if rather over-dressed young lady, her once-unruly hair tamed by a poodle cut. "Oh," she exclaimed, "I thought you were studying at Oxford or Cambridge or something."

"My father had a heart attack."

Rifka was to be a bridesmaid at the wedding. However her fiancé, Sheldon Kaplan, had been struck with one of his allergy attacks. Rifka, her mood sentimental, asked Moses to escort her instead.

"Only if you promise to sing your song," he said.

Anita Gursky had met her first husband on the ski slopes of Davos. A New Yorker, the wayward son of a German-Jewish banking family, he hoped to make his name as a tennis player. *Life* came to the wedding at the Ritz-Carlton.

Becky Schwartz leaned closer to Harvey. "Don't look now," she said, "but the Cotés just walked in looking like they smelled something bad. How can she wear a backless dress with those shoulders like chicken wings? *I said don't look.*"

"I'm not."

"I thought I told you to cut your nose hairs before we went out. Feh!"

Plump, double-chinned Georges Ducharme, parliamentary secretary to the minister of transport, winked at Mimi Boisvert. "I'm going to be the first to boogie-woogie with the rabbi's wife."

"*Tais-toi, Georges.*"

"Do not talk in the language of the peasantry here. Speak Yiddish."

Cynthia Hodge-Taylor was there, so was Neil Moffat, Tom Clarkson, a Cunningham, two Pitneys, and other insouciant young Westmounters. Their far more punctilious parents would not have blessed a Gursky wedding with their presence, but for the young set it was sport, and possibly, just possibly, a chance to see their photographs published in *Life*.

Jim MacIntyre said, "My father, you know, was one of the government prosecutors in the trial. When Solomon was confronted by a particularly damning piece of testimony all he could say was I AM THAT I AM, and right there, my father swore, the temperature in the courtroom dropped by twenty degrees. The judge looked like he was going to have a stroke."

There were thousands of red roses in vases all over the ballroom. At the appropriate moment, Guy Lombardo and his Royal Canadians swung into "My Heart Belongs to Daddy", and Mr. Bernard took to the floor for the first dance, tears streaming down his face as he fox-trotted cheek-to-cheek with Anita.

Moses danced with Kathleen O'Brien, whom he had chatted with more than once at The Lantern. "Come on," she said, "We're going to get some fresh air."

"I'm not drunk."

"Your dad wrote a poem for the bride and groom. In exactly five minutes Becky Schwartz will step up to the microphone and read it aloud."

Outside, Moses said, "Well, he always wanted to be a poet laureate."

"I hope you don't drink like this in Oxford. I believe your father is counting on you to come home with a First."

"Actually nothing would delight him more than my being sent down."

"Now now now."

Back in the ballroom she led him to the table where Mr. Morrie was rooted with his wife, Ida, and their enormous pimply daughter, Charna. "He's the sweet one," Kathleen whispered before making the introductions. "Be nice."

"How's your father?" Mr. Morrie asked.

"Getting better."

"Thank God for that."

"Is his father the writer?" Charna asked.

"And how."

"Big deal," she said, glaring at Moses. "I could write a book too. I just wouldn't know how to put it into words."

"Bless you," Ida said.

Mr. Morrie squeezed Moses's arm. "Don't think I don't know all about you from your father, Mr. Rhodes Scholar."

Responding to a kick from Kathleen, Moses said, "Oh yes, thank you," but he was watching Barney, who was flirting with Rifka Schneiderman on the dance floor.

Barney, they said, still hoped to be the one to draw the sword from the stone, becoming McTavish's next CEO. Certainly he had done everything possible to establish his claim. While Lionel fiddled, he had driven a truck for McTavish. He had spent a summer in Skye, working in the Loch Edmond's Mist distillery, starting out by raking the barley floor, absorbing what he could in the mash house and then moving on to tend to the worm tubs in the stillhouse. On his return to Canada, he had become an expert on cooperage, and travelled out west to sit in on grain purchase negotiations.

Rifka quit the dance floor, leaving Barney standing there in the middle of a number, laughing too loud. Then Barney joined Lionel, the two of them swooping from table to table, drawing closer.

Lionel had bet Barney five thousand dollars that he could drink the most champagne without upchucking and that he could get laid before midnight without having to pay for it. Bottle in hand, he bounced from table to table, Barney trailing after. Lionel saying, "Hi, Jewel, want to stroke my cock?" And at another table, "Any of you girls want to fuck?"

(Years later a best-selling hagiographer of the family wrote, in a chapter titled "Lionel as Prince Hal", that though many took Lionel to be a vulgarian at the time, lacking the royal jelly, the truth is "he was a lonely young man, lonely as a lighthouse keeper on Valentine's Day, overwhelmed at a tender age by the secret knowledge that one bright dawn his would be the keys to the Gursky kingdom, even though he would have preferred breeding horses in Elysian fields." An abiding passion, a footnote pointed out, that led to the establishment of The Sweet Sue Stables in Louisville, Kentucky, the name changed to Big Cat after his first divorce.)

Finally the Gursky scions swayed over the same table and Barney heard his cousin say, "But everything's settled. It's all going to be mine one day. So think carefully before you turn me down, honey."

Barney grabbed Lionel by the lapels and shook him. "What are you talking about?"

"Didn't your father tell you?"

Barney, the colour drained from his face, descended on Mr. Morrie's table, but he wasn't there. Barney found him in the men's room, washing his hands. Blind to the presence of another man in one of the cubicles, Barney began to curse his father for allowing Mr. Bernard to swindle him out of his patrimony. Soaked in sweat, his chest heaving, Barney said,

"If Uncle Bernard put a saucer of milk on the floor you would get down on all fours and lick it up."

"Please, Barney, don't be angry with me. I love you."

"Big fucken deal."

"When you are thirty-one years old you will inherit millions."

"I'll have the money right now or I'll sue. In fact I might fight this in court anyway."

"But, *yingele*, I signed the papers years ago," Mr. Morrie said, reaching out to touch him.

"You think it would be difficult to prove that you were mentally incompetent even then?" Barney asked, knocking his father's hands away and fleeing the men's room.

Moses, in the cubicle, heard the door slam and thought both men had left. But when he came out Mr. Morrie was still there, looking dazed.

"Oh, my. You must have heard everything."

"Sorry about that."

"Barney's a good boy, the best, he just had too much to drink tonight."

"Can I get you anything?"

"I'm feeling, well, a little dizzy. You could help me back to my table maybe."

Moses took his arm.

"Barney's an outstanding person. I want you to know that."

SIX

$\blacklozenge$

1973. Following his humiliating altercation with Beatrice at the Ritz, the insufferable Tom Clarkson behaving impeccably, which only exacerbated matters, Moses had gone out on a bender. Ten days later he found himself being shaken awake by a black cleaning lady. He was lying in a puddle of something vile in the bathroom of a sleazy bar in Hull, his hair knotted and caked with blood, his jacket torn, his wallet open on the cracked tiles, emptied of cash and credit cards. Carleton dismissed him.

Idiot. Blind man. Cuckold. Driving back to the Townships, Moses missed exit 106 and had to continue on the autoroute as far as Magog, backtracking to his cabin, his Toyota riding low, laden with hastily packed suitcases and all the books he had accumulated in Ottawa. A telegram was tacked to his front door. From Henry. The ravens were gathering. Well, the hell with that.

Moses got right back into his car and went to pick up his mail. Legion Hall, who fetched it for him, usually dumped it at The Caboose when he was away.

Legion Hall was an imaginative man. According to Strawberry, Legion Hall and his two brothers, Glen and Willy, had joined the army in the spring of 1940. They were sorting out the barn for their father, shovelling cowshit, black flies feasting on them, blood streaming down their faces, when suddenly Glen threw down his pitchfork. "This guy on the radio this morning said democracy was in peril or some crap like that. He says our way of life is threatened."

"About time too."

"I'm joining up."

"Good thinking. Me too."

"Mister Man."

Glen's head was shot off at Dieppe and Willy was blown apart by a land-mine in Italy. Legion Hall, however, saw real action only once, in Holland, and decided it wasn't for him. The next morning a colonel found him on his hands and knees with a hammer and chisel outside the field mess tent. "What are you doing, soldier?"

"What does it look like I'm doing, you prick? I'm cutting the grass."

It was the guardhouse for him. "And then," Strawberry said, "this bunch of tests he done for a Jew doctor before Legion Hall was discharged with a twenty-five percent mental disability pension. I woulda scored him fifty percent easy."

Now Legion Hall, wearing his regimental beret at a jaunty angle, worked all the bars on the 243 and 105 on Remembrance Day, selling poppies, possibly even turning in some of the money.

For the most part, Moses's mail was made up of magazines: *The New York Review of Books*, the *TLS*, the *Economist*, the *New Republic*, and so on. He retrieved it, retreated to his cabin, flopped down on his unmade bed, and slept for eighteen hours, wakening at seven the next morning. Following his second pot of black coffee, fortified with cognac, he sat down at his desk. Sorting out papers he stumbled on a letter he had been unable to find for weeks. It was from the lady of the eyes of a different colour. "Having rambled on at such unpardonable length and to no point, let alone catharsis," Diana McClure's letter concluded, "I have taken the liberty of having Mr. Hobson send you a memento. Consider it compensation for my having been elusive for so long and finally proving such a bore. Are you, perhaps, a reader of detective fiction? Patricia Highsmith, Ruth Rendell, P.D. James. I am addicted to their work,

but I have always found the mysteries far more compelling
than their resolutions, and most assuredly that is also the case
with my belated 'confessions.' The cherry wood table I have
arranged to have sent to you (delivery pre-paid no matter
what they tell you) is the one Solomon finished for me on the
Friday that I was unable to pick up the bookcase. Central
heating tends to suck the moisture out of the wood. It should be
treated regularly with beeswax (available from Eddy's
Hardware, 4412 Sherbrooke St. W.).

"To this day I still vacillate between considering my failure
to appear for tea with Solomon that Friday as most
unfortunate or, conversely, a blessing for both of us. Of course
this is all idle conjecture, quite useless now, but seated in my
wheelchair overlooking the garden I can no longer tend, I am
much given to it. The roses are badly in need of deadheading,
the pods swollen. A boy with a fishing pole has just passed on
his way to the brook, his eyes understandably averted. Dr.
McAlpine says my hair will grow in again, but I doubt that
there will be time enough. I must stop this rambling right
away. Goodbye, Moses Berger, and do please remember to
treat the table as instructed. Perhaps you could make a note in
your desk diary or wall calendar."

Moses continued to rummage through his desk. In a bottom
drawer filled with angry letters-to-the-editor he had written
but never mailed, he came across his silver cognac flask and a
cheque for one hundred pounds from the *TLS*, payment for a
book review that he had given up for lost. Then, under
everything else, he found Mr. Morrie's handwritten memoir.
Getting him to compose it, Moses recalled, had required some
fancy footwork. The result was pathetic, a masterpiece of
evasion. But things could still be learned from it, even as
Kremlinologists pried the occasional pearl of truth out of
Pravda. The analogy pleased Moses. For after all was said and
done what he had become, if anything, beyond a degenerate
drunk and cuckold, was a Gurskyologist. The only one armed
with flint among all the hagiographers in the woodpile.

Moses moved to the cherry wood table, his most prized
possession, shook the pages free of mouse droppings and began
to skim through them. Mr. Morrie, in his opening paragraph,
ventured that it was his intention to hit the high spots in his

history of the development of the Gursky empire, begging indulgence in advance for any omissions, which could be blamed on an old man's faulty memory. So in 122 closely written pages there was not a single mention of Bert Smith. Mr. Morrie started out by saying that his father, Aaron Gursky, had decided to emigrate to Canada in 1897 (with his wife, Fanny, who was five months pregnant with Bernard) "so that he could raise his family under the British flag, which was famous for fair play." But in fact that wasn't exactly how it happened.

Raw, illicit whisky was not only the well-head of the Gursky billions, it was also what indirectly floated Ephraim's legal descendants to Canada in the first place. Moses was able to establish as much through a close study of the Royal Commission Report on the Liquor Trade, circa 1860–70, and by chasing down every available history of the formative years of the North West Mounted Police. This led him to RCMP headquarters in Ottawa, where he sweet-talked his way into the archives by flaunting his Rhodes scholarship, his First in History at Balliol, and pretending that he was researching an essay on Fort Whoop-Up for *History Today*.

Sorting through old diaries, journals, and charge sheets until his eyes ached, Moses had been rewarded by the discovery that, in 1861, Ephraim was ensconced in a log cabin in the foothills of the Rockies with a Peigan squaw and three children. He turned his hand to making Whoop-Up Bug Juice from a recipe that called for a handful or two of red pepper, a half-gallon of Jamaica ginger, a quart of molasses, say a pound of chewing tobacco, and a quart of whisky. This lethal brew was then diluted with creek water, heated to the boiling point, and carted off to a tent outside Fort Whoop-Up, hard by the Montana border. Ephraim peddled it by the cupful to Blackfoot Indians in exchange for fur and horses. It was the unhappy combination of unquenchable Blackfoot thirst and an endless need for horses to satisfy it that led to a problem. The Indians were driven to stealing horses from settlers and Hudson's Bay forts. Crazy drunk they also burned down a trading post or two for sport. They robbed and they raped, and Ephraim, according to one report, had to shoot a couple of them as an example when they had the effrontery to demand undiluted whisky, that is to say firewater that could be ignited by a match.

There were other skirmishes, more shootings and burnings, and eventually news of the unrest reached Canada's first prime minister in faraway Ottawa. Sir John A. Macdonald, a prodigious drinker himself, created something called the Mounted Rifles to cope with the trouble. However, Washington took umbrage at the aggressive Canadians imposing an armed force of three hundred men so close to the border. The resourceful Sir John A. reached for his pen and renamed the force the Mounted Police. The fabled riders of the plain were born:

> We muster but three hundred
> In all this Great Lone Land
> Which stretches from Superior's shore
> To where the Rockies stand;
> But not one heart doth falter,
> No coward voice complains,
> Tho' all too few in numbers are
> The Riders of the Plains.
>
> Our mission is to raise the Flag
> Of Britain's Empire here,
> Restrain the lawless savage,
> And protect the Pioneer;
> And 'tis a proud and daring trust,
> To hold these vast Domains,
> With but three hundred Mounted Men,
> The Riders of the Plains.

Before the North West Mounted Police ever finished their punishing eight-hundred-mile-long march to Fort Whoop-Up, rampaging American whisky-runners slaughtered a band of Assiniboines at Battle Creek. Ephraim, at this point, was being supplied with rotgut whisky out of Fort Benton. Rather than wait to explain himself to the newly formed police corps, possibly being required to answer for the death of two Blackfoot, he obviously thought it more politic to skedaddle.

And then, for a long while, Moses lost him, unaware of where he went next.

An enigma that was resolved when Moses came by the journal wherein Solomon recounted the tales he had been told by his grandfather on their journey to the Polar Sea. Tales filtered through an old man's faulty memory and written down by Solomon many years later. Tales that Moses suspected had been burnished in the service of not one, but two outsized egos.

In any event, according to Solomon, his grandfather next ventured as far as Russia, disposing of a cargo of beaver pelts in St. Petersburg, and then carrying on to Minsk, where his parents had escaped from. Walking out, early in the reign of Nicholas I, when among other decrees it was ruled that Jewish children should be forcibly taken from their parents at the age of twelve and be compelled to serve in the czar's army for as long as twenty-five years.

Ephraim, wandering into the synagogue in Minsk in time for the Friday evening service, discovered that his father was still remembered fondly. "The best cantor we ever had," an old man told him.

A week later Ephraim served as cantor for the sabbath services, the congregation amazed by the soaring golden voice of this Jew who didn't wear a capot, but dressed like a Russian prince and was rumoured to frequent *their* taverns, demanding service. Wary of his reckless behaviour, they nevertheless offered him his father's old post in the synagogue. Ephraim declined the honour, but lingered in Minsk long enough to impulsively marry a certain Sarah Luchinsky, who bore him a son called Aaron. Then there was an incident in a tavern and Ephraim was obliged to flee again. He settled his wife and child in reasonable style in a *shtetl* in the Pale of Settlement and soon, bored with both of them, left the country, but continued to send them funds from France and England and finally Canada.

Ephraim continued to wander, running guns to New Orleans during the American Civil War, he told Solomon, and then dropping out of sight until 1881, the year a swirl of pogroms followed the assassination of Alexander II by terrorists. Ephraim, his nagging wife safely dead, his son now married, eventually sent the feckless Aaron steamship tickets and enough money to come to Canada with Fanny. But Ephraim did not care for the adult Aaron any more than he had for the simpering child, and neither did he warm to Fanny. So he dumped them on a homestead he had acquired on the prairie and disappeared again.

"My dear father," Mr. Morrie wrote, "had been poorly advised about the Canadian climate and brought cherry and peach tree saplings and tobacco seeds with him."

They arrived in April, greeted by snow and frost, obliged to retreat to a hotel in the nearest railway town until the thaw. Then Aaron built himself a sod hut, acquired a team of oxen and a cow, and planted his first wheat crop. It froze in the field. So Aaron bought pots and pans, tea, kerosene and patent medicines from a wholesaler and peddled to the farmers. Bernard was born, and then Solomon and Morrie.

Meanwhile Ephraim scaled the Chilkoot Pass into the Klondike. "He told me," Solomon wrote in his journal, "that he found work as a piano player in a saloon in Dawson, doubling as a cashier. The drunken prospectors paid for their booze and girls with gold dust, Ephraim usually the one to handle the scales, joshing the men, distracting them, even as he ran his fingers through his Vaselined pompadour. Then, before going to bed every night, Ephraim washed the gold dust out of his hair. Eventually he put together a stake of $25,000, most of which he lost in a poker game in the Dominion Saloon."

It was spring before Ephraim returned to the prairie and settled down in a tarpaper shack on the reservation with Lena Green Stockings. From time to time he looked in on Aaron and his family, mocking him, a Jew peddler; needling Fanny; and teasing the children. His visits, Solomon noted in his journal, were dreaded. But Mr. Morrie wrote, "My grandfather was a very colourful man, more interesting than many you've read about in my favourite *Reader's Digest* feature, The Most Unforgettable Character I've Ever Met. How we looked forward to his joining us at the sabbath table! His had been a very hard life, filled with adversity. The poor man lost his beloved wife while he was still in his prime and never found anybody to replace her in his heart. He could speak Indian and Eskimo and set bones better than any doctor. Sadly, though he lived to a very ripe old age, he didn't last long enough to see his grandchildren succeed beyond his wildest dreams. He would have been very proud for sure."

On his visits Ephraim reproached his grandchildren for their ignorance, saving his worst sarcasm for Solomon, because he had Ephraim's hair, his eyes, and his nose.

Ephraim waited and watched and when he adjudged Solomon ready, he was there as the boy came tumbling out of school into the thickly falling snow; he was there standing on the stern of his long sled, stinking of rum, his eyes hot. Instead of turning right at the CNR tracks he took a left fork on the trail leading out to the prairie.

"I thought we were going to Montana," Solomon said.

"We're heading north."

"Where?"

"Far."

SEVEN

◆

It depended on whom you talked to. Some said certainly six, seven million, others swore ten, maybe more. Anyway in 1973 that was the scuttlebutt on how much Harvey Schwartz had already made for himself hoeing the hundreds of millions ripening in Jewel, the Gursky family investment trust, as well as riding shotgun over Acorn Properties, the Gursky international real-estate company, its estimated value a billion plus at the time. Mind you, a good chunk of Harvey's fortune was tied up in vested shares. But it was the weight of the money, they said, that explained why Harvey chewed his fingernails and suffered from insomnia, dyspepsia, and agonizing bowel movements. The gossips, as is so often the case, were wrong. Even before Harvey had accumulated his millions, he had been consumed by the secret fear that one day they would come for him. He would be falsely accused of a crime. Robbery, rape, murder, take your pick. One day he would be framed and they would come for him, his protestations of innocence unavailing *unless he had a foolproof alibi*. So Harvey, who knew he could be arrested when he was least expecting it (any time, any place) constantly worked at clearing his name. Once, at ease by the poolside of the Tamarack Country Club, on the verge of snoozing, Harvey came quickly alert when he grasped that everybody else was discussing the Kleinfort murder case. "You know," Harvey said, as soon as he had the group's attention, "I wouldn't even know how to handle a gun."

Harvey's obsession crystallized when he saw *The Wrong Man*, an Alfred Hitchcock movie inspired by the true story of a bass-fiddle player at the Stork Club, who was mistakenly identified in a police lineup and charged with robbery, only to be saved at the last moment when the real culprit struck again. Harvey, who had seen the movie three times, suffered with Henry Fonda throughout.

Harvey knew. Harvey understood. So naturally he took precautions.

If, for instance, he went to a movie with his wife, Becky, (whose testimony in his favour wouldn't count), he not only held on to the stubs, filing them with the date, but also did his best to make his presence felt. He might thrust a hundred-dollar bill at the ticket seller, apologizing for not having a smaller banknote with him, *but making himself known*. Once inside, he would look for anybody he knew, greeting even the slightest acquaintance effusively.

— Yes, on the night of the rape I definitely saw Mr. Schwartz at the Westmount Square cinema.

Checking into a hotel in New York, Chicago, or wherever, Harvey donned surgical gloves as soon as the bellboy had set down his bags and departed the suite. He searched the closets, the shower (since *Psycho*), and every dresser drawer, unwilling to leave his fingerprints about until he was satisfied that no bloodied knives or incriminating guns had been left behind by a previous occupant, *setting him up*. Harvey also insisted that his chauffeur obey all traffic regulations, especially speed limits, lest some disadvantaged mother, crazed with greed, throw her baby under his wheels, *intending to sue for millions*. Then, in the days when he was still obliged to fly commercial, he never accepted a seat next to an unaccompanied lady, *lest she was a plant*, set in place to hit him with an indecent assault suit. Happily, nowadays, he enjoyed access to the Gursky jets, thanks to Mr. Bernard's largesse.

The truth was Mr. Bernard could be surprisingly caring, treating Harvey like his most favoured acolyte, thinking aloud in his presence. He told him that if he were prime minister he could settle the national deficit one-two-three. He felt strongly that there was too much screwing without rubbers in the Third World and he would put a stop to that. If the Israelis only had the sense to call on him he would also settle the Arabs' hash.

"You know, Mr. Bernard, we should keep a record of your table talk."

"For future generations?"

"Yes."

So the sessions began, Mr. Bernard pontificating.

"You know what's the greatest invention of western man?"

"No."

"Interest."

Mr. Bernard munching cashews, sipping Mascada Blanc, reminiscing.

"Abraham Lincoln (I'm not knocking him, he freed the niggers) he was born in a log cabin in a warm climate, which couldn't have been that bad. But for Bernard Gursky it was a sod hut on the freezing prairie, which was all my poor father could afford at the time, Ephraim he wouldn't give him shit. I was Ephraim's favourite, you know. Big deal. Ephraim always had money for whores and gambling, yesirree, but for his own son? *Bupkes.* How do I know your tape recorder is working?"

Harvey shifted briefly into playback. It was working.

"You think Westmount can be cold? I'll tell you cold. When it drops to sixty below, even with the kitchen stove roaring all night, the water pails would be solid ice in the morning. Then it's spring, and no matter how good you fill in the chinks in a sod hut when it rains it pisses on your head. Never mind. You also collect the rain-water in barrels off the sod-and-poplar roof to help with the water supply. Otherwise, kid, you are dragging water up from the spring in galvanized pails day after day.

"In the winter my mother, God bless her soul, she used to melt snow in tubs for water. For heating we collected buffalo chips. The buffalo were long gone, but their skulls were still everywhere. Hey, how did Bernard Gursky, that empire-builder, make his first money? Ordinary people might like to know. I made my first money catching gophers, but now," Mr. Bernard said, slapping the table and laughing until tears came to his eyes, "now I have my own, eh, you little runt?"

Harvey's freckled cheeks shone stinging red.

"Hey, I was only teasing. I made a funny. No hard feelings, eh?"

"No."

Another day.

"Every family has a cross to bear, a skeleton in the closet, that's life. Eleanor Roosevelt, she's been to our house, you know. Couldn't her father afford a dentist? Her teeth. *Oy vey*. Her people were in the opium trade in China, but you wouldn't read that in *The Ladies' Home Journal* or wherever she wrote 'My Day'. Joe Kennedy was a whoremaster from day one and he swindled Gloria Swanson, but they never sang about that in Camelot. Take King George V even, an OBE was too good for me. One of his sons was a hopeless drunk, another was a bum-fucker and a drug addict, and that dumb-bell the Duke of Windsor he threw in the sponge for a tart. You want the Duke and Duchess for a charity ball, you rent them like a tux from Tip-Top. Royalty they call that. Me, my cross to bear was Solomon, though God knows I tried my best for him, it's on the record. He was what they call a bad seed. You think it doesn't grieve me? It grieves me plenty, my brother to die like that, besmirching the family name to this day. Hey, that Solomon Gursky he ordered Willy McGraw shot dead at the railway station. And those Gursky brothers were once bootleggers. Oh me oh my. Oh dearie me. We can't have them here for tea and cucumber sandwiches on bread made from Lepage's glue.

"Did I ever tell you what happened just before I bought our first railroad hotel, and if anybody says that was Solomon's doing just look it up, eh, and see whose name the deed was in. All we've got to our name at this point is my father's general store and maybe four thousand dollars in the *pushke*. Correction. We *had* four thousand dollars until Solomon stole it so's he can sit in on the biggest poker game in town. He's going to risk the family's hard-earned money at the table, everything, and win or lose the bastard's going to run. Bye bye family. Bye bye family savings. My poor mother and father, and Morrie it goes without saying, are going sob sob sob in the kitchen. Nobody knows where the game is but I know where Solomon's whores can be found. The old Indian one on the reservation and the Polack with the big knockers at the hotel. I give them a message for my darling brother. Tell him he runs as far as Timbuktu and I'll find him and have the cops put him in prison and he can rot there. He got the message all right and he comes home but he's so ashamed to face us he runs away the next day and joins the army. And while he's making his paid tour of Europe, ending up an officer in the flying corps yet by forging a university degree, I'm putting together a chain of hotels, working eighteen hours a day for me was nothing, putting a third of everything in his name because that's how Bernard Gursky is built. Family is family. He comes home, does he say, Bernard, I don't deserve such a big share? Does he observe I've done real good? Forget it.

"You know in the bad old days hijacking was a problem we had to contend with. Gangsters. Other people's greed. Well one day he sends out Morrie, of all people, with a convoy, himself he's too scared. Morrie's in the last car, you know, the one that drags a fifty-foot chain behind, it makes one hell of a dust cloud in case anybody is chasing after. The men in this car also have a searchlight they can shine into somebody's eyes through the back window and they carry submachine guns, but only for self-defence. The shooting starts before they even hit the Montana border. Morrie shits his pants. That's no disgrace, you know, if you've read up on the Great War. Me they wouldn't take because of my flat feet. I was heart-broken. This country I love it and everybody in it. Anyway I read that happened to men at Vimy Ridge the first time they went over the trenches and they came home some of them had the VC, not VD like Solomon. Big hero Solomon. Did he ever go on about Vimy Ridge. The mud. The lice. The rats in the trenches. You ask me the closest he ever got to those trenches before he transferred to the flying corps was a whorehouse in Montmartre.

"Where was I? Oh yeah. Solomon starts to tease Morrie something awful about what happened to him. Boy, did I ever fix him. I shoved Solomon into the next convoy out, he's white as a sheet of paper. He's sweating. A truck backfired he hit the floor. Everybody breaks up. They're laughing at him, the hero of Vimy Ridge. He doesn't bother Morrie any more, you bet your ass."

Yet another day.

"Each generation produces a handful of great men, raised in log cabins or sod huts, who reach to the stars to grasp at impossible dreams. Einstein, Louis B. Mayer, Henry Ford, Tom Edison, Irving Berlin. Men in different fields of endeavour and what they have in common is that they never rest. But how did it all start in Bernard Gursky's case? Well, I'll tell you. We were living in Fort McEwen now (hoo boy, plank sidewalks) and among other things my father was dealing in cattle. My father had an understanding with this guy and one week instead of cattle he brings him forty wild mustangs. I had to break them in a corral behind the old Queen Victoria Hotel. My father auctioned them off and after each sale he invited the customer into the hotel bar to seal the deal with a drink. I watched this, sitting on a corral fence. I watched and I thought, which was always my way. Paw, I said, the bar makes more profit than we do, why don't we buy the hotel? There, right there is where it started. I led the Gurskys across the Rubicon into the liquor business. Have I got the river right?"

"Yes."

"There are so many lies being told about Bernard Gursky already somebody should be hired to listen to the truth from me and write my biography."

"I was thinking the same thing, Mr. Bernard."

"For this job I don't want a Canadian. I want the best. The hell with the expense."

"I could consult Becky and draw up a list of names."

"What about Churchill, who wrote his stuff?"

"He did, Mr. Bernard."

"Oh yeah?" Mr. Bernard drummed his plump fingers against his desk. "Maybe yes and maybe no. Now this Hemingway fella, how much can he earn?"

"He's dead."

"Of course he's dead. You think I don't know? You're getting on my nerves, Harvey. Haven't you any work to do?"

Yes, yes, certainly he did, but Becky, just back that morning from a two-day trip to New York, phoned to say, "I want to see you *and I mean right now*."

Harvey, home within the hour, found Becky seated behind her Louis XIV *bureau-plat*. The contents of an asbestos-lined box that had been lifted out of Harvey's wall safe were spread out before her. "I want to know why your precious life as Mr. Bernard's poodle is insured for three million dollars with various companies while the value put on mine, a published writer, is a piddly one hundred thousand?"

"Actually, I made a note to myself to review the situation this weekend."

"Let's see it."

"I mean a mental note."

Becky threw the deeds and policies at him and flew out of the room, charging up the stairs to their bedroom. Harvey pursued her as far as the hall, where he stumbled over a stack of boxes from Gucci, Saks, Bendel's, and Bergdorf Goodman. He retreated into the living room, sinking on to the sofa. The truth was the day he had done his annual review of their life insurance portfolio, intent on fattening her coverage, the newspapers had been full of a Toronto murder case that had given him pause. A real-estate developer, who seemed to have led a blameless life, was on trial for the murder of his wife of twenty years. His story was that driving to Stratford after dark he had wobbled into a rest area off the 401 to attend to a flat tire. While he was bent over a rear wheel another car pulled up behind, two druggies got out, knocked him senseless and shot his wife, who had foolishly put up a struggle. They made off with his wallet, her handbag, and all of their luggage. His defence was compromised by one bit of evidence. Only a month earlier, he had insured his wife's life for a cool million. Harvey, understandably alert, now balked at doing the same for Becky . . . because what if a week later, God forbid, she was run down crossing the street or lost in an airplane crash? *He would be suspect number one, that's what*. Led out of his own home in handcuffs before the TV cameras. Incarcerated with salivating faggots. His body violated like Peter O'Toole by that creepy Turk in *Lawrence of Arabia*. Harvey, his heart thudding, started up the stairs in search of an aspirin, and there, lo and behold, was Becky standing in the bedroom door, all smiles. "What do you think, buttercup?"

About what, he thought? *Give me a hint.*

She twirled around, her hands fluttering round her neck, and then he saw it. A diamond-studded choker.

"From Van Cleef & Arpels," she said, and then she indicated a little parcel, tied with a golden bow, lying on the bed. "I also brought you something."

Harvey tore open the wrapping.

"I know you could use a dozen, but I just couldn't *shlepp* any more parcels."

Holding the socks against his chest, Harvey said, "They're just the right size."

EIGHT

———◆———

Tim Callaghan hoped that Bert Smith would be drawn to Mr. Bernard's funeral, ending his twenty-five-year-old hunt for him. He must be sixty-five years old now, Callaghan calculated, maybe more. Smith, the righteous rodent. In his mind's eye, Callaghan saw him in a tiny basement kitchen that reeked of rot and cat piss and Presbyterian virtue. There would be a calendar with a photograph of Queen Elizabeth II on horseback tacked to the wall, the corners curling. The linoleum would be split and worn, the teapot chipped. He would be sitting down to a supper of macaroni or baked beans on toast at a table with a Formica top, sustained by the red-hot coals of hatred. Yes, Callaghan thought, providing that he was still alive, Smith would come to the funeral even if he had to be carried there on a stretcher.

Callaghan, a child of the century, had survived gunshot, two heart attacks and a prostate trim, none of which distressed him so much as the loss of his teeth, an intolerable insult. He was a tall man, an old coin worn thin, his once-blond hair reduced to a fringe of wintry straw, his eyes pale blue, his shoulders stooped, his liver-spotted hands with the busted knuckles prone to trembling. But at least he wasn't incontinent. He didn't shuffle like some of the others who had overstayed their welcome. Once he found Bert Smith, and made the necessary arrangements, he himself would be free to die, a prospect he contemplated with a sense of relief. He would leave the rest of his money to the Old Brewery Mission and his mementoes to Moses Berger.

"My God," Moses had said, the first time he had seen the photographs in Callaghan's apartment.

Over the mantel there was a faded snapshot of the young Solomon strolling down a country lane with George Bernard Shaw, and another one, somewhat out of focus, showing him seated on a verandah with H.L. Mencken, a malacca cane held between Solomon's knees, his hands clasped over the handle, his chin resting on his hands.

1956 that was, and Callaghan had shown Moses one of his most cherished souvenirs of that era when he had been most vibrantly alive. It was his edition of the Holy Bible as purified by the incomparable Dr. Charles Foster Kent, professor of biblical history at Yale. The abstemious professor had revised Samuel 6:19 from, "And he dealt among all the people, even among the whole multitude of Israel, as well to the women as to the men, to every one a cake of bread and a good piece of flesh and a flagon of wine," to read, "And he distributed to the whole assembled multitude a roll of bread, a portion of meat, and a cake of raisins."

Those were the days when Callaghan seldom saw his bed before four A.M., if at all, but, instead, sat enthralled at Solomon's table, listening to him pronounce on Trotsky's forging of the Red Army, or Edward Gordon Craig's theory of the actor as marionette, or the art of breaking a mustang. More often than not the table was festooned with fawning society girls. A de Brisson, a McCarthy, one of the Newton girls. And you never knew what was coming next, what a driven Solomon would decree. A midnight dinner thrown for whatever tacky touring company was playing His Majesty's Theatre, Solomon flattering the inadequate performers with caviar and champagne, dandling the middle-aged Juliet on his knee, flirting with the girlish Macbeth, and finally dazzling the company with his parody of Barrymore's Hamlet. Or Solomon crashing a supposedly secret Communist party meeting in some professor's apartment, playing the speaker like a kitten with a skein of wool before pouncing with his

superior knowledge of dialectics, slapping him down with
Marx's *Theses on Feuerbach*: "The philosophers have only
interpreted the world in various ways: the point, however, is to
change it." Or Solomon opting for a breakneck run to Albert
Crawley's hotel in the Townships, playing the piano with the
Dixieland band, luxuriating in their astonishment at his skill.
Or Solomon disappearing, retiring to brood on that bend in
the Cherry River where Brother Ephraim had once set his
traps for game and, come to think of it, men as well. The
abandoned shafts of the New Camelot Mining & Smelting Co.
were still there, the rotting rafters a perch for bats. Or Solomon
suddenly turning on his flutter of society girls, seducing one
of them into submitting to outrageous sexual acts and
then sending her back to her mountainside mansion, himself avenged but also, he would complain to Callaghan,
diminished.

"Gerald Murphy got it wrong," he once said, "living twice,
maybe three times is the best revenge."

Callaghan, sprung from Griffintown, hard by the Montreal
waterfront, had once been a club fighter. Possibly because he
displayed more spunk than talent in the ring, he developed a
following in the west. Solomon, who had watched him lose a
semi-final in Regina, invited him to dinner afterward. He fed
him beef and banknotes and started him out driving a Hudson
Super-Six, laden with booze, to just short of the North Dakota
border, where the switch would be made with the waiting
Americans. Callaghan proved so proficient that Solomon soon
had him managing the Detroit River run, armed with what
Eliot Ness once called "The Canadian Print Job", that is to
say, B-13 clearance documents that stipulated the liquor on
board was bound for Havana. Because Callaghan had so
much on Mr. Bernard he survived at McTavish following
Solomon's death, serving for years as vice-president in charge
of nothing for Loch Edmond's Mist.

Cancer claimed Callaghan's wife in 1947. He saw her
through her last months at home with the help of a night nurse
and Kathleen O'Brien and cases of Loch Edmond's Mist,
tolerating the comings and goings of the officious Father
Moran for her sake. Kathleen O'Brien read to her every
afternoon. Belloc, Chesterton. Then she sat with Callaghan,

praising him for proving such a devoted husband.

"But the truth is I wish she'd die and leave me in peace," he said.

"Shush."

"And then there's the nurse."

"She doesn't know."

"I do."

Frances, Frances. Each time he looked down on her bed, her once-fine flowing mane of black hair reduced to dry scorched patches, her eyes sunken, he was consumed with rage. What he wanted back was his once-glowing Frances, the girl he had first caught a glimpse of emerging from the Cathedral of Mary Queen of the World on a perfect spring morning. Frances, utterly unaware that all the men had turned to look, but not one of them whistled or made a coarse remark. She told him that he would have to speak to her father, a sour plumber with telltale broken veins in his nose. Callaghan told him that he was in transport, which made her blush because she understood and prayed for him. When the RCMP investigators came in the weeks leading up to the trial, she proved surprisingly tough. "But what does your husband do?" one of them asked, smirking.

"Mr. Callaghan provides. Do you take sugar and cream?"

Only a week before she died, swimming out of a morphine undertow, she said, "You shouldn't have lied at the trial."

"We owed Solomon everything."

"You did it to save your own skin."

"Why bring that up now, after all these years?"

"Find Bert Smith. Make it up to him. Promise me that."

"I promise."

She died in his arms, and for a while Callaghan became a drinker to be avoided, seeking out fights at two A.M. in the Normandy Roof or Carol's or Rockhead's. Then, stumbling out of Aldo's late one afternoon, turning into Ste. Catherine Street, Callaghan saw him. He saw Bert Smith. His chalky pinched face filling the window of a number 43 streetcar, staring right back at him without expression. Callaghan, the back of his neck prickly, took off after the streetcar, catching up with it at the corner of Peel Street. One stop too late. Bert Smith was no longer on board.

Callaghan found 153 Smiths listed in the telephone book, none of them with the Christian name Bert. Probably Bert is still rooted in Regina, he thought, and he was in Montreal only to attend a wedding or an Orangemen's convention. Something like that. Callaghan sent for the Regina phone book and, on a hunch, the one from Winnipeg as well, but he couldn't locate any relatives. So he tried another ploy. He had his lawyer place notices in newspapers in Toronto, Montreal, and throughout the west, announcing an unclaimed legacy of fifty thousand pounds for Bert Smith, a former customs agent, residing in Regina. None of the many bothersome claimants who came forward, several of them threatening lawsuits, turned out to be the real Bert Smith. So Callaghan, remembering that he had been drunk at the time, concluded that it had not been Bert Smith's face filling the streetcar window. It had been an apparition. That's what he decided. But he didn't believe it. He knew it had been Bert Smith.

Tim Callaghan retired in 1965 on a necessarily generous pension and moved into an apartment on Drummond Street. A creature of habit, no matter how late he turned in he wakened at six-thirty every morning, shaved and showered and ate his bacon and eggs, ploughing through the *Gazette*. Then he took to the streets, searching for Bert Smith in Lower Westmount and N.D.G. and Verdun, sometimes wandering as far as Griffintown, circling back to The Hunter's Horn or stopping at Toe Blake's Tavern to chat with the detectives from Station Number Ten, including his nephew Bill.

After a solitary supper in his apartment Callaghan would go out again in the futile hope of running into Bert Smith or at least tiring himself out sufficiently to sleep through the night.

Increasingly, striding those downtown streets, Callaghan mourned for the glittering city he had once known, the fine restaurants and bookshops and watering holes that had been displaced by the ubiquitous fast-food joints (Mike's Submarines, McDonald's, Harvey's) and garish clothing stores, video gamelands, bars where vapid girls danced nude on your table, gay clubs, massage parlours and shops that peddled sexual devices. There were no more cubbyhole shoeshine parlours where you could also get your hat blocked and maybe bet on something good running at Belmont. The last honest barber had retired his pole years ago. Gone, gone were Slitkin's and Slotkin's, Carol's, the Café Martin, the Eiffel Tower, Dinty Moore's and Aux Délices. Tramping the streets Callaghan sometimes wondered if he were the last man in town to have heard Oscar Peterson play at the Alberta Lounge or to have ended a long night with an obligatory one for the road in Rockhead's Paradise. Certainly he must be the last Montrealer to have seen Babe Ruth pitch for the Baltimore Orioles in Atwater Park, now a sleazy shopping centre.

If Moses was in town Callaghan usually met him for lunch at Magnan's or Ma Heller's, carrying on from there into the night. Years ago an agitated Moses had told him, "I was in Winnipeg last week and dropped into the *Tribune* and asked the librarian if I could see the Gursky file. But all the newspaper accounts of the murder of Willy McGraw and Mr. Bernard's arrest and trial had been stolen. I contacted other newspapers and found out that the old bastard had one of his minions go through the west and sterilize all the files."

"Moses," Callaghan said, "your father wasn't drafted, he volunteered. He didn't have to write those speeches for Mr. Bernard."

Moses was young then, already a considerable drinker, but able to handle it. Callaghan found him interesting, but he was not sure that he liked him. Moses was too nimble, ever ready to rush to judgement, and there was, Callaghan suspected, too much self-display there, born of insecurity perhaps, but tiresome all the same. Callaghan was also put off by Moses's silly determination to pass for the perfect British gent. The Savile Row suit. The Balliol College tie. The furled umbrella. Callaghan didn't understand that Moses, having already adjudged himself ugly, unattractive to women, felt better playing the peacock, his strut defiant. As far as Callaghan was concerned, what redeemed the young Moses, so quick to anger, was that he had not yet grasped that the world was imperfect. He actually expected justice to be done.

Callaghan tried to warn him against pursuing Solomon's story, but had he anticipated the ruin Moses's quest would lead him to in the years to come, he would have frogmarched him clear of the Gursky quagmire. "I know damn well why you are so enamoured of Solomon," Callaghan said, "but you haven't got it nearly right. Mr. Bernard is vulgar, but all of a piece. Totally consumed by his appetite for riches. But Solomon . . ."

"Betrayed hopes?"

"Yes."

NINE

———◆———

"Good time to invest. Bad time to invest," Becky said. "*I want it.*"

So, in 1973, when most of his friends, fearful of French-Canadian unrest, were going liquid, Harvey Schwartz bought an imposing limestone mansion on Belvedere Road in Westmount. Westmount, dug into the mountainside and towering over the city of Montreal, was a traditionally WASP enclave, the most privileged in Canada. Many of its great houses, hewn out of rock, had been built by self-made grain and railway and beer barons and shipping and mining tycoons. Most of them were originally Scots, their mansions constructed to rival the grandest homes of Edinburgh, colonial sons triumphant, the progeny of crofters, ships' chandlers and Hudson's Bay factors chiselling shields of the dimly remembered clan into the stonework. Harvey bought the mansion, with its spectacular view of the city and the river below, from a stockbroker. Tall, stooping, the broker insisted on showing them through the place himself, smiling acrimoniously all the while. He led them upstairs, past a wall of Harvard Classics and a set of Dickens, Becky pausing to admire the leather bindings. "My articles have been published in *The Jewish Review*," she said, "and the *Canadian Author and Bookman*. I'm a member of the P.E.N. Club."

"Then Mr. Schwartz has reason to be proud."

"You bet," Harvey said.

The broker ushered them into the master bedroom, opened a cupboard and said, "Now here's something that should interest you, Mr. Schwartz. The wall safe. Of course," he added, "you'll want to have the combination changed now."

"We wouldn't think of it," Becky said.

Downstairs they met the broker's wife. The elegant Mrs. McClure, her smile cordial but guarded. Maybe seventy years old now, Harvey figured, but still a beauty. Her ashen hair, streaked with yellow, cut short. She seemed fragile and favoured a cane. Harvey had noticed her crippled leg at once. The leg was as thin as his wrist — no, thinner — and caught in a cumbersome brace. She offered him a sherry, set out on a cherry wood table on which there was a vase of Sweet Williams. Indicating the cheese and crackers, Mrs. McClure apologized for not being able to offer them more, explaining that their maid and chauffeur had preceded them to St. Andrews-by-the-Sea. Westmount, she told them, had once been an Indian burial ground. The first skeletons, discovered in 1898, had been unearthed on the grounds of the St. George Snowshoe Club. "This street," she said, "wasn't laid out until 1912. When I was a little girl I could toboggan from here, through Murray Hill Park, all the way down to Sherbrooke Street."

A portrait of McClure, kilted, wearing the uniform of the Black Watch, hung over the mantelpiece. On the mantelpiece itself, there was a framed photograph of Mackenzie King. It was inscribed. The largest portrait hanging in the room was of the saturnine Sir Russell Morgan, Mrs. McClure's grandfather.

"I understand that you are retained by the Gurskys," McClure said.

"He runs Jewel," Becky said, "and serves on the board at McTavish. He is a recipient of the Centennial Medal and a — "

"Do you know Mr. Bernard?" Harvey asked.

"I haven't had that distinct pleasure."

"He's a great human being."

"But Mrs. McClure once knew the brother who died so tragically young. Solomon, if memory serves."

Mrs. McClure, favouring her thin misshapen leg, limped three steps toward a chair, managing the move with astonishing grace. Immediately she sat down, her hand sought out the knee-joint of her steel brace and clicked it into place. "I do hope," she said to Becky, "that you care for tea roses?"

"Are you crazy? We love flowers. Harvey buys them for me all the time."

"Why don't you show Mrs. Schwartz the garden? I'm sure she'd appreciate that."

"Allow me, Mrs. Schwartz."

Mrs. McClure offered Harvey another sherry, but he declined it. "I'm driving," he said.

"He made this table."

"I beg your pardon?"

"Solomon Gursky made this cherry wood table."

Harvey smiled just a little, but he was not really surprised. Strangers were always lying, trying to impress him. It came with the territory. "He did?"

"Indeed, but that was many years ago. Ah, there you are," she said, smiling at McClure without dropping a stitch. "Back so soon?"

"Mrs. Schwartz was worried about her high heels."

"Quite right, my dear. How foolish of me."

His blue eyes frosted with malice, McClure raised his sherry glass. "For generations this was known as the Sir Russell Morgan house, and then mine. Here's to the Schwartz manse," he said, with a little bow to Becky, "and its perfectly charming new chatelaine."

Outside, Becky said, "Now that we've got it, where are you taking me to celebrate?"

He took her to Ruby Foo's.

"Mrs. McClure," Harvey said. "Did you notice?"

"That she's a cripple. You must think I'm blind."

"No. Not that. Her eyes."

"What about them?"

"One is blue, one is brown."

"Don't look now," Becky said, "but the Bergmans just walked in."

"I've never seen that before."

"How can she wear such a dress, she just had a mastectomy, everybody knows. Oh, I see. They make them with nipples now."

"What?"

"The plastic boobs. *I said don't look.*"

"I'm not!"

"And don't use chopsticks. People are staring. You look like such a fool."

TEN

◆

"What did you think, Olive?"

"He should go on a diet. Like yesterday. Brando used to be so sexy. Hubba hubba!" Mrs. Jenkins didn't dare mention *Last Tango in Paris*, which she had slipped out to see alone. Imagine Bert Smith there when Brando reached for the butter. "But," she added, "I really go for that Al Pacino."

"He's Italian."

"Yeah, but cute. Those bedroom eyes. Remember Charles Boyer? Come wiz me to ze Casbah. Those were the days, eh, Bert? What did you think?"

"I thought it was shockingly immoral from beginning to end."

"Said the prioress to the Fuller Brush man. But didn't you just die when that guy woke up with the horse's head in his bed?"

"In real life he would have wakened when they came into the bedroom with it."

Squeezing her beady little eyes shut, puffing out her lower lip, Mrs. Jenkins said, "And what if they put it there while he was out, smarty-pants?"

"Then he would have been bound to notice the bump at the foot of his bed before getting into it."

"Oh, Bert, it takes seventy-two muscles to frown but only twelve to smile. Try it once."

As usual, they went to The Downtowner for a treat after the matinee. Smith ordered tea with brown toast and strawberry jam.

"And for you?" the waitress asked.

"Make me an offer I can't refuse."

"The lady will have a banana split."

"One bill or two?"

"Mr. Smith and I always go Dutch."

No sooner did the waitress leave than Mrs. Jenkins snatched all the little tin foil containers of mustard and ketchup on the table and stuffed them into her handbag. "When that waitress wiped the table with that yucky cloth she leaned over for your benefit."

"I don't get it."

"*Her jugs.*"

"Please," Smith said.

"And maybe, just maybe, that guy didn't hear them put the horse's head in his bed because he had taken some sleeping pills before retiring like they all do in Hollywood, if you read up on it."

"Then why did he waken later?"

Mrs. Jenkins sighed deeply and rolled her eyes. "Oh, come off it, Bert. Do cheer up."

But he couldn't. The world was out of joint, every one of his cherished beliefs now held in contempt. Once the G-Men, say Dennis O'Keefe or Pat O'Brien, were the heroes in the movies, but today it was *Bonnie and Clyde*. The guardians of law and order, on the other hand, were portrayed as corrupt. Even in westerns, when they still made one, it wasn't Randolph Scott or Jimmy Stewart who was the hero, but *Butch Cassidy and the Sundance Kid*. The memoirs of whores and swindlers became best-sellers. Young Americans with yellow streaks down their backs were being welcomed by a fat Jewess in hot pants at a store-front office on Prince Arthur Street, the book brazenly displayed in the window — *Manual For Draft-Age Immigrants To Canada* — telling them how to lie to gain entry into the country. Uppity French-Canadians wanted the sons of anglophones who had beaten them on the Plains of Abraham to speak their lingo now, a patois that made real Frenchmen cringe. The shelves of Westmount Library were laden with filth and to go for a stroll in Murray Hill Park on a balmy summer evening was to risk tripping over copulating foreigners.

Since his wrongful dismissal from the customs office, Smith had never gone on welfare. He had always managed somehow. He had worked as a bookkeeper for an auto-parts outfit in Calgary until he gathered that he was expected to help Mr. Hrymnak diddle his income tax. He had been employed for eight years as a cashier at Wally's Prairie Schooner, trusted with the bank deposits, and then a new manager came in, a young Italian who wore his hair in a pompadour. Vaccarelli fired Smith and put a young Polish girl with bleached blonde hair in his place.

Through the wasting years Smith consulted lawyers again and again, the reputable ones nervously showing him the door once he began to rage against the Jews, and the other ones bilking him. Each time a new minister of justice was appointed, he wrote him a voluminous letter, trying to have his case reopened, unavailingly.

Smith first drifted to Montreal in 1948. Answering a want ad in the *Star*, scraping bottom, he actually found himself working for a Jew. Hornstein's Home Furniture on the Main. Smith's first day on the job, he discovered that he was one of six rookies on the floor. Gordy Hornstein gathered them together before opening the doors to the crowd that was already churning outside, jostling for position, rapping on the plate-glass windows. "You see that three-piece living-room set in the window? I took a half-page ad in the *Star* yesterday advertising it for $125 to our first fifty customers. Anybody who sells one of those sets is fired. Tell those bargain-hunters outside whatever you want. Delivery is ten years. The cushions are stuffed with rat shit. The frames are made of cardboard. Tell them anything. But it's your job to shift them into pricier lines and to sign them to twelve-month contracts. Now some words of advice because you're new here and only three of you will still be working for Hornstein's once the week is out. We get all kinds here. French-Canadians, Polacks, guineas, Jews, hunkies, niggers, you name it. This isn't Ogilvy's or Holt

Renfrew. It's the Main. You sell a French-Canadian a
five-piece set for $350, ship him only four unmatched pieces
from cheaper sets he won't complain, he's probably never been
into a real store before and he buys from a Jew he expects to be
cheated. I trust you have memorized the prices from the sheets
I gave you because none are marked on the actual items. You
are selling to Italians or Jews, you quote them double, because
they don't come in their pants unless they can beat you down
to half-price. One thing more. We don't sell to DPs here."

In those days DP was the Canadian coinage for Displaced
Persons, that is to say, the trickle of European survivors that
had recently been allowed into the country.

"Why don't we sell to refugees?" one of the rookies
asked.

"Oh shit, a DP by me isn't a *greener*, it's a nigger. We call
them DPs because all that interests them is the Down
Payment. They fork out for that, load my furniture on to their
stolen pickup, and it's goodbye Charlie. Tell them we're out of
anything they want. Whisper they can get it cheaper at
Greenberg's, he does the same to me, may he rot in hell. But do
not sell to them. Okay, hold your noses. I'm now gonna open
up dem golden gates. Good luck, guys."

Smith, who didn't last the week, promptly found a better
job, this time as a floorwalker in Morgan's department store.
He had only been at it for a month when, riding a number 43
streetcar, he saw Callaghan staring at him from a street
corner. *The liar. The Judas.* And shortly afterward the Gurskys
made a serious attempt to snare him with an obviously
spurious notice in the *Star*, the bait an unclaimed legacy of fifty
thousand pounds for one Bert Smith. *They must think I'm stupid.
Really stupid. Looking to be found lying in a puddle of blood on a railway
station floor, like McGraw. Or to be discovered floating down the river.*
Too clever to be caught out by such a transparent ruse, but
alarmed all the same, Smith packed his bag and quit
Montreal, fleeing west, his cherished photograph of Archie
and Nancy Smith posing before their sod hut in Gloriana,
wrapped in a towel to protect the glass. Smith comforted
himself on the train by imagining the Gurskys in conclave,
fabulously wealthy, yes, but frightened by the knowledge that

there was a poor but honest man still out there who had their measure and could not be bought, a man watching and waiting, writing to government officials in Ottawa.

Smith worked the phone for a small debt-collection agency in Regina, he was a department-store security officer in Saskatoon, and rose into a bookkeeping job again, in Edmonton, until his employer discovered that he had once been discharged from the customs office as a troublemaker, maybe worse.

Then, in 1963 he was drawn back to Montreal, wandering up the mountainside to survey the Gursky estates, passing the high brick walls topped with menacing shards of glass, peering through the wrought-iron gates.

> The tabernacles of robbers prosper,
> and they that provoke God are secure;
> into whose hand God bringeth abundantly.

Driven by extreme need, Smith approached his bank for a three-hundred-dollar loan. The clerk he was sent to see, a slinky black girl less than half his age, seemed amused. "My God," she said, "you're sixty years old and you haven't got a credit rating. Haven't you ever borrowed money before?"

"I would like to speak with the manager, please."

"Mr. Praxipolis doesn't deal with small loans."

"And at the Royal Bank I expected to deal with my own kind," Smith said, fleeing the office.

Fortunately, the affable Mrs. Jenkins accepted a post-dated cheque for his first week's rent, and now he had been lodged in her house for ten years.

A decade.

Smith darned his own socks, but Mrs. Jenkins did his laundry and, after their first year together, only charged him a token rent. In return, Smith did minor repairs, kept the rent books, made the bank deposits, and filled out Mrs. Jenkins's income tax returns. He was able to survive on his pension and the occasional odd job, filling in here and there as a temporary night watchman, dishwasher, or parking lot attendant. Mrs. Jenkins allowed him a shelf in her refrigerator. They watched

TV together. And then, retiring to his room, Smith often went through his Gursky scrapbooks, thick with the family's activities.

Over the years Smith saw buildings endowed by the old bootlegger and bearing his name rising everywhere. He read that the prime minister had had him to lunch. Only a few months later Lionel Gursky succeeded in having St. Andrews, the home of the British Open, accept a two-hundred-thousand-pound purse for the Loch Edmond's Mist Classic Tournament. Lionel's latest concubine was featured in *Queen*:

" 'Some spend on things they can use, I splurge on paintings,' says dazzling Vanessa Gursky, the English beauty, wife of Lionel Gursky, likely the next CEO of the James McTavish Distillery Ltd. Chatelaine of a castle in Connemara, but equally at home in her Fifth Avenue penthouse ('My crash pad in the Big Apple,' as she so charmingly puts it) or her Nash terrace flat in Regent's Park, the peripatetic Vanessa's portrait has been painted by both Graham Sutherland and Andy Warhol. Here, left, she is seen standing before her favourite, the portrait painted by Annigoni, a picture of beguiling elegance."

On the occasion of Mr. Bernard's legendary seventy-fifth birthday party at the Ritz-Carlton, in 1973, the *Gazette* printed a list of those fortunate enough to be invited. And within months the old bootlegger was dead. Cancer. Smith went to the funeral, mingling with the mourners, and there he was confronted by the Judas himself.

"I'm Tim Callaghan. Remember me?"

"I remember you."

One morning only a week later Mrs. Jenkins rapped on the door to Smith's room. "There's a gentleman here to see you."

"I'm not expecting anybody."

"He says it's important."

And he was already there, sliding past Mrs. Jenkins, his smile benevolent. "Bertram Smith?"

"What's it to you?"

"I'd like to speak to you alone."

Mrs. Jenkins, her massive bosom rising to the insult, didn't budge. "What's black and white and brown," she asked, nostrils flaring, "and looks good on a lawyer?"

"How did you know I was a lawyer?"

"Aren't you?"

"Yes."

"Well, then?"

"Black and white and brown and looks good on a lawyer?"

"Uh huh."

"Sorry."

"A Doberman," Mrs. Jenkins said, marching out of the room, slamming the door behind her.

"Now tell me what you want here," Smith said.

"Providing that you are Bert Smith, the only issue of Archibald and Nancy Smith, who came to this country from England in 1902, and that you can produce the necessary documents to prove your identity, what I want, sir, is to tell you that we have been looking for you for years. You are the beneficiary of a considerable legacy."

"Hold it," Smith said, inching open the door to his room. But she wasn't listening outside. "All right, then. Go ahead. Tell me about it."

THREE

THREE

ONE

◆

Strawberry was descended from United Empire Loyalists. The name of his great-great-grandfather, Captain Josiah Watson, was inscribed on a copper plaque embedded in a boulder on the shores of Lake Memphremagog, a memorial dedicated to the pioneers "who braved the wilderness that their progeny, et al, might enjoy the advantages of civilization in one of Nature's wonderlands."

One day Strawberry took Moses to see the boulder. It stood on a height that had long since become a popular trysting spot for local teenagers. Strewn about were broken beer bottles and used condoms. Standing alone when it was first set in place, the boulder now overlooked VINCE'S ADULT VIDEOS on the roadside and, directly below, a billboard announcing that the surrounding terrain would shortly be the site of PIONEER PARK CONDOMINIUMS, complete with state-of-the-art marina. Yet another ACORN PROPERTIES development under the supervision of Harvey Schwartz.

Moses found Captain Watson's name mentioned in *Settling The Townships* by Silas Woodford. "The first permanent location of what we now call Watson's Landing was made by Capt. Josiah Watson, U.E. Loyalist from the province of

New York, who came from Peacham, Vt., sometime during the later years of the 18th century."

Perhaps it was the likes of the captain that another local historian, Mrs. C.M. Day, had in mind when she wrote in *History of the Eastern Townships, Province of Quebec, Dominion of Canada, Civil and Descriptive*: "Generally speaking, the class of men who comprised our earliest population were anything but religiously inclined: indeed, it has been said, and we fear with too much truth, that a really God-fearing man was a rare exception among them."

No sooner did these ruffians harvest their first crop than they distilled the surplus grain to make spirituous liquors, which prompted Mrs. Day to note with a certain asperity, "The way was thus gradually but surely prepared for drunkenness, poverty, and the various forms of vice which often culminated in crime and its fearful penalties."

Such was certainly the case with Captain Watson who, staggering home from a friend's cabin one rainy spring night, managed the difficult feat of drowning in a ditch filled with no more than three inches of water. His son Ebenezer, also a prodigious drinker, seemed destined to follow suit until he was literally plucked out of a Magog gutter one day by that interloper known as Brother Ephraim.

" 'Behold,' " Brother Ephraim said to him, " 'the day of the Lord cometh, cruel both with wrath and fierce anger, to lay the land desolate: and he shall destroy the sinners thereof out of it.' "

Brother Ephraim, sole author of *Evidence from the Scriptures of the Second Coming of Christ in the Eastern Townships about the year 1850*, later revised the date to 1852 and, finally, February 26, 1853.

Thrusting his demons behind him, Ebenezer Watson joined Brother Ephraim and his two leading converts, the Reverends Columbus Green and Amos Litch, preaching against the tyranny of hootch and spreading fear about the coming of Judgement Day.

Many of Ephraim's followers, Ebenezer Watson prominent among them, taking to heart his warning about camels and rich men, signed over their livestock and the deeds to their properties to the Millenarian Trust Company. In preparation

for the World's End, they also bought ascension robes from
Brother Ephraim. The men weren't concerned about the cut
of their loosely fitted robes, but many of the women, especially
the younger ones, had to return for innumerable fittings in the
log cabin that Brother Ephraim had built for himself in the
woods. They came one at a time and only much later did they
speculate among themselves about the ridges and deep swirls
and curving hollows carved into his back.

The Millenarians never numbered more than two hundred
and were subject to ridicule in some quarters. Say, in Crosby's
Hotel or round the hot stove at Alva Simpson & Co., dealers
in Proprietary Medicines, Perfumery, Rubber Goods, Hair
Preparations, Druggists' Sundries, &c., &c., &c. The laughter
of skeptics heightened after the world failed to end as predicted
on June 2, 1851. It was plain to see that the Millenarians,
gathered in their robes in the Magog Town Meeting Hall, had
been stood up by their Maker. A journal popular in the
Townships at the time, *The Sherbrooke Gazette*, also proprietor
of SMITH'S PATENT EGG BEATER (will beat a pint of
eggs in five seconds), noted, "From the failure of calculations of Brother Ephraim as to the 'time of the end', many
of his followers apostatized, but a large number continued
steadfast."

They could hardly be blamed. The land they were
attempting to cultivate, once the hunting ground of the
Algonquin nation, was ridden with unmanageable humps and
strewn with rocks. The first settlers, their grandparents, had
organized themselves into groups of forty to petition for a
township ten miles square, splitting the forest between them,
the agent grabbing the choicest site.

The grandparents set out with a camp-kettle, an axe, a gun,
ammunition, sacks of seed, and maybe a cow or two or an ox.
There were no roads. There were not even trails. Until they
managed to build their first log shanty with a bark roof and an
earthen floor, they were obliged to sleep out in the woods,
making a bed of hemlock branches, using the largest ones for a
windbreak. Without matches they were dependent on flint,
steel and spunk. Come June they had to keep smudge fires lit,
in the dim hope of fending off moose flies big as bumblebees.
There was no hay. So they destroyed the dams in the beaver

meadows, drained the flooded land, and relied on the wild grass that grew there. They learned to eat cowslips and nettles, pig-weed, ground-nuts, wild onions. They coped with panthers and catamounts, black bears killing calves and carrying them off. Once they acquired lambs and turkeys and chickens, they discovered that these were hostage to lynx and wolves. Most of the clothes they wore were spun and woven by the women who learned to master hand-card, distaff, wheel, and loom. If they were lucky, only three years passed before they brought in their first harvest. If the crop failed, the men felled trees and made black salt, tramping forty miles to market their sacks of potash, for which they were paid a pittance.

By Ebenezer's time the families lived in real cabins, with a cavity for a root cellar, a stone fireplace, floors of hewn planks, and furniture of a sort. Roads had been opened and covered bridges thrown across rivers and streams. There were grog-shops, saw and grinding mills, general stores, a doctor (struck off the register in Montreal) who could be sent for, churches, newspapers, a whorehouse, and plenty of home-brew whisky. But some things remained the same. For six months the settlers endured isolated and savage winters, enlivened only by the occasional brawl or suicide or axe-murder. They stumbled out of bed at four A.M. to tramp through the snow to milk their cows. Then there were spring floods and black flies and mosquitoes and work from sunup to sundown, and after that the accounts to be done. Usually they were obliged to plant late, because the fields were frozen hard as cement until the end of May. Often they never got to harvest what they planted, because there was an unseasonal hailstorm or the frost struck late in June again, or the fierce summer sun withered the corn in the fields. Idiots and malformed children were plentiful in villages, where marriage among first cousins was the rule rather than the exception. The women who didn't die in childbirth were old before their time, what with all the cooking and canning and sewing and milking and churning and weaving and candle-making. The men who rose before dawn to clear their poor hilly fields of rocks and stumps and tend to their crops and livestock had to start chopping winter wood in May. The harder they worked, the deeper they seemed to sink into debt. No wonder, then, that they welcomed a prophet who offered them an end to the only world they knew.

Brother Ephraim, consulting with the Reverends Litch and Green, went back to his calculations, leaning heavily on the Book of Daniel, and came up with a brand new date, March 1, 1852, which was happily not too far off. Yet again he exhorted his flock to cleanse itself. So more Millenarians signed over their holdings. Neglecting their farms, they flocked into the Magog Town Meeting Hall once more and were stood up once more. A headline in *The Townships Bugle* ran:

HUNDREDS IN TOWNSHIPS ARE PLUNGED INTO DIFFICULTIES

Brother Ephraim set a new and irrevocable date: February 26, 1853. More property was signed over. While the Millenarians were preparing for the World's End, however, a twice-disappointed, despondent Ebenezer Watson slid back into drinking, clearing the kitchen shelf of his wife's supply of the Rev. N.H. Downs' Vegetable Balsamic Elixir, highly recommended for the cure of neuralgia, rheumatism, headache, toothache, colic, cholera-morbus, and diarrhoea. Once again Ebenezer became a fixture at Crosby's Hotel.

"Hey, Eb, when you get there if there are no blizzards or bankers or pig shit, would you be kind enough to drop us a note?"

Understandably fed up with ridicule and impatient for the end, Ebenezer one morning consumed a jug of homebrew, donned his ascension robes and climbed to the roof of his barn. At exactly twelve noon he jumped, heading for heaven solo. He didn't make it. Instead he fell, slamming into a boulder jutting out of the snow, dying of a broken neck.

Ebenezer left his wife and six children no more than the original eighty-acre farm, which, through a fortunate oversight, he had neglected to sign over to the Millenarian Trust. And that night, even as the Watsons grieved, lakeside residents were wakened by the yapping of dogs. They figured that Brother Ephraim was going out to check his traplines on the Cherry River, but he was never seen in Magog again.

Ascension, without Brother Ephraim, was not going to be much fun, so only seventy-odd Millenarians turned up at the Town Meeting Hall on February 26. When they were grounded for a third time, they turned on the Reverends Green and Litch. Both men of God were beaten and tarred and feathered and then driven out of Magog on a sled. News of the swindle was reported with glee in the Montreal *Witness*, the writer enjoying a good laugh at the expense of the yokels. The next thing the dispossessed Millenarians knew was that three middle-aged strangers, obviously men of substance, came all the way out from Montreal. The strangers put up at Magog House, keeping to themselves, whispering together. They ate dinner with "Ratty" Baker, the local banker, studying surveyors' maps and consuming a good deal of wine, especially the plump, red-faced fellow, a lawyer.

The next morning the Millenarians were invited to a meeting by the lawyer, who offered to represent their interests in court, saying it was a dead cinch he could recover their property. Pausing to sip from a sterling silver flask, he assured them that they were looking at a grandson of a tiller of God's green acres himself. He understood what land meant and how it got into a man's blood. Often, he went on to say, even as he argued a case successfully in the supreme court of the land, he wished he were back on his grandaddy's farm, cutting hay, the sweetest smell in creation. But even before he began talking nonsense to them, Russell Morgan, QC, just wasn't the sort to gain the Townshippers' confidence. He wore a beaver coat and spats and sported a silver cigar cutter, riding a big bouncy belly.

"Yeah, but if you got our land back the mortgages would come with it you betcha."

"No, sir," he said, refreshing himself from his flask. Before quitting town Ephraim Gursky — for that, he told them, was the Hebrew scoundrel's proper name — had paid off all the mortgages with gold nuggets the size of which the bank had never seen before.

The lawyer's two confederates, Darcy Walker and Jim Clarkson, seated at the back of the hall, immediately grew restive. One of them pulled out an enormous linen handkerchief and did not so much blow his nose as honk it. The other one banged his cane against the plank floor.

"Mind you," Russell Morgan, QC, added hastily, betrayed only by a rush of blood to his jowls, "Gursky certainly didn't find those nuggets in Township streams. He brought them with him."

"He wasn't a Hebrew," a boy called out. "He was a Four by Two."

"That happens to be Cockney argot for Jew, young fella, and Ephraim Gursky is one of the worst of that nefarious race. He is not only wanted by the police here, but also by the authorities in England and Australia."

A murmur rose among the Millenarians, a murmur that a gratified Russell Morgan, QC, took for outrage, but was actually prompted by naked admiration.

"No shit!"

"Tell us more."

"Ephraim was transported from London, England, to Van Diemen's Land in 1835, a forger of official documents. The rest is understandably murky. We don't know how he came to this great land of ours."

"What would your services cost us, Mister Man?"

"Why not a penny, sir."

"We may be stupid," Abner Watson said, "but we ain't crazy. How much?"

Russell Morgan, QC, explained that if he lost the case, which was unthinkable given his brilliant record and fabled courtroom eloquence, then his services — much sought after, he needn't point out — would come to them *pro bono publico.*

"Come again?"

"Free."

But if he proved to be their saviour, all the timber land adjoining the Cherry River — including mineral rights, he put in quickly — would be signed over to him.

Once saved, twice shy, the Millenarians began to walk out one by one, drifting over to Crosby's Hotel. Watching from a window, they saw Russell Morgan endure a tongue-lashing from his two confederates, one of whom actually reached into a pocket of Morgan's beaver coat, yanked out the sterling silver flask, and flung it into a snowbank. As a contrite Morgan retrieved his flask, "Ratty" Baker rushed up, said something, and the three Montrealers immediately set out for Sherbrooke. On arrival, they repaired to the bar of the Prince of Wales Hotel, and there they discovered a short fierce man with hot eyes and an inky black beard drinking alone at a table in a dim corner. They did not so much approach the table as surround it.

"What can I do for you, my good fellows?"

Morgan wagged a finger at him. "You are Ephraim Gursky!"

The fierce little man, his eyes darting, tried to rise from his chair but was quickly knocked back, wedged into place, the three men having joined him at his table. Morgan, charged with glee, took his time lighting an Havana, watching the little wretch begin to sweat. Cornered, they were all the same. That lot. Laughing aloud, his belly bouncing, Morgan blew smoke in his face. "I am trying to decide," he said, "whether to escort you back to Magog, where you would undoubtedly be hanged from the nearest tree, or whether I should show you a modicum of Christian charity and merely hand you over to the authorities. What do you think, Hugh?"

"Oh, heavens, what a conundrum."

"Please," a tearful Ephraim whined just before he slumped forward in a faint.

The waiter was hastily summoned. "I'm afraid," Morgan said, "that our companion has overindulged himself. I assume that he is a guest of your establishment."

Darcy retrieved the room key from the desk and the three men, supporting Ephraim between them, led him back to his room, dumped him in a chair and slapped him awake.

"Well, my little man," Morgan said, "I'd say, not to put too fine a point on it, that you are a rat caught in a trap."

Darcy began to go through Ephraim's suitcase. Hugh searched the bureau drawers.

"What little money I've got is under the mattress. You can have it, if you let me go."

"Now isn't that rich, boys. He takes us for common thieves."

"You are obviously gentlemen of quality. But I don't know what you want with me."

"Possibly we wish to buy your illicitly gained properties on the Cherry River."

"They're worthless, sir."

"Oh, why don't we just take him back to Magog and be done with it?"

Ephraim watched, his eyes bulging with anguish, as Darcy pulled out a heavy pine chest from under the bed. "It's locked," Darcy said.

"The keys, Gursky."

"Lost."

Morgan dug the keys out of Ephraim's jacket pocket.

"I collect rocks," Ephraim said. "It's a passion of mine."

"That's rich. That's very rich. I should tell you that Mr. Walker is a geologist, and Mr. Clarkson a mining engineer."

The pine box unlocked, the rock samples lay bare.

"You will find a gold nugget or two in there," Ephraim said, "but I swear they do not come from any creek near here."

"Where from, then?"

"The north, my good fellows."

The men passed the rocks from hand to hand.

"You can beat me," Ephraim suddenly lashed out. "You can turn me over to the police or take me back to Magog to be hanged, but unless I'm offered a fair price I will not sign over deeds to properties that took me three long years of hard work to accumulate."

The Millenarians, their properties lost, were in a hallelujah mood. Brother Ephraim, who had promised to save them, had been as good as his word so far as they were concerned. No sooner did the snows melt than most of the dispossessed packed their wagons and headed south. Free free. Free at last. Free to put the unyielding wintry land behind them. Some struck out for Texas, which they had read so much about in dime novels, but others made it no further than the "Boston-States", where eight years later a few accepted money to replace rich Yankees in the Union Army.

One of the volunteers, Hugh McCurdy, had been related to Strawberry on his mother's side. A letter of his survived on three-coloured newspaper from a *Magnus Ornamental and Glorious Union Packet*. It had been written on the eve of the battle of Shiloh, where McCurdy fell, and one night Strawberry brought it to The Caboose to show Moses.

Dear Bess,

Bess, there is grate prospect of my Being Called into Battle Tomorrow — And for fear of it and not knowing how I may come out I will incloes 15 dollars and in Cayse of my Being Short of Money, which I may be, I will rite you if Necessary. You better give Father the little pocket Charm in Cayse only if its necessary. Tell Amos to Be a good boy and take Care of him Self, and I advise him as a Brother never to inliss for this is not a place for him. Tell Luke to Be Contented where he is and never to inliss and Battle all day. Bess! will you kiss little Frankie for me for I may never have that ocasion to do so my Self. I don't think of Enything more very important. This is from Your Dear Husban,

HUGH MCCURDY

The next morning Moses had hiked to Strawberry's house on the hill and together they had rooted through an attic trunk, surfacing with other intriguing items, among them a traveller's account, from an 1874 issue of *Harper's Magazine*, of a trip through the Lake Memphremagog country following its short-lived mining boom. "From Knowlton to South Bolton extends a wilderness. Small bears have been seen, foxes are often killed and the trout brooks yield up their treasures. From there we moved on to Cherry River. Gold was once thought to be abundant in the streams feeding the Cherry River, a Magog banker having displayed several large nuggets as evidence. But sadly for the many investors in New Camelot Mining & Smelting this turned out not to be the case. Therein, however, lies a tale. We sought out Sir Russell Morgan at his Peel Street residence in Montreal, the proud family coat-of-arms emblazoned over the portico. We hoped Sir Russell might enlighten us over what still remains a subject of some controversy. Unfortunately, he was unavailable."

New Camelot Mining & Smelting was the rock on which three considerable Montreal family fortunes were founded, that of the Morgans, the Clarksons and the Walkers. The mining stock, originally issued at 10¢, soared to $12.50 before it crashed. Radical members of parliament called for an inquiry at the time, arguing that Morgan and his partners had sold before the bubble burst, but nothing came of the protestations.

Sir Russell Morgan, in his privately printed autobiography, *A Country Gentleman Remembers*, dwelled at length on his progenitors, whom he had no difficulty tracing back to the Norman Conquest of 1066, even though — or just possibly because, some wags ventured — surnames had not yet been introduced in England. But he devoted only two paragraphs to the short, febrile life of New Camelot Mining & Smelting, the company he had founded in partnership with Senator Hugh Clarkson and Darcy Walker, MP. The three of them had been misled in the first place, he noted, by an Israelite renegade who had assured them that the hills were veined with gold. He deeply regretted that many investors had endured a beating. Mining, alas, was a risky business. Mind you, he added, he had never heard so much as a peep from the many more who had made money trading the stock or from those who had profited on his later ventures, but — he reflected — *c'est la vie*, as our charming habitant friends are so fond of saying.

TWO

◆

Hungover, unable to concentrate, Moses reckoned the day would not be utterly lost if he put the books in his cabin into some kind of order, beginning with those scattered on the floor. The first book he picked up was *The Unquiet Grave; A Word Cycle by Palinurus*. "The more books we read," it began, "the sooner we perceive that the true function of a writer is to produce a masterpiece and that no other task is of any consequence. Obvious though this should be, how few writers will admit it, or having made the admission, will be prepared to lay aside the piece of iridescent mediocrity on which they have embarked!"

Well, fuck you, Cyril, Moses thought, flinging the slender volume across the room and then, because he held Connolly in such high regard, promptly retrieving it. There was a Blackwell's sticker on the first page and a notation in his own handwriting: "Oxford, 1956"

That, of course, was the year Moses caught his first glimpse of the fabulously rich Sir Hyman Kaplansky, seated at Balliol's High Table, chattering with two of the most tiresome of the dons. Several weeks passed before Moses ran into Sir Hyman again, this time in Blackwell's bookshop, a malacca cane tucked under the old man's arm. Sir Hyman introduced himself. "I read your essay on Yiddish etymology in *Encounter*," he said. "Excellent, I thought."

"Thank you."

"So I hope you won't take offence if I point out a small error. I fear you missed the mark on the origin of 'kike'. Mind you, so did Partridge, who cites 1935 as the year of its first usage in English. As I'm sure you know, Mencken mentioned it as early as 1919 in his *American Language*."

"I thought I said as much."

"Yes. But you suggest the word was introduced by German Jews as a pejorative term for immigrants from the *shtetl*, because so many of their names ended in 'sky' or 'ski.' Hence 'ky-kis' and then 'kikes'. Actually the word originated on Ellis Island, where illiterates were asked to sign entry forms with an 'X'. This the Jews refused to do, making a circle or a *'kikel'* instead, and soon the inspectors took to calling them *'kikelehs'* and finally 'kikes'."

Another month passed before there came the summons from Sinai.

"There's no accounting for taste," Moses's history tutor said, "but it seems that Sir Hyman Kaplansky has taken a fancy to you."

Sir Hyman, the tutor explained, was a collector of rare books, primarily Judaica, but also something of an Arctic enthusiast. He owned one of the largest private collections of manuscripts and first editions dealing with the search for the Northwest Passage. A Canadian university, the tutor said, McGill, if memory served, had asked to exhibit his collection on loan. Sir Hyman acquiesced and now required somebody to compile a catalogue. "I imagine," the tutor said, "that you could manage the job nicely in a fortnight. He will pay handsomely, not that you were about to inquire."

On his next trip down to London, Moses made directly for Sam Birenbaum's office in Mayfair. Sam, overworking as usual, if only to prove himself to the network, had barely time for a quick pint and shepherd's pie in the pub section of the Guinea. Then, back at the office, he had the librarian feed Moses the thick file on Sir Hyman.

The elusive Sir Hyman was reported to have been born in Alexandria, the son of a cotton broker, and seemed to have made his fortune speculating on the currency market in Beirut, before settling in England shortly before World War Two. He was knighted in 1945 for his services to the Conservative party, it was said, and went on to amass an even greater fortune as a merchant banker and property developer. The immediate post-war period, however, appeared somewhat murky, Sir Hyman entangled in at least two botched ventures. In 1946, operating out of Naples, Sir Hyman bought two superannuated troop ships and a number of freighters of dubious seaworthiness, incorporating a shipping line. In the end, he had to write off his fleet, selling his tubs for a pittance. Then one of the freighters, still bearing the emblem of his defunct line, a raven painted on the funnel, was caught trying to run the Palestine blockade and diverted to Cyprus by a British destroyer. Fortunately Sir Hyman was able to prove that he had unloaded the ship in question six months earlier, and said as much in his letter to the *Times*.

Then, in early 1948, there was another unsuccessful flutter, this time in film production. Sir Hyman, known to be an aviation buff ever since he had learned to fly in Kenya, confounded his admirers in the City again, acquiring a villa in Valletta and announcing that he was going to produce a film about the air war over Malta. With this in mind, he began to recruit former World War Two pilots and to assemble a small air force, comprised largely of Spitfires. But the film never went into production, Sir Hyman unable to settle on a satisfactory script. He returned to London in May, assuring a reporter from the *Financial Times* that he would not plunge into unfamiliar waters again, and allowing that his air force had ended up in a knacker's yard, costing him a pretty penny. A day later David Ben-Gurion proclaimed the State of Israel, which he said would be "a light unto the nations." The new state was immediately attacked by troops from Syria, Lebanon, Transjordan, Egypt, and Iraq.

The most recent addition to the file concerning Sir Hyman was actually no more than a typed memo from a researcher, requesting a comment regarding an interview Guy Burgess had given when he had surfaced in Moscow only the day before.

"The Bolshie who did a bunk?" Sir Hyman had said. "I

hardly knew Burgess and, furthermore, I do not appear on television."

The file included magazine articles about Sir Hyman's country estate not far from Bognor Regis on the Sussex coast. The estate, its art treasures and antiques, its garden statuary, had been featured in both the *Tatler* and *Country Life*. Lady Olivia was an accomplished steeplechase jumper. She also bred corgis.

Moses longed to see the estate, but, as things turned out, he was summoned to Sir Hyman's flat in Cumberland Terrace. Moses arrived punctually at four and was shown into the library by the butler.

Left alone, Moses scanned the shelves encountering, for the first time, names that would come to be embedded in his soul: Sir John Ross, Hearne, Mackenzie, Franklin, Back, Richardson, Belcher, M'Clure, M'Clintock, Hall, Bellot. . . . Then Moses drifted over to take a closer look at a painting that hung over the fireplace. An Eskimo primitive. Against a stark white background a yellow ball of sun bled red rays. Below, a menacing raven plucked at a floating human head.

"Ah," Sir Hyman said, entering the library, "I see that you've been seduced by the deceitful raven."

"Is that what it is?"

"Once a raven swooped low over a cluster of igloos and told the people that visitors were on the way. If the people did not encounter the travellers before nightfall, he said, they were to make a camp at the foot of the cliff. The visitors did not turn up and the people built new shelters at the foot of the cliff, as instructed. When the last stone lamp in the igloos was put out the deceitful raven flew straight to the top of the cliff that loomed over the igloos. On the summit, perched on an enormous overhang of snow, he began to jump, run, and dance, starting an avalanche. The trusting inhabitants below were buried, never to waken again. The raven waited for spring. Then, when the snows melted, revealing the bodies of the unfortunate people, he amused himself emptying their eye sockets. According to legend, the raven did not lack for tasty provisions well into summer. What would you say to a sherry?"

"Would you mind if I had a Scotch instead?"

"Of course not."

They were interrupted by Lady Olivia. Considerably younger than Sir Hyman, blonde, with a daunting jaw, she held up a map of their dining-room table on a clipboard, flags protruding from each setting. "Henry's secretary just phoned to say he's iffy for tonight. The House will be sitting late."

"Then we'll simply have to do without him."

"But don't you see? That means I'd have to sit Rab next to Simon."

Sir Hyman glanced at the flags. "What if you moved Rab over here?"

"I've seated Lucy there. She'll love it. After all, it's a coronet she's shopping for over here, isn't it?"

"Lucy Duncan?"

"The little Canadian girl."

"Oh, Gursky. Couldn't we discuss this later?" Sir Hyman asked, indicating Moses. "I shan't be very long."

Moses was reading a book that lay open on a pedestal. *The Diaries of Angus McGibbon, Hudson's Bay Company Chief Factor, Prince of Wales's Fort*:

> A young white man who is unknown to the Compy. or opposition is living with a wandering band of Esquimaux in Pelly Bay and appears to be worshipped by them as a manner of Faith-healer or shaman. He goes by the name of Ephrim Gor-ski, but possibly because of his dark complexion and piercing eyes the Esquimaux call him Tulugaq, which means raven in their lingo.

A half hour later an irritated Lady Olivia was back, clipboard in hand.

"Our problem is solved, darling," Sir Hyman said. "Mr. Berger will be joining us for dinner. He's also a Canadian. He met Lucy when he was a child."

That was hardly sufficient for Lady Olivia.

"He's at Balliol. A Rhodes scholar. His father is a poet."

"Oh, how sweet," Lady Olivia said. "I didn't know they had any."

THREE

◆———

Lucy.

Their first morning together Moses came to shortly before noon, trying to sort out whose silken sheets he was lying on, when he isolated the sound that must have wakened him. It was the sound of retching and flushing. Surfacing, but still far from shore, he pried open his eyes and followed the sound through an open door to where a nude Lucy reclined on her knees before the toilet bowl. She struggled to her feet, wobbly, touchingly thin. "What would you like Edna to bring you for breakfast?"

"Black coffee. Oh, and a vodka with orange juice would be nice."

Still nude, Lucy pressed a button embedded in the wall and then stood on her scale. A fat, surly black lady drifted into the room without knocking. Lucy didn't bother to turn around. "Bring us a huge pot of black coffee, a jug of freshly squeezed orange juice and two yogurts. Oh, and Edna, this is Mr. Berger. He's moving in with us."

Moses waited until Edna left before he said, "Am I?"

"Well, if you don't remember you can bloody well leave right after breakfast."

"No, I want to stay." And have Aunt Jemima bring me the newspapers and a yummy yogurt in bed every morning.

"I've gained three-quarters of a pound."

He could, if he chose, count her washboard ribs. "I figure you weigh no more than a hundred." Maybe one ten, he thought, if she was wearing her jewellery.

"You don't understand. They need you to be thin. Or don't you remember anything about last night?"

"I most certainly do."

"Then who am I testing for this afternoon?"

"Manchester United."

"Ho ho ho."

"Remind me, then."

"Sir Carol Reed."

"It was on the tip of my tongue."

"So was I for a good part of last night."

Moses blushed.

"You'll find I can be rather coarse, but I come by it honestly. A satyr's daughter, they say. Do you own a dinner jacket?"

"Of sorts," he said, figuring he could borrow money from Sam to rent one.

"Good. You'll need it tonight." They were, she explained, going to the opening of a new play at the Royal Court and then on to a black-tie party at Sir Hyman Kaplansky's place. "Can you stay sober until I get back?"

He promised.

"Ken Tynan will be there and Oscar Lowenstein and Joan Littlewood and Peter Hall and God knows who else. Hymie invited them all for my sake."

Once she was gone, Moses immediately poured himself a straight vodka and then wandered about her bijou flat. Her bookshelves were crammed with play texts, actors' memoirs, studies of Hollywood greats and near-greats. A wicker basket overflowed with old copies of *Stage*, *Variety*, *Plays and Players*, *Films and Filming*. Moses decided that just one more little vodka, say three fingers, wouldn't do any harm, and then he collapsed into a velvet-covered wingback chair. Something bit into the small of his back. He pulled out a pearl necklace, long enough for a fishing leader, which he reckoned must be worth thousands of pounds. Suddenly aware that he was being closely watched from a kitchen porthole, he sent it clattering into the nearest ashtray.

"Can I get you anything, Mr. Berger?"

"No, thank you."

Lucy returned in a foul mood. "If it ever comes down to a choice between me and some tart in a bed-sitter, she gets the part. I'm being punished for being rich."

The play, a kitchen-sinker, proved interminable. Charged with significance. If, for instance, somebody turned on the radio it was never to catch the Test Match results or a weather report. It was unfailingly Chamberlain announcing peace in our time or somebody snitching that they had just dropped it on Hiroshima. Outside, her driver waited in the Bentley. Harold drove them to Sir Hyman's flat, which was awash with important producers and directors, all of whom Lucy pursued relentlessly. Moses, who didn't know anybody there, retreated to the library and pulled out a familiar title, the book which convinced him that Ephrim Gor-ski, or Tulugaq, had been fruitful during his sojourn in the Arctic. It was a first edition of *Life with the Esquimaux, A Narrative of an Arctic Quest in Search of Survivors of Sir John Franklin's Expedition*, by Capt. Waldo Logan. Logan, a native of Boston, had set sail for the Arctic on the whaling barque *Determination* on May 27, 1868. A month later, entering Hudson Strait, he wrote: "The next day, June 29th, we once more stood in toward the land, but it still continued foggy, and we were unable to get near until about 4 P.M. having just before again sighted the *Marianne*. At the time two Esquimaux boys were seen coming at full speed toward us. In a few moments more they were alongside, and hoisted — kyacks and all — into the ship. Their names were 'Koodlik' and 'Ephraim,' each 5 foot 6 inches in height, with small hands, small feet, and pleasing features except that both had some of their front teeth gone. These boys had brought an abundance of salmon, caplins, sea-birds, &c. and eagerly began to trade with us. Speedily we were on the most friendly terms, and merry-making was the order of the day. On entering the cabin to supper their conduct was most orderly. But Ephraim, the younger one, would not eat before salting his bread and mumbling a blessing over it. I couldn't catch most of it, but I did learn that the Esquimaux word for bread is *lechem.*"

Drink betrayed Moses yet again, the print doubling on him. He replaced the book on the shelves and went to a mullioned window, worked it open, and sucked in the night air. Then, feeling marginally better, he wandered over to examine the picture that now hung over the fireplace, displacing the deceitful raven.

"It's Prince Henry the Navigator."

Startled, Moses turned around to find that Sir Hyman had come up behind him once again.

"How old are you now, Moses?"

"Twenty-five."

"Well now, in 1415, when Prince Henry was twenty-one, he severed all connections with the court and became the Navigator. He retired to Cape Vincent, Portugal's Land's End, and from that promontory he sent out ships to chart the coast of Africa, but, above all, to seek the legendary Kingdom of Prester John. But you must be familiar with the story."

"Sorry, no."

"Ah, the mythical kingdom of the just, a veritable earthly paradise. A realm of underground rivers that churned out precious stones and the habitat of an astonishing breed of worms that spun threads of the most exquisite silk. It was purported to lie somewhere in the 'Indies', and it was said that Prester John combined military acumen with saintly piety and that he was descended from the Three Wise Men. It was anticipated that he would help to conquer the Holy Sepulchre as well as defend civilized Europe from the Anti-Christ, the hordes of cannibals to be found in the lands of Gog and Magog. News of the kingdom was first circulated in a letter supposedly written by Prester John in 1165 and sent to the Byzantine emperor of Rome. Unfortunately the letter proved to be a forgery. There is no just kingdom, but only the quest for one, a preoccupation of idiots for the most part, wouldn't you say?"

An agitated toothy Lady Olivia cantered into the library. "There you are, Hymie! Everybody's asking for you."

"Coming, my dear." He paused at the door and turned

back to Moses. "I'm sure you appreciate that Lucy is a
troubled young lady. Do be kind to her."

To begin with, they were actually kind to each other, playing
house together, tended to by Edna and Harold and provisioned by Harrods, Paxton and Whitfield, Fortnum &
Mason, Berry Bros. & Rudd.

Looking after each other was a game they came to cherish.
Lucy, for her part, astonished that she could be concerned for
anybody else's welfare and Moses gratified that somebody
gave a damn. Teasing, cajoling, abstaining from wine, she
seduced him into abstinence. After he had gone without a
drink for a fortnight, lying to her, pretending he didn't miss it,
she pleaded with him to resume work on his study of the
Beveridge Plan and the evolution of the British Welfare
State.

Out with Harold one afternoon, flitting from Harrods to
Asprey's to Heal's, she purchased a box of the creamiest bond
paper available; an electric typewriter; file cards that came in
a darling velvet case, each drawer with a brass pull; a leather
armchair; and an antique desk with a tooled leather top.
Then, while Moses was out for an afternoon stroll, counting
each pub he passed, his own Stations of the Cross, she had her
sitting room made over as a study. He found it all more than
somewhat pretentious, but he was also pleased, especially by
the Fabergé humidor filled with Davidoff cigars. There were,
he figured, only two things missing. A portrait of M. Berger,
Esq., pondering the mysteries of the cosmos, enduring its
weight, and of course cork lining for the walls.

Lucy, he discovered, had come to London (on the first
overseas flight anywhere out of Idlewild with her lucky seat
number five available) immediately following the breakup of
her affair in New York with a South American Grand Prix
driver. Her next lover, a beautiful boy encountered at the bar
in Quaglino's, absconded with a necklace of gold, diamonds,
and pearls that had once belonged to Catherine the Great.
RADA wouldn't have her, neither would the London Academy, so Lucy stitched together a school of her own. She
took acting lessons from a dotty disciple of Lee Strasberg,

dance and movement from a drunk who had once performed with Sadler's Wells (a bitchy old queen, whom Moses enjoyed having lunch with occasionally) and singing from a one-time tenor with La Scala, who claimed to have fled Mussolini, but more likely, Moses thought, scathing reviews. A McTavish Distillery executive arranged for her to be represented by a reputable agency before he realized that she was not Mr. Bernard's daughter, but Solomon's, and that he needn't have bothered.

The morning of an audition Lucy would waken convinced that she looked a total wreck, which was usually the case considering how poorly she had slept. She would patch herself together and hurry off to Vidal's, her analyst, her masseuse, and her voice teacher, though not necessarily in that order. Then, clutching her portfolio of photographs by David Bailey, regretting that she didn't look as good as Jean Shrimpton or Bronwen Pugh, she would join the other girls, also clutching portfolios, on the bench outside the sleazy rehearsal hall, waiting for the oily fat man with the clipboard to call her name. Why Lucy, with all that money, humiliated herself, going to market determined on the dubious prize of a bit in some mediocre movie, utterly confounded him. He wished, for her sake, that everybody would turn her down, bringing her to her senses. But unfortunately she was tossed a misleading bone from time to time, sufficient to inflame her fantasies of stardom. Say, the part of a sassy secretary in a Diana Dors vehicle. Or in yet another movie the gum-chewing long distance operator in a call put through to America by no less than Eric Portman or Jack Hawkins. Moses tried to reason with her. "It's not as if you're being offered Masha or Cordelia. What do you need this for?"

"Oh, go read a book, you prick."

Those were actually their sunshine days together. A time when staying at home with him, rather than dashing off to Les Ambassadeurs or the Mirabelle or the Caprice every night, offered her a chance to play a Celia Johnson role. Most evenings he seemed content to settle into the sofa with a book. She tried it herself, but her attention span was short, so she made do with magazines, jigsaw puzzles, or flicking from one TV channel to the other. All the while doing her utmost to squelch an inner voice that kept protesting these were to be your salad days and here you are, wasting in a cave, growing older with a morose reformed drunk, not much good in bed, the real fun elsewhere. No, no, she corrected herself. He will write something stupendous and everybody will point to her, like Aline Bernstein, that voluptuous Jewess whom her college instructor had said made it all possible. Yeah, sure. The trouble is Thomas Wolfe was a big tall *goy* and Moses, let's face it, is a little Jewy intellectual with pop eyes and thick lips. *Of Time and the River* is a classic, it's in the Modern Library, but a study of the Beveridge Plan with graphs and charts? Forget it.

What she failed to understand was that he loathed staying in every night, reading on the sofa, a habit not answering some dearly held predilection of his but born of penury. A good part of her attraction for him was that she could take him to Les Ambassadeurs or the Mirabelle, a world he longed to experience but couldn't afford. However, having ventured out with him two or three times she swore never again. Moses, insecure in opulent surroundings but absolutely adoring it, coped with the contradiction by indulging in snide remarks about the glittering couples at the other tables. He embarrassed her in fine restaurants where her arrival had once been treated as an occasion, the maitre d' strewing flatteries like rose petals in her path, by never settling the bill before checking each item as well as the addition.

Bored, he laid his book aside one night and said, "Tell me about Solomon."

"I was only two years old when he died."

"Didn't your mother ever tell you anything?"

"He drove her mad. What more is there to say?"

Her clothes, acquired at the Dior boutique or from the Rahvis sisters, were strewn everywhere, left for Edna to retrieve. Lying on the sofa, absorbed in the latest issue of *Vogue*, she was given to absently picking her nose. Even more disconcerting, her thumb might find its way into her mouth and she would suck it avidly, unaware of what she was at. Her appalling table manners were explained, he thought, but hardly pardoned by the mad mother, the absent father. For all that, she had a way of teasing him out of his bouts of depression, increasingly frequent now that he was supposed to make do without drink.

"What are we going to do for excitement this afternoon, Moses?"

"What would you like to do?"

"Maybe there's another Arctic nut with rotten teeth lecturing at the ICA?"

"Would you settle for tea with Hymie, if he's free?"

Sir Hyman seemed delighted to see them, but they had no sooner settled in when the butler interrupted with a whispered message.

"Really," Sir Hyman replied. "I wasn't expecting him today."

A tall gangly man with a tight little mouth sailed into the room. Sir Hyman introduced him as the Deputy Director of the Courtauld Institute and the Surveyor of the Queen's pictures.

Though Sir Hyman pleaded with them to stay, Moses made his excuses and led Lucy out, but he wasn't ready for another night incarcerated in her flat in Belgravia. "Why don't we go to the Mirabelle for dinner?"

No answer.

"I shouldn't be alienating you from all your old friends."

"What do you do in that room all day? I never hear your typewriter any more."

"I am pondering the mysteries of the cosmos, enduring its weight."

"Edna found an empty bottle of vodka hidden in the bottom of the cupboard."

For all their bickering, she came to depend on him. Her anchor, she thought. Somebody who could dissect a script, or explain a character that she longed to play, in a manner that allowed her to dazzle many a director with her insights. But she, too, had begun to find their evenings together in the flat unendurable. Even so, she wasn't going to treat him to a night out until she heard the hum of his typewriter again. So she began to lie, pretending that she was working late with a girlfriend on a scene when she was actually at Annabel's, and he, grateful for some solitude, began to sneak drinks in earnest, topping the Scotch and cognac bottles with cold tea when Edna wasn't looking. Then one morning she returned from her agent's office flushed with excitement. One of the proliferation of new young directors had seen her in something on TV and had invited her to audition for a small but telling part in a new play by a writer whom even Moses had said was not utterly without merit. Her audition was scheduled for the afternoon but it was midnight before she returned to the flat, kicking over an end table, sending a bowl of pot-pourri flying. "He told me I was perfection. Born to the role. Why, he wouldn't even bother auditioning anybody else." Then, she said, he asked if she would find it too boring to join him for a light supper. Harold drove them to Boulestin's.

"Oh, isn't this fun," the director said, rubbing his chubby little hands together. "It calls for a proper celebration. Wouldn't you say, my dear?"

"Yes."

"We could start with masses of beluga and a bottle of Dom Perignon unless you object?"

"Certainly not."

He told her wicked stories about Larry and Johnny G. When admirers stopped at their table he introduced her as his latest discovery. "What would you say to lobster?" he asked.

"Why not?"

"Good girl."

"Oh, and we'll have to give Vincent a warning right now if we want the baked Alaska."

"Wonderful idea."

He called for a bottle of Chassagne-Montrachet. Finally, when he was into his second snifter of armagnac, she said, "Forgive me if I'm being pushy, but when do we begin rehearsals?"

"Glad you asked me that because there is a wee problem."

"Tell me about it."

"It's nothing, really," he said, deftly shifting the saucer with the bill on it closer to her place, "but we do have to raise another fifteen thousand quid before we plunge ahead."

"Is that all?"

"I knew you'd understand."

She asked him if he'd like another bottle of bubbly.

"Well, do you think your driver would be able to take me home, or is that too much to ask?"

"Of course he will."

"It's in Surrey, actually."

"So?"

"Damned good of you too."

Then Lucy told Moses, "Once Mario had popped the cork, I yanked the bottle out of his hands, pressed my thumb against the lip, pumped it three or four times, and let him have it right in his fat face. Then I fled the restaurant, shouting at Vincent to mail me the bill. And now if you don't mind you can pour me a cognac and you might as well have one yourself. I know what's going on here. Let's not pretend any more."

They drank through the night and well into the next afternoon. Between crying jags Lucy told him tales of Mr. Bernard, Henry, and her mad mother. Mr. Bernard, she said, had turned against Nathan when he discovered that his son, then only seven years old, had run away from a fight at Selwyn House. "I'm going to phone the Jewish General Hospital right now," he had said, "to see if they'll exchange you for a girl."

But the call had been unsuccessful. "I'm stuck with you. They don't take cowards."

And then, Lucy said, when they had still been allowed to play with the other Gursky children, Mr. Bernard had told them that when he was a boy jumping into a corral churning with wild mustangs was nothing for him.

"And look at the Gursky children now," Lucy said, "every one of us a basket-case. Except for Lionel. A worse son of a bitch than his father. Henry's God-crazy. Anita buys a new husband once a year. Nathan's afraid to cross a street. Barney has broken my Uncle Morrie's heart, he won't even talk to him, and will probably end up behind bars one of these days. I don't understand Morrie. The more my Uncle Bernard rubs his face in the dirt, the more devoted he is to the old pirate."

After Solomon had been killed, Lucy said, when his

airplane had exploded, a weepy Mr. Bernard had come to the house to assure her mother that he would be their father now. "I swear on the grave of my saintly mother that I will treat Solomon's children like my very own."

"Murderer," she had cried. "Get out and don't you dare come here again."

"Murderer?"

"To the day of her death she believed the explosion was no accident. But the truth is my father didn't deserve her loyalty. He married my mother because she was pregnant and when she miscarried he took that as licence to come home only when it suited him."

"Why didn't she divorce him?"

"Well they didn't in those days. Or she might have if Henry hadn't come along. Or me. Oh, my father was such a bastard. She once told me that he would leave his journal on his desk where she could read about his other women."

"Solomon kept a journal?"

"Yes. No. So what?"

"What happened to it?"

"It's none of your business. Morrie, that creep, has it maybe."

"Would you like to get your hands on it?"

"You and Dr. Hersheimer. Some pair. No, I wouldn't. I know more than enough about him as it is."

"But he was your father."

"And you're so fond of yours, right? Remember the first time we met?"

"Yes."

"And there was that blank space for a picture on the wall — the portrait of that lady with the eyes of a different colour — the one that was stolen."

"Yes."

"It was a mistress of his, obviously, and he had it hung where my mother could see it every day."

Finally Lucy and Moses fell asleep, wakening to a breakfast of Bloody Marys and smoked salmon. Lucy was violently ill and consumed by remorse. "I lied to you," she said.

"About what?"

"The champagne in his fat face. I wanted to do it, but I didn't have the guts. But I did leave him stranded in the restaurant."

Lucy phoned her agent and was told he was in a meeting. She called again at noon. Her agent was out to lunch. She and Moses moved on to Scotch and Lucy called her agent again at five. He was unavailable.

"There are other agents," Moses said.

She fled the flat and didn't return until noon the next day. "I got in touch with the director," she said, "but I'm too late. He found the money elsewhere."

Only then did she notice Moses's packed suitcases.

"You can't walk out on me now. I'm going crazy. Look, you can drink as much as you want. I won't say a thing. Stay. Please, Moses."

In the morning she hurried to a gallery on New Bond Street to buy Moses a Hogarth etching he had once admired and, in another shop, a first edition of Sir John Franklin's *Narrative of a Journey to the Shores of the Polar Sea*. She fired Edna the same afternoon.

"But I thought you adored her," Moses said.

"I did. I do. But haven't you read about the bus boycott in Montgomery, Alabama, you *shmuck*? Everybody's talking about that Martin Luther King now. I found out people are saying it's just typical of Miss Moneybags to have a black maid. I had to let her go."

"I hope you told her why."

"She's so thick, that one, she'd never understand."

A couple of days later Lucy rented an office on Park Lane, hired a secretary and a script reader and began to option novels and plays and to commission hacks to turn them into film scripts in which she could play the lead. Soon avaricious agents and inept writers began to beat a path to her door, shaking the legendary Gursky money tree. She was consulted. She was listened to. All she had to do in return was scribble cheques. Fifteen hundred pounds here, twenty-five hundred there, two thousand somewhere else. It was amazing how little it took to satisfy them. Baffled, she asked Moses, "How much does a writer earn?"

"One of your screenplay spivs or a real one?"

"Okay, a real one."

He told her.

"Boy, am I ever dealing with a bunch of jerks."

But one of them, a former juvenile lead in more than one West End farce, caught her eye. Jeremy Bushmill, in his forties now, was trying to carve out a place for himself as a writer and director. The first draft of a screenplay that she had optioned from him actually attracted the attention of Sydney Box's story department. Lucy, armed with the notes that Moses had fed her, invited Jeremy to dinner. To her delight, he insisted on paying the bill. They carried on from Wheeler's to the Gargoyle Club, which wasn't the same, he said, now that poor Dylan was gone. But a sodden Brian Howard was there and Jeremy told her that he had been the model for Ambrose Silk. Lucy didn't get home until two in the morning. Moses, pretending to be asleep, didn't stir. But when he heard her pouring herself a bath he understood. He switched on the bed lamp and went to find himself a drink and a cigar and then waited for her to emerge from the bathroom. "Have fun?" he asked.

"He's a bore." She fetched herself a drink and sat down on the floor. "What if we got married and had children together?"

"I'm an unredeemed drunk. I also think you ought to complete your own childhood before thinking of taking on kids of your own."

"Who was Ambrose Silk?"

"A character in one of E.M. Forster's novels."

"Which one?"

"*Captain Hornblower*."

In the week that followed, Moses found himself a satisfactory flat in Fulham, but it wouldn't be available until the first of the month. Lucy was absent a good deal, usually coming home late and slipping into her tub. Later she clung to her side of the bed, careful that their bodies didn't touch anywhere, her thumb rooted in her mouth. Then one evening, even as she was applying her makeup in the bedroom, the bell rang. It was Jeremy, tall and handsome in his deerstalker hat and Harris tweed coat; Jeremy bearing roses.

"I'm afraid she's still getting ready. Shall I put these in a vase, do you think?"

"Bloody awkward, isn't it?"

"How goes the scriptee?"

"She's a marvel. Her notes are always bang on."

Lucy came home earlier than usual. "I have something to say to you," she said.

"You needn't bother. I'm moving out tomorrow morning."

She wanted him to join her production company as script editor for an annual retainer of ten thousand pounds. "We would have lunch together every day."

"Lucy, you continue to amaze me."

"I hope that means yes."

"Certainly not."

"Oh Moses, Moses, I'll always sort of love you. But I need him. It's the physical thing."

"I understand."

"I have something else to tell you." As no director, she said, would give her a chance, she had decided to mount a showcase production of her own and invite a selected group of directors and producers and agents to see her. She had acquired the rights to revive *The Diary of Anne Frank* for three performances only and had rented the Arts Theatre for that purpose. Jeremy was going to direct, play Mr. Frank himself, and put together the rest of the cast. "What do you think?"

"I think you should hire an audience as well and pay them to applaud."

"I want you to come to rehearsals and make notes and tell me what I'm doing wrong."

"The answer is no."

"Will you at least come to the opening performance?"

"I wouldn't miss it for the world."

"We're always going to be friends." She snuggled into his lap, cuddling. But he could tell that something was still troubling her.

"Moses, who wrote *Mr. Norris Changes Trains*?"

"P.G. Wodehouse."

"Should I read it?"

"Why not?"

Sir Hyman Kaplansky came to the opening night. So did some producers, directors, and a surprising number of performers at liberty. Some had come out of curiosity, others because they were pursuing Lucy's production company for outlandish deals; there was also a Bushmill claque, but still more were there in a perverse spirit of fun, anticipating the worst. Bushmill played the mushy Dutch condiments dealer, Otto Frank, as if he had wandered into the doomed attic out of a Tory garden fête. The other performers were competent at best. But Lucy was intolerable. A natural mimic, but clearly no actress, she played her scenes like an overwrought Shirley Temple with a disconcertingly gay Peter Van Daan. When that didn't work, she switched to the Elizabeth Taylor of *National Velvet*.

Moses wandered into the theatre dangerously drunk, but determined to behave himself. Unfortunately the excruciatingly banal play outlasted his resolution. Nodding off briefly in the first act he was confronted by Shloime Bishinsky in his mind's eye. "What I'm trying to say, forgive me, is that such princes in America are entitled to their mansions, a Rolls-Royce, chinchilla coats, yachts, young cuties out of burlesque shows. But a poet they should never be able to afford." *Or a theatre. Or an audience.* "It has to do with what? Human dignity. The dead. The sanctity of the word."

They were being noisy up there on stage, which wakened him to the troubling sight of an attic and its denizens trebling themselves. Poor Bushmill, emoting about something or other, now had six weak chins stacked one on top of another and maybe twenty-two eyes. Moses shook his head, he pinched himself, and the stage swam into focus again. Damn. It was that maudlin Hanukkah scene, overripe with obvious irony, wherein the pathetic Mr. Frank Bushmill seated with the others at the attic table — all of them hiding from the Gestapo — praises the Lord, Ruler of the Universe, who has wrought wonderful deliverances for our fathers in days of old. There were no *latkes*, but insufferably adorable Anne (the bottom of her bra stuffed with Kleenex) came to the table armed with touchingly conceived pressies. A crossword-puzzle book for her sister. "It isn't new. It's one that you've done. But

I rubbed it all out and if you wait a little and forget, you can do it all over again." There was some hair shampoo for the horny Mrs. Van Daan. "I took all the odds and ends of soap and mixed them with the last of my toilet water." Two fags for Van Daan's oafish husband. "Pim found some old pipe tobacco in the pocket lining of his coat . . . and we made them . . . or rather Pim did."

Once more the images on stage throbbed, trebling themselves. Moses squinted. He made fists, driving his fingernails into the palms of his hands. And there were four Anne/Lucys, each one of them out of tune, rising to sing:

> Oh, Hanukkah, Oh, Hanukkah.
> The sweet celebration.

Suddenly there was a crash from below the attic. The Green Police? The Gestapo? Everybody on stage froze. Straining to hear. For a few seconds there was a total silence and then something in Moses short-circuited. Not rising, but propelled out of his seat, he hollered, "Look in the attic! She's hiding in the attic!"

The next morning the telegram came from Moses's mother and he immediately booked the first available flight to Montreal.

FOUR

—◆—

"Not that I have anything to hide, but does my brother know that you're here?"

"When I asked if I could see you I had no idea that it was necessary to clear my visit with Mr. Bernard."

"Nonsense necessary. I'm not Bernard's keeper and he's not mine. I was curious, that's all. Are you parked outside?"

"I walked."

"From which direction?"

"Downtown."

"Good for you. It's such a lovely day it makes a man grateful to be alive," he said, drawing the blinds. "Oh, forgive me. What a thing to say to a young man in mourning. My brother was in tears. Such a loss to the community and of course to you and your mother it goes without saying. How long will you be in Montreal?"

"I'm flying back to London the day after tomorrow."

"You think I don't remember what a nice boy you are? Something to drink maybe?"

"Coffee, if it's not too much trouble?"

"You're not living up to your reputation. But I'm relieved to see that. Moderation in all things, that's the ticket. Hey, if I'm smiling like an idiot it's because I look at you and what do I see? L.B. as a young man."

"Maybe I'll have a Scotch after all."

"My pleasure. You know, before you were born even I attended one of his readings."

"Not many people did."

"Let me tell you something, as if you didn't know. You were blessed with a great man for a father. And you think we weren't aware how much he suffered in private, never able to take your poor mother anywhere."

"I beg your pardon?"

"*Oy vey*, have I let the cat out of the bag? Please, it's not something he talked about, a man of his natural dignity, but it slipped out, you know, when my brother asked how come L.B. never brought his wife to dinner. You're upset. I can see that. Listen here, it's nothing to be ashamed of. Look at Solomon's widow. What's the mind? A muscle. Doctors will tell you it's an illness like any other. But who will take care of your mother now that L.B.'s gone? Don't tell me. I know. You are as devoted to her as he ever was."

"Would you mind if I topped up my glass?"

"Isn't there more where that came from?"

"Thank you."

"I want to tell you that when your father came here to dinner with us and sat in this very room it was a real honour for Ida and me. Such a *goldener yid*. A true idealist. But, please, don't get me wrong. A great artist dies and suddenly everyone who shook hands with him once is his best friend. Unfortunately I wasn't close to him like Bernard. I'm not the reader in the family with the big library."

"I'm told it was Solomon who was the prodigious reader."

"You know what I wish? I wish I had your education. But your father, may he rest in peace, my, my, was there a book he hadn't read? In his presence I was tongue-tied. Once, you know, he came to tea with one of his admirers. What was her name, that sweet young girl?"

Moses reached for the bottle again.

"Peterson. Marion Peterson. He wanted her to see my brother's paintings, but he wasn't home. So they came here, he was kind enough to inscribe his books for me, every one of them, and to this day they rest in that glass bookcase over there."

There was also a concert piano that had once belonged to Solomon in the living room. The surface was covered end to end with photographs of Barney and Charna mounted in sterling silver frames. Barney and Charna, still toddlers, romping on the grass in Ste.-Adèle. Barney on horseback, a beaming Mr. Morrie holding the reins. Charna in her white Sweet Sixteen gown. Barney raking the barley floor in the Loch Edmond's Mist distillery in Skye.

"Now tell me what it is I can do for you," Mr. Morrie said.

"Actually I'm here because of Lucy. She was only two years old when Solomon died and she'd like to know more about him."

"A little birdy told me that you and Lucy are living together in London."

"Lucy is convinced that you've got her father's journals and she would be grateful if she could have them."

"How did you meet? Come on. Spill the beans. You're looking at a real sucker for a love story."

"We knew each other as children, as you know, and Henry and I have been friends for years."

"Does he still stutter so bad that poor boy?"

"No."

"I'm glad. Now tell me how you met Lucy after so many years."

"At a dinner party at Sir Hyman Kaplansky's."

"I'll bet if Canadians were still allowed to accept titles my brother would be number one on the list."

"Solomon's journals would mean a good deal to Lucy."

"Poor Lucy. Poor Henry. Poor Barney. It's a shame that their generation had to be caught up in family fights over what? Money. Position. Power. I'm not surprised that Lucy became an actress. She'll be a star. I'd bet money on it."

"Why are you not surprised she wants to act?"

"Because it's in her blood, it's got to be. That's what Solomon really should have been. A stage actor. When we were kids he was always dressing up, writing little plays for us to perform. He could do accents. It was amazing. Later, you know, we had our first hotel already, the bar is filled with girls of a certain type; what were we supposed to do? Throw them out into the snow? Bernard was never a pimp, and if anybody ever says that, I'm just a little fella, I'll still punch him in the nose. Anyway Solomon comes back from the war, a flier yet, and he phones Bernard at the hotel and pretends to be the RCMP. He was letter perfect, let me tell you. Cruel too, of course, but we're talking Solomon here. He did a Chinaman, he even walked like one. The German butcher. The blacksmith, a Polack. He could do anybody. He also had a gift for languages, but I suppose he inherited that from my grandfather." Mr. Morrie leaped up. "I think I heard a car. Bernard must be home. You walked here you say?"

"From downtown."

"Was my sister-in-law in the garden?"

"No."

"Libby's a wonderful wonderful woman. You know when Bernard married her, *she* was considered the catch. Her father was president of the *shul* and the Beneficial Loan Society. Nobody suspected him."

"Of what?"

"Listen here, I'm not one to carry tales. He was unlucky in the market, but he meant to return every penny and it's no reflection on Libby. She presides over so many charities because she has a heart bigger than the St. Lawrence River and you could open the books on any one of them and I'll bet they would balance perfectly. Libby isn't trying to prove anything."

"Did you know that your grandfather is mentioned several times in Lady Jane Franklin's letters?"

"You don't say? Hey, I'm sitting with a scholar from the scholars. Why I'll bet even Bernard doesn't know that."

"Twice in letters to Elizabeth Fry and once in a letter to Dr. Arnold of Rugby."

"To think that rascal couldn't have been more than sixteen years old at the time and still he caught that good lady's eye."

"It started with the snakes, you know. Van Diemen's Land was infested with snakes, which appalled her. So she offered convicts a shilling a head for them and he came up with so many the first day she just couldn't stop laughing."

"Some kid he must have been. But, if you don't mind my asking, what is your interest in our family history?"

"Lucy."

"Ah. I was worried maybe you were thinking of writing something. Bernard wouldn't like that. And digging up the past would be painful to Lionel, God bless him, who is striving so hard to make his way in society. So just between you, me, and the lamp-post, what are you up to, Moses?"

Moses reached for the bottle.

"Don't worry. It doesn't stain. Just pour yourself another."

"Didn't Ephraim ever tell you anything about his stay in Van Diemen's Land?"

"Let's be frank. If he talked to anybody in those days it was Solomon. Once he kidnapped him, you know. What was that?"

"I beg your pardon?"

"Sh." Mr. Morrie went to the window and peeked out from behind the blind. "Bernard and Libby are going out. That's odd."

"Is it?"

" 'Dragnet's' on tonight. Oh, I get it. He must have got them to send him a copy of the film in advance. Once, you know, he couldn't wait to see how a Dick Tracy turned out, it was killing him, and so Harvey Schwartz had to fly down to see the people at King Features and bring back the comics before they were even printed in the newspapers. Oh you should have seen Bernie after Harvey came back with the goods, nobody the wiser. We were in the middle of a board meeting. Should we buy this vineyard just outside of Beaune for X million or should we build the office tower in Houston for Y million? Everybody's making their pitch, quoting facts and figures, watching Bernard's face. 'Hey,' he says, suddenly perking up, 'I've got a hunch how Dick Tracy bails out of his latest jam and about exactly what happens to Pruneface. I could be right, I could be wrong. But I'm willing to bet a ten spot on it. Who's coming in?' Well, naturally, everybody forks out their ten bucks, not because they're afraid of my brother, that's nonsense, but because they adore him. And then

Harvey, that little devil, he says, 'I raise you twenty, Mr. Bernard.' So everybody digs into their pocket again. I suppose you know Harvey Schwartz?"

"Yes."

"Such a brilliant boy. Loyalty should be his middle name. I can't tell you how lucky we are to have him here. And devoted to his lovely talented wife? You better believe it. You know she couldn't get her book published at first. So Harvey goes to Toronto, meets with the number-one publisher there, invests in the company out of his own pocket, and that beautiful book comes out. *Hugs, Pain, and Chocolate Chip Cookies*. But Ogilvy's book department here orders only four copies. Becky's in tears. She's got cramps. Her period is late. Harvey gets on the phone rat-tat-tat to the chairman of Ogilvy's board and he says ahem ahem this is Harvey Schwartz speaking. I'm in charge of special projects for Jewel Investment Trust, and my boss Mr. Bernard Gursky just asked me how come your book department has taken only four copies of my wife's book? Bing bango bongo. They order another four hundred and display them in the window. I understand that in the end they had to burn just about all of them, but I don't have to tell L.B.'s son that art isn't the fastest moving commodity in this country. Don't worry. It doesn't stain. Just pour yourself another."

"Did you say Ephraim once kidnapped Solomon?"

"He sure did. Solomon is only nine years old and Bernie and I get out of school just in time to see Ephraim riding off on his sled with him. Okay, why not? Only now it's seven o'clock at night, we are sitting down to supper, there's a blizzard blowing out there, and where are they? God forbid an accident. Finally a messenger comes from this Indian fella, George Two Axe, saying Ephraim said to tell us Solomon is spending the night with the Davidsons. Fishy. Very fishy. Because only an hour earlier the Mounties have paid us one of their friendly visits. There's been trouble out on the reservation where Ephraim is shacked up with this young Copper Indian woman. Let me tell you she was something to look at. Anyway Lena has been stabbed and somebody has shot André Clear Sky's father dead. Have we seen or heard from Ephraim, the corporal wants to know. Why? Just asking, he says. Yeah, sure. The next question is does Ephraim have any friends in Montana?

How in the hell would we know? To make a long story short, my grandfather has taken the boy all the way back to his old haunts in the Arctic with him. They are gone for months, and that's where Solomon learned how to speak Eskimo and hunt caribou and God knows what else. And that was the last we ever saw of my grandfather, aged ninety-one, buried out there somewhere, according to Solomon, who also expects us to believe he made his way home all alone. From the Polar Sea? Tell me another one, my father says. Well, Solomon says, he had a map with him and he had marked a tree with a gash in each of their camps on the way out. Sure, my father says, *and what about before you reached the tree line*? A raven led the way, Solomon says with a straight face. Ask a foolish question, my father says, *and what did you eat all that time*? I hunted and I fished and, besides, Ephraim had left food caches for me underneath each of my marked trees, and before we parted he gave me this. Ephraim's gold pocket watch. Tell me if I'm boring you. Ida says that once I get started I'm worse than a broken record."

"Did Solomon ever mention anything in his journals about that first trip north?"

"Boy, speak of the third degree. You know, you could tell me something. What's poor Henry doing out there?"

"Poor Henry is happier than you know."

"My mother used to say that there's nothing like a religious education, but Henry, my God." Mr. Morrie sighed. "The children, the children. We made all that money, more than you can spend in three lifetimes, and my Barney just can't settle down and my Charna now lives in a commune with a bunch of nut-cases and calls herself Sunflower Dark-Crystal."

"I suppose control of McTavish will eventually fall into Lionel's hot hands."

"Listen here, I love Barney. I understand what a blow it was to him that McTavish would never be his to run. So I forgive him his mistakes. He walks in here right now I'd hug him. Wait till you're a father. But, let's face it, Lionel is the only one of his generation with a touch of Bernard's genius and I don't blame him he doesn't trust anybody. The thing very few people appreciate is the rich have their problems too. You come from our kind of money you're a marked man. If Lionel hadn't had Fenella followed how could he have known that she was having an affair with a *schwartze* yet, which must have been very humiliating for such a proud fella. And have you any idea what that marriage cost him, it didn't even last a year? The alimony. The diamonds. The sables he never got back. Some people say it's bad taste, but I don't blame him for one minute that he now has each new wife sign a divorce settlement before he marries her. All that gossip about receipts for gifts, however, is highly exaggerated. I can assure you Melody doesn't have to sign a return-on-demand voucher for anything valued under one hundred thousand dollars. But that's not why she insisted on the cheaper tiara at Winston's. She did that because it's not in her nature to be a grabber. Now tell me something. Is it true that Henry has some *meshuggena* theory about a new ice age, a punishment for the Jews?"

"Certainly not," Moses said.

"To be orphaned so young. *Oy vey.* You know it breaks my heart to this day that Solomon died in the prime of his life in that frightful plane crash. I still suffer from the nightmare. I dream of that Gypsy Moth exploding, Solomon's body blown to bits, the white wolves of the Arctic carrying off his bones."

"What if he wasn't blown to bits, but parachuted out before the explosion and walked out of the barrens?"

"What are you talking?"

"He'd walked out of the barrens once before, hadn't he?"

"Oh come on. Please."

"And I'm told he had to parachute twice out of his Sopwith Camel during the First World War."

"So where has he been all these years?"

"Damned if I know."

"His bank accounts were never touched, not a penny withdrawn. I'm surprised to hear you talk such foolishness. Listen!" Mr. Morrie leaped up and peeked out from behind the blinds again. "The car's back. They're going to watch 'Dragnet' after all. I think I'd better switch it on. Moses,

I've been keeping you too long. I'm sure you have more important people to see."

"What do I tell Lucy about Solomon's journals?"

"If I had them," Mr. Morrie said, "it would be my sincere pleasure to pass them on to her. Tell her that and give her a big kiss for me."

"What do you think happened to the journals?"

"God knows. But I'll tell you the best thing that could have happened is that they were burnt in the plane crash. I got a peek at some pages once and boy oh boy Solomon could tell some real whoppers in his day. If those journals, should they still exist, ever fell in the wrong hands they could be dynamite. Do you mind if I turn on the TV?"

"No."

"Bless you. And now I'm going to ask you a favour. May I?"

"Of course."

"My Barney, he has had such bad luck in so many of his ventures, poor boy, has decided to become a writer and has written a book. But nobody in New York will print it for him. Do I have to explain to L.B.'s son how difficult such things are?"

"Certainly not."

"It's a detective story, maybe a little too sexy for my taste, but what do I know? Barney's in Mexico now, partners with this doctor in some kind of cancer clinic, and he has asked me to try the manuscript on publishers in Toronto. But first, what I'd really appreciate is somebody of your education, not to mention the literary background, to read it and tell me what you honestly think."

"I'd have to take it with me to London."

"I knew I could count on you. Now come down to the garage, I'll give you the manuscript, and my driver will take you back to your hotel."

"I can walk."

"No, it's my pleasure. Ida will be jealous that she missed you. L.B.'s son in our house. You know what they say, don't you?"

"The apple doesn't fall far from the tree."

"Such a nice boy. To be your uncle one day would be a genuine honour for me. Don't stand in front of the lamp, please. It casts a shadow on the blind. Come, Moses, and let me hear from you soon."

FIVE

It was sort of Friday afternoon, late, time to close down the office. Send Myrna home. Pile into my heap and tool down to Nick's Bar & Grill on the main stem for a quick snort. Nick and I have been through hell and back again together. Sweeping Normandy clean of Nazi punks.

Normandy.

Where Nick's right leg is buried and they pinned the Military Cross on my chest, to go with the rest of the fruit salad, forgetting that I was a Hebe, born and bred. "For valour beyond the call . . . " Forget it, kid. War's over. With my MC and fifty cents I could buy myself a burger and fries and a cup of java.

Time for a snort.

Maybe two.

Trouble was my tab at Nick's was already longer than a night in a fox-hole and my cash box emptier than my .45 after I had pumped six of the best into Spider Moran's fat gut. But that's another yarn.

Anyway there I stood, six foot two, reaching for my chapeau, when Myrna opens the door. "There's a dame here to see you."

I was in no mood for another splitsville case, tailing some henpecked sucker until I caught him with a bimbo in a motel room. "Tell her to come back Monday morning."

"She's got gams that go all the way and then some, and I think she's in trouble, Hawk," she opinioned.

Next thing I knew in sashayed Tiffany Waldorf, smelling like the day the swallows came back to Capistrano. Flaming red tresses you want to walk through barefoot. Blazing green eyes. Class written all over her, but stacked. Breasts fighting her tight silk dress. Hour-glass waist. Curves in all the right places.

"Sit down," I said.

Tiffany shook off her sable wrap and poured herself into a chair, crossing those million-dollar legs. Then she opened her handbag that cost some poor alligator its skin and peeled off five c-notes. "Will this do as a retainer, Mr. Steel?"

"That depends on how many rats you want me to exterminate. Tell me about it, kid."

"There's a body lying on my bedroom floor with a shiv planted where his heart used to go pitter-patter."

"Then you've been a naughty girl."

"I am a naughty girl," she said, tossing her head high, "but I didn't do it."

"Then why don't you go to the cops?"

"Because that shiv happens to belong to yours truly. It's a priceless, diamond-studded sixteenth-century dagger worth one hundred thousand dollars. It was presented to me by Crown Prince Hakim at Monte Carlo last season."

"For services rendered?"

"I ought to slap your face," she said, casting her eyes at me.

"You look good when you're angry."

"I didn't get in until very late last night and there he was lying on my bedroom floor. The body was still warm."

"I take it you recognized the hombre?"

"I was his chick until I found out what a louse he was."

"What's his monicker?"

"Lionel Gerstein."

I had bought myself trouble. A ton of it.

Lionel Gerstein was the number-one son of old Boris Gerstein, a former bootlegger, worth zillions, who had crawled out of his sewer and gone legit some years back. But he was still connected. You could bet the farm and your beloved Granny's Maidenform bra on that one. Old BG was meaner than a rattlesnake with a hangover and just as dangerous.

Originally there had been three Gerstein brothers. Boris, Marv, and Saul. Marv, no more than knee-high to a mouse in his elevator shoes, was

*weaker than a bar Scotch. A born boot-licker. But Saul was a hell-raiser.
So old BG, who didn't care to share the wealth, had him taken out.
Erased. He had a bomb planted on Saul's private airplane.*

*"I hope," Tiffany said, "taking on the Gersteins isn't too much for
you, Hawk."*

"I think we'd better go and take a gander at that stiff, kid."

*But my feelings were mixed. Whoever had planted that shiv in Lionel
had done a good deed. The Gersteins were a bad bunch. Except for
Marv's boy, Brad, who had fought with me in Normandy, but wasn't
ever coming home. Lost an argument with a Nazi machine-gun nest.*

*"If I ever get God in a corner," I said to Tiffany, taking her arm,
"I've got a hot one for him. Namely, why do the good and the beautiful
die young?"*

SIX

Madness, Moses thought. Unforgivably loopy. A fifty-two-year-old man turning his cabin inside out searching for a salmon fly. A bloody Silver Doctor that could be replaced for three dollars. Yes, but the missing one had been lucky for him, once hooking him a sea-bright eighteen-pound hen on the Restigouche and another time an even friskier fish on the Miramichi. Reaching under his bed, Moses found his other slipper. He caught his finger in a mouse trap. He retrieved a mouldy pizza carton, an empty bottle of Macallan Single Highland Malt, a broken glass, a pair of Beatrice's panties (sloppy bitch, that one), a letter from Henry, his baseball glove, and the copy of *Encounter* with his essay on Yiddish etymology.

Excellent, I thought.

Thank you.

Fool. Moses considered banging his head against the stone fireplace. My God, how could he have been so naïve when he was at Balliol? Manipulated in the first place by Sir Hyman and later by Mr. Morrie. The calculating Mr. Morrie — spontaneously, as it were — foisting Barney's manuscript on him. *But Saul was a hell-raiser. So old BG, who didn't care to share the wealth, had him taken out. He had a bomb planted on his private plane.*

Gurskys. Gurskys.

"If you have to go to the toilet, you ask me and I'll show you where there is one for the guests."

As L.B. had been indentured to Mr. Bernard, so Moses acknowledged, he had come to be in thrall to Solomon, Ephraim's anointed one. Furthermore, he had been led like a lamb to Ephraim by Sir Hyman. At the time, Moses had been vain enough to believe that McGibbon's diary had just happened to be open on the pedestal and that Ephrim Gor-ski had been his discovery.

Ho ho ho.

"Has it ever occurred to you," the doctor in the clinic in New Hampshire had once said, "that your obsession with Solomon Gursky can be explained by your self-evident search for a father, having dismissed your own as unacceptable?"

"The food here is abominable. Do something about it."

"You seem to require the admiration," the doctor said, "even the love, of older men. Take your friendship with Callaghan, for instance."

How to explain, Moses thought, emptying a cardboard carton on the bedroom floor, that it had all started years ago as an attempt to discredit the Gurskys, digging up dirt to shove at L.B.

Then there had been Henry.

Lucy.

Sir Hyman Kaplansky, as he then styled himself.

Two A.M. Collapsing onto his unmade bed, sinking into sleep, Moses dreamt he was in New Orleans again, not there to see if he could find any record of a Civil War gun-runner called Ephraim Gursky, no, no, but as a treat for Beatrice. He was in New Orleans again, splurging on a breakfast with Beatrice at Brennan's, restitution for last night's sins. Only this time the waiter didn't return his American Express card. "Sorry, sir, but — "

A humiliated Beatrice saying, "Take mine," and then turning on him. "I suppose you threw out the bill with the junk mail again or your envelope with the cheque in it is in a jacket pocket somewhere."

Only this time a small embarrassment didn't escalate into tears and recriminations. He dreamt he was in New Orleans with Beatrice again only this time he didn't disappear after lunch, turning up at the hotel three hours late in a sorry state. Only this time they got to Preservation Hall, where benign old black musicians were doing nothing more than going through the motions until a saucy little white man rested his malacca cane against the wall and sat down to the piano, stomping his foot one, two, three, four ... and suddenly the band was transported, digging deeper. Moses, his quarry in sight at last, just out of reach, was set to make a grab for him, but his legs wouldn't work. He couldn't budge. Then, even as he was gaining control over his limbs, the gleeful piano player faded and Moses came awake, sweaty and trembling.

It was still dark, but he got up all the same, reheating what was left of the coffee and lacing it with a shot of Macallan. Then he dug into the bedroom closet again, emptying another carton, and out tumbled the Fabergé humidor that Lucy had once bought him. Inside he found the letter Henry had sent him a week after he had ruined Lucy's debut at the Arts Theatre. A clipping from the Edmonton *Journal* was enclosed.

NEW ICE AGE THREATENED
AFTER 10,000 YEARS

GENEVA (Reuter) — Many scientists believe a new ice age is coming but they cannot agree when or how hard it is going to hit us.

Some climate specialists studying clues as varied as volcanic dust, the earth's wobble, tree rings, and sunshine have concluded the world is about due for a big freeze after 10,000 years of comparative warmth.

If they are right, countries like Canada, New Zealand, Britain, and Nepal could be covered by ice sheets and France would look like Lapland.

But others predict no more than a mini-freeze, like the "little ice age" which seized Europe between 1430 and 1850. It froze all the rivers of Germany in 1431 and iced up villages near the present French alpine resort of Chamonix in the early 17th century.

During the American War of Independence nearly 200

years ago, British troops were able to slide their guns from Manhattan to Staten Island across the ice.

A report by the CIA in May spelled out the possible effects of a little ice age throughout the world.

In India 150 million people would die during droughts if the average temperature dropped by one degree centigrade. China would face a major famine every five years. Soviet Kazakhstan would be lost for grain production and Canada's grain harvest would drop by 50 percent, the report said.

The report stated the world is already cooling, but scientists will not answer how near is the next ice age. "We just don't know. Nobody knows," said a leading climatologist.

SEVEN

◆

In his prime, nibbling cashews or sucking on a Popsicle, pontificating for the benefit of a *Fortune* reporter or a hotshot from the *Wall Street Journal*, Mr. Bernard had been fond of saying, "Lewis and Clark, Frémont hoo ha, my grandpappy Ephraim was right up there with them. He came to this country to help Sir John Franklin in his search for the Northwest Passage. My enemies — I know you will have to listen to their slanders, it's your job — will tell you Bernard Gursky he came out of nowhere. Not like them, eh? Don't make me laugh. Westmount *oy vey*. It doesn't fool me that they get into a skirt once a year for the St. Andrew's Ball, pretending they come from quality and that they didn't get the shit kicked out of them at Culloden.

"And the Frenchies? The higher one of them holds his perfumed nose in the air the more likely it is that his great-grandmama was a *fille de roi*, a little whore shipped over by the king so that she could marry a soldier and have twenty-five kids before she was forty. To this day you know what a French-Canadian family gives the daughter for a wedding present she's only sixteen years old? Hold on to your hat, fella. They send her to a dentist to have all her teeth yanked out and to fit her with false ones, which they consider prettier. Where was I? The Gurskys, yeah. Well the Gurskys didn't come here steerage fleeing from some *drecky shtetl*. My family was established here before Canada even became a country. We're older, how about that?"

But in a more mischievous mood, dandling one grandchild on his lap, the others gathered round his chair, he would say, "Your great-great-grandpappy, hoo boy, he was something else. I was his favourite, you know. But I have to say that Ephraim, that old son of a gun, why he never did an honest day's work in his life."

Actually that was not the case. Ephraim's first job, after he had run away, was in a coal mine in Durham. He was a scrawny thirteen-year-old at the time and his duties were two-fold. Working deep underground, near the heading of a new road, he had to convey oxygen from the shaft by opening and closing ventilator doors, regulating the air current. He also had to maintain traffic on the courses, clearing the mullock for the man labouring at the face. The area he was obliged to crouch in was only three feet high and wide. The coal dirt was loaded into sledges known as dans with an iron ring welded to each end. It was dark down there, dark as a raven's wing, the only available candles fixed to the ends of the stages. And in those days the sledges didn't ride the rails, but had to be dragged along wet clayey soil to the gob, where they would be emptied. Ephraim, stripped to the waist in the heat and the dark, wore a sturdy rope belt with a chain attached. Hooking the chain to the sledge, sinking to all fours, mindful of scuttling rats, he would crawl along, dragging his load, singing the songs he had learned at his father's table:

> Strong and Never Wrong is He,
> Worthy of our Song is He,
> Never failing,
> All prevailing.
> Built the Temple in our days.
> Speedily, O speedily,
> Built that all may sing Thy praise.

Twice a day at fixed times during his twelve-hour shift he would stop to gorge himself on huge chunks of pulpy white

bread, a gristly beef bone, and cold coffee gulped out of a tin
canteen that unfailingly tasted of anthracite grit. The crash of
shifting rock and coal above his head was alarming, but the
pay was excellent — ten pence a day, five shillings in a good
week. When he got to the top, panting, sucking air, he could
always flirt with the pitbrow girls, who sorted and graded the
coal at the surface. Among themselves the girls called him
Little Lucifer. They were afraid of him. Not Kate, however.
Once a week Ephraim paid Kate, one of the County Clare
girls, a sixpence to go with him to the leaky shack at the far end
of the slag heap. Standing on a box, he would have her against
the wall, the earthen floor too mucky for such sport.

Ephraim had only been employed in the mine for six
months when he became a trapper-boy, minding the doors to
allow putters to pass with their ponies and coal-tubs. This
called for quickness of feet as empty tubs came hurtling down a
steep incline toward him in trains of sixty.

The miners taught him bawdy songs.

> Even randy little duchesses have lured
>   me to their arms,
> And crumby little countesses have yielded
>   me their charms.
> Then, only give me leave to go a-fishing
>   in your pond,
> I've got a rod so long and strong, and
>   such fine bait, Mrs. Bond.

Ephraim became a putter himself. His new job was to push,
or put, the trains of coal that had been filled by the hewers as
far as the crane, where they were hoisted on wagons to be
hauled the rest of the way by ponies. The average heft of a
loaded tub was six to eight hundredweight, and Ephraim,
paid by the number of tubs he put, now earned as much as
three shillings, six pence a day. He supplemented this by
delivering newspapers for a newsagent in an adjoining village,
which is how he came to meet the affable Mr. Nicholson, the
schoolmaster. Mr. Nicholson was astonished to learn that
Ephraim could read and write. In spite of Mrs. Nicholson's
objections, he began to lend the boy books. Charles Lamb's

Tales from Shakespear. Robinson Crusoe. "Tell me, boy," Mr. Nicholson asked one day, "did you know that your namesake was the second son of Joseph, born of Asenath, the daughter of Potipherah?"

Confused by the names pronounced in English, Ephraim refused to commit himself.

Mr. Nicholson brought out the family Bible, turned to Jeremiah, and read aloud what the Lord had said unto his prophet. " 'I am a father to Israel, and Ephraim is my first-born.' " Moving his finger lower down the page, he found the other passage he wanted. "Jeremiah, you know, foretold the coming of Christ. 'Behold, the days come, saith the Lord, that I will sow the house of Israel and the house of Judah, with the seed of man . . .' "

Ephraim leaped up as Mrs. Nicholson brought them tea with bread and strawberry jam.

" '. . . and with the seed of beast,' " she said.

Considerably younger than Mr. Nicholson, she was pale, her manner severe, disapproving.

"Joshua, the son of Nun, was descended from your namesake," Mr. Nicholson said, all twittery.

Mrs. Nicholson set down her teacup, shut her eyes, and swaying just a little in her chair recited, " 'And Joshua the son of Nun sent out of Shittim two men to spy secretly, saying, Go and view the land, even Jericho. And they went and came into an harlot's house, named Rahab, and lodged there.' "

The colour rising in his cheeks, Mr. Nicholson said, "When Jacob was ailing he acknowledged the two sons of Joseph, blessing Ephraim with his right hand and Manasseh with his left."

"Do you know why, boy?" Mrs. Nicholson demanded.

"It was to show that the descendants of Ephraim would become the greater people."

"Hip hip hurrah," Mr. Nicholson said, "you have read your Old Testament."

"Only in Hebrew, sir."

"Fancy that."

Shutting her eyes, swaying again, Mrs. Nicholson declaimed, " 'Gilead is a city of them that work iniquity, and is polluted with blood. And as troops of robbers wait for a man, so the company of priests murder in the way by consent: for they commit lewdness.' " Her eyes fluttered, they opened, and she stared at Ephraim. " 'I have seen an horrible thing in the house of Israel: there is the whoredom of Ephraim, Israel is defiled.' "

"Yes, yes, my dear. But surely not this sweet little Ephraim. Where are you from, boy?"

"Liverpool."

"Is that where your parents be?"

"They are dead, sir."

"Or have been transported, more likely," Mrs. Nicholson said.

"And where did they come from?"

"Minsk."

Mrs. Nicholson snorted.

"I would like to study Latin and penmanship with you, sir, providing you set a fair price."

Mr. Nicholson rocked on his heels. "Oh dear me," he said, shaking with laughter, "a fair price, is it?"

Mrs. Nicholson managed to convey her disapprobation by the manner in which she swept up the tea things, and then retreated into the kitchen.

"I will take you on, boy," Mr. Nicholson said, "but I cannot, in conscience, accept an emolument."

"I will do chores for Mrs. Nicholson."

"You will find," Mrs. Nicholson said, her face hot, "that I am most particular."

Mr. Nicholson proved kindly to a fault, irrepressibly jolly, and Ephraim's lessons with him went exceedingly well. He earned pats on the head, playful little jabs and tickles, and exclamations of joy. "Well done, my pretty one!" But when Mrs. Nicholson chose to join them, seated darkly behind their deal table doing needlework in her rocking chair, Mr. Nicholson would become abrupt, impatient, his back stiffening each time her rocking chair creaked. One evening Mr. Nicholson, having quite forgotten his wife's presence, covered Ephraim's hand with his own to guide him in a penmanship exercise. Ephraim, fully aware that she was there, contrived to draw his head closer to Mr. Nicholson, their cheeks brushing. Mrs. Nicholson spoke out: " 'The woman shall not wear that which pertaineth unto a man, neither shall a man put on a woman's garment: for all that do so are an abomination unto the Lord thy God.' "

Mr. Nicholson's eyes filled with tears. His lower lip trembled. "That will be sufficient for today, boy. Now you run along and see that you make yourself useful to Mrs. Nicholson."

Following his first lesson, Mrs. Nicholson had set Ephraim to cleaning the living-room carpet. After he had beat it, sent back twice before it was done to her satisfaction, she had him lay it out on the flagstones in the little back yard, where hollyhocks thrived in spite of the soot. Then he sprinkled it with a thick layer of salt mixed with used tea leaves, annoying her by singing the Hebrew songs he had learned at his father's table.

> Who knows One? I know One: One is God in Heaven and
>   Earth.
> Who knows Two? I know Two: Two the Tablets, One is
>   God in Heaven and Earth.
> Who knows Three? I know Three: Three the Fathers,
>   Two the Tablets, One is God in Heaven and Earth.

Next she had him clean the kitchen range with black-lead, burnish a copper pot inside and out, and clean and trim the oil lamps. Then he returned to the carpet, clearing it of every single tea leaf with a hard brush, and going over it with a wet cloth laced with vinegar to restore the fading colours. His efforts brought out damp patches under his armpits. He stank of sweat. Sniffing to show her displeasure, Mrs. Nicholson helped him hang the carpet on a line to dry. Then she brought him a slice of bread fried in dripping and two rashers of bacon and sat down to watch him eat it. " 'And the swine,' " she said, " 'because it divideth the hoof, yet cheweth not the cud, it is unclean unto you: ye shall not eat of their flesh, nor touch their dead carcase.' "

Ephraim looked her directly in the eye and smiled.

"In the first house where I worked," Mrs. Nicholson said, lowering her eyes, "all I had for dinner every night was a herring with bread and dripping. I had to leave after the master's son, who had served with Gough in Bangalore, came home on leave. He tried to administer laudanum to me. Do you understand why, boy?"

"No, madam."

"It was his vile intention to make me subservient to his passions."

Following his lessons and increasingly onerous chores Ephraim was allowed to curl up on the stone floor next to the fireplace and sleep there in one of Mr. Nicholson's old nightshirts until he rose shortly before dawn to walk five miles to the pithead. The nightshirt had been Mrs. Nicholson's notion. Once she had been taken to a zoo and there she had seen a gazelle with its perpetually swishing tail. She had expected as much of him or at least cloven hoofs, but he had neither. The first night that he had been allowed to stay, Ephraim had barely fallen asleep when he felt a bare foot probing his face. An indignant Mrs. Nicholson loomed over him, wearing a crocheted black shawl clutched tight over her long flannel nightgown. "Have you said your prayers yet, boy?"

"No, madam."

"I thought not. I worked once for a certain Mrs. Hardy, who was related to the Duke of Connaught. I had to climb dark stairs to my little iron bed in the attic, but each night, heedless of the cold, I remembered to fall on my knees and say my evening prayers. So long as you are taking advantage of Mr. Nicholson's charity you will most certainly do the same in this house, boy."

His smile, which cunningly mingled compliance and insolence, infuriated her.

"I will leave my chamberpot outside my bedroom door and you will empty it before you leave in the morning. Quietly as you go, mind you."

She had him tend to the sterling silver, inherited from Mr. Nicholson's uncle, returning the candlesticks to him for a second and even a third polish before it gleamed to her satisfaction.

"Where is Minsk?"

"It is in Russia."

"I'm glad you at least know that much. How did your parents get from there to here?"

"They walked."

"Stuff and nonsense."

She ordered him to dust the furniture and when he was done she inspected the chair legs and under the tables. "What possible need," she asked, "has somebody of your dubious origins and modest expectations for Latin and penmanship?"

"It interests me."

A pattern developed. Once Ephraim's lessons were done, an aroused Mr. Nicholson fled the cottage, charged across the heath, blind to passersby, and retired to The Wagon and Horses for a pint. Ephraim would put himself at Mrs. Nicholson's disposal. She had him wash down the paintwork and do the ironing and then she served him a hardboiled egg and toast. "Once I had a post in Cheyne Walk, Chelsea, which is in London. And there I enjoyed excellent daily fare, augmented by occasional delicacies left over from grand dinner parties. I daresay that for all your cheek and singular lack of humility you have never tasted quail's eggs?"

"No, madam."

"Or venison or partridge?"

"No, madam."

"Or smoked salmon?"

"No."

"I thought not. But I have partaken of all of them more than once and we were also allowed a quart of ale for its nutritional content. Alas, my mistress's brother kept trying to corner me in one bedroom or another. He thought me fair game, but he was sadly mistaken. Do you understand, boy?"

He smiled.

"I know very well why you have come here. Undoubtedly you intend to prey on Mr. Nicholson's weakness and expect to profit from it."

Each time he slept over next to the fireplace, he no sooner drifted off than he was prodded awake by her bare foot and reminded to say his prayers. The seventh time she came to him, he reached out to snatch her slender ankle and took all her toes into the warmth of his mouth. Scorched, she fled from him. But some weeks later she was back. Covering her face with her hands, moaning, she let him do it again. When he let go, she promptly served him the other foot. He drew the toes apart, driving his tongue between them. Standing over him, her eyes rolled upward, she was seized by shuddering. Once it subsided, she pulled herself free and whacked him hard on the nose with the heel of her foot, stunning him. "Auntie's little sodomite," she cried, fleeing.

She had learned what they called Mr. Nicholson after she had gone to buy a quart of ale in The Wagon and Horses and had overheard those mincing voices drifting through the shutters of the private bar.

"Where's Auntie tonight?"

"Cuddling with his little bit of stuff from the mines. The dark Israelite with the hot eyes."

During the week she was afflicted with spells of dizziness, and the camisoles she had worn for years without complaint were suddenly an irritation to her breasts. The next time Ephraim came to the cottage she sat in her rocking chair throughout his Latin lesson and then had him scrub the tiled floor in the kitchen with hot soda water three times before she was satisfied. "I am going to instruct Mr. Nicholson that you are not to come here any more. I know what the two of you are about."

But she came to him later, offering her foot, and he obliged her once more, steadying her by pretending to make a game of it, panting, growling like a pet puppy with a bone. She presented the other foot. Emboldened, as her breath began to come short, he let his hand fly up her leg. She withdrew, gasping. But she didn't flee. Instead, after a pause, she drew close to him again. Rolling over on his back, he slipped a hand under her nightgown to fondle her. But he couldn't quite reach. Keening, she had to squat. Afterward, her eyes charged with rancour, she said, "You are not to come here next Sunday. Mr. Nicholson will be away. A poetry reading."

"Leave the bolt off the door and I will come after dark."

"Oh, no," she pleaded, rocking her face in her hands, sniffling; and he had to move smartly to avoid a kick in the groin.

The following Sunday, a misery to her, she paced up and down the cottage, wringing her hands, bumping into things. She bolted the back door immediately before sunset and lay down to rest, fighting another dizzy spell, a pillow squeezed between her thighs, weeping. It was no good. She started each time she thought she heard him on the cinder path. She unbolted the door and made herself some tea. She couldn't keep it down. She tried needlework, but her hands wouldn't stop trembling. She shot the door bolt again, angrily this time, but still he didn't come. She set her rolling pin on the kitchen table and unbolted the door. It didn't matter any more. He wasn't coming. It was too late. Probably he was with Mr. Nicholson. Imagining postures that disgusted her, she filled a basin with water and washed, remembering to bolt the door first. When she heard him on the path, singing one of his mournful synagogue songs, she blew out her candle and didn't move. Her eyes filled with tears. Silence. Then cinders flew against the kitchen window. The neighbours, the neighbours. She relit her candle and quickly unbolted the door and let him in. "You must leave at once," she said.

But he was already inside, smiling. She retreated to her rocking chair, her eyes rimmed red, the family Bible on her lap. "Do not comfort yourself, boy, thinking hell is an abstraction. It's a real place waiting on disgusting little sinners like you. If you have ever seen a swine roasting on a spit, its flesh crackling and sizzling, squirting fat, well that's how fierce are the eternal flames in hell's coolest regions."

He sat down in Mr. Nicholson's chair and shook off his wooden shoes.

"There is laundry stacked and ready," she said, "and it appears to me that these tiles have lost their sparkle."

He did the laundry, seemingly more amused than angry, and then he got down on his hands and knees and tackled the kitchen floor. Coming close to her rocking chair, he startled her, nuzzling her legs, growling. She jumped free, tore chunks out of a loaf of bread and tossed them in the air, making him leap for them. When he missed, she reached for her rolling pin, threatening him. He sank to all fours, pawing at the stones with his head bowed, whimpering. She laughed, which he took as an invitation to nuzzle her between the legs again, somewhat higher this time. She stumbled backward, appalled, suddenly seeing him not as a playful pup but as a menacing goat. She reached for her rolling pin and struck him with it, the blow glancing off his shoulder. Incensed, he tore it from her, sending it bouncing off a wall. She retreated hastily behind a chair, panting, and once more asked him to leave.

"No," he said.

Only then did she notice the parcel he had brought with him. It was wrapped in old newspapers and tied with a string. "What have you got there?" she asked.

"A surprise for you, Mrs. Nicholson."

"That would be most improper. You will take it with you when you leave, boy."

"After I have emptied the slops?"

"Yes."

Subdued, apprehensive, she swept the remaining chunks of bread into a corner and then led him to the deal table and introduced him to the New Testament of Our Lord and Saviour Jesus Christ. " 'Again,' " she intoned, swaying her eyes shut, " 'the devil taketh him up into an exceedingly high mountain, and showeth him all the kingdoms of the world, and the glory of them; And saith unto him, All these things I will give thee, if thou wilt fall down and worship me. Then saith Jesus unto him, Get thee hence, Satan: for it is written, Thou shalt worship the Lord thy God, and him only shalt thou serve.' "

Finally she showed him his usual place, reminding him of his prayers and the slops, and then she retired to her bedroom, leaving her door ajar. But he didn't follow. Instead he slipped into Mr. Nicholson's old nightshirt and waited on the stone floor, hands clasped behind his back, singing:

> I should like to have a youth, who me
> Would in his arms enfold,
> Who would handle me and dandle me
> When my belly it was cold;
> So I will be a mot,
> I shall be a mot,
> I'm so fond of Roger,
> That I will be a mot.

He heard her thrashing about. She called out to him, but as if possessed, his name plucked from a nightmare against her wishes. He didn't answer. He sang:

> I love that magic member
> That men have 'neath their clothes,
> I love squeezing I love Roger,
> And I love his ruby nose.
> So I will be a mot,
> I shall be a mot,
> I'm so fond of Roger,
> That I will be a mot.

Soon she called out again, peremptorily this time, demanding a fresh candle. He brought it to her, lit it, and retreated to his place. Within the hour she stood over him. "Are you diseased?" she asked.

"No, madam."

"Well, then."

He padded after her into the bedroom and the first thing he did was to show himself and piss into the chamberpot. "Empty it," he said.

Retreating into a corner, she began to weep.

"Do as I saith."

She emptied the chamberpot and then blew out the candle. He thrust her on to the bed and she would not remove her long flannel nightgown but raised it, hiding her face. He let that go the first time, which was quick for both of them, but before he took her again he relit the candle and made her shed her nightgown and look on him. Afterward, even as she wept softly, he retrieved his package, undid the string, and dumped his coal black laundry on her sweaty body. "I will not leave here before dawn," he said, "if it is not ready for me."

The following Sunday, with an especially jolly Mr. Nicholson there, Ephraim mortified her by teasing her with his foot under the table when they sat down to supper together. He was more than somewhat surprised when she did not come to him by the fireplace once Mr. Nicholson had begun to snore. But then, in the early hours of the morning, she was there, rousing him from a deep sleep with her foot. "I had expected you earlier," he said. "Go back to your room."

Stung, she turned to flee.

"Wait."

She paused.

"Here," he said, tossing her his parcel.

The next Sunday no sooner did Ephraim sit down to the deal table for his lesson with Mr. Nicholson than Mrs. Nicholson swept into the room, her needlework to hand.

"You will not sit here through my lessons any more," Ephraim said.

Mrs. Nicholson fled.

"Oh dear," Mr. Nicholson stammered, "what have you done now?"

"You are a sweet man, sir, of kind and gentle disposition, but I am not of your sort." Unbuttoning him, he added, "In payment for these lessons and because I hold you in high regard I will do this much for you, but no more."

Afterward Mr. Nicholson took off through the back door, charging across the heath in a turmoil.

Ephraim took Mrs. Nicholson by the hand and led her toward the bedroom.

"Are you mad?" she demanded, hanging back.

"Mr. Nicholson will not be back until the morning. It is arranged."

Monday, and through the rest of the week, Mr. and Mrs. Nicholson did everything possible to avoid each other. They ate in silence. If their eyes met, she blushed and his lower lip began to tremble. On Saturday he pretended not to be aware of her weeping over the kitchen sink. Peeling potatoes, she cut herself. The sight of her blood was too much for him. He repaired to The Wagon and Horses and lingered there until closing time and had to be helped home by two of his young friends. "Easy does it, Auntie."

Sunday was intolerable.

"Bolt the door. We won't let him in, Mr. Nicholson."

"Yes."

But when they heard him singing on the cinder path they

both leaped up. She raced to undo the bolt, but he managed to be the first to greet him.

Because she was knitting him a sweater he presented him with the gold pocket watch that he had inherited from his uncle. When she splurged on a joint for Sunday night dinner he hurried out and bought a bottle of claret for them to share at their lesson. Other accommodations were made, but not spoken of. She, for instance, would wind into her shawl and go out for a stroll while they were at their lessons. Then he would leave the cottage and not return until Monday morning. In return for his consideration, on Wednesday nights she now retired early to her bedroom and allowed him to entertain his young friends from the poetry society. In preparation for these visitations he sometimes borrowed one or another of her garments, but she did not taunt him with Deuteronomy, Chapter 22, verse 5. Neither did he remark on the scent she trailed on Sunday mornings.

Ephraim carried on until he grasped that his knowledge of Latin and penmanship far surpassed Mr. Nicholson's ability to help him further. There was something else. One Sunday night he observed how her breasts had begun to swell and the dark brown nipples trickled an unfamiliar sweetness. Only then did he notice the thickening of her waist.

The following Sunday Mr. and Mrs. Nicholson sat and waited until after dark and still he did not appear.

"He's not coming," she said.

"Nonsense, Mrs. Nicholson. He's been late before."

"You don't understand," she said, weeping, "your uncle's candlesticks are gone."

Pearls of sweat blossomed on Mr. Nicholson's forehead.

"It's your duty to inform the authorities," she said.

Wearing his new sweater, carrying a gold pocket watch, the candlesticks, and a purse with five pounds and twelve shillings in it, Ephraim quit the mine in Durham and started out on the road to London. He also had with him some mementoes from his father's house. Phylacteries, a prayer shawl, and a Hebrew prayer book.

Who knows Four? I know Four: Four the Mothers, Three the Fathers, Two the Tablets, One is God in Heaven and Earth.

Who knows Five? I know Five: Five the books of the Torah, Four the Mothers, Three the Fathers, Two the Tablets, One is God in Heaven and Earth.

Spring it was, the earth moist and fragrant, rhododendrons and azaleas in blossom.

Ephraim never saw Mrs. Nicholson again, or laid eyes on his son, the first of what would become twenty-seven unacknowledged offspring, not all of them the same colour.

EIGHT

"What did you think, Olive?"

"I'm not saying, because you'll just point out a boo-boo and spoil this movie for me too."

As usual, they went to The Downtowner for a treat. Mrs. Jenkins gave him what she hoped was a piercing look. "I'll bet you've had a wife stashed away somewhere all these years, Bert, with grown kids, and she's finally tracked you down for back alimony payments."

"What on earth are you talking about?"

"The shyster from Denby, Denby, Harrison and Latham who came to see you, what is it a month now? You still haven't told me what he wanted."

"It was a case of mistaken identity."

"Don't look now, Pinocchio, but your nose just grew another three inches."

"Mr. Hughes was looking for another Smith."

"Then how come you get all that mail from those lawyers and suddenly you keep a locked strongbox under your bed?"

"You've been snooping."

"What are you going to do about it? Move out. Go ahead. Make my day. For all I know your name isn't even Smith.

Bert," she said, covering his hand with her own, sticky with chocolate sauce, "if you're wanted by the cops you can count on Olive, your only pal in this vale of tears."

"I've never broken a law in my life," he said, sliding his hand free before anybody saw.

"Hey," she said, giggling, "what's the difference between a lawyer and a rooster?"

He didn't want to know.

"A rooster clucks defiance."

He didn't even chuckle.

"It's a play on words, Bert. I'll explain it to you, if you want."

"That won't be necessary."

"Said the farmer's daughter to the preacher."

Rattled, Smith paid both their bills for once and left a sixty-five cent tip in the saucer.

"I think somebody's ship has come in and he's not telling."

Pleading a headache, Smith did not join her in the parlour that night to watch "Kojak".

"Somebody saw you come home in a taxi last Tuesday, but you got out at the corner so that Olive couldn't see from her window."

"I was feeling dizzy."

"Bert, whenever you're ready to spill the beans, I'll be waiting. Meanwhile," she sang, "I'll tie a yellow ribbon round the old oak tree."

"Thank you."

"Loyalty is my middle name. Let's just hope it's yours too, old buddy of mine."

The legacy, which Smith was told had been left to him by his late Uncle Arnold, who had died childless in Hove, had come to $228,725.00.

"But I thought it was fifty thousand pounds," Smith had said.

"That was in 1948. It was invested on your behalf."

Trudging through the driving snow, Smith had taken the certified cheque right to the Royal Bank. Deposited it. Started home. Panicked. Hurried to the Westmount post office to rent

a box. Then back to the bank to tell them no statements were
to be mailed to his home address any more, but only to his P.O.
number. He was back first thing in the morning to test things,
drawing two hundred dollars in cash.

Smith decided that he was too old to have his teeth fixed. He
considered buying a Harris tweed jacket, some shirts that
weren't drip-dry, a pair of wingtip shoes, but Mrs. Jenkins
would demand to know where the money had come from.
Strolling through Eaton's, he saw a small refrigerator that
would do nicely for his room. He came across an electric kettle
that would be a blessing. He could fix himself a cuppa
whenever he felt the urge. Not Salada tea bags, either, but
Twinings Darjeeling. No, he didn't dare. Olive never missed a
trick.

"What do you make of Murph Heeney in number five,
Bert?"

Heeney, the new roomer next door to him, was a big bear of
a man, hirsute, a carpenter, never without a bottle of Molson
Export in his paw.

"He's not my type."

"Guessy guessy what I found under his bed? A stack of
Playboys. Certain pages stuck together with his spunk."

Olive Jenkins turned Smith's shirt collars. If he was feeling
poorly she climbed the stairs to his room with beef tea made
from an OXO cube. During the longest week of the month, the
week before his pension cheque came, she had fed him bangers
and mash or toad in the hole for supper. Well, now he could
buy her a new colour TV or treat her to a movie and Murray's
for supper once a week. No. She'd smell a rat. "Where did you
get the do re me, Bert?"

All that money in the bank. He could visit the Old Country,
see where his parents had come from. Lightheaded, he ventured into Thomas Cook & Sons and inquired about ships
to England, astonished to discover that now only Polish or
Russian liners sailed from Canada, which would never do. But
the insolent young clerk, his look saying you just stepped in
here to get warm, you old fart, still stood before him, reeking of
pansy aftershave, brandishing ship plans with cabin locations,
quoting fares.

"Would that include meals?" Smith asked.

The clerk, cupping a hand to his mouth, failed to squelch his laughter.

"I suppose you own this establishment," Smith said, fleeing.

Smith continued to draw two hundred dollars a week from his account. He stashed what he didn't spend, which was most of it, in a hiding place that he had prepared by sawing through a floorboard one night. He took to treating himself to solitary lunches at Murray's, requesting a table in the rear, but even so he started whenever the door swung open. Most afternoons he stopped at Laura Secord's for a half-pound of cashews or chocolates, and then he would move on to the lobby of the Mount Royal Hotel or Central Station, never going home until he had finished every last bit.

"Where have you been all day, old buddy of mine?"

"Looking at magazines in the library."

"What did you do for lunch?"

"Did without."

Not according to her information.

"As the vicar said to the rabbi's wife, I think we ought to have a little chat."

She made tea. And when he sat down she spotted his new socks at once. Argyle. Knee length.

"Bert, I want to know if you're shop-lifting."

He was stunned.

"If you're short, Olive will see you through, but you must tell me if you're in trouble."

He shook his head no, and started for his room. Mrs. Jenkins followed him to the foot of the stairs. "You never used to hold out on good old Olive."

"Maybe I'm not the only one who's changed."

Once Smith had been the only one favoured with a special place in Mrs. Jenkins's refrigerator, but now the shelf below his was crammed with bottles of Molson that rattled whenever the door opened or the engine started up. Saturday night TV with Olive, the two of them resting their tootsies, as she liked to say, sharing Kool-Aid and Twinkies, watching the Channel 12 movie, was now also a thing of the past. Olive no longer wore any old housecoat on Saturday nights, her hair in curlers. Now she was perfumed and girdled, Shirley Temple curls tumbling over her cheeks, wearing a candy-floss pink angora sweater a size too small and a green miniskirt, her fat legs sheathed in black fishnet stockings and her feet pinched into fluffy white slippers with baby-blue pom-poms. And it was "Hockey Night in Canada" on TV, the parlour stinking of spilt beer and pizza and White Owl cigars, Murph Heeney in attendance.

"Hey, Olive, how am I gonna concentrate on the power play when you're making me feel so horny?"

Olive shrieked with laughter, squirting beer. "You'd better clean up your act, buddy, because after these messages. . . . Here comes Johnny! Whoops, I mean Bert, my loyalest pal in this tear of vales."

"Am I intruding?"

"Naw," Heeney said. "Come on in and haunt the room for a while, Smitty, you old turkey you. Canadiens 3, Chicago 4, with eight minutes to go. Time is becoming a factor."

Smith fled to his room, scandalized, and the next morning he slipped out early for an Egg McMuffin breakfast at McDonald's. Then, stepping out into the slush, he searched for a taxi. He waved off the first to slow down, because it was driven by a black man, but got into the next one.

"Central Station, please."

"Hey, you know who once warmed their arses right where you're sitting right now, mister? Nathan Gursky and his wife. Big bucks that. So I asked him for his philosophy of life. I collect them, you know. He says his old man taught him all men are brothers and his wife laughs so hard he turns red in the face. Guess where he's going? Old Montreal. His shrink. How do I know? His wife says, 'At those prices please don't sit there for an hour saying nothing but um, ah, and er to Dr. Weinberg. Tell him the truth. Now it's Lionel you're afraid of.' Imagine that. All those millions and he's a sicko."

Smith bought yesterday's *Gazette* at the newsstand and sought out a bench that wasn't already laden with drug addicts. He dozed and then ate lunch at the Peking Gardens, indulging his one daring taste, an appetite for Chinese food. Then he wandered over to the Mount Royal Hotel and rested in the lobby. Next he drifted through Alexis Nihon Plaza, stopping for a Tab, and snoozing on a bench. Later he

splurged on an early dinner at Curly Joe's. Steak and french
fried potatoes. Apple pie. Bloated, more than somewhat
flatulent, he was back at Mrs. Jenkins's house before eight,
resolved to announce that he was moving out, but not before
giving the two of them a piece of his mind.

Murph Heeney was wearing a crêpe-paper party hat.
"Surprise, surprise! We thought you'd never get here."

"Said the curate to the go-go dancer," Olive shrieked,
blowing on a noisemaker.

Hooking him under the arms, they danced a shaken Smith
into the parlour, where the table had been set for three.

"For horse-doovers we got devilled eggs and then Yankee
pot roast and chocolate cake with ice cream," Heeney said,
shoving a chalky-faced Smith into a chair.

Smith managed to force an acceptable share of food down
his gullet while Olive entertained Heeney.

"This guy goes to the doctor he's told he has to have
his — his — " She stopped, censoring herself in deference to
Smith, and continued, " — his *penis* amputated, he hits the
roof . . ."

Smith begged off coffee and struggled upstairs to his room.
He wakened, his stomach churning, at three A.M., and raced
to the toilet down the hall only to run into that hairy ape
emerging in his BVDs. Heeney grabbed him by the arm,
possibly to sustain his own uncertain balance. "I'd wait a
while I was you," he said, holding his nose.

"Can't," Smith said, breaking free of Heeney's grip.

FOUR

ONE

◆

1973. September. Pulling out of Wardour Street, gearing down with a gratifying roar, Terry tucked his battered MG into the carpark. Then he walked swiftly back to the Duke of Wellington, mindful of the plump grey skies for he was wearing his new suit, jacket nipped in just so at the waist, patch pockets, trousers slightly flared. They were all at the bar, waiting. Des, Nick, Bobby.

"Hello, hello, hello."

"Saucy."

"Ta-ra, ta-ra!"

A grinning Terry, dimples displayed to advantage, lifted the corners of his jacket and twirled about.

"Oh, my dear," Bobby exclaimed, quaking with pleasure, "the wonders wrought by Cecil Gee."

"Not bloody likely. Three hundred nicker it was. From Doug Hayward," Terry announced, "tailor to the stars."

Des reached over to stroke the fabric; then, abruptly, his hand dropped to Terry's groin, fat fingers fondling. "And what have we here?"

"Forbidden fruit," Terry said, slapping Des's hand away as he leaped free.

"Bespoke, you mean."

"Piss off, son."

Nick, anticipating trouble, slid between them.

"Anybody seen Mother Foley?" Terry asked.

"Not to worry, Terry. Foley will be here. Got time for a nosh?"

"Not tonight, dear, I've got a headache." Cunningly lifting a jacket sleeve, Terry revealed his magnificent bulky black wristwatch. The face showing absolutely nothing until he flicked a tiny knob and 7:31 lit up in computer-type numerals. "Ta-ra, ta-ra!"

"Where'd you nick it?"

"It's not even on sale here yet. Lucy got it for me in New York."

Suddenly Foley loomed over them. Grey curls leaking out from under a broad-brimmed safari hat, wine turtleneck sweater, tie-dyed jeans. Terry slipped into the Gents' after him.

"You bring the bread, mon?"

"*Mañana.* No fear."

Foley rubbed his purple jaw pensively.

"Oh, come off it, luv. When have I ever let you down?"

Foley handed it over. Terry, blowing him a kiss, danced back into the bar. "I've got time for one more."

"And where are you off to tonight?" Des asked. "Pray tell."

"Oh, maybe Annabel's for a bit of the old filet mignon and some Dom P. Or possibly Les A. for a spot of chemmy." Actually she had yet to take him anywhere that she might be recognized. Infuriating, that.

"Shame on you, Terry, selling your body beautiful for such ephemeral trifles."

He reclaimed his MG, shooting into Hyde Park, emerging at the top of Sloane Street and cutting into Belgravia. He knew, without looking, that she would be waiting by the window of her mews flat, chain-smoking. So he took his own sweet time getting out of the car.

Wearing a black silk shift, the sleeves necessarily long, Lucy opened the door before he could ring the bell. The thumb on her right hand was wrinkled as a walnut, all the moisture sucked out of it. She had tried bandaging it at night, but it didn't work. She tore the bandage off in her sleep.

Lucy's large black eyes flickered with distress. Not quite forty-one, she looked older, possibly because she was so scrawny now. "The money's on the hall table," she said. Like he was the delivery boy from John Baily's.

"You haven't said a word about my suit."

"Don't tease me, Terry. Hand it over."

"Do you think the trousers are too snug?"

"They advertise. Shall we leave it at that?" And she disappeared into the kitchen, slamming the door.

Terry drifted into the bedroom, idly opening drawers. In the topmost drawer of her bedside table, a priceless antique no doubt, the surface pocked with cigarette burns, he found a half-finished Toblerone bar. More chocolates, these from Bendicks, were in the next drawer, as well as used tissues everywhere, rings he could risk saying the char had nicked. The next drawer yielded a bottle of Quaaludes. Other bottles. Uppers, downers. And a book, many pages dog-eared, passages underlined here and there. *The Collected Poems of Gerard Manley Hopkins*. The book was inscribed in a tiny scrawl. "July 12, 1956: To my darling Lucy, love, Moses." Terry's first impulse was to rip out the inscription and tear it into little pieces, but his instinct for self-preservation saved him. There were limits.

"You've got it," Lucy said, emerging from the kitchen, "haven't you, and you're teasing me?"

"Sorry, luv."

"Get me a drink."

"Please."

"I wouldn't go too far if I were you."

So he fetched her a Scotch. "Drink up. There's a good girl. Now let's go out and eat."

"I can't go out like this. I need something right now."

"Ta-ra," he sang out, leaping back as he flashed his envelope at her. "Ta-ra, ta-ra!"

"Terry, please."

"I want to go to Les A." Fending her off, he held tenaciously to the envelope. "Will you take me to Les A. for dinner?"

"Yes. Why not?" she said, startling him.

"Promise?"

"Yes yes yes."

"All rightee, then." Pulling her bodice away from her with a hooked finger, he rammed the envelope between her breasts. Then he stepped back, smirking, but smelling of fear. Lucy, beads of sweat sliding down her forehead, retreated to the bathroom. She trapped the little vein in her neck, pinching it between two fingers — it was either that or her tongue, the other veins had collapsed — and then she reached for the needle. When she came out again her manner was imperious. "Sit down, Terry."

He sat.

"You were never the only hunk of meat dangling on the rack, my dear. If I shop around I daresay I can find a less expensive, more obliging cut."

Cunt. But he didn't say it. He knew from experience that it would soon wear off, she would need more, and then she was the one who would be obliging. So he grinned, making an offering of his dimples. "Can't you take a joke any more?"

"A joke, yes. You, no."

"Aren't we going to Les A. together? Like you promised."

"We're not going anywhere together any more." Relenting a little, she added, "Come on, Terry. Surely you knew it had to end sometime."

"All rightee, then. Okay, ducks."

TWO

◆

Mr. Bernard died on a Monday, at the age of seventy-five, his body wasted. He lay in state for two days in the lobby of the Bernard Gursky Tower and, as he failed to rise on the third, he was duly buried. The family requested, unavailingly as it turned out, that instead of flowers donations should be sent to the Cancer Society. The flowers, some in the form of wreaths from sympathizers unfamiliar with Jewish ritual, were meticulously screened for compromising cards by a dutiful Harvey Schwartz. Most of them, Harvey was gratified to discover, came from celebrated people, achievers, names recognized beyond Montreal, around the world in fact, and this information he imparted to attendant newspapermen with his customary zeal.

Happily, there were no embarrassments. Lucky Luciano was dead. So were Al Capone, Waxey Gordon, "Little Farfel" Kavolick, Longy Zwillman and Gurrah Shapiro. Other cronies from the halcyon days did not send flowers or, with the exception of Meyer Lansky, were sufficiently tactful not to comment in the press. Lansky, unforgiving, told the reporter who surprised him in Miami with the news of Mr. Bernard's death, "Without Solomon that bastard would have ended his days like he started them. Sweeping up in a whorehouse." But, pressed by the news agencies, Lansky refused to elaborate. He insisted that he had been misquoted.

Fat Charley Lin rode to the funeral in a rented Rolls-Royce, passing out scented cards for his trendy Toronto restaurant, the House of Lin, to all comers. Stu MacIntyre, the former minister of justice, was also there, amused to see the son of the late Judge Gaston Leclerc in attendance. André Leclerc, who was in charge of public relations for McTavish in Europe, was rooted in Paris, but also, appropriately enough, maintained a château on the Loire. And just as Callaghan had anticipated, Bert Smith showed up to see Mr. Bernard buried.

"Mr. Smith?"

"Yes."

"I'm Tim Callaghan. Remember me?"

"I remember you."

"Yes. I thought you would. Well, he's dead. It's over now."

"Over? It's not over. It's just begun. Now he will have to face a Judge that he can't subvert."

"Well, yes, I suppose that's one way of looking at it."

"It's the only way of looking at it."

"I would like to talk to you, Bert."

"Call my secretary for an appointment."

"We're old men now, Bert, both of us. I would be grateful if we could go somewhere and talk."

"About the good old days?"

"I know how you feel, Bert."

"Do you now?"

"Let's talk."

The newspapers noted that Mr. Bernard, who began his life with nothing, was born in a sod hut on the prairie. The son of a peddler, Aaron Gursky, he owned his first hotel at the age of twenty-one and lived to preside over a distillery with estimated annual sales of more than a billion in fifteen different countries. Reporters observed that some two thousand mourners filed past Mr. Bernard's coffin. Among them were federal and provincial cabinet ministers, American senators, the Israeli ambassador, and numerous business leaders. The rabbi, in his eulogy, ventured "that Mr. Bernard Gursky's deeds would survive him locally, nationally and internationally at home and abroad. He was as good at giving away money as he was at making it. Though he supped with kings and presidents, he could also walk humbly with ordinary people, regardless of race, colour or creed. His sense of compassion was personal. We have lost a legend in our time, a man of world renown."

Obituaries the world over emphasized Mr. Bernard's generosity, his legitimate claim to being a latter-day philanthropist. They made no mention of his brother Solomon, the notorious Solomon, and, mercifully downplayed the Prohibition years.

Harvey, his mood expansive, his shoes new, handled his own interviews with surprising élan. He was grateful that no embittered employee — say old Tim Callaghan — surfaced with the most compromising story of his long tenure with Mr. Bernard. The day the merchant bankers of London were flown in for lunch in the Gursky boardroom to celebrate their underwriting of a five-hundred-million-dollar line of credit that would enable Mr. Bernard to acquire the McEwen Bros. & Ross Distillery in the Scottish highlands. The day that lived in infamy in Harvey's head, still polluting his dreams.

Mr. Bernard, intimidated for once, was determined that those establishment bankers, including one lord and two knights, would not wink at each other behind his back, putting him down for a reformed ghetto thug. He had gone over the menu endlessly and put on and discarded three suits before he settled on the charcoal grey, with the surprising help of a charming, disconcertingly pretty new receptionist. The young lady actually whistled as he passed, obliging a startled Mr. Bernard to stop and stare.

"It makes you look *very distingué*," she said. "Like you were on your way to Windsor Castle."

"What's your name, young lady?"

"Why it's Kathleen O'Brien, Mr. B."

Nobody called him that. He enjoyed the mischief in it. He chuckled. "Can you type?" he asked.

"Like the wind," she said. "I can also take shorthand, speak French fluently, and shoot a mean game of snooker."

"But do you know enough not to repeat what you hear?"

"Try me, Mr. B."

Transferred to his office for a trial run a week before the bankers' lunch she teased him into exchanging his diamond-studded, initialled cuff-links for something more subdued, and even managed to talk him out of his black silk socks. "Only for Hungarians of questionable origin," she said.

Rehearsing him for lunch, Miss O'Brien slapped his hand when he picked up a fork in his accustomed manner. "No, no, Mr. B. Like this."

"But you'd have to be a real horse's ass to hold your fork upside down."

"Ours is not to reason why, Mr. B. It's *comme il faut*."

With the bankers' lunch only two days away, Mr. Bernard began to pace his office frantically, his sinuses blocked, his stomach knotted, wishing that he had just a fraction of Solomon's style, Solomon's wit. The day of the luncheon he hollered at his underlings all morning, throwing ashtrays, kicking wastepaper baskets, chasing secretaries down the hall, lashing them with obscenities. Morrie, a born nose-picker, was banned from the building. In fact with the exception of Mr. Bernard's own sons and Harvey, whom he needed, only the gentile executives of McTavish were invited to meet the bankers. Even at that Mr. Bernard agonized over the invitation list into the early hours of the morning, crossing out a name, reinstating it, crossing it out again.

To begin with, everything had gone amazingly well, the bankers drawn to the compelling drawing of a radiant Ephraim Gursky that hung in a gold frame over the fireplace. "Of course you know," Mr. Bernard said, "we are hardly newcomers to this great land of opportunity. My grandfather first set foot in Canada in 1846. That's the young fellow you're looking at. Ephraim Gursky at age twenty-nine. He came over looking for the Northwest Passage. Shall we dine now, gentlemen."

Only a grieving Harvey Schwartz could tell that Mr. Bernard — his speech numbingly formal, Emily Post perfect — was under a terrible strain; and he knew from experience what kind of eruption that could lead to. Then, just as the bankers were sitting down to the table, Harvey pulling out Mr. Bernard's chair for him, Mr. Bernard relaxed prematurely. He let out a fart. A thundering fart. In the ensuing silence which seemed to last a decade for Harvey, but was actually a matter of seconds, Mr. Bernard, his eyes bulging, glared at Harvey.

"I'm — I'm — so sorry," an ashen-faced Harvey stammered. "Been up all night — upset stomach — something I ate — sorry sorry — excuse me, gentlemen." And he rushed off to his own toilet, where he slid to the floor, blinded by tears, quaking and raging and banging his head against the wall, trying to assuage his humiliation by quickly calculating the street value of his shares in Acorn and his McTavish stock options.

Harvey had not returned to the boardroom, but had fled the Gursky Tower, retreating to his bed for three days, pleading a migraine.

Now there was trouble of another kind. Only a day after Mr. Bernard was buried in the Temple Mount Sinai cemetery, his grave was desecrated. Fortunately, it was not the immediate family but Harvey who was contacted at once and hastened to the cemetery, uncomprehending but charged with concern by what he found there. A raven skewered and harpooned to the grave.

Harvey, his stomach churning, pressed a hundred-dollar bill into the cemetery custodian's hand. He swore the old man to secrecy, established an immediate twenty-four-hour vigil at the graveside, and took his discovery to Walter Osgood, the former museum curator who ran the Gursky Art Foundation.

Osgood, a portly Englishman, troubled by dandruff and halitosis, sported a bushy moustache; he had mocking blue eyes and a manner that Harvey found decidedly condescending for — as he put it — somebody who would never be anything more than a fifty-thousand-dollar-a-year prick. Aside from guiding the Gurskys in the acquisition of masters traditional and modern on the world market, Osgood also pronounced on literary matters in the Saturday edition of the Montreal *Star*. His widely read column, "The Bookworm's Turn," was larded with Latin quotations as were his frequent lectures to the St. James's Literary Society and the Pen Club, some of which were delivered in his apartment or *atelier* as he preferred, which was on the second floor of a converted warehouse in Old Montreal. He shared his *atelier* with a lady whom he was fond of introducing as his *inamorata*. "*Seulement*," he once confided to Becky, "*pour épater les bourgeois*."

"Good for you," she had replied, squeezing his hand.

Osgood, bulging out of his safari suit, suppressed amazement when Harvey burst into his office and slammed his burden down on his desk. The raven, Osgood said unequivocally, was *rara avis* indeed in Montreal, its natural habitat being the north. It was, of course, the royal bird. A raven croaked the warning of a royal death in *Macbeth*. The raven, he added, was consecrated to the Danish war god. Then, scrutinizing the harpoon, the shaft fashioned of caribou antler, the head made entirely of bear bone, the thong of bearded sealskin, he declared it to be clearly an Eskimo artifact, probably Netsilik in origin, but of a type that hadn't been in use for a good many years. "Bloody valuable I should think. Where did you get it, old boy?"

"That's of no importance," Harvey replied brusquely, "but you see this here," he said, indicating a symbol carved into the shank of the weapon, "that's a '*gimel*'."

Osgood, his slack facial skin splotchy at the best of times, reddened perceptibly. "I do beg your pardon," he said, rising slowly, "but I must micturate."

"What?"

"Pee pee."

Osgood rested briefly on the toilet seat, his head bobbing between his knees. Then he splashed his face with cold water and reached into the medicine cabinet for the little packet and his tiny silver spoon, snorting deeply before he confronted Harvey again. "You were saying . . ."

"This is a '*gimel*'. A Hebrew letter, Walt," Harvey added, as he knew Osgood found the diminutive offensive.

"Yes, yes, the third letter of the Hebraic alphabet. But that's impossible, old boy. It's simply not on. It may appear to be a '*gimel*' to the uninformed eye, but it's the maker's sign, actually. And the maker, beyond a doubt, was an Eskimo or, more properly, an Inuit. Eskimo, don't you know, is an Indian word that means 'eater of raw meat'. It's pejorative." Osgood grinned. "Like kike, to take a random example," he said, reaching for the harpoon.

Harvey snatched it back from him. "I think I'll hold on to this, if you don't mind?"

"Oh, Harvey, just a minute. I've had my amanuensis transcribe my notes for the up-and-coming *souk* in London. The Sotheby auction. Would you care for a copy?"

"Yes. You do that."

"Harvey, um, I can't quite put my finger on it, but you've changed. You seem taller now that — "

"Don't get smart with me, Walt."

Once back on the forty-first floor of the Bernard Gursky Tower, Harvey, all things considered, was not surprised to find Miss O'Brien lying in wait for him in Mr. Bernard's office. Into the Scotch again, the bottle open on the desk. Loch Edmond's Mist, Gursky's twelve-year-old malt. The best. She was drinking it neat.

"Will you join me in a farewell salute, Mr. Schwartz?"

Years ago he had asked her to please call him Harvey, but she had turned him down. "I prefer to call you Mr. Schwartz." Years ago she had only to sail down the hall on those long slender legs, auburn hair flowing, a crucifix nestled maddeningly between her breasts, for every man's head to turn. Just about everybody in the office, but certainly not Harvey, had tried it on with her at least once, learning no more than that she was an expensive tease. She would drink with them at The Lantern, her manner silky, and sometimes even agree to an intimate dinner at the Café Martin, but nobody ever got into her apartment on Mountain Street.

Miss O'Brien, Harvey had to allow, had certainly kept her figure, but she no longer turned any heads. Look at her neck. Her hands. "Why 'farewell'?" he asked, relieved.

"Isn't it?"

"You're family, Miss O'Brien."

"Neither of us is family. I never made that mistake, Mr. Schwartz. Don't you."

Bristling because she had the effrontery, that whore, to suggest that they had ever been in the same boat, he smiled tightly and said, "I'd expect you to take a computer course.

We all have to keep up with the times. But you're always welcome here. A lady with your proven talents."

"He used to say I'll bet Harvey is peeking through the keyhole. Did you, Mr. Schwartz?"

"Meanwhile I have some good news for you. You were remembered in Mr. Bernard's will. A bequest. Twenty thousand dollars."

"Let's not drag this out unnecessarily, Mr. Schwartz. I've come for the envelope he left in the safe."

Harvey opened Mr. Bernard's top desk drawer, plucked a file from it, and thrust it at her. "Here, if you are interested, is a list of the complete contents of his safe, properly notarized."

"And were you there when the safe was opened, Mr. Schwartz?"

"There was no envelope addressed to you."

"Mr. Bernard wouldn't lie to me about a thing like that. I'm fifty-three years old now, Mr. Schwartz."

"Time flies."

"Mr. Bernard was right about you. You are a little runt. Goodbye for now."

For now. After she had gone, Harvey brooded over the implied threat, weighing the possible consequences, when he was startled by the ghostly clack of snooker balls. The door to the billiards room was open. Harvey approached it cautiously, but smiled broadly when it turned out that it was only the pathetic Morrie in there. Mr. Morrie in a mood to reminisce.

"Did you know, Harvey, that I was shot at twice? I'm talking about the old days when hijacking was our biggest headache. The second time I was shot I soiled my pants. Bernie used to tease me about it something awful until Solomon found out. He grabbed Bernie and shoved him into the cab of the first truck in the next convoy out and that, *boychick*, was when 'Nigger Joe' Lebovitz and Hymie Paul, the Little Navy guys, were really catching it from the Purple Gang. Bernie was shaking like a leaf. A truck backfired and he hit the floor. So he never mentioned my embarrassment to me again." Mr. Morrie paused to chalk his cue and then lined up a tricky shot. He failed to make it. "Hey, you know what I wanted when I was a young fella? To own a bar. Morrie's. A nice, classy joint in a refined neighbourhood. Panelled walls. Old wood. Local artists could hang their pictures I wouldn't charge a cent commission. I wouldn't put pretzels or dried-out peanuts on the bar, but at six o'clock, bowls of freshly chopped liver. Devilled eggs. Spicy little sausages. I would cash personal cheques. You had a problem I'd be a good listener. That Morrie, they'd say, he's some sweet guy. He pours you a drink it's a drink."

"Of course you realize," Harvey said, trying not to show his distress, "that you couldn't do that now."

"It wouldn't be dignified."

"No."

"I'm Bernard Gursky's sole surviving brother."

"Yes."

"So, *boychick*, how do you think you will rate with the new generation? The homogenized Gurskys. My brother's children."

So that was it. Morrie must have heard that he was to be dismissed from the board, the first decision of the new CEO at McTavish. "Lionel and I couldn't be closer if we were brothers. Ask anybody."

"You know what my poor brother really wanted he never got. What he wanted was to be accepted, really really accepted by *them*. Maybe to be appointed an ambassador. Like Joe Kennedy. Come to think of it, we didn't do any worse. How do you figure it, Harvey?"

"By any standard you can think of Mr. Bernard was a great human being. A giant."

"You're such a smart fella, Harvey. Really you are. I've always admired you for that."

"I sincerely appreciate the compliment."

"But what did you do with the envelope?"

"There was no envelope. I can bring witnesses to support that statement."

"Bernie assured me that he was making provision for Miss O."

"I swear there was no envelope. Either he forgot or he was lying to her. With all due respect, he could be hard, you know. Look how he was to you for so many years."

"You think he didn't talk to me for all that time? *Oy* Harvey, when we were alone you know what? Some afternoons those last weeks he was still coming into the office he would lock the door to this room, raid the fridge for Popsicles, take out the cards, and we would get down on our hands and knees, playing nearest-to-the-wall, just like when we were kids. Tears came easily to him, you must know that, but in the last months there was no turning off the tap. Solomon, forgive me, Solomon. The truth is only Bernie could have made us so incredibly rich. I was obviously too dumb and Solomon would have destroyed McTavish just like he destroyed everything and everybody he touched. Lansky shouldn't have said what he did. Solomon was a bandit. Guns. Whores. Runs across the river. Prohibition was made for him. Only Bernie could have built what we are sitting on now. But, you know, toward the end it was the early days that obsessed him. He told Miss O. plenty."

"Who would listen to such an embittered old maid?"

Mr. Morrie chalked up his cue again and sank a red ball in a side pocket. "Moses Berger, maybe."

Harvey began to pace. Should he ask Morrie about the harpoon, the raven? Naw, Morrie was teetering on the cliff edge of senility. *Popsicles. Nearest-to-the-wall. Imagine.* "There was no envelope." Harvey's eyes filled with tears. "But maybe I should find an envelope and fill it with plenty."

"You're such a clever fellow, Harvey. You think of everything."

The next morning Harvey asked his secretary to find out where that flunk Moses Berger was hiding out these days. There was no answer in his cabin in the Townships. Harvey supplied his secretary with a list of bars.

"But it's not even noon yet," she protested.

"Late in the day for that one."

Next Harvey told his secretary to try a salmon-fishing camp on the Restigouche.

"They're expecting him on Tuesday."

There were no further incidents at the graveside, but a week after Mr. Bernard died Harvey was called upon to deal with yet another conundrum. The Monday following Mr. Bernard's death, his children had studied the newsweeklies for comment on their father's passing and then conferred together, uniformly outraged. Lionel phoned Harvey from his perch high in the Gursky building on Fifth Avenue. "I need you here," he said.

Harvey hastened to the airport and boarded one of the Gursky jets, a Lear. His lunch, ordered in advance and consumed at 28,000 feet, consisted of cottage cheese salad, a bowl of bran, and a sherbet of stewed prunes washed down with a bottle of Vichy water. Even as he flossed his teeth, Harvey pondered financial reports, but his mind was elsewhere. He knew that Lionel was giving a dinner party for Jackie Onassis that night. Harvey had packed his magenta velvet dinner jacket just in case. He no sooner landed at LaGuardia than a helicopter settled alongside, swallowing him, ascending again, and easing him on to the pad on the roof of the Gursky building, Harvey hurrying to Lionel's office. Lionel thrust a copy of a newsweekly at him, open at the offending page. "Do you have a ball-park figure for our annual ad budget with *Time* and *Newsweek*?"

Reconciled, Harvey placed a call to the publisher while Lionel listened on the extension on his side of the desk.

"Mr. Bernard died last Monday after a long illness."

"Yes. We know that. Please convey our condolences to Lionel."

"He was a great human being. I say that not because of my continuing unique relationship to the family, but from the heart."

"Nobody doubts that."

"During his lifetime, you know, I had many offers to go elsewhere for more money. But as he was loyal to me, I was loyal to him. His children appreciate that."

The publisher didn't know what to say.

"From nothing he built one of the world's largest liquor businesses. Wasn't that truly remarkable?"

"Certainly it was."

"Then why does his unfortunate passing rate no more than five lines in 'Milestones'?"

As the publisher explained to Harvey that there had been a big break in the continuing Watergate story during the week and, consequently, the back of the magazine had been

contracted to accommodate it, Lionel flipped the magazine
open to another page, scribbled a note, and passed both to
Harvey. The note read: "Ask him about the nigger."

"Oh, I can understand that," Harvey said to the publisher.
"Only how come an Afro-American dies and he gets a full
page?"

"Louis Armstrong was famous," the publisher said.

Lapsing into pleasantries, Harvey continued to chat as
Lionel hastily scribbled another note. Taking it, Harvey
swallowed hard and interrupted the publisher. "But thinking
aloud, if I may, why don't you make up for overlooking Mr.
Bernard's death by doing a story on Lionel taking over, which
is absolutely wonderful. I love him. I love him like a brother.
I'm not ashamed to say that. But I think a lot of people are
eager to know more about him, like what makes him tick and
what are his future plans for McTavish."

The deal made, or so he hoped, Harvey hung up; and then
he raised his enormous expressionless brown eyes to Lionel,
searching.

Lionel, his grin boyish, responded with a clap on the back.
Harvey had seen him do that to manicurists and parking-lot
attendants, just before fishing into his pocket for a tip.

"Join me in a drink?" Lionel asked.

"You go ahead. I'll have a Vichy, please."

Harvey subsided into a leather chair, spent, as an ebullient
Lionel took to the telephone, calling one friend after another,
letting it drop that over his objections the newsweekly was
doing an in-depth story on him. "They'll be calling all my
friends, you know how they operate. Hey, you won't tell them
about Rumania, right?"

Rumania, Harvey remembered, sighing.

A year earlier Lionel had been included in a chartered jet
laden with fifty corporate leaders who were flown to eastern
Europe by the newsweekly to meet with communist leaders.
Afloat on champagne and caviar, Lionel and a couple of the
other middle-aged magnates had started in goosing the
stewardesses as soon as the seat-belt-sign blinked off. If some
of the girls had been compliant, the longlegged straw-haired
one Lionel fancied had clearly taken umbrage. She spurned
his red roses and champagne in Warsaw. She slapped his face

in the lobby of the Hotel Metropole in Moscow. And come Bucharest there was an embarrassing incident. A drunken Lionel, the stewardess claimed, had forced his way into her room, attempting indecent assault. Not so, Lionel protested, he had been invited. Once back in New York, however, the girl had consulted a lawyer, Harvey had been sent for, and the out-of-court settlement had not come cheap, all things considered.

Girls recalcitrant or unresponsive, but consumed by avarice, had been Lionel's problem even at McGill. A terrified Harvey had unfortunately been present the first time a financial settlement had been demanded and Mr. Bernard had flown into one of his legendary rages, spewing obscenities.

Mr. Bernard, in his forties then, rocking on his tiny heels before the towering marble fireplace, seething. Young Lionel seated on the sofa, unperturbed, riding it out with a supercilious smile. When without warning an exasperated Mr. Bernard strode toward him, unzipped his fly, yanked out his penis, and shook it in his son's face. "I want you to know, you whore-master, that in all my years this has only been into your mother, God bless her," and, zipping up again, tearful, adding "and to this day she has the only cunt still good enough for Bernard Gursky. Respect. Dignity. That you still have to learn. Animal."

Coming off another telephone call, Lionel looked up, surprised, "I didn't realize that you were still here, Harvey."

"Yeah, well, I was wondering if you needed me for anything else."

"Nope."

"Hey," Harvey said, brightening, "would you like to join me for dinner tonight?"

"Sorry. I can't."

"Busy busy?"

"Bushed. I thought tonight I'd turn in early for once. Harvey, you look different. What is it?"

"I do not look different."

"Harvey, I loved my father. But he was also something of a tyrant, wasn't he?"

"We've got a problem, Lionel." Miss O'Brien's unfulfilled expectations. The envelope.

"Good for you, Harvey. How much was in it?"

"You were there when we opened the safe. There was no envelope."

"Was the old goat screwing her for all those years?"

"No, but there were intimacies of a kind."

"Hell, if that's what he wanted, we could have afforded much better."

"He also appears to have told her a good deal about the old days. It might be prudent to discover an envelope with, say, a couple of hundred thousand dollars in it."

"I don't want to have anything to do with it."

"That's exactly what I said to Morrie."

"What in the hell has that idiot got to do with it?"

"It was his idea. I told him it was ill-advised. Once you start on a thing like that, you could be paying out for years."

"I didn't say there should be an envelope or that there shouldn't be an envelope. All I said is I want nothing to do with it. You do what you think best, Harvey. I'd like to be able to count on you."

A copy of the drawing of a radiant Ephraim Gursky that hung over the fireplace in the boardroom of the Bernard Gursky Tower in Montreal hung in a gold frame in Lionel's office. Harvey was so familiar with it that he hadn't looked at it for years, but he did now. Ephraim, no taller than Mr. Bernard, was, unlike him, all coiled muscle, obviously ready to spring out of the frame and wrestle both Lionel and Harvey to the ground. Ephraim was drawn alongside a blow-hole, with both feet planted in the pack ice, his expression defiant, his head hooded, his body covered with layers of sealskin, not so much to keep out the cold, it seemed, as to lock in the animal heat lest it melt the surrounding ice. He held a harpoon in his fist, the shaft made of caribou antler. There was a seal lying at his feet, the three masts of the doomed *Erebus* and jagged icebergs rising in the background, the black Arctic sky lit by paraselenae, the mock-moons of the north. Harvey, unaccountably distressed, looked away from the drawing and indicated the whalebone sculpture resting on a pedestal in the corner. "That's Eskimo, isn't it?"

"You want it, it's yours."

"No. But where did you get it?"

"I can't remember how it got here, but I think it belonged to my Uncle Solomon once. Why?"

"Nothing. Just asking," Harvey said, lifting the piece off the pedestal to examine its underside, where he espied what, to his uninformed eye, appeared to be a '*gimel*'.

THREE

◆

Each time he reached that point on the 132 where it overtook the St. Lawrence River and hung in there, twisting with the shore, hugging it — past Trois Pistoles, winding beyond Rimouski — Moses's spirits soared. In his mind's eye, he would obliterate the straining Winnebagos and swarms of black-leather motorcyclists and roadside signs: TARZAN CAMPING ICI . . . BAR BQ CHICKEN CHEZ OCTAVE . . . 10 DANSEUSES NUES 10. He would shut out the slapdash little riverside towns with their souvenir shops mounted on cinderblocks, windows choked with machine-tooled carvings of cute spade-bearded habitants. He would ignore the houses framed by multi-coloured lights, the owner's initials woven into the aluminum storm door. Plastic reindeer staked in mid-prance on lawns already adorned with geranium beds set in worn whitewashed tires, the Quebecker's coronet.

Blinding himself to what we had made of our provenance, he would try to see the countryside as it must have looked to Cartier and his crew of sea-weary fishermen out of St. Malo in 1534. The year that they first ventured beyond the gulf, sailing into the estuary and up the fjord, anchoring at Ile Verte to scamper after hares for the pot, putting in at Ile aux Coudres to

shake wild hazelnuts free of the trees. Sailing into the
Kingdom of the Saguenay and beyond, drifting past beluga
whales and walrus and unbelievably thick schools of salar the
leaper, as the king of freshwater fish was first known. Though
the river would fail to lead them to La Chine — a
disappointment to François I no doubt — how the poor and
pinched men of Brittany must have marvelled at the
cornucopia on either shore. The abundance of virgin dark
green forest and the river-enriched black soil. The moose and
deer and beaver and geese and ducks. The cod. The salmon,
the salmon. The silvery, sea-bright salmon rolling in the
ripples and leaping free.

At Mont-Joli, grateful to be exactly where he was for once,
even without her, Moses dropped sharply right into the Gaspé
on the winding 132. Rising and dipping he spun into the valley
of the Matepédia, riverbanks soaring like canyon walls, the
spruce and cedar and birch not so much rooted there as scaling
the cliffs on which they held no more than a tenuous toe-hold.
Then he crossed into New Brunswick at Pointe-à-la-Croix,
taking the bridge into Campbellton and then making straight
for the camp of the Restigouche. Vince's Gulch was made up
of a dining lodge and a sleeping lodge and a spread of
outbuildings, including an ice-house.

Bouncing into the parking space in his Toyota shortly after
five P.M. Moses noted two cars, with North Carolina licence
plates, already in place in the shade, a Cadillac and a
Mercedes 450 SEL with a Playboy bunny mounted on the rear
bumper. Big chunky Jim Boyd, the head guide, walked slowly
toward Moses, his catcher's hand extended but his eyes
troubled. "They got here about an hour ago," he said.
"Barney Gursky and his girlfriend Darlene Walton and Larry
and Mary Lou Logan. The Logans have a teenage boy with
them. Rob. A real doozer. He didn't know there wasn't going
to be any TV and he suffers from allergies." Jim allowed that
to sink in before he added, "They never fished for salmon
before. They're in furniture, very big, looking to set up a
factory, maybe two hundred jobs, either here or in Ontario.
They're guests of that horse's ass who passes for our minister of
trade and he wants them to have one hell of a good time. So we
don't want any trouble, Moses. Where's Beatrice?"

"We're not together any more."

"You're no damn good, Moses, and you're going to die all alone like me in a tarpaper shack somewheres."

Moses handed over his traditional gifts, a pound of Twinings Ceylon Breakfast Tea and a bottle of Macallan Single Highland Malt.

"You've already had two phone calls," Jim said. "One of them was from England."

"I'm not even here."

Moses unpacked his things and then stepped out on the lodge porch to look at the water. The screen door to the adjoining bedroom whacked open and out sailed a real life Barbie doll, thirty maybe, blonde, drenched in perfume, her blue eyes not so much made up as underlined and set in italics; everything glowing, twinkly, her confident manner redeemed somewhat by badly chewed fingernails. She was wearing a corn-coloured raw silk top, a necklace ending in a pentangle in the cleft between her high perky breasts, and skintight designer jeans. She was barefoot, her toenails painted black. "Blessed be," she sang out in a drinker's husky voice, "I'm Darlene Walton. And what, may I inquire, is your rising house?"

"Why, I do believe I have a stationary Mercury rising in Pisces," Moses said. Then he tried to take her arm to help her down from the porch, but she withdrew abruptly from his touch. "There's a step missing," he pointed out, irritated.

She shrugged fetchingly, crinkling her sweet little nose and rolling her eyes, her alarm signals overlarge, like that of a silent movie actress, all to warn him against the man watching from the porch of the dining lodge.

Barney Gursky might have been forty or sixty. If you didn't know, it would be difficult to tell, for he was the manner of man who after forty didn't age but settled into himself. His black hair hadn't been cut but sculpted. He was bronzed and tall, not a hint of flab on him, with hard blue eyes and a sullen calculating mouth. Had Moses not known him he would have taken Barney for a golf pro who had failed to qualify for the tour, or a local TV morning host still waiting for that network offer. Darlene hastily introduced Moses, explaining, "I opened the screen door and there he was."

Either Barney didn't remember Moses, or he wasn't allowing that he did. "Do they call you Moe for short?"

"No. They don't."

"Well, glad to meet you anyway, buddy boy."

Barney was the Gursky cockatrice. A week after Anita's first wedding, he had acquired a Lamborghini, shifted into overdrive, and lit out for California and then Florida, rumoured to have invested in turn in a roller-derby team, film production, oil exploration, the international arms market, a wet T-shirt girls' basketball league in which he held the rights to the Miami Jigglers, et cetera.

Wanted, at one time or another, on various charges including fraud and alimony payment arrears, by the authorities in Florida, California, New York, and British Columbia, he hadn't even attended his sister's funeral in 1963. Charna had been discovered drowned in a swimming hole at the Friends of the Earth commune in northeastern Vermont four o'clock one morning, wearing nothing but a pair of snakeskin boots.

The Logans were waiting in the living room which, to Moses's astonishment, was festooned with red roses and actually had a bartender in attendance, something he had never seen before. The middle-aged Logans seemed an ill-matched pair. Mary Lou looked happily plump, wearing harlequin glasses with the sort of lenses that both magnified and blurred her eyes. But Larry was a scrawny bird, his bald head shiny, his dentures gleaming. Had he been a customs inspector he would have searched the bags of anybody that he considered saucy or younger or more privileged than he was. Their enormous son, who wore a Rolling Stones T-shirt over an immense belly and outsize faded jeans, sat apart. His button-nose cherry red, Rob held a box of Kleenex and two large Lowney's Nut Milk chocolate bars on his lap. The Logans were casually dressed, but Barney Gursky was even more fashionably turned out than his dishy girlfriend — Ralph Lauren polo shirt and dungarees and Tony Lama boots. Summoning the bartender with a flick of his manicured fingers, he asked Moses, "What can I offer you to drink?"

"A soda water, please."

"Shucks, I think we got us a teetotaller, Larry. Bring this

admirable fella a soda and the former Miss Sunset Beach here," Barney said, indicating Darlene, "will have a vodka on the rocks, but just one before dinner. She's watching her calorie intake." The Logans were from Chapel Hill, Barney said, furniture manufacturers, very big, and Barney's investment group was backing them in a venture that was willing to bet some twenty million plus on a Canadian plant. "And, hey, the fishing's going to be just great, because Jimbo here won't be holding us to the legal limit of two measly salmon a day, will you, boy?"

"We can't do anything illegal, sir."

"Now isn't that nice," Mary Lou said, "really nice. Jim here must have been told that we're very important VIPs, but he won't bend the law none for us. I respect that. Where do you hail from, Moe?"

"He doesn't like being called Moe for short," Darlene said, wandering in narrowing circles, closer and closer to the bar.

"Forget it, baby."

"Holy Toledo, I was just going to put my glass down."

"Montreal."

"We stayed at the Le Château Champlain there," Mary Lou said.

No sooner did Moses begin to unwrap a Monte Cristo than Rob leaped up and pointed a fat trembling finger at him.

"If you intend lighting that thing," Mary Lou said, "you'll have to step outside pronto."

Jim Boyd, tying a fly at the corner table, pricked his finger on a hook.

"And what," Barney asked, "would be your chosen field of endeavour, Moe?"

"*He likes to be called Moses*. He must think we're simply *dreadful*."

"These days you could say I don't do much of anything."

"Well, something tells me the former runner-up to Miss Flowering Dogwood has taken a shine to you, Berger."

"Oh boy," Darlene said, "here we go round the blueberry bush again."

"Mulberry."

Dinner at Vince's Gulch was usually something to be endured. Steak fried grey to the core served with potatoes boiled past the crumbling point, followed by "homemade" apple pie from Delaney's General Store, usually still frozen solid in the middle. But tonight a chef had been brought in from the Tudor Room of the Queen Victoria Hotel in Chatham. There was sweet corn and boiled lobster. Barney reached over to relieve Darlene of her corn — "More cellulite would be a real turn-off, baby" — and then called for another Scotch. Larry leaned forward so that Mary Lou could knot the napkin behind his neck. "Mercy bowcoop, Mummy." And Rob lunged for the bread basket, stacking four hunks at his place, then swooping on the butter dish, appropriating it. He gathered his plate in, leaving his plump arm curled on the table, sheltering what was his by right. Lowering his head as if to charge, he decimated his first corn cob and started in to strip the next one.

Jim explained that at Vince's Gulch the guides went out in the morning and again in the evening. There was no fishing in the afternoon. Everybody, he said, gets one turn at all the different pools during their three-day stay. He threw little twisted pieces of paper with the guides' names on them into a hat and asked everybody to draw one. Barney, who went first, drew young Armand. Larry got Len, or Motor-Mouth, as he was known on the river, and Rob drew Gilles.

"Well then," Jim said, "I guess that leaves me and Mr. Berger."

"He'll have the edge going out with the head guide, won't he, boy?"

"We don't call Jim or anybody else around here 'boy'. Furthermore, it is not a competition."

Barney accepted a large cognac and swished it around in his snifter. "I know you don't drink, Berger, but are you a gambling man?"

"What did you have in mind?"

"You, me, and Larry here each write out a cheque for a thou and tack it to the bar. Come Thursday top rod takes the pot."

"I'm an old hand, Barney. It's more difficult than you think."

"He's been fly-fishing for years," Darlene said.

"Okay. We've got a bet."

Thick unyielding clouds lay overhead as the Logans waddled down the dirt track to the river laden with bug sprays and cameras and expensive-looking movie equipment. Rob lugged a portable radio and his Kleenex and a big bag of candy. Barney carried a bottle of cognac. As Darlene raised a long slender leg to sidestep off the little floating dock into their long canoe — Armand reaching out to help, his eyes on her panting bosom — Barney immediately knocked her off balance with a proprietorial whack on her bottom. "Oh, man, do I ever go for those buns!"

Allowing everybody else a head start, Moses lighted a Monte Cristo and settled into his canoe with Jim.

"What can I say, Moses?"

"Don't come this week is what you could have said."

Over the hum of the outboards, The Rolling Stones began to ricochet off the river walls, scattering the crows. Fortunately Rob was heading a good mile downriver to the Bar Pool.

Once Jim had anchored at their first drop, out of sight of the others, Moses started out with a Silver Doctor, went to a Green Highlander and then a Muddler without getting anything to rise. Things were no better on the second drop. On the third drop they saw a big salmon roll and another leap, maybe thirty feet out. Moses laid every fly he could think of over their heads, but they weren't taking. Then there came a hollering and a squealing from the Fence Pool. "It's probably only a grilse they got," Jim said.

A half hour passed and then the deer flies came out and it began to drizzle. Covering the far fast water, stripping his line quickly, Moses got his strike. A big fish, maybe thirty pounds, taking so hard Moses didn't even have to set the hook, his rod already bent double. Immediately the line screeched and the fish shot downriver, taking most of Moses's backing before it paused and he started to reel in the slack. Jim lifted anchor and began to paddle gently toward shore, his net within reach. The fish came close enough to look at the canoe and raced downriver again, breaking water about fifty feet out. Flipping in the air. Dancing on its tail.

"Hey there, Moses. Hey there."

The fish struck for the bottom and Moses imagined it down there, outraged, rubbing its throbbing jaw against the gravel, trying to dislodge the hook. It couldn't, obviously, so it gave in to bad temper, flying out of the boiling water once more, shaking its angry head, diving, then resting deep, maybe pondering tactics. After Moses had played the fish for another twenty minutes, he heard and then saw the others in their canoes returning from their pools. Approaching Vince's Hole, Gilles and Len both cut their outboards back sharply, as courtesy required, but not Armand, whom Barney had instructed to actually accelerate into the opposite bank before killing his engine. Frank Zappa bounced over the water at God knows how many decibels. Cursing, Moses reeled the fish in close. It was lying on its side on the surface now, panting desperately, but good for one more run. Moses vacillated only briefly before leading the exhausted fish toward the net. And that's when Mary Lou stood up to take pictures, her flash attachment exploding again and again. Distracted, Moses didn't notice his line tangling round the butt of his rod. The fish bolted, running his line taut and jerking free of the hook. Moses's rod sprung upright, his line going slack.

"Well now," Barney said, "like the old hands say: it's more difficult than you think."

Back in camp, Moses was told soon enough that Barney had killed two salmon, a total of twenty-four pounds, Larry had landed a five pound grilse, and Rob had lost a fish.

As the bartender had gone home it was an exuberant Barney who served the drinks, allowing Darlene another vodka and asking Moses whether he would like his soda straight up or on the rocks. Har, har, har. Moses, pleading fatigue, allowed that he would have just one and then retire to his room to read in bed.

"Didn't I tell ya, Mary Lou? Moses is a *real* highbrow."

"Well, I've read a whole stack of novels myself this year, both fiction and non-fiction. I never bother with TV."

"In my humble opinion," Darlene said, "TV is just one big waste of time. I only watch PBS."

"Yeah," Barney said. " 'Sesame Street.' "

Rob shook with laughter, retrieving a trail of snot from his upper lip with a lizard-like dart of his tongue.

"I'm going to turn in now," a tearful Darlene said. "Will you be long, Barney?"

"I won't be long here; but I sure will when I get there. So there'll be no call for you to unpack your vibrator tonight, baby."

The telephone rang, Barney scooping it up before Jim could reach it. "It's for you, Moe."

Jim rubbed his hands against his trousers. "You can take it in the kitchen," he said.

It was London on the line.

"Lucy, is that you?"

"Yes," a thick voice came crackling back.

It was, Moses reckoned, three o'clock in the morning in London. "What's all that racket in the background?"

"I'm moving."

"At this hour?"

"You're such a nag, Moses."

"Why are you slurring your words?"

"It's my jaw. It's still swollen. The dentist yesterday. Oh, you and Henry are both going to be sent some photographs. I don't want either of you to open the envelopes. You are to put them right in the fire. Do you understand?"

"Are you in trouble again, Lucy?"

"Will you please do as I ask for once and not bother me with any stupid questions."

"I will throw the envelope in the fire without opening it. Have you spoken to Henry yet?"

"Obviously you are more worried about him than you are about me."

"There's a delicate sensibility at play there."

"But not here?"

"No."

"You think I'm disgusting?"

"Yes," Moses said, hanging up. Then he dug a couple of pills out of his pocket and swallowed them without water.

Approaching the bedroom lodge some fifteen minutes later, Moses saw moths dancing in the cone of light coming from Darlene's bedroom. Darlene was waiting on her side of the screen door, wearing a Four Seasons Hotel towel robe belted loosely over a wispy black negligee with a red lace trim.

"You're not a teetotaller," she said. "You had to give it up, but you continue to nurse some secret sorrow. My daddy was a boozer too."

Moses laughed, delighted with her. Darlene was sucking on a joint. Opening the screen door, she handed it to him. Moses inhaled deeply before passing it back, not letting go of her hand, but drawing her close and whispering a suggestion to her.

"Why, Moses Berger, you are a simply *dreadful* man," she said, all twinkly. "But if he sees your car gone as well he'll figure it out and go absolutely apeshit."

The banging screen door of the dining-room lodge warned them of Barney's unsteady approach. Darlene thrust the joint at Moses, hastily adjusting her towel robe, and then began to spray her bedroom with deodorant. Retreating to his own room, Moses collapsed on his bed, gratified that he was still capable of mindless lust. Then the bickering flared in the next room, Darlene declaring with some vehemence, "I'm not getting up to brush my teeth and rinse out again. If that's what you want go find yourself a whore."

Moses quit his room and headed for the dirt road to walk off his rage. He made it as far as the turnoff for Kedgewick before he started back. Once in camp again, he didn't return directly to his room. Instead he slipped into the dining room and dialled Clarkson's number in Montreal. Clarkson, he knew, was in Toronto. Beatrice answered on the seventh ring.

"I'm at Vince's Gulch."

"Moses, it's one A.M." She sighed. "Did Jim ask after me?"

"Possibly he hasn't inquired because he has yet to catch me alone."

"You mean to say you're with somebody up there? It was our place."

"Get into your car and drive straight out here. You should make it by morning."

"Don't humiliate yourself, Moses."

Stung, he didn't speak again until he could trust his voice. Then he said, "What in God's name can you see in him?"

"Solomon Gursky isn't his obsession. I am. Oh, and this will amuse you. He thinks I'm intelligent."

"Beatrice, he's going to bore you."

"I've had quite enough of not being bored. What you call boring would be refreshing. At least if he goes out to fetch a pack of cigarettes at ten P.M., I can count on his not being gone for a week or ten days without a word, me going out of my mind, and then you phoning to say I'm in Paris or back in the clinic again. Is it somebody I know?"

"What are you talking about?"

"With you there."

"Yes. It's somebody you know. Why not somebody you know?" he asked, slamming down the receiver.

Barney was waiting in the bar, a glass half-filled with cognac to hand, his eyes shiny and unfocused. "Pussy trouble?" he asked.

"Good-night, Barney."

"A word of advice, buddy boy. You never should have let your hair go grey like that. Have it dyed. We've been together two years and she still doesn't know my real age. I keep my passport hidden."

"Did you see your father when you were in Montreal?"

"Take my advice and have it dyed. Pump iron. Look at you. Shit."

Everybody was at breakfast by the time Moses got there.

"Well," a red-eyed Barney said, mopping up the eggs on his plate and shoving back his chair, "I'm for an early start, baby."

"I'm not going out with you this morning. It's going to be buggy as hell out there and I don't want to pick any more hooks out of my sweater."

"You worry too much about your tits springing a leak."

"Maybe there are some folks *who don't know yet*. Why don't you put an ad in the newspapers or on TV?"

Mary Lou flung her napkin down on the table. "Come with me, Rob."

"My eggs weren't turned over easy like I asked," Rob said. "I'm bitten everywhere." He banged his radio down on the table. "And something's wrong with my Sony. I told you we shoulda bought a Sanyo."

"There are fresh batteries in the car," Larry said.

"It's not the batteries. It doesn't work. It's fucken broke. Shit. My asthma. I shouldn't get excited."

"There's a Radio Shack in Campbellton that would probably fix it," Moses said. "It's not such a long drive."

Rob lost another fish in the rain that morning. Larry didn't bring back anything and Barney, who had to settle for what looked like a nine-pound fish but weighed in at eleven, waited impatiently at the dock to see how Moses had made out. But when Jim motored into camp he was alone in his canoe. Moses, he explained, had been invited to lunch with an old chum, Dan Gainey, at the Cedar Lodge; and then he held up a twenty-six pound salmon for Barney to admire. Which was when Darlene came skittering down the hill to join them. "I need the car keys," she said.

Barney grabbed her by the buttocks, driving her against him. "I know what you need, but I could do with something to eat first."

"While you're having your nap I'm going to drive into Campbellton and get Rob's radio fixed."

"Okay, okay," he said, tossing her the keys, which were weighed down by a heavy brass disc bearing the initials B.G.

When he undressed her Moses had no doubt that he would find a little cord with a catch on the end dangling from her back. He would yank it and she would blink her eyelashes and chirp, "What's up, doc?" Meanwhile he settled in to wait for her in the dark of the Marie Antoinette Room of the Auberge des Voyageurs in Campbellton. Three sodden Micmacs, seated at the bar, were watching a wrestling match on TV. An hour passed. Moses was about to give up when Darlene flew into the room, arms fluttering, eyes signalling fire and flood and emergency exits, her full petulant mouth forming a huge startled O. "*Surprise, surprise*," she shrieked. "You'll never guess who's here, MARY LOU!!"

Mary Lou, stumbling in the unaccustomed dark, couldn't even find Darlene at first. Squinting, she finally got her bearings. "Why if it isn't the highbrow," she said.

"*What a* COINCIDENCE!" Darlene pleaded, eyes darting from one to another, settling on Moses. "She needs the powder room *right now*."

Moses indicated the door marked COURTESANS and Mary Lou toddled off obediently. Darlene's explanation came in a rush. "He took the car keys with him this morning *I could have died*. When he got back, it seemed like CENTURIES. I said I would drive here to get Rob's radio fixed and she insisted on coming along. But she won't tattle on us. Mary Lou and I belong to the same coven. In a previous incarnation she was my son and in ancient times, when I was king of Egypt she was my queen."

"Obviously you've been through a lot together."

"I'll say. But what are we going to do *now*?"

"There's a bottle of vodka sitting in an ice bucket in the room I rented for the afternoon here."

"Oh, you are such a *dreadful* man!" She offered him a quick hug. "But I couldn't go that far now. I'm too scared. Mary Lou is *very* sensitive ever since her first husband, blessed be, was lost in the mail."

Moses doubted that he had heard right.

"It was a very severe blow at that point in time. She should have sued the post office for *plenty* is what I told her. *Some* Christmas. All the family was gathered together but it just wasn't the same opening the presents without Lyndon there."

"How was he lost in the mail?"

"*Cheezit*," she hissed, bashing his ankle under the table hard enough to make him wince.

Mary Lou settled into her chair, shed her glasses, and stared at Moses with big blue eyes as blank as Orphan Annie's. "I can tell that you are a very well educated man just by looking into your third eye. If you ask me," she said, her mouth puckered with suspicion, "your wife is a very lucky lady."

"Actually, I'm not married."

Making his excuses, Moses directed them to the Radio Shack. He retrieved Gainey's Ford pickup and returned to the cabin on the river where Gainey kept watch over the Shaunnessy pools. Then he canoed back to Vince's Gulch.

Jim, standing on the shore, greeted him with a perfunctory nod. "What in the hell can you see in her, Moses?"

"She makes me laugh. Never underestimate that."

Entering the dining lodge in search of a coffee, Moses found that Barney and Larry were being entertained by a deputy of New Brunswick's minister of trade, an obsequious young man wearing a tartan jacket and canary yellow Bermuda shorts. The deputy had come equipped with information on local land and labour costs. Larry, taking notes on a legal pad, needed to know what kind of sweetener they could expect investment- and tax-wise from the provincial government. The deputy assured them they could expect New Brunswick to be generous, but he was not authorized to talk numbers. Barney didn't like that. "The trouble with you Canadians," he said, "is that you're always sitting on the fence. Look at it this way, buddy boy, you can't catch a dose pulling your meat, but it sure as hell ain't as much fun as pussy."

"I will certainly advise the minister of your feelings," the deputy said, and then he reminded them that a lot of important people were waiting to meet them at the country club, but if they didn't leave soon they wouldn't be back in time to fish.

Barney called for another Scotch. "We're waiting for the future Mrs. Middle-Aged Spread to get here."

But when Mary Lou led Darlene into the dining lodge she was obviously in no condition to go anywhere. "I think I'd better lie down," she said.

"Shit."

"Shall we be off, then?" the deputy asked.

Barney looked hard at Moses sipping coffee in a far corner of the room.

"I promise to get you back by six, sir."

Moses retreated to his room, aching for a nap, but no sooner did the cars pull out than he was startled by a rhythmic tapping on his wall. "Boo," Darlene said.

She was waiting on the porch when he got there. All twinkly again, she drove him back into his room, thrusting against him. A perplexed Moses was weighing the two hundred jobs at possible risk against his so-far frustrated lust when the screen door banged open behind them. Rob, munching on a Lowney's Nut Milk, asked, "Were you at least able to get it fixed?"

"The man said you must have banged it real hard against something because the innards are all fucked up, pardon my French, and he couldn't do anything with it."

"Uncle Barney said that you were feeling poorly and that I should stay with you in your room until he got back, in case you had to vomit or something."

After they had gone, Moses opted for the public school boy's remedy, a cold shower, and then he decided not to join the others for dinner. Instead he ate a cold roast beef sandwich in the kitchen with the grizzly Motor-Mouth. Motor-Mouth's wife ran a florist's shop that they both owned in Campbellton. "Having a good summer?" Moses asked.

"Terrific. We're averaging three funerals a week."

Short-tempered, his casting jerky, Moses lost a big fish in the Bar Pool and never got another strike. Barney came back with a fish that looked to be no more than ten pounds, but — according to young Armand — it had weighed in at twelve.

Moses retired early, but he was too restless to sleep. So he slipped into his clothes, went down to look at the water, and then climbed to the dining lodge to see if there was a Perrier in the refrigerator. Barney was standing at the bar. Drunk again.

"I'm developing a property for Warners. Dustin's crazy for it, but I'm thinking Redford and Fonda. It's a baseball story, the greatest ever told. I've got to keep it under wraps, but let me describe the big scene to you. Redford's a pitcher, see, the greatest southpaw since Koufax. Only he can no longer throw red hot. He's got arm trouble. Each time he's gone to the mound this season the other teams have shelled him. So the manager, played by Walter Matthau, has benched him. Now we are into the deciding game of the World Series and the team's young hotshot, Al Pacino, has been throwing and he is suddenly in trouble. His team is leading 7 – 4, but it's the bottom of the ninth, the bad guys have the bases loaded, and up to the plate steps this big buck, a Reggie Jackson type, *who can murder southpaws even when they're at their best.* What does Matthau do? He takes the ball away from Pacino and turns to the bullpen *indicating his left arm.* The crowd begins to murmur. No, no. Is he crazy? He's bringing in Redford. Redford takes his warm-up pitches and then Reggie steps into the box. Tension? You can cut it with a knife. Reggie spits and Redford just grins at him. He rears back and pitches. Ball one. Reggie steps out of the box, looks at the third-base coach and steps in again. The catcher gives Redford a signal and he shakes it off. He throws. Ball two. The crowd is roaring. They are cursing Matthau. The windup. The pitch. Holy shit, *it's ball three!* The fans are going bananas because they know Redford just has to throw a strike now. He's won maybe two hundred games for them over the years and now some of those bastards are booing him. Cut to the stands, where Jane Fonda is weeping. She's eight months pregnant, but the kid isn't even his. It's Reggie's, which will be very controversial as well as give the picture a redeeming social value. Cut to Reggie at the plate. Imitating Babe Ruth, that cocky jigaboo points at the flagpole out there. He's going to hit a dinger. Cut to Redford's baby-blues and they say you fucked my wife. Now it comes. This is it. The catcher trots out to the plate *and hands Redford another glove and Redford puts it on his left hand. The fucker has been practising a secret pitch for just such a spot as this.* HE'S AMBIDEXTROUS! A SWITCH-PITCHER! THE FIRST IN THE HIS-TORY OF OUR NATIONAL PASTIME SINCE ABNER DOUBLEDAY INVENTED IT! But can he deliver? Sixty thousand fans in the stadium and you can hear a pin drop. Redford rears back. He throws. STEE-RIKE! Reggie calls time out and asks for another bat. A lot of good it will do him. STEE-RIKERINOO NUMBAH TWO! Reggie asks to see the ball. Catcalls. Boos. Laughter. He steps back into the box and this time he's swinging for downtown you bet, but he's out of there. STEE-RIKE-OLA NUMBAH THREE! Game over." Barney, who had been acting out all the parts, slumped exhausted at the bar and poured himself another drink. "I'm going to call it *The Big Switcheroo.*"

"How old were you when Solomon's plane went down?"

"Old enough to know that it was mighty convenient for

somebody." Barney stretched. He yawned. "You know, Berger, I've got you figured out. Lionel sent you down here after he found out I was coming. You're a paid snoop."

"Good-night, Barney."

But Barney followed him out on to the porch. "Hold on a minute. It's copyrighted."

"What?"

"*The Big Switcheroo*. And remember what I said. Have it dyed."

Moses took his pill and slipped into bed. He didn't hear Barney come in. Neither did he appreciate how deeply he must have slept until a subdued Darlene turned up for breakfast. The last to appear, her eyes were puffy and her lower lip swollen.

"See you later," Barney said, "I've got to go and catch me a big fish."

Outside Moses ran into Jim. "A Mr. Harvey Schwartz has called three times from Montreal. He knows that you're here and he says that it's urgent."

There was not a cloud in the sky and the sun had already burnt the mist off the winding river when Jim anchored at their first drop on the Cross Point Pool.

Moses took a grilse and a big fish before noon. While Jim went to weigh them, he slipped away to have a few words with Darlene.

At lunch Jim reported that Moses had taken a five-pound grilse and a twenty-four pound salmon. Barney had only managed to kill a small fish that weighed in at nine pounds. Rob took his first fish and Larry never got a strike. So Moses was now top rod, if only just. "Yeah," Barney said, "but he's shot his legal wad for today and I intend to take a whopper tonight."

Moses didn't turn up for dinner.

"Where's the old hand?" Barney asked.

"Like you said, he's not allowed to fish any more. I lent him my canoe so he could visit with Gainey downriver."

"Well, let's hope his cheque is good."

Moses waited on the road, exactly where he had promised, and as soon as Darlene spotted him she slowed down, pulling up and letting him take the driver's seat.

"How was he lost in the mail?" he asked, immediately.

"Oh, him. Holy Toledo!" Lyndon had been killed in a hunting accident in Vermont and Mary Lou arranged to have him cremated, the skull left intact so that it could sit on the mantelpiece each holiday season. "If only for little Rob's sake," she said. "But he was lost in the mail. The undertaker man swore up and down that he had sent him off in a box they had made especially because of how the bones stuck out of regulation size. Some of them didn't crumble in the fire. He was a Baptist, you know." A tear slid down her cheek. "Mary Lou wrote to the postmaster-general in Washington and phoned our congressman I don't know how many times, but to this point in time nobody could ever find him. So poor old Lyndon is lying in some damp ratty post office basement somewhere, unclaimed after all these years because of insufficient postage or some shit like that."

Moses turned the Mercedes on to a narrow bumpy track and eased it down a steep incline, tucking it among the trees where it could not be seen from either the road or the river. Then he led Darlene to where he had laid out the quilted blanket.

"Oh, you're such a *dreadful* man," she squealed, setting down her camera.

Moses lifted the vodka bottle out of the ice bucket, dipped in for some ice cubes, and poured her a long one. He sat down and watched enviously, his heart aching, as she gulped it. Then she contrived to tumble into his lap, the glass rolling away, her drink spilling on the blanket. He was still mourning the lost liquor as she squirmed out of her jeans and he slid her jersey over her head. He began to fondle and kiss her breasts.

"Oh boy, do I ever go for *that*," she said, swaying from side to side, her pentangle clipping him in the nose as she jiggled her breasts and cooed, "You never guessed, didja?"

"How Lyndon was lost in the mail?"

"*Nooo*! How I had them made as a fortieth-birthday surprise for Barney."

"Your breasts?"

"They're implants, you silly."

A troubled Moses retreated from her, unwrapped a Monte Cristo and lighted it with a shaky hand. "Did he pick the size?"

"He didn't *exactly*, but hint hint, he did show me pictures from magazines of the kind of tits that turned him on. I'm such an airhead. Nothing could happen. I knew *that*, the doctor assured me, but for the first few months I wouldn't let anybody squeeze too hard and I didn't dare sit close to the fireplace at the ski lodge, because I was scared they might — Well, you know. *The heat*."

Moses inhaled deeply, wishing that he were somewhere else, somewhere alone. Sensing that he had begun to drift, a pouting Darlene got him out of his shirt and began to probe between his legs, fishing for him. "There isn't a manual I haven't read," she said. "Talk as dirty as you want. Order me to do things."

She bit his ear. Moses yelped and bit right back.

"Hey, there! Hold your horses. *Woa!*" she said, thrusting him from her with surprising strength.

"What's wrong?"

"It's my fault. I shoulda told you right off that there's to be no scratching or biting or even hard pinching, honey, because he checks me out for bruises every night." She had him out of his trousers now, but stopped abruptly short of descending on him, her face clouding. "How many times can you come at your age, honey? I should know that before I risk spoiling any multiples for me."

Possibly, he thought, back in Chapel Hill, where they were very big in furniture, she did door-to-door surveys.

"Are you still there?" Reaching down to root out his testicles, she discovered, to her consternation, that he only had one. "Holy Toledo," she said, a shopper short-changed.

"What did you expect? A cluster?"

"FAR OUT!" she exclaimed, running her tongue from his groin to his throat like he was an envelope to be sealed.

But now her camera had become painfully lodged in his back. Moses pried it free. "What did you bring this for?" he asked, holding it up.

"Silly. I brought it along because I thought you'd surely

want to take some pussy pictures for a souvenir to remember me by. Look!"

Leaping up, she turned her back to him and bent over to clasp her knees, ass riding high, and then she hooked one finger through her black bikini panties, tugging at them. Shifting to an upright position, her back still turned to him, she shot him an over-the-shoulder naughty wink, licked her lips and then popped her thumb into her mouth, fellating it. He was reminded of the Goldberg Brothers Auto Parts calendar stapled to the wall in the Texaco station on Laurier Street. Unable to help himself, Moses shook with appreciative laughter. "Oh, Darlene, you are perfection. Honestly."

"Then why aren't you snapping any pictures?" She struck another Playmate pose, this one obliging her to at least partially dress. "Go ahead and shoot the whole roll, but please remember to take it with you."

Only then did she notice that he was also dressed.

For her, he hoped, it would not be passion frustrated or, God help us, unrequited love so much as gym class cancelled for today.

"Maybe it's better this way," she said, "our being, well you know, platonic friends . . . but I did think we had come here to fuck our brains out and I never did it with a *real* highbrow before."

"Maybe we should start thinking about getting back."

"Not yet. Jim Boyd says you can make a salmon dance on its tail. Show me," she said, her eyes taunting. "Show me."

"Okay, but it will be strictly catch-and-release."

"Like me," she said, startling him.

He led her down the steep embankment to where he had beached Gainey's canoe on the edge of one of the Shaunnessy pools.

"If Barney comes by now and sees us together," she said, "he'll beat the shit out of both of us."

"He's on the other side of the camp way upriver."

"Lucky for you."

Lifting Gainey's rod out of the canoe, he took his anger out on his casting, whipping the line harder than was necessary, straining for the far shore before he even covered the near water. Within minutes he had hooked a big one, but it didn't bolt downriver or break water. Instead it made for the bottom and sat there. Moses tightened his line, jiggling his rod, sweeping it to the right and then to the left.

"Can't you finish anything you begin?"

"It's a sulker. Hand me your car keys."

"What are you going to do?"

He fed the key ring with the heavy brass disc on to his line. "Bop him over the head."

"*But what about* THE KEYS?" she asked, wide-eyed, as they shot down the line.

"There's nothing to worry about." He would retrieve them as he released the fish in shallow water near the shore. "Hey, there he goes."

His line screeched. About sixty feet out the silvery, sea-bright salmon came thrashing out of the water, sailing high. Twisting, flapping. It snapped the leader. The keys, flying free, caught a glint of the failing sun before they plopped into deep water and disappeared. "I'm afraid we've got something of a problem now," Moses said, reeling in.

"*A problem?* Holy Toledo! Ass-hole! I don't *believe* it. This isn't happening to me. It's a *dream.* You know what Barney's going to do? He's going to kill me *and then he's going to cancel all my credit cards again.*"

"But not necessarily in that order."

"If I were you right now I wouldn't be coming on smart-ass. I'd be hoping I was covered by Blue Cross. And how!"

"Right now I'm not worried about me. It's Jim I'm worried about." He would never forgive him. "The two hundred jobs. The furniture factory."

"You're not only crazy but for a highbrow you sure take the airhead prize." She explained. "*How about that, Moe?*"

Moses didn't answer immediately. Instead he slowly unwrapped a Monte Cristo, bit off the tip, and smiled at her. "I'm going to tell you exactly what to do."

Barney should have been jubilant. He was top rod. The salmon he had caught, while it was certainly not a whopper, had been sufficient to allow him to tip the scales five pounds better than Moses. But only the Logans and the guides were there to witness Barney's triumph at the weigh-in outside the

ice-house, and Jim seemed somewhat troubled by it. Barney
was not surprised that Moses, obviously a sore loser, had yet to
return from wherever he was visiting, but he was beginning to
worry about his car. He had forgotten that Miss Calculation
still had the keys. She never should have driven off without his
permission.

"Maybe somebody ought to go out and look for her," Mary
Lou said.

Rob cleared his nose of snot with one wipe of his sleeve.
"Daddy's smoking," he said.

Larry ground his cigarette into the gravel with his heel.
"Where would we look?" he asked.

"The nearest pit stop is where," Barney said. "She drives
back here drunk she could slam into a tree. You know what
that car cost me?"

Larry passed Barney his flask. His eyes burned bright. "I
think she's with Berger somewhere."

"You're crazy, Larry."

"That's exactly what you said the last time."

"Okay, okay, let's go. We'll take your car."

Jim was waiting on the shore when Moses came in to beach the
canoe. "How could you do this to me, Moses?"

"Hasn't she come back yet?"

"You better believe it. With some cock-and-bull story
too."

"What did she say?"

"She went out for a drive and parked on the Kedgewick
road, leaving the keys in the ignition, and walked down to the
river to snap some pictures of the sunset. When she got back
some no-good Micmacs had made off with her car. Goddamn
it, Moses, I hope you enjoyed yourself, because this could cost
me my job and maybe two hundred other jobs for the people
around here."

"There weren't going to be any jobs. They had no intention
of building a factory here or in Ontario, but it got them a free
fishing trip with all the trimmings. Last year they pulled off the
same scam in Mexico and went bone fishing for a week without
it costing them a dime. Where are they now?"

"Fat boy and his mommy are in the lodge and the men are out looking for the car. Darlene's with them."

"They'll run into Gainey on the road and he'll show them where it was abandoned by those no-good Micmacs who took it for a joy-ride. However, there is a problem. No keys. Barney will have to jump the wires."

"Oh, I forgot to tell you. He's top rod. The son of a bitch weighed in some five pounds better than you did."

"Shall we check it out?"

"Damn right."

So they slipped into the ice-house where Barney's catch lay in a row on last winter's shrinking snows, and Jim knelt to probe their bellies one by one. "I'm going to have to fire Armand," he said.

Then the cars rolled back into camp, the Cadillac followed by the Mercedes. Darlene jumped out, not looking right or left, but running to her bedroom, pursued by Barney.

"Is he going to beat up on her?" Jim asked.

"Just check her out for bruises."

Mary Lou had poured herself a beer in the dining lodge. "They didn't steal anything or do any damage. Even Barney's camera was still on the front seat. Isn't that nice?"

Moses was drawn to the radio. The late news. Watergate again. The tape that had been mysteriously erased. General Haig, speaking at a press conference, suggested that there was a sinister influence at work in the White House. Moses was still pondering that, dismissing his initial gut reaction as crazy—well, at best unlikely—when Barney came striding into the lodge. "The best man won," he said, "or haven't you heard?"

"Congratulations."

"Fuck you too," Barney said, and when the telephone rang he lunged for it. "Yeah, right. Sure he's here. He's been here for days. It's for you, Moe. Your boss wants you to file a report on me. Boy, did I ever have you figured."

Moses took the call in the kitchen.

"Moses, this is Harvey Schwartz. Of course you've heard that Mr. Bernard has died. No matter what you think, he was a great human being. I say that not because of my unique relationship with the family but from the heart." Harvey told him what had happened. The raven, the harpoon. "In your opinion could this have been Henry's doing?"

"Henry wouldn't besmirch himself doing such a thing."

"If it wasn't Henry, who was it, then?"

"Henry would quote Ben Sira to you. 'Seek not things that are too hard for thee, and search not things that are hidden from thee.' Was there a *'gimel'* carved into the harpoon?"

"Yes. Now tell me why anybody would commit such an obscene act?"

"You wouldn't understand, Harvey," he said, hanging up. Then, his heart thudding, Moses went to pack. *The ravens gathering. A sinister influence at work in the White House. A "gimel".* I'm crazy, Moses thought. But he had already decided to fly to Washington. What else could he do?

The next morning Jim and Moses stood by the dining-lodge window, sipping coffee, as they watched Barney pose for picture after picture with his catch.

"He belongs to some kind of sportsman's club back in Chapel Hill," Jim said, "they meet once a month, and when he gets back he shows them his slides. This time he's going to boast about how he came out here, fishing salmon for the first time, and came out top rod. The least you could do is cancel your cheque."

Moses left Vince's Gulch after breakfast, stopping at the post office in Campbellton to mail a small box to Chapel Hill.

"You'll have to fill out a customs declaration," the clerk said, taking the box. "Hey, this is awful heavy."

"It should weigh exactly five pounds."

"What's in it?"

"Pebbles."

"Pebbles?"

"Pebbles."

FOUR

◆

Harvey, an insomniac, could sleep comfortably these days, knowing it was not a total waste of time. Even while he drifted off, ostensibly an idling engine, his stocks were working in overdrive for him. His burgeoning shares in Acorn and Jewel. His fattening private portfolio.

Harvey's day started out like a bell-ringer. Becky didn't make one rude remark to him at breakfast. Picking up the front section of the *Gazette* at the table, he saw that it was Watergate, Watergate, Watergate everywhere. Harvey, as usual, waited until he got to the office to read the sports section. Bad omen. Turning to the box scores, he was brought up short by an item on the opposite page:

I WAS JAILED
BY MISTAKE
MAN SAYS

A Montreal West man who was thrown into jail when he went to bail out his brother-in-law has filed a $200,000 lawsuit against three Montreal Urban Community police, a provincial policeman, the MUC and Quebec's solicitor general.

Hector Lamoureux is claiming for moral damages, humiliation, loss of freedom, anxiety and anguish after his illegal arrest and more than 48 hours behind bars. His problem began —

Miss Ingersoll buzzed to say Lionel Gursky was on the line from New York.

"My father's only been in his grave for a week," Lionel said, "and it's started again."

"Not necessarily."

"I'm talking millions of dollars in shares, all of which were acquired in Montreal this time, through Clarkson, Frost & McKay. Isn't Tom Clarkson a neighbour of yours?"

"Yes."

"Then you'd just better find out who his client is and what he's after and call me back."

Harvey had now been rooted in his house high in Westmount long enough for him to have grown familiar with his street. Its rhythms, its moods. Eight o'clock every morning, rain or snow, as his chauffeur backed his Mercedes out of his garage, the Jamaican Clean-Up Brigade, eyes swollen with sleep, began to lumber resentfully up the hill. One sullen, parcel-laden cleaning lady following another. And if Harvey was early starting out for the office he was bound to run into the Italian gardeners, a ferocious swarm, blasting compulsively on the horns of their pickup trucks as they swooped from house to house, ploughing the driveways clear of snow in winter and laying in beds of impatiens and petunias in summer, bellowing each to each, no matter what the hour, over the roar of their power mowers or snowblowers.

Further down the street was that most esteemed of Belvedere residents, Tom Clarkson, with his second wife, his surprising bride of a month, a girl called Beatrice. Tom was tall and thin, almost delicate, with sandy hair and piercing blue eyes. He had about him the manner of a man who would have been disappointed rather than angry with a *maître d'* who didn't show him to the best table. He served on symphony and museum boards because it was clearly his duty. He was also a collector: jade, nineteenth-century porcelain.

Tonight Tom Clarkson had a problem. Over the past three days Tom hadn't returned four phone calls from Lionel Gursky's office and now Harvey, the family's pet cobra, was coming to the house, having been impulsively invited to the party by Beatrice. Mind you, she hadn't had much choice in the matter. On Monday she ran into him at Dionne's, Harvey introducing himself, explaining they were neighbours now. "I'll bet you're an Expo fan. Any time you want to use my box, just let me know."

Tuesday she met Honor Parkman for drinks at the Ritz and when she called for the bill she found that it had already been paid, which baffled her until Harvey leaped up from another table and waved frantically.

Out to walk the corgi on Wednesday, Beatrice found Harvey lying in wait. "You're going to have to cope with a lot of cars on Friday night. I know. We entertain a lot too. In fact, as soon as you're settled in you and Tom simply must come to dinner."

"Thank you."

"Anyway I just wanted you to know you can direct as many cars as you like into our driveway. We won't be going out Friday night, so it doesn't matter if they block the garage entry."

Beatrice, of whom Tom's old friends knew distressingly little, was considerably younger than he was. One night when the Clarksons' Volvo had broken down on Champlain Bridge, she astonished everybody by leaping out in spite of Tom's protests, diving under the hood, calling for a rag and a wrench and setting things right. Laura Whitson had once seen her striding down Sherbrooke Street biting into an apple. Betty Kerr, though she couldn't quite put her finger on it, felt that she was somehow too *experienced* for her age. There was something about her, a suggestion that she hadn't been bred but had scratched to reach her present position, that made the other wives uneasy if not yet censorious. It didn't help that they were unable to place her, not having been to school with her. Or that their husbands, once having been introduced, gratuitously protested that they found her a tich vulgar, but couldn't they have her to dinner next week, if only for good old Tom's sake.

Her freshly styled bouffant hairdo towering over her like a lacquered black helmet, her fingers swollen with rings heavy as knuckle-dusters, Becky wiggled into a shimmering silvery sheath especially acquired for the party.

The Clarkson living room was filled with chattering strangers, the sort on whom it only rained capital gains. The men, flat of stomach, exuding confidence, their wives languorous, fetching, understated in clothes and manner, easy with each other, but quick to sniff out an intruding outsider. Tom greeted Harvey with a forced smile. "I think it's awfully good of both of you to come on such short notice."

"We'll talk later," Harvey said, moving on.

Tom turned to Beatrice. "I thought he was bringing his wife, not a hostess from Ruby Foo's."

"Now now now. That's a Saint Laurent she's wearing."

Trailing a morose photographer, the ubiquitous Lucinda, of the *Star*'s Lifestyle section, thrust past Harvey, obviously seeking better bets. Pert, bright-eyed, she flitted from group to group, notebook poised. Finally she settled on Nathan Gursky, who immediately froze, like a squirrel caught by headlights as it attempted to cross the highway. "I'm turning tomorrow's column into the most delicious game, Mr. Gursky."

"Oh."

"If Hollywood were to film your life story, who would you want to play Nathan Gursky?"

"Er."

Nathan confronted Harvey with his problem.

"Tell her George Segal," Harvey said.

"What about, um, Dustin Hoffman?"

"I'm picking him."

Tom Clarkson had only tolerated Nathan Gursky and the *Star*'s Lucinda in his home because the party, being held just before a federal election, was actually a fund-raiser for Westmount's cabinet minister. A most discreet fund-raiser, nobody mentioning the size of the cheque they had brought and the cabinet minister never acknowledging an envelope. He was a lean hound of a man. His wife was a MacGregor. Tom's Uncle Jack owned a property next to his in Bermuda. Leaning against the mantelpiece, the cabinet minister neatly parried questions about the desirability of a price and wages freeze. Then Becky thrust herself forward, leading with the elbows, as if she were seventeen again and jumping a queue for a table at Miss Montreal. "My name's Rebecca Schwartz. I'm a published writer. My husband is making a personal donation of ten thousand dollars to your campaign tonight. Now can you tell me if the government favours further wheat deals with Russia while so many Jews, falsely accused, languish in prison there?"

Holy shit. Before the cabinet minister could answer, Harvey retreated into another room, grabbing Moffat and telling him what he needed to know.

"Damn it, Harvey, he's the soul of discretion. How in the hell am I supposed to find that out?"

Then Harvey, recognizing Jim Benson (CEO, Manucorp), broke into his circle. Since he had last seen him, Benson must have lost thirty pounds. Rubbing his own modest paunch, Harvey winked and said, "Boy, could I ever use a copy of your diet. How did you manage it, Jimmy?"

An appalled silence settled on the circle as it broke up, leaving Harvey stranded. And all at once Becky was there. "McClure is here," she said. "He said I looked very *soignée.*" Becky beamed, pancake cracking. "Oh, something else I picked up. Jim Benson's on chemotherapy now. They say he's got six months. Maybe."

McClure smiled at Beatrice over the rim of his bifocals. "I must say Tom has done splendidly for himself, but I do hope the children won't become a problem, devoted as they are to poor Charlotte. Charlotte's a Selby. Her great-uncle Herbert was my godfather. Her father and I served in the Black Watch together. Are you a Montrealer yourself?"

"No."

"I thought not. Would you be from Toronto then?"

"Wrong again."

"But even a creature as enchanting as you must be from somewhere, my dear."

"Yellowknife. I was brought up a Raven kid."

"I don't understand."

"In those days, in Old Town, you belonged to one mine or

another. Raven or Giant. That's how the kids were known in Yellowknife."

"And is that where you met Moses Berger?"

"Oh my, you are inquisitive, aren't you?"

"I only ask because my wife left him a letter and a cherry wood table in her will. I suppose you would no longer know where Mr. Berger can be reached?"

"Try The Caboose."

"What's that?"

"His club," she said, sliding away from him.

Portly Neil Moffat finally caught Betty Kerr alone. "What about Wednesday?" he asked.

"I told you not to talk to me here."

"It would look a lot more suspicious if I didn't."

Becky was here, there, and everywhere. Busily picking up table lamps to peer at the imprimatur on the underside. Flicking her nails at china pieces. Running the palm of her hand over side-table surfaces. Easing the corners of paintings free from the walls, making a note of the dealer's name.

Joan St. Clair kissed Beatrice on both cheeks. "I haven't seen Tom look so young and fit in years. You're the best thing that ever happened to him. I understand you're an Ottawa girl?"

"No."

"But you met there?"

"Yes."

"How nice for you."

"Don't you mean for both of us?"

Becky sailed into a group that included the *Star*'s Lucinda. "Hello. I'm Becky Schwartz and, talking one writer to another, I think your stuff is wonderfully wicked. If Hollywood were to make my life story, I'd want to be played by Candice Bergen."

Quack quack quack. Harvey, who had been stalking Tom Clarkson all evening, finally saw him alone and closed in quickly.

"Oh," Tom said, "excuse me, there's Beatrice."

Approaching her from behind, Tom slid his arms around Beatrice's waist. He kissed her neck. "You're not being very nice to my friends."

"If you mean McClure, he's insufferable."

"He's so lonely now, darling. His wife was a Morgan. My Aunt Hattie's cousin."

Harvey found the toilet door unlocked, but Moffat was on the seat, his head held back, a bloody handkerchief clamped to his nose. Betty Kerr stood over him. "Get out, you little snoop," she hissed at Harvey.

Joan St. Clair retreated to a corner of the hall with Laura Whitson. "She may be God's gift between the sheets, but the child can only talk in monosyllables and there's no family there."

And Harvey finally cornered Tom in the kitchen. "Your firm put in a huge order for McTavish shares on Monday."

"I don't get to see all the slips."

"I'm talking millions and millions of dollars. I want to know who you're acting for."

"That would be privileged information, Harvey."

It was three A.M. before a portly Neil Moffat, the sole surviving guest at the Clarkson party turned it into a dirge, lamenting the future of the city, their patrimony.

"The party's over, Thomas m'boy. Montreal Piss Quick is not where it happens any more. It's all Toronto now, perfectly awful Turrono. Outright separatism doesn't matter. What we're going to get is *de facto* separatism. We're going to be Boston in the new order of things. Or maybe even Milwaukee."

Then, overwhelmed by nostalgia, Moffat recalled the good old days, the days when the civil service was still theirs. Not mismanaged by French-Canadians washed and hung out to dry by L.S.E. or the Harvard Business School. Or pushy jewboys out of Winnipeg's North End. Look at McGill now. Old McGill. Or the Mount Royal Club. In my father's day they turned down the importuning Mr. Bernard three times. Now Nathan, the old bootlegger's simpering son, is actually a member. Last Christmas that timorous little twit sent the doorman a case of Crofter's Best. Compliments of the season. Nobody knew what to say. Where to look.

Moffat began to tick off possible departures from Montreal on plump pink fingers. All the head offices with contingency

plans, prepared to sneak out of town tippytoe if the Parti
Québecois ever rides into office. "The Gurskys, I hear, are
already abandoning the sinking ship, shifting key personnel
into Hogtown. And they know those boys, those clever Semitic
mice, they can feel balance sheets in the seat of their pants. It
agitates the Jew's sphincter. Like sex for us, eh, Thomas?"

Tom yawned. Beatrice began to empty ashtrays.

"Mind you," Moffat said, "now that the old bastard's dead,
McTavish is vulnerable. I wouldn't be surprised if there's a
takeover bid."

Tom glanced pointedly at his wristwatch.

"Even before the old man died," Moffat said, "once it was
clear he had begun to slip, maybe six seven years ago, our
office had a huge buying order."

"Oh, that's interesting. Do you remember who from?"

"A Brit. A Sir Hyman Kaplansky. Is that your client?"

"Mine's one of those off-shore funds based in Geneva.
Corvus Investment Trust."

"Preparing to mount a raid, no doubt."

"Don't be ridiculous, Neil. It would take billions to dislodge
the family."

"Providing they hang together."

Moffat, his nose throbbing, his bladder fit to burst, finally
consented to being led to the door, showering benedictions on
Tom and his ravishing bride. "You old tomcat, you."

Tom found Beatrice in the solarium. Self-absorbed,
bending to water the plants, her breasts full. He hurried away
to get his camera and began to snap pictures of her, just as he
had taken pictures of her reading, combing her hair,
descending the stairs in an evening gown.

"I wish you wouldn't do that," she said.

He salvaged a chilled bottle of Montrachet, floating in ice
and corks and cigarette butts, and brought her a glass. "I'm
told Moses Berger can now usually be found in a bar called
The Caboose."

"We're going to be fine, Tom. Honestly we are. I have no
interest in seeing Moses again."

When Harvey got home, he was told that Mr. Gursky had
phoned twice in his absence. Glaring at him, Becky peeled
off a glittering silver slipper and threw it against the wall

"*Shmuck*. Why didn't you tell me they'd all be so underdressed?"

Then the phone rang again.

"That must be the massuh," she said. "Take it, Rastus."

But it was Moffat.

"That doesn't tell me anything," Harvey said. "You've got to find out more."

Harvey retreated to his study, sat down at his desk, and fished a file out of a bottom drawer. There was a killer shark out there somewhere who went into a feeding frenzy, say once every six seven years and then, unaccountably, swam away. A predator of infinite guile and patience who was bound to make a lethal move, sooner or later sinking his teeth into Lionel's jugular. Well, Harvey reflected, considering his own stake in McTavish, possibly he could be a big gainer in the heat of any takeover bid.

Harvey waited until ten o'clock in the morning before he phoned Lionel. "There's nothing to worry about," he said.

Then Harvey phoned his banker in Geneva. "I want to know who's behind something called Corvus Investment Trust."

"You aren't the only one," the banker said.

FIVE

———◆———

"Here, if you are interested," he had said, "is a list of the complete contents of the safe, properly notarized."

"And were you there when the safe was opened, Mr. Schwartz?"

"There was no envelope addressed to you."

So Kathleen O'Brien, who had been in charge of transcribing the tapes Mr. Bernard had made with Harvey, slipped the lot into her tote bag when she left the Bernard Gursky Tower on Dorchester Boulevard for the last time.

Tim Callaghan took her to the Café Martin for lunch and listened to her story with interest.

"But what was supposed to be in the envelope?" he asked.

"A certified cheque. Shares. I don't know how many. All those years of my life. God in heaven." She lit one cigarette off another. "You don't understand, Tim. It isn't the money."

"I never thought that."

"I adored the old bastard. Go ahead. Laugh."

"You've hardly eaten a thing and you're drinking far too much."

"We held hands in the movies. Once every summer we

sneaked off to Belmont Park together. The Hall of Mirrors. Dodge 'em cars. The House of Horrors . . ."

Her voice broke. Callaghan waited.

"There was a side of him the rest of you didn't know."

"Only you."

"Yes. Only me. Christ."

"Easy now."

"He wouldn't lie to me. Somebody stole the envelope. The little runt, probably. He didn't like you."

"Schwartz, for God's sake."

"Mr. B. Because you were Solomon's man, he said. His brother's death haunted him."

"I wonder why."

"I want to know what Moses Berger is up to out there in the woods."

"Wrestling with his Gursky demons. Hoping to justify man's ways to God."

"He's been here, there, and everywhere, digging up dirt on the family."

"He'd like to talk to you."

"No way."

Kathleen phoned Mr. Morrie. He invited her over to his house and sat with her in the garden, where he knew that Libby could see him from her bedroom window.

"I want to know if you were there when the safe was opened, Mr. Morrie."

"It pains me right here to tell you this," Mr. Morrie said, hand on his heart, "but there was no envelope."

"Couldn't Harvey have pinched it earlier?"

"He didn't have the combination to the safe."

"Maybe Mr. B. just never got the time to put the envelope in the safe and it's still among his papers in the house."

"Didn't I look?"

"Libby could have it."

"Kathleen," Mr. Morrie said, tears welling in his eyes, "forgive me, but I can't stand to see you suffering like this. I have to tell you something hurtful. He also promised an envelope to a young lady in the New York office."

"The hell he did."

"I'm sorry."

"Christ."

"I'm so ashamed."

"Who?"

"I can't say. I gave my word."

She began to sob. Mr. Morrie took her in his arms. "Bernie, may he rest in peace, was a complicated man."

"Was it Nora Weaver?"

"Why torture yourself?"

"Shit."

"You know what? I'm going to go through his papers in the house again tomorrow. From top to bottom. And I bet you I find the envelope, just like he promised."

"Did Lionel have the combination to the safe?"

"I'm such a fool. Why didn't I think of that? I'll phone him."

"Forget it."

"Let me give it a try."

"There never was an envelope, and even if there was, I don't want it any more."

"I appreciate your feelings in this matter," Mr. Morrie said, freshening her drink.

"I'm fifty-three years old now."

"You don't look a day over forty."

Kathleen burst out laughing. She blew her nose and wiped her eyes. "And what will you do now that Lionel has cut you out?"

"Say, why don't we open a bar together downtown? Right on Crescent Street. Kate's and Morrie's."

"Seriously."

"Can I let you in on a secret?"

"Please."

"After all these years my Barney came to see me on his way to the Maritimes. He was going salmon fishing. A guest of the minister of trade. Isn't that something?"

"I hope he didn't come to borrow money."

"Barney is an outstanding person. Let me tell you that boy has more ideas . . ."

"So I've heard."

"He's in the furniture business in North Carolina. Very big. But, now that the ice has been broken, I'm hoping that he'll come in with me in oil and other investments I can't speak about yet. You come to work for us you name the salary."

"Thank you," Kathleen said, kissing him on the cheek, "but I think not."

"Hector will drive you back to your place. But you know what? This is your second home. You're feeling blue you hop into a taxi and come to dinner."

Five minutes later the phone rang in Mr. Morrie's study. "What did she want?" Libby demanded.

"I was hoping to get rid of her before you saw her here."

"Money?"

"A letter of reference."

"You give her a letter of reference it should be to the madam of a whorehouse."

"You think I don't appreciate your sentiments in this matter?"

"I don't want to see her on the property again."

"Whatever you say. Now would you like to come over tonight and watch 'Dragnet' with us?"

"It would hardly be the same," she said, hanging up.

Mr. Morrie unlocked the top desk drawer and took out his private address book. He reached Moses at The Caboose. "Poor Kathleen O'Brien is very depressed," he said. "I think it would be nice if you took her to lunch."

SIX

◆

Moses knew that he could stay with Sam and Molly Birenbaum in Georgetown, but he opted for privacy, checking into the Madison instead. An hour later he took a taxi to Georgetown.

Sam, his caramel eyes shiny, hugged Moses. He held him tight. "Moishe. Moishe Berger. Shall I offer you a drink?"

"I'm on Antabuse."

"Glad to hear it. Tea, then?"

"Please."

Looking to warm the coals, Sam reminisced about the table with the crocheted tablecloth in the cold-water flat on Jeanne Mance Street. Then he got into London, their halcyon days, starting into a story about Lucy Gursky. Remembering, he stopped short.

"Sam, relax. It's okay to talk about Lucy. Now tell me about Philip and the others too of course."

There were three children. Marty, Ruth and Philip. Ruth was putting in a year at the Sorbonne. Neither of the boys, knock wood, were in Vietnam. Marty was at MIT and Philip, having dropped out for a couple of years, working as a bartender in San Francisco, was at Harvard. "He's visiting us now."

"Terrific. Where is he?"

"Out."

"Oh."

"He's gay," Sam said, slapping down the gauntlet and waiting for Moses's reaction, pleading with his eyes.

"Well, he isn't the only one."

"I could be appropriately liberal about it if it were another man's son, but it's an abomination in one of my own."

"I understand."

"No, you don't understand. It's not that I'm prejudiced against faggots, it's just that I don't like them." Sam poured himself a Scotch. A large one. "He wouldn't come home for the weekend unless he could bring his Adams House sweetie-poo with him. What could I say? We hadn't seen him in months. I was determined to behave myself. I wasn't going to make a crack about his boyfriend's earring or his black silk shirt open to his *pupik* at breakfast. We had words this morning. I don't think it necessary for them to skinnydip in the pool. Molly looks out of the window it breaks her heart."

"There's a pool?"

"Hold tight. There's a pool and the black maid you've already seen and a cook and stock options and a condo in Vail and a tax-shelter scam I don't understand, but I'm sure will land me in the slammer one day. That's the way it is, Moishe."

Suddenly Molly was there. "Moses, it's unfair how you never answer a letter but drop in and out of our lives once in five years."

They ate at Sans Souci, senators and congressmen and others in search of prime-time exposure on the network stopping at their table to pay obeisance, whispering in Sam's ear, delivering the latest Watergate scuttlebutt. *He's going to be impeached. No, he's resigning. He's no longer playing with all the dots on his dice. Henry told me. Len says. Kay assured me.* Sam, Molly sensed, was not so much pleased as apprehensive at such a tangible display of his importance. He was waiting for Moses to pronounce. The less he said the more Sam drank. Liquor, as had always been the case, rendered him foolish. Three publishers, Sam let out, were pursuing him to do a Watergate book. Moses nodded. "So," Sam said, deflated, "I didn't become the Tolstoy of my generation. . . ."

"Did you, Moses?"

Moses shook his head, no.

"Do you still write short stories?" she asked.

"Canada has no need of another second-rate artist."

"Gerald Murphy," Molly said, pouncing.

"Clever Molly."

"Hey, we've been through the fire together," Sam pleaded. "We're all friends here. What brings you to Washington? You still haven't told us."

Moses explained that he wanted to see raw tapes, everything available at the network, shot at the Watergate hearings or during Nixon's press conferences. He wasn't interested in the footage that had actually been shown, but the out-takes, especially panning shots of onlookers. "I'm looking for somebody who might have been there."

"Who?"

"You wouldn't know even if I told you."

Sam asked Moses to return to the house with him as they had hardly begun to talk. He would play his Yiddish music hall records for him: Molly Picon, Aaron Lebedeff, Menasha Skulnik, Mickey Katz. But Moses, complaining of fatigue, asked to be dropped off at his hotel.

Once back at his place, Sam poured himself a Remy Martin.

"God knows you're not a braggart," Molly said, "but there was no stopping you tonight. Why do you feel you have to justify yourself to him?"

"You know when Moses was only twenty-one, he found an error in the OED. A first usage. We wrote them and they sent back a letter thanking him and promising to correct it in the next edition."

"You still haven't answered my question."

"I have, only you don't know it. Okay, okay. The *emes*. I envy him."

"*You* envy *him*? He's an alcoholic, poor man, and who knows how many tranquilizers he takes he slurs his words now. Let's face it, Sam, he didn't amount to much."

"And me? Hoo haw. Sam Burns né Birenbaum can call Cosell Howard to his face. Mike Wallace sees me he waves."

"The truth is he's a failure."

"Oh, yeah, a failure absolutely. But he's an enormous failure, a tragic waste, and I'm a little trendy horseshit TV mavin, the trustworthy face that comes between the Preparation-H and Light Days commercials."

Sam wandered into the bathroom, knocking into things, opening the medicine cabinet, pulling out her jar of Vaseline and holding it up to the light, squinting.

"What are you doing?"

"I marked the level it was at with a pencil before we went to dinner."

"Sam, you're disgusting."

"I'm disgusting? When they leave burn the sheets." He shook his fist at the ceiling. "It's an *averah* what they're doing up there. *Makkes* they should have! A *choleria* on them! *Faygelehs! Mamzarim!*"

"Please Sam. Philip is not responsible for tonight. Lower your voice."

"He plucks his eyebrows. I caught him at it. Maybe you should never have taken baths with him."

"He was three years old at the time."

"Okay, okay."

"What did you and Moses talk about when I went to the ladies'?"

"This and that."

"He's your oldest friend. You've known each other since you were nine years old. What in the hell did you talk about?"

"The Mets. Moses thinks they can take Cincinnati in the playoffs. Pete Rose. Johnny Bench. Tony Perez. He doesn't know what he's talking about."

"Raw tapes. What's he after?"

"All I know is that he has that crazy look and I've seen it before." And then Sam, breaking an old vow, told her the story, making her swear never to say anything to Moses. "In the spring of '62 I think it was, I was drinking in the Algonquin with Mike, shortly after he started with *The New Yorker*, and we were soon joined by a couple of other editors.

They were sharing a private joke about something they called the Berger Syndrome. What's that, I asked? Well, it seems that in the early fifties some kid called Berger, a Canadian, sent them a short story that everybody liked and wanted to publish. They wrote him, asking for a few minor revisions, and he wrote back a nutty letter saying *The New Yorker* regularly prints crap, so long as it is written by their friends, they couldn't tell Pushkin from Ogden Nash, and he was withdrawing his story. When I met Moses the next afternoon for drinks at Costello's, I got up sufficient nerve to ask him about it and he said, no, it was certainly not him. But he was lying. I could tell just looking at him. I thought he was going to pass out on the spot."

"Why would Moses do such a thing?"

"Because he's crazy." Settling on the edge of the bed, depleted, Sam asked, "Was I really bragging tonight?"

"A little," she said, bending to help him out of his trousers.

The bodice of her dress came away from her. Sam peeked. It was still nice, very nice. "Was Moses ever your lover?" he demanded, jerking upright.

"Philip's his son. Now you know. The cat's out of the bag."

Sam forlorn, his eyes wet, said, "I want the truth."

"Remember when you were working for the *Gazette* and there wasn't enough money and I said I could give French lessons?"

"Yes."

"Some French lessons. Moses and I were making pornographic movies together. Now can we get some sleep?"

But he couldn't sleep. He was thirsty. He was dizzy. His heart was hammering. His stomach was rumbling. "They can take everything. The works. I would have settled for writing 'The Dead'. Never mind *War and Peace* or *Karamazov*. Am I greedy? Certainly not. Just 'The Dead' by Samuel Burns né Birenbaum."

" 'The best of a bad job is all any of us can make of it,' " she recited, hoping she had got the lines right. " 'Except of course, the saints . . .' "

"I wasn't kidding about the sheets, you know. I want them burnt. I want the room fumigated."

"Sam, he's our son. We've got to play with the cards that we were dealt."

"Molly, Molly," he asked, lying on her breasts, weeping, "where has all the fun gone?"

Uninvited, her manner truculent, Molly turned up early at the Madison. She steered Moses into the dining room, slamming her PBS tote bag on the table. "Ever since he got your call saying you were coming he's been on a high. Boy, were the two of you ever going to light up the town. He went through all of our books to make sure there were no compromising best-sellers on the shelves. The signed pictures of him with Kennedy were hidden in a drawer. His framed honorary degrees went into a cupboard. He must have made up and crossed out eight dinner-party lists, saying no, Moses wouldn't approve of them. He laid in a case of Macallan. Our fridge is stocked with smoked salmon. Then you show up and stick him with the fact that he has a swimming pool. Count on Moses. You don't tell him once — it would really cost you — how damn good and honest he is on TV. Or that he should write that Watergate book, he's dying to, but it scares the bejesus out of him. Philip with that boy in his room is breaking his heart. I find him sobbing in the toilet, but you have nothing reassuring to say to him. I could wring your miserable bloody neck, you self-centred son of a bitch. Then last night he gets drunk, also to please Moses, and he actually asks me if we ever had an affair. He's so pure of heart he doesn't even know that he's a much better man than you are. What are those cuts in the palms of your hands?"

"Some people grind their teeth in their sleep. I clench my fists. It's a bad habit."

"Read your paper and don't look at me. I'll be all right in a minute."

Moses ordered more coffee for both of them, stirring five spoonfuls of sugar into his own cup.

"What are you doing to yourself?"

"I crave sweets now. I can never get enough. Please don't start crying."

"I won't. I won't."

"The last time I was in the clinic there was a beautiful girl there I still can't get out of my mind. I mean genuinely beautiful. A fawn. Maybe only nineteen years old. She would drift into my room, shrug out of that awful starchy gown, and do an arabesque, a pirouette, a *tour en l'air*. She never leaped, she soared. Then she would smile like a naughty girl, squat, and shit on my floor. It's all right, I'd say. I don't mind. She danced and shat on my floor every day for a week and then she was gone. We weren't allowed cutlery, but somehow or other she got her hands on a fork and it was enough to do the job. I don't know why I'm telling you this. If I had a reason I forgot."

"Have you tried A.A.?"

"Yes."

"Antabuse won't do it. Can't you cut it out whenever you feel like it?"

"Clever Molly."

"When Marty's in town he brings his friends around, really bright kids, and Sam adores drinking beer and horsing around with them. But they don't know who Henry Wallace was or Jack Benny or Hank Greenberg. Sam's Yiddish music hall records don't do a thing for them. It drives him crazy. He's going to be fifty soon. He's jowly. He overeats. It's the tension, you know, all that travelling. His new producer, he's only thirty-two — he discos — he's on coke half the time — he wants Sam to get a facelift. He's done viewer surveys, demographic studies, may he rot in hell. Sam told him when I was with the *Times* I was nominated for a Pulitzer for my Korean stuff. Kiss my ass, sonny. But there are rumours that they are testing younger faces and I don't think they'll renew his contract."

"He ought to do the Watergate book."

"Sam still collects 78s. You wouldn't believe what he came home with the other night." She sang, " 'Chickery Chick cha-la-cha-la, Check-a-la romey in a bananika.' "

"Molly, he's a lucky man. You're a good woman."

"Good bad. I love him."

"So do I."

"Hey," she said, brightening, her old jauntiness and loopy logic shining through, "in that case maybe we should have an affair."

"Let's save it for our dotage."

"Come to dinner," she said, fleeing, because she knew that she was going to cry again.

Sam, hurrying home early from the office, changed quickly and made a dash for the pool. He found Philip and his boyfriend sunbathing on the back-yard terrace, sipping champagne. His champagne. "Celebrating something, boys?"

"You really are *quelque chose*, Dad," Philip said, producing a glass for him.

Immediately regretting it, but unable to help himself, Sam said, "Gay was a perfectly good word until it was appropriated by your kind. Our hearts were young and gay. The gay hussar. Et cetera. Gay means cheerful, merry, sparkling. According to my thesaurus its opposite is joyless, glum, dreary. Whoever gave you the right to pass such a judgement on heterosexual love? Real *chutzpah*, that's what I call it."

"Oh, Dad, about those hussars. When the Austro-Hungarian empire was still intact no officer below the rank of colonel was legally allowed to wear makeup."

"How does your family handle it, Steve?"

"They don't."

For the next four days Moses sat in a small stuffy screening room looking at footage of the Watergate hearings, circling sections on certain frames and having the lab blow them up, unavailingly. Then on Moses's fifth day in the screening room there he was, seated immediately behind Maureen Dean, smiling that smile of his, a gold-tipped malacca cane clasped between his knees. Moses fled to the washroom and splashed cold water on his face. He went for a walk. He stopped for a hamburger somewhere. Then he returned to the screening room and sat staring at the frame, sliding in sweat, for the better part of an hour.

Back in his hotel room, Moses pulled the blinds and collapsed on his bed, chain-smoking through the rest of the afternoon. *Once by air*, he recalled, *and once by water*. He washed the blood off the palms of his hands and had already begun to pack when the phone rang. It was the front desk.

"Will you be checking out today, Mr. Berger?"

"Yes."

The assistant manager had a letter for him.

"It was left here by a most distinguished-looking gentleman who said you would be turning up eventually."

"Why didn't you give this to me before?"

"His instructions were most explicit. We were not to let you have it until you were checking out."

Moses opened the letter in the bar.

If the Catholic Church could outlast Pope Innocent IV, Auto-da-fé, and Savonarola, why can't Marxism survive the Georgian seminary student and his acolytes. For the record, I didn't erase the tape.

When the waiter approached his table, Moses ordered a Macallan. A double. Neat.

SEVEN

◆

The next morning Sam sought out the editor who had worked with Moses. "I understand that you were a great help to my friend. Now show me what he wanted."

So Barry screened the pertinent out-take for him, a panning shot of observers at the Watergate hearings, including many familiar faces, among them Maureen Dean and, immediately behind her, an old man with a gold-tipped malacca cane clasped between his knees. "It was either Mo Dean or the old guy seated right behind her who turned him on," Barry said. "He shot right out of his seat to have a closer look, and then he lit out of here like he had been badly burnt."

"Blow up the old guy for me. Big and bigger."

Sam ate lunch at his desk, pondering the photographs Barry had brought him. I know that face, he thought. But where and how eluded him.

Later Sam took the photographs home with him and retreated to the library, but once more how and where he knew that face remained tantalizingly out of reach. So he began to pull down scrapbooks that Molly had put together in spite of his objections, poring over old newspaper stories that he had churned out on four continents, hoping something would evoke that face for him. It didn't work. In fact all his efforts only muddled him, rendering the face even more elusive, and he went to bed wondering if he was mistaken after all.

Unable to sleep, he tried to play a game that had worked for him before. Think of something else, anything else, and the right brain circuits would connect without effort, putting a name to the face. He replayed Ralph Branca's home-run pitch to Bobby Thomson, striking him out in his mind's eye. Once again he savoured Ron Swoboda's ninth-inning catch in the fourth game of the '69 Series. Then, sinking into sleep, other images drifted into his mind. Moses saying, "Oh come on. Let's take a peek."

"I don't think we ought to."

"It's probably the new Bonnard he bought."

Lifting a cloth revealing what, at first glance, appears to be the most conventional of portraits, the sort that would be welcomed by the Royal Academy. A lovely young bourgeois lady seated in a wicker chair. Long blonde tresses, flushed cheeks. She wears a broadbrimmed straw hat with a pink bow, a multi-layered chiffon dress, also with a pink bow, and holds a bouquet of sweet williams in her hands. But there is something quirky about the portrait. The young lady's eyes are of a different colour. One eye brown, one eye blue.

EIGHT

North, Moses knew, is where he would find him.

"Where north?"

Far.

On his return from Washington, Moses picked up his Toyota at Dorval, and set out for his cabin in the Townships to pack his northern gear. Then he collected his mail at The Caboose, drank for a couple of hours with Strawberry, and drove back to Montreal, where he had recently rented a *pied-à-terre* on Jeanne Mance Street. Every bottle in his flat was empty. So Moses took a taxi to Winnie's, and carried on from there to Big Syl's and when all the bars shut down for the night, he moved on to the Montreal Press Club, floating between tables to a dim corner and falling asleep almost immediately.

"Moses?"

Drifting awake, he was claimed by a fuzzy raven-haired figure, sweetly perfumed, throbbing in and out of focus. Her smile, tainted with benevolence, irritated him.

"Beatrice?"

"Yes. Are you pleased?"

The raven-haired figure, possibly Beatrice, subsided softly into a chair, silk rustling.

"Don't let me fall asleep again."

"I won't."

"Say your name."

"Beatrice."

"Imagine. Beatrice."

He squinted, concentrating, grudgingly reducing the multiple breasts, each one exquisite, to two; the comically trebled mouth to a more satisfying sensual one.

Unable to cope with his idiotic gaze, she asked, "How do I look?"

"Harder."

"Count on Moses."

"You asked."

"Yes."

"I don't think I can make it back to the bar again," he said, pointing at his empty glass with a certain cunning. "You go, please."

Enabling him to watch Beatrice, his heart's desire, stride to the bar, obviously nourished by the stir her presence was creating among the men in shiny suits gathered there. She took too long. Head slumping, he drifted off to sleep again.

"Moses."

"Go away." Then he recognized Beatrice, the proffered drink, and he smiled again. "I want to ask you a question of the most intimate nature."

"Please don't start on me, Moses."

"Do you wear pantyhose now?"

She shook her head, no, flushed but amused.

"Garters still. I knew it. Ah, Beatrice." Satiated, he slid into sleep again, his smile serene.

"Moses?"

"What?"

"You said you didn't want to snooze."

Slowly, deliberately, he relit his dead cigar, enormously pleased with his accomplishment.

"Strawberry says you're heading North of Sixty."

"Tomorrow afternoon. Could I see a garter?"

"Oh, Moses, please."

"Just one little peekee."

"Where are you staying in town?"

"Why, Mrs. Clarkson, whatever are you thinking?"

"Stop playing the fool."

"I rent an apartment here now."

"I'll drive you there and we can talk. It's too depressing here."

"It's my club."

"You belonged to better clubs once."

"And a better woman."

"Let's go."

"Only if I can have a peekee first."

"Not here. There. Let's go."

He gave her his address before staggering out with her, toppling into her Porsche, and falling asleep again. But they had only gone a few blocks when he started to tremble. "Stop the car!"

Alarmed, she braked. Moses, fumbling with the door handle, tumbled out, lurching blindly into the middle of Sherbrooke Street.

"Moses!"

Circling, he scrambled to the curb, sinking to his knees beside a fire hydrant, his stomach heaving. Beatrice pulled up alongside and waited in the car for him to finish. She was wearing a new dress. A Givenchy. "Do you feel better now?"

"Worser."

While Moses showered, she made coffee and then wandered restlessly about the apartment. Bay windows. Old-fashioned bulky radiators. The Persian carpet, worn threadbare in the middle, reminded her so vividly of home that she found herself searching for the walnut RCA radio cabinet and the sticky Peer's Cream Soda bottle supporting the window with the broken sash. Then, clearing the dining-room table of old newspapers, she caught her first glimpse of the crocheted tablecloth. She slipped on her hornrimmed glasses to have a better look just as Moses emerged from the bathroom in a towel dressing gown.

"Where did you get this?" she asked, stroking the tablecloth.

"My mother made it years ago."

"How come you never brought it out when we were together?"

"I was saving it for your vintage years," he said, accepting a black coffee and adding a couple of fingers of cognac to it. Then he bit off the tip of a Monte Cristo and lit it. "To think that I had once been so foolish to believe that you would be the one, as the old human question mark put it, who could 'help me through this long disease, my life.'"

It was, she knew, his way of putting her down. She was supposed to recognize the quote. "You think I'm stupid," she said.

"Of course you're stupid, but it hardly matters in the circles you frequent now that you are so insufferably rich."

"I didn't marry him only for that."

"I want my peekee now."

"Go to hell."

"Just the quickest of peeks, a mere flash, what would it cost you?"

"Why are you determined to make me feel cheap?"

"Aren't you?"

"I loved you, Moses, but I couldn't stand it any more. You have no idea of how insufferable you are when you're drunk. I want my peekee. Just one little peekee. Fuck you."

"At least I haven't changed."

"I'll give you that much."

"Actually, I would have left me a lot earlier than you did. I *am* impossible."

"Are you going north to visit Henry?"

"I have a hunch the ravens are gathering. Damn it, Beatrice, why did you flush me out? What do you want with me now?"

"I needed somebody to talk to. Somebody I could trust."

"Well that somebody isn't me. Not any more."

"Tom goes both ways. He has a boy. I'm not supposed to know but they're in Antibes together now."

"Then you'll get an even richer divorce settlement than you were counting on when you decide it's time to trade up again."

"Take me north with you."

"Certainly not."

"Can I stay the night?"

"Yes. No. Let me think."

"Bastard."

"No."

"Why?"

"Because fool that I am," he said, sinking into an armchair, "I sometimes rush to the door of my cabin, thinking I've heard a car and that it will be you." He knocked over his coffee cup, half full of cognac. "Get out, Beatrice. Leave me alone," he pleaded, before his head slumped forward and he began to snore.

Beatrice went into the kitchen and washed the dishes and then it came to her. She dug a pen and paper out of her purse and wrote, "The human question mark was Alexander Pope. You are as smug and pompous and hateful as ever." She left the note on the dining-room table. Then she stood before him, hiked her dress, revealing her garters, and fled the apartment, weeping. Outside, she stopped, cursed, and retraced her steps, determined to retrieve the note. But his apartment door was locked.

NINE

◆

Isaac, who had once tagged everywhere after his father, clutching the hem of his parka, now avoided him. Shirking his Talmud studies, pleading a headache. Declining to join him in saying grace after meals. Giving up on his Hebrew lessons. "Who speaks it here? Only you."

Nialie anticipated that he could hurt Henry badly, but Henry claimed not to be distressed. "It's a stage they all go through," he said. "You are not to worry."

Only twelve years old, Isaac's face was already encrusted with angry red pimples. He bit his nails. His voice was cracking. Once inseparable from his schoolmates, always up to mischief, he now eschewed their company as well.

"What happened to all your friends?" Nialie asked him.

A shrug.

"I asked you a question."

"So?"

"Answer me."

"They're always asking me for money."

"Why?"

"That's what you've got, they say, isn't it?"

Cleaning his room, Nialie didn't quite know what to make of the changes. The pinups of hockey players pasted to the wall

(Guy Lafleur, Yvan Cournoyer, Ken Dryden) had been displaced by a row of McTavish labels peeled carefully off bottles that had been soaked in the sink, and a photograph of the McTavish building on Fifth Avenue, scissored out of the last quarterly report.

"What does an 'adjusted dividend' mean?" he asked at the sabbath table.

"Search me," Henry replied.

" 'Amortization of goodwill and other intangible assets'? "

"I'm afraid your father is a prize *klotz* in these matters."

" 'A covenant'? "

"Ah. Now we're talking turkey. We are *Am Berit*, 'The People of the Covenant.' A covenant is what *Riboyne Shel O'lem* made with us at Mount Sinai, choosing Jews over all the other peoples in the world, liberating us from slavery in Egypt. Now how would you say Egypt in Hebrew?"

"I don't remember."

"Come on."

"Eretz Mitzraim."

"Yes. Excellent. Now in every generation, each person should feel as though he himself had gone forth from *Eretz Mitzraim*, as it is written: 'And you shall explain to your child on that day, it is because of what the Lord did for me when I, *myself*, went forth from Egypt.' "

Hypocrite, Isaac thought, his only response a smirk. Hypocrite, hypocrite.

"Don't make such a face to your father."

"I can't help how I look."

"Leave the table."

Henry waited an hour, tugging absently at his sidecurls, before he went to Isaac's room. "Is there anything wrong, *yingele*?"

"No."

"If there's a problem, I'm here to help."

"There's nothing wrong, I said."

But when Henry leaned over to kiss him good-night, Isaac slid away from him.

"Do you think I should buy us a TV set?" Henry asked.

"Only if we can afford it."

Nialie found Henry in the living room. She brought him a cup of lemon tea. "Was he bad to you again?"

"No."

"You look terrible."

"I'm fine. H-h-h-honestly."

A few days later Nialie startled Isaac going through the papers on Henry's rolltop desk. "What are you looking for?" she demanded.

"A pencil," he replied, leaping back.

"There's plenty in your room."

"Do you know how much he gives to the *yeshivas* in Jerusalem, never mind the Rebbe?"

"It's his money."

"Millions and millions."

"Shame on you."

"Yeah, sure. Go to your room. Don't worry. I'm going."

Then, his ear to the door, Isaac heard her say, "You ought to lock your desk every night."

"What have I got to hide?" he asked.

Plenty, Isaac thought. If only she knew. But he wouldn't tell her. He didn't dare. Henry, whom everybody took for a holy man, a saint even, hid filthy photographs in his desk. Photographs more revealing than anything Isaac had ever seen in *Playboy*. They had come in a plain brown envelope from somebody in England and showed a naked woman, a really skinny one, doing amazing things with one man and sometimes two of them.

Nialie confronted Isaac at breakfast the next morning. "How can you be so rude to your father?" she asked.

Because he's a hypocrite, he thought. But he didn't say it. Instead he glared at her.

TEN

◆

Condemned to a night in Edmonton before he could catch his morning flight to Yellowknife, Moses checked into the Westin, and then settled into a stool at the bar. Sean Riley was on TV. He was in Vancouver, peddling *Bush Pilot*, the book about his thrilling adventures in the Land of the Midnight Sun. The pleasantries didn't last long and then the interviewer, a former Miss B.C. Lion, took a deep breath, swelling her bosom, and asked about Riley's celebrated crash in the winter of '64. His passenger, a mining engineer, had died on impact. A month later Riley, who had been given up for dead, limped out of the barrens right into the Mackenzie Lounge in Inuvik.

"As you know, it was rumoured in Yellowknife at the time that you survived your terrible ordeal by resorting to, um, cannibalism. If that's the case," the interviewer suggested, flushing, "and, darn it, who's to say any one of us would have done different — if that's the case — I'm looking at a guy who has had a *very* unusual experience, eh?" Then, glancing hastily at one of her index cards, she added. "Now what grabs me is how such an unusual experience has affected you personally and psychologically?"

"Say, I don't get to appear on TV that often. Do you mind if I say hello to Molly Squeeze Play in Yellowknife?"

"What?"

"Hiya there, Molly. See you in The Gold Range tomorrow. Meanwhile keep your legs crossed, ha ha ha."

"Does it haunt your dreams?" Shirley Anne asked.

"Molly?"

"Cannibalism."

"Well, I'll tell ya, it kind of puts you off your prime rib. Like, you know, it's so good and sweet. Hardly any gristle."

The bar was rocking with chattering men and women wearing name tags, educators gathered from all ends of the continent to ponder WHITHER THE GLOBAL VILLAGE? But, as Moses started into his fourth double Scotch, most of them had dispersed, only a handful of dedicated drinkers surviving. Then a lady came flying into the room, out of breath, obviously too late for the party. She snuggled into the stool immediately beside Moses and ordered a vodka on the rocks. "Prosit," she said.

MY NAME IS CINDY DUTKOWSKI wore a snug woollen dress and carried an enormous shoulder bag. Fierce she was, black hair unruly, petite, forty maybe. She taught Communications 101 at Maryland U. "Say, do my eyes deceive me, or didn't I see you in Washington last week, rapping with Sam Burns at the Sans Souci?"

"You're mistaken."

"I'll bet you're also a media personality and I should know your name."

"Sorry about that."

"If you tell me your name, I won't bite."

"Moses Berger," he said, signing his bar bill and starting to slide off his stool. She shoved him back.

"Hey, you're really shy. It's a form of arrogance, you know. It also protects you against rejections in highly charged social encounters. I was a psych major." Hers, she said, was an open marriage, which allowed both partners a life-style enabling them to explore their full sexual potential.

"That must be awfully convenient for you."

"Oh come on. Do I have to spell it out? I'm interested if you are."

MY NAME IS CINDY DUTKOWSKI scooped up her enormous shoulder bag and they went up to his room, not hers, because she was sharing with a real square, she said, a lady from Montana who undressed in the bathroom. "I'm willing to act out your favourite fantasy, so long as it isn't too kinky."

"The usual," an intimidated Moses said, "will suit me fine."

In that case, she had a menu of her own. "I'm going to be your laid-back, but secretly horny high-school teacher and you are the nerdy little teenager. I've asked you to report to my office after classes, pretending that we have to go over your latest assignment, but actually because I caught you peeking up my skirt when I sat on your desk this morning and it really turned me on. Now you go wait out in the hall and don't knock on my office door until I call out 'ready'. You dig?"

"I'm not sure exactly how you want me to behave."

"Well, you know. You don't know from nothing. Like Canadian will do."

"Gotcha," he said, slipping out of the room, tiptoeing over to the elevator bank, and then grabbing a taxi at the front door of the hotel. "Take me to a bar where they don't play loud music."

Seated on yet another bar stool, Moses pondered Beatrice's baffling note again. It was three A.M. in Montreal now, but he phoned her all the same. "What did you mean," he asked, "that the human question mark was Alexander Pope?"

"Are you telling me," she replied, her voice hard, "that you don't remember?"

He began to sweat.

"You mean I've been sitting here, unable to sleep, crying because the note I left must have hurt you, *and you don't even remember last night?*"

Moses hung up, mortified, and when he got back to the hotel he was confronted by another problem. His open suitcase on the floor was half empty. As it turned out, however, she hadn't stolen anything. He found his shirts, socks, and underwear in the bathroom, floating in a tub full of water.

Once out at the Industrial Airport the next morning, Moses knew, without asking, which was the right gate for the PWA flight to Yellowknife. The familiar northern flotsam was already gathered there. A knot of chunky young Eskimos with their hair slicked back, wearing heavily studded black leather jackets, stovepipe jeans, and vinyl cowboy boots. Ladies in beehive hairdos and fat coats, lugging plastic bags filled with goods from Woodward's. There was also a group of northern workers obviously returning from leave, heading back to the oil rigs or DEW line stations, their stakes blown on whores, satisfied that women were shit, life was shit, everything was shit. Bruised and fleshy they were, one of them with his eye badly blackened.

On arrival in Yellowknife, Moses took a taxi directly to The Gold Range, where he knew he would find Sean Riley. Sean ordered two and a juice, but Moses settled for a black coffee.

"It's like that, is it?" Riley asked.

"Yes. How's your book doing?"

"When I was a kid, my old man caught me in a lie, it was a visit to the woodshed. Now I get paid for it."

Moses placed a photograph on the table. "I'd like to know if you saw this old man around here last week, possibly shopping around for a charter."

"The naturalist from California. Mr. Corbeau?"

"That's right."

"Cooney flew him out to King William Island last Wednesday, I think. He figured the old coot was crazy, wanting to camp out there, but there was something about him. Anyway, according to Cooney, he built himself a snow house in a jiffy. Had plenty of supplies."

"Could you fly me out there?"

"I could find him if I had to."

"Tomorrow morning?"

"I charge ten dollars a mile for the Otter, six for the Cessna, if you agree to help with the pedalling."

"We'll take the Otter and we'll put in overnight at Tulugaqtitut to look in on Henry."

Henry and Nialie, given only short notice that they would be blessed with guests at their Shabbat table, enabling them to celebrate the *mitzvah* of hospitality, *Hachnasat Orechim*, happily stayed up most of the night preparing delicacies. *Challah*. *Gefilte* fish. Roast chicken. *Tsimmes*. *Lokshen* pudding with raisins. Honey cake. The very best linen was set out on the table and and, as a concession to Moses, a prized bottle of fifty-year-old cognac on a side table. Isaac was ordered to bathe and put on a white shirt and tie and smartly pressed trousers before he went out with his father to meet the incoming Otter, Henry's sidecurls dancing in the breeze.

"*Sholem aleichem*," Henry sang out, embracing Moses.

"*Aleichem sholem.*"

Riley, not wishing to impose on two old friends who seldom got together any more, agreed to drinks at Henry's house, but would not stay to dinner. "Could be I'm running a fever," he said. "I think I'll look in on Agnes McPhee."

"*Abei gezunt*," Nialie said.

After she had blessed the candles, they sat down at the table and Henry pronounced the traditional blessing over his son. "*Yesimecha Elohim keEfrayim vechiMenasheh.*" May God inspire you to live in the tradition of Ephraim and Menasheh, who carried forward the life of our people.

Henry waited, expectant, but a sulking Isaac didn't respond until prodded by Nialie.

"*Harachaman hu yevarech et avi mori baal habayit hazeh veet imi morati baalat habayit hazeh.*" Merciful God, bless my beloved father and mother who guide our home and family.

Isaac, just short of hostile at the table to begin with, soon found himself giggling in response to Moses's teasing of Henry, amazed that anyone could get away with cracking irreverent jokes about the Rebbe, astonished to see his father drinking more than one cognac. To Henry's delight, he even joined in when the two men began to sing Shabbat songs, slapping the table with their hands to keep time.

"You know," Moses said, "the first time I met your father he was just about your age, and we sat on his bedroom floor and refought the Battle of Waterloo with toy soldiers."

Then, forgetting himself, Moses lit a Monte Cristo. Nialie was about to protest this desecration of the sabbath when Henry silenced her with a wave of his hand. It was, however, too much for Isaac. "How come," he demanded, "Uncle Moses is allowed to smoke on Shabbat here and I'm not allowed to play hockey with the guys or even watch TV without being scolded for being such a bad Jew."

"Moishe is not so much a bad Jew," Henry said, "as a delinquent one."

"I'll put it out," Moses said.

"No," Henry said, and turning back to Isaac, he added, "And, furthermore, he is not my son. Remember, it is a *mitzvah* to teach one's child Talmud Torah, as it is written: 'Set these words, which I command you this day, upon your heart. Teach them faithfully to your children; speak of them in your home and on your way . . .'"

"Everything is written," Isaac said, fighting tears, "even that I'm supposed to have a lousy time, because if it isn't Shabbes it's Tishah Be-Av or Shavuot or the Fast of Gedaliah or the Seventeenth of Tamuz or some other shit out of the stone ages. I know. Leave the table. I'm going. Good-night everybody."

"*Oy vey*," Henry said, dismissing Isaac's outburst with a nervous giggle. "What a difficult age for a boy. Forgive him, Moishe, he didn't mean to be rude. Excuse me for just a minute."

Nialie waited until Henry had gone to Isaac's bedroom, shutting the door behind him, before she spoke up. "He steals," she said.

"Does Henry know?"

"You mustn't say a word to him."

"Why not?"

"Don't."

And then Henry was back, laden with weather charts, other documents, and a recently published book, many passages underlined. "According to Dr. Morton Feinberg, a really outstanding climatologist, we are in for it. The new ice age, which is almost upon us, will bring an end to civilization in the northern hemisphere as we know it."

"Thank God for that," Moses said, reaching for the cognac bottle.

"Fifty years from now, maybe less, the equatorial countries will dominate the planet."

"Henry," Moses said, irritated, "as there was once a School of Hillel and a School of Shamai, so there are now other experts who believe we are in for a different kind of judgement day. They say all the evidence points to the earth's gradually warming because of the increased amount of carbon dioxide in the atmosphere, which tends to trap a good deal of the earth's heat. But the hell with all of them. Maybe you should worry less about the world coming to an end and more about Isaac."

"I want you to look at these ch-ch-charts," Henry said.

"There are better places to bring up a boy who will soon be an adolescent."

Henry waited until Nialie had retreated to the kitchen. "I hope that he will attend the *yeshiva* in Crown Heights."

"And what if he isn't cut out to be a *yeshiva bucher*?"

"Look at these charts, please," a tearful Henry pleaded, "and then tell me the earth is warming."

Before flying out with Riley in the morning, Moses took Isaac to the Sir Igloo Inn Café for breakfast.

"Can I have bacon with my eggs?" Isaac asked.

"Don't be a pain in the ass, please."

"You mean it's okay for you, but not for me."

And then Riley was there, his eyes bloodshot. "If we don't take off within ten minutes we could be weathered in here for days."

"Isaac, why don't we write to each other? Maybe you might even come to visit me during your summer holiday," Moses said, immediately regretting the invitation, and then, turning to Riley, he added, "I'm coming, but I've got to say goodbye to Henry and Nialie first."

Isaac went to join a group of boys at another table. They immediately closed ranks, making no room for him.

"See that old fart who just left here?" Isaac asked.

"So what?"

"He got my father pissed last night."

"Like shit he did."

The boys began to get up one by one.

"He used to fuck my aunt in London," Isaac said.

"Big deal."

Blocking their exit, Isaac flashed a hundred-dollar bill. "And he gave me this," he said.

"Bullshit. You swiped it."

"He gave it to me," Isaac said, flushing.

"Then we'll meet you here after school and everything's on you."

"I was just going to say that."

Finding Mr. Corbeau's camp on King William Island did not turn out to be difficult. A runway of sorts had been cleared at Victory Point, some sixty-five miles from where the *Erebus* had last been seen. As the Otter lowered into it, Moses made out a snow house hard by the shore. No sooner did Riley slide to a stop than Moses flung open the cabin door, jumped on to the ice, and ran to the snow house. Dropping to his knees to crawl through the entry tunnel he got one of his feet tangled in a trip wire, flipping on a cassette.

There came a clap of thunder. The sound of a crackling fire and another thunder clap. Then a baritone voice, oozing self-importance:

"Moses, Moses, draw not nigh hither: put off thy shoes from thy feet, for the place whereon thou standest is holy ground."

Bastard. Son of a bitch.

"But here I am not any more."

Moses, who had made out the tracks of four dogsleds leading away from the snow house, should have known as much. However, he couldn't have been that late. The snow house, heated by a Coleman camp stove, was still reasonably warm. A caribou skin was laid like a carpet on the floor and on it rested a bottle of Dom Perignon, a tin of beluga caviar, a loaf of black bread, two volumes of Solomon's journals, and a note: "If not me, who? If not now, when?"

FIVE

ONE

◆

Shortly after his arrival in London, Ephraim was accosted on Regent Street by a girl with sable skin. She was young and saucy, wearing a pork-pie hat with a jaunty red plume and a brown mantle and a heavily flounced crinoline skirt. On any other afternoon Ephraim would readily have accompanied the girl to her lodging house, risking the bully bound to be hidden there, but on his first day in London the ferment of the streets was sufficient for him. The din, the din. Rattling omnibuses, broughams and chaises, hackneys and saddle-horses. He saw ragged boys turn cartwheels, sweeping pedestrian crossings free of dung for elegant ladies, all rustling satins and silks. Grim men in bobbing black top hats seemed to be everywhere. As one of them emerged from a pub, his face flushed, he was confronted by an emaciated old beggar offering boxes of lucifer matches and small sticks of sealing wax in trembling hands.

Ephraim sought out a remote corner of Hyde Park, and satisfied that he was concealed by shrubbery, dug a deep hole with his trowel and buried the leather purse with his gold watch, his prayer shawl and phylacteries, and all of his money, save ten shillings. But he kept his candlesticks secure under his shirt, intending to dispose of them at a pawnbroker's in Whitechapel or Spitalfields.

Ephraim lost his way briefly in the maze that made up the
rookery behind the Strand, emerging hard by St. Paul's, an
unfamiliar stench leading him to the street-level maw of an
open underground abattoir, its thickly caked walls sweating
fat and blood. As he stopped to gaze, he was thrust aside by
workers who were hurling protesting sheep into the pit so that
they would break their legs before being set upon with knives
by the slaughterers below, already ankle deep in slippery
entrails and excrement. Close by other men, heedless of
buzzing flies and scuttling sewer rats, were busy boiling fat,
rendering glue and scraping tripe.

Mindful of dippers and *ganefs*, moving on smartly whenever he saw a peeler, Ephraim finally reached Whitechapel.
Two sodden sailors lay in a pool of their own piss outside a
gin mill. One of them had a purply eye swollen shut, the
other a broken bloodied nose. And suddenly there were
stalls, stalls everywhere.

The stalls of Petticoat Lane offered apples and oysters,
cheap jewellery, boots, toys, whelks, herring and cutlery and
firewood. Ephraim pressed on as far as the Earl of Effingham
Theatre, joining the rambunctious mob inside. Jenny
O'Hara, wrapped in gauze twinkly with sequins, her
enormous rouged bubbies all but plopping free of her corset,
settled on a swing and sang:

> Bet Mild she was a servant maid,
> And she a place had got,
> To wait upon two ladies fair
> These ladies' names was Scott.
> Now Bet a certain talent had,
> For she anything could handle,
> And for these ladies, every night,
> She used a large thick candle.

Hopping off her swing, approaching the front of the stage
with mincing little steps, Jenny continued:

> Now Betty had a sweetheart got,
> It was their footman Ned,
> Who slipped into their room one night,
> And crept beneath the bed;

And there he saw them at the fun,
And he his tool did dandle.
Says he, "I'll give them a thing
Much better than a candle."

The sum Ephraim was offered for his candlesticks in the first
pawnbroker's shop he entered did not tempt him; he also
declined the pittance proffered in the second jerryshop he
visited. Unfortunately, coming out of yet another shop, he was
nabbed by a peeler.

Shedding hot tears, Ephraim fell to the gutter, kicking his
legs, hoping to attract the sympathy of passersby. He protested
that he was an orphan, driven by hunger to pawning his
beloved granny's candlesticks, but his story wouldn't wash.
Ephraim spent his first night in London incarcerated in the
gassy bowels of a rotting hulk on the lower Thames and within
a week he was sentenced to six months in the notorious "Steel"
(so-called after the Bastille) in Coldbath Fields.

On arrival, the lags sized him up and assumed that once
Sergeant Walsh had wearied of him, he would be sequestered
in the harem until things sorted themselves out and he found a
protector. But the obdurate Ephraim refused to lower his
trousers for Sergeant Walsh. As a consequence, he was obliged
to ride the cockchafer every morning, treading down a wheel
of twenty-four steps that sank away from him at an infuriating
fixed rate in stifling heat. When that failed to do the trick
Sergeant Walsh sentenced him to a week of shot-drill on the
square. For this exercise he joined other offenders in a row, the
men posted three yards apart. On a shouted order from
Sergeant Walsh each man picked up a twenty-four-pound
cannon-ball, lugged it as far as his neighbour's position and
hurried back to his own place, where another cannon-ball left
there by his other neighbour was waiting for him. The drill
usually lasted an hour, sometimes longer, depending on how
urgently Sergeant Walsh needed a beer. When Ephraim still
resisted the sergeant's advances, he earned himself some time
on the crank. This required him to turn a sand-filled drum
with a crank handle, the drum's revolutions recorded by a
clock mechanism. He was birched again and again. Then one
morning Sergeant Walsh was found squatting in an outhouse,
his throat slashed from ear to ear. Detectives descended on the

Steel, questioning all the lags, putting everybody on short ration, flogging indiscriminately, but the culprit was never discovered. Ephraim, a prime suspect, was vouched for by Izzy Garber, who swore that the boy, troubled by a fever, had slept by his side all through the night.

The impudent, astonishingly resourceful Izzy Garber, a hirsute, barrel-chested master of magic, was a born scrounger for whom nothing was impossible, even within the bleak confines of the Steel. At the right moment Izzy's loosely worn shirt would yield salamis, coils of stuffed derma, roasted chickens or rounds of cheese acquired who knows where, God knows how. He also never lacked for tobacco and gin and Indian hemp and soothing salves to heal the lacery of cuts burnt into Ephraim's back. The other prisoners, even the turnkeys, treated Izzy with deference, calling upon him again and again to extract teeth, set broken bones, or stitch knife wounds, no questions asked. Izzy, never without his *yarmulke*, embossed with the inscription, "Honour the Sabbath, To keep it Holy," was the most triumphantly Jewish man Ephraim had ever met. "Look at their God, or son of, as those sods would have it. Turn the other cheek. The meek shall inherit the earth. Codswallop. Nancyboy horseshit. But our God is truly vengeful," Izzy once said, thrusting his *siddur* at Ephraim. "So say your evening prayers, because it doesn't pay to mess with Jehovah, that old Jew fucker."

Izzy aside, Ephraim's sojourn in the Steel proved an invaluable learning experience. From coiners who normally operated in the Holy Land rookery of St. Giles he learned how to take a counterfeit with an unmilled edge and work it into acceptable coin. Practising with pickpockets of his own age he was soon adjudged sufficiently adroit to become a dipper, although he had no intention of putting himself in the hands of a kidsman when he got out.

"*Nischt fur dich*," Izzy Garber said.

From a member of the swell mob out of Seven Dials Ephraim absorbed all he needed to know about garroting. But Izzy proved Ephraim's most beneficial teacher. One night he told him how he had used to work village greens as a prater, or bogus preacher, raising funds for a mission to the savages of the Gold Coast. " 'Behold, the day of the Lord cometh, cruel both with wrath and fierce anger, to lay the land desolate: and he shall destroy the sinners thereof out of it.' " Another night Izzy recalled his days as a professional beggar. He told Ephraim how, posted outside a church, waiting for the Christians to emerge, he would promptly fall to the ground, simulating convulsions: foam, produced by soap shavings under his tongue, bubbling pathetically to his lips. Then, as soon as sympathetic members of the congregation had flocked around, he would whip out his letter.

THIS IS TO CERTIFY, to all whom it may concern, that the EXEMPLAR, Captain Staines, was returning to Liverpool Dock, from the Canadas, laden with beaver pelts from Rupert's Land, and that said vessel encountering a prodigious GALE and ICEBERGS off the banks of Newfoundland, and was dismasted and finally wrecked on the ice. That the above-mentioned vessel foundered and only the second mate and three of the crew, the bearers of these certificates, escaped a watery grave. These survivors were humanely picked up by the brig GLORIANA, Capt. Wescott, and landed at Tilbury Dock. That we, the Masters of Customs, and one of Her Majesty's Justices of the Peace for the said dock, do hereby grant and afford to said ISRAEL GRANT this vouchment of the truth of the said wreck and do empower him to present and use this certificate for twenty-eight days from the date thereof, to enable him to acquire such temporal aid as may be essential to reaching his wife and children in the Outer Hebrides. And this certificate further sheweth that he may not be interrupted in the said journey by any constabulary or other official authority, provided that no breach of the peace or other cognizable offence be committed by the said Petitioner.

As witness to our hands,
   Magnus McCarthy, M.C.   £1-0-0
   Archibald Burton, J.P.   £1-0-0

Given at Liverpool Dock, this 27th day of January 1831.

GOD SAVE THE KING

Given his skill in penmanship and Latin, and the connections he had made in the Steel, Ephraim envisaged setting himself up as a screever once his sentence was done. Izzy was pleased with his protégé. "It wouldn't be nice for a Yiddisher boy to be a footpad or a dragsman. Remember, *tsatskeleh*, we are the People of the Book."

"How will I find you after I get out?"

"Don't worry," Izzy said. "I'll find you."

On his release, Ephraim dug his money out of its hiding place in Hyde Park, acquired the necessary quills and inks and parchments, and moved into a lodging house in Whitechapel. Within months he was prospering. After dark he drifted from gin-shop, through bordello to gaming-house, seeking Izzy Garber, unavailingly. But during the day he was hard at it. He wrote letters for ruined clergymen. "Milady — I held the rank of Captain in the Peninsular War. I have struggled exceedingly hard, after being discharged from the service on account of my crippling wounds, but unhappily. . . ." Keeping a sharp eye on the death notices in the *Times*, he would send an appropriately dressed dollymop, a pillow bound to her belly, to the fashionable home of the newly bereaved family of a gentleman. She would carry a letter saying that the bearer had been seduced by the deceased and was now with child but utterly without means, cast off by her own family, and though she did not wish to publicize the affair. . . .

His letters, the penmanship exquisite, were signed with the names of sea captains, rectors, major generals, and lords of the realm; and they were garnished with heart-rending appeals, nicely turned Latin phrases and suitable biblical quotations.

Such was the demand for Ephraim's inventive pen that he soon acquired an opera hat, a white waistcoat, an elegant snuff box and a silk handkerchief. He was brought to the attention of a theatrical producer, who offered him a position in his combine of brothels. Ephraim declined, but he did accompany him to a boxing match and saw Ikey Pig, a Jew, badly mauled. However, one taste of the fancy was enough to make him a victim of boximania. He was with the producer again when an American Negro, an escaped slave, had the effrontery to challenge for the enviable title of Champion of England. As

Pierce Egan wrote of this match, "that a FOREIGNER should have the temerity to put in a claim, *even* for the mere contention of tearing the CHAMPION'S CAP from the British brow, much more the honour of wearing it, or bearing it away from GREAT BRITAIN, such an idea however distant, never intruded itself into the breasts of an Englishman."

Ephraim, despairing of ever finding Izzy, became a regular at Laurent's Dancing Academy in Windmill Street, the Argyll Rooms, and of course Kate Hamilton's night house, flourishing there as a favourite of Thelma Coyne, whom he considered establishing in a flat in Holborn as his very own *poule-de-luxe*.

Wandering through Piccadilly one night he was drawn into his first, admittedly spurious, acquaintance with Canada through a theatrical poster.

EGYPTIAN HALL

Piccadilly

JUST ARRIVED

Canadian North American

INDIANS!

Will perform at the above hall, at

2 o'Clock in the afternoon, & 8 o'Clock in the Evening

A Grand Indian Council

In front of the Wigwam, when the whole

Party will appear in FULL NATIVE COSTUME,

Displaying all the Implements of War.

THE CHIEF

Will Shoot An Apple Off A Boy's Head!

A Facsimile of Scalping!

Never before attempted in this country

THE WAR DANCE

In which the Indians will give a true

Specimen of the FURIOUS RAGE with which

feelings are aroused against their adversary

at an approaching conflict.

BURYING THE HATCHET, AND SMOKING THE

CALUMET (OR PIPE) OF PEACE.

A slash glued to the poster announced:

Entirely due to *Sacred* ABORIGINAL RITES
There will be no Performances,
Wednesday, Oct. 8 or Thursday, Oct. 9.

Thrilled by the events in Egyptian Hall, but naggingly
suspicious of the chief, Ephraim slipped backstage after the
performance. Voices were raised in the chief's dressing
room.

"*Paskudnyak*! *Mamzer*!"

"*Hok mir nit kayn tchynik.*"

"*Ver derharget*!"

His doubts happily confirmed, Ephraim kicked open the
door. The hirsute, barrel-chested chief instantly dived behind
a screen. His plump raging wife scooped up a hatchet.

"Izzy, come on out of there."

"Ephraim!"

The two old lags embraced. "I told you I'd find you," Izzy
said, and then turning to his wife he added, "This lad here can
set bones almost as well as I can. You can't teach these things.
You've got to have the touch."

They repaired through greasy fog to a garlicky, smoke-filled
basement kitchen in Soho that kept open late to cater to
the troupe as well as other dubious night people. Buxom
waitresses in stained lowcut blouses sailed through the jostling
crowd, hoisting tankards of ale even as they slapped probing hands, their curses drowned in a cacophony of Yiddish,
Greek, and Italian. In a gas-lit corner, an old jeweller, one
eye sprouting a magnifying glass, bargained with a solemn
moustachioed Sikh. At Izzy's table, platters of chopped liver
and shmaltz herring were followed by steaming trays of stuffed
derma, boiled *flanken*, *kasha* drenched in chicken fat and
potato *kreplach*. Shouting over the din, Ephraim congratulated
Izzy on the full house at the Egyptian Hall and then asked why
there would be no performances on the Wednesday and
Thursday of the following week.

Affronted, Izzy replied, "I think it would be most
inappropriate for us to perform the war dance on Yom
Kippur."

"*Gottzedank*," Mrs. Garber said.

What finally brought Ephraim down, as it would many times in the future, was a dangerous admixture of vanity, lust, and recklessness. Many a night he entertained two particularly pert Irish girls, the Sullivan sisters, in his attic rooms. The obliging sisters, who lived in the same lodging house as he did, thrived as palmers by day, prostitutes by night. On occasion Ephraim, in a mood to go on the randy, would treat the two of them to an evening at the Eagle, splurging on a box. Not for the small profit involved, but because he enjoyed the sport of it, there were nights when Ephraim would go out bug-hunting with them. The sisters, posted under a gas lamp, would lure a likely, prosperous-looking drunk, preferably a country bumpkin, into buying them a tot in a gin-shop where Ephraim waited. Jammed tight against the crowded bar, Dotty would stroke him, lick his ear, and sing softly:

> Tell me, what it is I spy,
> Frisky Johnny, randy Johnny,
> Hanging down beside your thigh,
> Frisky Johnny, randy Johnny?
> Have you got a swelling there,
> Frisky Johnny, randy Johnny?

Meanwhile Kate would pick his pocket and usually that's all there was to it. But if the victim caught on to what was happening, making a fuss, then Ephraim would be called upon to act as the sisters' stickman. Simulating outrage, he would elbow through to the victim, vociferous in his defence, assuring him that he had seen everything. Then, as soon as Kate had slipped him the booty, he would rush off, ostensibly to fetch a peeler, but actually hurrying back to his lodging to await the girls, a bottle of claret uncorked on his bedside table. If necessary, back in the gin-shop the girls would submit to a useless search, protesting their innocence, bawling at their offended modesty, until the embarrassed victim would flee into the fog.

Bug-hunting became such a plague that questions were raised in parliament. Irate citizens wrote to the *Times*, inveighing against Scotland Yard's ineptitude. And so, inevitably, one night the sisters' victim turned out to be a police detective, working with an accomplice of his own. The accomplice, another detective, followed Ephraim out of the gin-shop, nabbing him as he was about to enter his lodging house. Even so, Ephraim might have got off with another six-month sentence, but the detective insisted on a visit to his rooms.

"You don't understand, sir," Ephraim said. "I don't live here among the Ikey Pigs and I had no idea that those girls had slipped that gentleman's purse into my pocket."

"Why did you stop here, then?"

"You will think badly of me, sir, but I had come to await those wicked girls in their rooms. My father was taken from us at Trafalgar and now my poor widowed mother will be undone. I am a victim of my own lust."

But a closer search of Ephraim's waistcoat yielded one of the calling cards he had foolishly had printed and the address was the same. The detective and Ephraim proceeded to his attic rooms, where the work table was strewn with begging letters awaiting pick-up by clients. Burglar's tools, actually not Ephraim's but held by him for a ticket-of-leave man of his acquaintance, were discovered in the closet. A brace and bit fitted with a large, adjustable cutting head; a jemmy; a set of pick-locks and a peter-cutter. A desk drawer turned out to be filled with forged official seals. Another drawer contained a harvest of silk handkerchiefs, the property of the Sullivan sisters, but no matter. As the detective began to make notes, Ephraim lunged at him, knocking him off his feet, and flew down the stairs right into the waiting arms of the other detective, who had just entered the lodging house with the Sullivan sisters in tow.

"There he is," Dotty squealed, "the fancyman who forced us into a life of sin."

"He takes all our money," Kate hollered.

TWO

◆

The fat pulpy man from the DEW line station offered him twenty dollars, but Isaac wouldn't do it. Instead he continued as before. For five dollars he met the man once a week in the toilet of the Sir Igloo Inn Café and pumped his thing until it squirted. This time, however, the man gave him two hand-rolled cigarettes as well. "It's a special kind of tobacco, kid. If you like it, and you want more, maybe we can talk again about the other deal."

Isaac couldn't spend his earnings going to a movie because they didn't have one. They didn't have anything in Tulugaqtitut. Bored, an irritated Isaac drifted through the settlement, cursing it. He paused at his customary vantage point, the one that offered him a view of Agnes McPhee's bedroom. She seldom drew the curtains, and more than once he had seen Agnes going at it with one of the bush pilots, her quivering naked legs reaching for the ceiling. But today he couldn't even catch her undressing. So Isaac wandered into the Hudson's Bay trading post, Ian Campbell instantly alert, setting aside his ledgers to watch him. "Hey, Isaac," Campbell called out, playing to the other customers, "has your father decided on which kind of boat yet?"

Everybody, but Nialie, knew Henry was crazy. "Mind your own business," Isaac hollered.

"Just asking, kid, because it looks like rain."

Each mail plane would bring Henry elegant packages from boat-builders. C. vanLent & Zonen Kaag, Abeking & Rasmussen, S.E. Ward & Co., Hitachi Zosen. Each package came with encomiums from satisfied sheiks and international arms dealers and Hollywood moguls. There were colour photographs, elaborate deck plans, and, invariably, a personal letter from the designer.

None of them understood. Henry was not unreasonable. He didn't expect a boat built of gopher-wood, or that the length would be three hundred cubits, the breadth fifty cubits, and the height thirty cubits. But he was not interested in Twin MTU main engines or U25 HP Caterpillar D-353s. When the time came he was not so foolish as to think his descendants would send forth a dove — or, more appropriate to the generations of Ephraim, a raven — but neither would a pad for a Bell Jet Ranger III helicopter be required. The likelihood was that there would be no fuel and they would be dependent on the wind in their sails for power. So Henry was thinking of a three-masted ship modelled on turn-of-the-century schooners or possibly a windjammer or the sort of square-rigger that had once been built in the Maritimes.

"Please don't do it," Isaac said.

"Why not, *yingele*?"

"Don't do it!"

"Give me a reason."

"Everybody is laughing at us already. Is that reason enough for you?"

"Are you ashamed of me?"

"Maybe for more reasons than one," Isaac said, fleeing.

Seated at his rolltop desk with the two bullet holes in it, awash in estimates and brochures, Henry turned to his Pentateuch for solace, rocking over it, reading, "And the Lord said, I will destroy man whom I have created from the face of the earth; both man, and beast, and the creeping things, and the fowls of the air; for it repenteth me that I have made them."

Of course that could never happen again. God had

established a covenant. He had set his bow in a cloud. But the conditions that prevailed today, the wickedness of man great in the earth, were as bad as those of Noah's time. God's punishment, Henry was convinced, would be another ice age. Then there would be floods and a properly equipped ship would be crucial to survival. Meanwhile, Henry continued to study the entrails.

A CIA report predicted catastrophic changes that would return the world climate to a condition similar to that of one hundred to four hundred years ago. The report, leaked to the Washington *Post*, anticipated famine in the near future.

> The earth's cooling will lead to increasingly desperate attempts on the part of the powerful, but hungry, nations to get grain any way they can. Massive migrations, sometimes backed by force, will be a live issue and political and economic instability will be widespread.

Henry's file also included a recent item clipped from the Edmonton *Journal*.

> The proposition that the planet is cooling has been advanced most articulately by Reid Bryson, professor of meteorology and geography at the University of Wisconsin.
>
> Between 1880 and 1940, the mean global temperature rose about one degree Fahrenheit. Since then it has fallen by about half that amount.
>
> Bryson argues that the period of 1930–61 was a time of extraordinarily benign weather that has been mistaken for normality. The earth's declining temperature and the historical evidence persuade him that the weather in the coming years will be more unpredictable than ever — and quite possibly devastating.

Once his parents had gone to bed, Isaac lit his handrolled cigarette in his own little bedroom, switching on a tape.

A gale-force wind screamed across the Arctic. "Last week," the narrator said, "we left Captain Allan Cohol lying in a fish net inches from death. Frightened by the golden-haired stranger's escape from a coffin of ice after centuries of entombment, the men of the Eskimo village have overcome him and are preparing now to thrust a harpoon through the giant stranger's heart."

"No!" Kirnik cried. "We will take him by sled to Dr. Fantom. The doctor has things to cause sleep. When he sleeps we will send for the police."

"So the men of Fish Fiord," the narrator said, "manhandled the mighty man of muscle onto a dogsled, his fabulous frame still entangled in the coils of the net. Their destination was the sinister quarters of Dr. Fantom, renegade refugee from the world of medicine, practising his nefarious skills in the hiding of the high north. Fantom looked down at the giant in the net."

"I am Captain Allan Cohol. Inter-galactic 80321. I demand my rights."

Chuckling malevolently, Fantom said, "Come now, relax. My name is Frederick Fantom, MD. You may call me Fred. I will call you Al. Well, isn't that amusing, gentlemen? Meet our new friend. Al Cohol. What a truly intoxicating pleasure to make your acquaintance. Now then, your arm, my friend. This won't hurt a bit."

"Don't touch me with that needle, you foul physician. This is medical mayhem," Captain Al Cohol protested, already in a daze.

"Let's get some stimulant into you. Overproof rum. Just what the doctor ordered, Al. Now open your mouth like a good patient."

Sounds of struggle. Gurglings, splutterings, liquid being swallowed.

"Look," Kirnik cried, alarmed. "Look at his eyes. Look at the way his face is changing."

Captain Al Cohol began to roar. "Kill! I'll kill you all. A-a-rgh-h-h-h!"

There now came the terrifying sounds of tearing and rending. The Eskimos shout and scream as Captain Al Cohol hurls himself at them.

"What is this?" the narrator asked. "Captain Al Cohol, the hero of the inter-galactic fleet, driven into madness by a glass of rum?"

Then another voice proclaimed, "The ordeals of Captain Al Cohol is a radio adaptation by E.G. Perrault of a comic-book series written by Art Sorensen for the Alcohol Education Program of the Northwest Territories Government."

His tape done, Isaac reached under his mattress to dig out his folder of New York photographs, cut from the pages of *Time, Newsweek* and *People*. Photographs of the world out there where the main event wasn't the arrival of an Otter from Yellowknife and the sun didn't sink below the horizon for month after chilling month. Photographs of film stars and tycoons and fashion models. He had written to his Uncle Lionel, reminding him of his visit and inviting him to come again, signing himself, "Your admirer, Isaac." In response, he had been sent an electric train set with a card signed by Lionel's private secretary.

The next evening a resolute Isaac delighted Henry at the dinner table, joining him in saying grace and asking if they might resume their Talmud studies. They had only been at it a week when Isaac burst into tears at the table.

"What is it, *yingele?*"

"Please don't send me to school in Yellowknife. I want to attend the Rebbe's *yeshiva* in Brooklyn."

Henry, his eyes sparkling, danced his son around the room, singing, "*Shteht oif, shteht oif, l'avoidas haBoiray.*" Wake up, wake up, to do the work of the Creator.

Nialie watched without expression, frightened for both of them.

THREE

◆

September 1916. Solomon, seventeen years old now, short for his age, wiry, his skin burnt nut-brown by the prairie sun, was perched on the corral fence behind the Queen Victoria Hotel with Bernard and Morrie. Plump Bernard, who parted his hair in the middle and already owned a three-piece grey serge suit and a homburg and spats, sucked on a caramel. Morrie, whittling away on a chunk of wood as usual, was apprehensive as Solomon had joined them on the fence for once, familiar as he was with Solomon's need to bring Bernard to the boil. Slapping at flies, squinting against the sun, the Gursky brothers were waiting for the sale to start. Aaron had bought a snorting, restive herd of wild mustangs from Hardy, overpaying again, and now hoped to sell to the farmers, most of whom were already in debt to him at the store. By this juncture the Gurskys had moved into town, living above

A. GURSKY & SONS
GENERAL MERCHANTS
Importers of Stable and Fancy
DRY GOODS
Sole Distributors of
DR. COLBY'S celebrated ANTI-COSTIVE
and TONIC PILLS, unequalled in the
Promotion of Regular Evacuation.

Cajoling, sweaty, Aaron bantered with the farmers at the corral, laughing too hard at their inane jokes. The farmers feigning indifference, most of them waiting for sundown when the jumpy Jew's prices would drop.

No sooner did Aaron cut a deal on a horse, realizing a small profit, than he would invite the buyer into the hotel bar for a ceremonial drink. The farmer would not order a beer like Aaron, but would spit on the sawdust-covered floor, wink at the bartender, and demand a double shot of the hard stuff, saying, "Both of my boys have already enlisted, but I suppose yours will be staying put."

Then a breathless Aaron would zip out to the corral again, counting the shiny rumps of the remaining horses, calculating likely losses in his head, mingling with the other farmers, thrusting gifts of coloured hair ribbons at their wives and children. Panicky at sundown, he would drop prices drastically.

Solomon prodded Bernard with his elbow. "Now that you're such a man of affairs, a student of correspondence courses, what do you make of all this?"

"Whatever I make of it is strictly my own business."

"Why can't we be like the three musketeers," Morrie asked, "all for one and one for all? The Gursky brothers."

"Well," Solomon said, "I'll tell you what I think. The bar's turning over a bigger profit than Paw is sucking up to that bunch of farmers. What Paw ought to do is buy the hotel and sell drinks and let somebody else worry about the horses."

And then Solomon, terrifying Morrie, jumped down from the fence right into the flow of wild nervy horses in the corral. Solomon, Ephraim's anointed one.

Bernard didn't credit most of his brother's tales about his trek to the Polar Sea with their grandfather. But whatever had really happened out there, Solomon had returned blessed with a certain grace, an inner stillness. And watching him now, at ease with the wild mustangs, Bernard grasped that had he been the one to jump into the corral, probably stumbling in the dust, they would have smelled his fear and reared up on their hind legs, snorting, looking to take a chomp out of him. Bernard understood for the first time that he was a coarse, tubby little man with wet fishy eyes, and that he would have to scratch and bite and cheat to get what he wanted out of life, which was plenty, but that Solomon would sit, expecting the world to come to him, and he would be served. He watched Solomon crossing that corral, he watched choking on envy and hatred, and yet, for all that, he yearned for Solomon's approval. Then Solomon spoiled it by pausing to taunt him, calling back, "Follow me, Bernie, and I'll buy you a beer."

"Go straight to hell."

"Aw, you two," Morrie groaned. "Hey, you're crying."

"I am not. He's going to *shtupp* Minnie Pryzack now."

Minnie, comfortably ensconced in the Queen Victoria Hotel for years, was only seventeen when she first went west, working the first-class carriages on the train from Winnipeg to the coast and back again.

"He's going to *shtupp* Minnie and then he's going to join the poker game."

"They'd never let him play in the big autumn game. Besides, he's busted."

"I wasn't afraid of jumping into the corral, but then you would have had to come after and you could have been hurt. Is he really broke?"

"They cleaned him out last Thursday."

Aaron, sprawled at the kitchen table, smelling of manure, his ears and nose clogged with dust, his back aching, counted out his money twice, calculating that he had turned a profit of fifty-five dollars, provided two of the farmers honoured their notes.

Morrie stooped to remove his father's boots and then brought him a glass of lemon tea and a bowl of stewed prunes.

"Paw," Bernard said, "if you ask me, you work too hard for too little."

"You're a good boy," Aaron said. "Morrie too."

Rather than risk throwing everything into the pot in the heat of the game, Solomon gave Minnie his valise, as well as his railroad ticket out and five ten-dollar bills, which would see him through, if things turned out badly. Then he drifted through the kitchen of the Queen Victoria Hotel, climbed the back stairs to the third floor, and rapped three long, two short, and one long on the attic door.

McGraw shot the bolts. "You can't play. Not tonight."

Solomon didn't budge.

"It's different rules tonight, kid. You know that."

Not including Solomon, there were five of them gathered together for the big autumn game, the betting soaring so high it could only be risked once a year. McGraw, the owner of the hotel and the blacksmith's shop, a recent acquisition; George Kouri, the Lebanese, who had owned the five-and-ten-cent store and a shop that sold buggies and wagons; Ingram, Sifton's man, who dealt railroad land to the Slavs in their sheepskin coats; Charley Lin, who had owned the laundry and the butchershop, but since last autumn's big game only a couple of bedbug-ridden rooming houses; and Kozochar, the barber and fire chief. A side table was stacked with cold cuts, potato salad, and bottles of whisky and vodka. There were two cots in an adjoining room, in case anybody needed to take a nap or wanted to send down for one of the girls, maybe changing his luck.

Last year's big game had ended acrimoniously after forty-eight hours, one of Charley Lin's rooming houses, the blacksmith's shop, two cow pastures, six heifers, three Polish whores and one Indian one and $4,500 changing hands. The men involved in the big game enjoyed the status it conferred on them by dint of the enormity of their winnings or losses. The game, a curse on the wives, had once been broken up by three of them marching on the tables. Since then it convened at a different place every year. The basement of Kouri's five-and-ten. The back room in the fire station. And this year the attic of the Queen Victoria Hotel. Weeks before the men sat down to the table, the game was the subject of speculation in town, and was denounced from the pulpit by the Reverend Ezekiel Shipley, who blamed it all on the harlots of the town.

McGraw was adamant. "It just wouldn't be right to deal you in," he said.

McGraw had been against allowing Solomon into the weekly game in the first place. He was hardly a man of substance, like the rest of them, but merely a snooty kid.

Besides McGraw liked Aaron, a dummy maybe, but an honest and hardworking Jew. Kouri had been indifferent, but Ingram was also opposed and Kozochar dead against it. "It would be like taking candy from a baby."

"His money's as good as yours or mine," Charley Lin said with appetite.

Ostensibly it was the need to teach Solomon a lesson that was his ticket of admission, because the men resented him without knowing exactly why. But there was another consideration. They wanted to impress him with their money and their moxie. That little son of a bitch.

His grandfather had been a squaw man, his father was a peddler, and, for all that, the boy, a mere seventeen-year-old, a squirt, a Jew, strode through the streets of town as if he were a prince-in-waiting, destined for great things. Unfailingly polite, considerate, it was difficult to fault him. If a fire broke out at four o'clock of a sub-zero morning, he was there at once to join the bucket brigade. When Miss Thomson was poorly, laid low with one of those feminine ailments, he took over the schoolhouse, enchanting the children. The Reverend Shipley, who could sniff evil in a year-old babe born to fornicate, sought out Solomon for discussions of the Holy Scripture. He was also more welcome on the reservation than any one of them, and could be gone with the Indians, God knows where, for ten days at a time. But there was something about him that riled the men and made them want to rub his nose in fresh dog shit.

Unlike pushy Bernard or Morrie (a really nice, polite kid), he didn't deign to serve in his father's store. But it was because he could be found there on occasion that the daughters were drawn to A. Gursky & Sons in swarms, blushing if he greeted them, the one he picked out for a buggy ride all but swooning on the spot. And, remarkably, the other young men in town, far from being jealous, vied for his favour, competing to recruit him as a hunting or drinking partner.

Once Solomon just happened to be passing in his buggy when McGraw's wagon was stuck in the mud. Immediately he jumped down and offered help. "No, no," McGraw protested, kneeling in the muck, his own shoulder to the wheel, "you'll only get dirty." Then McGraw turned pale, amazed at himself, because he would not have said such a thing to anybody else in town.

Solomon brought two hundred dollars to his first game, his pool-room earnings, and was promptly stripped of it. But he didn't sulk. He didn't complain. Instead he joked about it. "My initiation fee," he said.

So when he turned up again he was made welcome, the men digging deep for old hunting stories and gilding tales of past sexual triumphs, determined to prove to him that far from being a bunch of big-bellied hicks they were, if the truth were known, a band of hellraisers.

Solomon did reasonably well in his second game until he foolishly tried to bluff Kouri, showing three ladies, with what turned out to be no better than eights over deuces. He lost a third time and a fourth and now he was back, demanding a seat at the autumn game. McGraw didn't like it one bit. If they cleaned him out people would say they had taken advantage of a kid, but if he won it would be even more embarrassing.

"I must have dropped five hundred bucks at this table," Solomon said. "You owe me a chair."

"We don't owe you shit," Ingram said.

"No IOUs tonight. You want to sit down," McGraw said, sure that would be the end of it, "you got to show us at least a thousand dollars."

Solomon laid out his money on the table like bait immediately before Charley Lin.

"What can I get you to drink, kid?" Charley Lin asked.

Bernard brought his father a slice of honey cake. "Paw, I've got an idea."

Aaron, dazed by fatigue, itchy everywhere from horsefly bites, only half-listened.

"We could bring in a fiddler on Friday nights. Salt the pretzels more. Start a darts league. I know where we can get mugs with bottoms an inch thicker for the draft beer. Morrie could handle the cash register."

"And how would we raise the down payment?"

"McGraw buys his beer from Faulkner's. If we switched to

Langham, signing a contract with them, they'd lend us some money. So would the bank."

"Sure. The bank."

"This isn't Russia, Paw."

"Neither is it Gan Eden."

Aaron, his money in hand, shuffled over to a corner of the kitchen, lifted a plank floorboard, dug out his strongbox, unlocked it, and howled and stumbled backward, a stricken man. Fanny, who had been tending to the pots simmering on the wood stove, was instantly by his side. "Aaron!"

His eyes had gone flat. All he could manage was a croak. "It's gone. The money."

"Some of that money's mine," Bernard yelled, seizing the box, turning it upside down and shaking it.

Out tumbled citizenship papers, a marriage licence, birth certificates, but no cash and no deed to the general store.

"Should I go to the police?" Aaron asked in a failing voice.

"Only if you want to put your son in prison," Bernard said.

"How can you be sure it was him?" Morrie asked.

"I'll kill him for this," Bernard said. And he was off and running, pursued by Morrie. Bernard didn't stop before he stood red and panting before Boyd, the porcine clerk in the Queen Victoria Hotel. "Where's the fucken poker game?" he demanded.

Boyd, his smile bright with malevolence, pointed at the sign behind his desk: no cursing, no spitting, no games of chance allowed.

"Listen, you little shit, if you don't tell me where I can find Solomon I'm going to try every room in the hotel."

"You go right ahead, shorty, but there are some awful big guys in a number of them rooms, some of them entertaining company."

A tearful Morrie stepped between them. "Please, Mr. Boyd, we have to find Solomon."

"If I see him I'll tell him you're looking for him."

The Gurskys sat up all through the night waiting for Solomon to come home. Fanny moaning and Aaron seated in a chair with his hands folded, his eyes turned inward. "I'm too old to start over again," he said to nobody in particular.

It was dawn before Bernard slipped into the bedroom he shared with his two brothers and discovered that two of Solomon's drawers were empty and his valise was gone. Win or lose, he wasn't coming back.

"I've seen dead men look better than you do right now."

"Unfavourable winds," Solomon said to Minnie in the adjoining room. "How much did you bring?"

"Your fifty and the railway ticket and eight hundred of my own and my rings."

"What happens if I lose that too?"

"Then you must promise to marry me."

"Minnie," he said, inclined to be generous, "you must be thirty years old."

"Take it or leave it."

"It's blackmail," he said, scooping up the money.

"Now that's what I call a proposal."

It was time to open the store.

"What we should do," Bernard said, "is hire wagons and move all our stock somewhere safe, because tonight this place may no longer belong to us."

"He's a minor," Morrie said.

"Prick. If he signs over the deed and we don't honour his gambling debt, we're asking for a fire."

Bernard figured he wouldn't run away without saying goodbye to Lena Green Stockings, so he took the buggy and rode out to the reservation. Kids with scabs on their faces wrestling in the dirt, one of them with rickets. A drunk slumped against a tree trunk outside George Two Axe's store, scrawny chickens pecking at his vomit. Flies everywhere. Crows fluttering over the entrails of a dead dog, flying off with the ropey bits.

Bernard entered the tarpaper shack and was enraged to find it stocked with goods that could only have been swiped from A. Gursky & Sons, General Merchants. Tea. Sugar. An open ten-pound bag of flour on a high shelf. He found her out in the back yard, seated on a wicker chair with a broken seat, dozing.

"Lena!"

No answer.

"Lena, Solomon left in such a hurry he forgot to give me his new address."

When she finally raised her head, wizened as a walnut, he saw that she no longer had any teeth.

"It's important that I have it," Bernard said, pulling a bottle of rum out of his jacket pocket and waving it in front of her.

Lena smiled. "It's the boy with the two belly buttons," she said, remembering.

"Jesus Christ! Son of a bitch! Fuck! Everybody looks like that coming out of the swimming hole."

Her head began to slump again.

"Your shack is full of stolen goods. I could tell on you and then they'll come to lock you up."

Lena swatted a fly.

"Where's he going?"

"To see the world."

Passing through her shack again, Bernard paused to leave evidence of his passage, and then he went to see Minnie, taking the bar entrance to the hotel to avoid another encounter with Boyd. "I want you to give Solomon a message. Lena Green Stockings told me where he's planning to run to."

"How did you get that flour all over your suit?"

"Maybe my father won't go to the police, but I will. You tell him that."

Solomon came home three o'clock the next morning and went right to the kitchen sink, stooping to pump cold water over his head. He turned around just in time to see Bernard making a run at him, his arms outstretched, his fingers curled, ready to scratch. Solomon slapped him away and then went to his father and dropped the deed to the general store and a bundle of money tied with an elastic band on to his lap.

"Some of that money you stole was mine," Bernard said.

Emptying his pockets one by one, Solomon piled banknotes on the kitchen table, more money than the Gurskys had ever seen at one time.

"Big shot," Bernard said, "it's a good thing you were lucky for once."

Morrie went to make coffee and Bernard sat down to count the money.

"We are the new owners of the Queen Victoria Hotel and the blacksmith's shop on Prince Albert Street and a rooming house on Duke. The hotel comes with an eight-thousand-dollar mortgage, now our responsibility. Sell the rooming house. It's a fire trap. The blacksmith's shop is for André Clear Sky."

"I don't see any hotel deeds here," Bernard said.

Solomon reached into his jacket pocket and tossed the deeds on the table.

"You're a good boy," Aaron said.

"Like hell he is. He was planning to run away. Me, I stopped him."

Solomon waited until his mother had left the kitchen. "I want somebody to wake me up in time for the noon train. I'm going to Winnipeg. I'm joining the army. But please don't any of you say anything to Maw. I'll tell her myself."

Bernard stood apart, fulminating, as everybody fussed over Solomon at the train station. Minnie and the other whores, Lena, some farm girls whose names he didn't even know, a drunken McGraw, and Fanny Gursky awash in tears. Then Bernard ate lunch with his father. "I'm registering the hotel in my name, because I'm the eldest."

Wearing his homburg, his three-piece suit and spats, Bernard went to see the notary and then had a word with Morrie. "You know Boyd, the fat clerk at the hotel?"

"Yeah, sure."

"Go tell him he's fired. You're taking his place."

Next Bernard went to the hotel and arranged for a box of chocolates and a victrola to be sent to room twelve, and then he sailed into the bar and sat down at Minnie's table.

"If I invited you to sit here," she said, "remind me."

"You better learn to talk nice if you want to continue here. I'm boss now."

"It's Solomon's hotel."

"My kid brother left me in charge. Go to room twelve at once and wait for me there."

Minnie was waiting when Bernard entered the bedroom.

"Help yourself to a chocolate," he said. "It's for you. The whole box. The largest on sale."

"Thank you."

"Do you read the funnies?"

"I look at the pictures," she said, blushing.

"My favourite is Krazy Kat, but I also like Abie Kabibble. How's the chocolate?"

"Very nice."

"It breaks my heart, but the army turned me down. Flat feet. I don't mind if you tell that to the other girls, but if you repeat anything else that happens here you will not be allowed into the bar again. Now tell me what you like better, waltz or ragtime?"

"Ragtime."

Sweaty, his hand trembling, Bernard nevertheless managed to set the record on the victrola: "Alexander's Ragtime Band".

"Are we going to dance first?" Minnie asked.

"Just you. Taking things off. But not your garter belt or stockings. And you mustn't look at me, not even a little peek," he said, reaching for a towel. But the record was finished before he was satisfied.

"What do I do now?" she asked.

He put on another record. "I Love My Wife, But, Oh, You Kid."

"Now you can get dressed and don't forget to take your chocolates."

"Would you like to do it, honey?"

"Don't honey me. I'm Mr. Gursky to you."

"Mr. Gursky."

"Do what?"

"Dress me."

"Shit, I know you can't read, but surely you know how to put your clothes on at your age."

"*Sorry.*"

"Well, hold on a minute. If I could do the brassiere I wouldn't say no."

"Oh, Mr. Gursky, chocolate makes my skin break out, but

do I ever love Frenchy perfumes and scented soaps and anything made of silk."

Once she had gone, Bernard immediately washed his hands with soap and water, using a different towel. Then he curled up on the bed, hot with shame. Later he picked up the incriminating towel with two fingers and took it to room fourteen, which he knew was empty, and left it there. And he decided to punish himself for his indulgence. For the rest of the week, when he popped into Susy's Lunch to meet Morrie at four o'clock, as was his habit, he took his blueberry pie without ice cream.

FOUR

◆

While Solomon was overseas, during the First World War, Bernard acquired hotels in Regina, Saskatoon, Portage la Prairie, Medicine Hat, Lethbridge, and Winnipeg. Shrewdly, he followed wherever a railway extension was planned, buying hotels close to the yards. The hotels provided beer and breakfast at six, before the railroad men went to work, and solace more appropriate to bachelors when the men drifted back in the evening, their shifts done. The Gurskys' burgeoning fortunes could be measured by the escalation of the down payments they made on hotels, conscientiously recorded by Morrie, which leapt from $10,000, through $35,000, to $150,000 paid to a certain Bruno Hauswasser for the New Berlin Hotel in Winnipeg, telephones in each of its one hundred rooms, an elevator to every floor, but unfortunately cursed with a restaurant that specialized in *wiener schnitzel* and *sauerbraten*, and a bar which had done little business since the Kaiser marched on Belgium. Bernard placed an ad in the *Tribune* announcing the hotel's new name, The Victory, and that, as a patriotic gesture, the new Canadian ownership was offering one free beer an evening to nurses.

The family sold the general store and moved to Winnipeg. Manitoba had already been declared dry, except for Temperance Beer and alcohol "for use for medicinal, scientific, mechanical, industrial or sacramental purposes." Fortunately, there was a convenient loophole in the law. As interprovincial trade in liquor was still allowed, Bernard acquired a mail-order house in a small town in Ontario, and Morrie became a distributor of something called Rock-a-Bye Cough Cure, which enjoyed an understandably huge sale.

The outraged drys began to apply more pressure on Ottawa. A Presbyterian minister, back from a visit to the Canadian troops in England, declared that innocent boys were being "debauched by British booze, and by the immoral filth of London." The Reverend Sidney Lambert sniffed even more iniquity at home. "I would rather Germany wins this war," he said, "than see these get-rich-quick liquor men rule and damn the young men of Canada."

In 1917 the Gurskys were struck not one, but two blows. Ottawa introduced income tax, a nuisance that Bernard chose to ignore. Then, on Christmas eve, the importation of intoxicating liquors over two-and-a-half-percent proof was banned until after the war's end by an Order-in-Council. Only three months later, in March 1918, another Order-in-Council abolished interprovincial trafficking in liquor.

Morrie's memoir of the years that followed was uncommonly evasive, even for him, but, surprisingly, also a touch poetic. "This is no tale of woe," he wrote, "but as we climbed out of the prairie of toils into the garden of plenty, enjoying our first tasty chunks out of the roast beef of life, Solomon and Bernard began to quarrel bitterly, and I had to intervene more than once. It was in that acid soil that seeds of my future nervous breakdown were planted."

Solomon came home in the spring of 1918, wearing a flying-officer's uniform, favouring his left leg, and sporting the first of his malacca canes. Bernard sat down with him and laid out all that he had accomplished during his absence. The family holdings, he said, now included nine hotels and two mail-order houses, one in a small town in Ontario and the other in Montreal, and then he looked up, hungering for praise, entitled to it, but gaining only an impatient nod. "Okay," Bernard roared, "you want me to give it to you straight? In spite of my working sixteen hours a day, since the introduction of the new laws, the mail-order houses aren't worth a dry fart. And you know what those fucken hotels are good for now? A fire. Insurance money."

Solomon sent for copies of the Orders-in-Council, studied them in bed, and the next morning summoned Bernard and Morrie. "We're going into the wholesale drug business," he said.

Wearing his uniform, Solomon took the Manitoba Liberal party bagman to dinner at The Victory Hotel.

"How I envy you," the bagman said. "I was desperate to join my regiment, but the prime minister insisted I could do more for the war effort in Ottawa."

A girl was provided for the bagman, a considerable tribute was paid, and the necessary licence was forthcoming. An abandoned warehouse was acquired and The Royal Pure Drug Company of Canada was born. Within weeks it was producing Ginger Spit, Dandy Bracer, Dr. Isaac Grant's Liver & Kidney Cure, Raven Cough Brew, and Tip-Top Fixer among other elixirs. The brew was blended by pouring sugar, molasses, tobacco juice, blue stone and raw alcohol into washtubs and letting it sit overnight. In the morning, once drowned rats had been scooped out with a fishing net, the solution was stirred with an oar, strained, tinted different colours, and bottled.

Then Solomon discovered another loophole in the law. Given a drug licence, a wholesaler could import real whisky from Scotland without limit, providing it was stored in a bonded warehouse, imported for re-export. Another girl was washed and scented for the bagman, more money was fed into the voracious maw of the Liberal party machine, and warehouses were promptly bought in Manitoba, Saskatchewan, Ontario and Quebec. Railroad carloads of whisky were imported from Scotland.

And then Solomon had another idea. "Why are we selling other people's booze when we could make our own?"

Morrie was sent out to buy mixing vats and bottling equipment, and Solomon set to designing labels and commissioning a printer to produce them. Highland Cream, Crofter's Delight, Bonnie Brew, Pride of the Highlands,

Balmoral Malt, Vat Inverness, Ivanhoe Special Brand. Bernard, armed with a book he had stolen from the library, insisted that he be put in charge of the blending that was to be done in one-thousand-gallon redwood vats and Solomon, amused, agreed to it. But the initial carload of 65 overproof ethyl alcohol shipped to the Winnipeg warehouse presented them with a conundrum, and it was only the first of many carloads expected. If the overproof were to be used in the making of beverage alcohol it would be subject to a tax of $2.40 a gallon, but if, on the other hand, it was to be used to make vinegar the excise tax would be only 27¢ a gallon. Lloyd Corbett, the obese, affable Winnipeg customs agent, explained the problem.

"What time is it, my good friend?" Bernard asked.

"Eleven twenty-three."

"Come," Bernard said, and taking him by the arm he led him to the window and pointed at the big, endlessly blue prairie sky. "I tell you what, I'm such a crazy fool, I'm willing to bet you a thousand dollars it rains before noon."

Lloyd Corbett sat down again, sorting out his genitals, and then lit his pipe. "Jeez, Bernie, I'm crazier than you are. I'll bet you two thousand dollars and give you until one o'clock before the first drop falls."

While they waited, Bernard fished a bottle of Scotch out of his desk drawer and poured Corbett a large shot. Among them, it was never too early.

"I'm retiring next month. Going to settle in Victoria. Had enough of these damn winters."

"Will Frobisher be taking your place?" Bernard asked, suddenly alert.

"Nope. He's going to Ottawa. They've already sent in a new fella. Just a kid. His name's Smith. Bertram Smith."

"Well, let me have his address and I'll send him a case of Johnny Walker Red to welcome him into town."

"I wouldn't do that, Bernie, if I was you."

"What are you trying to tell me?"

"Smith's a teetotaller."

"Married?"

"Nope."

"I bet I've got just the girl for him."

"He's a regular church-goer, Bernie. A troop leader with the Boy Scouts."

Three weeks passed before Bert Smith made his first appearance at the warehouse. At first glance, Bernard took him for another unemployed farm boy looking for a day's work, he walked so softly and seemed so unsure of himself. Smith was scrawny, dry brown hair parted in the middle, pale as a plucked chicken, grey eyes with pupils like nailheads, blade of a nose blackhead peppery, hardly any lips, just a line there clamped shut, and a receding chin. His suit, too large for him, was neatly pressed and his black leather shoes shone. Once he introduced himself, Bernard grasped why he kept his mouth shut so tight. His crowded teeth were not so much irregular as running off in every which direction, the puffy gums an angry red. And his breath came hot and smelly. "I'm the new customs agent," Smith said.

"It's very thoughtful of you to come by to say hello. What do you say we grab a coffee and a blueberry pie at The Regent?"

They sat together in a booth.

"Where are you from?"

"Saskatoon."

"Isn't that my favourite town?"

"I came to inquire about the four carloads of bonded whisky you've got lying on a railroad siding."

"You got a hero, Bert? Jesus aside."

"Jesus was not a hero, Mr. Gursky. He is our Saviour."

"Goddamn right he is. I meant no disrespect."

"Those who do not accept him can never enter the Kingdom of Heaven."

Or the Manitoba Club, you little rat, Bernard thought, but never mind. "Risky risky," he said, "that's life. And death too, if I take your point correctly."

"Yes."

"Me, my hero is Baden-Powell. You know, the best years of my life were in the Boy Scouts and it really pains me that the troops here haven't got a proper meeting hall. We'd like to contribute to that, the Gurskys, and we'd be honoured if you served as treasurer, taking charge of the funds at the committee's disposal."

"I would like to know if your bonded whisky is really for re-export and, if so, I want to see evidence of its final destination."

"Papers papers. When it comes to paperwork you're looking at a guy who takes the booby-prize. Give me a couple of days and I'll find the documents."

"I'll be back next Wednesday," Smith said, and on his way out he paid for his own coffee and blueberry pie.

Bernard, sniffing trouble, was filled with unease. Then, returning to the office, sifting through the monthly bank statements, his unease flared into red-hot anger, and he hurried over to The Victory Hotel, pulling Solomon away from the poker table, and presenting him with the evidence. "I've found you out," he hollered, waving cancelled cheques at him, cheques endorsed by Solomon. "Look at this. $3,000 to Billy Sunday. $3,500 to the Anti-Saloon League. And here's another one. $2,500 to Alphonso Alva Hopkins. You invented that name. Admit it."

"Why, Mr. Hopkins is a writer and editor of great distinction. In 1915 he campaigned to have the name of German measles changed to victory or liberty measles, and now he is even more adamantly opposed to the scum of besodden Europe — people like us, Bernie — corrupting the Christian youth of this once-pure continent with booze."

"If you ask me none of these cheques are going where you say, but they are covering your poker losses right here in the hotel."

"I'll get back to my game now."

"The hell you will. Tell me what the fuck is going on!"

"We're investing in the future."

Two days later Nebraska became the thirty-sixth state to ratify the Eighteenth Amendment. Prohibition would be enforced a year later.

"Bernard, you driven, greedy bastard," Solomon said, "Bernard, you're going to be richer than you imagined in your wildest dreams."

In his excitement, Bernard forgot to tell Solomon about Bertram Smith, and that he would be coming back the following week.

FIVE

◆

The necessary customs documents for the bonded whisky were not produced, contrary to Bernard's promise, so Smith had no choice but to report the infraction to the Regina office. He was rebuked for his zeal. Then, patrolling a border road one evening, Smith saw two "Whisky Six" Studebakers racing south, riding low on their springs under a full load of booze. The bootleggers promptly switched on their rear windshield searchlights, trying to blind their pursuer, but Smith pulled ahead and cut them off at the border. The bootleggers turned out to be three defiant, unemployed construction workers out of North Dakota. They giggled at the sight of their scrawny, snaggle-toothed captor. "Jeez, sonny, you ain't gonna shoot us, are ya?"

Smith established that the three Americans had crossed the border illegally the night before and, consequently, had to be detained until they paid double duty on their cars, some $1,850, that would be reimbursed once they returned to the States.

"Hey, why don't you just be a good boy and take us to town, where the Gurskys will straighten you out."

Bernard arranged for Smith to meet with him, Solomon,

and Morrie in the warehouse office, Tim Callaghan also in attendance.

"It was good of you to come here today, Mr. Smith," Solomon said. "May I pour you a drink?"

"He doesn't."

"Such a nice boy," Morrie said.

"A *putz* you mean," Bernard said, "just like you."

"Is there anything I can offer you?"

"No."

"How about money. Plenty of it," Bernard sang out, opening the safe and tossing bundles of banknotes on to the desk. "You could get your teeth fixed. Buy a suit that fits. A car. A house, even. The girls you could get. Wowee!"

"Precisely how much money is on the table?" Smith asked.

"Ten thousand dollars," Bernard said, brightening.

Smith took out his fountain pen and made a note on his pad.

"But maybe if I counted it again it could come to fifteen."

"I intend to see you and your brothers in prison."

"Would that give you pleasure?" Solomon asked.

"You and your sort will have to learn once and for all that not everybody has his price."

"You know what you're asking for, Mr. Fucken Boy Scout Troop Leader," Bernard shouted, "Mr. Eighteen-Dollars-a-Week Pipsqueak, you're asking for trouble, eh? Big big trouble."

"I intend to report your threats verbatim," Smith said, scribbling on his pad again.

"You heard that? Threats yet. Well fuck you, sonny, I don't threaten cockroaches. I squash them," Bernard said, rubbing his heel into the floor, "like this."

"Mr. Callaghan, you are a witness to this attempted bribe and to the threats to my person. I expect you to testify accordingly in court."

"I'm Tim's boss, not you, *cacker*. Jeez, why didn't you ever do anything about those teeth of yours? Look at him, guys," Bernard said, heaving with laughter, "I'll bet he hasn't even busted his cherry yet."

"You're disgusting."

Solomon said he wished to speak to Smith alone. Grudgingly, Bernard stepped outside, followed by Morrie, Callaghan starting after.

"I'm leaving too," Smith said, "unless Mr. Callaghan stays."

"You want a witness?" Solomon asked.

"Yes."

So Callaghan remained behind.

"I want to assure you, in the presence of Mr. Callaghan, that even if you choose to testify against us nothing will happen to you."

"I'm not afraid."

"I admire you for it, honestly, but the deck is stacked against you. Your superiors, grossly underpaid, are not nearly so fastidious. Far from appreciating your ardour they will crush you for it. Don't testify, Smith."

"I was both threatened here and offered a bribe."

"Yes, but circumstances will oblige me to deny it, and Callaghan will lie for my sake."

"But he'll be under oath."

"Swearing on a Bible?"

"Yes, sir," Smith said, infuriated with himself for the "sir," but there was something in Solomon that compelled it.

"Oh Smith, Smith, if it's justice you're after, don't bother looking for it in this world, wait for the next. I've got enough on my conscience without you. Take the money or leave it, as you see fit, but don't stick your neck out."

Once he had gone, Solomon poured himself a Scotch and then passed the bottle to Callaghan. "Did you know, Tim, that John Calvin attended the same school in Paris as Rabelais? Le Collège de Montaigu."

"And what if I don't care to swear on a Bible and then lie for your sake on a witness stand?"

"That would really make things interesting."

Bernard was back, Morrie trailing after. "Softsoaping him got you nowhere, eh?"

"He's a man of principle."

"So you're sending for somebody."

"I promised that nothing would happen to him."

"Hey, that was big of you, but I didn't. Meyer would help. Little Farfel owes us. Phone him. Or maybe Longy better."

"Forget it."

"Good good. We'll go to prison and learn how to sew mailbags or stamp licence plates. Why should other guys have all the fun? *Say something, Morrie.*"

"What should I say?"

"Say you don't want to go to prison."

"I don't want to go to prison."

"With him for a brother who needs a parrot? Come on, Solomon. Send for somebody."

"What did you make of Smith, Tim?"

Callaghan shrugged. He looked troubled.

"What if that's the size the saints are now? Bad teeth. Boils on their neck. Consumed with hatred."

Morrie approached Solomon. "In your honest opinion," he asked, "is he dangerous?"

"Yes."

"Watch," Bernard said, "he's going to run to the toilet now."

Morrie froze in the middle of the room.

"What are you going to do? Wet your pants just because I called the shot? Go, for Christ's sake." Then Bernard turned on Callaghan. "I'd like to have a word alone with my brothers, if you don't mind."

"Sure," Callaghan said, leaving.

"Tim could testify against us to save his own neck."

"Wouldn't you?"

"Speak to Meyer. Send for somebody."

Solomon poured himself another drink.

"You think it doesn't go against my nature?" Bernard asked.

SIX

◆

Among the dusty stacks of Gursky memorabilia that cluttered Moses's cabin was a copy of *The Cunarder* for May 1933. Featured articles included "In Havana, Gay Capital of Cuba" and "Czechoslovakia's Winter Jollity". There was also a double-page spread of "Some Trans-Atlantic Personalities" posing on the decks of the *Berengaria*, *Aquitania*, *Caronia* and *Mauretania*. Among them were the Duchess of Marlborough, the former Miss Consuelo Vanderbilt; Madame Luisa Tetrazzini, a star of the New York Metropolitan Opera House; and Mrs. George F. Gould, "*Filiae pulchrae, mater pulcherior* might have been coined to describe Mrs. Gould." The photograph next to that of Mrs. Gould was one of Solomon Gursky. "Nothing at the moment is more in the public eye than a possible end to the enforcement of Prohibition in the United States. Above is seen a prominent Canadian distiller intimately connected with the looming wet invasion of America. He is smiling against the deck plating of the *Aquitania*, where he allowed himself to be photographed on a recent trip to England."

Moses had noted on a file card, attached to *The Cunarder* with a paper clip, that several months earlier — on February 27, 1933 to be precise — the American House of Represen-

tatives and the Senate had passed a resolution to repeal the
Eighteenth Amendment. The resolution called for ratification
of Repeal by a majority vote of state conventions in thirty-six
states. Franklin Delano Roosevelt, an acknowledged wet, was
sworn in as the thirty-second president of the United States on
March 4 and early in April it became legal to sell 3.2 percent
beer. H.L. Mencken sampled a glass of the new brew in the bar
of the Rennert Hotel in Baltimore. "Not bad at all," he said.
"Fill it again."

Solomon sailed for England in May, ostensibly bound for
Edinburgh, where he was to seek a partnership in the
American market with the powerful McCarthy Distillers
Limited of Lochnagar, just above Balmoral. But over the next
three months there was nothing but the occasional teasing
postcard from Solomon. Postcards from Berlin and Munich
and London and Cambridge and finally Moscow. Meanwhile
a fulminating Mr. Bernard was not idle. He acquired a
distillery in Ontario and another in Tennessee. Solomon
returned to Montreal early in October.

"What happened in Scotland?" Mr. Bernard demanded,
his eyes bulging.

"You know damn well I never got there. You go,
Bernie."

"I need your permission? Like hell I do."

Mr. Bernard sailed late in October only to find that the
Scots liquor barons considered him not quite the right sort to
represent their interests in America now that Prohibition was
about to end. In fact, they seemed amused by his presumption.
A bristling Mr. Bernard was in London, staying at the Savoy,
when Utah became the thirty-sixth Repeal State, making the
news official. November 20 that was, and the headline in the
Evening News read:

PROHIBITION IS DEAD—
THE MORMONS KILLED IT—
WHOOPEE
HAPPY DAYS ARE HERE AGAIN

Solomon, to Mr. Bernard's bewilderment, did not mock
him for coming home empty-handed. Solomon had put a

short-wave radio and a cot into his office. Unsavoury, shifty-eyed little strangers, wearing funny European-style suits, dribbling cigarette ash everywhere, met with him there and left with their pockets bulging with cash.

"What are we buying?" Mr. Bernard asked.

"Kikes."

"You'll make fun of me once too often."

Solomon had already made the first of what would become many infuriating trips to Ottawa, this time to see Horace MacIntyre, the deputy minister of immigration. MacIntyre, a bachelor and church elder, was celebrated throughout the civil service for his rectitude. If he mailed a personal letter from his office he dropped two cents into a box for the postage.

MacIntyre listened to Solomon's plea for the refugees with some impatience. "Let's not hide behind euphemisms, Mr. Gursky. By refugees you mean Jews."

"I had been told that you were a most perspicacious and forthright man."

"Jews tend to be classified as 'non-preferred immigrants' not because of their race, which prejudice I would find repugnant, but because they consider work in agriculture or mining beneath their dignity."

"My grandfather worked in the mines in England before he came here in 1846, and my father was a farmer on the prairies."

"But I understand that you have since found more profitable employment."

Solomon smiled his gleeful smile.

"It is because your people are such confirmed city-dwellers, and would usurp positions that could be filled by the native-born, or immigrants from the Mother Country, that we simply cannot open the flood-gates."

"As the population of this country is presently constituted, the Jews make up no more than 1.5 percent," Solomon said, and then he went on to describe some of the things he had seen in Germany.

"As it happens," MacIntyre said, "I am an admirer of the writings of Mr. Walter Lippmann, a co-religionist of yours though somewhat demure about it. He is of the opinion that the persecution of the Jews serves a useful purpose by satisfying the German need to conquer somebody. In fact, it's his considered opinion that it is a kind of lightning rod which protects Europe. Of course it's a nuisance, Mr. Gursky, but there is no need to panic."

Come summer Mr. Bernard was on the boil. It was rumoured that the prime minister intended to put the Gursky brothers in jail and throw away the key. The government case against them pending, the Gurskys bound to be charged with, among other things, avoiding customs duty on smuggled liquor, Mr. Bernard huddled with his lawyers every night, enraged with Solomon who sat silent throughout the sessions, seemingly indifferent to their fate. And now it was Mr. Bernard who flitted between Montreal and Ottawa once, sometimes twice, a week, lugging large sums of cash in his attaché case and returning with paintings by Jean-Jacques Martineau, which he threw into a cupboard. Such was the state of his nerves that a month passed before he noticed Morrie's absence.

Charging into their original Montreal offices on Sherbrooke Street one morning, kicking open office doors, searching toilets, he demanded, "Where's my brother?"

"Take it easy, Mr. Bernard," Tim Callaghan said.

Irish drunk. Christ-lover. "Oh yeah. Why?"

"Because the way you're carrying on these days, you're asking for an ulcer."

"I don't get ulcers. I give them. Where in the fuck is Morrie?"

Solomon was sent for.

"Did you actually hit him with an ashtray?" Solomon asked.

"Only a fool wouldn't have ducked."

"Morrie's had enough of you. He's tired of bringing up his breakfast every morning. He's retired to the country with Ida and the kids."

Mr. Bernard descended on Morrie's secretary. Terrified, she drew a map that would enable him to find Morrie's place in the Laurentians. Threatened, she told him about Morrie's workshop. Cursed, spat at, she snitched about the furniture-making. Mr. Bernard fired her. "Take your handbag and that nail file, the sound drives me crazy, and take your ten-cents-a-gallon perfume from Kresge's and your Kotex box and get the hell out of here." Then he called for his limousine and sped out to Ste.-Adèle.

Morrie, forewarned, waited in the living room, his head resting on Ida's lap. Then he roused himself and stood by the window, cracking his knuckles. When Mr. Bernard finally pulled into the long driveway and pounced out of his limousine, he did not start immediately for the large renovated farmhouse on the hill overlooking the lake. Instead, a startled Morrie watched him make straight for the vegetable garden. Yanking out tomato plants. Trampling on lettuce beds. Kicking over cabbages. Jumping up and down on eggplants, popping them. Pulling a pitchfork free of a manure pile and swinging away at corn stalks. Then he rushed to the front door, pounding on it with his fists. "Look at my suit! Look at my shoes! I'm covered in farm shit."

He squirted right into the dining room, pulling a linen cloth off the table, sending a vase of roses crashing to the pine floor, and wiping his hands and then his shoes clean of eggplant pulp.

"Tell him that you're not going back!" Ida shrieked.

"What was your father? A little Jew in a grocery store with a scale that gave fourteen ounces to the pound, living in a shack that didn't even have an inside toilet. You went into the outhouse for a crap, you had to guard your balls against bumblebees. Now you wear diamonds and mink I risked life and limb to pay for. Go to your room at once. I have to talk to my brother."

Ida fled, pausing at the top of the stairs to shout "Hitler!" before slamming the bedroom door and locking it from the inside.

"If God forbid she was my wife I'd teach her some manners let me tell you. What did you pay for this dump?"

Morrie told him.

"How many acres?"

"Thirty."

"Big deal. If I wanted a place in the country, I'd have a hundred acres at least and I'd be on the sunny side of the lake in a bigger house, where the floors didn't creak." He shook with laughter. "They must have seen you coming, you *putz*."

"I suppose so."

Mr. Bernard went to the window. "Is that," he asked, pointing at an obviously new clapboard building, "the workshop where you make the furniture?"

"Yes."

"I'm told that you accept orders for bookshelves and that you actually sell the stuff through a shop in Ste.-Adèle." Mr. Bernard scooped up a delicate side table. "You made this itsy-bitsy fuckshit table?"

"Yes."

"How much are you asking for it?"

"Ten dollars."

"I'll give you seven," Mr. Bernard said, counting out the bills, "because if you sell direct to me, you don't have to cut in the goy shopkeeper in Ste.-Adèle." Then he kicked over the table and jumped up and down on it. "You are my brother, you cuntlapper, and if the rich anti-Semites in Ste.-Adèle are buying your shit, it's only because they can say, hey, you know who made that crappy lopsided little table for me for ten dollars? Mr. Bernard's brother. You can't do this to me. I want you back in the office eight o'clock tomorrow morning, or I'll take an axe to that woodshop."

Morrie gathered together the remains of his table and set them down beside the fireplace.

Out of breath, Mr. Bernard subsided to the sofa. He wiped his face with a handkerchief. "What have you got for dinner?" he asked.

"Veal chops."

"What with?"

"Roast potatoes."

"I had that last night. Would she make me some *kasha* instead?"

"I could ask."

"Better say it's for you. Hey, remember Mama's *kishka*? She always had the biggest piece for me. But I was her favourite, eh?"

"Yes."

"What have you got for a starter?"

"There's some *borscht* from last night."

Mr. Bernard yawned. He stretched. He raised a buttock and farted. "Eddie Cantor's on tonight. You got a radio here?"

"The reception is not very good in the mountains."

"I suppose we could play some gin. Aw, forget it. I can eat better at my place. But a Popsicle would hit the spot. You wouldn't have any in the ice-box, would you?"

"Didn't I know you were coming?"

Morrie brought out a couple of Popsicles, crumpling the wrappers.

"Hey, what are you doing?" Mr. Bernard asked, retrieving the wrappers and flattening them out. "You fill out the coupon in back you can win a two-wheel bicycle. What time can I expect you back in the office tomorrow morning?"

Morrie began to crack his knuckles again.

"Morrie, be sensible for once. Without you, how am I going to settle my quarrels with Solomon? I need your vote so that I can beat him fair and square."

"I'm tired of being pressed in a vice between the two of you."

"Good. Tell him!" shrieked a voice from the top of the stairs.

An outraged Mr. Bernard shot out of the sofa, his arms extended, his fingers curled. Ready to scratch.

"If I ever made you *kasha* , you *oysvorf*, it would be sprinkled with arsenic," Ida shouted, scooting back into her room and this time shoving her dresser against the door.

"You have no idea what Solomon's like now," Mr. Bernard said, sinking back into the sofa, "our crazy brother. We were better off when he was chasing nooky. Now he stays overnight in the office, sometimes with Callaghan, the two of them knocking back a quart each, and he listens to the shortwave radio, fiddling with the dial all night. Hitler makes a speech, he never misses it."

"I'm not coming back to the office any more."

"I'll give you until Monday morning out here, but that's it."

Mr. Bernard got home after dark, but he knew better than to telephone Solomon at his place. There was no point. He was

never there. And in the morning Mr. Bernard discovered that
Solomon was in Ottawa again, stirring things up, at a time
when the last thing the Gurskys needed was more enemies in
high places.

Solomon told MacIntyre, "I have acquired two thousand
acres of farmland in the Laurentians as well as — "

"Where in the Laurentians?" MacIntyre demanded.

"Not far from Ste.-Agathe. Why do you ask?"

"Oh, Ste.-Agathe," MacIntyre said, relieved. "For years
now I've taken my holidays winter and summer at Chalet
Antoine in Ste.-Adèle. Do you know it?"

"No. I've acquired two thousand acres, as well as a large
herd of beef and dairy cattle, and I have a list of people who
promise to settle there."

"Mr. Gursky, are you seriously asking me to consider
placing more Jews in the province of Quebec?"

"And why not?"

MacIntyre sent for a file. "Look at this, will you?" It was
an editorial page clipping from *Le Devoir*. "The Jewish
shopkeeper on St. Lawrence Boulevard does nothing to
increase our natural resources." Then he passed him a copy of
a petition that had been delivered to parliament by Wilfred
Lacroix, a Liberal MP. The petition, signed by more than
120,000 members of the St. Jean Baptiste Society opposed
"all immigration and especially Jewish immigration" to
Quebec.

"If it would facilitate matters, I could buy land in Ontario
or the Maritimes."

"I am overwhelmed by the prodigality of your purse,
Mr. Gursky, but there is a problem. Yours is a race apart
with — how shall I put it? — an exasperating penchant for
organizing their affairs better than other people. This endless
agitation to flood this country with relatives and friends or
so-called farmers must stop. My hands are tied. I'm sorry."

When Solomon returned to the old McTavish building the
next morning, he discovered Mr. Bernard lying in wait for
him.

"How did you make out?" Solomon asked.

"Morrie wouldn't listen to reason."

"Let him be, Bernie."

"Listen, there's a trial coming up. Bert Smith is spilling the beans everywhere. I get on the witness stand, prejudiced people think I haven't got an honest face. You get on the stand you will be so fucken arrogant the judge will hate you. Morrie's a sweetheart. Everybody loves him. But he's got to be coached. So pull yourself together and bring him back here."

"I have business in Ste.-Adèle a week Wednesday. I'll look in on Morrie, but I'm not making any promises."

Solomon's business was at the Chalet Antoine, the most elegant resort in Ste.-Adèle, rising from a hilltop thick with pine and cedar and silver birch, commanding a view of Lac Renault that the travel brochures described as ravishing. A notice posted on the gate read:

RESTRICTED CLIENTELE ONLY

It was late on a fine summer's afternoon when Solomon got there. He made right for the bar that was tastefully done in natural pine with a low beamed ceiling. There was a painting of Howie Morenz cutting in on the net. There were also photographs of Red Grange, Walter Hagen, and Bill Tilden. French doors opened on to a flagstone terrace bordered by beds of gladioli, overlooking the tennis courts and the lake. There were six guests in the bar. A stout middle-aged couple at one table, obviously just back from the golf course. She wore a tartan skirt and he was in knickerbockers. A man, alone, pondering the stock market pages in the *Star*. A man and woman at another table. He, staring stonily into the middle distance; she, intent on her copy of *Anthony Adverse*. And then a lovely young lady seated alone, sipping white wine, writing a letter on rice-paper stationery, the sort that could only be ordered from abroad. Honey-coloured hair caught in an ivory clasp. Red painted mouth full but severe. She wore a striped beach shirt, a pleated navy blue skirt and tennis shoes. Magazines littered her table top. *Vanity Fair, Vogue*. When Solomon sailed in, she looked up — squinting just a little, obviously near-sighted — and then returned to her letter. Interloper dismissed.

Solomon sat down, unfolded a Yiddish newspaper, and summoned the waiter. "*Du whisky, s'il vous plaît. Glenlivet.*"

The man who had been staring into the middle distance leaned over to say something to his wife. She set down her book and reached for her handbag, securing it on her lap. Distress darkened the golfers' table like the wind before a violent rain. But the young lady who was seated alone continued to write her letter.

Paul, the burly, hirsute waiter, went to fetch the manager and led him to Solomon's table. M. Raymond Morin. A capon with a handlebar moustache.

"Ah," Solomon said, "*le patron.*" And he repeated his order.

"I must ask you to leave."

"Oh, don't be so fatuous, Raymond," the young lady seated alone called out, "serve him his drink and be done with it."

"There are other bars . . ."

"*Dépêches-toi, mon vieux,*" Solomon said.

Then the man who had been pondering the *Star*'s stock market pages said, "I can appreciate your finding this hotel's policy offensive, but I can't grasp why anybody would want to drink where they are not welcome."

"Your argument is not without merit," Solomon said.

"Paul, call the police."

"You needn't bother, M. Morin. They're on their way," Solomon said, and then he repeated his order.

"It's against our policy to serve your kind."

"You tell him, Ray," the golfer's wife said.

"I bought this hotel yesterday afternoon."

"Don't make me laugh."

"And, as for these two," Solomon said, indicating the golfer and his wife, "I want them out of here before dinner."

"Cheek."

The young lady seated alone put down her pen. "Ah well then, in that case the hotel's policy hasn't changed, only the nature of the clientele prohibited." Then she gathered her things together and retreated to the terrace.

The reader of the stock market pages smiled.

"Are you a lawyer?" Solomon asked.

"I'm afraid I'm already committed to representing the other side, Mr. Gursky."

"The law was an ass."

"But it's all we've got. And there's still a body or two unaccounted for."

"But not Bert Smith's. Wasn't that decent of me?"

"More likely foolish."

"This country has no tap root. Instead there's Smith. The very essence."

Two provincial policemen arrived: Coté and Pinard. "What can we do to help, Mr. Gursky?"

"I am the manager here," M. Morin protested.

"Don't make a fool of yourself, Raymond," the lawyer said. "If Mr. Gursky says he has really bought this white elephant, I expect it must be the case. Somebody has put one over on him."

"Actually the hotel's completely booked from Friday afternoon, but I do appreciate your concern."

"Glad to be of help. Incidentally I'm Stuart MacIntyre. I believe you're acquainted with my brother Horace."

"Indeed I am!"

"He's joining me here on Friday."

Solomon slipped out to the terrace. She sat at the far table, the sun in her hair and on her bare arms. "Have you really bought the hotel?" she asked.

"Yes. May I sit down?"

"Are you sufficiently wealthy to buy all the restricted hotels in the Laurentians?"

"I ought to introduce myself."

"I know who you are and what you are, Mr. Gursky. I'm Diana Morgan. And there's no need to stare. You're quite right. One eye is blue and the other is brown. Will they send you to prison?"

"I doubt it."

"Don't underestimate Stu MacIntyre."

"You know him, of course."

"His wife's a Bailey. She's my aunt. Stu and my father go duck hunting together."

"How long will you be staying here?"

"I come here for tennis lessons. We have a cottage near by."

"Have dinner with me."

She shook her head, no. "Your brother is making a bookcase for me. He's such a sweet man."

Rising, Solomon said, "I apologize for what happened in there."

"You were looking forward to a real donnybrook, weren't you?"

"Yes," he said, surprised.

"You don't understand. Those boring but nice people in there abhor a scene even more than they dislike Jews."

"I don't give a damn about the people in there."

"What do you give a damn about?"

"I'm looking for the Kingdom of Prester John," he said, retreating back into the hotel.

Prester John. She wanted to call him back. Stay, she thought, talk to me some more, Mr. Solomon Gursky. But bloody Stu was sitting in the bar. Even as things stood, he was bound to report to her father. Her luck. Oh well, she thought, if she hurried home there would still be time for a swim before dinner.

Solomon, standing by the window, watched her stride toward her car, a dark green Biddle and Smart sports phaeton. He lingered by the window until she drove off.

"Couldn't get to first base with her, could you, Gursky?"

And then Solomon turned back to the room and found himself face to face with the golfer, the latter's eyes dancing with malice.

"Don't you dare condescend to me," Solomon said, lunging, grabbing the golfer by the throat and slamming him against the wall. *More than a hundred years after Maimonides had written his* Guide for the Perplexed, *your ancestors, pledging each other's health in cups of their own blood, were living in mean sod huts, sleeping on bare boards wrapped in their filthy plaids.*

"Let go of him," the golfer's wife screamed.

Spinoza had already written his Ethics *when your forebears still had their children wearing amulets to ward off the evil eye and carried fire in a circle around their cattle to keep them safe from injury.*

"Please, Mr Gursky. He's choking."

Solomon yanked the golfer forward, then shoved him back hard, bouncing his head against the wall. His wife screamed again. Then the two provincial police moved in, breaking Solomon's grip on the golfer. "Hey, that's enough," Pinard said. "Enough."

SEVEN

◆

Plump, foolish Ida, her makeup too thick, greeted him at the door. Solomon had come bearing gifts. A flask of scent for her. An enormous teddy bear for Barney. Then he presented Morrie with a complete set of bench stones in an aromatic cedar box; a set of rasps and rifflers, imported from England; and a jack plane made of red beech.

"He's not going back to the office," Ida said.

Solomon rocked Ida in his arms, kissing her pulpy cheeks. "My God, Ida, you look ten years younger. If you weren't married to my brother I'd be chasing you around the room right now."

"We could always give him a quarter and send him to the movies, that one."

"How long can you stay?" Morrie asked.

"A few days maybe."

"Wonderful," Morrie said, frightened.

Solomon brought them up to date on Montreal. How difficult it was to sleep, it had turned so hot. "Honestly," he said, "you're better off right here."

"You should have brought Clara and the kids with you," Ida said, fishing.

King Kong, with Fay Wray, was playing at the Palace,

Solomon said, and there was a new Jean Harlow at the
Loew's. Everybody was singing the hit song from the new Moss
Hart and Irving Berlin show. Solomon, who had brought the
record with him, put it on the victrola.

> She started a heat wave,
> By letting her seat wave.
> And in such a way that the customers say,
> That she certainly can can-can.

Ida played the record again and shimmied along with it.
"Isn't anybody going to dance with me?" she asked.

"No," Morrie said.

At dinner, Ida warned Solomon to not so much as dip his
little toe into the lake. It hadn't been quarantined like the
North River in Prévost. It wasn't nearly as bad as Montreal,
where all the children's day camps had been shut down. But
there were already nine polio cases confirmed in Ste.-Agathe,
six in Ste.-Adèle. "Don't even brush your teeth with water
from the tap. I'll bring a jug of freshly boiled to your bedroom
in the morning."

"Solange can bring it to him."

"Hey there, Barney McGoogle, ain't he my brother-in-
law?"

Solomon refilled Ida's wine glass and then demanded a tour
of the woodwork shop. Morrie vacillated.

"Well, I'm not afraid of what will happen to *me* in the dark.
I'll take him," Ida said.

"You wait here."

"Secrets," Ida called after them. "Dirty jokes maybe. You
think I couldn't do with a laugh?"

The workshop was fired by a wood-fed boiler. The craftsman's bench was built in the traditional European style,
made of steamed beech with a rubbed-oil finish. There was a
large front vice, bench dog holes in front and a recessed tool
trough running along the back. Solomon wandered into the
rear and passed his hands over the planks stacked neatly in
steel trays. Pine, oak, cedar, butternut and cherry wood. He
went on to admire all the tools mounted just so on pegged

boards or resting on shelves. Mallets, moulding and scrub and block planes, skew and butt chisels, roughing gouges, special bow and fret saws, dowelling jigs and pins and a threading kit.

"I know I have to testify at the trial," Morrie said. "Don't worry. I'll get everything right."

"Did you make this yourself?"

A kitchen chair. Solomon sat on it.

"You've seen enough. Let's go."

"And this bookcase?" Solomon asked, passing his hand over the one slightly jagged edge.

"It was ordered by a customer. A lady. Let's go now."

Solomon sat down at the craftsman's bench and toyed with the vice. "Will she pick it up or do you deliver?"

"She's supposed to come for it a week from Friday with her caretaker. They have a small truck."

"Invite her to tea."

"I knew something was up. Listen here, Mr. Skirt-Chaser, she happens to be Sir Russell Morgan's granddaughter. Please, Solomon." He cracked his knuckles and sighed. "You only just get here practically and already my heart is hammering. Okay, okay, I'll invite her to tea. But only if you swear you won't try any monkey business."

"Would you let me try my hand at making something in here?"

"You've got to be kidding. It takes training. A lot of my tools are very delicate."

Ida hollered from the kitchen window. "Have I got B.O. and even my best friends won't tell me?"

"I'll be careful with your tools."

Early the next morning Morrie drove Barney to Count Gzybrzki's stables for a ride on a shetland pony. Ida, perfumed and powdered, hurried to Solomon's bedroom. "Ready or not here I come with a jug of water," she called out, all giggly. "But no funny stuff, eh?"

The bed was empty.

Ida was brooding over a third cup of coffee with toast and strawberry jam before Morrie got back.

"I thought he was with you," Ida said.

"You'll never believe this, but Solomon's in the workshop trying to make something. Whatever it is, let's tell him it's wonderful."

"I'll take him lunch."

"Neither of us is to even go near the shop until he's finished in there. He took the keys. He says what he's making has to be a surprise."

"Oh, for me!"

"Don't be ridiculous."

"Don't be ridiculous. He looks at me I can tell he's undressing me with his eyes."

Solomon had begun work at six-thirty, firing the boiler. Then he rooted about for some framing squares and sorted out mallets and chisels and other essential tools. He retrieved four drawer pulls mixed up with other fixtures from a large bucket. They were flush-fitting and made from cast brass. Exactly what he wanted. Sifting through the lumber that was stacked on the steel trays, he was tempted by the bird's-eye maple, but finally settled on the wild cherry wood. Difficult to work with, but strong. It was light brown, but of an amber hue at the heart that would darken further with age, its pores following the outline of the growth ring boundary. He sorted out the planks, sniffing and stroking them, and then he studied them for checking and warping. There was more than sufficient lumber for his needs. A good thing, because Solomon anticipated a lot of wastage. Except for the drawer pulls, not one nail, not one screw, would compromise his work. All the joints would be tongue-and-groove or else mortise-and-tenon. The piece he had in mind for her was a dressing table. She would keep her diary, rich in girlish surmise, in one drawer, and the jewels he would astonish her with in another. There would, no doubt, be fragrant sachets in each drawer. On the surface, a silver candlestick, a crystal bowl filled with pot pourri, her vanity set. On a hot summer's evening, the window open to catch the breeze from the lake, she would sit there brushing her thick honey-coloured hair, counting the strokes.

Solomon was determined to finish the table by Friday noon, but the first day he was content to square his lumber, smoothing the edges with a joiner plane.

He had met her father once. A big man, barrel-chested. My name is Russell Morgan, Jr., K.C., look on my inheritance, ye mighty, and despair. He was active in the Empire League and a colonel in the Black Watch. He was the inept, hard-drinking senior partner in Morgan, MacIntyre and Maclean, whom the younger partners tolerated only because of his esteemed name and useful Square Mile connections. He was a notorious snob. But, to be fair, there was also something quixotic in his nature. Twice he had stood for parliament in Montreal as a Tory and twice he had gone down to inevitable defeat. Once, a Liberal heckler planted at one of his meetings put a question to him in French. Russell Morgan Jr. tried to dismiss him with a wave of his hand, but the heckler persisted. "Is it possible," he demanded, "that your family has been here all these years and you still do not speak French?"

"It is no more necessary for me to speak French, my good man, than it would be contingent upon me to understand Chinese if I lived in Hong Kong."

Mr. Bernard, terrified by rumours that the brilliant Stuart MacIntyre might be representing the government in court, had foolishly approached the firm himself. Russell Morgan, Jr. had never heard of anything so outrageous. So Mr. Bernard, compounding his folly, tried to seduce him with numbers.

"Oh, isn't that rich, boys?"

Finally Mr. Bernard played his ace in the hole. "I wonder if you are aware that your grandfather and mine were once involved in a business negotiation? The New Camelot Mining & Smelting Company."

"Miss Higgins will show you to the door, Gursky, as surely as Stu MacIntyre will see you and your brothers behind bars where you belong. Good-day."

The light was failing when Solomon slipped into the kitchen to find a sour Ida waiting for him.

"Ida, you look adorable."

Her shoulder-length permed hair had been gathered into a flat rolled chignon. She wore a black lace dress by Chanel, that threatened to split at the seams. "It's nothing," she said, sucking in a breath.

Barney had already eaten and been put to bed when Ida served dinner by candlelight. Morrie, bubbling with good humour, said, "Maybe I should take him on as an apprentice. What do you think, Ida?"

Solomon was out of the house at six-thirty every morning and didn't return until nightfall. But he didn't spend all of his time in the workshop. He also went for walks. Once he saw her from a distance. At ease in her rose garden, cutting blooms for the table. She wore a broadbrimmed straw hat with a pink bow. *She will keep the book she is reading on the surface of her table. It will be encased in a tooled leather slipcover with a red silk bookmark. Say*, Sense and Sensibility *or Dr. Johnson's* Lives of the Poets. *He will read aloud to her at night. He would tell her about Ephraim in Van Diemen's Land and on the* Erebus *and how her grandfather had held him prisoner in that hotel in Sherbrooke.*

"Say," Ida said, "could you use a sweeper-upper in there? I charge two bits an hour, but no pinching."

"It's a surprise," Morrie said. "I told you. We're not allowed in there."

"Oh, did you remember, Morrie?" Solomon asked.

"Did he remember what?"

"Miss Diana Morgan is coming to tea," Morrie said, averting his eyes.

"Hey, I live here too. Why wasn't I told?"

"He's telling you now."

"If you think you're going to screw her, mister, you've got a surprise coming."

"Ida!" Morrie said.

"Ida! Pish pish. I'll bet even a milk bottle isn't safe alone in a room with Solomon. Poor Clara, that's all I can say." Ida shoved her chair back from the table and marched out of the dining room, pausing at the door. "She won't come, Solomon. At the last minute she'll have to shampoo her horsey-worsey or go to church for confession. Forgive me, Father, but on the hay ride last Saturday night Harry McClure kissed me on the lips and slipped his hand under my skirt. Describe it, my child."

"She's not a Catholic," Morrie said.

"Big deal. Neither am I."

"And who is Harry McClure?" Solomon asked.

"Just one of the many *young* men who are after her. I

mean talk about *naches*. She's by Sir Russell Morgan a granddaughter. I'd be practising my curtsies right now only I know
those people and she ain't coming to this house, her father sees
me on the road you'd think he'd stepped in dogshit."

The wild cherry wood table was finished by Friday noon.
Solomon covered it with a blanket, locked up, and went into
the house to bathe and change his clothes. Punctually, at 4:30,
a Ford pickup twisted into the long winding driveway leading to the house. Emile Boisvert, the Morgans' caretaker,
had come to collect the bookcase. "Miss Morgan sends her
apologies," he said. "She is not feeling well."

Solomon went directly to the workshop, picked up an axe
and, at the last minute, drove it not into the table but the floor.
Then he carried the table into the house, still covered with a
blanket.

"My surprise," Ida exclaimed, jumping up and down.

Solomon announced that he wouldn't be able to stay for
dinner, he had to get back to Montreal, and then he pulled the
blanket free and revealed the table.

"Now that's what I call a cabinet-maker," Ida said.

Morrie ran a hand over the surface of the table. He stooped to
stroke the legs. He opened and shut a drawer.

"Say something," Ida said, nudging him.

"It's beautiful."

Early the next morning Morrie trudged out to his workshop,
sat down at the craftsman's bench and held his head in his hands
and wept. He packed his tools away and covered both the bench
and his foot-pedal lathe with a sheet and then padlocked the
workshop from the outside, intending never to return again.

Ida had taken her bread and jam into the living room, where
she could admire the table as she munched.

"We're going back to Montreal," Morrie said.

Ida wiped her sticky fingers with a napkin and put the record
on the victrola again.

> She started a heat wave,
> By letting her seat wave.
> And in such a way that the customers say,
> That she certainly can can-can.

She shimmied. He watched.

EIGHT

◆

By the time Moses got to the Chalet Antoine, early one spring afternoon in 1968, it had changed hands many times. In its most recent reincarnation the chalet was a nursing home, septuagenarians sucking up sun on the flagstone terrace where Solomon had once told Diana about the Kingdom of Prester John. Moses didn't linger, but drove right on to the cottage on the lake that was still owned by Mr. Morrie. Happily, the French-Canadian caretaker, a convivial old man, was pleased to join Moses for a *crêpe aux pommes* and several beers in the village and then show him around the estate and the cottage.

"The family doesn't stay here any more," he said, "but Mr. Morrie keeps an eye on things. He may not come out for months at a time and then he's here twice in the same week."

The furniture was covered with sheets.

"What does he do when he visits?"

"Sometimes he can sit on that swing out there under the maple tree for hours, thinking about things."

The wood-workshop was locked. "Have you got a key?" Moses asked.

"Sorry, Mr. Berger, but I'm the only one allowed in there."

"I don't understand."

"Well, to keep all the machinery oiled, you know, the wood fed and polished, and to make sure there are no uninvited guests. Squirrels. Field mice."

"Does Mr. Morrie ever use it?"

"Funny you should ask. I caught him peering in that window once and I could swear he was crying. Hey, hold on a minute, Mr. Morrie, I'll run and get the key. No, no, he said. Not yet. But one day."

Then Moses continued on to what the locals still referred to with pride as the Sir Russell Morgan estate, where the elusive Diana had finally agreed to see him. Following a long meandering driveway, Moses drove slowly past a small apple orchard, a stand of sugar maple trees, stables, a barn, a tennis court, an immense greenhouse, a potting shed, an asparagus bed, a raspberry patch, and many more tilled beds, separated by brick walks, already planted with flowers and vegetables he imagined. There were clusters of daffodils here, there, and everywhere before the main house. White clapboard. Wraparound porch. Solid oak door with polished brass knocker. A maid led Moses into the solarium, where Diana McClure sat in a wingbacked wicker chair surrounded by greenery. One eye brown, one eye blue.

"It needn't be tea, Mr. Berger. I can offer you something more invigorating."

"Tea would be fine, thank you."

"As you pulled up, I couldn't help noticing that your front tires look distressingly soft. You must stop at M. Laurin's garage on your way back and have him check the pressure. First left just before you reach the bottom of the hill. If he's the least bit officious do tell him that I sent you."

"I'll do that," Moses said, mumbling something flattering about her gardens.

"It's a form of tyranny. Self-imposed, but tyranny all the same. I dare not leave here this time of year when everything will soon be coming up in such a frenzy."

"Including the black flies."

"Do you garden, then?"

"I'm new at it and not very good."

"Take my advice, then, and don't read too many books.

They will only discourage and confuse you. Get yourself a copy of Vita Sackville-West's *A Joy of Gardening* and follow her."

"I'll do that. Thank you."

"Shouldn't you write it down?"

"Yes," he said, fumbling for his pen. "It is very kind of you to let me intrude like this, Mrs. McClure."

"Not in the least, but I doubt that I can be of much help. May I ask you a direct question?"

"Certainly."

"You wrote to say you were working on a biography of Solomon Gursky. I do admire your industry, Mr. Berger, but who would be interested after all these years?"

"I am."

"The only valid reason for embarking on such a project. Now tell me why."

"Oh my. That's such a long and convoluted story."

"I'm in no hurry, if you aren't."

An apprehensive Moses gathered that he was being weighed on the scales of her intuitions, its measures unknown to him, and, all at once, found himself gabbing away like a silly schoolboy. Telling her about L.B. Lionel's birthday party. Ephraim Gursky. His involvement with Lucy. Henry in the Arctic. Then, suddenly, he stopped short, amazed at himself.

"Is the family co-operating?"

"No."

"There was no love lost between Solomon and Bernard."

"Why do you say that?"

"Oh come now, Mr. Berger. You'll have to do better than that," she said, laughing flirtatiously.

He blushed.

"If I may be so presumptuous, I think an excellent model for you might be *The Quest for Corvo* by A.J.A. Symons. Brilliant, I thought."

"Yes."

"Have you a publisher?"

"Um, no. I mean it's premature."

"I think McClelland & Stewart are the most adventurous of the lot here, though a touch vulgar in their promotions.

However, the likelihood is that they would be more interested in a biography of poor Mr. Bernard."

"Why 'poor' Mr. Bernard?" Moses asked, stiffening.

"I suspect," she said, smiling, "that you think I am badly disposed to him because he is a Jew."

"No," Moses lied.

"Don't you find it exhausting?"

"I beg your pardon?"

"I would."

"I'm not sure I understand."

"Being Jewish. For all its gratifications it coloured Solomon's reactions to everything. Like you, he always had his hackles raised. I am not an anti-Semite, Mr. Berger, and neither did I consider the bootlegging such a disgrace. On the contrary. It was frightfully clever and quite the only interesting thing about Mr. Bernard. I said 'poor' Mr. Bernard, because all he ever wanted out of our pathetic, so-called establishment was a seat in the senate. A modest enough demand. I would have awarded him two, happily."

"About Solomon."

"And me?" she asked.

"Yes."

"You have been told that we had an affair," she said, surprising him.

"Yes. But I don't mean to pry," he protested, stumbling.

"Of course you do, young man, or why are you here?"

"Sorry. You are absolutely right."

"This is hardly what I would describe as an age of discretion, Mr. Berger. I have seen the president of the United States pull out his shirt and lower his trousers on television to show us his abdominal scars. Public figures, if they be drunkards or womanizers or even swindlers, seem compelled to write steamy, self-pitying best-sellers about it, beating their breasts for profit. What I'm getting at," she said, her voice softening, "is that I'm afraid, much as I'd like to be helpful, that I couldn't tell you anything that might be hurtful to Mr. McClure or my son."

"At the risk of being rude, why did you agree to see me?"

"A reasonable question. A most justifiable question. Let me

think. Possibly because I'm a bored old lady and my curiosity got the better of me. Wait. There is something else. I have read your occasional book review in the *Spectator* or *Encounter* and I was not unimpressed by your intelligence. I took it that you were a young man of sensibility and I have not been disappointed."

Moses, beaming, wondered if it would be pushy of him to slip in that he had once been a Rhodes scholar. He decided against it.

"I need time, Mr. Berger. I must think about this very carefully."

Before he left, she had the gardener bring him a bundle of fresh asparagus. "Don't throw out the water you cook them in—for no longer than twelve minutes, as I'm sure you know, the crowns kept out of the water—and you will have the beginnings of a nourishing broth. And please do remember to see about your tire pressure or I shall worry about you on the road."

Driving back to Montreal, Moses was suffused with a feeling of well-being, unusual for him.

> Say I'm weary, say I'm sad,
> Say that health and wealth have missed me,
> Say I'm growing old, but add,
> Jenny kissed me.

Well, not quite. But Diana McClure née Morgan did describe me as a young man of intelligence and sensibility. Not bad, he thought.

NINE

◆

Instead of heading directly back to his cabin in the Townships, Moses drove in to Montreal, stopping at Callaghan's apartment. Inevitably, they fell to talking about Solomon.

"Solomon's jokes were always at somebody else's expense," Callaghan said, "but he was indifferent to the damage. Take that prank of buying the Chalet Antoine in Ste.-Adèle, for instance. Far from being overjoyed, the bunch from Fancy Finery were intimidated the minute they came spilling out of those chartered buses and saw what kind of hotel they were being put up at. Tennis courts. Lawn bowling. Croquet. Canoes. Instead of a bottle of seltzer at each table, a snobby waiter presenting them with a wine list and a menu they couldn't understand. *Pâté de fois gras. Ris de veau. Tournedos.* A couple of the more enterprising husbands piled into a pickup truck, drove out to Prévost, and came back with a sack of kosher chickens and briskets, gallon jars of sour pickles, stacks of rye bread and so forth, and their wives took over the kitchen. But then there were those bastards who gathered in boats offshore, come to gawk at the fat ladies taking the sun in their bras and bloomers and the men playing pinochle in their underwear. So the beneficiaries of Solomon's largesse, confined to the hotel for the most part, longed for nothing so much as the corner cigar & soda or the familiar front-door stoop. Moses, there are some eggs in the fridge if you're hungry. Mrs. Hawkins marks the hardboiled ones with an X for me."

Moses groaned.

"Okay, next time you flatter me with an unannounced visit I'll see to it that the larder is properly stocked. Pass the bottle."

"Here you go."

"If I had to mark the map I'd say it wasn't the trial, but Ste.-Adèle. Everything changed between the brothers after Ste.-Adèle. This is conjecture on my part but I think it was only then that Bernard grasped he would have to shaft Solomon if he was to survive himself. As for poor Morrie, castrating him would have been more merciful than humiliating him before his wife with that perfectly made cherry wood table. And Solomon, the insatiable Solomon, got his come-uppance at last. 'I know who you are and what you are, Mr. Gursky.' "

"I was out to see her in Ste.-Adèle this afternoon."

"Diana McClure?"

"Yup."

"And what did you find out?"

"That I'm in love."

"Seriously."

"It was incredible. She interviewed me, not me her. She was awfully polite, but she wouldn't say anything. There was her son to consider. Her husband."

"The son is worthless and Harry McClure's a boor. He's a regular at those appalling Beaver Club dinners. All got up in whiskers, goatee, frock coat and beaver hat. Excuse me," Callaghan said, rising, "but my bladder isn't what it used to be."

When Callaghan returned, he settled into his chair, reached for the bottle, and said, "Let me put it this way. Canada is not so much a country as a holding tank filled with the disgruntled progeny of defeated peoples. French-Canadians consumed by self-pity; the descendants of Scots who fled the Duke of Cumberland; Irish the famine; and Jews the Black Hundreds. Then there are the peasants from the Ukraine, Poland, Italy and Greece, convenient to grow wheat and dig out the ore and swing the hammers and run the restaurants, but otherwise to be kept in their place. Most of us are still huddled tight to the border, looking into the candy store window, scared by the Americans on one side and the bush on the other. And now that we are here, prospering, we do our damn best to exclude more ill-bred newcomers, because they remind us of our own mean origins in the draper's shop in Inverness or the *shtetl* or the bog. What was I talking about?"

"Solomon."

"Okay. Solomon. There are some things even a man of genius can never overcome and that's his origins. He was not her sort. Sure, her grandfather was a swindler, but he was knighted for his efforts. Like Sir Hugh Allan. Had the Jesuits or the rabbis got their hands on Diana she would have been the better for it, left with mysteries to conjure with, real baggage to check. But her school was Miss Edgar's and Miss Cramp's and what she learned there was never to cross her legs, and not to laugh out loud in the theatre or eat in public. She was brought up to believe that a lady only had her name in the newspaper three times: when she was born, when she married, and when she died. And hello, hello, along comes this notorious thundering Jew, who will not be denied, and she was both fascinated and terrified. She didn't turn up at the trial and he never forgave her for that. And she's just one chunk of the wreckage Solomon left in his wake. Damn him."

"I thought he was your friend."

"You don't understand anything. I count myself blessed that I knew a man of such roaring. I loved him."

Moses cooked the fresh asparagus for the two of them, supporting the crowns with crumpled foil to lift them out of the water, and then he asked Callaghan if he had an empty jar he could borrow.

"Whatever for?"

"The water will make a nourishing broth."

TEN

◆

Diana McClure's second letter, the one delivered post-humously, began:

Having rambled on at length once, and bid you a somewhat self-pitying adieu, here I am again, pen in hand.

Forgive me.

There was no boy with a fishing pole passing on his way to the brook, averting his eyes from my peeled egg of a head. But I thought it a permissible indulgence, a nice literary touch. Look at it this way. As an old lady sits in her wheelchair, grieving over what might have been, waiting for death, Huck Finn passes with his fishing pole. Life goes on. On reflection, most assuredly an image more maudlin than original. A lie, in any event.

You inquired about my first meeting with Solomon at the Chalet Antoine, when I was young and silly but passably pretty and he charged with such audacity and appetite and, above all, rage.

At the time, I would have sworn that I quit the bar for the terrace because I knew that Solomon's intrusion would culminate in violence and wished to avoid it.

Another fib. I was flirting, sending a signal. I wanted him
to join me on the terrace. But first I wanted him to follow
me with those hot eyes, watching me stride on limbs that
had not yet betrayed me and I still took for an
entitlement. Look, Solomon Gursky. Look look. Diana
Morgan is different. Not only intriguing to look at, one
eye brown, one eye blue, but also reasonably intelligent.
The things you recall in your senescence. The curse of
memory. I had two magazines with me at the time, *Vogue*
and *Vanity Fair*. I hid them, lest he consider me flighty,
and wished that I had brought my copy of *Ulysses* with
me, because that would have impressed him. So why,
once he joined me on the terrace, did I turn down his
invitation to dinner? I was scared of what the others
would say if they found out, especially Stu MacIntyre.
But, above all, I was frightened of the turbulence
Solomon evoked in me.

No sooner did I return to our cottage than I looked up
the entry on Prester John in our Encyclopedia Britannica.
Then I went for another swim in that lake that would be
my undoing.

I learned from a shopkeeper in the village that
Solomon had not left Ste.-Adèle, but was staying with his
brother. When the invitation to tea came from Morrie I
understood and began to count the hours, deliberating on
what I should wear and imagining our conversation,
polishing phrases that would do me credit. I also got into a
horrid row at the dinner table with my father and Stu
MacIntyre. My father, I should explain, was in a
justifiably vile temper. The day before the invitation to
tea came he had had to drive into Montreal, because our
house had been burgled in his absence. He did not yet
know that the police would recover everything within a
week. Everything, but a portrait that had been painted of
me that I, for one, considered no great loss.

According to Stu MacIntyre, Solomon was not only a
notorious bootlegger, but a killer whom he intended to see
behind bars. My father reminded me that his father, Sir
Russell Morgan, had been swindled by Solomon's
grandfather Ephraim. "That Jew sold him properties in

the Townships that he claimed were veined with gold and then disappeared."

In the end, the fever struck and I couldn't lift my head, never mind go to tea. Emile Boisvert, our caretaker, explained that I was unwell, but Solomon didn't believe it. Deeply insulted, he almost destroyed the cherry wood table he had made for me. I assume that it has arrived safely and that you are treating it with beeswax, as requested.

The opening days of the trial compounded the initial misunderstanding. Solomon scanning the courtroom every morning, disappointed that if nothing else I wasn't sufficiently curious to attend. Then he spoke with Stu MacIntyre, who told him that I had been crippled by polio. Solomon sent a car round to my house and the two of us met in a suite he kept under another name in the Windsor Hotel. We met again the following night and the night after that we became lovers, Solomon astonished by the evidence of the sheets. I not only had eyes of a different colour, but I was also a virgin. This prompted a measure of tenderness from him, but I suspected that it was forced in the hothouse, and I had my first glimpse of his vulgar side, a tendency to strut just a little.

Our stealthy meetings in that suite, festooned with red roses, adrift in champagne, were fraught with difficulties. Solomon was well known in town, to say the least, and my condition made me conspicuous. My father and his cronies favoured the hotel bar and so did Harry McClure to whom I was more or less engaged. I could never stay the night, which infuriated Solomon, and led to my turning on him. "And how can you manage it so easily," I asked, "married, with two children?"

"They mean nothing to me," he said.

I reproached him for being callous.

"I suppose. Yes. But it's the truth."

He immediately dismissed any show of concern on my part about the trial.

"On balance," he once said, laughing, "there are more important trials going on right now in Moscow."

But, prowling the suite, he raged against his accusers.

"You people. You people. My grandfather sailed here with Franklin and hiked out of the Arctic. A mere boy, I once made my way home from the Polar Sea. How dare you sit in judgement. MacIntyre. R.B. Bennett. Bloody fools. Only Smith is not a hypocrite."

His mockery of his brother Bernard, whom he abhorred, was far from enchanting to behold, but he lashed out at me on the one occasion I made a deprecating remark about him.

"Three hundred years ago in England, even a hundred years ago, *fifty* — or in the France of the Ancien Régime — the peregrinations of my devious brother would have secured the family a title rather than criminal charges. You people. You people. Dig deep enough into the past of any noble family and there is a Bernard at the root. The founder with the dirty fingernails. The killer. No better, possibly a lot worse, than my brother. Besides, Bernard is blessed. He is foolish enough to think that everything that is important to him *is* important."

So we had our time together, our pathetically few evenings of the only true love I have ever known and, as I write, I am a lady of seventy-three years. A melancholy confession, possibly. But I could name many others who haven't had as much.

Yes, but why didn't I run away with him, as he asked, even implored, fly away to a new and dangerous life, a question I have turned over and over in my mind ever since.

"I will come for you at six tomorrow morning. We will take nothing with us. We will travel as we are."

Yes, yes, I said, but I phoned his suite at five A.M. to say, forgive me, but I can't do it.

"I thought as much," he said, hanging up, passing sentence on me, flying off to his death.

Mine too, in a manner of speaking, though I will linger for a few months yet.

I was left with the cherry wood table and the photographs I scissored out of the next day's newspapers and still look at most days. Solomon in his flier's uniform, standing before his Sopwith Camel, on an airfield "somewhere in France." Solomon seated with "Legs" Diamond in the absurdly named Hotsy-Totsy Club.

I believe what tipped the scales against my flying away with him was our last night together in the Windsor Hotel. That night I felt his eyes on my misshapen limb as I lurched to the bathroom, those hot judgemental eyes, and I have never felt such a chill before or since. All at once I understood that there was something dark in him, something Gursky, and that he would come to resent my imperfection, his passion for me yielding to pity. There would be no growing old gracefully together with a man who was bound to crave variety and renewals with other women and who had always to be in the eye of the hurricane. I was heartbroken, but in some ways just as calculating and understanding of my own nature as Solomon. Put another way, I knew that I would be able to tolerate the inevitable infidelities of a Harry McClure, but that Solomon Gursky could destroy me.

I was disqualified or, conversely, saved by my twisted leg from flying away to a new and dangerous life in quest of the Kingdom of Prester John. I couldn't, as he had asked, travel without baggage.

Look at it this way, Moses.

Do you think Paris would have abducted Helen if she hobbled or, if he had been so blind, that Menelaus wouldn't have said good riddance, leaving Troy intact? Consider Calypso. If she had suffered from an infirmity such as mine, surely Odysseus, far from being detained, would have put his shoulders to the oars. Or imagine what two families would have been spared if Romeo had seen Juliet lurching on to that balcony, her leg brace going click click click.

Cripples are not the stuff of romance.

Only Lord Byron, dragging his club foot, springs to mind as an exception to the rule, but such a failing in a man is regarded as interesting, even provocative, rather than disfiguring. Women must submit to a more exacting measure.

Of course in today's parlance I am no longer crippled

but handicapped, a possible participant in wheelchair Olympics were I younger. In the new idiom, Solomon, the most defiantly Jewish man I have ever known, would be adjudged a member of a "non-visible minority". Solomon non-visible. Imagine that.

Realist (and possibly coward) that I am, I settled for my library and my music and my garden and Harry McClure and the children we would have together. Obviously I would have flown closer to the sun with Solomon. However, the likelihood is that I also would have been burnt to a crisp long ago.

Harry keeps a mistress in an apartment on Drummond Street and is sufficiently unimaginative to consider that sinful rather than banal. But he continues to be a solicitous husband and no doubt he will miss me when I'm gone. Harry has been cursed with bad luck in his business affairs and has had to turn to me for help on more than one occasion, which possibly accounts for the popsy on Drummond Street. Once he risked most of our joint savings on an ill-timed property development in the suburbs. We surely would have been ruined had he not been able to unload the lot on the representatives of a British investor, a Sir Hyman Kaplansky, who was happily ignorant of local real-estate conditions. More recently his partnership in the brokerage firm founded by his father was in question, which was humiliating. Then, as luck would have it, a Swiss investment trust (its patrimony unknown, naturally) chose Harry to broadcast their millions here. Only I know that he is restricted to buying shares as directed by Zurich, and such is the acuity of those people that his reputation as a shrewd trader has soared. I dearly hope it isn't Mafia money.

Enough.

This letter will be forwarded to you by my executors, after the fact, as it were. I wonder if Solomon would say that I brought the cancer on myself, saying no. Then why didn't he come round anyway and carry me off? Why didn't he insist?

It seems to me that our lives are consumed by countless

wasting years, but only a few shining moments. I missed mine. Yes is what I should have said. Of course I should have said yes.

With fondest regards,

DIANA

P.S. Quite the best of recent gardening books is Christopher Lloyd's *The Well-Tempered Garden*. I'd send you my copy but I have written in the margins.

SIX

ONE

◆

1973. Following his hurried descent on Washington and his frustrating trip to North of Sixty, a weary Moses returned to his cabin in the woods. Strawberry, he discovered, was in a sorry state. He had put in ten days painting the Catholic church in Mansonville and had yet to collect for it. He was not only out his pay, but also the cost of the paint and the fifty dollars he had forked out to rent a spray gun. The new priest, a sallow young man, had assured him, "Your money is safe. It's in the vault."

"Let's get it out, then."

"There is a problem. The cleaning lady has thrown out the paper with the combination written on it."

"Doesn't anybody know the combination?"

"Not since Father Laplante, who preceded me here."

Father Laplante was locked up in the Cowansville jail.

"But don't you worry, Straw. I have written to the good people who installed the vault in 1922. Meanwhile your money is safe."

Legion Hall rolled into The Caboose, bellied up to the bar, and asked Gord to bring him a quart.

"You buying?" Strawberry asked.

Without bothering to turn around, Legion Hall lifted a fat

droopy cheek off the bar stool and farted. "I got good news for you, Straw. I just dumped a load of gravel at the church in Mansonville. Father Maurice is real upset. The company that installed that vault for them went bust in 1957."

Moses was no longer listening. He was totally absorbed in a page of *Time* he had opened at random.

ALASKA'S SPEEDING GLACIER

A wall of ice seals a fjord, endangering nearby villages

The first person to report that something was amiss was Guide Mike Branham, 40, a strapping six-footer who each spring flies a pontoon plane full of bear hunters into a cove on Russell Fjord, in Alaska's southeastern panhandle. This year he discovered that things had changed: Hubbard Glacier was on the move — at a most unglacial pace of 40 ft. per day. "We saw the glacier advance like it never had before," says Branham. That was in April. Within weeks, the leading edge of ice had sealed off the fjord at its opening, turning the 32-mile-long inlet into a fast-rising lake and trapping porpoises, harbour seals and the salt-water fish and crabs they live on.

The immediate danger, explained USGS Glaciologist Larry Mayo, is that the lake, now rising about 1 ft. a day, will spill out of its southern end into the Situk River, a salmon-spawning stream that is the economic lifeblood of Yakutat. "In another 500 to 1,000 years," says Mayo, "Hubbard Glacier could fill Yakutat Bay, as it did in about 1130."

"You'd better drive me home, Straw," Moses said, staggering to his feet.

Moses curled right into bed and slept for something like eighteen hours. Waking before noon the next day, he settled his stomach with a beer bolstered by two fingers of Macallan. He showered, shaved with his straight razor, nicked himself only twice, ground some beans, and drank six cups of black coffee, shivers breaking through him in diminishing waves. Then he defrosted a couple of bagels, shoved them into the oven, and prepared his first meal in three days: an enormous helping of scrambled eggs with lox and potatoes fried in onions. Later he made another pot of coffee and sat down to his desk. A good start, he thought, would be to blow the dust off his pile of mimeographed copies of *The Prospector* and file them in chronological order. *The Prospector* (a weekly, price ten cents) was Yellowknife's first newspaper. In the issue of February 18, 1939 Moses read that *Mountain Music* with Bob Burns and Martha Raye was playing at the Pioneer Theatre. The Daughters of the Midnight Sun were planning a dance at The Squeeze Inn.

Moses found the item he wanted in the issue of February 22, 1938. A big banner headline announcing:

RAVEN CONSOLIDATED POURS FIRST BRICK
   Considerable ceremony attended the pouring of the first gold brick from the Raven Consolidated plant in the Yellowknife gold fields. The brick weighed 70 pounds and was valued at approximately $39,000.
   Several company officials and a number of out-of-town guests attended a banquet Tuesday night to celebrate the event. Prominent among the out-of-town guests was Raven's major shareholder, British investment banker Hyman Kaplansky . . . .

No imp leaning on a malacca cane appeared in Cyrus Eaton's biography and there was no mention of him in all the material Moses had collected about Armand Hammer, another tycoon who had made his first millions peddling cough medicine during Prohibition.

Fragments. Tantalizing leads. Tapes, journals, trial transcripts. But so many pieces of the Gursky puzzle missing. Take Aaron Gursky's case, for instance. Moses had been out west many times, seeking out old-timers who might remember Aaron, who had died in 1931.

Such a nice Jew.

A real good guy.

Some hard worker.

So far as Moses could make out, Aaron had been no more than a hyphen, joining the Gursky generation of Ephraim with that of Bernard, Solomon and Morrie. A shadowy presence, inhibited in the first place by his father's mockery and then by the turbulence between his sons.

Then there was the problem of Ephraim. The Newgate Calendar entry aside, Moses could find little hard evidence of his sojourn in London or his voyage out with the doomed Franklin.

Ephraim couldn't have been at ease in London, circa 1830. Henry Mayhew wrote of that time and place, "Ikey Solomons, the Jew fence, buys in the cheapest market and sells in the dearest." He noted two distinctive races among the London poor. The Irish street-sellers, a numerous and peculiar people, with "low foreheads and long bulging lips, the lowest class of costermongers, confined to the simplest transactions," and then of course there were the Jews. Mayhew deplored the prejudice that saw the Jews only as "misers, usurers, extortionists, receivers of stolen goods, cheats, brothel-keepers," but he did allow there was some foundation for many of these accusations. Gambling was the Jews' chief vice, he observed, just as the extreme love of money was their principal characteristic. But the Jews, he wrote, were also known for their communal spirit, contributing generously to Jewish charities, so that no Jew ever had to die in a parish workhouse. Remarkable, he concluded, "when we recollect their indisputable greed for money."

Once, while he was still living with Lucy, Moses took her to Westminster Abbey to show her the memorial to the foolish but intrepid Franklin, the epitaph composed by the explorer's nephew, Alfred, Lord Tennyson:

> Not here: the white North hath thy bones, and thou
> Heroic Sailor Soul!
> Art passing on thy happier voyage now
> Toward no earthly Pole.

An afternoon in Sir Hyman Kaplansky's library had been sufficient for Moses to determine that luxuries of a sort were not unknown on the *Erebus* and the *Terror*. Each of Franklin's ships had a hand organ, capable of playing fifty tunes, ten of them psalms or hymns. There were school supplies for instructing illiterate sailors, mahogany desks for the officers. The *Erebus* boasted a library of 1,700 volumes and the *Terror* 1,200, including bound copies of *Punch*.

For the voyage through the Northwest Passage the officers packed all the finery appropriate for a ball. But, unlike the natives, they had no animal skins that could be worn in layers, providing ventilation to prevent sweat from freezing on a man's back. Putting in at Disko Bay, on the west coast of Greenland, they did not bother to acquire any teams of sled-dogs. Neither did they take on board a translator or a hunter, though none of their company knew how to take a seal or a caribou. So, in their last extremity, Franklin's men were driven to boiling each other's flesh. And seemingly not one of them, save for Ephraim, survived their northern ordeal.

A framed copy of the notice that appeared in the Toronto *Globe* on April 4, 1850, hung over Moses's bed.

SIR JOHN FRANKLIN'S EXPEDITION

Copies of the following advertisement have been
forwarded by the admiralty to the authorities
in Canada:

£20,000

REWARD WILL BE GIVEN BY

Her Majesty's Government

To any Party or Parties, of any country, who shall
render efficient assistance to the crews of

DISCOVERY SHIPS

Under the Command of

SIR JOHN FRANKLIN

1. — To any Party or Parties who, in the judgement of
the Board of Admiralty, shall discover and effectually
relieve the crews of Her Majesty's Ships *Erebus* and
Terror, the sum of

£20,000

OR

2. — To any Party or Parties who, in the judgement of
the Board of Admiralty, shall discover and effectually
relieve any of the Crews of Her Majesty's Ships *Erebus*

and *Terror*, or shall convey such intelligence
as shall lead to the relief of such crews or any of
them, the sum of
£10,000
OR

3. — To any Party or Parties who, in the judgement of
the Board of Admiralty, shall by virtue of his or their
efforts first succeed in ascertaining their fate,
£10,000
W.A.B. HAMILTON
Secretary of the Admiralty.
Admiralty, March 7th, 1850.

Why, Moses wondered, returning to the riddle again
and again, hadn't Ephraim told his tale, claiming the ten-
thousand-pound reward? Why did he deny intelligence of
either the *Erebus* or *Terror* to McNair, pretending to be a runaway off an American whaler?

There was another problem.

Neither Ephraim Gursky nor Izzy Garber were listed in the
Muster Books of the *Erebus* or *Terror* (available at Admiralty
Records, Public Records Office). But they had been there
Moses knew, oh yes Ephraim Gursky had been there, and Izzy
Garber as well.

TWO

◆

Following his arrest, after his ill-fated bug-hunting expedition with the Sullivan sisters, it was Newgate for Ephraim; and in that dark and fetid hole — as he told Solomon some seventy years on, a raven perched on his shoulder, the two of them warming themselves under the shifting arch of the aurora on the shores of Great Slave Lake — he met the man who met the man who would lead him and now Solomon to this place. Ephraim shrunken now, but still frisky, saying: "He was an old Orkney boatman with a bad milky eye and a spongy grey beard and he stirred me as never before with his tales of his journey to the shores of the Polar Sea with Lieutenant John Franklin, as he then was."

It began innocently enough, Ephraim explained, when he cursed the jailer who once again had served them rancid sausages. This roused what at first glance appeared to be a sack of bones flung into a corner of the communal cell in the felons' yard, causing it to splutter and sort itself out, assuming the shape of a tall emaciated man, his lips chalky, his hair matted and his beard a filthy tangle. "Young man," the boatman said, "you are looking at somebody who was once grateful for the putrid powdered marrow bones and horns of a deer that had already been picked over by the white wolves and the black ravens of the barren land."

"Tell the lad what brought you here, Enoch. Why it's bound to be a leap into the dark for you."

"A Jezebel of a daughter bore false witness against me."

"I thought it was poaching on the Tweed," another voice called out.

"Poaching," somebody else put in, "but not on the Tweed."

"His son-in-law's slit it was."

Ignoring their lascivious laughter, the boatman sucked sausage into his all but toothless maw. "Why, when there was no *tripe de roche* to be had we boiled scraps of leather from our boots and praised the Almighty for providing it. And such was the cold that when we still had it our rum froze in its cask. Aye, and all that time we had to keep watch on the Canadian *voyageurs*, a thieving lot, and that Iroquois heathen, the treacherous Michel Teroahauté. But the worst of it was we did not know whether poor Mr. Back, lusting after that Indian harlot, had perished on his trek or would return to us with supplies."

Seizing Ephraim by the elbow, turning his own face aside the better to fix him with his good unclouded eye, he told him how the white wolves bring down a deer. "Those ferocious predators," he said, "assemble in great numbers where the deer are grazing. They creep silently toward the herd, and only when they have cut off their retreat across the plain do they begin to race and howl, panicking their prey, tricking them into fleeing in the only possible direction—toward the precipice. The herd, at full speed now, is easily driven over the cliff. Then the wolves, their jaws dripping saliva, descend to feast on the mangled corpses."

The boatman's eyes flickered upward and in an instant he was asleep, his mouth agape. Ephraim shook him awake. "Tell me more," he said.

"Have you any tobacco?"

"No."

"Gin?"

"No."

"To hell with you then."

The next morning the boatman's only response to Ephraim's questions was a bilious glare. He was intent on the lice in his beard, flicking them into the flame of a candle.

Out for exercise in the men's courtyard Ephraim, ignoring his cellmates, strolled up and down, surveying the rough granite walls of the enclosure. He sighed at the sight of the revolving iron spikes near the summit, possibly fifty feet from the ground. It would be impossible, he calculated, for him to squirm between the *chevaux de frise* and the masonry. And even if he could manage it, the cunning bastards had implanted yet another barrier above. A row of sharp, inward-projecting teeth rising from the top of the slimy wall. Hopeless, he thought.

Later in the day an anxious Izzy Garber hurried to Newgate and arranged to meet with two of the turnkeys at the George. The chaplain of Newgate, the Reverend Brownlow Ford, was already in place, soused, lolling on the sofa with the hangman Thomas Cheshire. Old Cheese, recognizing Izzy, raised his glass to him, his eyes charged with rancour:

> By noose and gallows and St. Sepulchre's Bell
> Until we meet — I wish you well.

Ignoring him, Izzy fed the turnkeys ribald stories and stuffed their pockets with guineas. As a consequence, Ephraim was tossed a straw mattress that evening and discovered he now had a line of credit in the prison taproom. He promptly loosened the old boatman's tongue with gin and tobacco for his pipe.

The Orkney boatman, his voice hoarse, complained to Ephraim about the ruinous addiction of the Cree to spirituous liquors, and how they had become debased by their undying thirst for the noxious beverage, cursed to live out their days without any of the consolations which the Christian religion never fails to afford. A vain, fickle, and indolent race, he said, given to seducing each other's wives.

The boatman, given to fits of shivering, obviously feverish, would doze fitfully from time to time, coming abruptly awake to demand more gin and to resume his tale as if he had never let off. "I have seen reindeer too numerous to count, the herd extending as far as the horizon, and learned to eat its flesh raw." The staple food for the voyage, he said, was pemmican, buffalo meat, dried and pounded with melted fat. But there were times, the boatman allowed, when fish and fowl were plentiful. River salmon, jack fish, the singular and beautiful gold eye, which could be caught in nets in the spring at Cumberland House. There was also ptarmigan, Canada grouse, mallard and wild swan.

Ephraim, who had never heard of such things, hungered for more details, but dared not interrupt the cantankerous boatman's flow.

If the boatman disapproved of savages, he also pitied them, his unbridled contempt reserved for the Canadian *voyageurs*, a riotous lot, lazy and complaining, who thought nothing of wintering in the fur forts with Indian wives of twelve years of age, whom they often bartered for a season to one or another of their rude companions. "When the cold abates, which you — in your ignorance — might consider a mercy, and the sun prevails day and night on the barrens, then do the mosquitoes begin to swarm everywhere, flying into your ears and mouth, a hellish torment, and the only thing for it is to light a fire, dampen it, and fill your tent with stinging smoke. Without a doubt, it is the land God gave to Cain."

"Then why did you undertake such an arduous voyage in the first place?"

"I had no way of knowing."

"True."

"For my sins, of all the men assembled in Mr. Geddes's house on June 14, 1819, I was one of the four who agreed to join the expedition, tempted by the promise of adventure and a wage of forty pounds annually as well as free passage back to the Orkney Islands. I was most impressed with the Christian character of Mr. Franklin. He bore with him a translation of the Gospel of St. John in the Esquimaux lingo printed by the Moravian Society in London. He also carried with him gifts to conciliate any savages we might encounter. Looking-glasses, beads, nails, tea kettles and so forth."

In that stifling cell that crawled with lice, cockroaches, and sewer rats, that stank of excrement and urine and reverberated with the hacking of men already taken with typhus, Ephraim dreamt of a cool white land where the summer sun never set and herds of reindeer extended as far as the horizon. He was jolted awake when one of the boatman's tormentors crept close to him, pretending to be the Bellman on his eve of execution visit. Ephraim lunged at him, grabbing his hand. Then, even as the man cried out, Ephraim gave his hand an even sharper twist, seemingly determined on uprooting his arm from its socket. "Tell me the name of your companion in the far corner."

"Larkin."

"Well now, he was with me in the Steel and he can tell you about me."

In the morning, after another discouraging stroll through the exercise yard, Ephraim wakened the old boatman with gin and filled his pipe with tobacco.

"I want the sodomites' sausages when they come," the old man said.

"And you shall have them. Now tell me more."

"I would also find a straw mattress most beneficial."

"Take mine."

Coughing, clearing his faltering lungs of phlegm, the old man told him that they had espied their first icebergs some ninety miles off the coast of Labrador. A day later the brilliant coruscations of the aurora borealis appeared to them. "We did not encounter any difficulties until we quit York Factory in a small boat, bound for the interior. Then we couldn't make progress on that damned Steel River by sail. The current was running too fast for using oars so we were bloody well bound to commence tracking."

"I don't understand."

"Then you are blessed. What I'm saying is that we had to drag the boat by a line to which we were harnessed like beasts of the field. This is not easy at the best of times, but these were the worst for anybody but a mountain goat, considering the steep declivity of the high banks and the soft slippery footing. Aye, we were fortunate indeed to advance at the rate of two miles an hour. Are you for the dance upon nothing?"

"I'm too young. And then?"

"And then the water in the Hill River was so low we were obliged to jump into it, though it was freezing, and this we did several times a day to lift the boat over our shoulders. And next came the sprouts, and we were leaping in and out of the boat all day, working in wet clothes in freezing temperatures. I take it you're a Four by Two."

"Yes."

The old man began to chortle. "Gin. Tobacco. Steak-and-kidney pie. The turnkeys dancing attendance. I thought as much."

"Did you now?"

He held out his tumbler for more gin.

"You've had enough."

"I want more, lad."

"Then tell me more."

It was the long trek back from the interior that really exorcised the boatman; a time when they had to contend with fearful famine and cold, the thieving of rations by the Canadian *voyageurs* and the unspeakable treachery of Michel Teroahauté. "We ate the skin and bones of deer and the storms raged without and within. Don't you see? Mr. Franklin had to do it."

"Do what?"

"Separate them. Hood and Back. Sending Back on his long trek."

"Why?"

"How can you be such an idiot?"

"I wasn't there."

"Hood had already got a savage with child at Fort Enterprise and now he lusted after the little Copper Indian harlot — after Green Stockings — who couldn't have been more than fifteen years old. But Back, an even worse whoremonger, was also smitten. That brazen girl would bathe in cold streams, displaying her cunny to the officers on the bank, inflaming them. She lay with both of them in turn. They took her from behind, like a bitch in heat."

"And how would you know that?"

"Why, if not for me those two midshipmen would have fought a duel. I consulted with Dr. Richardson and then I removed the charges from their pistols. Then it was that Mr. Franklin sent Back away for the winter."

"You were spying on the girl."

"I did no such thing. Mind, I did stumble on them fornicating in the bush once. Aye, and it was a disgusting sight. Not to you or your kind, perhaps, who have denied Christ. But you must understand that my Christian upbringing stood me no matter how far from civilization."

"Though not necessarily when you came back to it."

"I am here falsely accused by my daughter and the court will see that soon enough. Now I must get some sleep."

Prowling the men's courtyard the next morning, cursing the *chevaux de frise*, Ephraim loitered once again under the water cistern that protruded immediately below the revolving spikes at the corner of the yard. And once again he saw that the turnkeys did not keep a constant watch on it. Back in his cell he roused the old boatman with gin and tobacco and pleaded with him to resume his tale.

"But where was I?"

"Mr. Back had been sent off to search for supplies and the rest of you were driven to eating deer skin."

"Aye, for we had been abandoned by vile Akaitcho and his band of heathens. And by this time poor Mr. Hood was much inconvenienced by dimness of sight, giddiness, and other symptoms of sin, and we had to make frequent halts. Now did I tell you that Belanger and Ignace Perrault, unable to go on, had been left behind in a tent with a gun and forty-eight balls?"

"No. You did not."

"That was the case. And then one morning Michel Teroahauté claimed that he had seen a deer pass near his sleeping place and he went off to chase him. He couldn't find him. But, he said, he had come by a wolf which had been gored by a deer and he brought portions of it back to camp. Only after we had eaten it did we grasp that it must have been a portion of the flesh of either Belanger or Perrault, both of whom the savage had slain, and then gone at their frozen bodies with a hatchet."

Such was the failing boatman's increasing agitation that the rest of his tale was too garbled for Ephraim to comprehend, but he did sort out that in the days that followed the gale was relentless. Teroahauté, left alone with Mr. Hood in a tent, apparently murdered him with a shot of his gun. The priapic

Mr. Hood died by the camp-fire, *Bickersteth's Scripture Help* lying next to his body, as if it had tumbled from his hand at the instant of his death. A raging Teroahauté then heaped scorn on the rest of the company. Dr. Richardson, alarmed to see Teroahauté now armed with two pistols, and an Indian bayonet, took advantage of an opportune moment and killed him with a shot through the head with his own pistol.

The boatman suddenly clutched at Ephraim, his good eye bulging, a rattle rising in his throat, and then fell back, dying, his tale incomplete. Searching his person Ephraim found a soiled and torn sketch of a beautiful nude Indian girl, whom he would learn years later was Green Stockings, the daughter of Kesharrah, the prize that made such unforgiving enemies of Hood and Back.

Also years later, once he himself had become familiar with the barrens, Ephraim would discover that it was the vile Akaitcho and his Indian band that ultimately rescued the starving party, bringing them dried deer meat, some fat, and a few tongues.

Before parting with the survivors of Franklin's party, Akaitcho, denied his promised reward of goods, said to them: "The world goes badly, all are poor, you are poor, the traders appear to be poor, and I and my party are poor likewise; and since the goods have not come in, we cannot have them. I do not regret having supplied you with provisions, for a Copper Indian can never permit white men to suffer from want of food on his lands, without flying to their aid. I trust, however, that we shall, as you say, receive what is due to us next autumn; and in all events it is the first time that the white people have been indebted to the Copper Indians."

Hours after the Orkney boatman had died his body was dumped into a cart and taken to St. Bartholomew's Hospital to be privately dissected.

The next morning in the exercise yard Ephraim saw that the wall by the water cistern was still unattended. Back braced painfully against the rough stone, he slithered up the wall, just as he had once been taught by a sweep's climbing boy. He grasped the cistern and shot over its crown. His back badly torn, he then made a grab for the rusty bar supporting the *chevaux de frise* and edged along it until he came to the Press

Yard buildings. There he risked a jump of nine feet to the roof, spraining his ankle, but still managing to hobble clear of Newgate and the adjoining buildings. Emerging on the sloping roof of a house on a nearby street, he rested briefly, concealed behind a chimney stack, hugging his throbbing ankle. Then he slid down a drainpipe to the street and made directly for Izzy Garber's lodging in Wentworth Street, where he could count on a healing salve for his torn back, a warming fire, meat pies and wine, and ribald stories.

THREE

◆

The
NEWGATE CALENDAR
IMPROVED
Being
INTERESTING MEMOIRS
of
NOTORIOUS CHARACTERS
Who have been convicted of Offences
AGAINST THE LAWS OF ENGLAND
During the seventeenth century; and continuing
to the present time, chronologically arranged;

COMPRISING

Traitors,	Highwaymen,	Pickpockets,
Murderers,	Footpads,	Fraudulent Bankrupts,
Incendiaries,	Housebreakers,	Money Droppers,
Ravishers,	Rioters,	Imposters,
Mutineers,	Extortioners,	And Thieves of every
Pirates,	Sharpers,	Description
Coiners,	Forgerers,	

WITH

Occasional Remarks on Crimes and Punishments,

Original Anecdotes, Moral Reflections and Observations
on particular Cases; Explanations of the Criminal
Laws, the Speeches, Confessions, and
LAST EXCLAMATIONS OF SUFFERERS.

EPHRAIM GURSKY

Several times convicted — sentenced once to Coldbath Fields, once to
Newgate — And finally, on October 19, 1835, transported to
Van Diemen's Land.

Perhaps never natural talents were more perverted than by
that notorious Jew, Ephraim Gursky, celebrated for his daring
escape from Newgate in *The Weekly Dispatch* and *The People's
Journal.* We could scarcely believe that even in the melancholy
catalogue of crimes, a young man proficient in Latin, Russian,
Hebrew and Yiddish (the patois of his people), could be found
descending to the degraded character of forgerer of official
documents and letters, ravisher, panderer, and gentleman
pickpocket.

Ephraim Gursky was born in Liverpool. By his own account
his father, Gideon Gursky, was a Jew of Russian origin. He
had been a well-known opera singer in Moscow until an affair
with the Baroness K., a favourite of the Czar, had led to a
scandal, and the lovers had been obliged to flee for their lives.
Ephraim claimed to be the issue of that ill-starred union. After
his mother died in childbirth, he was raised as a Jew by his
father's second wife, whose maiden name was Katansky.
Gideon Gursky earned his living as a cantor in a Liverpool
synagogue. Though not affluent, he sent young Ephraim to
school. Ephraim made indifferent progress, and gave early
evidence of a daring and wicked disposition. While among his
companions, if any mischievous project was set on foot, young
Ephraim was sure to be their leader, and promoted it as far as
in his power. Weary of the floggings he endured by the hand of
his cruel stepmother, who constantly reproached him for both
his bastardy and Christian blood, Ephraim ran away from
home at the age of twelve. He worked in the coal mines in
Durham and added to his income by delivering newspapers in
a nearby village. There he was noticed and patronized by a
gentle schoolmaster, Mr. William Nicholson, who taught him

Latin and penmanship. As a reward for such kindness, Ephraim absconded with Mr. Nicholson's sterling silver candlesticks and, consequently, a complaint to this effect was made to the local constabulary by Mrs. Nicholson.

Shortly after his arrival in London, young Gursky was apprehended trying to sell the purloined silver candlesticks and was sentenced to six months hard labour in Coldbath Fields. On his release, young Gursky set himself up in lodgings in Whitechapel, among the lowest class of the metropolis, as a forger of official documents and letters. He was in his eighteenth year, and though not handsome and small of stature, he became a favourite of young ladies of loose character and dissipated manners. He corrupted two hitherto respectable young sisters who had rooms in the same lodging house, working as seamstresses. They were Dorothy and Catherine Sullivan, recently of County Kilkenny, and when a constable was sent thither to inquire after their characters, he found them praiseworthy. Perverted by young Gursky, the sisters became bug-hunters, though they profited little from their crime, regularly turning their booty over to their mentor. When the three of them were apprehended the Sullivan sisters were sentenced to three years hard labour in Newgate, but Gursky, while awaiting what was bound to be a more severe sentence, made his daring escape.

Now a fugitive, he adopted the name of Green, and then commenced what is called a gentleman pickpocket, by affecting the airs and importance of a man of fashion. In this endeavour his helpmate for a time was Miss Thelma Coyne, of equal notoriety as a sharping courtèsan. This audacious lady was, in all, tried three times at the Old Bailey; two of which she was acquitted, and found guilty the other one, and sentenced to two years imprisonment in Newgate. About the expiration of her time, she caught the gaol distemper; and died in a fortnight after her discharge had taken place — thus yielding up her last breath, in perfect conformity with the infamous tenor of her life.

Hitherto our pickpocket hero and his faithful confederate in the execution of his plans visited the most celebrated watering places, particularly Brighton, as brother and sister. Gursky, being supposed a gentleman of fortune and family, was noticed by persons of the first distinction. He picked the pockets of the Duke of L. and Sir S. of a considerable sum; all of which he got off undiscovered. He also took from Lady L. a necklace, but the circumstances and purlieu of the theft were such that she declined to prosecute.

While the lawyers were outlawing him, and the constables were endeavouring to take him, Gursky evaded detection by travelling in various disguises and characters through the southern counties of the kingdom; he visited the great towns as a quack doctor, clergyman, etc. On his return to London, he became an even more daring pickpocket. He went to court on the Queen's birthday, as a clergyman, and not only picked several pockets, but found means, while strolling in the gardens with the Viscountess W., to deprive her of a diamond order, and retired from the place without suspicion.

He was at length apprehended at St. Sepulchre's church, when Dr. Le Mesurier preached a charity sermon on providing pasture land for superannuated dray horses that might otherwise be sold as provender in France. Herbert Smith, a constable, saw Gursky put his hand in Mrs. Davenport's pocket, and presently after followed him out of the church, and took him into custody near the end of Cock-lane, upon Snow-hill.

Having taken the prisoner to St. Sepulchre's watch-house, and found a gold repeater watch, and some other articles, in his possession, Smith returned to the church and spoke to Mrs. Davenport whom he had seen the prisoner attempt to rob; she adamantly informed him she had lost nothing. But Mr. Davenport was far from satisfied. Upon Smith's return to the watch-house, the irate Mr. Davenport advised that the prisoner might be more strictly searched, which caused his wife to unaccountably swoon and then to be led outside. Gursky was desired to take off his hat, and raising his left arm, he cautiously removed his hat from his head, when a metal watch, a pearl brooch, and a scarlet garter fell to the floor. At the sight of the latter article, Mr. Davenport had to be forcibly restrained from striking the prisoner with his walking stick.

Gursky was bound over to prosecute, his trial at the Old Bailey surprisingly attracting many ladies of the beau monde and demi-monde more commonly seen in Rotten Row, Hyde

Park. Even more surprising was the appearance of Mr. William Nicholson, who came to speak in the prisoner's defence. The gentle schoolmaster, mentioned heretofore, was now a widower, his demented wife having hanged herself a month after giving birth to their only child. The child was being raised with the help of a young nephew, of most pleasing countenance, who accompanied Mr. Nicholson to court. The prisoner, Mr. Nicholson said, had not stolen his candlesticks, but rather they had been presented to him as a farewell gift on his departure for London. Mrs. Nicholson's complaint that they had been stolen was the first indication of her oncoming dementia that ended so tragically. Furthermore, Mr. Nicholson said, had Ephraim Gursky, a most promising student, not been falsely accused in the first place and wrongly incarcerated in Coldbath Fields at such a tender age, it is possible his life would have taken a more commendable direction.

The prisoner then addressed the court with considerable animation, making a great display of elocution, and enlarging upon what he termed the force of prejudice, insinuating that calumny had followed from boyhood because of his father's faith.

"Gentlemen, in the course of my life, I have suffered much distress, I have felt something of the vicissitudes of fortune, and now from observation, I am convinced, upon the whole, there is no joy but what arises from the practice of virtue, and consists in the felicity of a tranquil mind and a benevolent heart.

"Gentlemen of the jury, if I am acquitted, I will quickly retire to Prince Rupert's Land to preach my mother's faith to the savages that pollute the barrens, cursed to live out their days without any of the consolations which the Christian religion never fails to afford. If my life is spared, I will retire to that distant land, where my name and misfortunes will be alike unknown; where harmless manners may shield me from the imputation of guilt, and where prejudice will not be liable to misrepresentation, and I do now assure you, gentlemen of the jury, that I feel a cheering hope, even at this awful moment, that the rest of my life will be so conducted, as to make me as much an object of esteem and applause, as I am now the unhappy object of censure and suspicion."

The jury found Ephraim Gursky guilty.

On Thursday, October 19, 1835, Ephraim Gursky was sent to the bar.

Mr. Recorder: Ephraim Gursky: the sentence of the Court upon you, is, that you be transported for the term of seven years, to parts beyond the seas, to such place as His Majesty, with the advice of his privy council, shall think fit to declare and appoint.

FOUR

◆

Ephraim showed Lady Jane the letters commending Isaac Grant's skills and Christian piety. "The surgeon I'm speaking of is also a naturalist of some distinction," he said, as he proffered yet another letter, this one signed by Charles Robert Darwin. "Mr. Grant has long admired Sir John and would endure any hardship to sail with him on this bold venture. And I, who am forever in your debt, most revered lady, would take it as my duty to serve Sir John."

Lady Jane, enchanted to see the redeemed lad again, was willing to plead his cause, but she explained that he was, alas, too late. "Unless," she said, warming to the prospect, "you made directly for Stromness Harbour."

"Exactly my intention. And I would be happy to wait," he said, "if you cared to address an epistle to Sir John."

The letter in hand, Ephraim hurried back to Whitechapel, where a desperate Izzy was hiding out. "We're for the Orkneys," he said.

"I dare not leave here. They're looking for us everywhere."

"They will be watching the ports, expecting us to make a dash for Ireland or the Continent."

"Even if we got there safely how could we expect to get ourselves included in the ship's company?"

Ephraim was already steaming open Lady Jane's letter. The ink, he established at once, would be easy enough to duplicate. He had the nib she had used in his jacket pocket. He practised her spidery script for more than an hour before he risked adding the *post scriptum*, imploring Sir John to accept Ephraim, their Van Diemen's Land foundling, and Mr. Isaac Grant, admirable as he was devout, among his ship's company.

The rap on the door startled Izzy.

"Not to worry," Ephraim said. "That will be the Sullivan sisters. Dorothy and Kate are coming with us."

Once in Stromness Harbour, the gloomy dockside public house where the crews gathered was easily found. Many of them were fearful they would never see home again. Dangling the Sullivan sisters like bait, spending lavishly, it did not take Ephraim long to ingratiate himself with the sailors. He settled instinctively on those he took to be the most jittery, regaling them with tales of his late father's overland journey to the shores of the Polar Sea with Franklin in 1819. "Why, there came a time," he said, "during their third year on the barrens, when they were driven to eating the putrid powdered marrow bones of a deer that had already been picked over by ferocious white wolves and black ravens. Mind you, my father was one of the few fortunate enough to survive, though my poor mother hardly recognized him on his return. His teeth lost to scurvy and all of his toes amputated. Not much use to her, which probably accounts for her running off with Mr. Feeney."

The night before they were to sail, Captain Crozier of the *Terror* wisely refused his crew shore leave, worried that some of the men would jump ship. But Captain Fitzjames of the *Erebus* allowed his lot the usual liberty. All of them reported back at the required hour, but then the randy assistant surgeon appropriated a small boat and had a sailor, a lad fortunate enough to be fancied by Kate, row him back to land. There the two of them joined the Sullivan sisters, the assignation having been hastily arranged while Ephraim was ostensibly busy elsewhere.

According to the official records, the miscreants rowed back to the *Erebus* at three A.M. The third lieutenant, whose watch it was, hardly recognized them, but then it was a dark night, the moon and stars obscured by clouds, and he was somewhat the worse for drink himself. The sailor, sporting a silk top hat, was jabbering in some unknown guttural tongue with the assistant surgeon, the two of them lugging sacks of personal provisions on board. Certainly against the rules, that, but they had been sufficiently thoughtful to bring the third lieutenant a bottle of rum.

Franklin had no luck. Unknowingly, he set sail for the Arctic in what would subsequently prove to have been one of the most relentlessly cold cycles of the last 1,000 years. He went to sea with some eight thousand cans of preserved meat, supplied by one Stephen Goldner, the lowest bidder, and canned according to his new-fangled process called "Goldner's Patent". The meat was vile. Cans found on Beechey Island by a perspicacious anthropologist more than 125 years later had imperfectly sealed seams and bulging ends, evidence of putrefaction, supporting his theory that expedition members had suffered from lead poisoning, which can lead to debilitating fatigue, anorexia and paranoia. But Ephraim and Izzy, given their secret hoard of Jewish soul food, were not as infected as the rest of the company. True, the bulk of their supplies gave out during the first year, but the schmaltz herring, an indulgence Izzy limited to the sabbath, lasted them well into the second. And even then, the ever resourceful Izzy, by now an intimate of the cook, was able to leaven their intake of poisonous meat with delicacies that he had shrewdly held back. So one Friday night they might gorge themselves on *kasha* fried in chicken fat and the next on rice prepared in a similar fashion.

Trying to reconstruct Ephraim's interminable winters in the high Arctic, the sun sinking below the horizon for four months, Moses had to rely on conjecture and the accounts of other nineteenth-century explorers. Then there were the fragments from Solomon's journals, those tales told by Ephraim on the shores of a glacial lake, man and boy warming themselves by their camp-fire under the shifting arch of the aurora.

Navigation in the Arctic Archipelago was limited to eight

weeks. Then, confronted with the melancholy prospect of yet another winter, the men would either blast or saw their ship's path into a safe harbour, where they would be held hostage in the pack ice for ten months. They would set to cutting the ice for fresh water and constructing an ice wall around the ship, piling snow against the hull for insulation, and erecting canvas housing on the decks. The officers, intent on maintaining morale, diverted the crews with foot races on the ice, cricket matches, schools, and theatrical performances, the temperature on stage below zero for the Christmas pantomime. "No joke," the saucy Lieutenant Norton complained, "when you are wearing petticoats." Cabin boys and the more comely of the able sailors and marines took to demanding exorbitant fees for their favours from smitten officers.

Solomon noted in his journal that Ephraim attended classes in astronomy, becoming proficient in reading the stars, and never missed a lecture by Mr. Stanley, the surgeon on the *Erebus*.

"The science of medicine has now arrived at such perfection in England," Mr. Stanley said, "that we have almost forgotten the crude beginnings out of which our present knowledge was evolved. But from our pinnacle of learning, it is interesting to observe the darkness in which the wild Esquimaux still tolerates a class of medicine man whose pretensions to perform all kinds of miracles are of the extravagant character. These shamans say they can and do make themselves larger and smaller at will, or change themselves into some other animal, or enter into a piece of wood or stone; that they can walk on water and fly through the air; but there is one indispensible condition — no one must see them."

The officers laughed appreciatively.

"Alas," Mr. Stanley continued, "the matter is serious. The shamans, to take one example, have absolutely no understanding of the nature of delirium. When a patient becomes delirious, as in severe fevers, they take him to be mad, possessed of an irresistible desire for cannibalism."

Franklin, his death foretold, was buried on June 11, 1847 in the British ensign Lady Jane had embroidered for him. And when the longed-for summer dawned at last, its feeble sun was insufficient to free the ships from the ice floes.

The men, their teeth swimming in their bloodied mouths, were put on even shorter rations, Ephraim told Solomon. Scurvy, Solomon noted in his journal, claimed twenty of them in the winter of 1848. And then the *Erebus* became the place of darkness between Earth and Hades. Men tore at each other's faces over a chunk of tainted meat and peformed acts abhorrent to them for the sake of a ration of tea or tobacco. Officers wept as they wrote letters of farewell. The captain of the forecastle sat at the organ for hours, playing hymns, praying for deliverance from the sunless frozen sea. A demented, feverish Philip Norton, wearing a wig, his cheeks rouged, his lips painted, paraded below decks in a ball gown, attended by admirers, pausing to pinch Izzy Garber's cheeks or caress Ephraim's buttocks, speculating aloud on which one would taste most tender in the pot, warning everybody that it would come to that soon enough. One morning he had Ephraim led forcibly into his tiny cabin where, in spite of the intense cold, he lay on his bunk wearing nothing but a black suspender belt and stockings, singing softly as he combed his pubic hairs with a toothbrush. "The time has come, my dear, to reveal where you and Grant have your secret store of food."

Hallucinating crew members, fearful of being butchered, were never without a weapon to hand. Those who had spit out their teeth long ago and were now too weakened to move, ridden with skin ulcers, coughing phlegm and blood, slid in pools of diarrhoea in their hammocks. Those who were still mobile but with gums already livid, their mouths tasting of death, split into rival gangs, each suspecting the other of nourishing themselves on hidden caches of food. On the prowl, armed, they organized flash searches. Officers were openly jeered. An alarmed Crozier and Fitzjames met in the wardroom of the *Erebus*, two Royal Marines standing guard at the door.

Moses Berger, his annotated Franklin library all but definitive, found that more than a hundred years later scholars were still puzzled by why the expedition men, having decided to abandon their ships, sickly and inadequately equipped as they were, elected to strike out, by way of Back's Fish River, for Fort Reliance, some eight hundred miles away. "Certainly only some grave factor or combination of circumstances," wrote Hudson's Bay Chief Trader William Gibson, FRGS, in *The Beaver* (June, 1937), "could have precipitated such a hazardous and daring decision."

The grave circumstance, according to Ephraim, was Crozier's conviction that mutiny was imminent.

Scholars were even more baffled by the amazing variety of articles strewn about the lifeboat found by Hobson near Victory Point. Silk handkerchiefs, scented soap, sponges, slippers, toothbrushes and hair-combs. That is to say, just about everything required for the toilette of the demented "Dolly" Norton and his entourage. Neither could scholars understand why the lifeboat was pointed in the direction of the abandoned ships.

Ephraim told Solomon: "Crozier and Fitzjames had departed with the men they adjudged to be loyal or at least sane. They induced Norton and his band to separate from the main body, bribing them with stores of tea and chocolate, and allowing them to take me and Izzy with them. Prisoners for the pot. But as God spared Isaac from the knife at the last moment, providing a ram in his place, so we were saved by that polar bear they shot on the ice. Norton and his bunch immediately set to gobbling the liver raw, sparing not a slice for us, and that was that."

Hypervitaminosis, a toxic reaction to an overdose of Vitamin A, its severity heightened by the absence of Vitamins C and E, is acquired by eating the liver of a polar bear or bearded seal. The disease is so rare it is not even listed in *Black's Medical Dictionary*. Its symptoms, Moses noted on one of his file cards, are as follows:

Headaches, vomiting, and diarrhoea, all of which appear promptly. And, within a week, scaling and stripping of skin, loss of hair, splitting of the skin round the mouth, nose, and eyes. This is followed by irritability, loss of appetite, drowsiness, vertigo, dizziness, skeletal pain, loss of weight, and internal disruption from swelling of liver and spleen, including violent dysentery. And, in severe cases, convulsions, delirium, and possible death from intercranial haemorrhage.

Ephraim told Solomon: "The Eskimos who had been with us for four days had gone, and we were still camped some seventy miles from the ships, unable to move on, the men vomiting and shitting themselves, blaming it all on the seal they had shared with the Eskimos. Izzy was feverish. And Norton, wearing his ball gown in the tent, warmed as it was by a feeble fire, swore he would have me for his catamite. When I began to curse, he ordered his followers to lower me to my knees, arms twisted behind my back. Thrusting himself at me, he raised his skirts and lowered his silk panties, and then it was he saw fragments of his own skin and hair fall into the snow. His privates were red and raw. Crazed now, he lowered his stockings, sobbing as strips of skin peeled off his legs. The other men, determined to examine themselves, let go of me. Oh, there rose such a wailing in that tent, and threats of murder for me and Izzy, who had not been affected. With the greatest of difficulty the quarrelsome, failing men managed to turn the lifeboat round on the sledge, intending to head back to the ship and rest there until they recovered, butchering me and Izzy for food. However, they were so weakened by dysentery by this time that it did not take much for me to leap at Norton from behind, topple him, slit his throat, and retreat from the others with Izzy in the direction the Eskimo band of hunters had gone, dragging our things with us on a makeshift sled."

There was a gap in Solomon's journal, and when he next took up Ephraim's tale it was to recount the story of his grandfather's contest with the shaman in the camp of the hunters. The hunters were Netsiliks. One of their number, Kukiaut, had served on an American whaler for two years and was able to both translate for Ephraim and teach him Inuktituk.

The contest was over a sickly child, keening women dancing around him in the igloo, crying, "*Hi-ya, hi-ya, hi-ya.*"

The boy had fallen through a scalp of ice into freezing water. His cheeks were burning hot, he was delirious, but Ephraim guessed he was suffering from nothing worse than a bad case of the grippe, and offered to treat him with medicines from Izzy's sea chest. But Inaksak, the wily old shaman, denounced the usurper, a bloodthirsty interloper, who would bring storms and death into their camp. The old man, mocking Ephraim, pranced about him, snarling, flaunting the amulets hanging from his belt: rows of seal and bear teeth, the head of a tern carved in soapstone, the penis of a walrus. The child, he proclaimed, was possessed by an evil spirit, but the mighty Inaksak, with the help of the ghost of Kaormik, would draw it out of his body, curing him.

"*Gottenyu*," Izzy said, "have they got dybbuks even here?"

Crouching, covering himself with a caribou skin, Inaksak went into a trance. Then he advanced on the boy, rolling his eyes, groaning, flashing his snow knife.

Izzy, recognizing another professional, nudged Ephraim. "Careful, old son. He's bloody good he is."

Sucking at the feverish boy's stomach, Inaksak reeled backwards as the evil spirit struck him. Staggering about the igloo — thrashing — thrusting with his snow knife — he wrestled with the spirit. Finally, blood trickling down his chin, he spit out a stone at Ephraim's feet, pronouncing the boy freed, and fell down in a swoon. But, within hours, the boy was worse, and a rueful Inaksak declared that he was possessed by too many *tupiliqs* for him to vanquish, the evil spirits having come with the *kublanas*. He ordained that the hunters must now build a small igloo and abandon the boy and the intruders there to freeze to death, lest the blight overwhelm everybody in the camp.

Once the sentence was translated, an outraged Izzy had to be restrained from leaping at the shaman. He appealed to Ephraim. "Explain to the silly buggers that the old fart drew the blood from his mouth by lancing his gums with the stone."

Instead Ephraim said that he and Izzy would be pleased to accompany the boy to the igloo, providing they were allowed a stone lamp and fuel and food for a week, and in that time Ephraim would cure the boy, proving that he could perform greater magic than Inaksak.

Ephraim told Solomon: "Worse luck. The day I brought the boy back, shaky on his feet, but obviously on the mend, our return was followed hard by a blizzard. Inaksak, that cunning old bastard, danced up and down, saying my magic was bad. I had angered Narssuk, god of the wind, rain and snow."

Narssuk's father, a huge double-toothed monster, had been slain in a battle with another giant. His mother had also been killed. When still an infant, Narssuk was already so large that four women could sit on his prick. He flew into the sky and became an evil spirit, hating mankind, restrained from mischief only by the thongs that held his caribou skins in place. However, if women kept silent about their menses or other taboos were broken, Narssuk's thongs loosened, he was free to move about, and tormented the people with blizzards.

"Now, because of the *kublanas*, I will have to fly into the sky," Inaksak said, "and fight Narssuk, tightening his thongs, or there will be no good weather for the hunt and we shall all starve."

But once the hunters and their women and children had gathered outside it became clear that Inaksak's flight had become unnecessary. The storm had abated as suddenly as it had started. Ephraim then noted the position of the moon bobbing on the horizon. Hoping against hope that his calculations were right, he said, "I am more powerful than this foolish old man, or even Narssuk, and to prove it to you I will soon raise my arms and lead the moon, who is my servant, between you and the sun, bringing darkness in the season of light, and then, unless you obey my smallest wish, I will turn myself into a raven and pluck your eyes out one by one."

Once this was translated by Kukiaut, the Eskimos, vastly amused to have such a braggart in their midst, sat down to wait.

Ephraim disappeared into his igloo and emerged again wearing his silk top hat and his *talith*. He sang: "Who knows one? I know One: One is God in Heaven and Earth. Who know Two? I know Two: Two is the Tablets, One is God in Heaven and Earth."

He rolled over in the snow, simulating convulsions, froth bubbling from his lips. Then he stood up, and at the rising of the moon he lifted his arms and the eclipse began. The astonished Eskimos cried out, falling to their knees, pleading with Ephraim not to become a raven and pluck out their eyes.

And Ephraim said unto them:

"I am Ephraim, the Lord thy God, and thou shalt have no other gods before me.

"Thou shalt not bow down to Narssuk, whose prick I have shrivelled, or to any other gods, you ignorant little fuckers. For the Lord thy God is a jealous God, visiting the iniquity of the fathers upon the children unto the third and fourth generation of them that hate me."

He enjoined them not to steal or kill, unless ordered to do so by Ephraim, and instructed them not to take his name in vain. "Six days shalt thou hunt, providing meat for me and Izzy, and on the evening of the sixth day thou shalt wash thy women and bring them to me, an offering—"

Izzy stamped his foot.

"—and to my priest here. And on the seventh day, which is my sabbath, thou shalt rest."

In the days that followed, the women lying with him under caribou skins on the snow platform, the men gathered round, Ephraim told them, "In the beginning I created the heaven and the earth."

Ephraim enchanted them with stories of the flood, Joseph's coat of many colours, and his ten plagues, the latter tale a favourite of the hunters.

Ephraim set and mended their broken bones, he tended to their sick, and when a female child was born he would not allow them to strangle and then eat it, and when a male child was born he showed them how he was to be circumcised.

Ephraim promised them that their seed would be as numerous as the stars above. He told them that one day he would have to leave them, but, if they continued to behave themselves, he would send them a Messiah in another generation. The Messiah, a descendant of Ephraim, would return their ancestors to them and make the seal and caribou so plentiful that nobody would starve again.

Ephraim also bestowed on his followers a version of Yom Kippur, telling them that this was his holiest of holy days, and that from the time the sun went down, until it rose and went down again, any of his flock who was thirteen years old or older was not to fuck or eat any food, but instead must pray to him for forgiveness of his sins. He laid down this law in a foolish and absent-minded moment, overlooking the fact that his faith provided for all contingencies save that of the Arctic adherent.

In the years to come, followers of Ephraim who wandered too far north in search of seal in October soon discovered that they were in bad trouble. Once the sun went down they were obliged to remain celibate and fast until it rose once more several months later, not sinking below the horizon again for many more months. As a consequence, some sinned against Ephraim, the men stealing out of camp to eat, their women seeking satisfaction among the unclean. But most stayed in place to starve, dying devout, unless Henry, that good shepherd, found them, and hurried them south to the sun and deliverance.

FIVE

◆

"You're taking it wrong, Bert. Nobody's asking you to leave. But as I now have a professional to handle all the repairs and you can't afford the going rent, it's only fair you should move into the small room in back." Mrs. Jenkins, standing on the throw rug, shifted her weight from one foot to another, her ear cocked to the floorboard's answering squeak. "Loose board," she said.

"I'll take care of it," Smith said.

"I've got a couple would take this room on Monday and pay me forty dollars a week in advance."

Quitting the house in a rage, Smith hurried down the street, passing neighbours, not one of whom greeted him with a wave or even a smile. Grabby cheeky foreigners. Bloody ungrateful, that lot. If one of their women got on the same bus as he did, never mind she was merely an ignorant cleaning lady, pilfering from her betters, he immediately offered her his seat. Why, once he had even carried parcels home from the Metro for Mrs. Donanto. But if he ever slipped on the ice, breaking an ankle, the neighbours would probably cheer. Certainly they would leave him lying there with the poo from the Reginelli dog who did his business anywhere.

Smith went to the bank, withdrew his weekly two hundred

dollars, and then treated himself to coffee and a blueberry muffin at Miss Westmount. He had his pride. He would not submit to the indignity of that two-by-four room with a slit of a window overlooking the rats feasting on the garbage in the back lane. Instead he popped in on Mrs. Watkins and inquired about the vacant room in her house. Then he splurged on lunch at Ogilvy's and went home for a nap.

"Thinking of moving out, are we, old buddy of mine?"

Smith, startled, felt the room begin to sway.

"Go ahead. Make my day. The reason Mrs. Watkins has a vacant room is an old guy conked out in bed. Probably froze to death. Or didn't you know she sets her thermostat at sixty-five?"

"I have no interest in your back room."

"Guessy guessy why Mrs. Watkins phoned the minute you left her cockroachy place? Because she's put up with old fusspots got one foot in the grave before and she wanted to know did you pee in bed?"

"Have you quite finished, Mrs. Jenkins?"

"Mrs. Jenkins is it now? Ha! I found an empty Laura Secord box in your wastepaper basket last week as well as a take-out bag from the Shangri-la and three Lowney's Nut Milk wrappers. Where did you get the do re me, Bert?"

"None of your business."

"Well it's my bee's-wax if you're shop-lifting or maybe peddling dope to school kids in the Alexis Nihon Plaza and the cops will be coming to my door to make inquiries."

Smith didn't emerge from his room until noon the next day. After looking at a number of places, he settled on something in N.D.G. in a rambling old house that had been converted into self-contained one-room flatlets, each with its own bathroom and a cupboard kitchenette with a two-plate electric burner. Feeling sinful, he bought a small refrigerator and a colour TV and an electric blanket. Then, exhausted, he took a taxi home, slipping out at the corner, only to be totally undone when he discovered that his key no longer fit the lock to his room. Worse news. His increasingly frantic struggling with what was obviously a new lock wakened somebody inside. A whining feminine voice. "Is that you, Herb?"

Before Smith, dizzy with despair, could answer, Mrs. Jenkins was there.

"We moved everything into the back room for you nice and tidy. Even your precious strongbox full of marijuana and dirty postcards I'll betcha."

"I've got to get into my room."

"But everything's here," she said, leading him to the back room.

"Please," Smith said, "I've got to get into my room."

"This is your roomy-doomy-do now. Besides, Mrs. Boyd is in bed with the grippe, poor kid."

Smith shut the door and subsided on to his bed. Shivering under his blankets even though the radiator was on the sizzle, he realized that he couldn't move out tomorrow as he had planned. He would have to wait until Mrs. Boyd got better, went out shopping with her husband, and he could break into the room to retrieve his money. Meanwhile, he calculated it was safe. They would never look under the floorboard. *But it squeaked.* Oh, God.

Early the next morning Smith opened his door a crack. Soon enough he was rewarded with his first glimpse of Betty Boyd, a frail creature in a faded nightgown, hurrying to the toilet, a hand cupped to her mouth. Morning sickness, Smith thought.

Betty couldn't have been more than seventeen years old. Herb, easily ten years older, was a big man, his hockey sweater no longer stretching over his beer belly.

MONCTON WILDCATS
Eat McNab's Frozen Peas

Herb had a job at Pascal's Hardware and came straight home from work every night with a pizza or a couple of submarine sandwiches, a six-pack of O'Keefe, and a quart of milk. Except for hurried flights to the toilet, Betty lingered in bed all day, playing her radio loud. The Boyds had only been installed in Smith's old room for a week when he contrived to run into Herb in the hall. "You ought to take her out one night," he said. "Put some colour in her cheeks."

"She don't like you peeping from behind your door when she has to crap."

Two nights later Smith saw them leave their room. He waited until he heard the outside door open and shut and then he reached for his hammer and screwdriver. Mr. Calder in number five was out. So was Miss Bancroft. Bingo night. Mrs. Jenkins was watching TV in her parlour, but what if she heard the door being forced? Or what if the Boyds had only gone to the corner store and would be back in five minutes? Smith decided to wait for a night he could be sure they had gone to a movie. Meanwhile, he would time how long they stayed out. But when he fell asleep at two A.M. there was still no sign of them.

It was seven A.M. before Mrs. Jenkins opened the door to the room with her master key and saw that the Boyds hadn't taken anything with them.

A stricken Smith joined her.

"Don't touch anything," she said. "Fingerprints. They could be the victims of foul play."

But Smith knew, without even looking, that the Boyds had lifted a squeaky floorboard and were now on the road to Toronto richer by two thousand three hundred and fifty-eight dollars.

Still mourning his loss, Smith arranged for his things to be picked up while Mrs. Jenkins was out having her hair done by Lady Godiva. He left a brief note and two weeks' rent on the table, but no forwarding address, and his last best hope was that she would slip on the ice, breaking an ankle, and there would be nobody to take care of her when she got out of the hospital.

Good riddance, Mrs. Jenkins thought, crumpling the note, and then she stepped right out again, stopping for a banana split at the Alexis Nihon Plaza and then going to a movie, *The Day of the Jackal*. It was ruined for her by two glaring flaws. The assassin, crossing from Italy to France, never could have spray-painted his sportscar so easily. Another scene began with the sun at twelve o'clock, but ended with it at three, though the scene only lasted a minute, if that. Filmmakers must think everybody is an idiot.

Installed in his new flatlet, his colour TV and refrigerator in place, the photograph of his parents in Gloriana sitting on the mantel, Smith prepared his breakfast, gratified that he no longer had to respond to how many Newfies it took to screw in a light bulb or how do you tell the bride from the groom at a Polish wedding. It was a pleasure to have his own *Gazette* delivered to the door, not a crumpled copy, pages stuck together with marmalade. There were other benefits. He didn't have to wipe the blood off his butter, because she had shoved her leaky lamb chops on the shelf above his own, instead of putting it in the meat drawer. Neither was he obliged to spread paper on the seat before sitting on the toilet. Tomorrow, he decided, he would have his phone disconnected. He didn't want Mrs. Jenkins coming round to snoop just because he was listed in the book. Let her worry about what had become of her best friend in this vale of tears.

Lionel Gursky beamed at him from the front page of the *Gazette*. His newly established Gursky Foundation (yet another tax dodge, Smith thought) would offer a hundred university scholarships to needy students across Canada. This, in everlasting memory of Mr. Bernard. "My father," Lionel said, "loved Canada and everybody in it."

Said the call girl to the judge, Smith thought, a pain shooting up his arm.

SEVEN

ONE

◆

Inevitably, Gitel Kugelmass's daughter and her husband, the dentist, joined the exodus of English-speaking people from Montreal, fleeing down the 401 to Toronto. The Nathansons did not take Gitel with them. Instead they secured a place for her in the Mount Sinai, an apartment-hotel in Côte St. Luc with everything for Jewish seniors. A kosher dining room, a *shul*, arts and crafts classes, a health-atorium where a nice young girl led them in aerobics, a convenience store, twenty-four-hour security, and a room set aside for lectures, pinochle, funeral services, and dances on Saturday nights. *Die Roite Gitel,* tricked out in a big floppy hat and a flowing black cape, was anathema to those wives still lucky enough to have husbands in this world. A coquette. A menace on the dance floor. She was also known to invite men up to her apartment who were not yet incontinent or confined to walkers, serving them peach brandy. According to rumour, that *choleria* received the men in her black negligee trimmed with lace, slipping a Mick Jagger disc on the record player, that *shaygetz* howling, "I Can't Get No Satisfaction".

Gitel's only other visitors were bouncy cemetery salesmen armed with lyrical graveyard photographs and casket price lists, urging her not to end up a burden to her family. Or round-shouldered rebbes in smelly caftans who guaranteed to light a memorial candle on each anniversary of her death for a mere twenty-five dollars. So once a week Moses drove into town to take Gitel to lunch. What began as a happy excursion, the two of them gabbing away in Yiddish, evolved into a melancholy duty. Following her second minor stroke, *die Roite Gitel*, who had once led the workers out against Fancy Finery, lost her compass. The first inkling Moses had that she was now somewhat addled came when she insisted he drive into Montreal a day early. "I'm calling from a pay phone," she said. "My own line isn't secure any more."

Once seated with him at a table in Chez La Mère Michel, she showed him the letter. It was from her daughter in Toronto, inviting Gitel out for the High Holidays, and enclosing photographs of the grandchildren, Cynthia and Hilary.

"Well, that's all very nice," Moses said.

"Can't you see this letter is an almost perfect imitation of Pearl's handwriting?"

"Are you telling me she didn't write it?"

"Pearl would die before inviting me to their house for Rosh Hashana. Either the CIA or the KGB is behind this letter."

"Gitel, please, you don't really think that."

"I don't think it. I know it."

"Tell me why."

"If it's the CIA it's because they know I was a Party member the same time as the Rosenbergs and if it's the KGB it's because they know I left."

Moses ordered another Scotch. A double.

"Were you followed to my place?" she asked.

"I took precautions."

"My apartment's bugged."

On occasion, however, Gitel was her adorable self at lunch. "Moishe," she said, "I only want one thing more, to live long enough to see you publish your biography of Solomon Gursky."

Then one night she wakened him with a phone call at two A.M. "I found it."

"What?"

"The bug."

Feeling foolish, but concerned for her sake, Moses drove to Montreal immediately after breakfast. Gitel, who had been pacing up and down, waiting, rolled back her living-room carpet. Protruding from the centre of the floor was an ominous copper cap. Gitel handed him a screwdriver and he got down on his hands and knees and unfastened it. Fortunately the Farbers, who lived in the apartment below, were in the kitchen when their living-room chandelier fell to the floor. Even so, it took a good deal of explaining.

Quitting the autoroute at exit 106 late the same afternoon, Moses pulled in for a drink at The Caboose. Gord Crawley's second wife, the former widow Hawkins, was drunk again. When Gord edged past her, lugging a trayful of beer, she called out in a booming voice, "First marriage I never had time to take off my stockings, now I could knit a pair easy."

Moses retreated to his cabin. He no longer kept regular hours. Instead he might work around the clock, or even longer, and then pass out, drunk, on his bed and sleep for twelve hours. And now, overcome by ill-temper and impatience, he lit a Monte Cristo, poured himself a Macallan, and sat down at his desk. Sorting, sifting, he came across a file card with a passing reference to Mr. Bernard, discovered in a biography of Sir Desmond McEwen, the Scots liquor baron. "Bernard Gursky struck me as just what one would expect a person of his birth and antecedents to be, intelligent, but without any personal charm that I could discover, in fact the reverse." The lost file card had been serving as a bookmark in Trebitsch Lincoln's scurrilous *Revelations of an International Spy*, which Moses had read hoping against hope that the notorious conman, a.k.a. Chao Kung, né Ignacz Trebitsch, had run into Solomon in China, but seemingly they had never met. Too bad.

Moses got up to stretch. He rubbed his eyes. Then he opened Solomon's journal to the pages that dealt with the trial, Bert Smith, the shooting of McGraw, and Charley Lin.

Fat Charley.

Once proprietor of Wang's Hand Laundry and two

bedbug-ridden rooming houses, a survivor of the big autumn poker game of 1916, Charley received Moses at his own table in the House of Lin on a wintry night in 1972. The restaurant on Hazelton Avenue adjoined Mr. Giorgio's showroom on one side and Morton's Men's Boutique on the other. An elongated, twisting papier-mâché dragon, breathing fire and smoke, was suspended from the silken ceiling from which there also hung a tracery of teardrop purple lights and bamboo-framed pink lanterns.

The House of Lin was favoured by Toronto's film crowd. Slender, scented Chinese girls, wearing brocaded silk sheaths slit to the thigh, led the short rolypoly producers and their willowy young ladies to The Great Wall of China bar, where gathered around the rickshaw, its centrepiece, they sipped kirs or champagne as they studied their menus. Eventually the producers and their girls were escorted to tables according to rank. On each table there stood an enormous snifter in which rose petals floated in perfumed water.

The House of Lin's menu, ostensibly mandarin, was shrewdly tilted to accommodate the palate of its clientele. The won ton soup, for instance, was reminiscent of mama's chicken soup with *lokshen*. The steamed dumplings were indistinguishable from *kreplach*, except that they were filled with pork. The General Kang minced beef on a steamed cabbage leaf could pass for an unwrapped *chaleshke*.

Lin, possibly ninety years old now, Moses reckoned, was plump and bright-eyed and reeked of cologne. "It was Solomon's doing, of course. I'm not saying he actually pulled the trigger on McGraw. He was far too, ah, you know . . ."

"Fastidious?"

"Far too what you said. But he brought in the killers from Detroit."

"There are people who say it was Solomon they had come to shoot. He was the one who was supposed to go down to the railway station, wasn't he?"

"But he sent McGraw in his place."

"McGraw was his friend."

"Until he discovered that he had been swindled at the poker

table by a boy who had stolen his stake from his family in the first place."

"And who told you that?"

Lin smiled his irritating wisdom-of-the-East smile.

"Was it Mr. Bernard?"

"Mr. Bernard is a great human being. King of the Jews. If not for him the family would be nowhere today."

"Ah, so Harvey Schwartz eats here, does he?"

"When he is in town with his enchanting wife I'm pleased to say, but never Mr. Bernard, though I have extended him the offer of my hospitality more than once."

"However, he did invest," Moses said, taking a stab at it.

"I am sole proprietor of The House of Lin."

"How did Solomon cheat?"

"Let me show you something," Lin said, dealing cards from a deck he had prepared. "Kozochar had folded and so had Ingram and Kouri. I went out even though I was sitting on nines back to back. It was the only thing to do. McGraw was showing two ladies and a bullet and had been betting those ladies from the start like he had another one in the hole, and let me tell you he wasn't one to bluff, McGraw. Solomon was sitting there with only sevens and a ten showing. He was not only seeing McGraw, he was raising him, shoving thousands into the pot. Then Ingram dealt McGraw another bullet, giving him a full house for sure, and Solomon a deuce, good for nothing. McGraw tossed the deed to the hotel into the pot and Solomon put up the Gursky store, the blacksmith's shop, and the two rooming houses I had lost. And when they turned over the cards McGraw was sitting on only two bullets over ladies, that's all, but that little son of a bitch was holding three sevens."

"It happens."

"If you had been sitting on back to back sevens to begin with would you have raised into two and then what looked like three ladies for sure? No, sir. Not unless you knew that all McGraw had in the hole was a lousy eight."

"And how in the hell would Solomon have known that?"

"Now let me show you something else," Lin said, motioning to a waiter who promptly brought him two more decks of cards lying on a painted enamel tray. Lin set the decks down on the table immediately before Moses. "Tell me on which one the cellophane and stamp have been steamed off and then resealed."

"But you weren't playing with Solomon's cards."

"No. Ingram's."

"Well, then."

"But where did Ingram buy them, Mr. Berger?"

"From A. Gursky & Sons, General Merchants."

"You're not as stupid as I thought."

"That still doesn't prove anything, least of all that it was Solomon who ordered McGraw shot."

"Then tell me why Solomon jumped bail, flying off to his death in that Gypsy Moth?"

"Because he knew that you had been paid to lie on the witness stand and, besides, he had other plans."

"Not long term, I trust."

"*Tiu na xinq.*"

TWO

◆

As defined by the Electoral Franchise Act of July 20, 1885, "Person" meant a male, including an Indian, but excluding anyone of the Chinese race, among them Charley's father Wang Lin, who was one of Andrew Onderdonk's lambs. More than ten thousand strong they were, these coolies plucked out of Kwangtung province to cut a swathe through the Rocky Mountains for the Canadian Pacific Railroad. Suspended over cliff faces in swaying baskets, they fed sticks of dynamite into crevices and blasted twenty-seven tunnels through Fraser Canyon. Then, their work done, their presence no longer required, many of them drifted into the settlement that was incorporated as Vancouver in April 1886. The same month white navvies employed at Hastings sawmill struck for higher wages. The mill manager responded by hiring more Chinese, rounding up coolies willing to put in ten hours a day for $1.25. This enraged a local drunk named Locksley Lucas. So one night he organized a bunch outside the Sunnyside Hotel and they marched on the tents of Chinatown, bent on breaking heads. Some of the Chinese were tied together by their pigtails and flung over a cliff into the sea, encouraged to swim the rest of the way back to the Middle Kingdom.

Wang Lin, a survivor, fled into the interior of B.C., then

over the Shining Mountains into the western heartland, finally settling in the small town where the best bargains were to be had at A. Gursky & Sons, General Merchants.

Wang's son Charley prospered. Then, in the big autumn poker game of 1916, Charlie, as well as Kozochar, Ingram, Kouri, and McGraw were humiliated by Solomon, who rose from the card table the new owner of the Queen Victoria Hotel.

Before Solomon went off to the wars he installed McGraw as bartender, which some said was good of him. But it was hard on McGraw. He took to the bottle. He began to brood. Seated in the five-and-ten with Kouri, Kozochar, and Lin, he complained bitterly about Bernard, who made a point of checking out the cash register every night. He watched, amazed, as that strutting little bastard parlayed Solomon's winnings into a bunch of hotels-cum-bordellos and a couple of mail-order houses that shifted booze from one province to another. Gathered around the hot stove with his cronies, McGraw allowed he never could have done it himself, he lacked the audacity. Yes, Lin countered, but neither could Bernard have managed it without the Queen Victoria as collateral. "And what if Solomon didn't beat you fair and square," Lin asked, "but he was cheating?"

Then Solomon sailed home and, without consulting Bernard, appointed McGraw manager of the Duke of York Hotel in North Portal, Saskatchewan, only a few feet from the border and immediately across the road from the railroad station for the Soo Line, which connected with Chicago.

Bernard was outraged when he discovered that McGraw had been promised twenty percent of the hotel's take. "In the future," he told Solomon, "such decisions are to be made by me, you, and Morrie together."

No answer.

"I am considering offering my hand in marriage to Miss Libby Mintzberg of Winnipeg."

Solomon whistled.

"Her father is president of the B'nai Brith synagogue. He's a *shoimer shabbos.*"

"In that case, we must introduce him to Levine."

Sammy "Red" Levine, out of Toledo, was strictly orthodox:

he was never without a *yarmulke* and didn't murder on the sabbath.

"Miss Mintzberg and I plan to have a family and then my needs will be greater than yours or Morrie's."

"Piss off, Bernie."

During the Prohibition years Solomon was out of Saskatchewan more often than not, looking in on Tim Callaghan who was competing with Harry Low, Cecil Smith and Vital Benoit on the Windsor-Detroit Funnel, running into disputes with the Little Jewish Navy or the Purple Gang that only Solomon could settle by calling for a meeting in the Abars Island View or inviting everybody to dinner at Bertha Thomas's Edgewater Thomas Inn.

Bertha Thomas died in 1955 and her roadhouse burnt down in 1970, but when Moses finally got to Windsor he managed to track down Al Hickley, who had once been her bouncer. In his seventies now, Al was rheumy-eyed, his speech thickened by a stroke, reduced to drinking what he called Ontario horsepiss, nesting in a rotting rooming house on Pitt Street. Al, who had been a rum-runner himself once he had quit the roadhouse, led Moses to a bar near the corner of Mercer Street that still reeked of last night's vomit. "Hey, when I worked the Reaume Dock at Brighton Beach we not only ran booze across the river, but Chinks too. We loaded the Chinks in big bags, see, weighted, so's a patrol boat got too close we had to throw 'em overboard with the booze. Shit, Moe, I think of all the booze lying at the bottom of the river it breaks my heart."

"Did you ever meet Solomon Gursky in the old days?"

"I shook hands with Jack Dempsey himself once and I still got Babe Ruth's autograph somewheres. The Yankees they was at Brigg's to play the Tigers used to drink at Bertha's. I talked to Al Capone a couple of times you never met a nicer guy. He could handle a thousand cases a day."

"Gursky."

"Used a cane and read books?"

"That's the one."

"Solly you mean. Why didn't you say so in the first place? Hell's bells, he was one of Bertha's favourites. You know, we had a system at the Edgewater. The spotter buzzes us the cops are coming, Bertha lays a trail of ten-dollar bills from the front entrance to the back and those lardasses they're bent over double going scoop scoop scoop. Pigs in a trough. Other times there's a raid the shelves of booze behind the bar slides down a chute and waiters and members of the band are emptying customers' glasses like crazy on to the thick thick carpet. But one time the fat little piano player he was, you know, a drug fiend, I'm dead against that, he misses naturally and there's booze all over the dance floor. The cops they mop it up and they're going to bring charges against Bertha, but Solly it was he saves her sweet ass. Why, Bertha, he says, I could have sworn you varnished the dance floor last night and didn't that stuff contain alcohol? The judge, a good customer himself, laughs the cops out of court. Didn't Solly die in an airplane crash?"

"Yes."

"But his brothers are rich rich rich now?"

"Right."

Or Solomon was in Chicago, consulting with Al Capone's financial adviser, Jacob "Greasy Thumb" Guzik. Or he was bound for Kansas City to cut a deal with Solly "Cutcher-Head-Off" Weissman. In Philadelphia, he handled the needs of Boo Boo Hoff and Nig Rosen and in Cleveland he supplied Moe Dalitz. Then he would meet with Bernard in Winnipeg or North Portal or the Plainsman Hotel, in Bienfait, and they would quarrel, Bernard spitting and cursing, and Solomon would take off again. He would check into the Waldorf-Astoria in New York for a couple of weeks, partying with Dutch Schultz and Abbadabba Berman at the Embassy or Hotsy-Totsy Club. Then he would drive to Saratoga to join Arnold Rothstein at the races, once wiring Bernard for fifty thousand dollars and another time for a hundred, sending Bernard into a rage.

The summer following the Chicago Black Sox scandal, Solomon joined with Lee Dillage, a North Dakota liquor dealer, in bankrolling an outlaw baseball team. The team that toured the border towns of Saskatchewan numbered among its players Swede Risberg and Happy Felsch, both former members of the notorious Black Sox. The games were a welcome distraction to the locals as well as the bootleggers, mostly out of North Dakota, who had to hang around one-horse towns like Oxbow and Estevan until after dark, before loading up their stripped-down Studebakers and Hudson Super-Sixes at the Gursky boozatoriums. Heading for the border without lights, their only problem the potholes prairie yokels had deliberately dug into tricky curves, hoping to shake loose a case of Bonnie Brew or Vat Inverness.

Meanwhile, a frustrated Bernard was on the boil, convinced that his courtship of Libby Mintzberg was foundering. Libby's father, Heinrich Benjamin Mintzberg, BA, principal of the Winnipeg Hebrew Academy, president of the B'nai Jacob synagogue, treasurer of the Mount Sinai Beneficial Loan Society, invited Bernard into his study. A pouting Mrs. Mintzberg served tea with sponge cake and sat down to join them.

"When you first solicited my beloved daughter's hand in matrimony," Mr. Mintzberg began, "a matter of some consequence to my spouse and I — "

"If there's a bigger catch in respectable Winnipeg society I'd like to know about it," Mrs. Mintzberg said.

" — it grieved me, a professional man, that a potential future son-in-law of the Mintzbergs hadn't even graduated high school."

"And our precious one with her head always buried in a book," Mrs. Mintzberg said.

"But then you assured me that you were the owner of The Royal Pure Drug Company, an impressive achievement considering your father's origins in the *shtetl* — "

"And your own lack of a formal education."

" — but now I hear that it's really Solomon who is the boss."

Putz. Mamzer. Yekke.

"Even though you're the eldest," Mrs. Mintzberg said.

Yachne. Choleria. "Well you heard wrong. I'm the real boss, but we've always had a partnership that also includes my brother Morrie."

"So the materialistic proceeds of your various endeavours are shared in three equal parts?"

"Something like that."

"Correct me if I err because I'm not well-versed in commercial arrangements, but I always surmised that the boss was somebody who owns more than fifty percent of the shares, the company properly registered."

"Which will certainly be the case, sir, once the legal partnership papers are drawn up."

"And when can we anticipate that auspicious day?"

"As soon as Solomon returns from Detroit, where I sent him to iron out certain bottlenecks in distribution."

"Then I suggest we resume our deliberations once this matter has been resolved with your siblings. Meanwhile, Libby will continue to see you."

"But no more than once a week."

"And not exclusive of other beaux of good family."

"Listen here, for shit's sake, I earn more in a week than that fucken Saltzman does in a good year. Excuse me. I'm sorry."

"Dr. Saltzman's dental practice will undoubtedly grow."

"And don't take this personal, but he's not shorter than Libby on the dance floor."

"Neither am I if she isn't wearing those goddamn high heels."

"You see, Bernard, I'm taking the long view. I am thinking of the Mintzberg grandchildren."

"God bless them," Mrs. Mintzberg said.

"In a partnership shared equally among three brothers who are merely mortal the progeny are bound to squabble over their inheritance unless the line of succession is as clear as it is in the House of Windsor."

Morrie was no problem.

"Bernie, if you say I'm entitled to no more than twenty percent it's hunky-dory with me, honest to God."

"I love you, Morrie, and I'll always take good care of you and yours."

Bernard waited until Solomon had been back from Detroit for a couple of days before he went to see him in his suite in The Victory Hotel. Noon, and he was still lying in bed that one, reading newspapers. "Marcel Proust died yesterday. He was only fifty-one. What do you think of that?"

Empty champagne bottles drifted upside down in a silver bucket and there came a splashing from the bathroom, a girl in the tub, singing "April Showers".

"We've got to talk."

"No, we don't. Shut the door after you and have them send up scrambled eggs for two and another bottle of Pol Roger."

"Put down that newspaper and listen to me for a change. I pay all your gambling debts."

"Do you think Boston did the right thing, trading Muddy Ruel like that?"

"You trust me. I trust you. Everybody trusts Morrie. But if any one of us was knocked down by a car, God forbid, nothing is clear, we have no legal partnership papers."

"So you've got some right there in your briefcase," Solomon said, reaching for it.

Even as Solomon scanned the documents, Bernard reminded him once more of how he had parlayed one hotel into nine, working eighteen hours a day while Solomon was gallivanting around Europe in an officer's uniform. Furthermore, he pointed out, he was the eldest son with certain traditional rights going back to biblical times.

"Fifty-one percent for you, thirty for me, and nineteen for Morrie."

"I could get him to settle for fifteen and I'd be satisfied with fifty point five-o, which would boost you to thirty-four and a half points."

Solomon began to laugh.

"You whoremaster, you gambler, what if I lost my Libby because of you?"

"Then you'd have something else to thank me for."

"I hate you," Bernard hollered, scooping up an ashtray and throwing it at him, kicking open the bathroom door, "Give him the syph, he deserves it," and taking a peek at the alarmed girl in the tub, slapping his cheek, amazed. "Oh, my God," he said, fleeing the room.

Clara Teitelbaum snatched at the robe that hung from a hook on the door and spun out of the bathroom, wailing. "My father will throw me out in the street now and I don't blame him one bit I'm dying of shame."

"Don't worry," Solomon said, his mind elsewhere.

"I'm a respectable girl. I never even let another boy kiss me, but you, you animal, even a nun wouldn't be safe with you."

"I promise you Bernie won't say a word to anybody."

"And didn't you promise me if I came here you'd know when to stop this time, you think I don't know what they say about you?"

Solomon waited until her tears had subsided. "You're not only ravishing, Clara, but you are so bright. Now tell me why I'm always so nasty to my brother."

"He'll blab to Libby and she'll get on the phone to Faigy Rubin and my father, oh my God, you might as well hire me for the bar that's all I'm good for now," she said, thrusting her head deep into the pillows and beginning to quake with sobs again.

"Clara, please, you're beginning to get on my nerves."

"At least if I could say, Paw, I know I shouldn't have let him, but we're engaged."

"If you don't hurry, Clara, you'll be late for your skating lessons. I'll pick you up at eight and we'll go to see *Dream Street* at the Regal."

"I saw it," she said, sniffling.

"The new Fairbanks then."

"Better seven-thirty. But I'll meet you there, I'll say I'm going with a girlfriend, my father could be waiting at the door with a horsewhip. I wish I'd never met you and that's the truth."

Four o'clock in the afternoon Solomon was wakened by a soft scratching on the door. "Come on in, Morrie, the door's unlocked."

Morrie was followed by a waiter wheeling a table heaped with bagels and lox and cream cheese and a jug of coffee.

"Morrie, would you do me a favour?"

"Name it."

"Would you marry the beautiful, but unbelievably dense Clara Teitelbaum for me?"

"Hey, what are you talking? She's some number, Clara, very hoidy-toidy too. Have you ever caught a look at her on the rink doing those figure-eights in that little skirt?"

"Unfortunately yes."

"Her father leans against the fence, making sure nobody even talks to her."

"What if I could fix you up with Clara tonight?"

"I'm glad to see you're in such a good mood."

"Oh yeah. Why?"

"Bernie's really, really in love with Libby, but the Mintzbergs are giving him a hard time."

"If you so much as mention those ridiculous contracts he's drawn up I'll throw you out of here."

"Hold on. Don't give me that look. But supposing that in order to win Libby's hand he has to show those contracts to Mintzberg, but he also gave you a covering letter, nullifying the contracts, which would be torn up right after the marriage."

"How could I be a party to deceiving the delightful daughter of such a worthy family of German Jews?"

So Morrie trudged back to the warehouse office and reported to Bernard that Solomon wouldn't budge.

"I should have known better than to trust you with such an important thing, you little *putz*," Bernard said, punching him in the stomach. Then grabbing his homburg and beaver coat, Bernard went flying out of the office.

Head lowered into the wind, Bernard went striding down Portage Street, cursing at anybody he banged into. Once more, in his mind's eye, he saw Solomon, Ephraim's anointed one, jump down from the fence into the flow of wild nervy horses in the corral. "Follow me, Bernie, and I'll buy you a beer." Turning a corner, tears freezing on his cheeks, he was confronted again by Lena Green Stockings. "It's the boy with the two belly buttons." Minnie Pryzack, seeing him reach for the towel, smiled at him, a tubby little man with wet fishy eyes who would have to scratch and bite to get what he wanted out of life, but never cheat, he thought, like Solomon certainly did in that card game, and yet to this day McGraw looks at me like I'm dog shit but would eat out of Solomon's hand.

Bernard sat down in a booth in The Gold Nugget and ordered coffee and blueberry pie with a double helping of vanilla ice cream.

My God Lanksy phones and asks for Mr. Gursky.

Speaking, Bernard says.

I meant Solomon.

Well last time I looked I was Mr. Gursky too I'll have you know.

Tell Solomon I called.

Click.

Hardly anybody in town could even qualify for a date with the unattainable Clara Teitelbaum, but Solomon was screwing her black and blue in the hotel. Yeah, sure. While he could win the Irish Sweepstakes easier than collecting a little good-night kiss from Libby.

"We all have to learn to control our desires," she said.

"Yeah, well maybe not all. I could tell you something about your friend Clara Teitelbaum guaranteed to turn your hair white."

"Like what?"

"Somebody is doing it to her."

"Shame on you for making up such a thing. She isn't even allowed out at night there isn't a chaperone with."

"So what about before lunch she's supposed to be shopping?"

"You're crazy."

"About you, yes."

"Then stop futzing around and get my father's approval for the match."

"There are problems."

"Listen, Bernie, I'd marry you if you didn't have even a dime to your name, but I can't go against my father's wishes. So get a move on, please, and you'll see how warmly I can respond to your caresses," she said, shutting the front door on him.

Goddamn it to hell. Working eighteen hours a day, Morrie more hindrance than help. Keeping the books. Sorting out cashier's cheques drawn on banks in New York and Detroit and Chicago, everybody scared to carry too much cash now because of the hijackers. Checking out the boozatoriums and watching the tills in the hotels, every manager born to steal. Keeping the drivers from Minnesota happy, they got nothing to do all day but wait for dark, so suddenly they've started to rob the small-town banks and the yokels blame the liquor trade in general and the Gurskys in particular for welcoming such lowlifes into town. And meanwhile if Solomon isn't *shtupping* Clara (her father finds out he'll kill him for sure) or putting together a poker game, he's in New York at Texas Guinan's or better yet Mr. La De Da Himself is stuffing his *kishkas* at the Jockey Club with Arnold Rothstein and then wiring me for a hundred thousand here, fifty there, to settle his losses. He's a menace. A *makke*. If I let him he'll destroy everything I worked so hard to build and there will be nothing for my wife and children yet to come.

The following Tuesday night Bernard, wearing his homburg, grey serge suit, spats, and new wingtip shoes with elevator heels, called for Libby, as arranged, to take her to see *The Kid* at the Regal. A grim Mr. Mintzberg greeted him at the front door. "I'm afraid Miss Mintzberg can't go out with you tonight."

"She isn't well?"

"God forbid," Mrs. Mintzberg said.

"So what's the problem?"

"Shame on you," Mrs. Mintzberg said.

And then Libby appeared behind her parents in the foyer, a wraith, her eyes red, twisting a damp handkerchief in her hands. "Gossips are saying your brother has dishonoured Clara Teitelbaum. I don't believe a word of it."

"I'm not like him, Mr. Mintzberg."

"Didn't I tell them you're always the gentleman," Libby said.

"You give the word, Mr. Mintzberg, I marry Libby tomorrow."

"Not under the present circumstances," Mr. Mintzberg said, whacking the front door shut, a tearful Libby calling out, "Do something, sweetheart."

"I have a hunch," Bernard said to Solomon a couple of days later, "that you wouldn't mind getting out of town for a while."

"I appreciate your concern."

"There are three carloads of whisky arriving at the CPR station at North Portal tomorrow night. Can you handle it?"

"Certainly."

"Don't accept cashier's cheques from the Nebraska boys, only cash, those crooks they use pads of blank cheques that were stolen from banks here. Can I count on you?"

"You're beginning to irritate me."

"You have to be at the station by midnight without fail because the drivers start arriving about that time. And you are not to blow the receipts in a card game, if you don't mind."

On arrival in North Portal the next afternoon, Solomon made directly for the hotel and started to drink with McGraw and the rum-runners. A bunch of them, including Solomon and McGraw, moved on to The Imperial Pool Hall to shoot snooker at a thousand dollars a game. Solomon, who was ahead twelve thousand dollars at a quarter to twelve, didn't feel it would be proper for him to lay down his cue and retreat to the railroad station, so he sent McGraw in his place.

Solomon was lining up a sharp-angled shot on the pink ball into the side pocket when the game was disrupted by two shotgun blasts that came from the direction of the railroad station. Everybody piled into the darkened street, reaching the station just in time to see a lone figure, shotgun in hand, dashing across the platform and taking off into the night in a Hudson Super-Six. Solomon bent over McGraw, dead on the station floor, shot from the window, once in the head, once through the chest. As the others gathered around, Solomon slipped away, retiring to his suite in the hotel. It was three A.M., and he had consumed half a bottle of cognac to no avail before he phoned Bernard. "McGraw went to the station in my place at midnight and somebody shot him."

"Oh, no. How is he?"

"Dead is how he is the last time I looked."

"Did they catch the killers?"

"No."

Bernard began to curse.

"I didn't want you to worry. I wanted you to know I was safe."

"Thank God for that."

"Something else while I'm at it," Solomon said, remembering to coat the blade with honey. "Mintzberg has been buying the wrong stocks on margin from Duncan, Shire &

Hamilton. Considering he has to be managing it on a parochial school principal's salary, I'd say he's heavily over-committed."

"With God's help he'll lose his shirt, that fucken *yekke*."

"Possibly he'd be grateful for a loan from an understanding son-in-law."

Afraid he might doze off in spite of himself, Solomon shoved his bureau against the door to his room and laid his gun on the bedside table, alongside his bottle of cognac and gold pocket watch that was inscribed:

From W.N. to E.G.
de bono et malo.

The murderer of Willy McGraw was never caught, but, so far as the RCMP was concerned, the motive was obvious. McGraw had been stripped of his diamond ring and, Solomon estimated, some nine thousand dollars in cash. However, within weeks, more than one cockeyed story about the murder was being floated in speakeasies as far away as Kansas City. McGraw, one theory had it, had been killed by hijackers in reprisal for his informing on a couple of them to the RCMP. Another theory ran that McGraw had been shot by mistake, the intended victim Solomon for having seduced the wife of a politician in Detroit. In support of that farrago there were witnesses who swore that the getaway car had a Michigan licence plate. Still others whispered that it was Solomon himself who had ordered the killing because McGraw had something dirty on him that went back years. Lending credence to that theory was the undeniable fact that it was Solomon who had sent McGraw to the railway station. Finally, some said that the killer had indeed been after Solomon, hired by the father of a girl he had ruined in Winnipeg.

In any event, Solomon was not seen on the prairie for months, and when he came back it was, to everybody's surprise, to marry a girl in Winnipeg. She was six months' pregnant at the time, living in seclusion in The Victory Hotel, her parents having disowned her. Solomon, they said, married her merely to give the child a name. An unnecessary gesture, as it turned out, because the baby girl was stillborn. Libby Gursky pronounced that a blessing in disguise, because otherwise the poor child would have been bound to live out her life under a cloud of shame.

THREE

◆

Moses Berger never visited a city without seeking out its second-hand bookshops, not satisfied with scanning the shelves but also rummaging through unsorted cartons in the basement. One of his most cherished discoveries was a memoir of R.B. Bennett, the New Brunswick-born prairie lawyer who led the Tories into office in Ottawa in 1930, ending a nine-year reign by Mackenzie King. The memoir, written by the prime minister's secretary, Andrew D. MacLean, began:

> The Right Honourable Richard Bedford Bennett, P.C., LL.D., D.C.L., K.C., M.P., Prime Minister of Canada, foremost statesman in an Empire of over four hundred million people, rises at seven-thirty, enjoys an ample breakfast, and is at his office, every morning, a few minutes before nine.
>
> At sixty-four years of age, he works fourteen hours a day, and plays not at all. His admirers fear for his health; his political enemies delight in spreading stories of his impending collapse; yet he carries on — for such has been his habit for twenty years — in his quiet way; occasionally complaining of the trials of public life; doing three men's

work, with little outward indication of the strain put upon his powerful mind or his clean body.

Struggling for clients in a little Western town — when the West *was* wild — and when clients were usually found in the bar room; "Dickie" Bennett did not drink, did not smoke, yet his friends were legion, and I should imagine that the majority of them are not averse to the uses of strong spirits, and of nicotine.

R.B. Bennett, descendant of United Empire Loyalists, a Methodist millionaire, a bachelor and former Sunday School teacher, was pledged to bring to justice the bootleggers who had been coddled by the Liberals for so long, but he didn't get round to it until 1934. By that time the Gurskys, directors of the thriving James McTavish & Sons, were happily ensconced on the Montreal mountainside. Mr. Bernard's mansion was dug into the highest ground, enabling him to look down on the adjoining homes of Solomon and Morrie as, one spring morning, he sat down to breakfast with Libby, three months' pregnant. The maid announced that there were two men at the door who wished to see him. "They're from the RCMP, sir, and wish to speak with you at once."

They had warrants for the arrest of Bernard, Solomon, and Morrie, who were taken to RCMP headquarters to be fingerprinted and photographed and then escorted to the Montreal Court of the King's Bench Chambers, where they were released on bail of $150,000 each. The Gursky boys, as the newspapers called them, were charged with the evasion of $7 million in customs duties and a further $15 million in excise taxes. Mr. Bernard was also charged with attempting to bribe Bert Smith, a customs officer.

It was the murder of Willy McGraw that ignited the prairie fire, politicians in faraway Ottawa sniffing the smoke that eventually led to the Gursky boys being scorched by a humiliating arrest. Following a plague of bank robberies instigated by bored American rum-runners, the murder of McGraw infuriated the law-abiding citizens of three prairie provinces, vociferous members of the Loyal Orange Lodge in particular. Prime Minister Mackenzie King heard the cry of his western children, consulted his crystal ball and the hands of his wall clock, and decreed an end to the export liquor trade in Saskatchewan, giving the Gurskys a month to shut down their operations there. However, King was too late to save the provincial Liberals from electoral defeat. A Tory candidate, taking to the stump, declared, "The Liberals have been in cahoots with the booze peddlers from the very beginning. Take Bernard Gursky, for instance, a millionaire many times over. He is alleged to have offered Inspector Smith a bribe of fifteen thousand dollars. Then how much do you think he and his brothers paid into Liberal coffers for immunity from prosecution all these years?" Next the Bishop of Saskatchewan, Cedric Brown, a former chaplain to the intrepid settlers of Gloriana, took to the pulpit. "Of the forty-six liquor export houses in Saskatchewan," the bishop proclaimed, "sixteen are run by people of the Hebrew persuasion. When the Jews form one half of one percent of the population, and own sixteen of the forty-six export houses, it is time they were given to understand that since they have been received in this country, and have been given rights enjoyed by other white men, they must not defile the country by engaging in disreputable pursuits." Then he quoted from a dockside sermon by the legendary Reverend Horn, who had led a company of God-fearing Britons westward ho to Gloriana. We are bound, the reverend had said, for the land of milk and honey. Not, the bishop added, for the fleshpots of Sodom and Gomorrah.

The bishop's condemnation of the Jew bootleggers swiftly turned into a chorus, joined by the United Grain Growers, the Loyal Orange Lodge, the Women's Christian Temperance Union, the Ku Klux Klan and the Tories. The Tories sailed into office in the provincial election, promising to bring the Gurskys to the bar of justice.

That had been tried before, of course, by Bert Smith, who claimed that, as a consequence, Mr. Bernard had attempted to bribe him. The charge would be vehemently denied by Mr. Bernard before the Royal Commission on Customs and Excise, but the commission ruled that in their view a prima facie case had been made sufficient to warrant prosecution being entered against Bernard Gursky. Unfortunately, such was the press of other business, the commission neglected to set a date for the trial.

The Royal Commission, as a matter of fact, did not convene until several years after the alleged bribe attempt, but only a week following Smith's confrontation with the Gurskys in the warehouse, he was, to his astonishment, reprimanded by his superiors and transferred to Winnipeg. He had only been in Winnipeg for a month when he discomfited the Gurskys again, this time impounding another bootlegger's car on a back road, the culprit fleeing into the bush. When Mr. Bernard heard the news, taking the call in Morrie's office, he ripped the telephone off the desk, flinging it out of the window. "I'm stuck with a little *goyishe* splinter under my fingernail."

"Aw, he's just a kid doing his job. One car. Big deal. You make a fuss and you'll draw even more attention to us from the newspapers."

"And I don't make a fuss the word will get out that a fucken Boy Scout can make trouble for Bernard Gursky and get away with it."

So Mr. Bernard went to Ottawa to meet the plump, rosy-cheeked Jules Omer Bouchard, chief preventive officer for the Department of Customs. Though Bouchard earned only four thousand dollars a year, he managed to maintain a mansion across the river in Hull, looked after by a niece; a retreat in Florida; and a riverside cottage in the Gaspé, a cabin cruiser tied up at the dock, the estate cared for by yet another of his nieces. He would end his days as a prison librarian, driven out of office by Tory scourges who pronounced him "a debauched public official, rolling in opulence like a hippo in the mud." Actually, he was a most affable fellow, prescient as well. Once having adjudged the liquor laws unenforceable, a Presbyterian perversion, he saw no reason why he shouldn't benefit from them. He was not avaricious, but savoured the good life, lavishing expensive gifts on his nieces and impecunious painters and writers whose work gave him pleasure.

A discerning art collector, Bouchard was an early patron of the work of Jean-Jacques Martineau, possibly the most prodigiously talented painter ever to emerge from French Canada. Alas, Martineau was unrecognized until years after the debt-ridden artist committed suicide in Granby in 1948. An event that led in 1970 to a seminal essay by a Parti

Québecois metaphysician, "*Qui a tué Martineau?*", in which it was charged that the painter had been murdered by anglophone indifference, which would be the lot of all Québecois artists, the white niggers of North America, until they were free to paint in their own language.

Bouchard paid Martineau four hundred dollars a month, and never descended to his cabin on the Baie de Chaleur without bringing a crate of Beaujolais, a quarter of venison or a freshly caught salmon, as well as a couple of his nieces. In exchange, he was allowed his choice of five canvases a year, one of which always hung behind his desk.

"Hey," Mr. Bernard said, after describing his troubles with Smith, "that's a wonderful painting you've got hanging there!" Pea-soup cod fishermen bringing in their catch. What a life, he thought. "You know, I'd give ten thousand dollars to own a picture like that."

"You must be joking."

"Fifteen. Cash," Mr. Bernard shot back grumpily, indignant because he had seen better on the cover of many a jigsaw puzzle box which would have set him back only twenty-five cents.

A week later the bootlegger's car that Smith had seized in Winnipeg was released by the Department of Customs and Excise and Smith was rebuked for having been seen driving the car for his personal use, a stain on the department's honour. A fulminating Smith wrote back to Ottawa to protest that he had been seen driving the car to the garage and that there had already been an attempt to bribe him by the Gurskys. Furthermore, his apartment had been burgled, documents stolen. Everything possible, he wrote, was being done to hinder his investigation of the Gurskys and their ilk.

Without waiting for a reply to his letter, an aroused Smith took it upon himself one evening to raid the United Empire Wholesalers, the Gursky warehouse in Winnipeg. He stumbled on Morrie, seated on a stool, straining a drum of alcohol through a loaf of rye bread.

"What are you doing?" Smith asked, coming up behind him.

"I have to. The stuff's rusty. Oh my God, it's you."

Smith found illegal compounding equipment on the premises, as well as a cardboard carton filled with counterfeit U.S. revenue stamps and a tea chest laden with forged labels for famous brands of American whiskies. He packed the evidence in a box, secured it with an official seal, and drove it down to the CPR express office to be shipped to Ottawa.

"What have you got there?" the clerk asked.

"Enough evidence to put the Gurskys in prison where they belong."

"Then I'd better keep a sharp eye on it and get it on the first train out."

Unfortunately by the time the box reached Ottawa much of the evidence was missing. Bouchard wired Smith to take no further action but to report directly to him in Ottawa at once. However, when Smith got to Bouchard's outer office he was told to wait. Mr. Bernard was already seated with the chief preventive officer.

"Holy cow," Mr. Bernard said, leaping out of his chair for a closer look, "where in the hell did you get another Martineau, my Libby is crazy for his stuff."

"Oh, I couldn't part with this one," Bouchard said. "It's a favourite of mine. His masterpiece."

A sugaring-off party in the woods, fat women lugging pails, men boiling the maple syrup, kids cooling the stuff off in a snowbank and eating it, an old fart playing the fiddle, everybody freezing their balls no doubt but for them a whoopee time. Some bunch.

"I'm talking fifteen thousand dollars," Mr. Bernard said, clicking open his attaché case.

"You've got to be joking. This one is a lot bigger than the first one you talked me out of."

Fucking frog chiseller. "How much bigger would you say, my good friend?"

"Twice."

"I'd say only as much again. Shake on it, Jules."

Mr. Bernard and Bouchard retired to a restaurant in Hull for lunch and then a dozy Bouchard stumbled back to his office, aching for his sofa, but reconciled to dealing with Smith first. "The fact is," he told Smith, "your action against the United Empire Wholesalers, while not constituting illegal

entry, has shown a failure of judgement that reflects badly on
this office and, therefore, I must tell you that you are
temporarily suspended from further duty in excise work. Until
we rule otherwise you are confined to customs work at the Port
of Winnipeg and you are not authorized to undertake any
outside investigations unless ordered by me."

On his return to Winnipeg, Smith composed a long letter to
the minister of justice asking why, after a Royal Commission
had established that there was a prima facie case against
Bernard Gursky for attempting to bribe him, no trial date had
yet been set. The minister wrote back to say, unfortunately
many of the Crown witnesses were ill and in any event the
matter was really the concern of Saskatchewan's attorney-
general. So Smith wrote to the attorney-general who replied
that in his humble opinion the problem was one of federal
jurisdiction. Smith also wrote to his MP. He wrote to the prime
minister. Several weeks later Smith received a letter
discharging him from the Customs and Excise service. A
cheque for three months' salary was enclosed.

Smith moved into a rented room, setting his photograph of
his parents standing before their sod hut in Gloriana on his
bedside table, his Bible alongside, and began pecking away
with two fingers at his second-hand Underwood, writing
letters to cabinet ministers in Ottawa, proffering evidence of
Gursky transgressions and querying the integrity of Jules
Omer Bouchard. He had proof, he said, that the Gurskys had
acquired a farm straddling the border in Quebec's Eastern
Townships, where one Albert Crawley had been wounded in a
gun fight. He speculated about the Gurskys' activities on the
Detroit River and observed that they owned a shipping
company in Newfoundland, with as many as thirty schooners
on charter, each one bound for St. Pierre and Miquelon.

Smith's letters went unacknowledged. Then, just as he
despaired of ever seeing justice done, R.B. Bennett was thrust
into office and soon had to contend with tin and tarpaper
shacks springing up everywhere and with farmers who called
their necessarily horse-drawn Model-Ts "Bennett buggies".
When thousands of the unemployed marched on Ottawa,
Bennett was convinced that the country was teetering on the
edge of a revolution. Unable to supply bread, he provided a

circus. The Gurskys were arrested in Montreal, charged with the evasion of customs duty and excise tax. Prominent photographs of their mountainside mansions began to appear in newspapers. Reporters revived interest in the unsolved murder of Willy McGraw.

The government put together an intimidating flotilla of lawyers to prosecute the case, the captain on the bridge Stuart MacIntyre of Morgan, MacIntyre and Maclean. Bert Smith proceeded to MacIntyre's office directly after his train from the west arrived at Windsor Station. MacIntyre heard him out and then met with his colleagues, his disappointment self-evident. "Unfortunately," he said, "the guy's not physically blessed, but an obvious nonentity who practically foams at the mouth at the mention of Bernard Gursky and is also out to get Bouchard, a member in good standing of both the St. Denis Club and the St. Jean Baptiste Society. Putting him on the stand is going to be risky."

The Gurskys also assembled a formidable legal team, shrewdly comprised of one lawyer, Bernard Langlois, who was a French-Canadian, and another, Arthur Benchley, with impeccable Westmount connections, their tactics orchestrated by Moti Singerman, who would never question a witness himself.

The trial, presided over by Judge Gaston Leclerc, the former chief bagman for the Quebec Liberal Party, got off to a promising start, so far as the Gurskys were concerned. MacIntyre, opening for the Crown, charged that the Gurskys had conspired to violate the statutes of a friendly country, smuggling liquor over the longest undefended border in the world. Langlois countered that it would be incredible for the courts of the province of Quebec to administer the laws of the United States. "If the prosecution wishes to charge the Gursky brothers with smuggling, let them prove it."

But in order for the Crown to make their case it was essential for them to have bank documentation proving that millions of dollars had passed between Ajax Shipping, the Gursky-owned company in Newfoundland, and Gilbraltar, a Gursky family trust. However, the RCMP raid on McTavish headquarters had been too late, the account books having been lost in a fire the day before.

Things took a turn for the worse once Solomon moved into the witness stand. Pressed about his activities as an alleged bootlegger, he asked MacIntyre, "When you invited people to dinner at your seaside cottage on the Cape, during Prohibition, did you usually serve your guests carrot juice or cocktails?"

"What possible concern is that of yours?"

"I'd like to know what I missed — if anything."

Had Solomon ever met with Al Capone? Yes. Longy Zwillman? Yes. Moe Dalitz? Yes again. "But," Solomon said, "I have also met with Joan Miró and George Bernard Shaw, but I am neither a painter nor a writer. I have talked with your brother in Ottawa more than once and I am not a bigot."

Judge Leclerc cautioned Solomon, not for the first time. MacIntyre, sorting through papers, feigning confusion, asked, "Can you tell me if the name Willy McGraw means anything to you?"

Before Arthur Benchley could protest that the question was irrelevant, Solomon replied, "He was a friend of mine."

That night a distraught Mr. Bernard, dismissing his chauffeur, took to the wheel of his Cadillac and drove out to Ste.-Adèle. Judge Leclerc was waiting for him there, having reluctantly agreed to open his country place, Pickwick Corner, the grounds landscaped and the interior decorated to honour his somewhat skewed notion of a country squire's cottage in the Cotswolds. True, the walled rose garden had been a failure, the rhododendrons had also yielded to frost, but there was a wishing well. Each spring, a host of golden daffodils. And the beautifully sculpted yews bordering his croquet lawn clearly showed the hand, according to one visitor, of a master choreographer.

Mr. Bernard joined Judge Leclerc in the living room, the fireplace wall adorned with paintings of the fox hunt, another wall lined with a grouping of backlit pewter plates and jugs. Both men sat in leather armchairs, Judge Leclerc filling his pipe with a fragrant mixture of tobacco imported from Fribourg and Treyer, in the Haymarket, his briar acquired from Inderwick's. "Bernard," Judge Leclerc said, smoothing his hairbrush moustache, tugging at his ascot, "we've jolly well got to give them something."

"How come Jules Omer Bouchard, making maybe five grand a year, owns a big house in Hull and another in Florida and an estate in the Gaspé, eighteen-year-old nieces coming out of the woodwork everywhere, if he isn't accepting bribes?"

"Jules is for it, anyway, the poor bloke, but that won't be nearly enough."

Mr. Bernard unlocked his attaché case.

"And that won't do it, either."

"Look here, you little prick, I go to jail, so do you."

"By Jove, are you threatening me?"

"Sure I am."

"Stu MacIntyre's keen for blood. If he wins this case he can choose between being the next minister of justice or a seat on the Supreme Court."

"What could he have against me?"

"Not you. Solomon. He tried to pick up Diana Morgan in that hotel he bought down here and he's been after her ever since, his intent undoubtedly priapic."

"I don't know about that, but he's got nooky on the brain that one. I'll tell him to stop. Consider it done."

"That young lady is a thoroughbred. She's a granddaughter of Sir Russell Morgan and a niece of Stu MacIntyre's. I hope to succeed MacIntyre as Master of the Ste.-Adèle Hunt Club. I would be the first French-Canadian to be so honoured. Fancy that." Judge Leclerc brought out a decanter of port and two large snifters. "Did Solomon order McGraw killed?"

"Oh, no. I couldn't."

"That's what I thought."

"My own brother."

"We've bloody well got to feed them something."

"Callaghan?"

"Not enough."

"My own flesh and blood."

"I understand."

"What could I get? Worst case."

"A heavy fine."

"I can handle that."

"And possibly ten years in prison."

The next morning Bert Smith was called to the witness stand, realizing a dream that had sustained him night after night for years, gnashing his teeth in bed, raging, waking in a sweaty tangle of sheets. In his mind's eye, given his day in court, Smith smote the Gurskys as David had Goliath, not with five smooth stones but with the truth. Then, the governor-general intervened on his behalf, reinstating him in customs and excise, the new chief investigating officer, seated in Bouchard's chair. But now, stepping up to be sworn in at last, dizzy, his throat dry, he was mortified to hear the squeak of the new shoes he had purchased for the occasion. His shirt collar choked, but he didn't dare loosen his tie. Although he had been to the toilet twice already his bladder was fit to burst. His stomach rumbled and he feared he might soil himself right there. Desperately trying to summon up MacIntyre's detailed instructions, instead he could only recall their lunch together at Delmo's, Smith, terrified of being caught out in a gaffe, waiting for the distinguished lawyer to order, mumbling, "I'll have the same, thank you, sir," to the waiter. Then disgracing himself, realizing too late that he was buttering his bread with the fish knife, his embarrassment compounded when MacIntyre magnanimously followed suit.

Responding to the simplest question, determined to please MacIntyre, such a fine gentleman, Smith instinctively raised a hand to his mouth to hide his snaggle-teeth, then, asked to speak up more clearly this time, he lowered his hand abruptly, blushing and flustered. Sliding in sweat, stumbling, all the speeches he had rehearsed again and again were lost to him. He heard himself talking, those were his lips moving, but he had no idea what he was saying. In fact, bleeding vitriol and incoherence in equal parts, painfully aware of MacIntyre's impatience and the grinning simians on the press bench, he did manage to blurt out that the accused, in the presence of his brothers and Tim Callaghan, had offered him a bribe of fifteen thousand dollars to let three American bootleggers go free. Then, even as he warmed to his tale, he grasped that MacIntyre, obviously annoyed, was distancing himself from him. "Thank you very much, Mr. Smith."

"But—"

"I have no more questions."

Later MacIntyre, pontificating in his boardroom before the firm's most recent law graduates, would explain: "I knew I never should have allowed that malignant little man to testify. No sooner did he take the oath than I felt the ill-wind on the back of my neck. You see, boys, it was no use. There wasn't anybody in that courtroom who hadn't once been stopped and had his baggage searched by just such a punctilious little turd."

MacIntyre's questioning of him done, Smith was suddenly aware of somebody else swimming into focus, the portly Langlois, raising titters as he established that Smith was a Boy Scout leader who didn't drink or smoke. And probably, Langlois ventured, didn't have a sense of humour either or he would have realized when he was being teased by Mr. Bernard, a well-known practical joker.

"No bribe was offered," Mr. Bernard testified, "but Smith came to the warehouse office when we happened to be checking out the contents of our safe, our monthly receipts out on the desk, maybe fifteen thousand dollars, and winking at my brothers, nudging Callaghan, I happened to say, hey, kid, how would you like some of this money? You could get those teeth fixed. Buy a pair of shoes that didn't squeak . . ."

Laughter rose from the reporters.

" . . . treat your Boy Scout troop to ice-cream sodas. Maybe take out a girl for once. Wowee!"

Morrie said, "I can't help but feel sorry for Mr. Smith, really such a nice, polite boy, but it was all a misunderstanding."

Callaghan swore that no bribe had been offered in his presence.

And then Solomon took to the stand, aware of Smith sitting there, rocking in place, a hand held to his mouth, his eyes empty.

"Am I correct in saying," MacIntyre said, "that you asked to speak to Mr. Smith alone?"

"Yes, but he wanted a witness."

MacIntyre chuckled.

"So Callaghan stayed behind," Solomon said.

"And was present when you warned Mr. Smith not to testify against you?"

"I did not warn him. I advised him not to testify."

"But to take the money that was still on the table?"

"To take it or leave it, as he saw fit."

"And then," MacIntyre said, smiling at the witness over his reading glasses, "possibly you even said unto him, All these things will I give thee, if thou wilt fall down and worship me."

Judge Leclerc looked up, amazed. Before Langlois could intervene, MacIntyre continued, "If you recognize the quote . . ."

"The New Testament?"

"Yes."

"I don't know about you, Mr. MacIntyre, but I've always found sequels something of a disappointment, especially Matthew."

"Just who do you think you are to say a thing like that?"

"I am that I am, if *you* recognize the quote."

Judge Leclerc hastily adjourned the court, announcing that it would reconvene at the usual hour the following morning.

And that night a troubled Mr. Bernard drove out to Ste.-Adèle again, where the judge was waiting.

"Guilty or not," Mr. Bernard said, "it goes against my nature to turn in my own brother. I'd rather take my medicine like a man."

"More's the pity."

"But if MacIntyre really, really wants to get at the truth I suggest that he get in touch with this man," he said, passing him a slip of paper. "He will be arriving at the Windsor Hotel tomorrow afternoon."

A couple of days later, Stu MacIntyre, questioning Solomon again, seemed to wander without point, defence lawyers leaping up to protest the irrelevance of his queries, Judge Leclerc overruling them, displaying uncharacteristic patience and good humour.

"I take it," MacIntyre said, "that you are something of a gambling man?"

"Yes."

"Horses?"

"Yes."

"Snooker?"

"On occasion."

"Like the night you sent Willy McGraw down to the railroad station, where he was killed by unknown gunmen?"

Arthur Benchley shot out of his seat, infuriated. Judge Leclerc, taking his point, reprimanded MacIntyre. MacIntyre apologized and was then allowed to proceed.

"Poker?"

"Yes."

"As a matter of interest, for high stakes?"

"I've got a feeling we're going to see a surprise witness here."

"You haven't answered the question, Mr. Gursky."

"Just because you indicate a garden path, sir, doesn't mean I have to follow it only to be confronted by a liar."

Following a caution to the witness from Judge Leclerc, MacIntyre put the question to Solomon again.

"For high stakes. Yes."

"Didn't you once wager your father's general store, as well as a good deal of cash against — "

"You're forgetting the blacksmith's shop and Charley Lin's two rooming houses."

"That as well then, against the deed to the Queen Victoria Hotel, then the property of the late Willy McGraw?"

"Yes."

"Did you win?"

"Fortunately."

"My own card-playing is limited to the occasional rubber of bridge, so please correct me if I'm wrong, Mr. Gursky, but I would imagine in games played for such stakes it is crucial that the players trust each other to both honour their debts and play strictly according to the rules."

"What you lack in subtlety, sir, you do make up for in prescience."

"Would you please — "

"Answer the question?"

"Yes."

"You are correct."

"Am I also correct in assuming that if a player were suspected of cheating he would no longer be welcome at the tables?"

"If you are looking for a game, sir, I could arrange it. Outside the confines of this courtroom, I'm sure you wouldn't dare play with a stacked deck."

"Would you please answer the questions as they are put to you, Mr. Gursky."

"Yes, an unscrupulous player would soon be discovered and find himself *persona non grata* at the tables, to say the least."

"So had somebody threatened to compromise your no doubt enviable reputation as an honourable player it would have been a serious matter?"

"A very serious matter."

"That's all for the moment, Mr. Gursky, and I do thank you for the patience and of course the unfailing courtesy of your replies." But as Solomon got up, MacIntyre motioned for him to sit down again. "Sorry. Just one more thing. Going back to that game in which you were lucky enough to win the Queen Victoria Hotel — "

"From *the late* Willy McGraw?"

"Yes. From the late Mr. McGraw. Can you tell me did you use new playing cards?"

"Yes."

"And where were they purchased?"

"Why, from A. Gursky and Sons, General Merchants."

Charley Lin wasn't summoned to the stand until late in the afternoon. He averted his eyes as he waddled past Solomon, who smiled and whispered something that made Charley stumble and then turn to the judge to protest that he had had a long journey and did not feel well.

Judge Leclerc, noting the late hour, adjourned the court, asking Mr. Lin to resume the stand at ten the next morning.

But the next morning Solomon Gursky did not turn up in court at the appointed hour and was not to be found at home, either. He had met with Mr. Bernard the previous evening, according to Clara Gursky, the brothers quarrelling bitterly, and then he had gone out for a stroll at six in the morning and hadn't been seen since.

"Did he take a suitcase with him, Mrs. Gursky?"

"No."

It was late in the afternoon before the RCMP established that Solomon had taken a taxi to Cartierville airport and flown off in his Gypsy Moth with the raven painted on the fuselage.

Bound for where?

North was all Mr. Gursky said.

Where north, for Christ's sake?

Far, he said.

Refuelling in Labrador, it was later discovered, heading still farther out in appalling weather conditions, a whiteout predicted.

The next day's newspapers featured page one photographs of the late Willy McGraw, lying in a puddle of blood on the railway station floor. There were interviews with Charley Lin. Photographs of Solomon seen seated with "Legs" Diamond in the Hotsy-Totsy Club; Solomon standing on a corner of Third Avenue, kibitzing with Izzy and Moe, the fabled Prohibition agents; and, finally, a photograph of Solomon in his flier's uniform, standing before his Sopwith Camel, on an airfield "somewhere in France."

Reporters speculated that McGraw had discovered Solomon was playing with marked cards acquired from his father's general store. Fearful of exposure, or possibly responding to blackmail, Solomon appointed McGraw manager of the Duke of York Hotel in North Portal and then had him murdered, his own alibi foolproof.

RCAF search planes hunted for Solomon's Gypsy Moth, which seemed to have disappeared after refuelling in Labrador, where the mechanic who had serviced the plane was sharply questioned.

"Didn't he tell you where he was heading?"

"North."

"We know that, damn it, but where?"

"Far, he said."

A bush pilot, consulted by the RCMP, said that the day Solomon had taken off nothing else was moving, because it was as good as flying through a bottle of milk. In a whiteout, he explained, there is absolutely no horizon, and even the most experienced pilot, riding it out, wheeling and turning, his sense of gravity gone, is inclined to fly upside down into the ground. And that, he felt, is what happened to Gursky somewhere in the barrens, where only an Eskimo had a chance to survive.

Shuffling into court three days after Solomon's disappearance, Mr. Bernard apologized to Judge Leclerc for being unshaven and for wearing a suit jacket with a torn collar and slippers. It was not, he assured him, out of disrespect for the court, but in deference to the tradition of his people when mourning the death of an immediate family member, in this case a cherished brother, no matter what his sins.

Five days later, the Gypsy Moth still missing, Judge Gaston Leclerc delivered his verdict to an attentive court:

"The Crown claims that the accused maintained agencies in Newfoundland and St. Pierre et Miquelon for the purpose of smuggling and that the sales made there were proof of an illegal conspiracy. However, the accused were jolly well within their rights. They were legally entitled to maintain such agencies in such places, and it is no secret that at the time many Canadian distilleries sold as many of their products as they could outside of Canada. These acts, I'm bound to point out, were legal and the vendors were not obliged to verify the destination of the goods they sold, nor was there any obligation upon them to inquire of the buyers what they intended to do with the goods." The judge concluded, "There is no evidence that the accused committed a criminal act. I am of the opinion that there is not, prima facie, proof of a conspiracy as alleged, and the accused are herewith discharged." However, he did add that if Solomon Gursky were to be found alive there would be other charges that he would have to answer to in court.

The next morning an RCMP inspector subpoenaed Judge Leclerc's bank records and raided his safety-deposit box. No incriminating evidence was found. In any event, Judge Leclerc retired the following year, stopping in Zurich before proceeding to the Cotswolds, where the estate he acquired had a walled rose garden, masses of rhododendrons, a labyrinth and apple and pear trees.

The long-awaited verdict on the Gurskys didn't even make page one, because the same day charred pieces of a disintegrated Gypsy Moth were found strewn over a three-mile area in the barrens. Many of the airplane parts were brought in by a wandering band of Eskimos, all of them wearing sealskin parkas with fringes hanging from the corners, each fringe made up of twelve silken strands. One of the Eskimos had found an attaché case embossed with the initials S.G. It contained Solomon's passport and close on two hundred thousand dollars in American banknotes. Solomon's body was never found. It was assumed to have been blown apart when the Gypsy Moth exploded, the pieces dragged off and consumed by the white wolves of the barrens.

The next morning Mr. Bernard summoned Morrie to his house. "Before Solomon ran away," he said, "he was good enough to sign these new partnership papers."

Fifty-five percent of McTavish for Mr. Bernard, thirty percent for Solomon and his descendants, and fifteen percent for Morrie.

"I thought my share was going to be nineteen percent."

"I fought for you like a tiger, but he wouldn't budge."

Mr. Morrie signed.

"There's only the two of us left now," Mr. Bernard said.

"Yes."

"But you mustn't worry about me. I've decided to start having regular check-ups."

"Should I do the same you think?"

"Aw. Why go to the expense? You look terrific."

FOUR

◆

Becky Schwartz's name was now a fixture in E.J. Gordon's Social Notes in the *Gazette*, most recently in a column celebrating an anniversary of the Beaver Club; Harvey, like the other achievers who had been invited, bedecked in a beaver hat and a tailcoat and sporting a goatee for one of the grandest nights on the city's high society calendar.

"Boy, do you ever look like a *shmuck*," Becky had said before they started out.

"I'm not going."

"We're going. But would you please line the inside of that hat with paper or something. It looks like you have no forehead."

The Beaver Club was founded in 1959 to recreate the riotous dinners held two centuries earlier by Montreal's fur traders. "Welcoming the guests," E.J. Gordon wrote, "were Caughnawaga Indians, clad in doeskins, the men wearing feathered headdresses, standing beside their tepee in an encampment in the lobby of the Queen Elizabeth Hotel." Seated cross-legged immediately before the tepee, beating the drums, was a fetching young girl, actually a great-great-granddaughter of Ephraim Gursky and Lena Green Stockings, who would later enchant the guests with her rendition of "Hava-negilla".

Becky studied E.J. Gordon's column in her four-poster bed the next morning, reclining against satin pillows, picking at a bran muffin. She was in a sour mood. Problems with the children. Bernard, into coke and God knows what else, was falling behind with his studies at Harvard. Libby, at Bennington, wouldn't come home until Harvey divested his shares in any company with holdings in South Africa. And Becky, her outsize donations to the art museum and symphony orchestra notwithstanding, had still failed to crack the right dinner-party lists. She insisted that Harvey take her to dinner at the Ritz.

"The Moffats are watching our table. Order caviar."

"But I don't like it."

"And don't you dare mash chopped onions into it." Then she told him what she had decided. "We're going to redecorate the house and then hold a masked ball and invite *le tout* Montreal."

Becky went after the best that money could buy, the much sought-after Giorgio Embroli of Toronto and Milan. Giorgio, a master of rectilinear circuitry, did not undertake commissions just like that. He had first to explore the physic boundaries of the three-dimensional space involved and to test the stream of kinetic energy bound to flow between him and his clients. Harvey flew him into town in a Gursky Challenger jet. He and Becky welcomed him to their house by cracking open a bottle of Pouilly-Fumé that came out of a Napa Valley vineyard only recently acquired by McTavish. Giorgio raised his glass to the light, took a sip, swished it around in his mouth and grimaced. "Sadly," he said, "most Californian wines are completely incapable of producing a sensory shock. They never surprise you. They tell you how they were made, but not how they came into existence." Then, patting his ruby lips with a handkerchief, he said, "Show me, please, where I can rinse out the palate."

Harvey didn't blink at Giorgio's fees. He stood by as the interior decorator floated out of the house, pausing at the front door, offering a pale scented cheek to Becky to be kissed. But once he was gone, Harvey threw out the Baccarat wine glass that had touched his lips and the Pratesi towel that he had used in the hall toilet. "I know they say that you can only get it from an exchange of bodily fluids," he said, "but until they know for sure we're not taking any chances."

Giorgio's live-in companion, Dov HaGibor, was a talented painter out of Ramat Aviv. He had started out as an abstract impressionist, determined to create work that celebrated a collision of ur-references as well as trapping infinity and assigning a linguistic function to colour. Recently, however, HaGibor had confounded his admirers by converting to high-voltage realism, his pictures interpreting fractured rather than unified space. He found his subjects by seeking out junk shops wherever he travelled, never knowing what he was looking for but recognizing it immediately he found it. An old photograph, discovered in a Salvation Army sale in Montreal, was the *causa causans*, as Walter Osgood, curator of the Gursky Art Foundation put it in his essay in *Canadian Art*, of the famous 14×8-foot canvas that was to dominate the redecorated Schwartz living room, its value escalating once HaGibor had died of AIDS.

There had been a barely legible inscription on the back of the original photograph that HaGibor had burnt once his painting was done: "Gloriana, October 10, 1903". And "Gloriana" is what HaGibor called what came to be recognized as his masterpiece, the title an enigma, a matter of contention. Some critics argued that it made the artist's satirical intent clear, but others insisted just as forcibly that HaGibor had meant his work to stand as a complaint against *la condition humaine*, as witness the Hebrew words flying off to the right. The words, translated, read: My days are swifter than a weaver's shuttle, and are spent without hope.

In any event, the undeniably striking canvas showed a bewildered couple, the husband dour, the wife looking stricken, standing before a sod hut, the landscape bleak as it was bare. Though the couple in the original photograph had hardly ever seen each other nude in thirty-two years of marriage, they were naked to the world in the painting, the woman's breasts desiccated and her genitals bald; the man pigeon-chested with a penis like a withered worm.

Harvey was determined to dump the canvas as soon as that

hysterical Italian faggot was out of their house for good, but he relented once Walter Osgood came to inspect "Gloriana" and clearly coveted it. Then "Gloriana" was photographed for the cover of *Canadian Art*. Westmount matrons who had cut Becky at the annual museum ball now vied for invitations to view HaGibor's last statement. The curator of the National Gallery in Ottawa requested permission to exhibit the painting, assuring Becky that a notice mounted alongside would read, "From the private collection of Mr. and Mrs. Harvey Schwartz." Dealers began to make unsolicited offers that would have enabled Harvey to quadruple his original investment, but he was not prepared to sell. Instead he increased the insurance on "Gloriana" five-fold. A risky move, as far as he was concerned, because if the picture were stolen anti-Semites would whisper that he had arranged it to collect the money. Harvey Schwartz would be blamed. Count on it.

EIGHT

ONE

—◆—

"According to the Haidas, of the unfortunately named Queen Charlotte Islands, more properly Haida Gwai, the Islands of the People," Sir Hyman once said to Moses, "according to them, before there was anything, before the great flood had covered the earth and receded, before the animals walked the earth or the trees covered the land or the birds flew between the trees, there was the raven. Because the raven had always existed and always would. But he was dissatisfied as, at the time, the whole world was still dark. Inky black. The reason for this was an old man living in a house by the river. The old man had a box which contained a box which contained an infinite number of boxes, each nestled in a box slightly larger than itself until finally there was a box so small all it could contain was all the light in the universe. The raven was understandably resentful. Because of the darkness on the earth he kept bumping into things. He was slowed down in his pursuit of food and other fleshly pleasures and in his constant and notorious need to meddle and change things. And so, inevitably, he took it upon himself to steal the light of the universe from the old man."

Moses and Sir Hyman were strolling through Regent's Park, en route to Prunier's.

"But I think I'll save the rest of the story for lunch, dear boy. A pity Lucy couldn't join us."

"An audition."

"In the end she will have to settle for being a producer, putting her inheritance and business acumen to some use. But don't you dare repeat I suggested as much."

From the time Moses first met Sir Hyman in Blackwell's bookshop, through his turbulent affair with Lucy and after, he had listened to the old necromancer pronounce on many things, but mostly politics. Mind you, they first began to see a lot of each other in an especially febrile year. A watershed year. 1956. Nikita Khrushchev denounced Stalin in a speech to the Twentieth Congress of the Communist Party, hinting that Stalin had been responsible for the murder of Kirov, his licence for the show trials that led to the execution of two more rivals, Zinoviev and Kamenev. After Khrushchev snitched, Nasser grabbed the Suez Canal. Then, in the autumn, Russian tanks rolled into Budapest. The British and the French, in collusion with the Israelis, attacked Suez.

Moses and Sir Hyman talked at length about these matters, strolling through Regent's Park or drinking late in Sir Hyman's library, the old man sitting with a malacca cane clasped between his knees, his chin resting on the handle. Moses also became a fixture at Cumberland Terrace dinner parties, Sir Hyman seated at the head of a dining-room table with an Irish linen tablecloth, lecturing tycoons and cabinet ministers and actresses. Moses was enchanted. He was spellbound. But he also came to feel possessed. He discovered, to his consternation, that he had picked up some of Sir Hyman's patterns of speech. Moses Berger, a Jeanne Mance boy born and bred, actually addressing people as "dear boy". Even more chilling, leaning against the bar in The Bale of Hay, he once found himself passing off a witticism of Sir Hyman's as his own. Another day he discovered himself drifting through the cane shop in New Oxford Street trying out various walking sticks for effect. He fled. He turned down the next invitation to dinner and the one after. Then, inevitably, he was drawn back to the flame.

Drinking together in the library one night, Moses and Sir

Hyman discussed the Khrushchev speech, Moses inveighing against the Nazi-Soviet Pact of 1939, recalling the sense of betrayal round the table with the crocheted cloth. Sir Hyman pounced, holding forth on the history behind that devil's accord. If not for the Germans, he said, there might never have been a Bolshevik revolution in the first place. They were the ones who slipped the silver bullet on to the sealed train to the Finland Station, counting on Lenin to seize power and take Russia out of the war. Then, in 1922, when the revolution was still in quarantine, the German delegation to the Genoa Conference signed the Rapallo Treaty with the Soviets, effectively ending their isolation. "The consequences of that treaty," Sir Hyman said, "are not without interest."

It enabled the Germans to evade the arms clauses of the Versailles Treaty, sending air and tank officers to Russia for training. In return, the Germans built airfields for the Bolsheviks and tutored them in the military arts. "With hindsight," Sir Hyman said, "we can say that the Wehrmacht that all but conquered Russia was trained there between 1922 and 1933, and instructed the army that destroyed them."

Each time they met, Sir Hyman inquired about Moses's progress with his study of the Beveridge Plan. Finally Moses confessed that he had put it aside. Instead he was thinking of writing something about Lucy's father, Solomon Gursky.

"Ah."

Sir Hyman, he allowed, had inadvertently led him to a great discovery. While cataloguing Sir Hyman's Arctic library, he had accidently stumbled on an unmistakable reference to Solomon's grandfather Ephraim Gursky, and now he suspected that Ephraim might have been a survivor of the Franklin expedition.

"But there were no survivors," Sir Hyman said.

"Certainly that would appear to be the case," Moses agreed, adding that he would soon be returning to Canada to pursue his researches.

"And will the Gursky family finance such mischief?"

Moses laughed.

"How will you manage, then?"

"I suppose I'll have to teach."

"I'll put you on an allowance, my dear boy."

"I couldn't," Moses blurted out.

"Why not?"

"I'm not sure."

"Coyness doesn't become you, Moses. Neither are you a bore. Yes or no. I haven't the patience to twist your arm before you condescend to accept a stipend from an indecently rich old man."

"Let me think about it."

Moses had only been back in Montreal for a month, filling in at McGill for a friend on a sabbatical, when he wrote to Sir Hyman, thanking him for his generosity, but turning down his offer of a stipend. Actually he was longing to take the money, but he suspected the offer was more in the nature of a test. If he accepted, he would be diminished in Sir Hyman's estimation, and what he wanted, above all, was for the old man to love him. For the old man to look upon him as a son.

Moses's letter went unanswered for months of anguish, convincing him that he had blundered yet again, offending Sir Hyman when his real intention, he acknowledged, had been to ingratiate himself. Then Sir Hyman was heard from at last. A letter from Budapest. Would Moses consider coming over for the summer to help with some unspecified chores, while Lady Olivia was cruising the Greek islands with some old friends? Moses leaped at the opportunity.

"And how is the work progressing?" Sir Hyman asked.

"By fits and starts."

"I was hoping you had brought me some pages to read."

Moses was put up in a spare bedroom in the flat on Cumberland Terrace, his initial chore to compile another catalogue, this time of Sir Hyman's collection of Judaica. He was sent to antiquarian book dealers in Dublin and Inverness to inspect and acquire specific Arctic titles, the price of no consequence. He flew to Rome and Athens to deliver packets that could not be entrusted to the mail. Most weekends he joined Sir Hyman at his estate on the Sussex coast, accompanying him for a swim before breakfast, and encouraged to roam at will through the rambling house and grounds.

Moses did not get over the following summer but, instead, flew out to the Northwest Territories, ostensibly to visit Henry and Nialie, but actually to seek out Eskimos named Gor-ski, Girskee, or Gur-ski. However, he did keep in touch with Sir Hyman. Moses's letters, polished again and again before he dared send them off, instantly regretted as too familiar or not sufficiently entertaining, were acknowledged by the occasional postcard from Havana or Amman or Saigon. And Moses was back in the summer of 1959, met by a Bentley at Heathrow and driven directly to Sussex. Sir Hyman welcomed him with champagne. "I can't tell you," he said, "how much I'm looking forward to reading the pages you brought me."

"Not yet."

"But you are making progress?"

Moses told him that he had acquired transcripts of the trial. He had been out west twice. He had spoken with Mr. Morrie again. "According to Lucy, her father kept a journal."

"And that would be a big help, would it?"

"If it still exists and I manage to get my hands on it, yes, certainly, an enormous help."

"Well, if you really haven't brought me any pages, I do hope you at least remembered to pack your dinner jacket."

Sir Hyman and Lady Olivia were expecting something like sixty guests that evening, some arriving by car and others in a bus chartered for the party in honour of a visiting American senator. Sir Hyman, waving his hand, had assembled the usual suspects for the occasion. A lively but potentially vitriolic mix of politicians, film and theatre people, men "who were something in the city," art dealers, journalists, and any American of consequence who happened to be in London. Included in the latter group, much to Moses's delight, was Sam Burns, en route to Moscow to cover Vice-President Nixon's visit for the network.

Moses, taking Sam by the arm, led him on a private tour of the gardens and then through a basement door, down a winding corridor, into a vast wine cellar. He sat Sam down at a table, fetched a couple of glasses, and cracked open a bottle of vintage champagne.

"Christ," Sam said, "are you allowed to do that?"

"Hymie wouldn't mind in the least."

"You call him that?"

"Sure."

Sam strolled down one of the wine cellar rows, scanning labels. "Not a bottle of Kik Cola anywhere. My luck."

"Remember Gurd's?"

"Orange Crush."

"May Wests."

"Cherry Blossoms."

"Who centred the Punch Line?"

"Elmer fucking Lach."

"The Razzle Dazzle Line?"

"Buddy O'Connor."

"How come RAF night-fighters can see in the dark?"

"Because they eat their carrots. Now tell me where your benefactor, if that's what he is, gets his millions?"

"This is nothing," Moses said. "Come. I'll show you some of the paintings he doesn't even bother to display upstairs."

Moses led him into another room, pressed one of the sequence of buttons under the wall thermostat, and out slid a long rack: a Francis Bacon, a Graham Sutherland, a Sidney Nolan.

"He's going to think we're snooping down here. Let's go, Moses."

A cloth covered a painting leaning against the wall. "Let's take a peek," Moses said.

"I don't think we ought to."

"It's probably the new Bonnard he bought."

Moses lifted the cloth and revealed what appeared to be the most conventional of portraits. A lovely young bourgeois lady seated in a wicker chair. She wore a broadbrimmed straw hat with a pink bow, a multi-layered chiffon dress, also with a pink bow, and held a bouquet of sweet williams in her hands. But there was something quirky about the portrait. The young lady's eyes were of a different colour. One eye brown, one eye blue.

"Oh my God," Moses howled. "Oh Christ!"

"What's wrong?"

"Let's go."

"I haven't finished my drink."

"*Let's go, I said.*"

Sir Hyman was chatting with a group in the living room.

"I've got to speak to you," Moses said.

"Now?" Sir Hyman asked, eyebrows raised.

"Right now."

"Oh. Well. Yes. Certainly. The library."

Moses waited an exasperating five minutes before Sir Hyman joined him there.

"How come, Sir Hyman Kaplansky, how come, Sir Hyman," Moses shouted, "that sitting on the floor downstairs there is a portrait of Diana McClure née Morgan?"

"Ah."

"Have you brought me any pages, *dear boy*. I can't tell you how much I'm looking forward —"

"I'd all but given up on you. I was beginning to think you'd never find it," Sir Hyman said, deflating him with a stroke.

"Does Lucy know?"

"Nor Henry. And you are not to say anything to them, now or ever. I want your word on that."

"Dear boy."

"*Yingele.*"

"Bastard."

Two couples, carrying champagne glasses, drifted into the library. "Oh dear, are we intruding, Hymie?"

"Most certainly not. I was just telling Moses about my latest acquisition," he said, indicating the picture hanging over the fireplace. A raven perched on a half-open sea shell, human beings struggling to emerge from it.

"This is the raven that stole the light of the world from an old man and then scattered it throughout the skies. After the great flood had receded, he flew to a beach to gorge himself on the delicacies left behind by the water. However, he wasn't hungry for once." Looking directly at Moses, a stricken Moses, he went on to say, "But his other appetites — lust, curiosity, and the unquenchable itch to meddle and provoke things, to play tricks on the world and its creatures — these remained unsatisfied. The raven, his wings crossed behind his back, strolled along the beach, his sharp eyes alert for any unusual sight or sound. Taking to the air, he called petulantly to the empty sky. To his delight, he heard an answering cry, a muffled squeak.

"Scanning the beach something caught his eye. A gigantic clamshell. He landed and found that the shell was full of little creatures, cowering in the terror of his menacing shadow. So the raven leaned his great head close to the shell, and with his smooth trickster's tongue that had got him in and out of so many misadventures during his troubled and troublesome existence, he coaxed and cajoled the little creatures to come out and play."

Sir Hyman paused as a waiter brought everybody more champagne.

"As you well know, Moses, the raven speaks in two voices, one harsh and dissembling, and the other, which he used now, seductive. So it wasn't long before one after another the little shell-dwellers timidly emerged. Bizarre they were. Two-legged like the raven, but without glossy feathers or thrusting beak or strong wings. They were the original humans."

Sir Hyman paused again for a sip from his glass and the two couples, more than somewhat bored, took advantage of the break to retreat from the library.

"I have so many questions," Moses said.

"And my house is full of guests. We'll talk on Wednesday."

"Why not tomorrow?"

"Because tomorrow noon you are flying to Paris. A package to deliver. You are booked into the Crillon for three nights. A certain M. Provost will join you for breakfast on Monday or the very latest Tuesday, and you will hand over the package with my compliments."

Provost did not appear on Monday morning. Tuesday morning Moses sat down to breakfast, opened the *Times*, and read that Sir Hyman Kaplansky, the noted financier, had apparently drowned in stormy seas. Sir Hyman, as was his habit, had set out early Monday morning for his pre-breakfast swim in spite of gale warnings, and did not return. His beach robe, slippers, and the book he was reading, were found abandoned in the sand. Lady Olivia told reporters that Sir

Hyman, who suffered from a weak heart, had been cautioned not to swim unaccompanied or in rough seas, but he was an obstinate man. Foul play was not suspected. Fishing trawlers in the area had been alerted and lifeboats were out searching in high seas.

They needn't bother, Moses thought, bitterly amused. Obviously the raven with the unquenchable itch was at it again, playing tricks on the world and its creatures. *Once by air*, he thought, *and now by water.*

Provost failed to appear again. A frustrated Moses retired to his room, lit a cigar, and considered the package on his bed for a long time before he tore it open.

It contained three morocco-bound volumes of the journals of Solomon Gursky and a letter addressed to Moses Berger, Esq. The letter advised him that he was the recipient of an income of thirty thousand dollars a year to be paid quarterly by Corvus Trust, Zurich.

Moses lay down on the bed, picked up a volume of the journals, and opened it at random.

"Fort McEwen, Alberta. 1908. Late one winter afternoon I found my grandfather waiting for me on his sled outside the school house. Ephraim stank of rum. His cheek was bruised and his lower lip was swollen . . . ."

TWO

◆

A ceiling-to-floor bookcase in the living room of Moses's cabin in the woods was crammed with books, newspaper and magazine clippings relating to the life of the elusive, obscenely rich Sir Hyman Kaplansky, as he then styled himself.

The index of the third volume of the celebrated diaries of a British MP with impeccable Bloomsbury bona fides revealed several entries for Sir Hyman Kaplansky.

May 17, 1944

Lunch at the Travellers with Gladwyn and Chips. We were joined by Hyman Kaplansky, his cultivated dandyish manner insufficient to conceal the ghetto greaser within. He allowed that he was frightened of the V.11s. I suggested that he ought to think of his loved ones on the battlefield who were at far greater risk than he was.

Hyman: "That wouldn't work for me at all, dear boy. I have no loved ones on the battlefield. They are all in firewatching right here. The buggers' battalions, don't you know?"

An earlier entry was dated September 12, 1941.

Dined at the Savoy with Ivor. When Hyman Kaplansky stopped at our table I told him how *triste* I felt about the martyred Jews of Poland and how after Eden had read his statement in the House we all stood up as a tribute.

"If my unfortunate brethren only knew it," he said, "I'm sure they would feel most obliged. Did the Speaker stand up as well?"

"Yes."

"How very moving."

The Jewish capacity for cynicism is really insufferable. Although I loathe anti-Semites, I do dislike Jews.

June 8, 1950

Lunch at the Reform Club. The beastly Sir Hyman is there with Guy and Tom Driberg. Driberg is carrying on about his favoured "cottages" in Soho.

"Why municipal vandals," he said, "should have thought it necessary to destroy so many of them I do not know. I suppose it is one expression of anti-homosexual prejudice. Yet no homo, cottage-cruising, ever prevented a hetero from merely having a whiz. While to do one's rounds of the cottages — the alley by the Astoria, the dog-leg lane opposite the Garrick Club, the one near the Ivy, the one off Wardour Street — provided homos, not all of whom are given to rougher sports, with healthy exercise."

June 7, 1951

Dinner at the Savoy. Sir Hyman Kaplansky at another table, entertaining some of the old Tots and Quots. Zuckerman, Bernal, and Haldane. Everybody is discussing the Burgess-Maclean affair. Sir Hyman says, "I know Guy to be a coward and a Bolshie and I'm not surprised he did a bunk."

The next entry for Sir Hyman dealt at length with that infamous dinner party in his Cumberland Terrace flat. A Passover *seder*, of all things, to which Sir Hyman — much to Lady Olivia's horror — had invited the MP and other noted anti-Semites. Among them, a couple of survivors of the Cliveden set, an unabashed admirer of Sir Oswald Mosley, a famous novelist, a celebrated actress, a West End impresario, a Polish count and a rambunctious cabinet minister who was an adamant opponent of further Jewish settlement in troubled Palestine. Why did they come?

The novelist, arguably the most gifted of his time, wrote in his diary:

March 21, 1953

All in order for our trip to Menton. I am assured that the villa has been furnished to my taste, the servants will be adequate, and there will be no Americans to be seen. We travel in a filthy carriage to Dover and then board the boat. The usual drunken commercial travellers and this time a number of Jews, presumably tax-evaders. This reminds Sybil that we are expected to dine at Sir Hyman Kaplansky's the evening after our return. The food and wine will be excellent. Certainly no problems with ration coupons in that quarter.

Another diary, this one kept by the actress, reminded her many admirers of exactly what she was wearing (an outfit especially created for her by Norman Hartnell) on the day the Bomb fell on Hiroshima. On another page she revealed for the first time that her only child lay dying in Charing Cross Hospital on the night theatrical tradition obliged her to open in *Peonies for Penelope*, a musical that ran for three years at the Haymarket in spite of the posh critics. An entry dated three days before Sir Hyman's dinner party described a lunch at the Ivy with the West End impresario, a noted sybarite.

April 12, 1953

Signs of the times. At one table a loud infestation of newly affluent proles. GI brides, Cockney accents. But I could hardly afford to eat here any more—if not for Hugh's kindness. Hugh is in a snit about the dinner party at Sir Hyman's.

"Will I be expected to put on one of those silly black beanies I've seen the men wear in Whitechapel?"

"Think of the caviar. He gets it from their embassy. Consider the endless bottles of Dom P. I am told there will be a whole baby lamb."

"Kosher, I daresay."

Hugh confessed how deeply he regretted casting Kitty rather than little me in *The Dancing Duchess*. Stuff and nonsense, I told him. I wouldn't hear a word against Kitty. She tries so hard.

Other diaries, memoirs, letter collections and biographies of the period were rich in details of that disastrous night. There were contradictions, of course, each memoir writer laying claim to the evening's most memorable *bon mots*. Other discrepancies related to Lady Olivia, who had been born and raised an Anglican. Some charged that she had treacherously been a party to the insult, but others were equally certain that she was its true victim. Both groups agreed that the Polish count was her lover, but they split again on whether Sir Hyman condoned the relationship, was ignorant of it, or—just possibly—had planned the scandal to avenge himself on both of them. Whatever the case, there was no disputing the main thrust of events, only their interpretation.

Including Sir Hyman and Lady Olivia, there were thirteen at the refectory table, which made for much light-hearted bantering, the mood darkening only when Sir Hyman—insensitive or vindictive, depending on the witness—pointed out that that had been the precise number gathered at the most famous of all Passover noshes.

Every diary and memoir writer mentioned the table setting, describing it either as opulent or all too typically reeking of Levantine ostentation. The wine goblets and decanters were made of late-Georgian flint glass, their hue Waterford blue. The seventeenth-century candelabra were of a French design, with classic heads and overlapping scales and foliated strapwork. The heavy, ornate silverware was of the same

period. Other artifacts were of Jewish origin. There was, for
instance, a silver Passover condiment set, its style German
Baroque, stamped with fruit and foliage. The *seder* tray itself,
the platter on which the offending *matzohs* would lie, was made
of pewter. It was eighteenth-century Dutch in origin,
unusually large, engraved with Haggadah liturgies, artfully
combining the pictorial and calligraphic.

An ebullient Sir Hyman welcomed his guests to the table
with a prepared little speech that some would later condemn
as grovelling and others, given the shocking turn of events, as a
damned impertinence. In the first place, he said, he wished to
say how grateful he was that everyone had accepted his
invitation, because he knew how prejudiced they were against
some of his kind. He hardly blamed them. Some of his kind,
especially those sprung from eastern Europe, were insufferably
pushy and did in fact drive a hard bargain, and to prove his
point he quoted some lines of T.S. Eliot:

> And the jew squats on the window sill, the owner,
> Spawned in some estaminet of Antwerp,
> Blistered in Brussels, patched and peeled in London. . . .

Such people, Sir Hyman said, embarrassed him and other
gentlemen of Hebraic origin even more than they were an
affront to decent Christians. In a lighter vein, Sir Hyman went
on to say that he hoped his guests would find the rituals
essential to the Passover feast a welcome little frisson. Each of
them would find a little book at their place. It was called a
Haggadah and they should think of it as a libretto. We should
tell — that is to say, "hagged" — of our exodus from Egypt, not
the last time the Jews did a midnight flit. The Haggadah
— like the libretto of any musical in trouble in Boston or
Manchester — was being constantly revised to keep pace with
the latest Jewish bad patch. He had seen one, for instance, that
included a child's drawing of the last *seder* held in
Theresienstadt. The drawing, alas, was without any artistic
merit, but — it could be argued — did have a certain maudlin
charm. He had seen another one that made much of the fact
that the Nazi all-out artillery attack on the grouchy Jews of the
Warsaw ghetto had begun on the eve of Passover. A man who

had survived that kerfuffle only to perish in a concentration
camp later on had written, "We are faced with a Passover of
hunger and poverty, without even 'the bread of affliction'. For
eating and drinking there is neither *matzoh* nor wine. For
prayer there are no synagogues or houses of study. Their doors
are closed and darkness reigns in the dwelling-places of
Israel." However, Sir Hyman hastily pointed out, we have
come here not to mourn but to be jolly. He beamed at Lady
Olivia, who responded by jiggling a little bell. Servants refilled
the champagne glasses at once.

Seder, Sir Hyman informed his captive audience, seemingly
indifferent to their growing restiveness, literally means
programme,which applies to the prescribed ceremonies of the
Passover ritual. Raising the pewter *matzoh* platter, he
proclaimed first in Hebrew and then in English: "This is the
bread of affliction which our ancestors ate in the land of Egypt.
Let all who are hungry come and eat."

"Hear, hear!"

"Goodo!"

It was now nine P.M., and though Sir Hyman's guests had
begun to arrive as early as six, there had — much to their
chagrin — been no hors-d'oeuvres served. Not so much as a
wizened olive or peanut or blade of celery. Stomachs were
rumbling. Appetites were keen. Sensing his guests' impatience,
Sir Hyman hurried through the reading of the Haggadah that
necessarily preceded the feast, skipping page after page. Even
so, he had to be aware of the shifting of chairs, the fidgeting
that verged on the hostile, the raising of eyebrows, the dark
looks. It did not help matters that each time the kitchen doors
swung open the dining room was filled with the most
tantalizing aromas. Steaming chicken broth. Lamb on the
sizzle. Finally, at ten P.M., Sir Hyman nodded at an
increasingly distressed Lady Olivia, who promptly jiggled her
little bell.

Ah.

There were gasps of pleasure as a huge, wobbly, gleaming
mound of beluga caviar was set down on the table. Next came
an enormous platter of pleasingly moist smoked salmon. The
salmon was followed by a silver salver heavy with baked carp
and a surround of golden jelly. Everybody was set to pounce,

but Sir Hyman, his smile gleeful, raised a restraining hand. "Wait, please. There is one more protocol of Zion, as it were, to be observed. Before indulging ourselves we are obliged to eat the bread of affliction. The *matzoh*."

"Let's get on with it, then."

"For God's sake, Hymie, I'm hungry enough to eat a horse."

"Hear, hear!"

Sir Hyman nodded and a servant removed the pewter *matzoh* platter, piled it high with the bread of affliction, and returned it to the table, covered with a magenta velvet cloth.

"What we have here," Sir Hyman said, "are not the tasteless, mass-produced *matzohs* you might expect to find on the tables of tradesmen in Swiss Cottage or Golders Green, their eyes on the main chance. These are the authentic *matzohs* of ancient and time-honoured tradition. They are called *Matzoh Shemurah*. Guarded *matzoh*. Baked behind locked doors, under conditions of the strictest security, according to a recipe first formulated in Babylon. Brought from there to Lyons in the year 1142, of the Christian era, and from there to York. These were made for me by a venerable Polish rabbi I know in Whitechapel."

"Come on, Hymie!"

"Let's get on with it."

"I'm starved!"

Sir Hyman yanked the magenta cloth free, and revealed was a stack of the most unappetizing-looking biscuits. Coarse, unevenly baked, flecked with rust spots, their surfaces bumpy with big brown blisters.

"Everybody take one, please," Sir Hyman said, "but, careful, they're hot."

Once everybody had a *matzoh* in hand, Sir Hyman stood up and offered a solemn benediction. "Blessed be God, who brings food out of the earth. Blessed be God, who made each *mitzvah* bring us holiness, and laid on us the eating of *matzoh*." Then he indicated that they were free to dig in at last.

The West End impresario, his eyes on the caviar, was the first to take a bite. Starchy, he thought. Bland. But then he felt a blister in the *matzoh* burst like a pustule and the next thing he knew a warm fluid was dribbling down his chin. He was about to wipe it away with his napkin when the actress, seated opposite him, took one look and let out a terrifying scream. "Oh, my poor Hugh," she cried. "Hugh, just look at you!"

But he was already sufficiently discomfited merely looking at her. A thick reddish substance was splattered over her panting ivory bosom.

"My God!" somebody wailed, dropping his leaky *matzoh shemurah*.

The fastidious Cynthia Cavendish cupped her hands to her mouth, desperate to spit out the warm red sticky stuff, then took a peek at it trickling between her fingers and subsided to the carpet in a dead faint.

Horace McEwen, smartly avoiding the sinking Cynthia, stared at his rust-smeared napkin, his lips trembling, and then stuck two fingers into his mouth, prying for loose teeth.

"It's blood, don't you know?"

"Bastard!"

"We're all covered in ritual blood!"

The Rt. Hon. Richard Cholmondeley knocked back his chair and, convinced that he was dying, began to bring up bile and what he also took for blood. "Tell Constance," he pleaded with nobody in particular, "that the photographs in the bottom left-hand drawer of my desk are not mine. Noddy gave them to me for safekeeping when he got back from Marrakech."

The cabinet minister's plump wife vomited all over his Moss Bros. dinner jacket before he could thrust her clear, sending her reeling backwards. "Now look what you've done," he said. "Just look."

The sodden novelist slid to the floor. Unfortunately he was clutching the antique Irish lace tablecloth at the time and, consequently, brought down some priceless wine goblets as well as the platter of smoked salmon with him. The impresario, with characteristic presence of mind, grabbed the other end of the tablecloth just in time to secure the sliding tureen of caviar. Torn between anger and appetite, he snatched a soup spoon and lunged at the caviar once, twice, three times before demanding his coat and hat. The Polish count, his face ashen, leaped up and challenged Sir Hyman to a duel.

Sir Hyman startled him by responding softly in fluent Polish. "Your father was a swindler and your mother was a whore and you, dear boy, are a ponce. Name the time and place."

Lady Olivia sat rocking her face in her hands, as her guests scattered, raging and cursing.

"You will pay dearly for this outrage, Hymie."

"You haven't heard the end of it!"

"Tell it not in Gath," Sir Hyman said, "publish it not in the streets of Askelon; lest the daughters of the Philistines rejoice. . . ."

The last departing guest claimed to have heard a stricken Lady Olivia ask, "How could you humiliate me like this, Hymie?"

He purportedly replied, "There will be no more assignations with that squalid little Polack. Now let's eat the lamb before it's hopelessly overdone."

"I despise you," Lady Olivia shrieked, stamping her foot and fleeing to her bedroom.

There was only one account, its accuracy dubious, of that infamous evening's aftermath. It appeared in *Through the Keyhole: A Butler Remembers*, a truncated version of which was serialized in *The News of the World*, the full text available only from Olympia Press, Paris. In a steamy chapter about his employment by Sir Hyman, Albert Hotchkins — remembering that Passover *seder* — wrote:

"After the Top People had fled faster than an Italian from the battlefront, and a tearful Lady Olivia had retreated to her bedroom, the old cuckold sat alone at the table, happy as a Jew at a fire sale, having himself a proper fit of giggles. Then he summoned the non-U people, including this yobbo, out of the kitchen and insisted we join him in a nosh. We were in there faster than the proverbial fox into a chicken coop. Caviar, smoked salmon, roast lamb. Now I knew Sir Hyman enjoyed his libations, but this is the first time I saw him pickled as a dill in a barrel. He was a veritable one-man Goon Show! He entertained us with side-splitting imitations of every one of his guests. He also did Churchill for us and Gilbert Harding and Lady Docker. He sat down at the piano and sang us one of ye olde time music hall songs. (Pardon me, Queen Victoria, I know you're not amused!!!)

> I should like to have a youth, who me
> Would in his arms enfold,
> Who would handle me and dandle me
> When my belly it was cold;
> So I will be a mot,
> I shall be a mot,
> I'm so fond of Roger,
> That I will be a mot.

"Then he sang us some Passover ditties in Hebrew or Yiddish or Rubbish, I'm not sure which, and something else in Chinese. Chinese? Yes. For that was the night Sir Hyman settled a mystery darker than a nigger's arsehole for us. He wasn't, as the *Telegraph* diarist had speculated, of Hungarian extraction. He had been born in Petrograd, as it then was, but had been raised in Shanghai, where his dad had fled to after the revolution had spread through old Mother Russia like wildfire.

"It was a night to remember! Eventually we rolled up the carpet and, to coin a phrase, danced in the dawn as if there was no tomorrow. If I hadn't known better I would have sworn on a stack of Bibles that that was the night the sly old nancyboy actually dipped his wick into Mary, the naughtiest lady's maid ever to come out of County Clare, as keen for a taste of roger any time as a Chinaman is for chop suey. (See Chapter Seven: 'Eat Your Heart Out, Fanny Hill!!') Certainly we didn't see hide nor hair of them for a couple of hours and when they rejoined us he was as quiet as a burglar and she looked as innocent as the cat who had just swallowed the canary, but it was his spunk more likely!"

It was generally assumed that Sir Hyman was a homosexual, but one of the most celebrated beauties of the era, Lady Margaret Thomas, didn't agree. Her biographer reproduced the following diary entry in full.

April 8, 1947

Dinner with the Kerr-Greenwoods in Lowndes Square. Everybody most *simpatico* when I tell them what an awkward customer Jawaharlal had turned out to be and that poor Harold is having a devil of a time trying to help Dickie sort things out and that he won't be back from India for at least another fortnight. Hymie Kaplansky, who is also there alone, is full of *jeu d'esprit*, very droll, enchanting us with tales of his South African boyhood. He was educated at their pathetic notion of Eton. The headmaster had the boys in several weeks before they were confirmed to tell them about sex. They were warned that masturbation would destroy the body and drive the sinner into the madhouse. For all that, he said, the most observant of the boys might have noticed the little tube dangling between their legs with the jaunty little cap at the tip. It was very flexible. In the bath, for instance, it was inclined to shrivel or retract. But, depending on a boy's proclivities, it would harden and elongate in response to certain stimuli, proving something of a nuisance.

After his father died in the siege of Mafeking, the family was left destitute. Hymie was obliged to leave school and his mother had to take in boarders until Hymie restored the family fortunes and then some, I daresay. Everybody joined in when Hymie sat down to the piano and played and sang, "We are Marching to Pretoria." Then Hymie offered to escort me home, pointing out that I would be safe with him and he owed it to dear Harold to protect me.

I invited him in for a nightcap. We gossiped shamelessly about the *affaire* Delaney and he speculated about Lady _____ and Lord _____ , which I assured him was all rot. Then he told me in detail about an awful evening he had spent with the wicked Duchess of _____ , who behaved so badly that night at _____ 's birthday party. This, in turn, got us started on the disgusting _____ and _____ . We were well into our second bottle of champagne when Hymie actually burst into tears and confessed how wretched he felt about the nature of his private life. Reminiscing about his school days again, he recalled, with particular pain, being "bum-shaved" by his prefect, who was eventually sent down for buggery and for producing a bastard with a servant girl. "He was rather a lusty fellow," Hymie said.

For bum-shaving, he explained, two boys were set back to back, bare bottoms touching, and then the prefect began to make cuts with a cane.

Hymie wished he were capable of loving a woman as ravishing and remarkably intelligent as I was, he said, but unfortunately he was unable to achieve tumescence with a member of the opposite sex. Hormone injections taken in a Zurich clinic hadn't helped and neither had his analyst in Hampstead. Poor, dear boy. I always thought he was awfully plucky for a pansy, but now he was desolate. There was nothing for it but to take him in my arms, my intention being to console. Soon we had arrived at a state of *deshabillé* and his hitherto perfunctory kisses and caresses took on a certain clumsy urgency. Unfortunately he was unfamiliar with the terrain, as it were. I was obliged to guide and instruct. And then, eureka ! To his astonishment, we stumbled on indisputable physical evidence of his ardour.

"Whatever are we going to do?" Hymie asked.

In for a penny, in for a pound.

"You are a miracle-worker," Hymie said later, overcome with gratitude. "My saviour."

But the next morning he professed to be troubled by doubts. "What," he asked, "if it was only a one-time thing?"

We laid that ghost to rest most satisfactorily more than once, but then we had to cope with the inconvenience of dear Harold's return from India. Happily it turned out that Hymie kept a darling little bijou flat in Shepherd's Market. Strictly for business affairs, he said.

One afternoon I discovered an antique gold brooch, inlaid with pearls, staring at me from a glass shelf in the bathroom. I knew it well. I had been with Peter when he had bought it at Asprey's for Di.

"Hymie, my sweet, I thought your people had but one saviour."

"Whatever do you mean?"

I held out the brooch.

"Oh that," he said, "thank God you found it. Di is in such a state. She must have left it here when she came to tea with Peter yesterday."

"Peter just happens to be at Cowes now."

Sir Hyman was mentioned again in the salacious diaries of Dorothy Ogilvie-Hunt, which were introduced as evidence in the notorious man-in-the-black-apron trial. It seems that the lovely but promiscuous Dorothy not only accommodated many lovers, but graded their performance from delta-minus to alpha-plus, the latter accolade seldom awarded. The events leading up to her initial tryst with Sir Hyman were described in some detail.

March 2, 1944

Dreary day wasted in the records office at Wormwood Scrubs. What we're doing here is supposed to be terribly hush-hush, but on my way out the bus conductor on the no. 72 clearly said, "All change for MI5."

Then drinks at the Gargoyle with Brian Howard and Goronwy. Guy is there, reeking of garlic as usual, and so are Davenport, McLaren-Ross, and that young Welsh poet cadging drinks again. Everybody blotto. Some of us move on to the Mandrake, and then I leave them, hurrying home to change, bound for dinner at the Fitzhenry's, which promised to be a frightful bore. As might be expected, given Topsy's proclivities, two of the Apostles were there as well as one of the Queen's "knitting brigade". The evening was saved by Hymie Kaplansky, of all unlikely people. His tales of his formative years in Australia were absolutely enchanting. His grandfather, it seems, had been an early settler. Hymie's father died at Gallipoli, leaving the family without a penny. Hymie's mother, once a principal dancer at the Bolshoi, had to work as a seamstress until her resourceful son went to Bombay, where he made his fortune. We all joined in when Hymie sat down at the piano and sang "Waltzing Matilda" and other songs of the outback, some of them very salty. When the party finally broke up at two A.M. it was too late for me to return to the country. I decided to check into the Ritz. But the gallant Hymie offered me the use of his flat in Shepherd's Market instead. "You'll be perfectly safe with me, my dear."

Mr. Justice Horner ruled the next four pages inadmissible evidence, but allowed that they concluded with the encomium ALPHA PLUS followed by four exclamation marks.

Many wartime diaries and journals, published thirty years later, were rich in references to Sir Hyman, a notable entry appearing in the diaries of the Duc de Baugé. The Duc, whose château was in Maine-et-Loire, had been a fixture at Hymie's celebrated dinner parties in his own château, just outside of Angers, also on the banks of the Maine. Hymie's château, surrounded by vineyards and parkland, had originally been built by a military family in 1502. Badly damaged during the revolution, left to crumble for more than a century, it had been lovingly restored by Hymie in the thirties. During the occupation it was the official residence of SS *Obergruppenführer* Klaus Gehrbrandt, something of a sybarite.

June 27, 1945

The charming Sir Hyman, whom we haven't seen since the occupation, is with us again. Nicole is delighted to see him. So am I. His château, he said, had suffered only negligible damage, but there had been some serious thefts. A precious wall tapestry was missing and so was the portrait of Françoise d'Aubigné, who became Louis XIV's mistress — Madame de Maintenon. Sir Hyman told us that Henri, his wine steward, had assured him that he had managed to keep the best bottles in his cellar out of the hands of Gehrbrandt, during his many dinner parties.

"As a matter of interest," Sir Hyman asked Henri, "who came to the *obergruppenführer*'s dinner parties?"

"Oh, the same people who used to attend your dinners, Sir Hyman."

Nicole burst into tears. "We had no choice but to accept his invitations. It was awful. His father was a pork butcher. He had no manners. He didn't even know that Pouilly-Fumé is not a dessert wine."

Sir Hyman, gracious as always, took her hand and kissed it. "Of course, my dear, we have no idea of what you went through here."

Cross-checking, Moses came upon an interesting gap. Sir Hyman, or plain Hymie as he then was, seemingly dropped out of sight in June 1944 and was not mentioned again, and then only in passing, until August of the same year. His name surfaced in the diaries of a Labour MP, a noted Fabian pamphleteer who had served as a junior minister in the coalition government but had been forced to resign his seat in disgrace in 1948. Apparently he had taken too keen an interest in discipline at a hospice for distressed young ladies that was the pride of his constituency; the so-called spanking *soirées* that *The News of the World* made so much of at the time, publishing a photograph of the MP in a gym slip.

Aug. 21, 1944

Dinner at Lyon's Corner House with a representative of the Anti-Vivisectionist League who is concerned about the damage to marine life by the wanton use of mines in the pursuit of U-boats. I take her point, but I am bound to remind her that innocent animals are often the first casualties of war. SS death squads have murdered all the animals in the Berlin zoo. Mindless, gum-chewing American pilots have been known to drop their bombs over grazing herds of cattle rather than risk the flak over Cologne or Dusseldorf.

Strolling back to the House I had to cross Whitehall hastily in order to avoid running into Hyman Kaplansky, looking unashamedly tanned and well fed. I understand that he has just returned from a holiday in Bermuda. Actually I'm surprised that one hadn't fled London earlier, during the worst of the Blitz.

Then, quite by chance, reading *The Berlin Diaries* of Baron

Theodor von Lippe, Moses was startled to come across the
following entry.

May 18, 1944

Berlin is being methodically destroyed by *Bombenteppich*
or what the Allies call "saturation" bombing. People have
taken to chalking inscriptions on the blackened walls of
crumbling buildings. *"Liebste Herr Kunstler, Lebst du noch.
Iche suche Sie uberall. Clara." "Mein Engelein, wo bleist Du? Ich
bin in grosser Sorge. Dein Helmut."* All that remains of the
Hotel Eden is the outside shell.

Last night, even as the bombs fell, Count Erich von
Oberg gave a small dinner party in his wine cellar,
attended by Elena Hube, Felicita Jenisch, Baron Claus
von Helgow, Prince Hermann von Klodt, and Countess
Katia Ingelheim. The goose was excellent. We talked
about nothing but the raids.

That little imp of a Swiss financier, Dr. Otto Raven,
was also there. His gleeful smile disconcerting, he said the
whole thing reminded him of a meeting of persecuted
Christians in the Roman catacombs.

I thought this bizarre coming from a Jew, but Adam
von Trott says he is to be trusted with details of coming
events.

This, of course, was sufficient to propel Moses into a search
of publishers' catalogues, German as well as English, but he
came up with only one more reference to Herr Dr. Otto
Raven. He found it in the Wiener Library, in the unpublished
journals of a Swedish princess who had passed the war years in
Berlin, married to one of the Hohenzollerns.

July 17, 1944

Lunched yesterday at Gabrielle's. Started with crab
cocktail and vol-au-vents filled with caviar. Not a word
has been heard of Gabrielle's Jewish mother since her last
arrest — this time for good. Nothing can be done about it

and I am desperately sorry. Presumably she has been sent to the ghetto in Theresienstadt in Czechoslovakia.

Today, at Potsdam, Otto Bismarck arranged a shooting party for boar. Only one was shot. Surprisingly the successful hunter was a little Swiss banker, Herr Dr. Otto Raven. He had learned to shoot, he said, on the pampas, south of the Amazon, where he had been raised by a rancher following his father's death in a duel. He sat down at the piano and played us a number of South American cowboy songs, but Otto Bismarck was not amused. He was, in fact, extremely irritable, disturbed by Churchill's latest speech, once more demanding "unconditional surrender".

"It's lunacy," Bismarck said.

But Herr Dr. Raven assured him the speech was for public consumption, *pour encourager les Russes*, and that under certain circumstances, anticipated with impatience. . . .

Later I heard them quarrelling about Stauffenberg in the library.

". . . wrong man," Herr Dr. Raven said. "He's missing two fingers of his left hand, which could be a fatal handicap."

"It's set for the 20th of July at Rastenburg and this time we won't fail."

When Hyman Kaplansky's name appeared on the King's New Year's Honours List some six months later hardly anybody was surprised. He was not the first, nor the last, heavy contributor to the Conservative party chest to be rewarded with a title.

THREE

◆

One Saturday morning in 1974 a flock of the Faithful gathered at Henry's house to celebrate the *bar mitzvah* of the great-great-grandson of Tulugaq. Nialie, who had learned to temper recipes plucked from her Jenny Grossinger cookbook with local produce, served chopped chicken liver moistened with seal *shmaltz*. Though most of the *knishes* were filled with mashed potatoes, there were others that were stuffed with minced caribou. In the absence of candy, a platter of succulent seals' eyes was available for the children. Among Isaac's gifts, there was a book from his father, a collection of sermons by the Rebbe who reigned over 770 Eastern Parkway, illuminating eternal mysteries, deciphering the code hidden within the holy texts:

"We can hasten the arrival of the *Moshiach* by intensifying our *simcha* or rejoicing. *Simcha* is obviously connected with the *Moshiach* or why do both words contain the Hebrew letters '*shin*,' '*mem*,' and '*ches*?' Similarly there is an inner link between Moses and *Moshiach*, as witness the verse, 'And the sceptre shall not depart from Judah, nor a lawgiver from between his feet, until *Shiloh* come . . . ,' which is clearly a concealed reference to the *Moshiach*, as the words '*yavo Shiloh*' and '*Moshiach*' are numerically equal. Also equal are the words

'*Shiloh*' and 'Moses', proof positive that the coming of the *Moshiach* is related to Moses. Furthermore, '*yavo*' is numerically equal to '*echad*', which means one; therefore we can deduce that the *Moshiach* = Moses + One."

When Isaac was to enroll in the *yeshiva* a month later, an elated Henry flew down to New York with him. Father and son made directly for Crown Heights. They stopped for a Lubavitch beef burger at Marmelstein's, on Kingston Avenue, and then went out for a stroll.

"We're being stared at," Isaac said.

"It's your imagination."

They paused to look in Suri's window, filled with glamorous wigs for the wives of the faithful who had shaven their heads to render themselves unattractive to men other than their husbands. Reflected in the glass, Isaac saw men across the street pointing him out, whispering together.

Sleek black hair. Brown skin. "They're going to take me for some kind of freak of nature here," Isaac said.

"*Narishkeit.* We're among good people," Henry said, taking him by the hand and leading him into the Tzivos Hashem store.

Garishly coloured portraits of the Rebbe, similar to the pictures of saints peddled at the kiosks outside provincial cathedrals in Europe, were on display everywhere, framed in plastic pressed and burnished to resemble pine. The Rebbe's graven image was also available in postcard and wallet-window size or embossed on canvas tote bags. Isaac overheard a bearded man say, "Don't look now, but it's the rich *meshuggena* from the northland."

"What can I buy for you?" Henry asked.

"Nothing," Isaac said, glaring right back at a couple of pimply boys of his own age. "Let's go."

Next Henry took Isaac to the *yeshiva* to sit in on a study session with one of the Rebbe's younger acolytes, swaying over his text:

"We look into the mirror," he asked the men gathered at the long table, "and what do we see? The self, of course. You see yourself, I see myself, and so forth and so on. If we have a clean face, we see a clean face in the mirror. If we have a dirty face, that is what the mirror reflects back on us. So when we see bad in another person we know that we too have this bad.

"Now looking up into the mirror, we see the face, but looking down, what? The feet. You see your feet, I see my feet, and so forth and so on. The Rebbe has pointed out to us that on Simchas Torah one does not dance with his head — he dances with his feet. From this our beloved teacher has deduced that a person's intellectual capacities make no difference on Simchas Torah and this is equally true for every Jew worldwide.

"Looking into the mirror you should also note that the higher is contained in the lower and the lower in the higher. But the reverse is also true. Chassidus teaches us that the lower is revealed in the higher and the higher in the lower."

Isaac yawned. He yearned to see Broadway. The Felt Forum. A hockey game in Madison Square Garden. The offices where *Screw* was published. The McTavish building on Fifth Avenue.

"Are we going to visit Uncle Lionel?"

"I think not."

But Henry, carrying charts, did take him to Columbia University. While Henry conferred with a climatologist, Isaac sat on a bench in the outer office. Bored, he dipped into the *Mishneh Torah* Henry had bought him at Merkaz Stam. The Messianic King, he read, will be a descendant of the House of David. "Anyone who does not believe in him or does not wait for his coming, denies not only the statements of the other prophets, but those of the Torah and Moses, our teacher. The Torah testified . . ."

Finally Henry emerged from the climatologist's office, looking chastened. "Tell me, *yingele*, do you think your father is nuts?"

They made another stop, this time at an address on W. 47th Street, where Henry had to see somebody about a pair of diamond earrings, a gift for Nialie.

"How long will you be?" Isaac asked.

"A half-hour maybe."

"I'll wait outside."

Bearded men in bobbing black hats seemed to be

everywhere, flying past, briefcases chained to their wrists. Sirens wailed somewhere. The traffic stalled. Isaac, moving along, caught up with a bunch of people gathered in a semi-circle at the corner of Eighth Avenue. Thrusting through to the front, he came upon a ragged black boy turning cartwheels, two of his chums dancing on their heads. Then he was accosted by a girl wearing a see-through blouse and a silver miniskirt. Her hair was dyed orange and purple. Isaac, frightened, started back.

Crossing Seventh Avenue, he made out Henry in the distance, pacing up and down, searching, sidecurls bobbing. On impulse, Isaac retreated into a doorway. Look at him, he thought. With his millions, we could be living in a penthouse here. He wouldn't have to keep dirty photographs of a skinny girl in his bottom desk drawer, he could afford the real thing, but, no, it had to be Tulugaqtitut. Shit. Fuck.

Henry, increasingly frantic, was stopping passers-by, obviously describing Isaac to them, asking if they had seen him. Five minutes passed before Isaac, taking pity on him, emerged from his hiding place. The instant Henry spotted him striding down the street he raced forward to embrace him. "Thank Hashem you're safe," he cried, even as Isaac wiggled free, embarrassed.

Two days later Henry returned to Tulugaqtitut, laden with books. Isaac didn't see him again until he flew home, two weeks before Passover, and the two of them set out on the journey that led to Henry's death only a hundred miles short of Tuktuyaktuk.

FOUR

◆

The first thing Isaac noticed when he flew home for Passover was the new ship with three masts locked into the ice in the bay. Damn. Just what he needed, in case the gang in the Sir Igloo Inn Café didn't already have enough to tease him about. The ship, which had been built in Holland, had its planking doubled, the bow and stern bolstered with steel plates. It was provisioned with sacks of grain and rice and dried vegetables, the immense freezer stocked by the Nôtre Dame de Grace Kosher Meat Mart. Crazy Henry's Ark, they called it.

"You just got home," Nialie said, "and already you are in a bad mood."

"Forget it."

Nialie soon had more to worry about. The night before Henry was to start on his journey a big menacing black raven pecked at their bedroom window, wakening Nialie with a start. She clung to Henry, pleading with him not to go, but he insisted. The trip was traditional. Every spring, two weeks before Passover, he and Pootoogook set out for a hunting camp of the Faithful, some 250 miles east along the Arctic shore. The Faithful counted on Henry to bring them boxes filled with the bread of affliction and wine appropriate to the feast days. Furthermore, Henry pointed out, this Passover's journey would be a special pleasure for him. Pootoogook, troubled by arthritis, would not be coming. Instead Henry would be taking Pootoogook's fifteen-year-old grandson Johnny and, for the first time ever, Isaac, whom he counted on to continue the tradition in later years.

A gleeful Henry roused Isaac out of bed early. "Wake up, wake up, to do the work of the Creator!"

To please Isaac, they were not taking the dogs with them this year. For a change, the sleds laden with supplies would be pulled by three red snowmobiles, the third snowmobile lugging a sled with sufficient fuel for the journey there and home again.

Given reasonable weather conditions, Henry was usually five days out, a day in camp, five days back. This enabled him to be home a couple of days before the first *seder*, in good time to search his pre-fab for any trace of *Bedikat Chametz*, leavened bread, and to observe the *mitzvah* of *Tzedakah*, distributing money among the poor. But this year, as Nialie watched Henry start out with Johnny and Isaac, she doubted that she would ever see her husband again in this world. So she was hardly surprised when Henry failed to turn up in time for the first *seder* and she did what he would have expected. She went through the house, covering all the mirrors with towels, and then took to a low stool, holding her head in her hands, rocking to and fro, keening.

Henry's party was five days overdue when Moses, gone to collect his mail at The Caboose, read in the *Gazette*:

GURSKY HEIRS
MISSING
IN ARCTIC

The story noted that Henry, a Hassidic Jew, the eccentric son of Solomon Gursky, had been rooted in the Arctic for years, married to a native woman. It was illustrated by a photograph of the ship with three masts locked in the ice. A vessel, the reporter wrote, that the locals called Crazy Henry's Ark, its estimated cost three million dollars.

Moses threw things into a suitcase, drove to Dorval airport, the other side of Montreal, and caught the first flight to

Edmonton. He had to wait three maddening hours before he could make a connection to Yellowknife, where he immediately set out for the Canadian Armed Forces search-and-rescue headquarters, volunteering to serve as a spotter. The search master, adding his name to the list, told him that two long-range Hercules transports had already been crisscrossing the area of the highest probability for three days, flying a mile apart at a height of 1,000 feet. The area of the highest probability was calculated to be 350 miles long and 250 miles wide. In the event of a siting, para-rescuers were standing by equipped with a long-range Labrador helicopter, prepared to take off immediately. The good news was that Henry's party had certainly reached their destination, remained in camp for a day, and then started back with sufficient food and fuel to get them home. A land search was also underway, Eskimos fanning out over Henry's most likely route home.

The next morning a whiteout grounded the search planes and Moses passed most of the day in The Trapline with Sean Riley.

"He should have taken his dogs," Riley said, "not those goddamn snowmobiles. You can't eat snowmobiles."

"What are their chances, Sean?"

"They're crossing some damn unforgiving country, but if Henry's okay, they're okay. If not, not. Henry knows the terrain, but Isaac's no damn good and Johnny's a druggie. If Henry's out of it, those kids could head off any which way, providing the snowmobiles haven't broken down."

"All three of them?"

"Bloody unlikely I know, but there's been an accident for sure. Somebody overturned or went over a cliff or into a crevice or how the hell do I know what, and maybe they've set up camp and they're waiting to be rescued."

"Didn't they take flares with them?"

"If I had to guess I'd say they lost the sled with the flares and what we got to hope is that it wasn't also the one with the food and the fuel. Look, Moses, they're good for ten days out there, maybe two weeks, before we have to worry."

Another two days passed before the search planes were able to take off again, this time flying at five hundred feet only a half-mile apart. Moses, like the rest of the volunteers, was only capable of logging ten minutes at a stretch as a spotter, harnessed into the open loading hatch at the rear of the Hercules, squinting at the ice and snow skidding past in temperatures that ran to forty below.

They flew out day after day, weather permitting. Then, on the twenty-third day, the camp was sited, a solitary figure scrambling out of a tent to wave frantically. The Hercules swooped low, dropping a survival pack, and the para-rescuers started out in their helicopter. Security was thick at Yellowknife airport, but Sean Riley managed to have a word with the helicopter pilot shortly after he landed, and then he hurried off to The Trapline to meet with Moses. "Henry's dead. A broken neck. Johnny starved to death. They've brought in Isaac and they've got him in the hospital now. The RCMP are guarding his room."

"Why?"

"They lost the sled with the food. Isaac survived by slicing chunks out of Henry's thighs," Riley said, ordering double Scotches for both of them.

"What about Johnny?"

"He refused to nosh on the great-grandson of Tulugaq, but what did he know? Little prick was just a savage. Are you going to be sick?"

"No."

"Look here, Moses, Henry was already dead. You might have done the same. Certainly I would have."

Moses ordered another round.

"Isaac swears he didn't dig in until the tenth day out there," Riley said, "but the helicopter crew told the RCMP they found little bags filled with cubes of meat hanging from his tent. If Isaac had waited ten days, like he said, Henry's body would have been harder than a frozen log. Splinters is what he would have got, not *boeuf bourguignon*. Something else. Bizarre, if it's true."

"Let's have it."

"Isaac says he was attacked by ravens one morning. Maybe he was delirious or he dreamt it."

Rumours of cannibalism were all over town. Reporters, attracted by the Gursky name, flew in from Toronto, London,

and New York. Convening in The Trapline, they concocted a
verse to commemorate the event:

> There are strange things done 'neath the
>   Midnight Sun,
> but the thing that made us quail
> was the night the Jew
> in want of a stew
> braised his father in a pail.

Moses decided not to stay on for THE CORONER'S
COURT INQUIRY INTO THE MATTER TOUCHING
UPON THE DEATHS OF:
> HENRY GURSKY, and
> JOHNNY POOTOOGOOK.

However, he was still in Yellowknife the morning they
released Isaac from the hospital, flanked by lawyers. "My
client," one of them said, "is still suffering from bereavement
overload and has nothing to say to the press at this point in
time."

FIVE

◆

Considering the nature of Isaac's sin, there were lengthy deliberations before the *yeshiva* agreed to take him back, and then only on sufferance.

"How could you do such a thing?" one rebbe asked.

Another rebbe said, "The other one maybe. But your own father, *alav ha-sholem*?"

"The other one was *trayf*," Isaac responded, glaring at them.

He had come home only once since he had been acquitted by the coroner's inquiry, grudgingly come to spend the *Aseret Yemei Tushuvah*, the ten days of repentance from Rosh Hashana through Yom Kippur, with his mother, avoiding the Sir Igloo Inn Café and the Hudson's Bay trading post, where the teasing was relentless.

"Have you come back to roast your mother for dinner?"

No answer.

"Nurse Agnes likes men to eat her. Try her."

Friday evening, he stood defiantly at the door of his father's house, waiting for the Faithful camped on the edge of the settlement to appear, beating on their skin drums, parading their traditional offerings before them, but nobody came.

"Any of them would have done exactly what I did," he

shouted at Nialie, slamming the door to his room, and collapsing on the bed that had the letters of the Hebrew alphabet painted on the head-board. A deadly *"gimel"* flying out of the raven's beak. Nialie brought him a bowl of soup.

"And if one more person tells me what a saint he was," Isaac hollered, "I'll punch him out! There was another side to him! Only I know!"

"Know what?"

He pitied his mother too much to tell. "Never mind."

Eventually the *yeshiva* principal found out about the marijuana and the Puerto Rican maid.

"It is written," Isaac argued, quoting Melachim, "that a king may take wives and concubines up to the number eighteen, and I am descended from the House of David."

Once Nialie discovered that her son had been expelled from the *yeshiva*, she stopped his allowance. An infuriated Isaac went to the McTavish building on Fifth Avenue.

"I want to see Lionel Gursky."

"Have you an appointment?" the receptionist asked.

"I'm his cousin."

A stocky teenager in a black leather motorcycle jacket, stovepipe jeans, and cowboy boots. Sleek black hair, hot slanty eyes, brown skin. "Sure," she said, amused.

Even as a security guard approached, Isaac slapped his passport on the counter. The guard snorted, incredulous, but put in a call to Lionel's office all the same. There was a pause, then he said, "Take the elevator to the fifty-second floor. Mr. Lionel's secretary will meet you there, kid."

Isaac trailed behind the young lady who led him to Lionel's office, his eyes on her legs.

"Mr. Lionel is already late for a board meeting. He can give you ten minutes."

She had to buzz him into Lionel's outer office, monitored by a TV eye and attended by an armed guard. Behind the guard, rising over a Ming dynasty vase laden with gladioli, there loomed a portrait of Mr. Bernard.

Another set of doors, seemingly solid oak but actually lined with steel, slid open. Lionel's corner office was the largest

Isaac had ever seen. Antique desk. Leather sofas. Matching wastepaper baskets fashioned of elephant's feet. Thick creamy carpet. Silken walls. A framed *Forbes* magazine cover of Lionel. A painting of cod fishermen in the Gaspé. Photographs of Lionel shaking hands with President Nixon, bussing Golda, embracing Frank Sinatra, dancing with Elizabeth Taylor, presenting a trophy to Jack Nicklaus.

"Your father was a saint and a role model for the rest of us poor sinners," Lionel said. "Please accept my belated condolences."

Isaac, his smile ambivalent, explained that he had left the *yeshiva* following a religious dispute, and now wished to enroll in a secular school, continuing his education in New York, but there were problems. When he was twenty-one he would inherit millions as well as a nice bundle of McTavish stock. Meanwhile, his mother controlled everything. She was determined that he return to the Arctic.

Lionel's secretary intruded.

"Thank you, Miss Mosley. I'll take that call in the library, but you stay here and keep my cousin company, will you?"

Isaac began to prowl about the office. He drifted behind the antique desk, sat down in Lionel's chair, and spun around.

"I don't think you should do that."

"Now I have to piss," he said, leaping up.

"There's a men's room down the hall," Miss Mosley said, tugging at her skirt. "First right and second left. Security will give you a key."

"Isn't there a can right here?"

"It's Mr. Lionel's."

"I promise to lift the seat."

At first glance, the medicine cabinet yielded nothing of interest, but a tray on the glass table was filled with cuff-links: pearl, jade, gold. Isaac pocketed a pair and plucked the most promising bottle of pills out of the cabinet.

Lionel's secretary had gone, displaced by the guard from the outer office.

"Hey, what happened to my baby-sitter, man?"

"You just sit there like a good lad and wait for Mr. Lionel."

But Lionel didn't return. Instead he sent a short man, plump and pink, with a full head of curly ginger hair. "Your father was a wonderful human being," Harvey said. "I say that from the heart. Mr. Lionel sympathizes with your situation and admires your ambition. He has instructed me to put you on an allowance of two hundred dollars a week, which we will credit to your bank once you fill me in on the details. Later there will be some papers for you to sign."

"When do I come back for them?"

"They will be mailed to you. Meanwhile, this envelope contains a thousand dollars in cash."

"Where's my fucken cousin?" Isaac asked, snatching the envelope.

"Mr. Lionel says you must come to see him again soon."

Isaac rented a one-room apartment on W. 46th Street near the corner of Tenth Avenue, supplementing his meagre allowance by picking up jobs here and there that didn't require a green card. Bussing tables at Joe Allen's. Washing dishes at Roy Rogers on Broadway. Passing out cards on the street for DIAL 976-SEXY.

Several months later, fifteen years old now, he stared at his ceiling, unshaven, his back adhering to his futon. The summer heat of his one-room apartment a torment, he reached for his tiger-striped jockey shorts on the floor and wiped the sweat from his neck and face. Then he rolled a joint and groped blindly for a tape, slamming it into his Sony. No sooner did he hear the gale-force winds raging across the barrens than he giggled fondly. There was the distant howl of a wolf, electronic music, the sounds of human struggle, and then the narrator faded in:

"The Ravenmen, man-shaped creatures from the ancient spirit world are attacking the good people of Fish Fiord; their fingers bearing the talons of an owl; their noses formed like the beak of a hawk; their great arms feathered and winged. Many of the villagers run in fear, but others fight on against fearful odds. In the forefront is Captain Cohol, pitting his prowess against the pitiless pillagers, fighting like ten men in a gleaming circle of death . . ."

Posters and bumper stickers were plastered to the walls of

Isaac's apartment. Posters of David Bowie, Iggy Pop, Mick Jagger. Sandwiched between Black Sabbath and Deep Purple was a garishly coloured picture of the Rebbe who reigned over 770 Eastern Parkway. A nude Marilyn Monroe, sprawling on a white rug, smiled at the Rebbe from the opposite wall. Glued to the poster was the crest Isaac used to wear on the breast pocket of his jacket, certifying that he was a foot soldier in the ARMY OF HASHEM. A car bumper sticker pasted on another wall read WE WANT THE MOSHIACH NOW.

Those days, Isaac thought, inhaling deeply. *Yeshiva* days. Waking in the wintry dark to say his *Modeh Ani*, the Prayer of Thanks Upon Rising:

> *Modeh ani lefaneha, melekh hai v'kayam.*
> I offer thanks to Thee, O Everlasting King.
> *Sheh hehezarta bi nishmati b'hemla.*
> Who hast mercifully restored my soul within me.

Fuck the *yeshiva*. And fuck the Gurskys too. Some family. Lionel, that scum-bag, had never agreed to see him again. Mind you, he was only a cousin. Lucy, his aunt, *his only aunt*, had treated him even worse. Not to begin with. No sir. To begin with she had thought he was the cutest thing since sliced bread. He had first gone to visit Lucy in her apartment in the Dakota while he was still studying at the *yeshiva*. He rang the bell clutching a beribboned box of Magen David Glatt Kosher chocolates, unaware that he was intruding on a cocktail party. A little Filipino in a white jacket answered the door and then an out-of-breath lady wearing a tent-like kaftan chugged down the hall to greet him. She was immense, bloated, heavily made-up, her glittering black eyes outlined with something silvery, her chins jiggly. Lucy grasped a retreating Isaac and held him at arm's length, bracelets of hammered gold jangling. Isaac, who still wore sidecurls, a wispy moustache and just a hint of beard, black hat, long black jacket, thick white woollen socks. "Oh my shattered nerves," she called out in a voice loud enough to command attention. "Look, everybody, it's my nephew. Isn't he super!"

Then, taking Isaac by the hand, she fed him to one guest after another, singing out again and again, "This is the son of my brother, the early warning system." Earning chuckles and going on to explain that her saintly brother lived in the Arctic, married to an Eskimo, waiting for the world to end. "Out there, he'll be the first to know, wouldn't you say?"

Finally Lucy abandoned Isaac to a group that included a couple of agents, a set designer, and the star of a long-running Broadway play. Isaac had seen the actor on the "Johnny Carson Show". Determined to make a good impression, he asked, "So, tell me, do you find it like a drag to have to repeat the same lines night after night?"

The actor rolled his eyes and handed Isaac his empty glass. "There you go," he said.

Backing away, Isaac collided with a pretty young girl wearing a miniskirt and a T-shirt with LOOKING FOR MR. GOODBAR emblazoned on it. He could make out her nipples. "Sorry, sorry," he said.

"Hey, you look really neat in that. Did you come straight from the location?"

"What?" he asked, beginning to perspire.

"Didn't you have time to change for the party?"

"These are my clothes."

"Come off it," she said. "I just happen to know Mazursky was shooting in the Village today."

He saw Lucy once more before Henry's death, this time in a building on Broadway, the young man who was her personal assistant ushering him into her office. Lucy, her kaftan hiked up to her apple-pie knees, her fat legs propped up on a hassock, was shouting into the phone. "Tell that no-talent cunt that the time is long past when she could play an ingénue and a year from now when her tits are hanging round her ankles she'll be grateful for any crumb, not that she will ever work for Lucy Gursky again." Then she hung up and shoved the huge platter of brownies on her desk toward him. "Oh, shit. Hold it. They're not kosher."

Though she had failed to return any of his phone calls, she seemed so pleased to see him that she cancelled her reservation for lunch at the Russian Tea Room and had her chauffeur take them to a kosher deli on W. 47th Street. Ordering a second mound of *latkes* — "I shouldn't but this is an occasion, isn't it?" — she regaled him with loving stories about Henry.

"You know, your father suffered from a bad stammer until he picked up with your lot, so the Rebbe can't be all bad."

Isaac, seizing his opportunity, his words spilling out at such a pace that she had difficulty following him, told her that he had an idea for a movie. It was about the Messiah. Locked in the Arctic ice for centuries, he explodes out of a pingo, his mission to waken the Jewish dead and lead them to *Eretz Yisroel*. He has a weakness, however. If he is fed non-kosher food he loses his magical powers, he goes berserk.

"I love it," Lucy said, and grasping what a hoot it would be to read aloud at her next party, she added, "You must send me an outline."

When he next got in touch with her, after he had been expelled from the *yeshiva*, she shrieked at him over the phone, "I'm surprised you even have the nerve to call me, you disgusting little cannibal," and she hung up on him.

One night only a month later Lucy dismissed her chauffeur, pretending that she was staying home, and then took a taxi to Sammy's Roumanian Paradise, a restaurant she frequented on rare nights when she was alone and so depressed there was nothing else for it, gorging herself on platters of unhatched chicken eggs, *kishka*, and flank steak, and then sliding into a troubled sleep on the drive home. Back at the Dakota, even as her taxi driver lifted her out of the back seat, she saw Isaac emerging from the shadows. "Go away," she said.

Gone were the sidecurls and black hat. He wore a filthy T-shirt, jeans torn at the knees, and sneakers.

"You can't come up with me. Bugger off. Animal."

"I haven't had a thing to eat in forty-eight hours."

She seemed to wobble in place.

"You're supposed to be my aunt," he said, beginning to sniffle.

Her breath coming short, sweat trickling down her forehead and upper lip, she sighed and said, "I'll give you five minutes."

But once in her apartment, she retired to her bedroom and didn't come out again until she had changed into a fresh kaftan, promptly sinking into the sofa and lifting her swollen legs on to a hassock.

"Are you willing to listen to my side of the story?" Isaac asked.

"No. I am not. But you'll find my handbag on the dresser in the bedroom," she said, unwilling to get up again. "I'll give you something this once. Wait. I know exactly how much money is in there."

It was a mistake. He was gone too long. So she hoisted herself upright and followed him into the bedroom.

Isaac was staring at the large photograph on the wall of a slender lady in a sexy black cocktail dress, her bra stuffed with Kleenex.

"Who's that?" he demanded, smirking, for he recognized her, even with her clothes on, and was only looking for a confirmation.

"Why that," she said, curtsying, "is a photograph of your Aunt Lucy in her prime, taken by a rather naughty boy in London in 1972, if memory serves. Or did you think I was born looking like a hippo?"

"No."

She fished a hundred and seventy dollars out of her handbag and handed it to him. "But, remember, you are not to come here again."

"Sure thing."

To be so rich and yet so broke. Denied by his own family. Maddening. Isaac wanted to scream, he longed to break things, it was so unjust.

His apartment stank. He opened the window, but there was no breeze. Not even the cockroaches stirred. In search of solace, he slapped another Captain A. tape into his Sony.

"Wrestled into submission by the rapacious Ravenmen, Captain Cohol has broken loose from the terrible table of death only to be cruelly clouted to the ice once more."

Toologaq, malevolent master of the Ravensmen, laughed fiendishly. "Brace yourself, space snoop, because this electric current will teach you watt's watt."

Shit shit shit. Isaac kicked his Sony across the floor. Only fifteen years old, he would have to endure another six years before the money and shares would be his. Groping for his can of spray paint, he treated the Rebbe to a squirt in the nose. Wobbly on his feet, he whirled around and took aim at Marilyn Monroe's coozy.

Then the doorbell rang. Three strangers. A little old man; a taller one, middle-aged; and a bleached blonde, all twinkly, reeking of perfume. "I'm your Cousin Barney," the middle-aged man said, "this is your great-uncle Morrie, and what we have here," he added, grabbing the blonde by the buttocks to propel her forward, "is the former runner-up to Miss Conduct. You can look but you can't touch."

Mr. Morrie sighed and clacked his tongue. "To think that a grandson of Solomon's would have to live like this."

"The first thing we're going to do," Barney said, "is buy you some decent threads."

"I'll bet a motorcycle would be more his life-style." Darlene crinkled her nose. "Mine too, honeychild. Vroom Vroom!"

"You ever eaten at the '21'?" Barney asked.

Their fingernails bearing the talons of an owl, Isaac remembered, staring at Darlene's fingernails. "What do you want from me?" he asked, retreating.

Barney took the spray paint can out of his hands. He aimed it at the bumper sticker on the wall that read WE WANT THE MOSHIACH NOW and squirted a line through it, crossing it out, as it were. Then he found a blank space and wrote:

WE WANT MCTAVISH NOW.

Mr. Morrie lingered in New York for a week, absolutely refusing to leave until he had established Isaac in a decent apartment, and had provided him with an allowance proper to his brother Solomon's grandson. They ate lunch together every day. "You know," Isaac said, "you are like the first relative ever to take an interest in me."

"After what you've been through. What about your Aunt Lucy?"

"Don't even mention that sex-crazed elephant's name to me."

"Lucy sex-crazed? You've got to be kidding."

So Isaac showed him his file of photographs.

Tears welled in Mr. Morrie's eyes. "To think that the poor child could have once been so unhappy," he said, stuffing the photographs into his briefcase. "Now tell me, Isaac, what is it you want to do with your life?"

"I want to make movies."

"You know what I say? I say why not, once things are settled."

SIX

◆

One night that same summer, the summer of 1976, Sam and Molly Birenbaum went bumping across the Aberdare Salient in a Toyota Land Cruiser. Their guide, a former white hunter, was pursuing a loping, slope-shouldered hyena. Soon they were overlooking a pack of them, their pelts greasy and bellies bloated, hooting and cackling as they fed on a dead hippo lying on its side in a dry riverbed. The hippo hide impenetrable, the hyenas were eating into the animal through the softer anus, emerging from the cavity again and again with dripping chunks of pink meat or gut, thrusting the scavenging jackals aside.

"I've seen all I can bear," Sam said. "I was raised on Rashi, not Denys Finch Hatton, so let us repair to our tent, *tzatskeleh.*"

Molly was delighted to see him in such high spirits. Only three months earlier, in Washington, he looked pasty and was growing increasingly sour. Obviously he had had his fill of hurrying to airports, flying hundreds of miles only to come back with another thirty-second sound bite from a politician or a film clip trivializing a disaster. "Judging by our commercials," he told her one night, "outside the beltway, the only people who watch our newscasts suffer from loose dentures, insomnia, heartburn, flatulence and, put plainly, they don't shit regular."

So, on the night of his birthday, Molly took him to La Maison Blanche for dinner and told him, "Enough." Lapsing into Yiddish because she knew it gave him pleasure, reminding him of Friday nights at L.B.'s, the men holding forth at the table with the crocheted cloth, he and Moses in the kitchen, overcome with awe as Shloime Bishinsky combed nickels out of their hair. She told him that when she had married him, a cub reporter on the *Gazette*, cultivating a moustache to make him look older, she had never dreamed that one day he would provide in such style for her and the children. But now the boys were grown, and Sam had more than enough money socked away, so the time had come for him to put in for early retirement. He could take a year off, maybe two, nobody was counting, and then he could decide whether to teach or write or join PBS or National Public Radio, both of which had made offers.

"Yeah, but what would I do for a year, never mind two?"

"We're going away," she said, presenting him with his birthday present, a safari for two in Kenya.

It worked wonderfully well for the first few days. Then, the morning after they had seen the hyenas feeding on the dead hippo, they stopped at the Aberdare Country Club for lunch, and Sam caught up with the news.

Air France Flight 139, originating in Tel Aviv on Sunday, June 27, bound from Athens to Paris, had been hijacked by members of the Popular Front for the Liberation of Palestine. The airbus had refuelled in Libya and was now on the ground at Entebbe Airport in Uganda, where His Excellency al-Hajji Field Marshall Dr. Idi Amin Dada, holder of the British Victoria Cross, DSO, MC, appointed by God Almighty to be saviour of his people, announced that he would negotiate between the terrorists and the Israelis.

"They'll fly out that no-nothing kid, Sanders, to cover for us."

"It's no longer any of your business, Sam."

The next morning they crossed into the Rift Valley, hot and sticky, the dung-coloured hills yielding to soaring purplish walls on both sides. Then they took a motorboat across the crocodile-infested waters of Lake Baringo to Jonathan Leakey's Island Camp. The camp overlooking the lake was hewn right out of the cliffside, embedded with cacti and desert roses and acacias. Sam made directly for the radio in the bar.

Wednesday, June 30. The hijackers demanded the release of fifty-three convicted terrorists, five held in Kenya, eight in Europe, and the remaining forty in Israel. If there was no Israeli response by three P.M., Thursday, they threatened to kill the hostages and blow up the airbus. Another report, this one out of Paris, revealed that forty-seven of the two hundred and fifty-six hostages and twelve crew members had been freed and flown to Charles de Gaulle airport. They said that the Jews had been separated from the others under guard in the old terminal building at Entebbe, this segregation imposed by the two young Germans who appeared to be in charge of the operation. Yet another report stated that Chaim Herzog, Israeli ambassador to the UN, had appealed for help from Secretary-General Kurt Waldheim.

Sam asked to use the office telephone. After endless delays, he finally got through to the network in New York, and then he stumbled out of the office ashen-faced, searching for Molly. He found her by the poolside. "Kornfeld, that coke-head, put me on hold. I hung up on him."

The next day they continued on to Lake Begoria. Sam, to Molly's chagrin, only feigning interest in the herds of antelope and gazelles and zebras they passed. Then, fortunately for Sam, there was to be a four-day break in Nairobi before they moved on to the Masai Mara. They no sooner checked into the Norfolk Hotel than Sam bought every newspaper available and drifted out to the terrace to join Molly for a drink. He was not altogether surprised to find that the terrace, usually thinly populated in the early afternoon, was now crowded with Israelis. A sudden infusion of tourists. Obviously military men and women in mufti. They talked in whispers, occasionally rising from their tables to chat with an old man who sat alone, a bottle of Loch Edmond's Mist before him. He was a short man, wiry, his hands clasped together over the handle of a malacca cane, his chin resting on his hands.

"You're staring," Molly said.

Sam hurried to the front desk, described the old man, and was told his name was Cuervo. "Mr. Cuervo," the clerk said, "is a dealer in Kikuyu and Masai antiquities. He has a gallery on the Rodeo Drive in Los Angeles. The Africana."

Sam returned to his table and told Molly to belt up.

"But we just got here."

They took a taxi to Embakasi Airport, where Sam saw an El Al Boeing 707. Refuelling, he was told, before proceeding to Johannesburg as scheduled. There were also two unmarked airplanes on the far end of the tarmac, another Boeing 707 and a Hercules, both being guarded by Israeli tourists.

Instead of returning directly to the Norfolk, Sam and Molly stopped at the Thorn Tree Bar at the New Stanley Hotel. And there he was again, the old man, and at tables on either side of him there were Israelis laden with camera cases that obviously held weapons. Mr. Cuervo was chatting with two other men, whom Sam later discovered were Lionel Bryn Davies, chief of the Nairobi police, and Bruce Mackenzie, a former minister of agriculture who now served as a special adviser to Jomo Kenyatta. Once the two men left, Mr. Cuervo motioned for Sam and Molly to join him.

"I thought we'd met before," Sam said.

"Oh, no. I've never had the pleasure. But of course I recognize you from television. What brings you to Nairobi?"

"We're on safari."

"Ah."

"And you?"

"Tomorrow night you and Mrs. Burns must be my guests for dinner at Alan Bobbé's Bistro, and then I will try to answer at least some of your questions. Shall we say drinks at seven?"

"Are you sure we haven't met before?"

"I'm afraid not."

That night, Saturday, July 3, following the ninety-minute raid on Entebbe, two El Al Boeing 707s, one of them a makeshift hospital, put in at Embakasi airport. They were joined in the early hours of Sunday morning by four Thunderbird Hercules. Waiting ambulances rushed ten of the more gravely wounded Israeli soldiers to Kenyatta State Hospital. Then the airplanes refuelled and were gone.

Sam read about it at breakfast in the *Sunday Nation*, which had to have had advance notice of the raid. The rest of the day passed slowly, Sam irritable, self-absorbed, but at last it was time to join Cuervo at Alan Bobbé's Bistro. The *maître d'*, who had been expecting them, reached for the bottle of Dom Perignon that floated in a bucket of ice on their table.

"Please don't open it yet," Molly said. "We'll wait for Mr. Cuervo."

"I'm afraid Mr. Cuervo had to leave Nairobi unexpectedly. He sends his apologies and insists that you are to be his guests for dinner."

Back in Washington, writing his piece about Cuervo for the *New Republic*, Sam checked things out in Los Angeles as a matter of form. As he suspected, there was no Africana Gallery on Rodeo Drive nor a Cuervo listed in the telephone book.

SEVEN

◆

1983 it was. Autumn. The season of the sodden partridges, drunk from pecking at fallen, fermented crab apples. Leaves had to be raked. It was nippy out there. The air smelled of oncoming snow, but Moses had not yet taken down his screens and set his double windows in place. His winter wood, dumped in the driveway by Legion Hall, needed to be stacked. Avoiding these chores, Moses — choking on dust — surrounded by overturned cartons — contemplated the interior of his cabin. A sea of disorder. All because he was determined to find his missing Silver Doctor, as if his life depended on it. Exhausted, Moses went to pour himself a drink. Then the phone rang.

"Hi, there. It's me."

The overdressed, fulminating divorcée he had picked up in Montreal on Tuesday.

"I'll be on the four o'clock bus to Magog. Is there anything I can bring?"

Oh, Christ, had he invited her out for the weekend? "Um, no."

"You don't sound pleased."

"Why, I'm delighted. I'll meet you at the bus station."

As soon as she hung up, Moses dialed Grumpy's and asked

to speak to the bartender. "It's Moses Berger. What's the name of the lady I met at your place on Tuesday?"

"Not Mary?"

"Yes. That's it. Thanks."

He collected empty bottles and soiled dishes. He emptied ashtrays. Then he began to stuff papers back into cartons. *Fool. Drunkard. Why didn't you say you were in bed with a fever?*

There had been a time when Moses had enjoyed the novelty of having a woman out to his cabin for the weekend, but now that he was fifty-two years old — grown increasingly cranky, according to Strawberry — given to rising and eating whenever it suited him, he found it an intolerable intrusion. The exception, for some years, had been Kathleen O'Brien, whom he adored. But eventually he came to dread her visits as well. Visits that unfailingly ended with the two of them stumbling about in a drunken stupor. Kathleen disposed to tears and self-pity and finally incoherence, lamenting the fate of what she called *Les Misérables*. The select club of Gursky casualties. She, a victim of Mr. B., and Moses undone by Solomon.

Each time she came out one or another of the tapes had to be played. Mr. Bernard, mouldering in his lead-lined coffin, coming back to haunt them: "Every family has a cross to bear, a skeleton in the closet, that's life. . . ."

The rabbi who had spoken over Mr. Bernard's casket had said, "Here was a man who was wealthly beyond our wildest dreams. He flew in his own jet. He sailed on his own yacht. He had been to Buckingham Palace as well as the White House. Mrs. Roosevelt and Ben-Gurion had both come to his house to eat Libby's boiled beef and *kasha* . Prime ministers of this great country regularly sought his advice. The truth is Mr. Bernard, may he rest in peace, founded one of the greatest family fortunes in North America. But what did this paragon, this legend in his own time, plead for on his deathbed? I'm going to tell you because it's such a beautiful lesson for all of us gathered here. Mr. Bernard asked for the one thing his millions couldn't buy. God's mercy. That was his last request. A plea for God's mercy. . . ."

But Mr. Morrie, who had been there, told Moses what had actually happened at his brother's deathbed.

Fading, his eyes filming over, Mr. Bernard had blinked

awake to see Libby taking his bony waxy hand, holding it to her powdered cheek. She sang:

> Bei mir bist du schön,
> Please let me explain,
> Bei mir bist du schön
> Means that you're grand. . . .
> I could sing Bernie, Bernie,
> Even say "voonderbar". . .

Mr. Bernard tried to scratch, intent on drawing blood, but he no longer had the strength. "No, no," was all he could manage.

"Bernie, Bernie," she sobbed, "do you believe in God?"

"How can you talk such crap at a time like this?"

"It's not crap, sweetie-pie."

"It's not crap, she says. Don't you understand? Don't you understand anything? If God exists, I'm fucked."

And then, Mr. Morrie said, he was gone.

Kathleen's visits, often unannounced, became a torment. The once fastidious and acerbic Miss O., a lady of quality, spilling out of her Subaru with the dented hood, puffy, her step uncertain, wearing a food-stained old sweater and a skirt with a broken zipper, bearing liquor commission bags that rattled, and then talking into the dawn, repeating her stories again and again.

Contemplating her one night, passed out on the sofa, snoring, her mouth agape, Moses remembered her leading him out of the Ritz, at Anita Gursky's first wedding, to spare him listening to the poem L.B. had written in honour of the bride and groom. He leaned over and wiped her chin, he kissed her on both cheeks, covered her with a blanket, and whispered, "I love you," assuming that she couldn't hear. But Kathleen stirred. "Me too you," she said. "But what will become of us?"

The missing manilla envelope still inflamed her. "He didn't lie. Not to me. The little runt took it or maybe Libby has it."

Gitel Kugelmass, who lingered on at the Mount Sinai,

never came out to his cabin, but phoned often. Most recently to report that Dr. Putterman was undoubtedly an RCMP undercover agent.

"Gitel," Moses said, "I want you to come with me to see a doctor I know."

"Maybe that Dr. Ewen Cameron at the Allan Memorial, where it was proven the CIA was paying them to experiment with mind-bending drugs on old people who had no idea what was going on."

Unfortunately he couldn't deny that.

"Or you could put me on the next plane to Moscow, where I could join the other dissidents in the loonybin."

The last time he had taken Gitel to lunch she had said, "Remember the letter L.B. sent me and Kronitz in Ste.-Agathe, pleading with us to think of the children? Not that my Errol Flynn of the north didn't already have his chess set packed. Well that letter is to be included in that young professor's book, you know the one I mean, he's always gabbing away on TV, he's against nuclear arms and wears Red Indian jewellery?"

"Zeigler?"

"That's the one. Isn't it ironic, Moishe? All those years hungering for fame and L.B. doesn't live to see his biography published?"

Three letters from Professor Herman Zeigler lay unanswered in Moses's cabin. The last one, a gem, had come with three enclosures.

1. A street map, detailing the exact route of L.B.'s afternoon strolls from the house with the garden and ornamental shrubs on a tree-lined street in Outremont, down to Park Avenue, past Curly's newsstand, the Regent cinema, Moe's barbershop, the YMHA and Fletcher's Field, cutting left at Pine Avenue to Horn's Cafeteria. He asked Moses to correct any errors or add variations to the route.

2. A photograph of "The Bard", a sculpture of L.B.'s massive head by Marion Peterson, CM, OC, that now rested on a pedestal in the foyer of *La Bibliothèque Juive de Montréal*.

3. Thoughtfully included computer printouts that tabu-
lated the frequency of rank-shifted clauses, tense
auxiliaries, nouns with attributive adverbs, total noun
phrase packers, et cetera in the poetry of W.B. Yeats,
T.S. Eliot, Robert Frost, W.H. Auden, Robert Lowell,
and L.B. Berger.

L.B., Moses was gratified to note, came first in the use of
personal pronouns.

In the letter itself, Zeigler requested an interview with
Moses in connection with a paper he was preparing for a
conference in Banff on *The Failure Syndrome of the Progeny of Great
Canadian Artists*. "Certainly," he wrote, "your co-operation in
this venture would be seminal."

He had not seen Beatrice for years, but he continued to
monitor her climb. An avid fan. She had already dispensed
with the biodegradable Tom Clarkson, divorcing him for a
pretty price. According to reports, she would soon be married
to the man favoured to be the next Canadian high
commissioner to the United Kingdom. From there it ought to
be only a hop, skip, and a jump to another marriage and a
coronet. Meanwhile, the urchin who had once been known as
a Raven kid in Old Town would be working garden parties at
Buckingham Palace. Moses, delighted for her, visualized
Beatrice telling Mrs. Thatcher how to dress and quarter a
caribou and reminding Prince Charles that they had met once
before, in the Elks Hall in fabled Yellowknife.

Lucy sent him newspaper clippings and magazine articles
about her that he might have missed. A photograph of her in
People hugging Andy Warhol, inscribed, "Look at your little
Lucy now!!" Reviews, largely favourable, of her productions
on and off Broadway. A profile in *New York* portrayed her as
foul-mouthed, notoriously bitchy about actresses who had
worked for her, but a perfectionist, no expense spared when
she mounted a production.

Lucy's last phone call had come a long time ago, maybe a
couple of years after Henry's death.

"The cannibal was here to see me last night."

"What?"

"Henry's boy. Isaac."

"How is he?"

"He gives me the creeps is how he is."

"Yes, I suppose."

"You sound drunk."

"Surprise, surprise."

"Come down to New York and I'll pay your fare. You don't have to stay with me if you don't want to. I'll put you up at the Carlyle."

"Say, I can remember when you suggested to Henry that he could pay for my company."

"We could have been married and had grown children by now."

"No, it would have been irresponsible. I'm an unredeemed lush and you have yet to complete your childhood."

"I weigh 280 pounds. I can't stop. I'm a monster. I'm going to explode one day like a sausage in a frying pan," she shrieked before hanging up.

Gitel, Beatrice, Lucy, Kathleen. For the rest, the kind of women Moses managed to attract to his cabin offered five minutes of release paid for with hours of irritation. There had been a lady of a certain age who couldn't abide cigar smoke and another out for a weekend who read a Sidney Sheldon paperback in his bed. Wet towels on his bathroom floor. Hairs clogging his sink. His records put back in the wrong sleeves. Women who expected chitchat at breakfast. And now, not Mary, as Grumpy's bartender had so aptly put it, out for the weekend. Fortunately, Mary insisted on leaving at once after he reprimanded her on Saturday morning.

"Not that I give a shit what you think," she said, "but I wasn't snooping. I have no interest whatsoever in your fucking papers. I was just foolish enough to believe you'd be pleasantly surprised if somebody tried to put this pig-sty in order."

Moses drove her to the bus station in Magog.

"I'll pay my own fare, *if you don't mind*. And this is for you. I sat on it last night. Do me a favour. Shove it up your ass."

His Silver Doctor.

EIGHT

◆

Moses pulled in at The Caboose on his way home.

"Wait till you hear what happened," Strawberry said. "It's 10:30 A.M. — yesterday — bank's been opened a good half-hour and Bunk ain't cashed his welfare cheque yet so's he can start on his monthly toot."

Bunk and his woman were now rooted in a shack up there somewhere in the hills beyond Lake Nick.

"So Hi-Test's worried and he loads a case of twenty-four into his four-wheeler and off he goes to check things out last night."

Entering the cabin, Hi-Test immediately sniffed something bad. He brushed past Bunk, snoozing at the kitchen table, his head cradled in his arms behind a barricade of empty quart bottles of Labatt's 50. He pursued the smell into the bedroom, bolted right out again, and shook Bunk awake. "Hey," he said, "your woman's lying dead in there."

"Oh, so that's it," Bunk said, relieved, "and I thought it was she was angry with me. She's sure been awful quiet since yesterday."

The bar was crowded, most of the regulars celebrating the arrival of their welfare cheques, but Legion Hall and Sneaker were nowhere to be seen. "They're hiding somewhere in the hills," Strawberry said.

Only a week earlier Legion Hall and Sneaker had set up a stall on the 243 piled high with quart cans, ostensibly filled with maple syrup. A placard nailed to the stall read:

HELP ANGLO FARMIRS
LAST OF A DYING BREDE.

They moved two hundred cans and skedaddled before any of their customers could discover that the cans were actually filled with a mixture of used motor oil and water, and now the provincial police were out making inquiries.

Moses sat staring at the salmon fly he had set out on the table. His Silver Doctor. After all his years on the rivers it finally struck him that he wasn't the angler but the salmon. A teasing, gleeful Solomon casting the flies over his head, getting him to roll, rise, and dance on his tail at will. Sea-bright Moses was when he first took the hook, but no more than a black salmon now, ice-bound in a dark river, the open sea closed to him.

Retrieving the fly, Moses returned to his cabin. Once dead by air, once by water, and now, Moses assumed, pacing, a shot of Macallan in hand, and now truly dead. If Solomon were still alive, he would be eighty-four years old, hardly impossible. But since he had last surfaced in Nairobi, Moses had heard from him only once. A telegram sent from Hanoi, in 1978, in response to a memoir Moses had published in *Encounter* about the group that had once gathered round the table with the crocheted tablecloth.

LOOK AT IT THIS WAY. THE SYSTEM WAS INSPIRED, BUT IT IS MAN THAT IS VILE. IT WON'T WORK. THE SERMON ON THE MOUNT. THE MANIFESTO. THE WORLD CONTINUES TO PAY A PUNISHING TOLL FOR OUR JEWISH DREAMERS.

Solomon, Moses suspected, didn't die of old age, but in the

Gulag or a stadium in Latin America. Wherever, the ravens would have gathered.

Dead, Moses. Extinct. You knew that back in 1980, the first year masses of red roses did not bedeck the grave of Diana McClure on the anniversary of her death. So the black salmon is now obliged to sit down, sort things out, and write Solomon's tale or what he knew of it. Or to risk the open sea, swimming out of his Gursky mausoleum never to return.

Problems.

"Hello there, Beatrice. Guess who? Yes. It's your favourite barrel of fun, Moses Berger. If you'll give up that oaf, I'll swear off drinking for life and take you to London myself."

Moses glanced at the portrait of L.B., contemplating the cosmos, enduring its weight, and turned away, surprised by tears. He freshened his drink. Then, badly in need of distraction, flicked on the TV, knowing it was time for Sam Burns to pronounce on PBS. Worrying about Lech Walesa. Disgusted by the massacre of the Palestinians in Sabra and Shatila. Instead there was an interview with the self-satisfied thug himself. Defence Minister Arik Sharon, and Moses switched off the TV impatiently.

Happily Henry hadn't lived to learn of the raids on the refugee camps, winked at by the party in power in the country that was to be a beacon unto the nations. Neither did he live to see the end of the world or to discover that if God did intend to punish us for our transgressions, we would fry rather than freeze, victims of the greenhouse effect. Once more he resolved to visit Nialie in the spring, possibly for Passover, and pardoned himself for not contacting Isaac, an abomination to him.

Moses lit a Monte Cristo, broke open a fresh bottle of Macallan, thrust Solomon's journals aside, and turned to his latest file of Gursky clippings. The family battle for control of Mr. Bernard's little cabbage patch was heating up, growing increasingly acrimonious. Competing appeals to shareholders appeared in full page ads in *The New York Times* and *Wall Street Journal* among other places.

Savvy investment analysts had long predicted that McTavish, given its under-valued assets but uninspired management, its vulnerability through sometimes ill-conceived diversification, was ripe for a hostile takeover bid that would wrest control from the family. What they had not anticipated was that it would be the Gurskys themselves who would be locked in a quarrel over the spoils. A dispute that became public knowledge after Isaac Gursky reached the age of majority, acquiring the shares that had been left in trust for him by his father. While these shares of themselves were not of intimidating consequence, and Isaac was considered a mere scratch player in the unfolding struggle, he began to attract attention once it was discovered that he was a protégé of the shy, self-effacing man the press had dubbed the Gursky jackdaw. The surprising Mr. Morrie who had been surreptitiously accumulating McTavish shares for years, parking them as far away as Tokyo.

Mr. Morrie, ensconced in a suite in the Sherry-Netherlands, was quickly established as a sentimental favourite of the press. He was, after all, the last survivor of the founding brothers. An observant reporter from *Money* noted the moist eyes and trembling hands when Mr. Morrie, whom he described as the Gursky leprechaun, read a statement aloud:

"It pains me, in my old age, to see the children and grandchildren fighting tooth and nail over the business my genius of a brother Bernard built with a little help from me and Solomon who died so young. There is more than enough money for all concerned. Nothing would delight me more than to have everybody meet with me to settle this embarrassing family feud in private. After all, we are a family. All I am asking for is seats on the board for my son Barney and my nephew Isaac. Lionel, bless him, is welcome to stay on at McTavish, though not necessarily as CEO. It is my fondest hope that he will come to realize that blood is thicker than water."

Lionel would have none of it. Heavily favoured in the betting if only because he was the CEO in place, he held the bulk of his late father's shares and was supported by his brother, Nathan, his sister, Anita, and, he claimed, his cousin Lucy, the Broadway producer. Lucy, barricaded in her apartment in the Dakota, refused to talk to reporters, but, according to informed reports, she so detested her nephew Isaac that she was willing to overlook an old family feud and throw in her lot with Lionel. Her shares, it was rumoured, might be sufficient to tip the balance either way.

Then an imponderable factor came into play. The shadowy Corvus Trust of Zurich. A spokesman for Corvus, custodians of 4.2 percent of the McTavish shares, only aroused suspicions by declaring that they were "friendly buyers, potential white knights, not hostile bidders."

Moses, following the struggle from his cabin, read of platoons of fabulously expensive lawyers, who were pelting the courts with charges and counter-charges; merchant bankers and brokerage houses at risk on both sides; and uncommitted raiders and greenmail enthusiasts circling the fray, ready to pounce.

Journalists rejoiced in what was undoubtedly the juiciest family feud in years, billions at stake.

Isaac babbled to one and all about his movie-making plans and Barney was turning up on talk-shows everywhere, gabbing about his future plans for McTavish, including a bid for a major league baseball franchise and a scheme to tow icebergs from the Arctic to the Middle East.

Responding to a tip, a New York *Post* reporter located a self-proclaimed former mistress of Barney's, the now disconcertingly plump, even matronly Darlene. This led to titillating photographs and a full-blown interview in *Penthouse*. Darlene wore her ankh ring for the occasion. "It's Egyptian," she explained, "and symbolizes life. Most Wiccans wear it with the point facing out to protect themselves against negative forces, but I've got a strong psychic shield. I wear it with the point inward." She said that she had been a witch since Camelot. "You know, King Arthur's time. I'm reincarnated every seven generations. I'm part Jew, part Mohawk, and part Seventh Day Adventurer. And did I tell you that I was once a good Jewish mother, you know, when I saw the Crucifixion? It was very, very moving."

The interviewer pointed out that Barney had denied that they had ever been lovers.

"Uh huh," she said, unsnapping the locket lying against her throat, "then how come I still got this?"

Purportedly a lock of Barney's pubic hair.

"In those bygone days he was very romantic and one night in the Ramada Inn we exchanged locks of pubic hair as a symbol of our enduring love ha, ha, ha. If you doubt my word I challenge you to have these hairs scientifically tested."

The cover of *New York* showed Isaac flying through the air over the McTavish building on Fifth Avenue in a red and blue Captain Al Cohol uniform, a *yarmulke* fastened to his hair with a paperclip.

Predictably even the *National Enquirer* got into the act, stung with a $200-million libel suit as a consequence. *The Enquirer* featured a front-page photograph of Isaac emerging from the rescue helicopter at Yellowknife airport.

THE CANNIBAL WHO WOULD BE A CROWN PRINCE.

Other, more fastidious publications obviously decided to eschew the Gursky family feud. An indignant Lionel discovered that *Art & Antiques* had temporarily postponed a photo essay on his collection of early North American banknotes. His wife took to her bed, seething, when *Town & Country* cancelled its piece on "Those Glittering Gurskys", which was to include a double-page Avedon photograph of Cheryl in her music room. "Dress: Arnold Scaasi. At Saks Fifth Avenue; Sara Fredericks, Palm Beach. Hosiery, Geoffrey Beene. Shoes, Stuart Weitzman. Makeup by Antonio Da Costa Rocha, New York. Asprey of London jewels."

An ailing Libby summoned Lionel to the family mansion in Westmount.

"Your father once told me that on Solomon's last night in Montreal, just before he flew off in that Gypsy Moth, he warned him that if anybody tried to diddle Henry or Lucy out of their shares he would come back from the grave if necessary and my Bernie was finished. A dead man."

"Daddy died of cancer, remember?" Lionel asked, dismissing his mother's foolish apprehensions.

"I remember it like yesterday. But who put that dead raven on his grave is what I'd like to know."

Back in New York, Lionel sent for Harvey Schwartz.

"There's a story I want to read in the columns, but it

wouldn't look good coming from me. I have it on the most reliable authority that Isaac suffers from delusions about being the Messiah. Moses plus one or some shit like that. Maybe the little prick was zonked out of his head, but that's what he told a bunch he took to dinner at the Odeon last night. I want to scare all the little guys out there who are wondering what to do with their proxies. I want to read about this in Liz Smith tomorrow. Understand?"

"Lionel, this is difficult for me to say, but I have decided it doesn't behoove me to take any further part in what is essentially a family quarrel."

"How much did Morrie offer you for your piddly pile of shares, you little runt?"

"Mr. Morrie is a great human being. I say that not because he has been kind to me since I was a youngster, but from the heart. However, I will not take his side in this matter either."

Then things began to crumble.

A spokesman for Corvus Trust declared that they had decided to cast their lot with a new management for McTavish, the next CEO, possibly an outsider, to be selected by a triad of three generations of Gurskys: Morrie, Barney, and Isaac.

Next Mr. Morrie went to the Dakota to talk to Lucy, who was irrevocably opposed to his takeover, according to most observers. That afternoon Lucy's Broadway office released a surprising statement. Barney and Isaac Gursky would be joining her board. In the future, LG Productions, shortly to become a division of McTavish Industries, would be mounting film as well as stage productions. Lucy, who had taken to her bed, was unavailable to answer questions herself.

Mr. Bernard's portrait was removed from the outer office of the McTavish building on Fifth Avenue and in its place went the drawing of Ephraim Gursky, all coiled muscle, obviously ready to spring out of the frame and wrestle anybody to the ground. Ephraim was drawn alongside a blow-hole, with both feet planted in the pack ice, his expression defiant, his head hooded, his body covered with layers of sealskin, not so much to keep out the cold, it seemed, as to lock in the animal heat lest it melt the surrounding ice. He held a harpoon in his fist, the shaft made of caribou antler. There was a seal lying at his feet, the three masts of the doomed *Erebus* and jagged icebergs rising in the background, the black Arctic sky lit by paraselanae, the mock-moons of the north.

An uncommonly serene Mr. Morrie announced his retirement from his estate in Ste.-Adèle.

"Barney and Isaac don't need any old fogies in the office, but if they want some bad advice they always know where to find me, those two outstanding young men."

Asking the reporters to wait, Mr. Morrie slipped into the house, opened his wall safe, and removed a set of keys that lay on a large brown envelope, addressed to MISS O., PERSONAL AND CONFIDENTIAL. Then he invited the reporters into his wood workshop.

"This is my new office, ladies and gentlemen. Anybody needs a nicely made table, a bookcase maybe, I'm accepting orders starting right now. Free estimates on request."

Autumn. The season of the sodden partridges, drunk from pecking at fallen, fermented crab apples. Moses, in need of fresh air, dropped his empty Macallan bottle into a wastepaper basket and drifted outside. Raking leaves, he wondered what Solomon would have made of all of it.

One of the journals Solomon had sent Moses some years back had come with a typically irritating note:

"I once told you that you were no more than a figment of my imagination. Therefore, if you continued to exist, so must I."

But he's dead, Moses thought, even as the sky above was filled with a sudden roaring, Moses ducking involuntarily, an airplane passing low enough overhead to clip the treetops. Straightening up, his balance uncertain, Moses couldn't find the airplane anywhere. Then it was back. A black Gypsy Moth wagging its wings at him. It made another pass at the cabin, wagging its wings again. Then, as Moses watched, it began to climb. He knew where it was going.

North.

Where north?

Far.

Watching the Gypsy Moth climb, Moses believed that he

saw it turn into a big menacing black bird, the likes of which hadn't been seen over Lake Memphremagog since the record cold spell of 1851. A raven with flapping wings. A raven with an unquenchable itch to meddle and provoke things, to play tricks on the world and its creatures. He watched the bird soar higher and higher, until he lost it in the sun.

Author's note

Years ago, following the publication of another novel, a television interviewer asked me, "Is this book based on fact, or did you just make it up out of your own head?"

I made the Gurskys up out of my own head, but I did not invent everything in *Solomon Gursky Was Here*. I dug deeply into Franklin, M'Clure, Back, Richardson and the rest on the doomed expedition to circumnavigate the globe through the Northwest Passage, putting my own spin on events. *Frozen in Time: The Fate of the Franklin Expedition*, by Owen Beattie and John Geiger, struck me as the most original of recent studies. I am indebted to *The Raven Steals the Light*, by Bill Reid and Robert Bringhurst, for the Haida myths. I found *The Victorian Underworld*, by Kellow Chesney, indispensable in my attempt to recreate nineteenth-century London. I have leaned heavily on James H. Gray's *Red Lights on the Prairie* and *Booze* for western history, and on Bernard Epps' *More Tales of the Townships*. I am also grateful to Christopher Dafoe, editor of *The Beaver*, for going through his files for me.

I should also come clean and admit that Captain Al Cohol is not my invention. He was conceived by Art Sorensen, then with the NWT Alcohol Education Program, and the radio scripts I have quoted from are by E.G. Perrault.

Finally, I would like to acknowledge the help of my wife. Over the years, Florence had to endure this novel in many drafts. Without her encouragement, not to mention crucial editorial suggestions, I would have given up on *Solomon Gursky Was Here* long ago.

Mordecai Richler

Pauline McLynn grew up in Galway and started acting while studying History of Art in Dublin. She has played many stage roles, but shot to fame as the inimitable Mrs Doyle in *Father Ted*. Her other television work includes *Aristocrats* and the sketch show *TV To Go* for the BBC and *Dark Ages* for ITV. She has appeared on cinema screens in *Angela's Ashes*, *Quills*, *When Brendan Met Trudy* and *An Everlasting Piece*. Pauline's first novel, *Something for the Weekend*, was a number one bestseller and received outstanding critical acclaim. She is currently writing Leo Street's third adventure.

Also by Pauline McLynn

Something for the Weekend

Better than a Rest

Pauline McLynn

HEADLINE

First published in 2001
by HEADLINE BOOK PUBLISHING

First published in paperback in 2001
by HEADLINE BOOK PUBLISHING

10 9 8 7 6 5 4 3 2 1

ISBN 0 7472 6398 1

Typeset by Letterpart Ltd
Reigate, Surrey

Printed and bound in Great Britain by
Mackays of Chatham plc, Chatham, Kent

HEADLINE BOOK PUBLISHING
A division of Hodder Headline
338 Euston Road
London NW1 3BH

www.headline.co.uk
www.hodderheadline.com

For Dominick McGrath without whom
things might well fall apart . . .

One

It is surely a given that a hairy big toe is not an attractive feature, on a man or a woman. Cats and dogs get away with it, as do otters, rabbits and what have you. Humans, no. That's what I was thinking at 12.30 a.m. as Michael O'Donoghue let himself out of another woman's house and set off for the southside of Dublin city where he lived with his wife, Miranda, and, occasionally, their two teenage children, Tara (15) and Ben (13). That's how scintillating the evening's mental activity had been, how interesting covert surveillance can get at times: hairy big toes.

I followed at a discreet distance. Sadly, not all of the motorists abroad that night had their full quota of discretion on board. As the O'Donoghue Mercedes slowed to a stop at traffic lights, and I began to do the same, a red banger hurtled out of a laneway, smashing into the side of my dark green banger. There was a sickening crunch, and my innards lurched as the cars scuttled sideways. After some moments of a macabre metal waltz, we screeched to a noisy stop and I realised that my journey this evening was just about over. In fact, I was going nowhere, fast.

As soon as I could, I extricated my trusty steed from the mess, and pulled in to the verge. I counted to ten, then calmly got out and walked over to the offending vehicle. The ninny in the other car was blubbering. She became incoherent when she saw the motorcycle cop who had appeared, *as if by magic*. They really do have the ability to fall from the sky. Black streams of mascara ran down the woman's cheeks, and saliva bubbled from her lips. If she hadn't messed my night up so badly, I might have felt some pity. I handed her a tissue as the policeman joined us. We had enough people for a small cheese 'n' wine do now. Worst of all, Michael O'Donoghue reversed to join us, and got out of his car with the immortal words, 'I'm a doctor, is there anything I can do to help?'

The crying heap shoved her face further into her handkerchief and began to pace up and down behind her car. The young Garda took off his helmet. He was just a kid, and could barely muster sideburns. When you've begun to think that teachers and the police look like babies, you know you're getting on. I was thirty now and felt every day of it. At least I wasn't old enough to be his mother, I thought. Or was I? I wondered with a shudder. No, biologically that wasn't possible. Even in these days of technological advancement. Surely? A nagging doubt lingered in my mind.

Michael O'Donoghue ascertained that his professional services were not needed and, lacking an inclination to involve himself in any other way, sped off to the south.

I envied him. Unfortunately, he was now familiar with my face and my car, although he did not know that I had been following him that night, and for the previous three, on the instructions of a worried and suspicious wife. I would need a major rethink of this case, no thanks to the stranger in the red car. And, inevitably, it would cost money to get back to the status quo. Money was in short supply. But then, what else was new?

My dance partner gathered herself sufficiently to begin the tedious exchanges that typified motoring in Ireland, April 1997. I didn't know the Garda, which was a relief. Many of his colleagues, who knew me all too well, would have relished a chance like this to put me on the spot to see how I reacted. When asked my occupation, I simply answered 'self-employed', and he was satisfied with that. For mischief, others might have pushed for a more detailed description, just to see me sweat. He was happy enough with the name Leonora Street, spinster of number 11, The Villas, Dublin 3. I could have offered 'insurance adviser', and it would not have been a lie; a lot of cases I work on involve insurance fraud. Equally, I might have given myself the title 'marriage consultant', because infidelity is the meat and drink of my trade. Only one thing was for sure, I was never going to admit to the real description, private investigator. Life was always easier when I avoided mentioning this.

When all of the relevant insurance details had been exchanged, the females of the group promised to stay in touch like the good friends we would never be, and the little party broke up. We all went our, now, separate ways. I headed back northwards, along the coast road, with a heavy heart and a limping, rattling car. I would need someone else to follow Michael O'Donoghue, at least in the short term. The problem was not so much that he'd seen me – a wig and glasses would have taken care of that. But I had no quick access to new wheels and the risk was that he would recognise my car now, with its distinctive, and unwanted, dent. I was going to need a new body with fresh transport. Best have a good night's sleep and tackle the problem with a clear mind in the morning.

I wasn't too worried about what my subject would get up to the following day during business hours. That was as predictable as my own moodiness coming up to a period. Michael O'Donoghue was one of the country's leading obstetricians, and held a clinic in his practice on Merrion Square on weekdays between nine and two. Then he had a quick lunch, usually a sandwich at his desk, before strolling across to do his daily round at the Fledgling Clinic, behind the National Maternity Hospital in Holles Street. The Fledgling also dealt in childbirth, but aside from that any similarity between the two institutions was hard to find. The latter was run by a private trust as a lucrative business and boasted a fertility clinic amongst its assets. It was a very expensive, and exclusive, facility with a clientele of the rich, the famous and the bankrupt. Michael O'Donoghue was one of its star attractions – in the medical sense, that is. Now, without our old friend 'the unforeseen circumstance'

turning up, I had until tea time to find someone else to
continue surveillance on him.

Noel peeked his cheeky face through the curtains as I
hiccoughed my jalopy over the speed ramps and clanked
to a halt outside my house. It was one of a series of
triangular dwellings, all in a row, known locally as The
Toblerone. The lights of the front room were on and I
could hear music being played on the stereo. I didn't
think that Noel or Bridie or Snubby was responsible for
the noise. They were cats. That left me with Barry, my
live-in boyfriend. Unless it had been No. 4, who was
partial to the Divine Comedy, the group I could hear
singing about Daddy's crashed car. Here comes Mummy
with her version, I thought, as I followed my cloudy
breath up the pathway and let myself in the front door.

Barry Agnew was draped lazily along the couch,
smoking a joint. Nothing unusual here. Barry had lived
either on the bed or on the couch since he had moved
in with me, three years ago. The only addition to this
familiar sight was the figure lolling in the opposite
armchair: Coleman Pearse, another actor. They
favoured the term 'wandering minstrel' to describe
their profession. I was beginning to prefer 'meandering
wastrel'.

'Leonora,' exclaimed Coleman, in deep theatrical
tones. 'What an unexpected surprise.'

'Coleman, I live here. But what an expected surprise
to find *you* in situ.'

'Of course I am, dear heart. This house of yours is an

5

oasis of the finest hospitality imaginable to a poor thespian.'

'Nice diction, Coleman,' I congratulated him, my voice lightly iced with sarcasm.

'Now, now, Leo,' said Barry, from the deepest reaches of his lair. 'Coleman is a guest, so play nice.'

'Okay, okay,' I agreed. 'Sorry to be a grouch, Coleman, but someone tried to take the side off my car tonight, and they very nearly succeeded. It's in a right mess.'

Coleman nodded his head sagely. 'All part of the derring-do of your profession. The risking of life and limb. Very brave of you, Leonora.'

This 'Leonora' business was beginning to get to me. Only my family used it with any regularity, and then it was usually reserved for occasions when they were angry with me, or winding me up for some reason. In them it was occasionally endearing, in Coleman I found it overly familiar, something I could not abide in a casual acquaintance. Coleman was very casual, particularly with my beer. And my food, for that matter. Oh, yes, and my spare bedroom, when he was too trashed to make it home to his own house.

Barry and Coleman had become the best of friends some weeks ago when they began work on the Dublin Literary Tour and Pub Crawl. They took to the job with marked alacrity, principally because it involved lots of thunderous oration and the drinking of, at least, one glass of stout in each of the many pubs they visited on the Crawl. And then getting properly shit-faced afterwards with the punters. It had been their vocation fulfilled. They finished most of these evenings with a brace of takeaway lagers, and smoking a load of dope. At my house.

Coleman liked to put it about that he was a cousin of the late Padraig Pearse, the Irish writer and revolutionary. I thought it more likely that he was as related to the famous Pearse as I was, which was not at all. But according to Barry, the boast worked a treat for pulling women, and Coleman was never short of a bedfellow in the shape of a foreign student, au pair or American tourist. That's when he was not bunking over at mine. I drew the line at him keeping company there, using the place like a brothel and giving me, effectively, another mouth to feed and water.

'Anyone for a beer?' I asked, foolishly.

'Did Rose Kennedy have a black dress?' replied Coleman.

I opened the fridge and saw two tins of Czech beer with an unpronounceable name. This brand was obviously the cheapest available locally; neither Barry nor Coleman believed in paying much for their drink, if they were using their own money. It didn't take a genius to figure out that three into two did not go. I announced as much.

'Well, you drink wine so,' suggested Barry. 'Anyhow, that lager is a terrible ring-stinger, and you'd regret having it as much as I'm going to tomorrow.'

'You're all heart, Barry, do you know that?' I said sweetly. 'And I would be delighted to drink some wine, if there were any. If seems the wine mouse has been to the fridge again, and had the lot.'

'Bad, evil, wicked wine mouse,' he slurred.

I looked back into the living room, saw the two languid beauties and made a decision.

'You've both been drinking all night, and now you're smoking your faces off. You don't need any more booze, so here's my revolutionary plan. Why don't I have *both* the cans that are left, and that way everyone is happy? Particularly me. Now who's a clever girl!'

The cream of Ireland's young actors looked shocked, but knew better than to argue; it was my house. As I closed the fridge door I noticed that the cat magnet poetry was getting more and more puerile, with over-use of the words 'pussy' and 'lick'. Kick rhymes with lick, I mused idly, and remembered that 'doggerel' is the word for bad verse, though it didn't seem appropriate in this case. As I made my way over to a chair, I looked around uneasily. The power of poetry had triggered a thought in my brain. Something was bothering me about the domestic set-up; something was missing. No. 4 was nowhere to be seen. He had come to live with us as a bizarre by-product of a case I'd worked on in Kildare. At that time I had been chosen for, perhaps even by, No. 4.

'Barry, where's the dog?'

'Oh, he's upstairs in one of the bedrooms. The cats and him were killing one another all evening, so I had to separate them.'

'Well, I hope you let him out for a pee before you banished him,' I said.

Realisation clicked behind his eyes, and I knew that he had not.

'Oh, for God's sake, Barry, can you not be trusted with anything?'

As I rushed up the stairs, I heard Coleman ask, 'Do you think that was the kind of green boat that the owl and the pussycat took?' followed by hoots of laughter. I opened the bedroom door and a yelping white-black-brown blur whizzed by and made for the cat flap from the kitchen into the back garden. It was still swinging to and fro when I got back downstairs.

'Doggone!' Barry hooted. Coleman enjoyed this and showed it noisily.

'Tossers,' I murmured to myself.

When the little Jack Russell had discharged his business, he returned and covered me with licks, before boisterously making friends with the bewildered felines.

After that I took great delight in cracking open the second last tin of lager in front of the lads. They looked on longingly as I slowly sipped the ice-cold brew. I gave a contented sigh and said, 'Barry, I don't know what you're talking about. I think this is delicious.' Then I squeezed on to the couch beside him so that he had to adjust his comfortable slouch to accommodate me. This was shaping up nicely, I thought.

We sat in silence for a while, and Barry rolled another joint. Then he and Coleman smoked it. I didn't partake. I never did. In a way there was no need. Unlike Bill Clinton, however, I did inhale. It would have been hard not to in the fumes that filled the air in the tiny room. I noticed that the cats, myself and No. 4 were like the Bisto Kids, our noses slightly upturned and inhaling the wafts of smoke though this was a different joint from the one the Bisto Kids would have been involved with, I guessed. We were all smiling although on No. 4's face this looked a little like a snarl. The expression on blond-haired Coleman Pearse owed more to Harpo Marx, but in a spirit of peace and reconciliation, I refrained from mentioning this.

'Leo, you'll love the latest standout advertisement we've found in the *Northsider News*,' said Barry, reaching for the local free paper. 'Myself and Coleman are very tempted to apply. We'd be just right for the job.'

In the Situations Vacant section, a drawing of a truck headed an ad declaring: 'Wanted – articulate drivers. Experienced HGV licence essential'.

'That old devil, the roving "d",' I laughed.

'If only I'd heeded me mammy and taken the heavy goods vehicle test,' wailed Coleman, dramatically, 'life would have been so different.'

'Yes,' I agreed, solemnly. 'You're only half qualified. You may be articulate, but you don't have the driving licence.'

'And your experiences may be of the wrong kind anyhow,' added Barry.

'Oh, I don't think so,' grinned Coleman. 'Trucking, and all that.'

The two actors began to discuss the finer points of a play we'd seen at the Abbey Theatre the week before.

This amounted to a fair bit of bitching about the younger members of the cast. Both Barry and Coleman had been up for parts, but had not been successful. As a result, they had long ago decided that the female director of the piece was a lesbian. I had enjoyed it very much, particularly as it starred my friend Maeve Kelly. She assured me that the director was as straight as ourselves, and married to a stunning, filthy-rich businessman.

I looked at Barry as he waved his arms about, explaining some complicated notion he had about the leading actor's lisp, which I had found charming in the extreme. Barry's long, square-jawed face was animated and therefore at its best. As he smiled dimples appeared in each olive-skinned cheek; his vivid blue eyes sparkled and crinkled good-naturedly. Every time he jerked his head, masses of black curls bounced up and down. He was gorgeous.

I had met him, and his friend Maeve, at a party in a house in Glasnevin on Dublin's north side. There was a catholic mix of people, ranging from air hostesses to brokers to teachers, with showbiz represented by actors and solicitors; a very good party. I ran into Barry, Maeve, and some more of their cronies in the kitchen as I foraged for beer. Of course, Barry had appointed himself Keeper of the Fridge, so I had to speak to him to cajole my way into the ice box. One sentence led to another, and when the night was winding to a close I found myself bundling him into a taxi and taking him home with me for a night of raucous sex and laughter. I called him Larry for the entire evening, having mis-heard his name in the noisy kitchen. He corrected me, gently, over a breakfast of beans on toast the following morning. He moved in three weeks later. There would be times over the next three years when I would miss Larry.

I had heard of a seven-year itch, but begun to think that Barry and I were going through a three-year ditch; some sort of a trough at any rate. Everything had become awfully routine. Sex was all too rare and drunken, and most other intercourse involved rows about hoovering and bill paying. The fun and adventure had disappeared, and somehow we had both grown too lazy and careless to rekindle those essentials. But at least Barry was working steadily again, even if he still hadn't had his big Hollywood break, and that meant he could run to his habits and social life without having to borrow money from me. He was also handy for trans-ferring the shopping from the supermarket trolley to the boot of the car. Occasionally he gave me a contribution towards the mortgage, but suffice to say it wouldn't have amounted to rent in even the smallest bed-sit imaginable in the area.

For all that, life was okay. We still had laughs, and rarely a dull moment. I met lots of people I would never have come across without Barry, including Maeve Kelly, whom I adored. The cats liked him, in their cat-like way, and when No. 4 had joined the household unexpectedly, he had adjusted fairly well. Barry, that is.

I had never lived with anyone before, apart from my family, so I had no comparisons to make, if these are ever a good thing anyway. I had had boyfriends, of course, but none had stayed over for more than a weekend at a time. Barry's moving in, although swift, was a gradual process. His clothes turned up in the wash pile, a toothbrush appeared in the bathroom. Then people started to leave messages for him on the answering machine, and he began to invite his friends around. Before I knew it his dole office had shifted him to my area, and demands for payment of his credit card began to plop through the letter box.

It took my family slightly longer than me to figure out that he lived at number 11, The Villas. And that was probably a good thing. I had two brothers, Peter and Stephen, respectably married to Anne and Angela respectively. Between them they had four children, all happily born into wedded bliss. My parents, who were by no means small-minded, would still have preferred their only daughter to be formally and legally hitched to the man she was living with. But that was glossed over quickly, and Barry became a regular fixture in the Street household, much to the delight of my teenage niece Lucy, who had a crush on him the size of Texas.

'Training, shmaining,' I heard Barry say, dismissively. 'If he hadn't gone off to London and got those letters after his name, no one would bother their arses with him. All he learned over there were fuzzy esses and a big attitude.'

'Agreed, agreed,' agreed Coleman. 'But,' he raised a

forefinger significantly, 'you know yourself . . .' His face drooped, but I felt that this had more to do with the grass he had been smoking than the perfidy of the Irish theatre world. The discussion would probably go around in circles from here.

As the two actors' melodious voices dissected their peers, I pondered my work problem. It was not unheard of for a private investigator to get someone in to help on a case. It happened for a variety of reasons. You might simply not have the time to do all of the leg work yourself. Or you might have been spotted, as I had been, although Michael O'Donoghue would not have known that I had been following him at the time. So, there was no disgrace in any of this. The problem was that I ran a very small operation of one, me, and avoided drafting in extras. I was moderately successful, but could ill afford to have another dependant on full pay. I racked my brain for a suitable replacement. And then, in a Road to Damascus revelation, it came to me; I actually slipped off the couch a bit as a name formed in my brain. I thought of Ciara Gillespie.

She had been part of our gang of four on a cookery course I had taken earlier in the year, a teenage minx who was driving her parents around the bend at home. Ciara was bored, aimless and full of mischievous intelligence. She was young, quick-witted and capable – I should have been writing her CV for her. I could train her in on this straightforward case, and she would be very useful in the future. She would also be cheaper than hiring another pro, and money was a consideration.

Ciara would be perfect. If it had not been so late, I would
have put the call in there and then. But the Gillespies had
enough to contend with in Ciara without some strange
woman rambling at them in the wee small hours about a
less-than-average job opportunity.

I was so delighted with myself that I opened the last
can of lager without even teasing Barry and Coleman. I
had gulped back half of it before I remembered to ask if
there had been any messages for me during the
evening. Coleman had to be cut off in mid-flow of his
treatise on Irish Theatre For A New Millennium as his
rapt audience reported that my mother had phoned to
remind me about lunch the following day. I was looking
forward to this. It would involve the Street women:
myself, my mother, her mother, my two sisters-in-law,
and our special guest Rose Street, who was the latest
addition to the family, and who would be mewling and
puking at her mother's breast for the occasion. Angela,
the mother in question, had even promised them both a
glass of champagne; she would drink it, and Rose would
have the filtered benefits.

I checked my watch and saw that it was close to
2 a.m. I hoisted myself into a standing position and
announced that it was very late and probably bedtime
for all of us.

'A lovely invitation, Leonora, my dear,' said Coleman,
'but I'm sure that Barry would prefer you all to himself.'

I looked at him, gobsmacked. Did he really think that
I had been suggesting a threesome, or was he taking the
piss? I caught Barry's eye and we both began to laugh.

15

'I'll just shuffle away,' Coleman continued.

Now I was very taken aback. Was he going home? I looked to Barry again. Huge tears were pouring down his cheeks.

'No need to be so sad,' slurred his cohort. 'I'm not going far.'

With that he made a lunge for the door, and before I could bid him goodnight, I heard his footsteps clumping upstairs to the spare room. Coleman might not have been going home, but he was certainly making himself at home.

As Barry wiped the tears of merriment from his face, he remembered something.

'Oh, yeah, there was one other call,' he said. 'Some man wants you to phone him tomorrow. I don't think he left his name. It'll be on the machine still. I'm off too, Leo. See you above.' He got to his feet and staggered slightly. 'Jeez, that latest dope is really strong stuff. I'm wrecked.' He stopped at the door. 'Have you seen my lucky underpants anywhere?' he asked.

Barry was as superstitious as any other actor I'd met. If he had an audition or an opening night, he had to wear a certain pair of Y-fronts. They were a bluey-grey from countless boilings and colour runs, no doubt a difficult shade to replicate if one had a mind to. I truthfully denied all knowledge of their whereabouts. He continued his unsteady progress to the stairs where he murmured what sounded like 'love ya, g'night', and disappeared. I could hear him bump softly off the walls of the stairwell at regular intervals before throwing himself on to our bed.

I slugged back the last of my beer as I pressed the 'play' button by the telephone. A deep and sexy voice said, 'Leo Street, you owe me and I'm calling in the favour. Ring me tomorrow.' He didn't identify himself. He didn't need to. I knew who he was. My heart gave an involuntary leap. Andy Raynor had called.

Two

I could not remember a time when Andy Raynor had not been around. He was older than me by a year, which would have made him Peter's friend initially, but since no one could remember when 'initially' was, he was just subsumed into the family as a friend of all of us. He had grown up across the street, and was in all of the photographs we had of children's parties, Holy Communions and Confirmations. And even if we were not running a social occasion at our house, he would be there. He was part of the Street furniture, and I treated him like that. Actually, I treated him as badly as I treated any member of my family. And in turn, he treated me as badly as one of his.

And then, in adolescence, something strange happened. Andy shot to his full height long before any of the other boys in the area, but without any awkwardness. He just blossomed. Gone was the pug-nosed rapscallion who was forever in some scrape or another, to be replaced by a suave ladykiller who charmed every parent for miles around, and was allowed free rein with their offspring. Or so it seemed to me and the gaggle of girls I hung around with, on corners and outside chip shops.

He was captain of his school's rugby team, and a crucial winger on the soccer team. He could also turn his hand to hockey, athletics and, God help us, *chess*, if required. He was a top debater both in Irish and English, and we were often pitched against one another as I was the captain of both of these teams in the girls' school. It was galling one year when they won the Dublin Regional Final of an Irish debating competition after an impassioned and totally baseless summing up by him, and we, the hot favourites, were left with our arms dangling by our sides. We were robbed. I could not be gracious in defeat, and did not speak to him for a month. I was never sure he even noticed that at the time; he was too busy fending off female attention. Or rather marshalling it, so that he was never without some stunner on his arm.

But busy as he was with his amours, he seemed to spend most nights in our house. Sometimes he would help me with mathematics, for which I had no aptitude and never would have. Or else we'd listen to the latest LP he'd bought and have some major difference of opinion about music, mostly just for the sake of it. I would deliberately champion the Police so that he could praise the UK Subs; I'd vote Madness, he'd say the Clash; we would agree on some common ground like the Specials and Thin Lizzy. I loved all of them and so did he; it was our game, these were our shared references. Sometimes he would just sit and watch telly with the family. If I was feeling particularly poisonous,

I would ask if the Raynors' own television set was broken, but he would always laugh me off. That's how he handled me, he laughed. It worked as well as any other way with the teenage Leonora Street.

But something else had changed between us, and I was the last to realise it. We became attracted to one another. Maybe we always had been. But this physical longing upped the ante considerably. I never trusted it. How could someone so cool be interested in me? I was a heap. My hair was too greasy, my face was too spotty, my bottom was way too big. I was moody; even I knew that. I had nothing to recommend me, I thought. My parents were horrified when I would go into one of my rants about how ugly I was. They couldn't understand how they had instilled me with so little self-confidence. I think, in fairness, they had just forgotten how awful and bleak it can be to be a teenager. One day my mother, close to tears, burst out with, 'It doesn't say much for myself and your father, does it, if we made you and you've turned out to be so hideous? Don't you think it's a bit of an insult to us?' So I toned things down after that. But I could not figure out what Andy Raynor wanted from me when he could have his pick of anyone in the area and beyond.

One early-summer's evening I was sitting in our back garden in quiet despair. It was nearing exam time and I was worried that I might not do well. I liked school, and I was academically sound. But I wanted to be one of the best because I wasn't much good at sport and felt I had very little else to recommend me. I was all of sixteen years old. I had also had a shaggy perm done in town the previous Saturday, and I wasn't sure that it was me. Andy came out for a breath of fresh air. I stuck my nose deep into the book I was studying, and ignored him. I tried so hard to read what was in front of me on the page but all I could see was a jumble of letters, and the light was a bit dim for reading anyhow. I could feel him close by and I began to shake.

'Are you cold?' he asked.

'No. And anyway, even if I am, what's it to you?'

'Just asking. No need to bite my head off. I was going to offer you my jumper if you were. No big deal.'

No big deal? I would have died at that moment to be swaddled in Andy Raynor's jumper. I began to shake even more violently at the thought of being so close and intimate with something that had touched him. What to do? I would be lynched at school the following day if I confessed to messing this opportunity up.

'Maybe I will take it, if you don't mind? I am a bit chilly.'

He took off the grey V-necked sweater and held it up for me to climb into. I did. He stayed right there beside me and said, 'It suits you, Leo. And, by the way, I like your hair.'

I was so sure he was lying that I began to cry. It came up on me from nowhere. Suddenly his arms were around me and he was saying urgently, 'Oh, please don't cry, Leo. What have I done? Please don't cry. What's the matter? Tell me.' And all the time he was stroking my hair, and its vile shaggy perm.

I sobbed into his white polo shirt for a while, and only stopped when I felt exhausted. He continued to hold me, then pulled back and asked, 'What's the matter? Did I do something to hurt you?'

I shook my head, fairly violently, and managed to stammer, 'I'm a bit worried about my exams, that's all.'

'As long as you're sure it's nothing that I've done,' he said. 'I couldn't bear that.'

I looked into his beautiful hazel-green eyes and smiled, shaking my head again, a little more gently this time. He magicked a handkerchief from somewhere and wiped away my tears. Then he held it to my nose and said, 'Blow,' and I obeyed. Then he leaned down and said, 'Kiss,' and we did.

We had an unspoken, unofficial arrangement after that. If we were in a group, we would oscillate towards each other. He would buy me chips at the weekends, and I would get him the *NME* if I thought I'd got to the newsagent's before him on the day it came out. These were blissful summer holidays, with no worries and nothing to do. We went swimming in a gang. We would go into town, or to the pictures, in a gang. But each evening Andy would come around to my house, sometimes to leave me home, sometimes to spend time in, always kissing me goodnight, at length. We grew hungrier and hungrier for one another. But with it came desperation on my part. As I fell deeper and deeper under this spell, I became more and more distrustful of it. I still could not believe he wanted the ugly duckling when there were so many beautiful girls in our group of friends.

I started to let my insecurities show. It began in little ways. I would tease him gently about how Karen Grealish looked at him, or ask him why he had never gone out with Maria O'Grady when she was so gorgeous and obviously had the hots for him. He gently brushed all of this aside. But I would not let up, and eventually he broke one night and told me that the teasing was boring now and would I please stop it. I accused him of being bored with me. He denied that he was. In retrospect, who could have blamed him if he had been? And then, like the lemming that I was, I declared one day that it might be better if we had a break from each other for a while. I meant it to be a test, and he should have said 'no' and convinced me that it was a bad idea and that we were meant to be together forever. But he was so worn out by my shenanigans that he thought I genuinely meant it. And, reluctantly, he agreed. I took to my room and cried for a week.

My family did not know what to do with me. I couldn't sleep. I wouldn't eat. I could not stop crying. In the end, they left me to my splendid isolation. I played every mushy track about love and loss that I had, over and over again. I waited hour after hour for a visit from Andy. Every time the front door opened, I was sure it was him. Each time the back door slammed, I felt certain it was in the wake of his arrival. I was wrong, each and every time. He did not visit my family, and he did not come to see me. I later found out that he had been so convinced by my assurances that separation was what we needed that he really felt he was not wanted any more in my life. He respected my space; he left me to it. He genuinely hoped that we could be friends again at some stage.

And by the time I re-emerged into teenage society he had an arrangement with Belinda Farrell, and that was that.

Life settled from torture into bearable torture after that. Another academic year came and went, and my parents deemed it acceptable for me to be allowed to go to the local youth disco. My brother Peter would keep an eye out for me, but I was never to know that. Of course I did. It made me feel both angry and safe, having a big brother to look after me. Weekdays were spent in feverish discussion of what to wear on Saturday night. Hours were spent trying on outfits and experimenting with make-up. Nothing was ever perfect, but by 9 p.m. on a Saturday evening, a compromise between fantasy and reality would have been reached, and the girls would be ready to descend on the Youth Centre. I would see Andy in the distance, chatting easily with both the males and the females of his group. We were on speaking terms again, actually quite friendly, after our old style, before romance had ruined everything. Which was to say that we had many sparky arguments, and were vicious to one another when pushing a point home. It was almost like the old days.

Then one balmy evening, Andy Raynor took me to a nearby field and showed me that kissing could be applied to more than the mouth area, and I was lost all over again. This time I was prepared, and, fall as I did, he never knew how bad my longing for him was. I even took a boyfriend, a lovely lad called Liam. Liam could not believe his luck with some of the things he was allowed to try out. I couldn't believe some of the things that I had learned.

When it came time for the young ladies of the Holy Faith Convent to have a Debutantes' Ball, excitement reached fever pitch. Liam and myself had parted company, but he still expected to be asked to this, the top social event of the school calendar. However, I knew that Andy Raynor was at a rare loose end, and decided to bide my time before pouncing. Everyone knew that this was my plan, including Andy, I suspect. But my timing was off, and I left it that tad too late. It was so close to the event that he assumed I had asked someone else. I had kept my cards so close to my chest that no one could confirm, or deny, his suspicion that I had intended invite him. Imelda Phelan saw her opportunity and made good with it. Liam was granted his wish and accompanied me on the worst night of my young life.

I was the picture of gaiety, of course. I looked great, because I was so miserable that I had lost at least a stone in weight. And my mother had bought me the most beautiful, classic gown. It was a long, flowing number in deep crimson, bias-cut, with an ever so slightly plunging neckline. She had also insisted on a special makeover in a salon in town. The Mammy did me proud. Andy and Imelda sat at the same table as Liam and me, and we all laughed and joked the night away. But I knew that it was all wrong, and so did Andy. Each time Imelda touched him, I died a little. She gazed into his eyes, she fed him morsels of her food, she even wore his bloody bow tie at the end of the evening.

He brought me out for a slow dance three-quarters of the way through. I shouldn't have gone, I knew it would be agony. But I had to grab any chance I could to be with him, no matter how painful and traumatic. As we swayed to the music, he told me that I looked lovely. I thanked him.

'You seem to be having a good time,' he said.

'Yes, I do, don't I?'

'Liam is a good bloke. He likes you.'

I made some sort of non-committal sound.

'Leo, I have something to tell you.'

My heart stopped beating, and my body wanted to fall to the ground. This did not sound good. He was solemn. Oh, sweet Jesus, please don't let him say that Imelda is pregnant and he has to marry her, I thought.

Or even if she is pregnant, please let him not marry her. If she is pregnant, please let him take me outside and make me pregnant too. Anything. But don't let him be taken from me so comprehensively. As it happened, he was taken away, but not by Imelda.

'You know I've been wanting to go to university,' he continued. 'Well, a place has come up.'

'That's great, Andy,' I murmured. 'Well done you. So, which one is it, Trinity or UCD?'

'Neither, I've decided to go to Galway.'

27

My world had ended. It was only marginally eased by the fact that he was not going to marry Imelda and become a father. At least if he did that, I would know where he was and what he was up to. This way, I felt sure I would never see him again. He would live the high life in Galway, sampling exotic delights that Clontarf could never offer or contend with. And I knew no one in bloody, bloody Galway; I couldn't just turn up out of the blue, and magically bump into him. I was out of the picture. I had ruined my life, by my own stupid, hormonal teenage hand. I was hollow with grief.

Andy did go to Galway to study for four years. We kept in touch. Every so often, during term-time, a postcard would arrive, usually a lewd one. I suspected that these delighted my mother every bit as much as they did me. Andy was always a favourite of hers; of all of the Streets', truth be told. And I did see him again, on a fairly regular basis. He returned at vacation time, and then we would go to the pictures, or to a gig. And we would argue, and kiss and make up. But never with abandonment, because that would have meant a commitment, and neither of us was in a position to make that. And neither of us wanted to upset the delicate balance it had taken us so long to find.

When he returned to Dublin to find work, I had started my apprenticeship as a private investigator and was more than a little preoccupied. After a few months of bunking out at his parents' house, he found his feet and moved to a wonderful bachelor pad near the Merrion Gates, right on Sandymount Strand. My mother assured me that it was the best place on earth to live, and that every woman in Dublin was queuing up to get in there with Andy Raynor. I didn't doubt it. The only thing that made her shut up going on about it, was when I accused her of being one of the women who had their sights set on it. And she'd only shut up then because she couldn't think of a good enough retort. Not, I suspect, because what I had said was untrue.

Andy moved in different circles. I tended not to move in any discernible circle at all, because of my work and the covert nature of my job. Oddly enough, once he moved back to Dublin we started to drift apart. In a way, because we could or might run into one another, we made less effort; if we did, it might acknowledge something that we could not sustain. *À la recherche du temps perdu*. It was, and would have been, too serious, and we had no real footing for that any more.

I contacted him whenever I needed information that I thought he might have. He worked as a journalist and part-time lobbyist in the Dáil. He kept his finger on the pulse of government and politics. My job often took me into that milieu, and if he could, or wanted to, he'd help.

Now that I lived with Barry, I felt that Andy and I could be proper friends again. As long as he didn't mention the stupidity in Kildare earlier in the year. I had slept with him, by accident. I was hardly even party to the event, given my unconsciousness through alcohol at the time. Andy assured me that my virtue was intact. He had been worried that I might come to some harm because of the state I was in, and had taken it upon himself to look out for me. It didn't count, but I still didn't mention it to anyone. I had been living with another man for three years now, and I was sure that Andy respected that. Even if he had little time for Barry.

So why was my silly heart so excited at the prospect of paying Andy Raynor's forfeit?

Three

It was doubtful Barry even noticed that he and I slept in the same bed that night. We had recently rallied ourselves in an effort to return to the heady, early days of our romance, and had been moderately successful, but things had fallen away again when he got distracted by the Pub Crawl. It seemed that he couldn't keep up with every option for pleasure at the same time. In the choice between a sex life with his girlfriend or paid fun and games with other thesps, I came off worst. But at least I had been moderately satisfied, even sexually, for a goodly number of weeks, and was no longer looking rabidly at any lengthy, bulbous thing that crossed my path. It had whetted my appetite, however, and now I was left with an amorphous notion that sexual activity should be a touch more regular. Swings and roundabouts, really. I wanted more.

The following morning started well. For once I didn't have to prise my face off the pillow. If I go to bed too knackered or too smashed to take off my make-up, it tends to act as a glue between me and the bedclothes. And if there's been a lot of alcohol involved, my saliva turns into Bostick too. Snoring can also enter the equation, and it's bad enough that Barry is talented in that area without our playing a duet. I hopped out of bed quite briskly, full of the joys. I was looking forward to the day ahead. This had a lot to do with one particular telephone call, but I resisted making it; at 8.30 a.m. it might have seemed a little needy.

A fresh hairball of cat vomit in the middle of the floor took some of the shine off my breakfast. The three lined up beside it as No. 4 pranced by. 'I know he makes you sick,' I said to them, 'but I'd really appreciate it if you could stage the protest outside from now on.'

If there is anything good about catchuck, it's that it doesn't smell and is relatively easy to clean up. That said, the day is always better without it.

I had a leisurely breakfast of cereal and coffee, taking good care to leave only just enough milk for one other person to have a hot drink. I knew this was a petty meanness, but giggled to myself as I sloshed the milk into my second cup. Perhaps it would help to strengthen the friendship between the two actors if one of them had to make a tiny sacrifice for the other. I giggled again. Honestly, it didn't take much to amuse me.

Maeve Kelly was on the radio telling me to buy a new brand of dishwasher tablet, but, persuaded as I was by her dulcet tones and brilliant delivery, I could not oblige; I didn't have a dishwasher. After some infectious pop music, I was treated to helpful home tips from a bouncy young Australian woman. She wanted to know if I was worried about fleas on my pets. And occasionally I was as they're a seasonal nuisance. She said she understood my reluctance to put chemicals on their fur, or to have it introduced into their bloodstreams, but those fleas were still a problem. Well, no more. The natural solution was to use a little urine, apparently. My own. I looked at the small menagerie in the kitchen, and decided that none of the creatures there would be at all pleased with that particular homeopathic remedy. Back to chemicals it was. Besides, I really did not think that any of them would stand still long enough for me to pee on them. And I wouldn't have known where to look while I was about it. All in all, both advice and marketing were wasted on me that morning.

I showered and dressed, humming all the way, then I set about the task of feeding the furry members of the household. As a dog, No. 4 felt it incumbent upon him to eat everything in sight. This habit, or *raison d'être* as he might have it, was beginning to piss the cats off mightily. If he had bothered to read the tins involved, he would have known that three-quarters of the food on offer was manufactured specifically for cats, but that was of little interest to him. After my third peacekeeping intervention, I separated them entirely by way of doors, and decided to bring the dog with me to work. A United Nations-style buffer zone would only work if it was in situ, and as I was that zone, and in situ, it seemed best to divide and conquer.

I rang the Gillespie household to hire Ciara. Her mother answered in a frail and weary voice. I explained who I was, and reminded her that we had met some weeks ago at the end of the cookery course Ciara had taken with me in Kildare. She relaxed a little then, but became agitated when I asked to speak to her daughter.

'Well, I don't know now. She doesn't like being disturbed too early in the morning. She's not really, you know, em, a . . . a morning person. And she was out late enough last night. So.'

Ciara pulled the wings off parents and toyed with them for sport. I could understand the poor woman's reluctance to waken her. I tried reassurance.

'Oh, believe me, I do know, Mrs Gillespie. But I may have some work for her. And if she does it, you'd be rid of her for hours on end each day.'

That did the trick.

'Really? Right. Here goes so. Wish me luck.' I could hear her walk slowly off to rouse the kraken.

Five minutes later a gruff voice said, 'Make it good,' into the phone. I did. Ciara agreed to be in my office in an hour's time.

Outside the weather had brightened, and a late spring was . . . well, springing. Miniature daffodils smiled and waved from every corner of my garden. I began to walk on air; that is what the colour yellow does to me. But air-walking is a tricky business, and after faltering above several of the concrete steps leading to my front gate, I reluctantly decided to stick to a more solid footing. In the confusion of righting myself I careered into the ancient, rusty fence and snagged my tights. Curses!

Mental note: buy new pair and put on before meeting family, particularly mother and mother's mother. With family, details are everything. So much for my grand gesture of wearing a skirt and blouse for them, rather than my usual jeans and jumper.

While No. 4 was busy de-fleaing the grass and hedge, I took note of the other types of yellow flowers blooming on my little patch. Dandelions were having something of a field day, as they tend to do. We called them 'pissy beds' when we were kids, because they were supposed to make you wet yourself if you slept with them under your pillow. Why you would want to do that in the first place was always lost on me. All of the weeds living in the garden were flourishing. I sighed. I'm under no illusion about who's boss out here. Slugs, snails, slaters, creeping buttercup, spiky thistles, velvet nettles, dandy lions, docks, they're in charge. I'm like a student tenant, very low on the evolutionary ladder.

Our street busybody, Marion Maloney, was standing vigil over my car.

'That'll cost you,' she murmured, inspecting the damage. She tut-tutted as she inserted her fingers into the grooves. St Thomas wasn't a patch on Marion. Did she really think the dents weren't there if she didn't touch them? If only. I thought of a question Barry was fond of posing of late (he was also fond of just posing): is the grass still green when you've got your back to it? I looked beyond Marion and saw that it was. Then I whipped around to check my own lawn. Even taken by surprise, it was one of the forty or more shades.

'No use looking for the culprits,' Marion said. 'They're long gone.'

'Oh, no, don't mind me, I was just checking something else.'

She gave me a look which confirmed that I had sprouted another head.

'It happened last night,' I explained. 'Someone ran into me.'

A silence stretched between us. I realised I would not be released until more information was forthcoming, so I glossed over why I was where I had been when the incident occurred, and gave her the low-down on the other woman and her car, even offering the make and registration number. Getting blood from a stone was second nature to Marion, no bother whatsoever. To be thorough, and Marion was nothing less than, she would probably check these details with the police. Finally, she was satisfied and returned to her lair. I was exhausted. I looked at the newly laid speed ramps on the road and wondered if we would make it intact to the corner at all.

'To the city and beyond,' I announced to No. 4. The engine *roared* into life (but not as we know it) and off we went.

The traffic lights were with me all the way, and I made excellent time from my house in Clontarf southwards to the city centre. Normally, this would have made me a little apprehensive, on the grounds that if something good happens, the inverse is lurking waiting to get me back. I'm nothing if not a fatalist. But with

Dublin glowing in a faint April sunshine, and healthy greenery popping out of every amenable crack in the concrete, it was hard not to grin. I passed hotels and office buildings and car parks, and found it hard to tell the difference between them most of the time. This morning that didn't bother me at all. I passed a shop called 'Inspiration' which was having a closing down sale, but even that didn't dampen my mood. Was it that phonecall to Andy Raynor, just waiting to happen? I laughed out loud at my girlish whimsy and dismissed the notion.

The car really was making a racket. Passers-by were staring, and every so often No. 4 would shoot me the look that said, 'Knock it off on the noise, okay?' I reckoned that the jolt the previous evening was responsible.

'It's sporty,' I told him. 'No mufflers, or squifflers, or bloofers, or . . . whatever,' I added, blinding him with automobile jargon.

He was mightily unconvinced.

My office was in an old building in the newly trendy Temple Bar area of Dublin. At one stage, the crazed municipal plan was to turn all of this 'Left Bank' into a giant bus depot, but a new spirit of Europeanism had put paid to that. Now we had coffee shops, craft outlets, *trattorie* and lots of pubs and hotels; themed or neo-traditional, spruce and expensive. I had managed to talk my way into a parking spot on a disused lot two streets away from base. It was only a matter of time before it was built on, and the word was that it would house a multimedia gallery space, cyber café, three bars, two restaurants, a bookie's and a dentist. All solar-powered.

For the moment, it was guarded by a gnarly old codger named Malachy, who could be kept sweet with a noggin of whiskey 'for the rheumatics', and £25 a week for the car. This is not to suggest that Malachy had any official capacity on the site; it was my opinion that he had happened on to a good thing and simply hung on to it. He had an entrepreneurial spirit, and good luck to him. I suppose whoever did own the place thought there were worse things that could be happening on it. Malachy, or Molly as he was also known, did a huge trade in the evening in theatre punters and restaurant goers. So much so that he had to enlist help in the form of a 'younger' chap called Gerry, who took this job very seriously and wore a peaked cap and changed his rolled-up newspaper daily. The paper was used as a pointer, along with the words 'lock hard, lock hard'. Gerry bore an uncanny resemblance to Molly, and as Molly was a bachelor boy all his life, rumour had it that Gerry was a lovechild. Romance is everywhere, and in all lives, you just have to know where to look.

'Grand day for it,' Molly said, by way of greeting. As this seemed to cover everything, I agreed with him. He shuffled over, all Sean O'Casey play, right down to the fingerless gloves.

'I heard you crossing O'Connell Bridge five minutes ago in that thing. You'd want to watch out, I think it's against the law to make that much noise in a car. Unless you're the President, maybe. And who is this little chap?'

'Malachy, I'd like to introduce you to Number Four. Number Four, this is Malachy.'

'No need to be formal,' he said to the dog. 'You can call me Molly.'

No. 4 was delighted with himself, and popped his front paws up on Malachy's knee so that the old man wouldn't have to bend down too far to pet him.

'They're grand company, aren't they?' said Malachy. Then he spotted the left wing of the car and shuffled over to inspect it. 'You've been in the wars since I saw you last.'

'It's a bit of a mess all right,' I acknowledged.

'Oh, it is that. And it'll be worse if you don't have it seen to a.s.a.p. If the rust gets in there, you won't be happy at all, at all. It's worse than the rheumatics, is the rust.'

I'd been treated to the long list of his ailments on many previous occasions, so I knew to nip this in the bud.

'Actually, Malachy, I'm just running off to ring the mechanic now about that. I'd need to hurry and get him before he books in a load of other jobs for the day.'

'Oh, you would. A mechanic is a hard man to find these days. Or a plumber, or a carpenter. There's no trades anymore, d'yeh see?'

Ailments and trades, a deadly combination of obsessions with Malachy. I had to run, quite literally; it was the only way to get away from him. I waved back and shouted 'see you later', then legged it with the dog. It's amazing how many obstacles have to be overcome before the working day can begin. And I wasn't past all of them yet.

My office building was once a Home for Indigent Chimney Sweeps, and given when it was originally built, those sweeps must have ranged in age from three to thirty. At that ripe old age, which I had attained myself recently, they would have been expected to die, having lived such a hard life. Well, life's still hard, there's just much more of it, I thought, as I decanted the mail from my post box. I turned hopefully to the elevator, reluctant, as always, to climb the many flights of stairs to my office. I know that it's all good cardiovascular exercise, but at that time of the morning, I just couldn't be arsed.

The lift was straight out of a thriller: an open-plan cage with latticed metal doors which accordioned open and shut. Unusually, it was ready and waiting, and not stuck on another floor full of the cleaner's equipment. Mrs Mack, the woman who 'does', likes to keep the lift for her own personal use, and you would need to be up very early in the morning to thwart her on that. I was delighted with myself, but Mrs Mack had a surprise ally up her sleeve. Or more accurately on my leash. No. 4 was terrified. Try as I might, I could not persuade him to go in. He whimpered, he cried, and when I went to carry him, he lay heavily on his side and whimpered and cried some more. I tried being cross with him, and he leapt to his feet and barked back. 'You cheeky pup,' I said, with some accuracy. He began to run around my legs, until they were well and truly bound. I spun around to free myself so fast I nearly turned into Wonder Woman. Leaning against a wall, I waited until the stairwell stopped reeling. Then I tugged on the leash once more to pull No. 4 into the elevator, but, as if instructed by Gerry, he locked hard on all four legs and began to howl loudly. I took the hint, and cursed just as loudly as we started up the stairs.

We were making a lot of noise at this stage, and several doors opened to check on the commotion. When we had all calmed down, and everyone had established that I was not being cruel to the dog, we set off again. In a knot of self-righteous indignation that anyone would think, even for a moment, that I might harm one hair on his disloyal little head, I caught sight of Mrs Mack looking down from her lair on the second floor. She was beaming with unexpected triumph. No. 4 was now dancing along merrily, his little claws scraping rhythmically on the wooden floor. 'Traitor,' I growled through gritted teeth. Hard to imagine that he was in league with the enemy on Day One of joining the firm. As someone once said, life is just one damn' thing after another.

I explained to No. 4 that he would have to behave himself in the office, as it was a place of work. He cocked his head from left to right, as if paying attention, then trotted over to the desk and cocked his leg against it to have a wee.

'Oh, no, you don't,' I said. 'No need to mark this territory, Mister. Anyhow, you went before we came in, so don't try it on.'

I began to have the inkling that inkles to you that you're behaving like a crazy lady. Or perhaps it's confirmation that you've become one. Here I was, talking aloud to an animal who probably didn't understand English, or even if he did, really didn't care what I was saying. So who was I trying to impress or convince? I rummaged in No. 4's bag, and took out his favourite ball and squeaky toy for him to play with. While he got to work with those, I fitted a box up with a blanket in which he could have his frequent snoozes, and wished that I had someone to do the same for me. This cur was a sharp operator; all of this was achieved without any overt instruction from him. I felt a conspiracy theory about mind control coming on, and decided to save it for a coffee break later in the day.

I was about to choose between calling Andy Raynor or retrieving my messages from a furiously blinking answering machine when a fierce kerfuffle in the hallway caught my attention. Like the canine incident earlier, it attracted the notice of the whole building. This time the voices in the stairwell were more or less human, two of them. I glanced at my watch: 10.06 a.m. and already we'd had major action at the Indigent Sweeps' place, so nothing poorly about that.

It was, of course, the Arrival of the Queen of Ciara. And small surprise that Mrs Mack would try to shoo her from the building. Today's sartorial ensemble was

Vampire, with a suggestion of drug-crazed thief thrown in for good measure.

'I'll have the cops on you, so I will, if you take one step further,' warned Mrs M.

'Listen, hag,' drawled Ciara, 'cut me some slack or face the consequences. I work here.'

'What?' shrieked the divine Mrs M.

'Yeah, you heard. I'm official. And if you don't let me pass, I'll have your sorry ass fired, OK?'

No one, and I mean *no one*, spoke to Mrs Mack like that. Every worker in the place retreated slightly into their respective doorways in order to enjoy some more of the sport, while it lasted. We all shared a common unspoken certainty that Ciara would suffer for this outrage. But for the moment it was bliss. And it seemed wrong to rob a young person of such a life-shaping experience, even if it would subsequently be filed under 'Learning the Hard Way'. It is hard to explain the gist of an argument when it's all gist, and this one was. After a few parries and thrusts, including a splendid 'you were dragged up, not brought up' speech from Mrs Mack, I decided it was time to intervene. Not for any noble reason, I just wasn't sure how far things could go before Mrs Mack did actually call the cops.

'Ah, you're here,' I shouted to Ciara, as I leaned over the banister. This passed into legend as one of the most unnecessary observations ever. But, in a roundabout way, I felt it could be used to strengthen and underline my deductive powers as a private investigator, even if I was unlikely to list it as a career highlight. I bounded cheerily down to the combatants. They were pulling an enormous black bag to and fro between them, and growling like two Rottweilers, though Mrs Mack looked like a beige poodle and Ciara resembled a dark Afghan hound with an unfortunate hair cut.

'Mrs Mack, I'd like you to meet my new assistant, Ciara Gillespie, and vice versa. I'm sure you two will be the best of pals.'

They gave me a long look of disdain that was united and terrifying. The older woman let go of the bag. Then, with almost ceremonial formality, they turned to one another and bowed their heads, ever so slightly. Time out. Mrs Mack fixed a steely gaze on me and said, 'Miss Street, I'm not sure that you're allowed dogs on the premises.' Before Ciara could thump her, I hurriedly interjected a 'she doesn't mean you' and swept her up the stairs. 'I'll have to check the rules,' warned the Mighty Mack. I shivered; I was in *such* trouble.

'You are in *such* trouble,' Ciara confirmed.

Four

'WHOAH! This is *so* retro . . . *man*!' Ciara took in the office; black-and-white-tiled floor, sturdy oak desk and battered leather chairs. It even had frosted glass in the door bearing the legend 'Leo Street and Company'. When you came in, you expected to meet Humphrey Bogart and a glamorous but down-to-earth, heart-of-gold secretary. They rarely turned up for work.

'Coffee? Tea?' I asked. Ciara nodded to both. Snap decision: coffee. 'It's not retro,' I explained. 'It's the real thing. It was like this when I arrived.'

'Yo! So *old*.'

No. 4 took time out from chasing his tail to dispense licks and love. Mmn, nice.

'It's cheap too, in comparison with the rest of the building,' I explained. 'The rent goes down the more steps you have to climb. I think the landlord must know that the lift is not an option. Because of Mrs Mack,' I added, darkly.

Ciara had now made herself comfortable by sliding sideways on to the big old brown chair opposite the desk. Clients had a choice of this or a slightly more modern upright, and the more uptight chose the upright, while those trying to appear cool, or business people about to nail an employee, usually perched or lolled in the armchair, with the cools perching and the nailers lolling, respectively. Ciara's head rested on one arm; her legs swung over the other as she addressed the ceiling. I'd never had a client choose that option.

'So, Streetsky, *meine kleine maestro*, what's the story?'

'Ciara, don't take this the wrong way, or do, whichever you like, but I hope you're not intending to keep this banter up all day? It really is enough that one of us in the office is barking.'

No. 4 duly obliged. Fair play to Ciara, she could nearly take a hint, however short-term and half-assed.

'CooLeo, *chill*. So who's the Spectre?'

'Oh, Mrs Mack. Well, she's officially the cleaner, but that's pretty much an honorary title. She doesn't believe in imposing herself or her cleaning products too much on the building. She sort of sprinkles disinfectant around, but stops shy of washing it in or out. It's some sort of weird illusion-of-cleanliness fetish. And far less work, of course. *But* she does actually run the place, so beware.'

'Too late for that now, boss. Duly noted, though. I wasn't referring to the Licence to Spill babe, who the fuck is that scary fucker?'

I followed her eyes. Ah, Mick. From the large photograph on the wall behind my desk a face hewn from rock, and thatched by a shock of wiry grey hair, glowered down at me. At both of us.

'Everyone is answerable to someone, and I'm answerable to him,' I explained. 'That's Mick Nolan. He's my boss, you could say. He trained me, and I worked for him for a few years. Now he's a kind of silent partner, I suppose, though not half quiet enough for my liking. He follows me around, giving me advice and berating me whenever he thinks I need it. He can be a right pain in the ass.'

All of this was true. Then I remembered a pertinent point.

'Oh, and he's been dead for a few years.'

Ciara had shifted out of her seat and was walking around the office, watching Mick as she went.

'That following thing is weird. No matter where I go in the room, his eyes are on me. You go over there, I'll stay here, and let's see how he manages that.'

I did as I was told, and sure enough, he was looking at both of us.

'Spooky,' I said.

'Yeah. *Man*, I never even met the guy and he's on to me already. You're gonna have to have words with him about that, boss.'

'I'll try, but I can promise nothing.'

I knew then that Ciara was exactly the right woman to join the firm, however short-term; she hadn't batted an eyelid at the prospect of being tailed by a ghost, and didn't seem to think it unusual that he was constantly on my case.

'Okay, let's get down to business. When do I start, what do I do and how much will you pay me?'

Succinct, to the point, my kinda goil.

'I need help,' I said.

Ciara began to laugh. 'Everyone knows that the minute they meet you,' she teased.

'Ha-ha. I mean, professional help.'

'Again, that's obvious, boss.' She laughed even harder.

'I need someone to take over a job for me, temporarily, you wagon.'

'And that's me. You've made a brilliant decision there, O, Streetwise one. Reveal the legend.'

On second thoughts, maybe I would just throttle her.

Instead, I told Ciara about Michael O'Donoghue, and his wife Miranda's fears of an affair. 'These are the cases I mostly get. Not glamorous at all, so you'll be starting at the bottom. I rarely do computer fraud, because I'm a turnip with technology, and I'm not brilliant with gadgets either.'

'I am, though,' said Ciara. 'When I've got this ordinary shit figured out, we may have to diversify as a company.'

'Steady on. I only need you for this case.'

'So far,' she interjected.

'I prefer to work alone, so don't get your hopes up.'

'You're not very good at delegating, are you? You don't trust people, do you?'

'What's with the hard philosophical questions?' I exclaimed. This whippersnapper was putting me on the spot. 'I see a lot of the darker side of human nature, so no, I don't always have a very good opinion of people. I'm a realist, that's all.'

We were getting side-tracked here, and in territory where I didn't feel comfortable. I wasn't particularly proud of the fact that I spent my days and nights trying to find people out in lies rather than saving the earth. I was in the grubby end of the PI's world, but hey, it was a dirty job and someone had to do it.

'Enough of the farting around,' I said, reaching into a drawer for pictures of Michael O'Donoghue, his wife Miranda, and his friend, special or otherwise, a Mrs Bernadette Flood, resident of Raheny on Dublin's northside.

'How did you find out the friend's name?' Ciara asked.

'I approached the postman while he was delivering one morning and asked if the O'Briens lived in number twenty-seven, and he said no, Mrs Bernie Flood lived there. She's a widow, her husband Joseph died last year.'

'Simple as that?'

'Yep, simple as that. A question is usually good for an answer, maybe eight times out of ten. Use your common sense and you'll be fine.'

Common sense is something that has always intrigued me. In a way it's an oxymoron. There's nothing all that common about sense, for one thing. And for another, is it one word or two? Or put it this way, should it be one word or two?

'The postman told you all that?'

I snapped back to the present. 'No, I also checked the electoral register, and births, deaths and marriages.'

'Wow, life is so formal.'

'Death too,' I pointed out.

'What if you ask a question and the answer is a lie?'

This girl was smart all right. 'Good point. Even if you don't get the truth, the form of the lie can be telling. It's up to you as a detective to establish the truth. That's what you're hired for.'

She gave an imperceptible nod, which was my signal that she understood and I was to continue.

'Let's see . . . yes, when in doubt, lie.'

'There's a lot of that around.'

'Yep. It's the three Ls really: Look, Listen and Learn.'

'Oh, so we just ignore the fourth "L", the Lie. Or do we count that as "F" for Fib?'

'Ciara, let's not get sidetracked so early. Now where was I? Oh, yes, never presume anything, just deal in facts; that's all we want, proof, not theories. And stay on the right side of the law. Okay?'

'And which would be the right side again?'

'The one that doesn't get you put in jail,' I explained.

'Riiiight. So, don't get caught doing anything illegal?'

'Mostly, yes. Also try not to do anything illegal either, if you know what I mean.'

She took a moment to contemplate that can of worms, then, sensibly, moved on. This girl was shaping up to be a natural, if there can ever be such a thing in a PI. It's not exactly a genetic trait to want to be in the grey area between law and disorder; to snoop furtively around other people's lives without any hope of a medal of honour or a public commendation at the end.

And with no real power to back you up. Not much back up at all, to be honest. It's just you and the power of nosiness to the nth degree, with a tough stomach for lies, corruption and abuse. Oh, and no state-supplied uniform either, which some might argue goes on the plus side for private dicks, and on the minus for public ones.

'What made the wife suspicious in the first place?' Ciara asked.

'Well, you'll see for yourself, this guy is very much a creature of habit. He keeps to an orderly timetable. But recently he's been coming home late, hasn't been where he says he was, or not for as long as he'd like her to believe. So, she confronted him, and he gave her a speech about how she'd have to trust him for the time being, that he'd explain everything soon, and there was nothing for her to worry about.'

'Now *that* would put the wind up anyone.'

'Exactly, and that's where we come in.'

I took her through the rudiments of my stills camera, the video, and the sound equipment she was to use. The latter was a directional microphone, which could be used to listen from a range of, say, a car parked close by. The essentials were point and record, though I could have dressed it up in more flattering terms. 'This and the camera with telephoto lens are good, because you won't be trespassing on the property,' I explained.

'And we'd never do that,' she teased.

51

'Nnnno. Or mostly never.'

I brought her up to speed on Michael O'Donoghue's clockwork routine during the day, and said that for now she might like to check that out herself, before beginning the more pertinent evening surveillance. The only half-excitement I encountered was when he gave a colleague a lift to her car. She was a petite thing with a dark Cleopatra bob. Nothing incriminating, but I took a photograph and I'll let you have it when it's developed.' His wife, Miranda, visited the clinic a few times, laden down with designer shopping bags. Looks like she knows how to spend money.

There were a few other details I might have mentioned, but I felt it more important that Ciara should ground herself in the mundanities of this case before progressing to some of its quirks, which I myself was not yet certain were relevant.

'One last thing. You'll need to be a bit less conspicuous than you are at the moment. Nosferatu is a noticeable look in the daytime.'

'But at night I am Princess of Darkness,' she pointed out. 'Actually, I'm ahead of you on that, I've brought a change.' She indicated the black bag from the tug-of-war with Mrs Mack.

'Why go to all that trouble?' I asked, somewhat naively.

'If I left the house dressed as a normal person just one morning, I'd never hear the end of it from my mother. She'd expect it every day. I can't let my rigorous standards of torture slide.'

'Sometimes, Ciara,' I said, 'I wonder where the good twin is.'

And then she genuinely surprised me.

'Oh, that eejit Ronan. Goody-goody is at college. He wants to be an engineer, for God's sake. I mean, how square can you get? See you in five.' She left for the loo.

I mulled over the Gillespies' plight: two Ciaras. Still, at least not identical girls, which would literally have meant a split egg. Ronan would have been a completely different one, if I remembered my biology correctly. There was, therefore, some hope that he would stay good and true, and, bless the mark, become an engineer.

I still had a strange feeling of wellbeing, which was bothering me. I should have been feeling all guilty about going into a supervisory capacity, as I now was. But I was not feeling guilty. There were in fact a few other avenues of Michael O'Donoghue's life to root around in, and now I had the time to do that. This assuaged my professional guilt. But I think I was relieved to find myself at one remove on this case. I was sick to death's door of pettiness. I was tired of the ugliness of cheating. And I was fed up with the paranoia that surrounded suspicion. Now it looked like I was going to get some distance. However, it didn't quite qualify for a victory dance around the room; for all I knew, some bags would walk in the door and offer me another job, and in truth I was in no financial position to refuse it. Subdued joy and a nascent smugness were the order of the day for now.

I thought of the other things I hadn't shared with Ciara. Last time I counted, there were upwards of sixty private detective agencies listed in the Golden Pages, or Yellow Pages, or Buttercup, or Sunshine . . . whatever you're having yourself. And that's before we even got to the 'security experts', another fertile area for ex-cops and private eyes who have hit lean times. I've been a bouncer in my day. I've collected 'bad' debts. I hate having to do that sort of work, but sometimes you're left without a choice. And you try telling a house full of cats that you can't afford their food and that you're on a diet yourself anyway; doesn't always wash. You takes what you gets sometimes. And often it sucks. Welcome to the real world.

Some agencies are listed as members of various Federations. In Ireland, where two or more of us are gathered together, a Federation can be founded. And like the seasons, they come and go regularly. I'm going out on a limb to say that a lot of those who advertise are chancers. And as I fall to the ground on my broken twig, let me also say that we all have our areas of expertise. I'm a people woman, so I've made that my remit. Big remit: the world is full of people. What I mean is, I'm best at observing, and I'm not great on the technicals. I'm not comfortable with technology. I prefer the worn shoe sole, a pen and paper, the dusty certificates that chart a life. And talk: conversational and inquisitorial. I do know my way around a bug, visual and aural, and the basics of an electronic search. I get by.

I also have a rule about death. I like to see as little of it as possible. I once heard a man on the radio say that when he is setting up a big business venture, he asks himself two questions: will anyone die if I do this, and will anyone go bust? If the answer to both is 'no', he goes ahead. I like those questions, and what they stand for. Unfortunately, when I take on a case I cannot know the answers, but I've been lucky that no one I've confirmed bad news for has felt so murderous about it that they've taken to fatal violence. So far. And, you know, so far so good.

I wondered if I should have talked to Ciara about the little I have learned during my time as a detective. Should I have mentioned that the truth and what you believe are often two different things; that people tell you what they want you to know, no more; that sometimes they tell you stuff which they believe to be true but which is completely false; that we are bred to lie and to cheat and to mould our morals to suit our situation of the week? If I had said any of this, I don't think Ciara would have been disillusioned; she doesn't seem to expect much of the human race.

Just as well.

Five

Staring at the walls of my office often leads me into a reverie, and sometimes from there into a doze. I decided it wouldn't look good if Ciara returned to find her new boss asleep, so I used the time to review the beginning of the O'Donoghue case in my head.

Miranda had arrived at my office on a filthy, rain-soaked afternoon, punctual for her four o'clock appointment and untouched by the weather. Even her coat appeared dry. She was composed as she described her problem, her voice a hypnotic, quiet monotone. Her steel-grey eyes considered me as casually as if I was an incidental, hardly there at all. Her coldness made me shiver, accompanied as it was by the howl of a late-spring storm outside. A deadly calm settled on the room.

She was a strange-looking woman. Her dark, shoulder-length hair was lustrous and expertly cut, framing features which didn't quite seem to match. Taken singularly, they appeared to be placed too high on her face, but together they gave the lie to that first impression. She was thin, painfully so, but this gave her a gaunt haughtiness, like a spindly aristocrat in the grips of poverty but too proud to admit it. A sharp nose descended from eyebrows held permanently in an arc of disdain. Cheekbones jutted out above a slender, fine jaw. Her mouth was surprisingly full, though she stretched it into a mean line as she spoke. If she had ever carried any weight on her spare frame, I imagined it had softened this harsh image. Here, in an uncompromising April light, she was frightening, formidable. But she was beautiful, too, and high on her high cheekbone was a magnificent scar, small and geometric. She wore it in the way a pirate would an eyepatch. 'I did that with a diamond ring,' she said, dismissing any further mention of the mark.

She did not loll or perch on the client chair, she inhabited it. Her story was told economically. Salient information, I felt, was that the O'Donoghue children, Tara and Ben were weekday boarders at Saint Columba's in the mountains.

'In that case, Miranda, I don't see why you can't follow your husband yourself. It really would save you a lot of money and waiting. You know him so much better than I do, you wouldn't have to go through the familiarisation I would. It makes sense.'

There is a certain school of thought which says that doling out this sort of advice is business suicide for a single woman with so many dependants. But I felt that it needed to be said, so I did just that. Dismissive was the kindest word for the look she bathed me in. I seemed lower than the lowest crawling thing on earth, which at last check was any government minister of the old guard.

'It is not appropriate,' she said, curtly. This was the closest to emotion she had come. An angry light almost manifested itself in those extraordinary eyes. Then she was back to the beauty and composure of a Renaissance Madonna. 'Money is not a consideration, Miss Street. I do not need to justify my decision on this to you. You will either take the assignment or not. I would appreciate a speedy answer. I cannot abide time wasting.'

Every nerve in my body said 'don't do it', while my brain reminded me that I needed the cash. I was on board. She handed me a five-hundred-pound advance in crisp, new banknotes, and told me she would forward her husband's mobile phone bills, which were now all handily itemised for the cautious and the curious alike. Then she shook my hand and made to leave. Her clasp was indifferent, but afterwards it burned on my palm.

Later, I reasoned that there are many ways of dealing with a problem. So Miranda O'Donoghue was not a shouter; she preferred to turn chilly and clam up. Who was I to say whether this was a bad or a good thing?

She stopped at the office door and turned back. 'Oh, yes,' she said, calmly, 'one last thing: he's been receiving death threats.'

I was agog. 'You didn't think to mention this before?' I gasped.

'Well, no. If you knew my husband and his business, you wouldn't be too surprised either,' she said. 'I'm sure it's nothing to worry about.'

'And I'm sure it is,' I protested. 'Have you informed the police?'

'Oh, there's no need. Michael deals with a lot of emotional people in his work, it all blows over eventually.'

'What form do these threats take?'

'They seem to be of two types. Sometimes he'll get a letter in the post, made up of newspaper or magazine clippings; you know the sort, very popular in television dramas. At other times, a woman's voice makes dire predictions on the telephone. But they've been going on for some time now, and we don't pay them much heed any more.'

'Do you have any of the letters, or the envelopes they came in?'

'No, no. My husband has taken them. I won't have them in the house.'

'I really do think this is a matter for the police,' I reiterated.

She laughed then, hollow though it sounded. 'I think you're over-reacting, don't you, dear?' She gave a limp wave of her hand, as if the gesture was beneath her somehow, and left.

Death is a big word, and a bigger event. So, if persons known or unknown threaten another person with it, this can quite reasonably be considered a serious situation. But I had not mentioned Michael O'Donoghue's *billets-doux* to Ciara. I justified it by telling myself that I didn't want to overburden her in these initial stages.

Perhaps the truth is that I needed her help, and wasn't prepared to look elsewhere: a crazy mixture of laziness and penny pinching without any regard for the outcome, no matter how potentially dangerous.

At the edge of my vision, and consequently my attention, a light was blinking hard enough to induce an epileptic fit. Real time was intruding. Basically, my answering machine was hopping mad that I had not consulted it to hear its treasures. I took a pad and pen and pressed 'play'.

Maeve Kelly wanted to know would I sell her mother some of my home-made bread. I laughed out loud. I am a terrible cook. In fact, it would be more accurate to say that I cannot cook. But I had recently taken a course in Kildare whilst on a job, and it was there that I had found both Ciara and the ability to make delicious bread. There was no scientific explanation for this, I just had 'the knack', like dowsing for water or being able to tell cars apart by the sound of their boots closing. Things had come to a pretty pass when I was selling something to Maeve, rather than her persuading me from my television or radio set.

'You would be the latest thing for my mother. There's *huge* competition between the Ladies Who Host Lunch to have a new and *marvellous* discovery. I mentioned you to Mum and she was *very* excited. *Do* say yes, and she'll pay *handsomely* for your wares.'

I wondered how many noughts there were in *handsomely*. Sold, to the lady with the golden tones, and her affluent mother. I phoned Maeve to tell her as much.

She was delighted to hear from me, for more than one reason. 'There is another little matter I need your help on,' she continued soberly. This was obviously serious. Maeve never usually spoke without sprinkling theatrical emphases liberally throughout. Now her voice was quiet and uninflected.

'I've been having crank calls, and they're beginning to get to me.'

'Right, don't panic, and don't let this sad fuck rile you, whoever it turns out to be. You're not alone, these calls happen to a lot more people than you'd think, unfortunately. Have you contacted the police?'

'Well, no. I didn't want to bother them. I assumed they'd take no notice anyway, just regard it as a nuisance.'

'Mmn, they might initially, but they will deal with it if things get out of hand.'

Maeve gave an involuntary cry.

'No, no, we'll nip this in the bud before it gets to that,' I reassured her. 'Do you have Caller Display on your phone?'

'No, I don't.'

'Right, I'll give you a handset that does. If we're lucky, this idiot won't have screened his or her number and we'll trace them that way. I'll bring something over to record the calls and that'll help give us a clue as to what we're dealing with here. One last thing, are you in the phone book?'

'No, I'm ex-directory. I thought that would ward off creeps. I was obviously mistaken.'

'What happens when you get one of these calls?'

'Nothing much, that's what freaks me. I suppose there's a bit of heavy breathing, but no obscene remarks or anything like that. I wait for a few moments, in case anything else happens, but it never does, and then I hang up. If a few calls come together, I take the phone off the hook for an hour or two. If someone wants me on business, they'll get me on the mobile.'

'What sort of sounds are in the background?'

'Not a lot really, maybe a television or radio, something like that.'

'Okay. I'm going to my parents' for lunch, so I'll drop off the stuff on the way. Don't worry, we'll get the sad bastard.'

By now Ciara had returned and was looking curious. So was I. I hardly recognised her. Gone were the chains, the rings, the piercings, the paraphernalia of the Goth. She had changed into a plain blue polo neck and jeans, topped by a black leather jacket and an ordinary, wispy hairdo, not the usual rock-solid hedgehog. Her face was naked, but for a sprinkling of freckles across her nose. She looked positively pretty.

'Don't mention the freckles,' she warned. 'I hate them.'

No. 4 began to bark and run at the door. Ciara opened it to reveal Sammy the Sandwich, who leapt back with a yelp.

'Call it off,' he cried, referring to the dog, we hoped.

'He's harmless,' I said. Sammy presumed I meant No. 4, and Ciara assumed I meant Sammy. Everybody happy. I introduced them all to one another.

'Have I got news for you?' said Sammy, reaching into his wicker basket. 'Not only did I manage to take the lift up here today, but look . . .' He flourished a cellophaned munchie. 'Dadah! This is our latest. It's a kind of Peking Duck in a three-grain baguette. It shouldn't work, but it's just so crazy – it does!' Then he sighed. 'These are the days that make this job worth living for.'

'Sorry to disappoint, Sammy,' I said. 'I'm off to The Mammy's for lunch. But perhaps Ciara can be tempted.'

'Damn' right I can,' said the youngster, diving in.

'What's with Mrs Mack today?' I asked Sammy. 'The elevator has been available to all.'

'Eshep mee,' Ciara pointed out, dribbling some masticated cucumber.

'Except you,' I acknowledged.

'It's sinister,' Sammy said. 'She's obviously looking for something.'

A chill ran through my body. If I had been religious I would have crossed myself. As it happened, religion was the right ball park.

We didn't have long to wait to find out what Mrs Mack's 'something' was. A light knock came on the door, followed by the All Powerful One herself, in hat and coat. The effect was all cream and off-white, and it was hard to make out where her face was.

'I hope I haven't disturbed you with a client, Miss Street,' she said, referring to Ciara, who was trying her best to disappear into the depths of the leather armchair. Mrs Mack darted looks, henlike, round the office. 'Is the other rip gone?' she asked. 'I didn't see her leave.' In fairness to Mrs M, she is as effective as Closed Circuit TV, so I had to let her off the hook.

'This *is* Ciara, she's cleaned her act up a bit.'

'Well, not before time,' said Mrs Mack, primly. 'I suppose there's hope for us all yet,' she added. Rather cryptically, it seemed to me. Isn't that one of those nonsense phrases people use, which means nothing really but presents the illusion of wisdom?

'What did you want?' I asked.

'Oh, yes,' she said. 'I'm knocking off early today because I need to go and get a few things for my pilgrimage. I'm off to Lourdes for a few days.' She hung her head in a suitably pious pose.

I'd been around long enough to know that this meant she would expect some cash to bring with her; sterling, francs, traveller's cheques, diamonds or gold bullion, all were acceptable. Now, if we'd been talking an appropriate bonus for work done, the amount would be nil. But this was Mrs Mack, and hard currency would have to change hands.

'Well, do make sure to call in before you go,' I said. 'Who'll be taking over from you?'

'That'll be a treat for everyone. My husband Kevin has agreed to dep for me. And he's a hoot, so he is. You'll all enjoy him. He's great *craic* altogether.'

With that happy thought she left us. My heart had now frozen over. If there's anything that frightens me rigid, it's people who are 'great *craic* altogether'. We obviously had a rocky trip ahead.

'I'm packing it in for the day,' I said to Ciara. 'I can't

take the excitement any more.'

'Now, now, Sarky,' she chided.

Of course, there was one excitement I could have treated myself to. I could have phoned Andy Raynor. But I didn't want to appear too eager. And, admittedly, I didn't want to do it with Ciara around. She would be on to me like a hot snot if she smelled any kind of intrigue. And though I knew there was nothing more than teasing going on between myself and Andy, I couldn't be sure that he'd be entirely the gentleman with me, and I didn't want to be caught in an inappropriate reaction or situation. I was The Boss now, and had to maintain my dignity.

'You've a huge ladder in your tights,' The Staff said, on cue, deflating my managerial bubble. 'It's been travelling in both directions all morning. That doesn't look good for the firm, so you might want to clean your act up.' No. 4 barked in agreement. I resisted the urge to kill them both, but only just.

I could feel Mick's eyes bore a hot hole in my back as we left the office. Ciara was getting the same treatment.

'Does he get out much?' she asked.

'Depends,' I said, grimly. Mick Nolan was far too free-range for my liking. He had been impossible in life, and death hadn't changed him all that much. I could hear him muttering darkly about how it would have been just as easy to borrow a car as it was to get in help. I ignored him. I was heartily sick of his moaning, and the ugliness of other people's lives.

We parted at Malachy's billet, with Ciara promising to check in later with a progress report. I loaded No. 4 into the car and said my goodbyes. Just then, Malachy had a coughing fit and hawked up a huge, green gob of phlegm on to the gravel of the makeshift car park. Good Golly, Miss Molly.

Six

'Legs Eleven,' was Maeve's greeting.

I had to set her straight. 'It's an optical illusion, I've only got the two.'

'And do I spot a deliberate mistake?' she asked, as I hauled myself, the dog and my equipment into her luxury apartment.

'If you're referring to the ladder in my tights, I can only presume that it won't work as a fashion statement.'

'Oh, *no*, *far* too grunge, *particularly* for a family lunch. *No*, not even close. *However*, help is at hand. I have a new pair that should do the trick, *and* lift that outfit all in one.'

Reasons To Be Nervous, Part 1.

Maeve disappeared into her bedroom, which housed her frighteningly extensive hosiery department while I installed her 'new' telephone and tape recorder. No. 4 had a good old sniff 'n' root. When she re-emerged, a glint in her eye made me uneasily prudish. I had erred on the side of conservative dress for the four genera-tions of Street women gathering today; keeping a low profile and all that. Well, it was what I was used to in my line of life and work. Maeve had a slightly different notion of the look I was going for, and it was embodied in the sparkling gun metal grey item she now brandished above her immaculately coiffed head. My thighs in shining armour, as 'twere.

'A bit flashy,' I demurred.

'Exactly. Live a little.'

'I don't suppose I have a choice,' I chanced, tentatively.

'Correct,' was the firm reply.

I went all obedient and struggled out of one pair of tights and into the other. Maeve Kelly was, and remains, mistress of the age-old art of timing, and as I was hauling the twinkling gusset into place, she made good her opportunity to ambush me.

'That handsome friend of yours, Andy Raynor, was in to see the show during the week.'

'Oh, yeah?' I said, diving behind the couch to fiddle with some cable.

'Yes. He stayed for a drink afterwards.'

I stayed by the skirting and tried to sound cool. 'I suppose he had some gorgeous woman on his arm?'

'Two of them, actually, one older, one younger. *Very* charming.'

I let slip a mewl of disappointment.

'*Ooh*,' Maeve purred, delighted with herself. 'And do I detect the merest *hint* of jealousy?'

I stayed down by a socket. 'Oh, don't be ridiculous. I've known Andy far too long to care what he gets up to.'

'And *that* would be why you are now a delicate shade of fuchsia?'

How could she tell from where she was standing?

I took a few breaths to calm myself. I did feel a bit hot. And bothered. I weighed up my options. There are times when you can win, and times when you can not, and this seemed the latter to me. So I gave in a little, and it was almost pleasurable to admit, 'Well, I am supposed to meet up with him soon. I guess I'll hear all about it then.'

'He *did* mention that I should tell you to phone him,' she said. 'So I am now *officially* reminding you to do just that. Oh, and by the way, he is *gorgeous* so why the delay?'

'It's a neighbour thing, nothing more,' I protested.

'Yeah, *sure*.'

'Look, Maeve, I know far too much about Andy to take anything he says or does seriously. He is so unreliable. And untrustworthy.'

'And gorgeous.'

'If you like that sort, yeah, I suppose.'

'All right, I can see that you *refuse* to be drawn so I'll tell you that he was with his mother and some other bit. *Fluff*. Not a patch on you.'

It was kind of Maeve to be loyal, and loose with the truth. Andy always had beautiful women hanging off him, I just wasn't in the same league. And, as he liked to remind me regularly, I was a huge pain in his butt. Before my heart could sink too visibly, I changed the subject.

'How is the show going?'

'Grand so far, we're all getting along. *But* Teddy Buckley, my father in it, is inclined to be a bit *fresh* with the younger ladies of the cast. Apparently, he was a *notorious* swordsman in his day, shagged everything and everybody. And he's *very* eager to prove that he's still active. There were fears for some panto ponies a few years back.'

Maeve let a silence descend, and fixed me with one of her looks. I knew what she was up to, and distraction was futile.

'Okay, okay, I'll phone him later,' I said.

There was a pause, accompanied by the Kelly gimlet eye. 'Promise?'

'I promise.'

'Atta girl.'

It was high time we got grounded again. 'These calls,' I began, 'you say you never get them on your mobile?'

'Not that I know of,' she answered, back down to earth too. 'If it's switched off people leave messages, and there have been no blanks, or silences if you could call them that, like the ones I'm getting on the landline.'

'Right. I don't want you to get overly worried about this, Maeve. Together we'll sort it, okay? Now, I suppose I'd better freshen up before facing the Street Tribunal.'

The bathroom in this apartment is where I want to live when I grow up. It is huge, with a claw-foot enamel bath in the middle of the floor. The sparkling steel taps are on the side, so as not to inconvenience the one or more persons who might be relaxing, or washing, or whatever. For those in a hurry, there is a power shower tucked discreetly in a corner beside a tower of towels, robes and fragrant fol-de-rols. It is lit by a huge, frosted window which manages to capture light all through the day, and is covered by a royal blue blind at night. Above the sink is an enormous mirror which bounces the light to any spot that nature finds hard to get to, and all of the ones on my face which don't need highlighting. And here on shelves are the unctions and salves of the modern girl. I swear that Maeve Kelly has enough to do a good mummification. And no matter what man is in her life, she manages to keep their presence discreet, if not invisible. Actually, she never lets them move in, perhaps that's her secret. That's the difference between Maeve and me. She's a serial dater, I'm more live and let live in.

If there is one feature that makes me nervous, though, it is the toilet. It's one of those modern jobs with no stem under it, so it juts out from the wall at an angle. I can never relax on it because I'm convinced that it will snap off while my large arse is enthroned. If there was a safety apparatus like, say, a seat belt, I'd be that bit more at ease. Still, I can change this when the time comes.

I noticed that one of the bubble baths had a quote on the label. I moved closer to read it. 'My hopes are not always realised, but I always hope,' it said. Fair enough. Then I noticed who the quote was from; Ovid, no less. What was the world coming to when these pearls of ancientness were turning up on mass-produced bath products? Still, maybe Ovid would be pleased that, although his genius had been reduced to a slogan, the message was reaching out to the wider populace who might not normally feel the need to check him out. The bubble bath was called 'Well Being'.

As I was surreptitiously dousing myself in a glorious Jo Malone cologne, Maeve knocked on the door and announced coffee, to fortify my spirits and make me just hyper enough to make a good entrance at home. 'I've given the mutt some water,' she added, ever the perfect hostess. As I joined her she said, 'More lippy, and toss your hair up a bit. That Jo Malone is divine, isn't it?'

'Em, yeah, I hope you don't mind?'

'Not at all. It's not mine, it's Mark's.'

Aha! In the past six months, Maeve had dated a copywriter, a cameraman, a Formula One racing driver (it made the tabloids for three days running, and she swears she's now allergic to champagne as a direct result of the excesses of that escapade), and a magician who specialised in children's parties, much to his own chagrin. I did a quick totting up and discovered there was not a single 'Mark' amongst them.

'A man leaving something in your bathroom? That is *so* serious. Tell all.'

Maeve was the cat who got the cream and had the t-shirt to prove it. She curled up on her designer sofa and stared dreamily into space.

'He's a lawyer or something. Whichever one does the theatricals in court.'

'A barrister then.'

'I suppose. He did that murder thing recently.'

The penny dropped in the amusement arcade of my brain.

'You mean, Mark Rolands? Only the most famous man in Ireland at the moment. The one who got Sara Fingleton off the charge of murdering her husband, even though she was as guilty as the prison day is long?'

'Yes, that Mark Rolands. He's divine.'

'*And* you've let him leave stuff here?'

'Worse than that, he's got his own key.'

'You realise you're going to have to kill him now?' This was as serious as a hardened criminal letting you see his face.

'I know!'

'I never thought I'd see the day, Maeve.'

'Well, in truth you haven't, yet. You know me and men, it may come to nothing. But I have to admit that I wouldn't mind with this one, he's special.'

'And he can defend me when I finally get nabbed by the law for something shady.'

'Which reminds me, *why* are you not at work? Are there no more bills in your life? Has Barry lost the *run* of himself and decided to support *you*?'

I laughed at the notion.

'No, I've had to get someone to take over for a while. I came face to face with the man I was following, so I'm having a change, which I hope will be as good as a rest.'

'Or, in *your* case, better than *arrest*.'

'Doesn't matter now, I've got a direct line to Mark

Rolands. Hang on to him, Maeve,' I pleaded, dramatically. 'I need him.'

She beat me with a cushion.

'Let me know when you have something on these
phone calls, and I'll hang by and have a listen,' I said.

Her mouth twitched, and I knew that she was putting
up a braver front than she had in her store.

'Maeve, the law is on your side. Making malicious
calls is considered a criminal offence, and we'll involve
the cops if we have to.'

Another twitch.

'Which we won't. Okay?'

She nodded and then she smiled. 'Ooh, but you're
forceful when you want to be.'

'All in a day's work, ma'am,' I said, in a woeful
American accent. 'Now don't you go worryin' your
purty little head 'bout nothin', ya hear?'

She was still nodding as I hitched me up ma dawg
and made fer ma wagon. Time fer this pilgrim to hit
injun country.

Although our family name is Street, we live somewhere
else entirely, the Close, Sycamore Close. I have no idea
whether this was far-sightedness on my parents' part or
pure serendipity. Whatever, it works for me. There is
nary a sycamore in sight, of course. I half recall the
helicopter seeds of sycamore trees from my childhood,
but it is only a half-recollection, and the trees might
have been elsewhere, like Larch Grove which is parallel
to the Close.

I passed the Raynors' house as I approached Casa Street. It looked a lot like our own, with the small exception that Andy's dad is devoted to hedging, carving it into whatever shape takes his seasonal fancy. This spring was all about Noah's Ark, it seemed. Two of everything, though the everythings were a little hard to identify. And I was certain that there were three unicorns on display, possibly to make up for the ultimate fate of the beast. Last year's effort had gone awry somewhere between idea and execution. He had intended giant acorns around the periphery of the garden, to make some complicated horticultural joke about oak trees, but the result was a phalanx of green penises, which his wife, Breda, quickly vetoed. Mind you, gardens are all about sex and reproduction so the scheme was perfectly sound thematically, and some might even have said a joy to behold; I guess it's all to do with the eyes that are beholding.

Frank Raynor was inspecting his handiwork as I drove by. He raised a head and waved, and I returned the salute. Andy has his father's dark, handsome features, coupled with his mother's fierce wit and way with words, graced by sparkling eyes that are all his own. A formidable combination. God, I wanted to make that call. But I held on to my dignity. And creamed myself.

I parked in a space opposite our driveway as my grandmother, Mary Ellen Doyle, rounded the corner, dragged by Fanny and Margot, two dogs who shared five hundred and thirty-one breeds between them. She was dressed in a red fleece, which she'd teamed with a knee-length emerald skirt and some very funky patterned tights. I complimented her on the latter.

'It's two pairs, the holes are in different places, so there's no need to waste them.'

My gran was a pioneer of recycling. On her back was a knapsack of indeterminate colour, for piccaroonying wherever she went; you never knew the hour or the minute when a top relic would present itself to be brought home. She was having a bit of trouble controlling the dogs, and had a look of Ben Hur about her.

'Did you forget your chariot?' I asked.

'Piss off,' she replied.

My granny had recently started a campaign of plain speaking, particularly with her family. She thought it was hip and modern, but I suspect she also enjoyed mortifying us all, and daring us to pull her up on her 'language'. She was inclined to tall tales of late, too, and again I suspected this was to tease out a reaction, and to worry us that she might be going a bit ga-ga. She loved the attention. In fact, there was nothing senile about this old lady, let me assure you. I could see my poor mother shaking her head, saying, 'She's hanging around with a bad crowd.' And she was. Gran's best pals were renegades, and none of them under seventy-five. They were a mixed bunch who got together to swap spells and potions, and sometimes to play poker for money or souls. Well, the sorcery was only suspected by the families, no one had the guts to tackle them directly on this. You never knew what life form you'd come back as after they'd finished with you.

No. 4, Fanny and Margot were now a tangle of leads and wagging tails. Mary Ellen Doyle handed me her two leashes and headed for the door, saying, 'I'll see you inside.' I tried protesting that I had an important phone call to make, but it didn't even merit a reply. I persuaded the knot of dogs to follow me around the corner of the house, through the side gate and into the back garden, where I unclipped any catch that looked viable and let the hounds run loose. Then I sat on a bench out of sight of the kitchen and rooted out my mobile to call Andy. My hands were clammy with nerves.

A luscious, deep voice answered, 'Andy Raynor. How can I help?'

'You get more mid-Atlantic by the day, do you know that?'

'Ah, Leo, that was quick. I thought you'd leave me hanging at least another six hours to prove how nonchalant you are about me.' There was a distinct merriment in his tone. DAMN! I thought I'd left enough of a time lapse. Well, he hadn't bettered me yet.

'Andy, I'm in a hurry, what did you want?'

'I need an escort.'

'That's not actually one of the services I provide,' I explained.

'I need your body, Street.'

'Mmm,' I murmured, coolly. 'In what way?' And gave myself a mental shake. What the hell was I doing flirting with bloody Andy? He was more trouble than any one woman could handle, particularly a woman living with another man, i.e. me.

'I've got to go to a Rugby Club dinner dance tomorrow night and I need someone along who doesn't crave attention and can look after herself. You may be a royal pain in the ass, but at least you can make conversation with strangers. And it's not a date, which is great, because I just don't have the energy for all that at the moment.'

'You surprise me, Andy,' I said. 'I can't believe you'd consider going out with a member of the opposite sex without the prospect of a shag at the end of the evening.'

'It's the new mature me.'

'And you've been let down at the last moment.'

'You are a very cynical woman, Leo Street.'

'Yeah, well, that's life.'

'So, are you up for it?'

My mind was thinking a hundred thoughts all at once. I was miffed that he didn't see me as a date, while at the same time reasoning that this was a good thing and what I actually wanted. We were friends and occasional sparring partners. It would surely be a laugh, at the very least. But I was insulted to be the last port of call in an emergency . . . or was that a compliment? And how dare he assume that I'd be available at such short notice?

'I'm not sure that I can make it,' I returned.

'Yes, you can, and you know you want to.'

'You are one cocky bastard, Andy Raynor.'

'Yep, and I know how to show a girl a good time, even you. Anyway, you owe me for helping you when you were on that case in Kildare.'

I gagged indignantly. 'I beg your pardon? All you gave me was some information, which was damn-all use anyhow.' I was spluttering now.

'And have we forgotten the little matter of me not letting you choke on your own vomit, because you were too pissed to know that you were unconscious?'

'That's dirty and low down and you know it. I was caught off guard!'

'You still owe me.'

My mind was racing now. But one fact clinched the deal for Andy, though he did not know it at the time. I knew that Michael O'Donoghue was a member of the same club as Andy, and might be at the dinner. That could yield something. So, it would be a work trip, as well as possibly assuaging some of my rampant hormones with a little window shopping.

'Oh, *okay*, I'll go.'

'I'm delighted that you've seen reason,' he said, laughing aloud now. 'Dress is informally formal, whatever that means. Something short and without knickers should do the trick.'

'*WHAT?*' I shrieked.

'Just joking, Leo. If you weren't wearing panties and your mother found out, I'd have to marry you, and God only knows where that would land us. I warn you in advance that it's a kind of fundraiser for some very worthy cause or other, so it'll probably be dull as dishwater.'

Ain't that the way of the world? Badness is spicy, goodness bland. I couldn't let it go.

'So it's sub-interest, and you're lining up the B-Team?'

'Leo, Leo, Leo,' he admonished. 'You are a sour woman at times. Choose those scanties, get primping yourself, I'll pick you up at eight. Ciao.'

I found myself staring at the phone with a mixture of horror and delicious anticipation. He had invested the word 'scanties' with such promise that I was in need of changing mine there and then. I made a note to wear two pairs of interlock knickers on the night.

According to Barry, the female equivalent of a hard-on is a wide-on. He can be utterly gross when he wants to. But as I struggled to walk upright to the kitchen door, I began to have an idea of what he meant.

Seven

I once saw my four-year-old niece Mary tackle the day.
It was 8 a.m. and she had dragged herself out of bed;
Mary loves her sleep. She descended the stairs, slowly
and gently, flakes of sleep stuck to her eyelids. As she
reached the door of the dining room, she stopped, gave
a big sigh, then *danced* sideways into the room, shouting, 'Mary's here, Mary's here!' She had to, you see. She
was a kid, and that was her job. I was now in a similar
situation, and though I had two foot four on her in
height, and twenty-six years, the demographics were
pretty much the same. I took a deep breath, then
bounced into the kitchen, saying, 'I'm here, I'm here!'

I needn't have bothered. There was no one to greet
me. Or should I say one member of the family was
lurking, but it was not strictly human. Smokey Joe
Street, our cat, sat in the middle of the table, and he
couldn't give a hang about any of us one way or the
other. He chose that moment to stretch a pantalooned
leg in the air, and lick his hairy white arse.

'You'd know you were a man, Mister,' I said, as I
made my way into the sitting room.

I never did get to make 'my entrance' because as I reached for the door handle a youngster exploded into the corridor and ran for the stairs. It was fifteen-year-old Lucy Street.

'Shouldn't you be at school?' I asked.

'Leo, you are beginning to sound like my mum. Day off. I'll explain in a minute, I'm bursting to go to the loo.'

She bounded up the stairs two at a time, though with her legs she could have managed three steps, no problem. At the top, she turned and said, 'Don't you think you should answer that?' And disappeared.

I could hear the strains of a highland jig, but didn't think that was anything to do with me until I realised it was coming from my bag. How could that be? I hate novelty rings on a mobile, and mine is programmed to the most boring sound available with my model. I fished it out and sure enough it was my telephone making the awful racket. When I answered, Barry's cheery tones yelled, 'Surprise!'

'Brilliant trick, Baz,' I drawled.

'Don't be so square, Leo. Live a little.'

This was the second time I had been told that today. If I'd had a moment I might have paused to give it some thought. Now was not that moment; I was on the cusp of the tribal gathering and didn't need any miscellaneous distractions. Instead I gave the Barry Boy short shrift, but not before he could say, 'Don't forget to get cat food and some milk on your way home.'

'Does that mean that you have no intention of

leaving the house at all today?' I asked, probably a little sanctimoniously.

'Who knows?' he said, airily. 'And I don't mean to excite you, but if I don't, I may not even wash myself.'

'Gee, there's something to look forward to.'

'Sarcasm, Leo. Unattractive in a lady. I will of course release myself into the community later, to bring culture and entertainment to the paying public. I have to do the Pub Crawl. But it'll be no harm if you get some provisions too. See ya later, babe.'

Lucy thundered back down the stairs, and paused long enough to tell me, 'You've a bit of froth at the side of your mouth, could be drool,' before crashing back through the sitting-room door. 'Leo's here,' she announced. 'She's got hose beast tights on.' That was my fanfare. Not the entrance I had intended, but sometimes you have to use whatever gets you to where you need to go. In my case, it was deep into the female bosom of the family, or 'boosum' as my granny likes to call it. She is also given to the word 'picturescew'. So you get the ... well, anyway, I wiped my mouth with the back of my hand and stepped in.

My grandmother popped a bottle of champagne as I entered, and I'll admit that I felt very flattered. Then she made it all the more special by saying, 'Jaysus, I thought you'd never get here, me brain thinks me throat's been cut. Who's for gargle?' When we'd all been dispensed our fizzy 'poo, my mother raised a glass to Rose and we toasted the little beauty. My gran grimaced and groaned, not her usual reaction to champagne. 'Me poor teeth are dancin' for want of a few fillings,' she explained. 'The cold kills them. And as for the neuralgia . . . oh, now, don't start me. Still, we'll soldier on.'

'Neuralgia?' I hooted. 'I thought that went out with the Ark.'

'No need for that sort of mockery, miss. You'll know all about it when you're my age.'

Angela popped her new daughter into my arms and said, 'This will be great practice for you, Leo.'

'Ah, now here,' I protested. 'I haven't a maternal bone in my body.'

'Oh, I don't know,' she said. 'You look after Barry pretty well.'

From anyone else, the comment might have held a barb, but this was Angela and all she spoke was the truth. I refrained from comment and, unusually, so did the older members of the family.

Rose Street was a dote. She locked you in her gaze with huge azure eyes, and waved her hands as if to tell you some important information. Sometimes, she gave an emphatic downward gesture that seemed to have a warning in it. You ignored her wisdom at your peril. I placed her flat on my thighs, with her feet to my stomach and her head at my knee, where she continued with a leisurely t'ai chi routine. I was as happy as mussels in garlic butter.

'It suits you, you know,' said Anne, Lucy's mum.

'Don't you start,' I warned. But it was too late, my mother was on to one of her favourite subjects.

'You're not getting any younger, Leo. The longer you

leave it, the dodgier it gets. And you don't want to miss out. When I see all the attention you pay to those cats of yours, and now that dog, it brings it home to me. It's a baby you should be having, and no more of this aul' nonsense with pets.'

I thought I might try a different tack. Normally I would argue with her, but now I went for enigmatic and vaguely agreeable.

'Well, you never know. Maybe you're right. Maybe one of these days I'll surprise you all.'

My grandmother snorted. She has a very well-honed bullshit detector. I guess she's heard a lot more of it in her lifetime, being the eldest of us. If she was going to undermine my newest plan, it was time to change the subject.

'Why are you off school?' I asked my niece.

Lucy was trying her best to like champagne, but each time she took a sip her face creased at the bubbles and the nasty taste. I had no doubt that, like her forbears, she would stick with it, and eventually reach a point in her life when she resented her parents for not having the surname Bollinger.

'Sister Mel died, so we got the day off.'

'Oh, no,' I blurted. 'Mel was great, she was one of the good guys.'

'She was?' Lucy's eyebrows were dusting the ceiling.

'Yes,' I insisted. 'I had her for Latin for three years, and then she started doing school plays and running the tuck shop. She was a mad little thing. I could never work out why she was a nun though.'

'I know that,' my gran said. 'She was brought up in the West. Her family owned a pub with a bit of land around it. But Mel was the youngest of two daughters, and there were no sons, so her sister got the family business, and she was sent into the convent. That's just what happened in those days. If she was growing up now I doubt she'd be a nun.'

'No, she'd be a writer or a theatre director or something like that,' I said.

'I thought she was a crazy old bat,' said Lucy. 'We used to call her Old Habits Die-Hard.'

'She'd have liked that,' I laughed.

'Wasn't Mel short for Melchisedech?' Anne asked.

'I hope so,' I said. 'I'd hate to think it was anything boring.'

We all took a moment to remember the dead nun. Except Lucy, who'd clearly decided that we'd all gone crazy. And Rose, who was set to grow up in a world where nuns were becoming obsolete. It didn't bother me that they were dying out, but I had liked Mel, and hoped that she'd got her due reward. That was the deal when you invested your life in the Catholic dream, wasn't it? I was so lapsed that the details were decidedly muzzy. And we had never been a devout household to begin with. *Carpe Dominum*, Mel, I thought, hoping that I'd remembered even a little of what she'd taught me. I added the proviso 'by the balls if you have to, to get what you want' in English, because my Latin studies had not continued to senior level.

Mothers have special powers which seem to come to

them by osmosis over the years. They gain the ability to read your mind, as well as your post, they can wrong-foot you, they can make you do things that you don't want to, they can tell what colour underwear you're wearing, and whether it matches, and of course they can smell lust and intrigue at a hundred paces. There's probably a simile in there somewhere, involving a wild animal hunting its prey.

'Did you ring Andy?' was all she asked. But this was no innocuous query. My mother was basically asking, 'What are you doing with your life and when are you going to get sense, or at least see things my way?' I wriggled in the bit between the rock and the hard place. (Amazing the way it's not site-specific, just turns up wherever it's not wanted.) I looked to Anne and Angela for moral support. All I met were grins, and the twinkle of expectation in their eyes. I looked down at Rose. She gurgled and gave me a wave. Lucy was curling up her nose, but this was more to do with a French château than my plight. And the vultures just perched and waited.

I tried, 'Oh, yeah, that, it was nothing.'

'So what are you going to wear?'

'Sorry?'

'What will you wear to the do?'

'Mammy, how did you know about that?'

'I'm your mother, of course I know.'

'This is a set up, isn't it? You've probably been planning this with Andy for ages, haven't you? You are so devious. No, I want to change that. You're evil, that's what you are.' I was on a roll now, so I waxed lyrical. 'He's a philanderer,' I added, summoning up a lorry-load of biblical denunciations, I hoped.

As if.

'Ah, calm down, would you?' my grandmother said. 'Sure he's gorgeous. I'd say he has a lad on him like a donkey's arm holding a child's orange.' There was silence in the room while everyone checked their hearing. Then the pronouncement sank in. I started to choke. Anne and Angela were holding on to one another for support. I'm glad to say that Lucy was bemused. But the look on my mother's face could have frozen peas. She squeezed out an indignant 'Mammy!' I was doubly delighted to know that I wasn't the only one in the house with mother-trouble. Mary Ellen Doyle finally asked me what was so funny.

'Nothing, Granny, I've just never heard it put like that before.' I tried gulping in some air to calm myself.

'So what did I get wrong?' she asked.

I cleared my throat. 'Well, I think the phrase you were looking for is "a child's arm holding an orange", I explained, not daring to catch anyone else's eye.

'And which of the two would be bigger?' she wanted to know.

'Em, I don't know really,' I had to admit. 'Probably your description.'

'That's what he is then.'

'I'm sure Andy's ears are burning, wherever he is,' my mother said.

'No, Mammy,' I corrected her. 'I'm certain it's another part of him entirely.'

The room fell about again.

There is a deviousness in all mothers that should never be underestimated. I'm not sure if it's an innate talent that's unleashed when parenthood is achieved, or whether it's something that's acquired stealthily over the centuries. Whatever the case, a Mammy can turn any situation to her advantage. Granted, when her own mother is there too, it's a little tricky, but not impossible. Geraldine Street, née Doyle, slalomed on a consonant, then proceeded to display her mastery by dominating the conversation from there on out. I was quizzed high up and low down about what I would wear, what I would eat and drink, and basically what my intentions were towards Mr Andrew Raynor. I eventually heard myself exclaim, 'His virtue is safe with me, for God's sake. You can come along to make sure, if you'd like.' And, do you know, for just a moment she considered the offer, rhetorical though it was. I found myself staring, horrified, as my mother and her mother looked at one another, sizing up the advantages and disadvantages of that particular scenario.

'It does sound like a fantastic night out,' my grandmother said. She was perched like some laughing troll on the edge of her chair.

'I could go with John Senior,' my mother calculated, referring to my father. 'And you could bring one of your cronies.' My grandfather, Nobby, is long gone.

My grandmother shuffled her round bottom forward in the armchair, stretching one leg out, then stretching the other past it, until she seemed on the brink of overshooting the furniture. Her eyes sparkled as she announced, 'We'll make a family night out of it.' To their credit, both my sisters-in-law had the decency to look taken aback. But I was saved by a double-pronged rescue from my nieces: Rose started to cry, and Lucy announced that she was going to be sick. They were both whipped away to be seen to, and I escaped to the kitchen.

Quite honestly, I was sweating by now. What crazed fever were we gripped by? I know that sexual politics is an inexact science at the best of times. There is no practical solution to infatuation, not even consummation. But what do you do when more than one of the women in a family is obsessed with one man, albeit in differing ways? Or what if the ways don't differ that much, just the generations under the grip of the infatuation? It's not only a nightmare, it's chaos.

So is losing your sense of humour.

The harpies followed me into the kitchen, laughing their heads off.

'Leo, you'll never learn. How could you be so easy to rise?' my mother asked.

'What do you mean?' I countered, tetchily.

'We can read you like a short story,' my gran said, shaking her head.

'I don't know what you mean,' I tried again. 'And anyway it's all a bit cruel, if you ask me.'

'Oh, for goodness' sake,' my mother exclaimed, 'would you loosen up and live a little?'

I was becoming entirely cheesed off with being told that.

'Go out and have a whale of a time, why can't you?' she continued. 'I only wish I had half the chance.'

Of course they had a point. I certainly was taking things far too seriously. But why? The frightening realisation was that a Pandora's box in my head would be opened if I admitted, even to myself, that I fancied the rocks off Andy Raynor. And that was not only undesirable but unethical in the relationships stakes. I was living with a man; had been for three years. We had had our ups and downs, but the arrangement worked, and what was commitment if it could be tossed out of the window at the first lusty imagining? 'Barry is not Andy,' Pandora whispered. I switched my brain immediately to neutral. I wouldn't listen to her. I could see the lid on the box lift ever so slightly, and I didn't think that I could deal with whatever was about to spew out.

'Is that your phone?' my mother asked.

We all paused to listen. The opening of Bach's Mass in C, 1997 remix, was repeating itself over and over, not my new and improved highland fling, so I denied it. I was about to do this again and make a liar of myself when it became apparent that it was indeed my mobile making this latest bizarre noise. How had Barry done that? Surely he couldn't have programmed it from afar? My answer came through the kitchen door just then, green of gill and dull of eye. She smiled sheepishly at me.

'Nice one,' I smiled back. The things we do for love . . .

'It's not lemonade, Lucy,' her mother Anne was saying. 'You shouldn't knock it back as if it was. No wonder you were ill.'

'Don't mind her, Luce,' I said. 'We've all been there in our time. As I recall, your mother had more than one run-in with cooking sherry, and cider, and other classy tipples like that. Sometimes all mixed together.'

'Oh, do you hear the queen of the hedges herself?' Anne laughed. 'I seem to remember many's the night you found your way home following a trail of orange puke you'd made earlier.'

'It was a system,' I shrugged. 'It worked.'

'I hope to God you're not still using it,' my mother said, with just the right mixture of superiority and mock outrage. She's good at being a mammy.

'Oh, holier than thou now,' said Über Mum Doyle, who was of course the Mammy of us all, and not to be undone.

'If you breathe a word about what I think you're referring to, I won't be responsible for my actions,' her daughter, Geraldine, warned.

I would have put myself deeply into hock to find out what she was talking about. But I should have known better. They grinned at each other, then settled into *Omerta*. They were shored up sheer, no questioners need apply.

My nose was itching with curiosity, and I had to scratch it somehow. Feeding it information (of any sort) was the only remedy here, so I accessed my message. It was Ciara. Short and to the point. 'I'm in the office. Phone me.' I followed instructions.

'What are you doing back there?' I asked.

'You know damn' well what I'm doing back here. You never told me I wouldn't get bloody parking on bloody Merrion Square. So how was I supposed to case the joint?'

I allowed myself a smile. Had she passed her first test? She was certainly working on the lingo.

'What did you do?' I asked, casually.

'I followed your advice,' she said. 'But in a much more effective way.'

'Of course. And which piece of my wonderful advice was it you remodelled so well?'

'I asked a question *and* told a lie, all at once,' she crowed. 'I telephoned, pretending to be our family doctor's receptionist, and checked on the good doctor's availability this week.'

'And?'

'Jammed solid. So he won't be going any place unusual any morning between now and Saturday. No need to sit on some bench like an eyesore attracting attention, or mess around in a bus shelter pretending to wait for the 46A.'

First test passed with flying colours. I glanced at my watch.

'Shouldn't you be back there now?'

'All in hand. I'll be hot on his tail to the baby factory within the nano-second. There have been some interesting developments in the doctor's life. I suggest you get an evening paper. Talk to you later. Over and out.'

A tingle of relaxation had been trying to establish itself between my shoulder blades since early morning; Ciara was doing well. She had sense, common or otherwise. She also had a sense of what needed to be done. It would be interesting to see this case through her eyes, unjaded as she was by the vagaries of the cheating classes. I say classes because in my experience being unfaithful is not a restricted activity. Anyone can get in on the act. Birds do it, bees do it, et cetera. And I wasn't worried about Ciara being damaged by the experience of spying on the unsavoury; for all her sense, she was not that kind of sensitive soul. Not by a long shot. But she had halted that pleasurable tingle's journey with her enigmatic remark. Instead of relaxation oozing through my muscles, I stiffened from my neck downwards again.

Eight

There were signs to be read all over this case. Treat them as omens, if you like, but that's not always a good road to go down. I try not to be superstitious because it's nonsense and you can end up spooking yourself and taking your mind off the proper focus of the work in hand. Also, it drives Mick Nolan completely mad, and he's not a man I like to piss off. But it seems to me that whenever I get relaxed, or even a little confident that things are going well, bad things are skulking around the corner waiting to run me down.

As it happens, I did have to run around the corner to get the newspaper in our local shop. Mrs Bradley had been running 'The Tip Top' since before I was a grope in my parents' romance. She still liked to press a sherbet upon me, and sometimes I didn't even have to pay for it. Today, as I dipped my liquorice stick into the vile, fizzy, white powder, I read the headline 'Scandal of Baby Shop', below which was a grainy photograph of my quarry. As I read the breaking news, I disengaged my tongue from my palate, where the sherbet had just glued it, with a loud smacking noise.

Department of Health officials today began investigating claims that one of Ireland's leading obstetricians is involved in a 'babies for sale' scandal. Unconfirmed reports suggest that Michael O'Donoghue is at the centre of the latest controversy to involve the beleaguered Fledgling private hospital and fertility clinic. Sources close to those involved say that complaints of overcharging and risky procedures have been received from members of the public. The Medical Council has refused to comment directly on the matter, saying only that Mr O'Donoghue has been a respected practitioner for many years, and that all allegations against him are hearsay until such time as accusations can be formally confirmed or denied.

This is not the first time that Michael O'Donoghue has attracted attention. In 1992 he was cleared of charges of performing abortions which are illegal in the Republic. And in 1994 his name was linked to research into DNA selection which was condemned by the Catholic Church. A spokesman for Mr O'Donoghue said that the doctor was unperturbed by the allegations as they were completely unfounded, and he would be vindicated by the results of any investigation into his practices. He also said that it was clear that elements within the wider community were attempting to block his researches and besmirch his name through a malicious misunderstanding of his work and its value.

The paper followed the story up with transcripts from a speech Michael O'Donoghue had made to medical students at Trinity College. They pushed his views that life was marketable, if genetic traits were isolated and patented. This, he maintained, could lead to cures for cancer and other diseases, and on a cosmetic level to eradication of baldness or choice of eye colour, for instance. He extrapolated that mortality itself might become a consumer choice, which had sent religious groups into a complete spin. It read like science fiction, yet he assured the students that within a decade this would all be available to us. And he was the one to deliver, it seemed.

Of course, the newspaper had also chosen the most demonic photograph of him they could find. Here was a glaring face with flared nostrils and unruly hair. His dark eyes burned out from the page and into some soft area of entrail protected by the reader's rib cage. Here was the bogey man.

I re-entered Château Street with my mind whirling yet none the wiser as to where this case was headed. Now that Michael O'Donoghue was pursued by half of Dublin, he was unlikely to notice me, even though we had met informally the night before. I could not have foreseen this, but I felt outwitted all the same. Did the unfolding news mean that he would change his routine in any way? Or would he keep his head down, maintain normality and wait for the brouhaha to blow over, on the grounds that the public has a notoriously short attention span? I was antsy about what else fate might throw at me, because I was clearly not in charge of what was happening here. And then war broke out between me and the animal kingdom.

All I did was try to move Smokey Joe off the table, because (a) he shouldn't have been up there, and (b) it was unhygienic for him to be in the middle of our lunch. I looked at the butter and was convinced that I could see the marks of a scaly tongue on one side. My mind summoned up a vision of him cleaning his hairy bum as I was arriving earlier, and I put two and two together. Elementary really, my dear Catson. So I made a shooing noise and flapped my hands close to his rump to shift him. Quick as a flash he nipped me on one wrist and swiped me across the back of the other. I often wonder if Smokey Joe has ever read his job description, which specifies that he is a house pet, not a hairy devil. I gave a gobsmacked 'Huh!' and looked for human support. No one had seen the incident. I could have sworn he was laughing at me now so I gave him a light smack on the bottom, at which he yowled in agony, and that got the attention of all. I might as well have been a vivisectionist at a vegetarian barbecue. Lucy rushed to the poor injured animal's side, cooing and petting him till he stopped his pitiful wailing. Barry could have taken acting lessons from this cat. Master Classes. He was fed some tidbits of smoked salmon as a reward for being so brave and went on his way, shoulders shaking with feline mirth. So, humiliating a human being is enough to make a cat laugh, in case you were wondering about the answer to that one.

No one mentioned the incident, probably because they couldn't find words to express the barbarity of it. My shoulder blades were joined up again, and my neck clicked into a rigor. I thought of famous people in history with a dread of cats, among them Napoleon, Shakespeare, Julius Caesar and Mussolini, and it seemed clear to me why: they knew what some of them were up to.

I suppose I was trying to make some sort of atonement when I offered to do the school run for Angela: a desperate attempt to come good after my transgression on to the dark side. (Anything to do with Smokey Joe Street is probably the Dark Side, whether he's with you or agin you.) I was also having an attack of that old favourite of mine, guilt; possibly the most powerful weapon for use on yourself, or others. My gran may have a finely tuned bullshit detector, my mum a gossip/intrigue one, mine is a highly trained guilt collector. A lot of people carry chips of regret around on their shoulders each day. I have a rock across my back made of sterner stuff: it's part conscience, part guilt and part regret, with a measure of mild self-loathing thrown in. But, hey, it ain't heavy, it's my boulder.

The job in hand was simple enough. I would collect Dominick and Mary, and two friends who were coming to tea, Dylan and Kylie. That way Angela got a bit more of a rest at home, and didn't have to deal with the pressures of after-school traffic, and hauling five kids around. I would only have to deal with four and a dog, because Rose would stay with her mum. At the back of my head rattled an idea that you should never work with animals or kids, but I suppose I thought that didn't apply to me, somehow.

On my way out, I paused to admire my mother's latest painting, and to re-ingratiate myself. It was a swirling mush of greens, brown and a dash of red. It was attractive, actually, and, as far as I could tell, abstract in the extreme. Or at least I couldn't make out any recognisable elements. I asked the stupid question 'What is it about?' and was told that it was whatever I wanted it to be. Duh.

'For me,' my mother said, loftily, 'it's about chaos and being a woman.'

'It's chaos all right,' my grandmother confirmed.

I could see my mother dart her a look, and decided that it was the perfect time to leave, while the heat was transferred to someone else. When aliens arrive from outer space, as they must, I believe the first skill my mother will learn is the ability actually to shoot with a glance of the eye. If they spare her. Which they will. She's a formidable weapon already, and is at least halfway to success on the look-shoot trick.

I often feel a pang of loneliness leaving a happy home, an urge to stay put and seek love and safety, away from the maelstrom of life and the hazards of earning a living. Not today. I hardly gave home a backward glance. I had been grilled, flipped and picked over. There was no point in hanging around for more. What else could they do anyway? Boil the bones and make some stock? Yes, was the answer, so I quickened my pace.

I gave Angela my injured banger to go home in and I took her four-door estate, which is like saying that I went from driving a moped to steering a tank. And why was the number four following me around? It wasn't even one of my Lotto choices. Maybe it should be. I consulted my own No. 4 as we stopped at a junction and he agreed wholeheartedly. So now I could look forward to an early retirement on a million or more pounds. All I had to do was identify the other five lucky numbers and Robert was my uncle. Actually I do have an Uncle Bob, but that's another day's work.

The Model School was relatively new and situated on a corner of Mountjoy Square, just to the north of the city centre. It's an imposing Georgian area that's seen better days. Merrion Square, where Michael O'Donoghue had his practice, would be a sister, but as it's on the south-side, it houses the Arts Council of Ireland, the National Gallery, the National Maternity Hospital, several film production companies, and the headquarters of the Red Cross. Mountjoy Square, being northside, is that bit seedier, and boasts two large electrical outlets, a few derelict spaces, lots of rackrented flats and a hostel for young people. And if it were on the southside, the greenery in the middle would have more dazzling floral arrangements.

The school shared its playground, which also acted as a pick-up and set-down point for parents and children, with a small crêche where a lot of the primary school candidates started off their education. In their day Mary and Dom had attended, then moved up the ranks and out next door at the age of four or five. I decided that the number five was stalking me a bit too so I added it to my list of lucky numbers.

The yard was packed with mums and the odd dad waiting for the end-of-day bell to go. I recognised a few faces from my own school days, women who were now married and bringing up families. I fixed upon two who'd been in my class, Lisa Farrelly and Colette O'Brien. They both had the look of people who don't get quite enough sleep: a vague frazzling about the edges of the soul, an absence of sparkle in the eyes (though a glass of plonk could usually restore this) and a certain looseness of detail. Lisa, for instance, had hastily plaited her blonde hair at the back, but the strands were working their way free from their anchor, and the hairgrips shoved in at the sides were about to surrender their flimsy purchase. She had a small blob of ketchup on her chin, or maybe it was a particularly proud pimple but I thought not, and a dribble of soft egg yolk was pointing southwards from the lapel of her jacket. She was there to collect her son Josh. She had a three year old by the hand and in a harness. I was reminded momentarily of my grandmother and her dogs.

'This is Beth,' she told me. 'Beth goes to the crêche normally, don't you? But she's had a nasty cold for a few days, so she's been at home with Mummy, haven't you?'

The little girl sent her ringlets dancing up and down in agreement.

'And will you be going to the big school when you get older?' I asked.

More dancing hair.

Colette O'Brien lit a cigarette, and gave a deep sigh. 'This is my favourite time of the day, the calm before the storm. Have you fallen foul of procreation yet yourself?' she asked me.

'No. But Angela had a baby girl a few weeks back, so I'm mucking in with whatever help I can.'

'Babies,' said Colette, 'so close to human, aren't they?' We all gave a giggle. 'I've fallen three times myself, like you know who and his cross. They're all here, between the school and the crêche.'

'Well, as long as you don't go for making up twelve apostles, you should be fine,' I said.

'Oh, no chance of that. I found out what was causing it and I cut that out. The husband has a lovely singing voice now.'

Colette was the wag of the old days, the school prankster, the house demon, and the street one too. Her family had arrived in Clontarf after her father lost the fortune he had made in home heating and their circumstances were reduced. Today, the direction of the move would probably be reversed. Now the nouveau riche are moving into the area, rather than the nouveau broke.

Colette had a talent for seeking out mischief. She could also invent it when required, and when not. She led expeditions into the local parish church trying to find the way into the vault, when she heard that Mickey

Freeney had found an open coffin there containing two eyeballs and a wooden spike. It was many years before we realised that Mickey Freeney had been born special and was very unlikely to have had that adventure. At Secondary School, she once locked all of the teachers into the staff room at coffee-break time and demanded money for charity before she would release them. We sat in blazing sunshine chanting for the donation until she judged that they'd given enough; this took two hours, during which time she took up smoking. And she delighted in fooling the relief teachers and student trainees into believing that she had a lisp.

Now she was married to a guy called Ray Leonard. He'd been a bit of a Jimmy Dean in his teenage years, but he charmlessly outgrew his biker's jacket when he started to drink too much, six months after his wedding, at which time he began to mislay his hair and acquire a belly. Rumour was that he still hit the sauce too much to hold down a job, which probably suited him in its way as he'd always been as lazy as sin but great fun with it.

Colette's hair was a shocked explosion of tinder-dry straw, the shape and attitude accentuated by a short cut. She ran a hand through it with some difficulty, scratching her scalp as she went. She caught my eye and confirmed, 'It's homage to Phyllis Diller.' Then she wiggled her nose, to chase off an itch. 'That's supposed to mean I'll have a fight with someone, isn't it? Give us a puck there, Leo, and I'll pinch you, and we'll be done with it.'

I did as I was told, though she pinched me harder than I'd hit her.

'Bitch,' I acknowledged. We weren't a million miles away from the old days now, right down to Colette smoking while we hung around a school yard.

'I suppose you heard about Mel,' she said.

'Yeah. I didn't even know she was ill.'

'She had a hole in her heart. Last week she decided enough was enough and stopped taking the medication. Then she just faded away. I saw her only a few hours before she died. She was genuinely happy. I'll miss the old bag. She was about the only good thing in that school.'

Her and you, I thought to myself.

'We despatched her earlier today.'

'Full metal jacket,' Lisa added. 'Nine priests concelebrating on the altar, and all the ancient nuns rolled out in their wheelchairs.'

'That probably confused them,' I said. 'They're normally only brought out to vote in elections, or against whatever referendum is on the go.'

'I really hope she was hovering around somewhere,' Colette said, 'because it was a hoot. Do you remember Mickey Freeney?'

'God, yes. That's freaky, I was just thinking about him.'

'Well, he's still going strong, I can tell you. He helps out at all the funerals and Masses in the local church. So today he was walking in front of the hearse and someone asked him who'd died, and he roared back,

"Nun in box, nun in box." Mel would've loved that.'

We were chuckling merrily, when I noticed both of my companions stiffen. I followed their line of vision to the gate, where a tall, pale woman in a designer coat had arrived. A hush descended on the playground. The woman tried to hide by a pillar, but all eyes were on her. She rummaged self-consciously in her bag, looking for something that she didn't need. In the false silence, I studied her. At first glance she seemed expensively turned out. And though she was, she was also three seasons out of date. Perhaps she was careful with her clothes, the sort of woman who can get real value from good things. She had some rings on her fingers, and possibly some bells on her toes, and a gold charm bracelet tinkled at her wrist. Her shoes had been costly when bought, but were now showing the wrinkles of age. Her make-up was natural and beautifully applied, but I was sure that the smudge on her right temple was a carefully disguised bruise. And there was one last fascinating detail: she was wearing a neck brace.

'Not a very popular person,' I said, indicating our latest arrival.

'You can say that again,' Lisa nodded. 'That's Carmel Lally.'

'I wouldn't piss on her if she was on fire,' Colette spat.

Before I could get embroiled in the ins and outs of the Lally intrigue, a bell rang and the double doors of the school opened and poured forth an army of little people. I located the two bobbing heads of the Street children, and pushed my way over to them.

'Hello there,' I said. 'I'm your chauffeur for today, so let's load up the car. Do we have a Dylan and a Kylie anywhere?'

Two kids close by nodded and I bundled them all off to the tank. There was a bit of commotion at the car, with neither of the visitors willing to get in, but I insisted and we hit the road for home. We also had an argument about who would get the front seat. In the end, No. 4 stayed where he was, paws on the dash-board, and the children sat along the back seat. I looked in the rearview mirror at the row of little heads and tuned loosely into their conversation. Dominick was doing his level best to annoy his sister.

'Mary, I'll be six soon. I'll be big then. You're not six, you're only four. You're a baby.'

'I am not a baby,' she wailed. 'Rose is a baby. I'm nearly five. I'm big.'

'Cut it out, you two,' I warned. 'I'm not having any of this fighting in my car.'

'It's not your car,' Dominick pointed out. 'It's our car.'

I had forgotten how logical kids can be. And he was right. But I couldn't let them see the whites of my eyes, otherwise I'd be overrun with bad behaviour.

'Well, I'm in charge, one way or the other, and I'm not going to put up with any of this carry-on from you lot. Especially in front of our visitors.'

The guests were very silent, so I tried to engage them.

'What would you like for tea, Dylan?'

'I want pasta,' he replied.

'We're not having pasta,' Mary said. 'We're having spaghetti.'

'Spaghetti is pasta,' Kylie chirped up.

'Yes, it is,' I agreed.

'Not spaghetti hoops,' Mary argued. The debate went into a bit of a loop then, with various philosophical pronouncements on pasta and its many guises.

'I don't want spaghetti hoops,' Kylie announced, finally. 'I want to go home.'

'Me too,' Dylan agreed.

'You will be going home later,' I explained. 'Your mummy will collect you from Dominick and Mary's house.'

'No, she won't,' Kylie said, tears welling. 'She doesn't know where we are.'

'I'm sure Dominick's mum has arranged it all with your mum,' I said. 'No need to cry.'

'We can have eggy bread, Kylie,' Mary said.

'I don't want eggy bread, I want pasta,' Kylie sobbed.

By any standards, this was excessive. I couldn't understand why she was so upset about what they were going to have for tea. But then again, I didn't have children, so I wasn't sure if this was commonplace. I was relieved when we hit the outskirts of Clontarf, where Angela and my brother Stephen lived. Now I could hand my cargo over to an expert.

Angela opened the door just as we drove in, and approached the car with Rose in her arms. I decanted the kids. She looked mildly puzzled.

'And who do we have here?' she asked.

I thought she was playing some sort of mock formal game, so I introduced the gang.

'Angela, I'd like you to meet Mary and Dominick, and Dylan and Kylie.'

She spluttered a little, looking from one visitor to the other, and said, 'I don't know how to put this to you, Leo, but you've got the wrong Dylan and Kylie.'

I looked at the impostors and felt my bowels loosen. I cursed Smokey Joe Street, and all of his seed and breed. This was the last time I would ever do a good turn. It was the last time I would be let for many years. Kidnapping. I was facing fifteen to life. And Mary Poppins could rest easy in her bed.

Nine

Strictly speaking, I should have been embracing the epitome of suburban life at that moment, rather than wondering how many pairs of socks to bring with me to prison. I had all the elements of standard happiness at my disposal here: comfortable home, noisy children frolicking, hopes and aspirations aplenty. There is still great pressure on anyone of my age to get settled and raise a family, to pass on genes, tradition, race memory (if you buy into that one), to strengthen blood lines, and sink into perpetuity. And some days, that all makes sense. But right now my shite magnet was pointed to top notch. The ley lines were clear. Any random crap could get to me without hindrance. Is this what having kids is all about? Especially if those kids are not your own, or even related? I didn't know. All I did know was that I would be lucky to walk the mean streets of Dublin ever again, cast as I was as the Child Catcher.

Back at the school, the lack of certain Dylans and Kylies had been spotted. By their mother, as it happens. And when a similar set of Dylans and Kylies was located, in the playground, asking where they could hitch a lift to their tea appointment on the northside, someone had the nous to call Angela and give some Librium to the distressed and dispossessed mum. I was spared a trip to the cop shop. And a long spell indoors at the Republic's pleasure.

The real Dylan emerged from a car fifteen minutes later asking Angela, 'Have you sexified every man you know?'

'He's a bit of a card,' she explained.

As the impostors were readied for return to their rightful place, a row broke out, with complaints from the kidnapped about having been promised eggy bread and spaghetti hoops for tea. The first Dylan bitterly renamed me 'Mrs Liar Woman'. If I was possessed of a biological clock, it had stopped.

'Never a dull moment,' I said to Angela.

'No, but sometimes they sleep, and that can be nice,' she said. 'Of course, they never go away. You can marry them off and so on, but they'll always come back. Just multiplied, that's all.'

'I don't think I'm ready.'

'No one ever is,' she laughed. 'They really are worth it though. I highly recommend the whole experience.'

'I can't believe you're back in the denial club so soon after having a bloody Caesarean, for godsakes.'

'I have to admit that it wasn't the most pleasant. And poor old Stephen had to wait outside because it was a bit of an emergency in the end. They came out with Rose in some tinfoil and plopped her on a radiator, and didn't tell him whether I was alive or dead. Apparently there was another chap pacing the corridor, smoking, waiting for news of his other half. When Stephen said how awful it was, yer man agreed and said, "Two years ago they would have allowed you to smoke *in* there." '

She was then approached by a hairy mountain of a woman, representing the Vaginal Birth Action Group, who was most anxious to sign her up for a 'natural' birth next time. Angela left her in no doubt about whether there would be a 'next time', and assured her that she would perform the vasectomy herself if she had to.

'I wouldn't mention that to my mother if I were you,' I said. 'She'll go all Irish Mammy, and accuse you of cruel and unusual practices. And she'll take to calling Stephen "Poor Stephen". Your life would be a misery. What she doesn't know won't bother her.'

The small folk tucked into their grub on a low table in front of the television. A cartoon alien was shooting all and sundry with a laser, and that seemed acceptable to them. In the relative calm, I made some tea for myself and Angela. A minor skirmish occurred amongst the children, with complaints about people 'looking' at other people. It didn't last long, due to a tremendously loud explosion from the thermo-nuclear anti-hero on the box.

'There was a bit of aggro at the school today,' I said, reminded of earlier. 'Or rather, silent malice,' I added.

'Ah, that'll have been the Carmel Lally situation.'

'What's the story?'

'Well, there's a lot of bad feeling around, because Carmel slipped in the crèche a few weeks back, and she's looking for compensation. And if the crèche has to pay, it'll go bust and there'll be a lot of inconvenienced parents. Finding decent childcare is a nightmare.'

'But surely the crèche is insured?'

'Oh, yes, but as far as I know the premiums will go sky high, and it won't be worthwhile on a business level. It's a terrible situation. Some of the mums are very angry with Carmel. She's getting a lot of hassle.'

Once upon a time insurance companies had titles with Fidelity, Mutual and Providence in them. Now the closest you'd get is an Alliance, an altogether colder arrangement and one to be watched in a climate of suspicion; a 'who'll do who first?' world. The big buzzword now is Compensation, and there can be no 'Mutual' gain there.

My antennae started to twitch, shifting about for information. 'I might keep an eye on things,' I said.

'You just can't resist, can you?'

'No, I'm a very, very nosy person,' I admitted. 'I have to be, it's my job. I am a professional snoop, though that's not the greatest job description to be filling in on the census. So, I suppose I'll be on duty again tomorrow, if that's all right with you?'

'Absolutely. But do try to avoid any more criminal behaviour.'

Sound advice.

Angela seemed fidgety as we made for the door. I

suspected an observation out of left field and braced myself accordingly.

'Leo, do you mind if I say something?'

'I don't know. You haven't said the something yet. Give it a whirl and then we'll see.'

'It's just that, mmm, how to put this . . .'

'Take a deep breath and let it out.'

'Right. You see, the thing is, it's not easy to stay with someone indefinitely. Me and Stephen have formality here, a system: you know, marriage, kids. It's one way. But if you don't *have* to abide by the rules that we've taken on, why apply strictures to yourself that you don't need?' She halted, briefly. 'I don't think I expressed that very well, but I hope you get the gist of what I mean. Go out and have a good time, you don't owe anyone half as much as you think.'

'Thanks, Angela. And now that you've let it out, no, I didn't mind the something.'

Outside, the day was waning, and the suburb was bathed in a misty, milky light. It was also deceptive. As I walked to my car, the wind whipped up and bit me, the height of bad manners. And I couldn't retaliate, which was maddening. Even an attempt at hitting the wind back might have resulted in being locked up as a lunatic. I settled for bearing it a grudge. As I crossed the road to my car, a woman with a shaved head and a 'Free Tibet' sticker tried to run me down in her Mini. Car, that is. I didn't feel I deserved it. Perhaps she hadn't seen me, she was wearing sunglasses. Maybe I didn't interest her. Unfairly, I began to feel sour about Tibet. No. 4 barked at the empty road where the Mini had been.

'That's told her,' I said to him. 'Good for you.'

Then he cocked his leg against a small tree and piddled on it, and beyond, on to my shoe. As I watched the steam gently rise from my black suede pumps, I thought about going home to bed.

I glanced at my watch and realised that I could not justify taking to the duvet because a set of flimsy circumstances had got up my long nose. A sprinkling of adversity can usually be worked off with activity, mental or physical. And all the better if money can be a by-product. It was time to skirt by the Fledgling.

Even if I'd had only a vague notion of the whereabouts of the private hospital, I would have had no trouble locating it that day. As I approached, I could hear the noises of a gathered crowd from a street away. The entrance to the building was swamped by newspaper hacks and a television crew. Photographers snapped anyone coming or going, and a small Garda presence tried to shield transient patients and visitors. I picked No. 4 up in my arms and we inched our way through. I positioned us behind a number of journalists and eavesdropped shamelessly. For all the use that was. They were talking sport. I quickly tired of the argument as to whether or not a major English football club would relocate to Dublin (it seemed a daft idea to me) and asked one of them what was going on.

'Did you not see the *Herald* tonight?' came the incredulous counter reply.

I took this to be a hint that he worked for the paper.

'Eh, no, I've only just come out,' I tried.

'There's a story brewing about shifty practices in this place.'

'Who are you waiting for?'

'Anyone we can get,' he said. 'Preferably the main man.'

'That's whatshisname, O'Donnell or O'Donoghue or something, isn't it?'

'O'Donoghue, yeah. And he's up to his neck in it this time.'

'How do you mean?'

'Read the papers and you'll find out,' he snapped, effectively ending our dialogue. Thanks for nothing, pal, I thought.

I looked around at the gathered public. Some were curious bystanders, some were protesting. One woman held up a placard which carried only one word: 'Disgrace'. Suddenly there was a surge forward from the reporters. Microphones were thrust into the face of a woman who had just left the Fledgling, others barked questions. The camera crew jockeyed with the rest for position. She held up both hands for silence, which she got, then began to read from a prepared statement.

'The Fledgling Hospital and Trust has provided excellent medical care for over a decade. We are proud of our service. We are also renowned for our research into fertility and childbirth, for which we have been commended many times at national and international levels. Our staff is of the highest calibre. Recently, unfounded stories and allegations have been given unjustified prominence in the country's media. It is not our intention to join in this circus. We have nothing to hide, and we are certain that any investigation into our affairs will prove this. Until we are vindicated, we will make no further statements.'

She surveyed the crowd for a reaction, then added, 'Ladies and gentlemen, we have patients inside who are distressed by this commotion. Please go home. There is no story here.' She gave a saccharine contortion of the face and retreated. I bet Michael O'Donoghue felt a shiver run riot on his spine as the management hung him out to dry.

The protesters began to jeer. It was then that I saw a familiar figure, half hidden in a nearby doorway. She was leaning against the doorjamb and sobbing openly. I edged closer. Some jostling in the crowd knocked me and No. 4 into a metal barrier, and when we extricated ourselves the woman was gone. I searched right and left along the avenues of exit and entrance available, but she had disappeared. I recognised her, though; she was Mrs Bernadette Flood, and she had been inconsolable.

Ten

'Barry,' I said, 'be very certain that I *will* kill you if you so much as look at these loaves. They're on order, they're not for us, and most particularly they are not for Coleman Pearse, whom I have every suspicion I'll encounter in this very house later on.'

For no good reason, Mick Nolan chose that moment to butt in and stick up for Barry. 'You should have baked two of everything,' he said. 'Preparation, Street. Look ahead.' I remembered he'd always loved his food. 'Grub first, then ethics,' I muttered, quoting some writer or other.

There was no reason for Barry to complain. I had been making my own brown bread for a few weeks now, and modifying the recipe with each attempt. It was disgustingly healthy stuff and was keeping our jaws exercised and our innards clear, laced as it was with all manner of roughage. We called it the 'Dublin Brick' and at that time, it was the most regular thing about our lives.

As Barry and No. 4 curled up on the couch to enjoy guests thumping the heads off one another on Ricki

Lake, I sat at the kitchen table for a coffee and a think. Snubby jumped on to my lap, and began to knead my thighs with her front paws. I hadn't the heart to stop her piercing my fatty deposits; with any luck the prickly massage might help shift some of the cellulite decorating those legs. I realised that the cats were feeling neglected because of the palaver of settling the dog into the household. I gave The Snub an extra special hug and kiss and was rewarded with loud purring. She also stopped hurting me for a moment. Noel sat on the chair next to me and Bridie boldly roamed the table. I let her, mindful of my run-in with Smokey Joe earlier. For all I knew, he'd been in touch on the feline bush telegraph and my name was muck here too.

I wondered at the dynamic between the three. Generally, they ignored one another, and we had peace. Now they had a tacit agreement to band together against the common foe. Bridie was a rinky-tinky-tinky cat, dancing like a kitten in a cartoon. Snubby was a toothless wonder with a placid nature and a strangely pungent bottom. Noel was the closest to macho, but even he had a wimpy habit: he sucked my hair, having been weaned too early from his mother. I looked at him now with his lovely black and white markings and a dark bandit mask about his eyes, and for no particular reason, I was reminded of Andy Raynor. He had never sucked my hair, but there were other areas of me that he had applied himself to, and I almost came in my pants as I savoured those memories.

I was squirming happily from buttock to buttock

when the telephone rang. God must have been watching me because Father Con Considine was on the line, in town and on the loose for the night. 'Let's hook up,' he said. I heard Barry laugh in the next room and had a brainwave.

'Con, how do you fancy an evening of enlightenment and pints? Barry is working on the Literary Pub Crawl and I haven't been yet. It's an evening of literary drinking.'

'Or literally drinking.'

'That's the one. Are you in?'

'Done. We should hunt out Ciara junior and bring her along.'

'Actually, she's doing some work for me tonight. I'll explain later.'

I hung up with a happy feeling in my heart. Second time today that a man had set me a-flutter, though in very different ways. Barry gave another chortle, and I reddened slightly. What was I up to, making dates with rogues and priests, when I had my own lad here at home? I did a Scarlett O'Hara, and promised myself that I'd think about it tomorrow.

'Barry,' I shouted, 'you've just sold two for tonight.' Then I had another thought. 'Make that three,' I added, dialling my dad to ask him along too.

'A what?'

'A pub crawl, Dad.'

'Yeah, yeah, I know that bit. But what was the rest?'

'Well, the two actors do bits from books by writers

123

that hung around Dublin back whenever.'

'Sure what's the point of that? Walking around the town like gobshites, or worse, tourists, instead of gettin' settled into a grand snug somewhere for a feed of pints. Hah?'

'It's supposed to be great fun,' I protested.

'Fun? Ah, no, I don't think so.'

'Right, well, I just thought you might enjoy it, that's all. Fair enough if you don't want to come.'

'Hold your horses there now. I didn't say I wasn't coming, I said it was a gobshite idea. Different thing altogether. And sure, I suppose I might as well have a look anyway. It'll make a change to see that other fella actually doin' somethin' with himself.'

I looked guiltily at Barry, who was oblivious to the trial ahead. He was laughing merrily as two of the television guests threw punches and slung insults. 'No way,' I could hear him say. Way, Barry.

'I saw that Brendan Behan once, you know,' John Street was saying. 'He was roarin' in at some poor barman that had probably thrown him out. He was as drunk as a lord. Terrible, the state of him.'

'Great, Daddy, you can tell me all about it later,' I said, and arranged to meet him at the set-off point.

If I had a pound for every person in Dublin who claimed to have known or seen or had a drink with Brendan Behan, Patrick Kavanagh or Myles na gCopaleen, I'd be a rich woman. Not to mention the people James Joyce owed money to.

★ ★ ★

I had barely replaced the phone in its cradle when it rang again. Maeve had something taped from earlier.

'It's nothing unusual, I'm afraid. Just some breathing, with a background of chat and music.'

'I'll drop by and have a listen before you leave for the theatre,' I said. 'Then I'm off into town for a little armchair drama. I'm going on the Crawl with a priest friend of mine and my dad.'

'What I wouldn't give to be a barfly for that one,' Maeve said. 'Barry will earn his money tonight.'

I was uneasy that I had not heard from Ciara, nor seen her at the Fledgling earlier. I tried her mobile but it went straight to voicemail, so I did what any normal person would do and left an urgent and worried message asking her to phone me with any news, or indeed views, on life, the universe, anything, but mostly the O'Donoghue case. She later played it back for me, and I sounded not only needy but incoherent. She had the best of times whipping me with that recording for weeks afterwards.

I had time to spare so I made for the bedroom I shared with Barry to check out an outfit for the following night. It seemed, absurdly, to be a small act of betrayal, so I headed back down the stairs to explain the situation to my boyfriend.

'Sure. Whatever.'

'You don't mind then?'

'Why would I mind? I'll be working, so I couldn't have gone with him.'

I laughed uneasily at his joke.

'Well, as long as it's no bother, I'll tell him I can go along,' I said.

Why the petty lie here? I had already agreed to accompany Andy, so why shroud it in fake approval from Barry? I didn't exactly need his permission anyway. I was a big girl and could decide where to go, and who with, all by myself. I was acting like a woman with a guilty secret. But I didn't have one, so why the subterfuge? Why the need for some sort of cloudy justification?

And, in my perfidy and double standards, I couldn't decide whether I was flattered that Barry was not in the least jealous, or if I meant so little to him that he couldn't even drum that up.

I beat a retreat before my mouth took charge and made a pig's arse of the now mountainous molehill.

My office is neat, of necessity. It's where I first meet most of my clients, and their impressions of the place have to be good. I like it to look reliable, approachable, well run, and not a tip which suggests that it belongs to some nutty professor. To keep it like that is my own business, of course, as Mrs Mack is *un*reliable, *un*approachable, *badly* run and wouldn't recognise a tip if it came up and bit her on the bum. Scotch that, the only sort of tip she knows is of the money variety, and even then she's fussy about what she'll accept.

Home is a different world, not least because it harbours so much wildlife. And most of the time, I'm afraid to open the wardrobe door in case I'm crushed beneath the accoutrements of my life which have no business being in there, or stored anywhere else for that matter. Much of the stuff involved was rescued from my parents' when room was being made for Peter, Anne and Lucy who now share their house. It was a peculiar time, to see my childhood dismantled, ready for the chucking. In a fit of sentimentality, I grabbed the lot and moved it to the painfully inadequate storage space of 11, The Villas. It never did get tagged and bagged, just shoved into this and that cupboard, amongst clothes and shoes and old coats past their best, ready for the never never of nostalgia whenever it would strike.

In today's case, the past took things into its own hands and struck me: as I rummaged for a decent pair of shoes, which were a distant memory in their own right, a naked Barbie doll spilled out at my feet, followed by some ancient magazines with pictures of long-forgotten pop stars with dodgy hairdos, and veiled references to sex; things are a lot more graphic these days. I grimaced at the fact that my body had not once achieved Barbie shape, and never would; but on a happier note, hair flicks were unlikely to return. A jewellery casket in the shape of a wooden heart opened to reveal a lack of treasures. And then came some school yearbooks. I opened up the pictures page of 1984, and there we were: Lisa Farrelly, Colette O'Brien and Leo Street, with three identical, atrocious perms, and the wide happy smiles of the hopeful, who don't yet have to worry about earning a living or finding someone for reciprocal love and cherishment. I sighed with resignation as I stacked the items of a past that could never be relived, and went in search of a cardboard box to put some order into the makings of a private investigator who was formally the proud owner of that truly awful hairstyle.

I began to wonder why I was not still friends with the girls I went to school with? Why had I not kept in touch? The answer was in my work. The world of a PI is a solitary one for the most part. You keep to the shadows, you skulk about, you don't strut, you never draw undue attention to yourself. You keep your clothes plain and your hair and make-up unremarkable. You blend. You never expose yourself unnecessarily. People talk, and soon everyone knows who you are and what you do. And if we are all separated by only a few degrees from any random person we meet during a day, no amount of disguise will allow the space needed for a detective to function.

Downstairs erupted into commotion. Barry had opened the door, with loud delight, to a roaring Coleman Pearse. After spurious chatter, intermingled with various 'you talkin' to me?'s, 'get up, you hump', and dodgy impressions of Al Pacino and Marlon Brando, they began to sing 'There's No Business like Show Business' with impressive lung power. No. 4 added his one and tuppence worth, and was surprisingly musical, I thought. When I looked out of the bedroom window into the back garden, I could see the cats taking to the hills in disgust. Then a low hum began, joined eventually by the thuds of two grown men jumping up and down. A chant of 'me, me, me, I, I, I, ego, ego, ego' resounded through the house: the thesps were doing their warm-up for tonight's show. Self-regarding sounds, apparently, work the mouth best. When the air cleared and uneasy calm descended once more, I chanced down the stairs.

Coleman was fashioning another crude rhyme on the fridge door with the magnets. How this would prepare him for sharing the works of some of our finest Irish writers with a bunch of strangers, I had no idea. Certainly, if the verse in question was anything to go by, their influence on him had been minimal. 'Harass is just one word,' I told him as I passed by. He swore a little under his breath, and rearranged some letters to form the words 'bad' and 'ass', but the magic was lost and he abandoned his project.

'So, Coleman, you're in charge tonight. I hope we'll be a good audience.'

'Every audience is a good one,' he said, sententiously. 'And although this will undoubtedly be more special, because of your own lustrous presence, I'd like to think that we always give of our best. We are such stuff as dreams are made on.'

Well, that sorted me out. You had to hand it to him, he talked the talk.

'I heard your warm up. I suppose it's important to do all that and keep in shape?' I said.

'Oh, yes, my body is an instrument,' he acknowledged.

'Yes, it *is* a tool,' I continued, childishly.

Barry could see that we were going nowhere in a hurry with this line of banter, so he butted in. 'I thought you had to go by Maeve's before hitting town?'

'Yeah, yeah, I'm outta here.'

Coleman suddenly clapped his hands and made for the sideboard with the words, 'Ah, supper.'

'Oh, no, you don't,' I yelped, flinging myself on him. 'Those loaves are for a customer, and if you so much as look at them, I'll rip your arms off and post them to China.'

'Get away from me, she-thing,' he shrieked melodramatically, raising his hands to protect his face (his livelihood).

Barry wedged himself between us, prying us apart in the process. I flailed about a bit, trying to make contact with some soft bit of Coleman's flesh. I snarled, for effect, hoping for a suggestion of lioness protecting her cubs. Elegant it was not. Dignified it was not. I did feel it was necessary, however, because Coleman can and will eat his own bodyweight at any meal, though his physique does not reflect this; another unfairness on the part of men. He was taken aback enough to ask, 'Are you having your period Leo? Because this is irrational behaviour, even for you.'

Even for me? The cheek!

'Let me at him,' I said to Barry. 'It's time he was taken out.'

Barry laughed and banished his acting partner to the sofa.

'I'll put these out of harm's way,' he said, moving the

loaves to one of the kitchen presses. Then he turned to me and asked, 'Are you, anyway?'

'Am I what?'

'Having your period?'

I really couldn't tell if he was joking or not, so I gave him a sharpish kick to the shin and headed off. As I passed Coleman, he shook his head and pronounced that I was 'one feisty lady'. So I booted him too; no point in assaulting the head area, as there was little or nothing in there. I felt infantile and fulfilled all at once. And who says that violence is not the answer?

At the door I stopped. 'Oh, nearly forgot,' I said, sweetly. 'Break a leg.'

Eleven

Maeve was right, there wasn't much of note on the tape. And even more disappointing was that no number was displayed for the caller.

'Don't be too despondent,' she said. 'I feel a lot better now that something is being done about the problem. It's a relief to know that you're on the case.'

'I'm supposed to be the one reassuring you,' I pointed out, ruefully. 'At least I've heard it for myself now. Whoever it is seems to be watching television or listening to the radio, so that narrows it down to some three to four million people. I'll check on everyone who's got a TV licence first, and if that doesn't turn something up, we'll go back to the drawing board.'

Maeve looked suitably shocked, so I added, 'Joke.'

She smacked her palm to her forehead and said, 'Twit! Leo, please don't tell anybody I was thick enough to fall for that. I'd never live it down.'

'It'll cost you, but your deadly secret is safe with me.'

'How about I make it up to you in some way by leaving you in to town? I've got a cab ordered, with Peter's lot.'

My brother, Peter Street, is a rascally coachman with Northways Taxi Company. They are now much patronised, in all senses, by ourselves and our friends.

Something about this was trying to push to the fore in my brain. An ill-fashioned thought battled to be heard. And then I had it.

'Maeve, do they have your home number?'

'Yes. They'll ring if there's a delay or whatever.'

We both paused, weighing this information up.

'Before we lose the run of ourselves,' I said, 'I'm not, for one moment, suggesting that it's someone at the base. And then again it could be, so I'm not ruling it out either. What I am suggesting, though, is that lots of companies would have this number, even though you're ex-directory. Think about it. Do you get takeaways delivered?'

She nodded.

'Did you fill in your number on the forms for electricity and gas and the telephone?'

She nodded some more.

'So, you see, your number's no secret to anyone with access to any of the above. We'll keep listening for the moment, and I'd like you to make a list of any of the companies you think might have got your number in this way. You can stop nodding now.'

She gave two more and that was that.

We were about to leave when the phone rang again. The recorder clicked into life, and Maeve answered. Through the speakers came the sounds of distant, tinny music and heavy, laboured breathing. I didn't dare inhale myself, as if that might break the eerie spell in the room.

'Who is this?' my friend asked.

The breathing became agitated, then a long hissing of the word 'Bitch!' seeped around us. It was impossible to tell whether a man or a woman had spoken. Suddenly, a cackle of laughter burst through and the line went dead. Maeve put the receiver back in its cradle and burst into tears.

I ran to the machine, but there was no caller number displayed, not that I really expected a break like that. I put my arms around Maeve and tried to comfort her. The situation had escalated and I began to feel angry. And when I'm angry, I like to think that I get things done.

'You know, now it's time to call in the cops,' I said.

'No, no. I don't think there's any need for that. Yet. Let's see how you do, okay?'

'Are you sure? This seems like a crazy to me. Whoever it is might be ill or dangerous, we don't know. I don't want you taking risks.'

'No, I'll be fine. I'm sorry about the tears, it's just a release of tension. I want you to continue.'

'Promise that you'll call the police if it gets in any way worse than this?'

'Right. As long as you promise not to tell Mum what's going on.'

'You got it.'

★ ★ ★

We travelled into town in silence, which was hardly surprising. I left Maeve at the stage door with assurances that everything was under control. I told myself to make sure that it was. She agreed to ask Mark Rolands to stay for the foreseeable, and that raised a smile.

'It's not exactly a hardship, is it?' she said.

I kissed her on both cheeks and waited until she was safely signed in. Then I proceeded to worry a lot as I set off for my night on the tiles.

Grafton Street is the main shopping drag just south of the River Liffey. It is a hive of activity at all hours, and tonight was no exception. I was slightly early and considered going into Bewley's Café to be ignored by the waitresses. Instead I did some window shopping and listened to the city's buskers; two young lads were murdering a compilation of the latest U2 songs, and close by a girl in an evening gown was lashing out a bad version of 'Annie's Song' on a flute, which is not to suggest that there can ever be a good version. In a doorway, a mime artist was noiselessly trying to escape from a very ungeometric cube.

I wondered at the fact that I now had a friend who was a Catholic priest. I am in no way religious, in spite or because of being moulded by the nuns. Gun to my head, I would probably confess to thinking religion a lot of mumbo-jumbo invented to make money and assuage mankind's vanity all in one fell swoop. That's the cynical me with the weapon of destruction held against my temple. Somewhere inside there's another woman who wants to give every philosophy and notion a chance. The cynical one says the other one is a wimp and is hedging her bets. I stay out of the argument because it can get pretty nasty between those two.

It so happens that Con's job is being a Catholic priest; he doesn't foist this unnecessarily on anyone. In the same way, I don't normally draw the public's attention to the fact that I'm a private eye. As a person, he is kind and funny, with a maddening line in puns and the quiet decency of a man who knows right from wrong and is prepared to act on it. I hope he hooks up with Sister Mel when he gets to heaven, and that they have a mighty laugh. I'll undoubtedly be roasting somewhere else, unable to join them.

I stopped outside the 'Dog and Divil' which was the kick off point for the Crawl. I was mindful that I hadn't heard from Ciara, so I texted her a message; the last thing she needed was her phone ringing if she was close to Michael O'Donoghue. I tapped in 'r u ok?' – 'yes' – 'n e news?' – 'no' – 'u sure?' – 'GO AWAY'. She seemed to be managing fine.

My father, John Street, was happily planted in front of his drink when I entered the pub. My heart warmed to the sight of his faded brown hair, speckled with the salt and pepper of age, style unchanged since the fifties, though not too bouffant now. His face bore the rosy glow of a man who enjoys a game of golf, a good dinner and a brace of pints thereafter. His familiar shape perched as if to the barstool born. He leaned the worn elbows of a green tweed jacket familiarly on the counter of the bar; you've leaned on one, you've leaned on 'em all. He had already made friends with the barman, vital for anyone who takes their drinking seriously. They were now on first-name terms.

'A pint of plain is your only man,' he declared as I approached, quoting Flann O'Brien, an accomplished drinker himself in his day. Then he raised his glass in a salute and downed the first half in one swallow. 'A grand pint, Joe,' he assured the publican. 'A darlin' pint,' he continued, more for my benefit this time. So he's brushed up on his O'Casey too, I thought. Or rather, dredged up the bits and pieces he could remember. I was dying to find out if he had any Joyce stowed away.

'Joe, this is my daughter, Leo. To tell you the truth, I'm afraid to order for her. I don't know what the young ones are drinkin' these days.'

'I'll have the same as yourself,' I said.

'A grand choice now,' my father said. 'But it's a terrible price here in town. That same pint in Kilbride's is tenpence cheaper. Would you credit that, hah? Two bob in the difference. Sure it's daylight robbery.'

I was waiting on a rant about how it's not right for women to drink pints at all anyway, but he resisted. My dad likes to wind me up on that and the issue of 'women drivers'; he takes great pleasure in remaining militantly unreconstructed.

We were nicely settled when the doorway darkened, filled as it was by the vast bulk of Father Con Considine.

In keeping with our evening, he was stately and plump like the bauld Buck Mulligan himself. He was thus at any time of the day, in fact.

'You have disgraced yourselves,' he said, echoing William Butler Yeats in a famous address to a rioting Abbey audience.

'Again,' we chorused.

Con was in the disguise of civilian clothing, and did not match his pint of stout as priests and nuns normally do. He was looking well, all the same. I introduced the men, and it was clear that they approved of one another. Then he got to his news.

'I seem to be in for a transfer,' he said. 'They need someone to head up a parish near the canal with a lot of drug and prostitution problems.' He laughed a moment, then said, 'Apparently that's me.'

'Do you get any say in where you're sent?' I asked.

'Oh, no,' he replied. 'I go where I'm told. I wouldn't mind this post though. I've grown a bit weary of the local carping where I am now. I feel a bit bogged down.' He laughed again, shrugging his shoulders and shaking his head. 'There are times when I have to remind myself of my Christian beliefs instead of descending into small-town bitchery.' He finished his drink quickly, slaking a long day's thirst, and we squeezed in another while the tour group expanded.

'Hearing confessions must be a hoot,' my father said.

The priest smiled. 'It can be a little too interesting at times.'

'Didn't one of our neighbours get excommunicated or

something for hearing confessions once in the local church?' I asked my dad.

'That can happen,' Con acknowledged. 'You have to leave all of that to us professionals.'

'It was Maurice O'Leary,' Dad said, remembering.

'Yes,' I agreed. 'He was eleven years old at the time.'

'Rodents,' my father said.

'Pardon?'

'Rodents at three o'clock.'

I was puzzled. Then I noticed a small knot of college types in a corner to our right. The Daddy has a thing about students, and believes that if you see one crossing the road, it's as well to run them down, thereby putting them, and society, out of considerable misery. He has also been known to expound the theory that they are God's way of telling us there are too many people in the world.

'He hates students,' I explained to Con.

'Ah,' said the priest, unwilling or unable to go further.

We were saved a scene by the arrival of Barry and Coleman, and quick as 'get out' the show had begun.

The actors debated the merits of going or staying until Godot arrived. Although the tramps in the play stay put, again and again and again, we headed out on to the mean streets of Dublin – or should that be that two mean Streets sallied forth, along with a handful of other culture seekers? Outside Davy Byrne's on Duke Street, we were exhorted to eat gizzards washed down with a fine burgundy, and I began to wonder if Hannibal Lecter was a fan of James Joyce. I decided that he probably was. As luck would have it, a drunk who had made a great deal of pissing in a nearby doorway, followed us shouting 'shite 'n' onions' as his contribution to the tour; everyone in this town is a Joycean, it seems. He got fed up when we hit Grafton Street thirty seconds later and lurched off in the direction of St Stephen's Green where he lived happily ever after, as in all of the best stories. The last we heard of him was a distant shout of, 'Yez are only a shower of hoor's melts 'n' anyway.'

The Dublin Pub and Literary Crawl was as camp as a row of Eurovision Song Contests. It afforded two performers the opportunity to show off vocal and physical skills to an excess that bordered on over-the-top; or perhaps it was just this pair. They blossomed in our attention, and that of the many passers-by who stopped to stare. We were halted outside McDaid's, listening to a piece by Patrick Kavanagh, when I spotted a woman I thought I knew moving towards the swish Westbury Hotel. It could have been Colette O'Brien, if Colette was blonde, wore glasses and short-skirted business suits over high heels. Before I had a chance to check out this döppelganger, she disappeared into the lobby and out of sight. I was back to Irish Literature and the promise of another glass of porter.

There is nothing more attractive than to see someone you love do their job well. I had been to a few plays in which Barry had starred and I knew he was talented.

But he had been through a lean patch of work recently and I had almost forgotten how good he was. Outside Trinity College, he was telling me of Oscar Wilde's trials and tribulations, and warming the cockles of many of my tender body parts. Every so often he shot a beatific smile my way, and I lit up like a candle.

We chattered happily, as a group and in our little sub-sections. My father was anxious to tell us about the various barstool poets he knew in his local. One of them wrote poems that actually rhymed, which my dad pointed out was where modern verse had gone so horribly wrong, in his opinion. Con said that parts of the Bible were as poetic as anything by Keats or Shelley, and the *Song of Solomon* was positively racy, with breasts likened to two goats in the moonlight and suchlike. I told him that I'd look up some of the aforementioned, as part of my spiritual education. My father said to let him know if they were 'any good'.

We made for the Palace Bar on Fleet Street where both actors treated us to Flann O'Brien's tale of a man becoming a bicycle, the various frictions between man and bike swapping ions and atoms from one to the other. I looked at my dad and surmised that he would, in time, become a pint of Guinness, if this theory were to hold true. As for Con, he would be an angel; but then again, he was one already, so no change there. I linked them both in happiness, with a little help from the brewery.

My own literary background consisted of a steady diet of Enid Blyton in my early years, followed by Nancy

Drew and Cherry Ames, Student Nurse. In all of these, sleuthing was to the fore. Though there was an argument which said that what I really wanted was Nancy's perfectly coiffed red hair, and the yellow silk clothes which set her looks off so well. Nancy did more for the Ginger Brigade than she has ever been given credit for. I moved on to Harold Robbins as a teenager, which meant lots of steamy sex – perhaps it was time to return to him. We were force fed obscure Gaelic writers at school, and Mr William Shakespeare who, as every street scholar knows, was an Irishman in reality. There are still some counties in Ireland which speak his English. I pondered suggesting his inclusion in the Crawl to the lads.

As we crossed O'Connell Bridge, a sub-human howl announced Coleman's rendition of 'The Auld Triangle', à la Brendan Behan. The herd stopped in its tracks to savour the spectacle. As he strangled the jingles and the jangles of that triangle, my brain begged for mercy in my skull. Top marks for effort, close to zero points for artistic endeavour. When he was done we moved on, as did the curious throng of onlookers we had acquired. I looked into the murky waters of the Anna Livia Plurabelle for response, but she gave none, which was probably for the best.

There was something about our inexorable march northwards which was bugging me. I hadn't thought that the Crawl followed this route. We stopped outside the Abbey Theatre, where Barry gave us Yeats, telling us to tread softly for we trod on his dreams, then announcing

143

that our last port of call was the handily situated pub across the road. Well, of course it was; the two actors were now right beside their bus stop for home, and only steps away from a handy taxi rank, and all it had taken was a song and two extra poems to get in there. Coleman warned us of the perils of drink. 'It is both a carrot and a stick,' he said, and, laughing, we all trooped to an upstairs lounge devoid of other customers. More pints and chat filled the agenda, life stories were swapped, jokes told and travel anecdotes related.

In a lull, Mary Lou Pheiffer, of Pennsylvania, Illinois, stood up to share a moment with us. We hushed to silence, awaiting her gem. She cleared her throat, gave a short hum, then began reciting aloud:

> My wound will not heal
> Now.
> Though it must,
> In time.
> I am woman.
>
> Heal me, Moon.
> Heal me, Life.
> Heed me.
>
> A wound.
> I am wounded.
> A woman wounded.
> The wound unhealing,
> Until middle age.

She nodded and sat down. The silence was palpable, painful, as we weighed up our responses as individuals and as a group. I am sure Mary Lou thought it profound, and so it was, in a way.

Then my father's voice rang out, 'Now for you, hah? Mighty altogether. Good woman yourself.' The crowd gave an almost animal cry of relief. We clapped our hands rapturously, the applause as much for my dad and his rescue as Mary Lou and her art. She held her hand up in self-deprecation. 'I am a mere wordsmith,' she said. 'A drone.'

'And that is what this night is all about,' declared Coleman. 'On behalf of myself and my partner, Barry Agnew, I would like to thank you all for coming along, and do tell your friends all about us.'

He grabbed his drink and sat beside the two prettiest girls he could find. I watched with curiosity over the next twenty minutes as he tried, valiantly but in vain, to get off with either of them. He was clearly puzzled.

'What do you think the problem is there?' I asked Barry.

He began to laugh. 'We live in politically correct times, Leo. I don't think Coleman has copped to it yet, but when he called me his partner, the girls automatically assumed he meant it in a gay way. He won't do that again in a hurry.'

Of course Coleman without a lady friend meant Coleman en route to 11, The Villas, but I let it pass and savoured his increasingly desperate attempts to win the hearts of the young ladies. When those didn't work, he moved on to the other older models, to no avail, and eventually admitted defeat.

Con had to leave. 'I'm staying by the Pro Cathedral down the road with a worry wart who wouldn't give me a key to get in. I'd better set a good example and go.' He shrugged on his jacket and knocked back the last of his whiskey. 'Isn't it great to think that you can get spiritual sustenance in two such different public houses, and so close together?'

'When you put it that way,' agreed my dad. He lifted his glass in salutation for the umpteenth time that night. 'Con, we'll see you again soon, please God.'

'Please God,' said the priest. 'Leo, I'll phone you when I know about the transfer. Take care, and ease up on yourself the odd time. There are plenty of people who'll give you a hard time in life without any provocation, particularly Ciara if she's given her head.' We laughed at the truth of this. He smothered me in a bear hug, shook hands with Barry and Coleman, waved to the rest of the stragglers, and left.

'Time to go home time,' I announced.

'Better call the bollocks so,' my father said. This was a charming reference to his eldest son, my brother Peter, taxi man *extraordinaire*. On a deeper level it was a term of endearment on my father's part, but a stranger would be hard pressed to spot this. In exchange for a set fee, somewhat lower than the going rate, Peter would leave us home, and put up with a lot of old guff on the way. This makes him patron saint of the travelling Streets.

Although he was in the area, my dad still managed to

squeeze in that last pint for the road before Peter arrived. There was nothing back-seat about my father's driving; he planted himself up front in order to be of maximum annoyance to my brother on the journey. With John Street issuing orders, I could be certain of shedding Coleman at his own house, so the trip was pure pleasure for me. I interrupted my father's flow only to make sure that he knew precisely where we were dropping Coleman. And so we had the villainy of city publicans and the price they were charging for a pint, how the country had gone to the bad and the state of the roads was a national disgrace, and how all of this was basically down to every living taxi driver, but mostly my brother. The last twist of reasoning required to make that point work was non-existent, but my dad was happy with the sound of his own voice, and so were we.

I am a city girl. I like the look of Dublin day or night, with the exception of the anonymous modern obstructions so beloved of town planners these days. But when push comes to shove, I have to express a preference for the night-time town. Perhaps it's a penchant for neon and flashing lights. Whatever the reason, it is the time most conducive to my movie-like dreams and imaginings. It can also lull a person into a feeling that these are gentler hours, whereas of course the opposite is true. The cloak of darkness has shielded many bad deeds. Happily, I was not following any of the night's skulduggerers or duggerees, so I snuggled into Barry instead. His arm wound around me and he gave my shoulder a squeeze. I looked up at him and he kissed me lightly on the nose. I had a warm feeling in my groin as I smiled and looked back out of the window.

We were stopped at a traffic lights in Fairview, and I was giving the other cars the once over; some habits are hard to break. 'Isn't that bizarre?' I said.

'What is?' Peter asked.

'You remember Colette O'Brien who I went to school with? Well, I haven't seen her in years, but today I met her at the Model School when I was collecting the kids, then I saw her double in town tonight, and now there she is herself in that car in the opposite lane.' She was putting on a jacket, as it happened.

'I see her quite a bit at nights,' Peter said. 'I think she must have a job somewhere.'

We gave a short beep on the horn, but either she didn't hear or didn't recognise us, because we got no return signal.

I tried really hard not to show my merriment as Coleman loped up his driveway. I congratulated him on the evening's entertainment, but it did little to lift his spirits. It must have been a long time since he'd got home to his own house from the Crawl without a companion for his bed. Whenever he had been unsuccessful before, he would end up at mine, where he could talk shite till the cows came home, or more pertinently this cow, Leo Street. He played his moment at the door beautifully, allowing us time to admire his wry and tired unhappiness, above which he would undoubtedly rise. Then we were treated to a plucky wave of the hand, a jaunty jut of the chin and he was gone.

'Is that fella a bit of a half-wit?' my dad wanted to know.

'Nah,' I said. 'Things didn't work out the way he'd hoped tonight, that's all'

'Mmm,' my father grunted, unconvinced.

Barry and I were next to be decanted. There was an uncivilised spat about the fare, which my father 'won', leaving Peter the biggest loser.

'Call me tomorrow and we'll sort something out,' I told my brother. 'And try not to kill him before you get home.'

'Or after,' Barry added.

'Jesus, Mary and Joseph, am I ever goin' to get to me bed?' the Daddy barked. 'I swear to God I'd be quicker walkin'. Would you ever rev up and fuck off or they'll have search parties out for us.'

Peter threw his eyes to heaven and drove away.

'I really enjoyed tonight,' I said to Barry as we climbed the six wide steps to the house. I thought I might add those to the lottery list I'd been compiling. So far I had four, five, six, and why not eleven as it was now staring at me from the front door? Two more numbers to go and I was sorted and would never have to work again.

'Your dad was in great form,' Barry said, as much in wonderment as anything else. 'He didn't even have a go at me. He was way too busy paying attention or chatting with your friend Con.'

'You don't think he's finally accepted you?'

'No. Can't happen. Not possible. It's completely against all the rules of Fathers and How They Treat Their Daughters' Live-in Boyfriends.'

I had to concede this point.

'Those legs are doing something evil to me,' he said, running his hand along the outside of my thigh. As he pressed the evil something against my buttocks I opened the door and let us into the small hallway.

'Lucy says they're hose beast carry-on,' I told him.

'She's not wrong,' he murmured, as he kissed me, running his tongue along my teeth. We both tasted of beer and desire.

I came up for air. 'Hold that thought,' I said. 'I'll deal with any calls, then you'll have my undivided attention.'

He sped up the stairs, warning me that he wouldn't wait for ever.

I checked on the animals, who were all present and correct. There was some evidence of a light contretemps, but they were settled into an accord now, so I didn't make a fuss; I had other more urgent matters to attend to. I had just one phone message, from Ciara.

'Secret Agent Number One reporting to management. Boring night, in spite of the press coverage. Nothing that won't wait till tomorrow morning. Talk to you then.'

There didn't seem much in there to suggest that I lose sleep over work that night so I rushed to the bathroom and performed some quick ablutions, checking for spots in the mirror and giving all of my relevant pits a wipe of a fragrant cloth. Then it was my turn to take the stairs at a leap. I presented my breathless self at the bedroom door. Barry gave a lazy smile from the bed. I undressed slowly, keeping as many of the sticking-out parts of my body as possible out of sight. I climbed under the duvet, enjoying the warmth he had created. Then I moulded myself to his familiar shape and we enjoyed a lingering caress before he moved his kisses along my throat and downwards. I writhed in delicious agony. After two or three minutes his movements seemed to get slower and his breathing more regular, so I stopped a moment. It was then that I realised he had fallen asleep on my chest. I was pinned on my back, like a bug in a rug.

Twelve

I could not believe that the workmen were back on the road. They had spent so many weeks building the speed ramps, we thought we'd had our lifetime's share of grandification and would never see them again. Two jackhammers drilled incessantly and though I tried my best to ignore them, I finally gave in and opened my eyes to the realisation that the Kango hammers involved were myself and the still sleeping body pinning me to the mattress. My throat was raw from snoring. My sinuses were dry as the Sahara. It was 7.42 a.m. and my life was on pause, so I stared at the ceiling awhile. A stain in the shape of Australia was spreading from one corner to the rhythmic housetrack of Barry Agnew. What the hell were we doing together if our arrangement was clearly a matter of companionship now rather than romance?

Australia began to distort before my exhausted eyes, so I abandoned it for the sanctuary of the kitchen. I spent the journey down the stairs repeatedly reaching for the cord to tie my dressing gown, but it was nowhere to be found. I gave up and wafted about like a tragic Victorian heroine, though the eggy yellowness of the robe undercut the image somewhat.

The kitchen was a chorus of complaint. Top of the list was that No. 4 had decided Noel's basket was better than his own. Well, of course he had. I mean, where's the fun in sleeping in your own bed when you can do over a cat by stealing his? The radio told me that one hundred and eighty people had died in a train crash in India, Northern Ireland was in a fragile state, and two gay celebrities had been married in a ceremony in California to which I had not been invited. Michael O'Donoghue did not get a mention, nor did his clinic. Could media interest have died so soon? Perhaps. We live in a disposable world.

I nursed a cup of instant as I thought about the evening ahead. I had not been entirely honest with myself about my motives for going to Bridgecross. For instance, although there was a possibility that Michael O'Donoghue would attend, a much simpler way of finding out would be to phone his wife and ask her. Mick Nolan was revving up a head of steam over that, so I explained that I would have to go now, one way or another, as I had made a commitment to Andy.

'I don't give a shite what you do in your private life,' he told me. 'Though you'd want to sort yourself out there, if you ask me.'

'Which I don't,' I replied, tartly.

'Oh, grow up,' was all he had to say to that.

I've never liked the word 'proactive'. I suppose it

conjures up images of life as a magazine article for me, with pumpy-jumpy phrases like 'strategy not stress'. But for all that, I thought I'd give it a go. And so I quickly fed the brood, showered and dressed, told Barry to go take a running jump when he asked for a cup of tea, and abandoned the car at 8.53 a.m. outside Mullaney Motors, with a note on the windscreen saying 'Fix this or else', and the keys in the letter box. Then I walked the rest of the way into town with my jolly canine companion, the inimitable No. 4.

We played a little game on the way. I tried to give him a new name, and he let me know which ones he liked, without committing himself to a choice. Top of the list were Englebert, Abelard and Tootsie, but the clear winner as we crossed the Ha'penny Bridge into Temple Bar was still No. 4. I was delighted to pass through various empty streets and small squares; I have an irrational irritation with people who insist on having their double-latte-espresso-hatchback-over-easy outdoors in the freezing cold, or the sort of light drizzle that drenches a person to the bone within forty seconds. We don't have the weather for a café culture, so let's just give in on that one, shall we?

I knew immediately that something was wrong at the Indigent Sweeps' place. It was in the air. I sniffed again and again to be sure. Normally, I would have been assaulted by the intermingled aromas of brewing coffee from the other offices, Piss Lite from the drunks who urinate against the outside wall when they can't make it to the next pub or club along the route, and the vague suggestion of Domestos courtesy of Mrs Mack. Yesterday I had spotted a brown streak on one of the walls, the origin of which I was loath to identify, but now it was gone. And the air was filled with a tangy, citrus odour which was downright pleasant. Someone had obviously broken in during the night and cleaned the building. What kind of conscientious, positive, breaking-and-entering was this? What splendid rehabilitation would lead a criminal to leave only good behind? Or, the most unlikely of scenarios, had Mrs Mack finally lost it and done her job? Her voice summoned me from on high; today it was a strange, happy falsetto. I was very afraid.

Kevin Mack was the reason for the glories manifest in our world. He was a small ball of a man, with a gleaming pate unadorned by more than the lightest burr of fuzz, and three actual hairs carefully plastered from one side of his head, over the top, to the other. He had an easy smile and happy brown eyes with which he delighted me as he handed over a mug of scalding tar and a digestive biscuit. It was enough to make a girl fall in love.

'I won't be a patch on herself, but she's put me on duty while she's away so I'll do my best,' he said, as he turned his adoring orbs on his wife. She was enthroned on a tall stool by the door of her tearoom, from whence she could check on her empire without any hindrance. 'It's a bit like learning to drive,' he went on. 'She believes in putting you in the hot seat from day one, so you can learn the proper way.'

'I'll bet,' I managed.

'And I keep reminding her that she'll have to tell all her sins, because it's a pilgrimage she's goin' on.'

'Stop it, Kevin, you have me all mortified in front of Miss Street. He's an awful man altogether.'

Oh, to be a fly on the wall of that confessional. Most of Mrs Mack's sins were those of omission, I guessed. Like omitting to do her job. Which in its way led to a charge of theft, or at least taking money under false pretences, i.e. her wages. But who was I to pass judgement? False pretence was second nature to me, and I often dealt a half-truth if I thought it would net me some information or release off a pointy hook. And while I was at it, hadn't I sent Ciara straight out into the field on her first day? Were we so different, Mrs Mack and I? I didn't want to answer that question, it was enough that it existed at all, so I gave myself a metaphorical shake by the scruff of the neck and cleared it away.

'There's a problem with the loo on your floor,' Mrs Mack told me. It was clear that I was to blame, in her books, for whatever aberration had caused this. 'The smell is only dreadful, isn't it, Kevin?' Again she looked the look which told me she knew what I was up to, and I would be dealt with accordingly.

'I'll have a butcher's later,' her husband said.

If it was left to the female of the Mack species, I would be found stultified by poisonous gases at my desk long before remedial action was taken by her fair beige hands.

'Thank you,' I said, meaning it.

Mrs Mack looked at her watch in an extravagant gesture. 'I'll take myself off to the Bureau de Change,' she announced pointedly.

'I'm glad you mentioned that,' I said, fiddling in my bag. I handed her an envelope. 'Get yourself something nice.' Inside was a twenty-pound note, which I hoped was enough of a tribute.

'Ah now, Miss Street, you *shouldn't* have,' she protested, putting one hand on her sternum to show how touched she was, while the other claw whipped the offering from me in double-quick time.

'Do you know, it's amazing how many people have been in to do the same thing this morning already,' her husband said. 'They all know what a treasure you are,' he told her.

Not for the first time I regretted shelving my first plan, which was to put a tea bag in the envelope, seal it and write on the outside, 'Have a drink on me'. Hindsight, you know? As always, it was about as useful as a pain in the eyeball. Ah, well, next time. In my dreams.

The stairwell did indeed fill with pungent air the higher I climbed. By the time I reached my office I had almost become accustomed to the overwhelming smell of fart. Almost. I unlocked the door, reached for an aerosol I keep for such emergencies, gave five generous sprays of 'Spring Meadow' and spent the next fifteen minutes sneezing.

When my sinuses clogged up and my breathing

became less emphysematic, I dialled the O'Donoghue household and was answered on the third ring.

'Yes, we'll both be attending the Bridgecross function this evening,' Miranda told me, in a tone that suggested I was a complete cretin not to know that.

'Sorry to have bothered you,' I said, in my own pissed-off tone, which wasn't half bad, if I may say so.

There was a minuscule pause, then she returned, 'I apologise for snapping. Michael did not come home until 12.30 last night, and we spent twenty minutes bickering before I went to the spare room for a sleepless night. But of course you'll probably know that already.'

Caught red-handed, Leo? Time for evasive action.

'You did promise to forward me his mobile phone bills, but I haven't yet received them.' Ball back in your court, Miranda.

'That is proving a little more difficult than I first anticipated,' she said, coolly. 'I am working on the situation.'

I've heard as many lies as truths in my time as a PI. My gut feeling here was that Miranda had just told a porky, or at least exaggerated the 'situation', as she so economically put it. Two could play at that game, and, believe me, when it comes to lies I can tell as good as I hear. It is not something that I am proud of.

'I'll be presenting an update shortly,' I glossed. 'And then we can assess what's best to do.' This was just meaningless jargon, but I felt I had to improvise, be seen to be doing something and so on. 'Now, if you'll excuse me, I have a call to take.'

Another casual juggling of the truth, and why? Because I did not want her to lose confidence in me. I needed the money and I needed to finish this job. I calmed my racing heart and looked around for something to do with myself. I ran my fingers along the desk and realised that it was dust-free. My office had been cleaned. I took this to be a majorly good omen.

Maeve had faxed through a list of companies which might have her home number. My initial thought was that this phone stalker was someone who knew her or had met her. I discounted the staff at the electricity and gas supply boards, because there are a lot of people with the name Maeve Kelly in Ireland, and when you see it on a bland form, there is no reason to believe that it is one of our finest actresses. If I had to I would return to them as suspects, but something told me to look elsewhere first. That left a list including her local Chinese and Indian takeaways, a hairdresser, a video store, a dentist, a doctor and two taxi firms, one of which my brother worked for. She had also jotted down the following: 'I've only just switched to Northways Taxis, because the previous lot had become so unreliable. I can't be certain, but I think the calls started before the switch, so I doubt it's anyone there (Northways). I've been with all the others, doctor, takeaways, etc. for years.'

Perhaps, perhaps, perhaps, I thought.

My plan, such as it was, was to frighten the life out of some, or all, of the companies on my short list to see if that produced any change in the pattern.

The office telephone rang with a soft electronic burr. I grabbed the receiver and chimed, 'Leo Street's office. What can I do for you?'

You really can't buy that sort of training.

A whispering voice said, 'My name is Tara O'Donoghue.' There was a pause, and if it was for effect, it worked. I sat up smartly in my seat and gave encouragement to Miranda and Michael's eldest child.

'Yes?' I ventured.

'I know you're involved in, like, *things*.'

'Yes?' I repeated, for good measure. '*Things*' were still a little vague for me to commit myself or break client privilege.

Throat clearing on the line suggested a mild fluster. Then she continued, 'Ehm, I might be able to shed some light on, well, *things*. But I can't talk now, so I'd like to come in to the office tomorrow afternoon.'

'Of course, Tara,' I said. 'Can you tell me a little more about what it is you want to discuss?'

She made an indiscriminate noise which sounded like 'feckit', then added, 'Look, I think I know who's been threatening my dad.'

I was hooked, complete with line and sinker. I gave her a time and a place to be the following day.

It's not good to wish your life away, according to my gran. I was now torn between a desire for tomorrow's meeting with Tara O'Donoghue and her intriguing information, and the expectation of a night out with Andy Raynor. And stuck there in the middle of the two was a need to get to work on tracking down Maeve's caller, which required a lot more time than I had available today. I felt helpless and inactive. I could not hurry events along, which left me feeling incapacitated and plain useless, to be honest.

I was scratching my head and feeling sorry for myself when I realised that I had no transport to deliver my bread order to Maeve's mum or to collect the kids after school. Mick Nolan began to laugh behind me; he is such a wise ass. I kept my poise, no way was I going to display weakness in front of him. 'Not a problem,' I said aloud. No. 4 looked up from his activities. I had made him a special ball to play with earlier on. Now it resembled a paper recycling kit, with shreds of the newspaper I'd used strewn across the length of the floor. No wonder he had been so quiet and content. I allowed myself one shallow sigh before scooping up as much of the mess as I could with my hands; I'm no vacuum cleaner, but it made some difference to the geography of the linoleum. Not a lot, but some. The dog found the exercise a real whizz, chasing between my legs, and even once climbing on to my back with a happy bark as I bent over his morning's work. I sat back at my desk, rubbed a furrowed brow and called Angela to arrange to pick up her tank for the afternoon's delights. Nearly back on track, I thought.

'Your face is covered in black streaks,' said the girl in the doorway.

'Jesus, Ciara, did you leave the house like that?'

'Don't be ridiculous. Mum was out, so I was safe enough. Ronan saw me, but he wouldn't dare squeal; I took some of his lecture notes hostage, and he knows I'll burn them if he says a word. What's with the camouflage?'

'It's a by-product of a perfect morning,' I explained.

Ciara was dressed as every parent's dream. She wore a pale pink shirt, buttoned to the top, faded but respectable blue jeans, and a navy jacket. Her hair was freshly washed and swept off her impish face where her jolly freckles sparkled. You might almost have thought her harmless.

'I need to type up my report,' she said, throwing the case file on the desk. 'Not that it's scintillating.'

'We're saving the world next week,' I said. 'That should liven things up a bit.'

'Yeah, I'll be looking forward to that. What have you been up to, now that you're one of the bourgeois leisured class?'

'Well, since I saw you last, I kidnapped two children, then went on a pub crawl with my father, my boyfriend and a priest.'

'You are such a pervert, do you know that? Saw you at the Fledgling, by the way. Pity there wasn't a riot, it could really have done with one. A few of the journos tried to give chase to Michael O'Donoghue when he was leaving, but it was all a bit half-hearted. I was the only one who stuck with him – lazy bunch of fecks.'

'So, tell me in a nutshell what I'll be reading in this report of yours?'

Ciara flopped into the old armchair and propped her feet up on the desk.

'The most interesting thing about yesterday is that I think I'm being followed,' she said.

Even No. 4's ears perked up.

Thirteen

Most people do not expect to be shadowed, unless they are a politician or a movie star with a shady past, present and possibly future, in which case a hounding Press Pack is *de rigueur*. It's one of the reasons a PI is ahead from the start. We have the advantage because we're not generally considered to exist by the public at large. And unless your subject is suspicious and trained, or very, very perceptive, you should go unnoticed. So maybe Ciara was just being paranoid. I said as much, but she was steadfast.

'No, I tried a few evasions, but the car stuck.'

'Car?'

'Yeah. I couldn't get it to come close enough to read the registration or get a make, but it's grey, a metallic grey. Nice saloon shape, for all the good that is to us. If it's around after me today, I'll try again to get it to come nearer.'

'But who would want to follow you?'

'I've been thinking about that. And I wonder if it's me or Michael O'Donoghue who's being followed.'

'Good point,' I conceded. I liked the way she was

operating here, nice lateral thinking.

'For instance, I wasn't followed from home to here this morning. So maybe it's him who's got the fan and not me.' Solid, logical analysis.

'Are you good at cryptic crosswords?' I asked.

'Yeah.'

'Thought so.'

'Why?'

'No reason, just testing a theory.'

'Anyhow, he had what I gathered from you was a normal enough day, apart from making the national news. He had his surgery, did his rounds in the hospital, and for all I know delivered a few babies. He's so boring he probably plans when his patients have them. When he dodged the journalists, he doubled back to his office for a few hours, though he wouldn't have had any patients then. Perhaps he was catching up on paperwork.'

'Or reading a novel,' I offered, warning lightly against making assumptions.

'Or having a wank. Who knows?'

I lifted a hand to indicate that we would go no further down that road.

She laughed. 'A pervert *and* stuffy all at once.'

'Meaning?'

'I'm not the one who was out with a priest last night.'

'It wasn't a priest,' I said nonsensically. 'It was Con.'

'Bitch! Why didn't you tell me? I'd have loved to have seen him. How is the big fatty anyway?' She took her feet off the desk in agitation, and leaned forward for more information.

'He's fine, possibly relocating to Dublin, I'll tell you later when you've finished your oral and written reports.'

'Jeez, hang on to your knickers. You can be really uptight sometimes.'

'There is a woman out there paying for our time, not our gossip.'

Even I knew I was being unbearably prim, but a little discipline in Ciara's life would not go amiss. 'Or in your own,' said sly old Mick Nolan.

Kevin Mack appeared at the door, prepared for battle. He held a giant plunger in hands decked out in black, industrial-strength rubber gloves. The rest of his body was encased in white overalls, not unlike a forensics suit.

'I'm just off to see to that toilet,' he said. 'If I'm not back by next Tuesday, send in the cavalry.'

Ciara looked quizzically in my direction. 'The new cleaner,' I revealed. 'And now a member of the Cisterncian Order.'

Ciara groaned, and who could blame her? 'You can tell you've been out with Father Punmeister Considine,' she said, shaking her head sadly. She swung her legs up on to my desk again. With ease. She had long limbs, and with that the height to go legit, should she choose to accept it.

I was too short to be a cop. Butty, weenchy, vertically challenged, squat; whatever description you like. So I fell into the world of the PI courtesy of Mick Nolan, ex-the Force. He took me apart and reassembled me as the Private Detective Leo Street. Eventually, he threw me out. On the occasion of his death, as it happens. And on my bad days I long for a badge, or even a uniform, and the official length and breadth to go after the baddies and make the world a better place. In essence, I sometimes want the Force to be with me, because on top of everything else, when they're against you, you're in deep shit.

Ciara flicked through a notebook with a spiral wire through the top, looking for all the world like a cub journalist.

'I'll type all this up for you,' she said. 'But the pertinent points are: he headed out to his fitness club at 7 p.m. then at 8.30, looking all squeaky clean and shiny, he set off for Bernie Flood's house in Raheny, on Dublin's less fashionable north side.' She checked me with cheeky eyes over the top of her notes. I gave the tiniest of smiles and she continued. 'They were arguing any of the time I could hear them. I caught phrases like 'stay away from me' and 'you won't rest till you've destroyed us all' from Bernie. Oh, and one 'stay away from her', too, but I'm not sure who that referred to. He did a bit of the 'you're an unreasonable woman' and at one point burst out with 'of course I know what's bloody well best', but they moved off again to a back room and I couldn't hear the rest. She didn't see him to the door at 9.30 p.m., which was in keeping with the tone of things between them. He drove home via the Bridgecross Sport and Social Club, where I observed him have a quiet drink with some of his mates. Then he went home, without passing go or collecting any money, and was safely ensconced in Sea View, Booterstown, by 10.45.'

'How did he get in?'

Ciara was clearly puzzled by my line of questioning. 'The lady of the house heard his car and had the door open by the time he'd parked. In he went, home sweet home.'

'It would be,' I said, 'except that's not where he lives. Michael O'Donoghue lives at Sea Point, Blackrock, ten minutes further down the road.'

'Shite!'

We all have to make that first mistake. Ciara's was an understandable one: two similar addresses only moments apart by road. She was also not as familiar with the case as I was, and could not be expected to grasp every little detail on day one. My job here, however, was to give her a good bollocking to teach her a lesson. Or so the gospel according to Mick Nolan went. I remember that he used the words 'shoddy', 'incompetent', 'unreliable', 'amateur' and 'waste of space' on the occasion of my first tongue lashing from him. Well, those were the words from his opening sentence, others followed, one borrowing another, until I was on the verge of tears. I would not cry in front of him, not because of pride, though I wish it had been: I knew he'd fire me on the spot if I cracked. It was one of my first tests, and even Hercules did not have to endure

as many as I did. Mick added to his tirade on each
subsequent roasting, and it was a formidable oration to
behold or endure. Oh, and I didn't need to fuck up to
deserve it, any old occasion would serve, one size fitted
all.

'What do you intend to do about this little turn of
events?' I asked Ciara, who, it must be admitted, was
pink with rage at herself. Or at least I can't believe that
it was embarrassment, she doesn't hold truck with that.

'I'm going back out there to find out who the hell he
went to see.'

'Correct,' I acknowledged. 'I know I shouldn't do this,
but I'll tell you that he did get to his proper home. At
12.30.'

How do you know that?'

'Never mind. I do, that's all. I am a detective, you
know.'

We let that hang in the air for a moment. Ciara
digested it and prepared to bounce back.

'Given journey times, he would have spent just over
an hour and a half in this house,' I said. Ciara nodded.
'Unless . . .' I continued.

'Unless he went somewhere else.' She put her head in
her hands momentarily. 'I was so sure I had put him to
bed,' she said.

'And perhaps you did. But whose bed was it?'

Ciara had a way with words. 'Fuck, fuck, fuck,' she
said.

★ ★ ★

I was no angel in all of this, so I came clean on the details I'd omitted to mention when I hired her.

'Death threats?' Ciara repeated.

'Yes, and the weird thing is that his wife doesn't seem to think this is unusual, or even relevant to what we're working on. She was positively dismissive about them. There is something decidedly strange about the whole set-up. I wonder if there are other details she's not sharing with us. And I don't want to put either of us in danger. We're not being paid enough for that.

I could have added a 'certainly' to the last statement because we were, in effect, sharing one wage then.

'Don't worry about me,' Ciara said. 'I thrive on the edge.'

'Ciara, I'm serious.'

'So am I,' she said.

I made a resigned noise. 'Just be extra careful. Now that the Fledgling is under scrutiny, things could get very mucky. If you feel, at any time, that you're not in control, back off. It's not worth getting hurt over.'

'Yes, boss.'

'For what it's worth, I'll be attending the same function as Michael O'Donoghue and his wife tonight,' I said. 'It would be best if you watched from outside in case he tries to sneak away. I'll keep an eye on him inside.'

'Why do I feel that I've got the rum end of this deal?' she asked.

'Because, as you've so rightly pointed out, I am the boss, and what I say goes. And as of now that's you.

Clear up your mess. Find out who he went to see last night. I don't want to hear from you until it's sorted. Goodbye.'

I got up and opened the door to show her out. 'Vamoose, scram, skedaddle, go.'

She left.

The hallway resounded to the flushing of a toilet. As one echo died, another flush took its place, and then another. The air smelled high, but I thought I detected an improvement. I secretly prayed for Mrs Mack to stay on her pilgrimage as long as the Knights Templar had on the Crusades. Perhaps I should have given her more money.

It was lucky that I turned back to my office at that moment, because I encountered a happy creature leaving with a package which I recognised as one of the loaves I had baked for Maeve's mum. I gave chase. This was dog heaven for No. 4 as he dodged in and out of the legs of the furniture. I ducked one way then the other, trying to trap him on open ground, but he was too wily. Eventually I got down on all fours and tried approaching him on his level. He still had the advantage. But ego was his downfall. Cockily, he came closer and closer on each of his forays, and eventually I got a hand to his collar. He let the package fall. By now I had manoeuvered myself into a coil around the front of my desk with my arse pointing towards the door. Kevin Mack reappeared. I could see him through my legs, in an upside-down way. I could not move. If I let go of No. 4 he would escape with the loaf again. If I stayed as I was, every story Mrs Mack had no doubt told him of my eccentricities would be borne out. I had a vision of her as Beelzebub on one side of me, and the deep blue sea on the other. I stayed put.

'I see you're busy,' he said. 'I just wanted to let you know that I've freed up the system. This was the culprit.' The red knitted glove was all too familiar. I didn't think it would help my standing in his eyes if I admitted ownership, particularly as we were conducting this conversation in less than ideal circumstances for me. 'Good for you,' I squeezed out. 'And thanks again.'

He loitered a little. 'Can I help at all?' he asked.

'No, no, everything under control,' I said. ''Bye now.'

As he closed the door behind him, I let go of the dog's collar and lunged for the bread. I won, but No. 4 was a close second, and had a piece of wrapping paper stuck to his upper lip to prove it. As I struggled from the floor he slurped a wet lick across my face, and left the torn shred flapping on my cheek.

Closer inspection revealed that the dog had not drooled too heavily on the merchandise, and the wrapping had performed beautifully as a barrier. Neither were there any teeth marks. 'You were *this* close to visiting the vet,' I warned him, holding my thumb and forefinger together. He jumped up and down at the news. There are times when I think that no one is listening to a word I say.

I re-wrapped the loaves and packed them into a basket with a few other sundries from my life. Then I tethered the dog, locked up for the day and made my bid for freedom. Mr Mack had nailed the red glove to a notice board on the ground floor. It was looking very sorry for itself, as any object removed from a blocked loo would. He had rinsed it, which was a small mercy. I wondered again about how it had made its unscheduled journey. I was not in the habit of wearing gloves, knitted or otherwise, for my visits to the bathroom, although the building can get very parky in bad weather. Toilet finger wear is not one of my fashion fetishes, though I'm not condemning it in any way; we all need our crutches to deal with life. Now, as the sorry red item hung exhausted from the board, I knew that I would have to remove its partner from the office under cover of darkness and dispose of it in a humane way. If Mrs Mack could pin the sewage crime on me, my life would go down the toilet in the very same manner as the ill-fated glove.

You have to wonder about taxi drivers, don't you? Are they really a microcosm of society? Are they a representative barometer of the way a country is feeling? And where do they get off with the idea that because you are captive in their car, a privilege you are paying for, they have every right to force their opinions on you? Eh, sorry, I'll pass on the special offer of free advice with every journey, thanks all the same.

I am usually careful not to complain too much as I am genetically tied to a taxi driver, my brother Peter.

Through him, I know not to ask stupid questions like 'Are you busy?' or 'What time are you on until?' Unless I deliberately want to annoy the driver, in which case great sport can be had. My hired hackney today was of the opinion that young people had gone to Hades in a handcart, and that too much zinc in the water was probably what had tipped them over the edge. And how were we to know what the government or other brigands were putting into the water supply anyhow? Fluoride was a villain, but zinc was just the worst of all bad things. And as for recycled effluent, that was worse than heroin. Without any warning, he started in on women. 'And as for the feminists,' he began. My annoyance meter was pointing way off the scale now. 'The feminazis, that's what I call them. Feckin' feminazis.' He gave a throaty chuckle, which only exacerbated how pissed off I had become. In retaliation, I found out that business was quiet and his shift finished at eight that evening, but he'd prefer to be working nights, because there was more money going around then. And that the cab was not his, he was cosying, because the price of a taxi plate had gone to hell in the same handcart as every young person in Ireland. I wanted to torture him more with talk of how brilliant it was that the government were issuing loads of new taxi licences, and that we would be awash with choice, but he had worn me down to a frazzle of my former self. I definitely preferred the quiet type who, by his very silence, had the ability to make you feel that you were worthless crud on the backside of humanity; that, I could relate to.

He started up a new whine about the evils of television. His voice had a strange frequency, annoying to all mammals, I guessed, and possibly injurious after prolonged exposure. 'It's all murders now,' he was saying. 'Of course in my day we only had the one channel.'

'That was murder enough,' I acknowledged.

By the time we reached Angela's even the dog was fed up with the incessant, nasal drone. In fact, he had started to bark any time the man opened his mouth in order to drown out the useless information spewing forth. If my dad wanted a taxi driver to call a bollocks, he should meet this guy and lay off Peter. I paid our fare and was treated to a homily on canine behavioural problems. There was a moment of danger when I thought I might burst, so I said, 'Shut *up*,' a little too loudly, and they both did. I was smiling by the time we got to the front door.

Angela stood, bleary-eyed, in the middle of chaos.

'The kids re-enacted the bombing of Dresden this morning before school,' she said. 'They won, of course. I fell asleep in the middle of clearing the mess up. Just nodded off on the floor. I sometimes feel that I'll never know a proper rest again.' Her hand reached up and scratched her scalp, distractedly. 'The big question is, where did I leave the car keys?'

For no logical reason, we found them in the fridge.

Fourteen

Maeve's family lived in Howth, a chichi peninsula further along the northern coastline of Dublin. It was, and still is, richly populated by the rich. Harvey, Maeve's dad, had made his money in packaging, and her mother, Sandra, was a retired nurse. They had a large, detached house with rambling gardens on the hill, overlooking the harbour. The view was a tranquil picture of two promenades embracing moored boats in the safety of their curved arms, and beyond, the Irish Sea. When they first viewed the property, Sandra had remarked she felt like she'd been there before. After the purchase was complete, a sign with the house name was hung on the front wall. It read 'Déjà View'.

Howth was sparkling in the gentle glow of the April sun, which is to say that the weather was mild. I recalled a summer's day I had spent here with Andy Raynor many years before. It was unremarkable by way or event, but it was one of the happiest of my teenage years. We walked and argued and ate ice creams, and laughed at the antics of various landlubbers as they struggled with their rudders and masts, and lay out on the hill looking at the clouds and enjoying the oneness of being together. Later, he put his arm around me and saw me to my door. Then he played havoc with my hormones and my underwear, and I was so happy that I nearly burst into tears. I did far too much crying then, and do far too much of it now. Things must change, I said to myself.

I crunched the tank to a halt on the gravel to the back of the house. A lurcher and a cocker spaniel came to investigate. There was much bum-sniffing before they decided that No. 4 was a jolly good type. Then I turned him loose to play with them. At this juncture he had more friends in Dublin than I did.

Sandra Kelly appeared, a vision in Ghost and Bruno Magli, enveloped by Chanel No. 19, and wearing the beatific smile of a contented woman. I felt another lottery number coming on: now I had 4, 5, 6, 11, 19, with just one more to find to win that jackpot. Then I too would dress beautifully and be calm in the bestowing of my largesse. She was carrying a Campari and freshly squeezed orange juice.

'Leo, you're very good to take on this latest task. And to deliver in person.'

'Not at all,' I told her. 'I'm always glad of a pleasant job and a nice drive.' I popped my basket on to the huge pine table that was the centrepiece of the kitchen. 'I've done you three loaves: a dark stout bread, which is delicious with some butter and cheese, a tomato with a crisp crust of fennel and sea salt, and an orange brioche for those ladies with a sweet tooth.' I felt unbearably proud of my work as I unwrapped it and enjoyed her obvious pleasure. I desperately wanted someone to take my picture as she paid me, but I affected an air of nonchalance, as if this were an everyday occurrence. Inside, I was churning.

Sandra Kelly did not smoke, and from a quick perusal of her wine selection, she drank only the best. Her face was remarkably unlined, a combination of quality skin-care products and an optimistic attitude to life. She was lean, but in a way that suggested good genes were responsible rather than constant dieting. Her elegance was a manifestation of pure class. If Sandra was an older version of her daughter, Maeve Kelly had a lot to look forward to.

'Is today a special occasion?' I asked.

'Yes and no,' she replied. 'It's a sort of reunion of some of the girls I used to work with.'

I wondered what the collective for nurses was, retired or active. On this occasion I thought it might be 'a feast'.

'Maybe you know someone I'm interested in,' I said, an idea forming in my head. It was a long shot, but I asked, 'Did you ever come across Michael O'Donoghue, the obstetrician?'

'Oh, yes,' she replied. 'He seems to be in a bit of a pickle, doesn't he? I can't say that I'm too surprised. He's had a fine reputation, I suppose, until now, but none of us ever liked having to deal with him. He was arrogant, a bit of a bully. Liked to rule the roost. Of course, that was years ago, when he was new on the scene and thought he knew everything. If the newspaper reports are anything to go by, his years in practice haven't chastened him. To be honest, I always thought him a little dangerous. He never heeded anyone's advice but his own. Had what we would call a God Complex.'

Ciara had overheard the phrase 'of course I know what's bloody well best' at the Flood house. And newspaper coverage of his writings and speeches made it clear that O'Donoghue felt he was a Saviour of Medicine and Mankind. Was this why his wife did not find it unusual that he would receive hate mail?

'I never did see the attraction in him,' Sandra Kelly continued. 'He dated quite a few of our batch; not me, I'm happy to say. Some of the others were completely smitten, though, and fell badly for him. He was a heartbreaker. A lab technician called Miranda, I think it was, got him in the end, and she was welcome to him.'

I felt I couldn't pump Mrs Kelly any more than I had without raising her suspicions, so I pocketed my money and my information, and felt absurdly successful. Driving back to the main road with No. 4, I pondered the notion of Michael O'Donoghue as manipulator, and wondered how that sat with a wife who was all edge. As I did, a metallic grey saloon passed the tank, and edged into the Kelly driveway. 'This town is only just big enough for the lot of us,' I told the dog, happily, as I jotted down the registration number. The car was driven by Mrs Bernadette Flood. I continued my journey back into the city centre with a satisfied hum in my craw. The building blocks were mounting one on the other.

★ ★ ★

Mick Nolan had had no room for passengers, or so the official line had gone. He did, however, have two sons, Jimmy and Jack, both of whom were vicariously blessed with their father's looks and their mother's brains – meaning they looked like cops but acted like airheads. Along with myself, they were trained by Mick to be Dublin's brightest and best. In the trade they were known as Dumb and Dumber. When Mick had died suddenly, of a bad bunker shot on the back nine of a golf course, I was surplus to company requirements and shed forthwith. I believe that Mick had it all planned, principally because he needed a change of scenery and could not bear to be in that office any longer. It was drastic action, undoubtedly, but once he made his mind up, that was it. He moved with me.

His son Jimmy was now standing in the yard of the Model School, casually posing with his hands in the pockets of his khaki raincoat. His thick, black hair was neatly parted to the side and slicked down with gel. His rosy cheeks matched the full red of his overblown, moist lips. He had overly long eyelashes for a man. If Central Casting had sent out their choice for the part of Paedophile No. 1 in the last television thriller, Jimmy would have been it. The sense of a lynch mob gathering amongst the waiting mothers and fathers was even greater than yesterday. I went to his side.

'Jimmy,' I acknowledged.

'Leo,' he said, without looking at me or moving his bow-lipped mouth.

'So you're on the Carmel Lally case?' I commented.

Now I had his undivided attention.

'How did you know that?' he gasped, forgetting to close his mouth when he finished the question.

I reached over and reattached his chin to the rest of his face. 'I'm a detective, remember?'

'You're not on the case too, are you?' he asked, his eyes narrowing suspiciously.

'That would be telling,' I said. 'Let's just say that I have a healthy interest in this one.'

He coughed into his hand and glanced around the playground, looking shiftier by the minute.

'I don't mean to be rude,' he whispered, 'but you're ruining my cover here. You're, you know, kinda drawing attention to me.'

'Jimmy, you fucking pillock,' I explained, 'I'm drawing attention *away* from you.'

'Leo, now is no time to get jealous. I'm just doing my job, you know?'

'Jimmy,' I said, summoning up imaginary reserves of patience, 'you are a strange man, alone in a children's play area, wearing a dirty mac and looking like you just got out of prison. How much more attention do you think you could draw to yourself?'

'Leo, everyone here thinks I'm just another dad waiting for his kids,' he explained, just as patiently.

'Right,' I said. 'You're on your own.'

I've always found close encounters with the Nolan boys unsettling. They look like their father, even speak like him, but they are fundamentally different from him. It's as if they are a shell of him. They are as close to proof as you'll get that *Invasion of the Body Snatchers* is not a work of the imagination.

Funnily enough, Mick had nothing to say about any of this.

'Do you know that weirdo?' Colette O'Brien asked as I joined her and Lisa Farrelly on what I now assumed to be their regular spot.

'He's nothing to worry about,' I said, wondering if this was the truth.

When the kids emerged on to the concrete heaven they had a letter addressed to each household. It said that a formal insurance claim had been lodged against the crêche, and that the nursery was now in danger of closing. With her strings pulled by the malignant Gods and all the Fates, Carmel Lally chose that moment to appear at the gates. Suddenly shouts of 'Bitch!' and worse, filled the air, along with adjectives to elaborate the general mood of the crowd. I turned to my friends and saw that their faces were as twisted in anger as any of the others. Suddenly the Model School was a very nasty place. I grabbed Mary and Dominick and made for the exit.

'Who's the little blonde you were talking to?' Jimmy Nolan asked as I passed. 'The one with the mean eyes.'

'Lisa Farrelly,' I replied. 'Why do you ask?'

'She let the air out of Carmel Lally's tyres earlier,' he replied. 'And what about the other one?'

'That's Colette O'Brien. Why?'

'Oh, no reason,' he said. 'Just keeping an eye. You know.'

If he was trying to bug me, he had succeeded. And not for the first time. I had experience of Jimmy being enigmatic, as he saw it, and it never involved enigma. Other times he might blab away, parting with all sorts of information without realising it. Which was not to call him a *naif savant*, or indeed an *idiot savant*; lose the *savant* and you get the general idea.

Jimmy tried to move off, but had difficulty with the manoeuvre. He gave a puzzled tug, and pulled his foot away, revealing a large gob of Wrigley's on the tarmac. 'Gum shoe,' I said, with some satisfaction, and much accuracy.

A problem shared is supposed to be a problem halved. In the case of Jimmy and Jack, it was a double trouble. They worked together, which meant that Jack was probably on nights, shambling about after Carmel Lally. Even if she didn't spot them, the Nolans had a way of making their subjects feel oddly wary; must have been an electrical charge they left in the air. Well, now they were back in my life, like it or not. I bundled the children into the car and took off.

'Leo,' Dominick was saying, 'you know we are all an animal?'

'Mmn, yeah,' I agreed. You never knew where this might go.

'Dominick, just because we eat bananas doesn't mean we're monkeys,' his sister pointed out, with nice deductive reasoning.

'No,' he conceded. 'But when a monkey does eat a banana he does do a poo. And so do we.'

They both shrieked with laughter, then repeated the word 'poo' a dozen times. I found myself admiring their abstract subjunctive, or whatever it was, and lamenting the day that they would shed it, in the interests of grammar, of which there is none any more if you believed arts programmes on the radio, or read any of the tabloids. I was experiencing a short-lived regret, as it happened.

'Leo, you are a poo head,' Dom told me.

Then we had a chorus of 'poo head'. No. 4 looked at me as if he thought I'd lost the plot altogether. When I analysed what they were saying, I realised why. Basically, the kids were calling me a shit head. Lovely. And grammar or no grammar this was not a joke. Which is not to dispute the truth or fiction of the statement.

I put a halt to the insults. Mary tried to make friends again.

'Leo,' she said. 'I did have a dream last night. I was up in the clouds and then I did reach into one of them and I was very happy.'

'Good for you,' I said, softening. 'How about you, Dominick?'

'I was a monkey and I did eat a banana and . . .'

'Right, right,' I said cutting him off. 'I think we can see where that story is going.'

'Your mother wants to know if you've got something nice to wear tonight,' Angela told me, as we nursed a coffee. She had given the children banana sandwiches for tea, and I found it a little disconcerting to watch them eat. They, in turn, rained angelic smiles upon me.

'I rooted out a decentish frock,' I replied as coolly as was possible under the circumstances.

'Thought so,' she said. 'It's one of the two you keep festering in your wardrobe, isn't it? Wait there.'

Angela was gone for two and a half minutes, which was precisely enough time for Rose to sick up on my black jumper. She was beaming at the acidic curdle when I looked, and Rose seemed pleased too.

'This used to fit me a century ago before that little vomit comet came along. One day, hopefully in my lifetime, I will fit back into it. In the meantime you may wear it for Prince Charming.'

The 'it' was a fifties-style, straight, raw silk dress, cherry red. I stopped short of dribbling, just.

'Lovely, Angela, but I don't have shoes to go with it.'

'Yes, you do,' she said, producing a pair of matching court shoes. 'And here are some hold-up stockings which I never got a chance to wear. They should do nicely with all the rest.'

'I can't wear those,' I protested. 'If anyone were to see, they'd think I was on the make.'

Angela gave me a teasing grin. 'You wear them to feel good for yourself,' she said, with mock-haughty emphasis, and more than a nod at the politically correct. The feminist cells in my head were cheering. They should get out more. 'Now, wipe that sick off your jumper, go home and spruce yourself up for a great night out.'

'It's just a favour for Andy,' I protested. 'He's hanging around with some leggy bimbo anyhow.'

'But not tonight. Have fun. Let your hair down. On second thoughts, put your hair up for that frock.'

'I presume my mother knows which dress you chose?'

'What do you think?'

'And does Andy's mother know?'

'As far as I know it was printed in this week's local newsletter.'

I sighed. 'As long as it's only the entire northside and its immediate environs that's in on the secret, I guess I can live with it.'

'She's very excited about this date,' Angela went on.

'Great. Better get cracking then. I don't want to let The Mammy down, along with tens of thousands of her closest friends. Not to mention Breda Raynor.' I turned at the door. 'And it's not a date,' I said.

'Of course not.'

People get the weirdest ideas; it's always best to keep things straight. This was only a pay-back, after all. Andy just wanted someone along as arm candy.

I decided to walk home. It was that or risk another cab, and I'd had enough lecturing from shiny, happy taxi people that day. If I called my brother out, I might run into more family interference, because the Street men are just as nosy as the Street women. There are times when it makes perfect sense to me that I became a detective, considering how curious my family are. So far we reckon that we're safer than cats are with it. I dialled my little helper.

Ciara had been busy, and was justifiably proud of her information.

'Her name is Maria Flood, she's twenty years old and she works as a laboratory assistant for, of all people, Michael O'Donoghue at the Fledgling Clinic.'

'You don't say. And Flood? Interesting coincidence or real-life relation?'

'Real-life relation: Bernadette's daughter.'

'And I have another interesting coincidence for you. Bernie Flood drives a metallic grey car. It's probably in Howth even as we speak.' I read out the registration number for her.

'Nice one.'

'Ciara, I know all of this information seems to point a certain way, but we should resist that. We want facts, not our own opinions.'

'Boss, I have no opinions. I'm paid not to have them, you made that perfectly clear. I think you're the one with the fertile imagination at the moment, not me. I haven't reached any conclusion at all about this.'

'You are one cool cookie, Ciara.'

'Believe it. You'll also be impressed to hear that I have captured Maria's lovely visage on film and you can feast your eyes on that shortly.'

I gave her the name of the photographic studio I use for this sort of work and told her to collect my latest film while she was delivering hers.

'Right, I have no more time to waste on you,' she told me. 'It's much more fun watching journalists try to doorstep Michael O'Donoghue, even though there's feck all of that today. See you later, though hopefully you won't see me.'

'Roger. Over and out.'

'What you do in your own spare time is none of my business,' she said, and hung up before I could retaliate. I found myself laughing.

I liked working alone, always had. And so Ciara's presence should have made me feel uncomfortable or crowded. But this was not the case. I enjoyed having her along. It was fun, actually. I think one of the reasons was that Ciara was fresh to me, as well as to the job. Come to think of it, she was fresh with me as well; she was lippy with everyone. We had no history, we were making it now, as we went along. And I needed her. Work was getting done, and the company marched ever onwards towards world domination. But I felt uneasy that my enforced leisure time was turning out to be busier than I could ever have predicted. I had miscalculated and didn't have enough of it left to be a proper back up to Ciara.

Part of me has always been a guilt-ridden purist. Now, the big 'G' tried to gain a foothold, and I needed to justify my existence. This was not something Barry ever seemed to worry about. Perhaps being an actor, or an artist, brought with it a different set of values. Barry relaxed when he was out of work, and got on with the strenuous business of dissing everyone in showbiz, as well as hours of old-fashioned bitching. Often he refused to work if it was 'not right' for him. And of course he had an agent, who held his hand at these times and looked after him; in loco parentis. Me, I fretted. I worried. I borrowed money to pay the bills. I looked around for ways to make ends meet.

I couldn't relax about the fact that I was going to have a bath and prepare myself for a night out. I was a good quarter of a mile from home, walking purposefully along with my red dress over one arm and a fearsome guard dog straining on a leash from the other, but I could still do business. I rang Maeve for an update.

'I had another call, but it wasn't like the others. It came in while I was out doing some voiceovers. Why don't I play it for you and you'll see what I mean?'

She was right. This message had a soundtrack: it was the shower scene from *Psycho*.

'That does it,' I said. 'This has officially gone too far. It's time to put serious frighteners on the companies we know have your number, see what that turns up. Is there any way it could be a friend or a work acquaintance?'

'I really don't think so, Leo. I'm not fighting with anyone or in the bad books anywhere that I know of.'

'I have to say again that I think we should tell the police about this.'

'I know, I know, so does Mark. But I don't want all that attention. And I'm worried that the press will get hold of it, and you know what they're like when they get the whiff of a story. I'd have no life.'

'Okay, we'll give my plan a go, but if that doesn't work and the calls continue, we go to the cops.'

'Agreed. Leo, I really am grateful for this. Also, I think it's time we discussed money.'

'No,' I said, firmly. 'I wouldn't hear of it.'

'Leo, you're running a business. Get sense.'

'We'll talk about it if I get a result. How about that?'

'Done. Incidentally, don't you have a date tonight?'

'Maeve, it's not a date. I am doing a favour for a friend.'

'Why don't you do *yourself* a favour? Go home and have a good time getting ready.'

'Just for you then,' I agreed cheerily, as I rang off.

A butterfly stretched its wings in my tummy. I relished the sensation, the expectation.

I let myself and the dog into the house. Although I had preparations to make for an evening's socialising, I was first to be an intermediary in a trans-species war. No. 4 barked thrice to alert the cat population of his presence. Bridie was the only resident feline at the time. She arched her back and puffed her fur out to twice its size, then hissed something of a symphony and gave a yeowl of encore. No. 4, in perfect harmony, lunged forward with a bass growl, while Bridie swiped a claw across his nose, before disappearing at graceful but high speed through the cat flap. All round, a beautifully judged performance.

It might normally have worried me, or at the very

least been jotted down for future reference, but all I could think of now was Andy Raynor. I kissed No. 4's injured snout and soothed his pride. Then I turned my attention to myself. I really can be a selfish cow sometimes.

Fifteen

I masturbated in the bath. It was the only way I could think of to reduce the mounting tension in my body, and I thought it might leave me less vulnerable to the charms of one Andrew Raynor, handsome man and knicker beast. I poured some drool into the water from an ancient Christmas present languishing on the shelf – a bit like myself, I thought at the time. It smelt plausible enough. By the time I finished, the bathroom was awash with suds; I hadn't realised that it was bubble bath, and I had been energetic. I searched for a wise message on the label, from Ovid or one of his cronies, but message found I none. Didn't really matter, I'd had a great time. I even stumbled a little blindly as I got out of the tub, so maybe there is a smidgen of truth in the old saying about wanking harming your vision. Then again I am notoriously clumsy, so . . .

No. 4 gave me 'a look' as I re-entered my domain.

'Don't you dare,' I told him. 'If humans could look after their arses like you can, they would. It's a wonder you don't have to walk with a white stick, now that I think of it.'

I had the house to myself barring the cats, who had returned en masse, and the dog, who decided on a snooze. It was bliss. I stood in front of the full-length mirror in the bedroom and posed a bit. Normally, Barry has exclusive use of this for preening purposes. My work calls for monochrome anonymity, so I don't have much call to fluff up the feathers. I did seem to be glowing, but the bath had been hot, and that could have resulted in this healthy flush I saw before me. I laid the dress and its accompaniments on the bed, putting the previous party choices to shame, and was reaching for the hairdryer when my mobile rang. This time the tune seemed to be a badly programmed version of the James Bond theme. I felt vaguely glad that Barry was going to so much trouble to follow up his ruse; I took it to be a sign of affection. But if he continued this for more than a week I would have to kill him.

'Good evening, Ms Street, this is your escort speaking.'

'Mr Raynor, how nice of you to call.' Andy had a fabulously rich voice, I decided. Pity he'd won Woman-iser of the Year for a decade and a half running.

'I just wanted to make sure that you had not forgotten our arrangement?'

'Andy, that would be difficult, seeing as how you've involved all of the women in my family, and yours too, probably.'

'I can't help it if your mother loves me. Can't blame her either. How is it I don't seem to have that effect on her only daughter?'

'Andy, leave it out. Tease someone else for a change.'

'Rightio. Now, to business. Do you have something wonderful to wear?'

'Of course.'

'Good. And are you dressed yet?'

'No, sir. I've just had my bath, and after I've dried my hair, I'll be climbing into full regalia.'

'Ah. So, a naked Leo Street, about to get into uniform. I have to confess that I am now thinking of touching myself in a rude way.'

I began to laugh. In the mirror I could see the reflection of a teenager from years past who had delighted in similar phonecalls from this same man. Be careful, said the older, wiser Leo, who was in my head somewhere. I shrugged her off, I was having fun.

'Are you naked?' he asked.

'Just about,' I replied, perhaps a little softly.

'Tell me more,' he purred.

'Well, I've had a bubble bath, and I smell of peach and orange, with just a hint of ylang-ylang, and a suggestion of sandalwood.'

'I can practically taste you,' he said, simply, to the point.

There was a pause between us, and I realised that my pulse was racing. To hear him so clearly on the other end of the line was so tactile, I imagined I felt his breath in my ear. Did he feel the same way too? After a time I continued, 'On the bed I have a red outfit with matching everything.'

'Uh-hunh. Why don't you lie on the bed beside those

clothes and I'll come over now and help you dress?' His voice sounded hoarse with desire, and I sat on the edge of the bed to steady myself.

Downstairs the front door banged shut. 'Leo, I'm home,' a voice called. My body jolted back to the present. 'Fucking hell,' I said, without meaning to. 'I'm upstairs, Barry,' I shouted. 'Eh, sorry, Andy, where were we?'

'I'll be over at eight,' he said, and hung up.

'Do I have any clean jeans?' Barry asked, as he invaded the bedroom. He paused briefly in front of the mirror to admire what he saw there. He was pleased with the reflected glory.

I crossed my still-shaking legs. 'If you've washed some, then yes,' I replied.

No one could accuse Barry of being handy around the house. Having said that, he was well able to do the laundry, and the washing up, and other sundry domestic chores, when the mood took him.

'Shite, shite, shite!' he said, punctuating the rifling of his chest of drawers, and the spilling of men's clothes all over the floor. 'I can't find my Butt t-shirt either,' he said. This was a frayed old grey thing with the words 'Bite my butt' emblazoned front and back. It had once been black, and reportedly magnificent; before my time. Like his favourite Y-fronts, he felt it was lucky for him.

'Can't help you with any of that,' I told him. 'If you didn't wash any jeans, you probably don't have a fresh pair. And I haven't seen Mr Butt in a long time.' I let the double-entendre hang in the air, but he didn't respond. Instead he spotted the party clothes.

'What's all that about?' he asked.

'I'm going out with my friend Andy, remember?'

'Oh, yeah, that, him. Well, have a good time.' He gestured to the dress. 'That's Angela's, isn't it?'

'Yes.'

I don't know how he did it, or if he had done anything at all, but I now felt completely second-hand. I was a sham. I began to feel angry with Barry, then calmed down; this was not his fault, I was mad with myself, surely, not him. I was the one feeling like a fake, his words were incidental catalysts. There was no point in taking any of this out on an innocent bystander.

But suddenly I wanted rid of the baggage in my life. I wanted to have the house to myself and my pets again. I wanted the freedom to allow a sexy man to come over and ravish me on my bed before we dressed ourselves in beautiful clothes and went out to enjoy ourselves some more about the town. I was fed up of having to pander to a heedless, selfish git – often more than one, given the open-door policy operated by Barry. What if I just threw him out, right now? I went downstairs to the bathroom and splashed cold water on my face. That brought me to my senses.

'Do you have work tonight?' I asked. 'Is that why you need fresh clothes?'

Barry had taken to the sofa with a forlorn look on his face. 'Yeah, what am I going to do?'

'Why don't you wear the trousers of your dress suit

and your white collarless shirt? You'll look fantastic.'

'I will, won't I?' he said, perking up. 'Thanks, Leo, I don't know what I'd do without you.' He pecked my cheek and ran upstairs to change. I felt drained, and my high good humour for going out had faded. I hauled myself up to the bedroom to finish my own preparations.

I often put off decisions. Sometimes it's because I'm unsure of the rights and wrongs of a situation. At other times, it's because I'm being cowardly. But now, I decided to defer any rash action, because haste might ruin a lot more than it preserved. It would be very easy to break up with Barry. But in the long run would that be a good thing? Was it right to smash up a relationship rather than work on it? Surely running away from our problems was the easy option; too easy. I was certain that my own parents had had hard times over the years of their marriage, but they hadn't packed it in. They had persevered. And so would I. And tomorrow, we would have a long talk and make a new beginning.

'We should spend some time together now that I'm freer during the day,' I said to Barry, as he grabbed his jacket to leave.

'Yeah, great idea,' he said. 'See you.'

And he was gone. I was exhausted.

I noticed that I had a message on my answering machine. It was Mull of Mullaney Motors. 'Leo, this is Mull,' he said, predictably enough. 'Your car should be ready late today, so I'll leave it over to your house then. Eh, I need a word with Barry anyway. On the vehicle front, I really do think you should get yourself something new, this one's in rag order. Oh, and it's dark blue now, I couldn't find a match for the green.'

Barry was the reason he was coming over. Mull and he had a stupid arrangement over dope. Barry maintained it was a favour between friends, but I hated it; it made him look like a dealer, and it was only a question of semantics whether he was or was not. I started to hyperventilate.

I needed something concrete to take my mind off my home life, and that was work, normally. I racked my brain, then remembered an unchased detail from earlier. I dialled Maeve Kelly's mum.

'Sandra, it's Leo Street here. Sorry to bother you again, but I wanted to ask you about someone I saw driving up to your house earlier on. It was Bernie Flood. Isn't she a friend of Michael O'Donoghue's?'

'Oh, was, Leo, *was*,' she said. 'It's interesting that you mentioned him to me earlier. I'd forgotten that she used to do a line with him, if that's not too old-fashioned a phrase to use nowadays. It ended badly, which was par for the course with him. He married Miranda shortly afterwards. Whether that was related or not, I've no idea. We don't talk about it generally, and anyway we don't see that much of one another as a group these days. I did mention his name today though, what with all the stuff in the papers, and she said something to the effect that he'd get his just deserts now, then clammed up. I get the feeling there's no love lost there.'

'Right,' I said.

'By the way, your breads were a great success. I took the liberty of giving your number to a few of the girls. I hope you don't mind? I think you can expect some orders soon.'

I was stunned. 'Er, thank you,' I squeezed out. 'Thank you very much.'

I stood rooted to the spot. My handiwork was a hit, and it had made me money. My, oh, my. And yet again, a simple question had yielded interesting information. Some things never change, and at the same time wonders never cease. Would that observation be any good on a bottle of balm? I wondered.

My landline rang. When I answered, my niece Lucy asked for Barry.

'He's gone, Luce. Anything I can do?'

'Eh, no, Leo, just he said that myself and a few friends could go on the Crawl tonight, and I wanted to check if that's still okay.'

I could feel an unreasonable, slow burn begin in the pit of my stomach.

'I'm sure if Barry said that, he meant it,' I told my fifteen-year-old niece. 'Actually, he seemed excited about tonight's show,' I continued. I neglected to mention the special effort with clothing, or costume, or whatever he wanted to pass it off as. 'Enjoy yourself,' I said, as I hung up.

I sat on the bed with legs shaking for the second time in an hour. No wonder Barry had taken so much care tonight; when a teenager had a crush, you had to dress to suit, to nurture it, and to burnish your own vanity. I was furious. I was beyond fury, I was jealous. I went to the bathroom, again, and splashed water on my face, again. I'm not sure if it worked a second time. What I do know is that I now took sensual pleasure in dressing my hair and my body, and scenting the whole package. When I looked in the mirror that last time, I found my hands stray to the tops of my stockings and linger as I revelled in the freedom they afforded me. And whoever was in that picture looked hot and ready for action.

When Andy Raynor rang my bell, I downed the last of a brandy I had been nursing and went to the door. He gave a low whistle and put his hands around my waist as I stood basking in his attention. A moment lengthened between us, delicious with tension and promise. Then he leaned in to kiss my cheek. It left an indelible burn on my senses. 'You look great,' he said.

I knew I was glowing, if only because a beautiful man had complimented me. And I didn't care a whit if it was the truth or not. I didn't feel second-hand any more, and I did not rush to explain that the dress was borrowed, as I normally would have. Tonight I was free of my self-imposed restrictions and self-deprecation; they were neither needed nor welcome. Tonight I could do and say whatever I liked. I decided that my final lottery number would be 1, in honour of myself. I would buy my ticket tomorrow, win the jackpot and piss off to somewhere wonderful while I decided what to do with my millions.

'That is one hairy house,' Andy also said, as he led me

down the garden path. I was not sure whether this was another compliment.

Marion Maloney just happened to be putting out her empty milk bottles at that very moment. She was wearing her night vision, which is even more accurate than her daytime sight. She could also smell interest in the post-dusk air. She dashed to my gate.

'Leo, I was just wondering how your poor car is?' she said, full of anxiety. I had a mental picture of the battered jalopy hooked up to a bleeping machine in intensive care.

'It's going to pull through, against all the odds,' I assured her, a little dramatically. I couldn't help it, her concern was catching. 'It'll be coming home tomorrow. And it has turned completely blue.'

'Blue?' she repeated, updating her data pool. 'Of course it must be costing you a fortune in taxi fares,' she said, pointedly referring to Andy's two-seater convertible Mercedes.

I let her off the hook. 'This is my friend, Andrew Raynor.'

'Pleased to meet you,' she said, extending her hand with a girly smile. Fair play to Marion, she knows a fine man when she sees one.

'Enchanted,' Andy said, flirting outrageously.

I laughed out loud. 'I didn't think anyone used that word any more.'

'More people should,' Marion said, in admonition of me in particular, for my bad manners, and people in general, for their ignorance. 'I can see that you're on your way out, so I'll not keep you youngsters. We'll talk again. Have a good time.'

She waved as we drove off, and stayed in her doorway until we had turned the corner.

'Nice bumps,' Andy said. It was hard to believe that he meant the speed ramps. He was not a man to miss some handy smut.

'You really are incorrigible,' I told him. And I smiled some more. I was happy. 'By the way, she means that. She really will want to interview you at some future stage.'

'I must make sure I have something interesting to tell her then,' he said as we sped into the night.

I felt a shiver run down my spine.

Sixteen

When a woman marries in the country, each of her neighbours lights a fire for her on her route to and from the church. With our mothers involved, I expected a conflagration on every corner, and at every set of traffic lights we stopped at. Luckily enough, no one was allowed to play with matches that night. Instead, the lights of the shore and the bay twinkled merrily, blessing us on our journey southwards. Oranges mixed with umbers, burnt and unscorched, speckled through with dots of white and cream from thousands of bulbs decorating the city. The waters of the sea and the river were still, as if holding their breath, and from within them a parallel universe gently waved, impressionistic in its undulations.

'A fiver for them,' said my companion.

'Oh, it'll cost you more than that, Andy Raynor.'

'It's a long time since I've seen that sort of smile on your face. What do you know that I don't?'

'Not a lot, really. I'm just relaxed, I guess.'

'Or happy, maybe?'

'Maybe.'

We drove on, over the river at the toll bridge, along by Ringsend and on to the Strand Road, with its panoramic view of the coast, before turning into Sandymount.

'I hope you won't get a nose bleed being so far over into Injun territory,' he said.

'Nah. I spend a lot of my time poking around this end of town. I could probably pass as a native now.'

'I appreciate this, Leo. Thanks for coming.'

'Don't mention it, a friend in need and all that. I think my mother's a lot more excited about it than anyone else,' I said, keeping my voice as neutral as possible. It was crucial that I believed this too, and if I passed this off as the truth, the night would be easier to deal with and to get through. There is nothing so unseemly as a grown woman with a crush on an ex from so far back that he probably can't remember that they ever went out together in the first place. This man had a girlfriend who was serious enough to get brought on nights out with his mum, and I lived with a partner. Sorted. No conflict of interest. No room for misunderstandings.

'That smile is back,' he said.

'Enjoy it, I am.'

He laughed and said, 'I will.'

When Andy smiles, the world brightens. When he laughs, it sings. He's just one of those guys.

'You're a very nice man,' I said, before I could stop myself.

'Thank you. You're a very nice woman.'

206

'I wonder, am I, Andy? I tell a lot of fibs, you know.'

'We all do, Leo. It's human nature. And now I have to insist that we have that smile back in place because we are within thirty seconds of the club.'

'As Sir wishes.'

'That's what I like to hear.'

We swung into the forecourt of Bridgecross. In the distance I could see the old railway after which it was named.

'Does this car turn into a pumpkin at midnight, or anything like that?'

'No, Cinders, it does not. And even if your wonderful dress turns to slavish rags at that time, you'll still look great to me.'

'Thanks.'

He came around to the passenger side to let me out. I know a few women who would swoon at such an action, thinking it chivalrous, and others who would deem it smarmy. I think he carried it off on this occasion.

'That could have been so cheesy,' I said, as I alighted from my carriage.

'Is there no romance in your soul?' he asked, in mock horror.

'This is not romance, Andy, it's persistence.'

'Still top marks,' he pointed out. I could feel that I was smiling 'that smile' again. Time to rein in.

'If it were romance, we wouldn't be out in a crowd of two hundred people of your acquaintance,' I added tartly.

'If I had asked you out on your lonesome, you wouldn't have come,' he replied.

This was true. We allowed a truce.

Bridgecross is the largest sports club in Dublin city. It has its own cricket pitch, indoor and outdoor tennis courts, all-weather pitches for hockey and rugby, and a five-a-side facility for weekend sports people. This evening the clubhouse, newly refurbished at a cost of trillions, was lit up to welcome us all. The well-heeled of the capital parked their expensive cars and escorted their trophy partners up the steps to the main door. We fell in step and Andy ushered me along with just the suggestion of an arm about my waist. It felt good; we fitted each other. We sauntered with the ease of two people who had known one another forever. And, for once, the goddess of grace had regarded me with favour: I did not stumble or go over even once on my sister-in-law's heels. Hallelujah.

Before we went in the door, I stopped Andy to ask, 'Will this be a night of "Agadoo" and "The Birdie Song"?'

'If that's what you'd like, I can arrange it.'

I stood with my mouth hanging open at that awful notion. It can't have been an attractive sight, but he leaned over and kissed me nevertheless. I recoiled and hit the door jamb with a vicious 'thwack'. It was all too sudden. It had the effect of closing my gob though. Guiltily, I realised that I had thought 'too' rather than 'so' with the 'sudden'. This would have to stop.

'Jeez, Leo, I didn't know you were that allergic to me,' Andy said, as he helped straighten me.

'I'm not – I mean, I am – I wasn't expecting that,' I burbled, rubbing the worst hit elbow.

'I'll give fair warning next time,' he said.

'You will not. There can be none of that carry on. It's not right. And neither is interactive shite music.'

'If you say so.'

'I do.'

'Do you need me to kiss that elbow better?'

'No,' I shouted. He held both hands up in mock surrender.

We walked through the door and I was a teenager again, in a room full of people determined to have a good time. The smells were different: no more Brut or Lynx, no more Lenthéric fragrances, or Charlie. Instead the air was steeped in Issey Miyake, Calvin Klein, Chanel, some Poison, and a dash of Obsession. The complexions of the anxious faces searching for a part-time thrill were clearer than in the old days, but the intentions were the same, and the promise of the dry grind against a thigh during the slow set was still an option after all these years. Heads turned. I blossomed. They may have been admiring Andy, but I was happy to share the attention from the side. He put his arm around my waist again, firmly this time, and we walked on. 'I'll introduce you to some people,' he said.

'Where do you get them from?' asked a man in a navy jacket, with the embroidered club crest and gilt buttons.

He was wearing *slax*. I immediately assumed that he called his wife 'the little lady', not particularly as an endearment, but because he couldn't be bothered to remember her name. My instant annoyance also suggested that he would hold his knife as if it were a pen, a habit I cannot abide. This, it turned out, was Bob Moran.

'I'll be with you both as soon as I've done my greeting duties,' he promised.

'Oh, no hurry,' we assured him, earnestly.

A woman in a pink confection fluttered up to see us. She was Mrs Bob Moran. She hung adoringly off Andy's free arm, cooing musically to him. Quite the coquette. But then he had a range of similar effects on most genders. I merited a nod. Meanly, I imagined her uttering phrases like 'heavens to Betsy' a lot. When Andy extricated himself, we headed for the sanctuary of the bar area and he explained that Mrs Bob was a relentlessly helpful woman who did a lot of good work for charity.

I scanned the room while Andy bought us a drink, but I did not see Michael and Miranda O'Donoghue. I checked my phone to make sure that it was working, in case Ciara wanted to call me. It was. I was as on duty as I could have been at that time. And the knowledge that I had a deputy in the field was a gift.

Mr Bob Moran turned out to be 'great gas', according to himself. He also thought that I had the funniest name he'd heard in a long time. 'The Streets,' he guffawed. 'Sure Dublin is full of them.' I should be paid for every time that I hear this; I could retire on the proceeds. 'And what class of a name is Leo for a gorgeous young lady like yourself?'

I creased my face into a pained grin, for Andy's sake. 'Oh, now,' I said, casting my eyes upwards, as if it would take an aeon to get through that one.

'Are you anything to that poofy lad, that ballerina, Wayne Street?'

'No, Mr *Moron*,' I replied, thinking that no 'oxy' need apply. 'I think you mean the dancer Wayne Sleep.'

'Do I? Well now, aren't you the clever one all the same? Oh, Andy is the boyo can pick them and no mistake.'

The 'them' stung; I was all too aware of how many women had accompanied Andy to similar functions over the years. Bob had reached a plateau of wit, as far as I was concerned, but before I raised my clenched hand to thump him, my phone rang and I excused myself.

'Yo, Management, it's the proletariat.'

'Ciara, you may have saved a man's life in here. I was about to punch a stupid fart's lights out when you called.'

'All in a day's work,' she said. 'Just to let you know that I saw you arrive with a most picturesque man: who is he? And the O'Donoghues have just pulled up, in a metallic grey car.'

'Curiouser and curiouser.'

'It might be, mightn't it? Don't worry, I'm not racing

to any conclusions. I can't tell if it's the one that's been following me because I haven't got it to come close enough to check the reg when I've spotted the tail.'

'We'll put it in the mix and see what comes up.'

'So, who is he?'

'Pardon?'

'Ooh, *pardon*, la di da. Who is the hunk?'

'He's an old friend of the family, nothing more.'

'Sure, boss.' I could hear her chortling on the other end of the line.

'I've got to get back to this party,' I said.

'I'll bet you do.'

'Ciara,' I growled.

'Talk to you later, or tomorrow, whichever. Be a good girl now. Remember, I'll be keeping an eye on you.'

Someone was watching me: a taste of my own medicine.

Andy was in conversation with the O'Donoghues when I returned. I don't know why, but I felt a little shocked by that. I was now right on the coal face. Miranda could sense my unease and relished saying, 'Are you sure we haven't met somewhere before? You seem so familiar to me.' Her cold, grey eyes dared me to engage.

'I have one of those faces,' I murmured, eschewing the challenge.

Her husband was also giving me more than the once over. 'It's funny, but I feel the same way too,' he said, agreeing with his wife, which was probably a first in a while. 'Of course, I see a lot of women from day to day,' he continued. He just stopped short of remarking that we all look the same after a while, I thought. Or was I tarring him, unfairly, with the same brush as Bob Moran? And he had 'met' me before, on the night of my car bashing as I followed him home. All of a sudden I felt hot and moist, which is good in some situations, not so in others; this was one of the bad times. I excused myself to visit the loo, or the 'Little Ladies' as I'm sure Bob would have called it.

The washroom was full of regular-sized women talking about a member who was steadily spreading glandular fever amongst the club. I waited long enough to ascertain that it was not Andy, and to learn that someone called Serenity had had twins the day before but planned to be back on the hockey team by the end of the following week. She had chosen the names Oswald and Thierry for the babes, and I took from this that they were boy babies; an iffy assumption in this day and age?

Bob had rejoined the growing band of Andy's company when I returned. Miranda's look of disdain for him could have been cut with a knife. He was remarking that fair was fair and fowl was chicken as I came within earshot, and with that she rolled her eyes and abandoned the group. Her husband looked relieved, Bob didn't even notice she'd gone. Andy was wearing a lazy grin as he watched me try to deal with the nonsense that was Bob Moran, now confessing that he was 'a rugby kinda guy'. Michael O'Donoghue just seemed intent on getting drunk, and after the day he'd had, perhaps this was no surprise. Out of sheer politeness, or perhaps loyalty to Andy, he asked what I did for a living, which I brushed off with 'office work, you know'. He told me that he was a doctor, and he made babies. I was interested in his choice of words.

'Like, in a test tube?' I asked.

'Oh, that. And I deliver and so on. I have that power.' He was so utterly casual that I wondered if his megalomania was imagined by others, or if his supposed God Complex sat so easily with him now that he hardly noticed it.

'I saw your picture in the evening paper,' I admitted.

It was the truth, of course, though somewhat short of the whole truth, given that I had seen much more than that of him over the last few days. He grunted and finished his drink in one gulp, then turned to the bar to order another. I took that to mean that he had nothing more to say to me on the subject.

Bob returned his attention to me, and his monopoly meant that I missed being introduced to a fun-looking group of Andy's friends. What was it about me, apart from my hilarious name, that attracted Bob? I wondered. And why couldn't he control it anyhow? I had about as much interest in this guy as I did in Quasimodo's jock strap. On reflection, the jock strap option was infinitely preferable.

Apparently no one is more than six degrees of separation from any stranger they meet. Move along a list of people you know, and you'll come up with a connection. And at the heart of this, often, is a 'hub' person;

someone who'll turn up on many lists. I looked across at Andy Raynor and decided that he was one of those central people. He moved in many circles; was as busy as any big London Underground station, and on more interconnecting lines than most. Given his profession, I also came to the conclusion that if we are normally separated from others by six degrees, none of us is further than two from a journalist at any given time. Which would be of no comfort to Michael O'Donoghue. He could take some solace from the fact that Andy was a political reporter, although like the doctor he was an expert on the female reproductive system. My warning bells tried a light tinkle at this point.

Bob was still invading my personal space, in spite of the fact that I was clearly not paying him any quality attention. I was rescued by a pan-fried man in an aloe vera sauce.

'I fell asleep on a sunbed,' he confessed.

The resultant blush on his cheeks gave him a perpetual air of embarrassment. The Moron wandered off, leaving Michael O'Donoghue sozzling away behind me and my new beacon friend.

'Don't mind Bob, he's not the worst. I'm Billy.'

'If he pats my ass once more, I'll break his arm,' I said.

Michael O'Donoghue let out an involuntary chuckle. Maybe he wasn't so bad after all.

The music had started and Andy was whisked on to the floor by a woman in her forties who writhed around him like a belly dancer. He had the knack of bringing out the eejit in all of us, it seemed. I looked at his tall, handsome form and was reminded of Barry. I know that comparisons are invidious, but I couldn't help but remember how inordinately proud Barry had been of a dump he'd taken recently. He'd weighed himself afterwards and discovered that he was eight pounds lighter. I could see him in my mind's eye, planted in front of Groundhog News, watching the same reports on the hour every hour, and smiling wistfully as he remembered his remarkable feat. Of course he wouldn't be there tonight, because he was too busy scrambling my niece's head and heart. It made sense in a way; he was really just an older teenager himself.

Andy came to take me away from my thoughts. His timing was flawless, as always. Just as we stepped on to the dance floor, the tempo slowed. He held one of my hands and used his other arm to encircle my waist. I put my spare mitt on his shoulder and tried to think pure thoughts. We swayed together in time to the music, and I was certain that he was edging closer with every beat. I tried in vain to stiffen, to send out a negative body signal, but the truth was that it was delicious. I could feel toned muscles under his shirt, and a very toned one in his pants.

Then, with even more impeccable timing than Andrew Raynor, real life interrupted.

At first I didn't notice the commotion over the noise of the music and the hum of my eager thoughts. But, little by little, events at the edge of the dance floor encroached on us. A woman was standing in front of Michael O'Donoghue, gesturing wildly and, it seemed, screaming at him. I craned my neck for a better view.

'You have to be the most curious woman I know,' Andy said.

'I hope you don't mean that as in odd,' I said. 'It's my job to be curious. I have an insatiable thirst for knowledge and information.'

He smiled indulgently. 'Here's the deal. I'll steer us closer, if you pay me full attention once the fracas is over.'

'Deal,' I said, drinking in those dark eyes of his.

As we approached, friends and acquaintances were trying to calm the situation. The woman yelled, 'You've ruined me! You promised me everything and you gave me nothing. You've destroyed me. I could kill you, you bastard.'

Miranda watched from the shadows, a smile flitting across her extraordinary face. When she caught my eye, she turned away and missed the rest of the action as a result. It was just then that the shouting woman shut up, and threw a pint of lager over Michael O'Donoghue.

A bouncer told everyone that the show was over, and escorted the assailant away. She went quietly, spent from her exertions. Michael O'Donoghue was aghast. He stood silently fuming at the incident, and quite unable to save face. He tried in vain to wipe away the drink drenching his suit and shirt, but gave up when he realised the futility of this and said his goodnights. I could see him ask his wife to leave, but obviously she refused. He took out a mobile, made a quick call and left. Ciara was back in business.

Something about the woman bothered me. She seemed familiar, but I couldn't put a name to her. The harder I tried the more buried the information became. There was nothing for it but to let my stubborn memory relax and choose its own sweet time to reveal all.

'Enough?' Andy asked.

'Sorry. You know I can't resist a scene.'

'Don't I just?'

By rights I should now have been following the unidentified woman while Ciara tailed Michael O'Donoghue, but these were not normal circumstances. And I am ashamed to say that reason was buckled to the floor as Andy swirled me gently to the middle of the throng of dancers, and we took up where we had previously left off.

It was exhilarating. We were back in the spotlight of our own emotions and the rest of the world was excluded. Work was forgotten. Bridgecross and its attendant function were forgotten. They receded further with each note of the music. We leaned together, slowly moving from foot to foot. He reached down to kiss the back of my neck and I was lost. Molten heat poured into every joint of my body and my ears filled with a ringing noise. His lips brushed lightly up and down, finding new erogenous zones, and I felt myself pushing against him with urgency.

'Come on,' he said, in a low voice laced with danger. 'We're leaving.'

We didn't bother with farewells, but grabbed our few possessions and rushed out into the night, and his car, and pleasure so long awaited.

Seventeen

I had often dreamed of speeding through the dark in a flash motor with a good-looking man who was about to make outrageous love to me. The dream and, I can report, the reality are exciting and vital, at the time. On mature reflection, it's nice when the man is your own live-in lover, but life does not always deal that hand. Then, in the dull grey pallor of hindsight, excitement and vitality disappear through a suddenly glimpsed window. But, happily, hindsight is just that, and can be ignored until later, when it is cued to make an appearance, whether you want it to or not.

Andy was nothing if not stylish. He blipped open the electronic gates to his house as we pulled up, with a timing borne of habit and panache. He steered me through his front door and on to a couch with effortless ease. We could not wait for the intense white heat of our first coupling, and so we did not. He even said my name as he came, which was a nice touch, I thought. Then we really got down to business, this time in his vast bed. I'm not sure that there are names for some of the things he did to me, as he brought me again and again to where I wanted to be. It was heavenly. And amusing, as he made me feel at ease with our love-making. We laughed and touched and kissed and licked and sucked, and plenty more besides. My groin usually ached from desire, now it was throbbing from sheer frantic exertion. I was sure that I would not sit easily for days. Great!

As I lay in the circle of his arms, cuddled and sated, I asked, 'Well? Worth waiting for?'

'Oh, yes,' he said, kissing me on my forehead, tenderly. 'But now that I know what I've been missing all these years, I'm raging I didn't do this sooner.'

Me too, I thought. I laughed involuntarily as I remembered something.

'What is it?' he asked.

'Nothing. My grandmother was right about you, that's all.'

'Is that a good thing?'

'In this case, yes.'

'Tell me more.'

'Can't, I'm afraid, it's a bit personal.'

He climbed on top of me, pinning my arms to the bed. 'Tell me, or I'll be forced to torture you.'

I thrashed about trying to get out from under him, but he was immovable. Finally, I gave in. 'She compared your penis very favourably with a donkey's,' I told him.

He guffawed and said, 'I want to reassure you that it's conjecture on her part, even if she is correct.'

I cuffed him lightly for his arrogance and snuggled closer.

'You do realise that this is the second time you've ended up in bed with me in a very short space of time,' Andy murmured.

'Mmm. But last time I really just *slept* with you, and I don't remember a thing.'

'And do you think this might be a little more memorable?'

'I guess.'

'Witch.'

'Mmm.'

We nuzzled together some more and I began to nod off. Then with a jolt I was awake and in a cold sweat. What had I just done? I must have taken leave of my senses. Andy held me tight, kissing my face and neck. 'You're fine, Leo,' he assured me. 'There is nothing to worry about.' I wanted to believe him. I returned his kisses and felt tension ooze away. I fell asleep.

We were spooned together when I woke with another start at 3 a.m. The room was in darkness, and Andy softly said, 'I'm here. It's okay.' And it was, you know. I felt happy and good. He stiffened behind me, and we began again. I abandoned myself to him, to us, and enjoyed each carnal moment. At 4.15 I stirred from my glow, which I was sure had lit up the bedroom. 'I have to go,' I said. 'I can't stay the night.'

'Yes, you can.'

'I can, but I won't,' I said. 'I'd better have a shower.'

These were some of the hardest words I'd uttered in years. I didn't want to go. I wanted to stay with this man. I felt safe and cocooned with him. But I also knew that I could not hide here, and that sooner or later I had to face the world and my life, and sooner seemed the better part of valour just then.

'I'll make us some coffee,' he said.

Of course he didn't, he joined me in the shower. And when I kissed him goodbye on his doorstep, thirty minutes later, he gave a groan and pressed me against the door jamb. He raised my dress, and caressed my thighs, then my buttocks, moving inwards to my clitoris. I was saturated for him again. As he thrust himself into me he moaned, 'What are you doing to me?' I might well have asked the same question.

When I was finally ready to leave he stood back and said, 'You look beautiful.' And, at that moment, I believe I was.

My heart started its *Titanic* routine as I told the taximan to take me to 11, The Villas in Clontarf. I dreaded going home. And rightly so; I was now no better than any of the cheats I'd followed over the years. The playing field had suddenly become all too level. I had betrayed someone I'd declared I loved. But are you *in* love with him? asked a small voice. I was a mass of confused thoughts and emotions. On one level I felt elated, untouchable; on another I was scum. The only plus I had going for me was that the driver stayed quiet for the entire journey.

The moon was a spotlight in the clear night sky. It lit

up The Villas, shining pure and pearl-like in the heavens. A soft, cold wind rustled the grass, making it whisper. I've heard in songs that this sort of grass is a gossip and likes nothing more than to pass on scandal and innuendo to the trees, who in turn broadcast it to the world. I followed my breath to the front door, quietly inserting my key in the lock, slipping in under a cloak of secrecy. The little house was at rest. No. 4 stirred, but was too immersed in his canine slumbers to announce that I was home. The cats weren't too put out by my arrival either. Barry's couch was empty, which was a relief. Silence bathed the house. I was grateful.

Stealthily, I washed myself in the bathroom, at once shivering to the memory of Andy and eager to remove evidence of my infidelity. I was deliciously sore, and my body felt joy at the remembered closeness of him. That old sack magic. It was my inner self which was having a hard time dealing with my night of passion. I felt exhausted and dragged myself up the stairs, where I saw that Barry was unconscious and wearing a t-shirt and boxers. I followed suit; it was April and nights were cold. I climbed into bed and fell into a deep sleep. If it was troubled I was not aware of it, I was literally too shagged to notice. Barry never stirred.

The next morning, or should I say later on, my body felt as if it had been put through a mangle. I was like an infirm woman of ninety as I tried to get out of bed. Barry was downstairs pottering around, and a glance at the clock told me that it was now 11 a.m. I was more alarmed than the alarm, horrified at the lateness, but unable to spring into action as many of my muscle groups appeared to be in spasm or actively locking. I lay for a few moments in the tranquillity of my duvet, which was warm and uncomplicated. I decided to stay there forever more.

Forever isn't what it used to be. In my case it lasted all of eight minutes. Then Maeve rang and my early retirement from the human rat race was over. I didn't move far, mind, just reached a hand out from under the bedclothes, but it was enough to acknowledge the rest of the world and one of man's greatest technological achievements, the telephone.

'I'll *not* beat around the bush,' she announced. '*How was it?*'

'Maeve, you're getting excited about nothing. I've told you before and I'll obviously have to tell you again, it was just a favour for a friend.'

'*Right*. We can do this one of two ways: *either* you give me *full* details over the phone, *or* I come over in person *now*.'

I was grinning from ear to ear. Was this it then, the thrill of the forbidden? How could betrayal leave me with such an exultant rush of adrenalin? If this was infidelity, was I now an infidel? I wanted to tell her that Andy Raynor had short circuited my electrics several times, and that I longed for more. I wanted to tell her that some of my inner workings had fused from the thermo-nucleic activity of my illicit adventure, and I could hardly stand for sore muscles. I wanted to scream and shout and dance around the room with delight. Most of all I wanted to tart the whole thing up to sound acceptable, which in my gut I knew it was not. But I couldn't. Barry had arrived with a cup of coffee.

'I'll call you later,' I said. 'I have to get going properly on your nuisance calls today, one way or another. THANKS, BARRY.'

'I *knew* it, I just *knew* it!' she squealed, but in a hushed way. 'I can't *wait* for the gorys. Ciao.'

I shuffled to a sitting position, duvet tucked tightly around me. I could still smell Andy on me, feel him in me.

'I don't mean to sound ungrateful, but what's all this in aid of?'

Barry shrugged. 'I suppose I must like you.' He flashed me a full-toother. Suspicion kicked in, which was a bit rich on my part, really.

'Is this some sort of guilty peace offering? You haven't done something awful to my niece, have you?'

A psychiatrist might have had a field day here, or at least a good couch morning: I wanted Barry to have a horrid secret to share with me, so that I could let myself off the hook I'd stuck myself upon. However, as is often the case, reality triumphed over hope, and he had nothing sordid to rescue me with. I gave it one last go, with reason as straight as a drunk's meander home after a skinful.

'She has the most awful crush on you, Barry, and I don't think it's a good thing to lead her on too much.'

'I know that, Marm. She's a nice kid and we have a bit of fun. I was dying for some adult attention when I was her age, but everyone treated me like an over-grown child. I think it makes her feel grown up to be having a laugh with me.'

I gave a little snort. 'And you're not much more than a big baby yourself still.'

He gave me a sing-song 'Takes one to know one', pulled an utterly childish face and ran down the stairs before I could retaliate. Then he released the hound, and I was faced with the choice of abandoning my bed, or death by affection, doggy-style.

No. 4 won and soon I was under a hot stream of shower water, washing that man right out of my hair. I became energised as I liberally applied the suds; I resolved to sort the Maeve situation, perhaps not for all but maybe for once, and allowed myself a frisson of anticipation at the prospect of Tara O'Donoghue's visit that afternoon. I emerged from the bathroom in a shroud of towelling, feeling great.

'That must have been some night out,' Barry said. 'You're glowing.'

I stopped in my tracks, did a guilty double take and lied. 'Nah, mixture of the shower and not drinking too much. I have a lot to do today, so I'm starting on a decidedly up note.'

For one awful, eternal moment, I thought he was going to ask me back to bed, but he was distracted by the news and I was saved by the world in general and Ireland in particular. The lead story was the ongoing investigation into the Fledgling Clinic. We heard a taped interview with a woman who preferred to remain nameless, telling a story of spending a fortune on in vitro fertilisation which hadn't worked. This in itself was nothing startling, the failure rate was high. But she went on to say that Michael O'Donoghue had promised further and even more expensive pioneering techniques, and after another year of failure she had begun to suspect that it was all a scam.

It seemed to me that this would be very hard to prove, if it were true, but it certainly meant that Mr O'Donoghue had a full plate with the Medical Council, the media and the Department all delving into his practices and ethics. Not to mention myself and Ciara. I did wonder, though, if the news people were just hyping a sad situation from which no one would emerge well. It was a depressing story of human desperation and manipulation and I felt the dark clouds of morality gathering over my head. I was firmly in their domain now, through work and play; rest would have to wait.

'Would I be right to suppose that we are without our full complement of actors today?' I asked Barry.

He raised his eyes at my continued pursuit of an old theme. 'Coleman changed his speech last night and scored,' he told me.

'Let's hope he has great luck every night from now on.'

'Relax, Leo,' Barry said. 'You'll live longer.'

Instead, I left the room which elongated Barry's life somewhat.

★ ★ ★

I was feeling a bit sniffly, so I put on my favourite woolly jumper in an effort to ape the comfort of a duvet. It must be admitted that it had the same shape as the bedclothes and was hardly flattering, but it did the trick. It was also nice to be back on the road in my own ratty old banger, now disguised as a blue car. I bumped out of The Villas with my trusty No. 4 at the dashboard, and headed for Maeve's old taxi firm. I might have stayed on for an argument with Barry about his part-time drug dealing, but I didn't feel I was on high enough ground after my evening of sin. A quick retreat for regrouping seemed a goodish plan. I gave my head a scratch, sneezed a few times and went on my way.

I don't think I have ever been in a taxi waiting room with a healthy atmosphere. This one was as musty as a marathon runner's underpants and had spots of mildewy damp in every corner, and all along the magnolia wall by the door. Some graffiti told me that Deano was a homo, and Lee luvs Candice, which was nice to know. The seats were a mixture of plastic chairs and some clapped-out cottage-style armchairs, ejected from a smelly bedsit and worn shiny by too many tired and/or drunken arses.

The controller sat behind a reinforced glass partition, warming herself in front of a Super Ser with all three bars blazing; her legs were a patchwork of purple brackets, or 'abc's' as we used to call them when I was a kid. I was vaguely surprised that her tights didn't melt from the proximity of the fire; there's the wonder of nylon for you. She was an eighties throwback, complete with Charlie's Angels hair and lurid make-up. She was also big into shoulder pads.

I introduced myself and explained that I was here on behalf of Maeve Kelly, and why. I also told her that we had every reason to believe that the malicious calls were coming from this office, and that if they did not stop immediately, the cops would be called in. I trusted that she would pass this message on to the rest of the staff. She suggested that she might. I didn't feel I'd hit pay dirt, however. For one thing, there was no radio or television in the office, so the background noise was minimal, and certainly didn't match what we'd heard on the recordings. Still, it was a start. The elimination process had begun. We left in a hurry when I noticed a steaming pool on the lino, fresh from No. 4's bladder, I suspected.

My next stop was Maeve's doctor where I asked an ancient retainer if there was any chance that someone could have rifled Maeve's records for her phone number. I endured a lecture on patient-doctor confidentiality, gave my own about police intervention being the next step, and left with the impression that I had not yet located the culprit. A trip to the Chinese takeaway proved entirely fruitless as it only opened in the evenings, but the Indian equivalent was doing a roaring lunchtime trade. I bought a sag aloo, a chana dhal and two peshwari naan, dropped my bombshell and had an impromptu picnic in the car. No. 4 liked the naans best: 'lightly cooked cloud' he seemed to say.

I had hoped that the heat of the food might dispel my impending cold, but if anything my nose was streaming even more after the feast. Between that, an itchy scalp, a sore arse and a troubled conscience, the day began to pall. I allowed myself a vision of Andy bearing down on me wearing nothing but a smile. I had been very naughty indeed, but, dammit, you only live once, unless you're a Buddhist.

I wasn't sure how to proceed with the Andy thing. Of course there could be no 'proceeding' in my current situation, I reminded myself. But I wanted to see him again. In actual and horrible fact, I wanted to shag him as soon and as often as possible. In order to do that I would have to streamline my life somewhat, and in stark reality that meant getting shot of Barry. I didn't know if I had courage enough to do that. And I was by no means certain that my being available featured anywhere on Andy Raynor's list of desirables. A ladies' man, by definition, is hard to pin down. Andy was a serial dater, perhaps even a speed one, and now that he'd had me, he was probably done with me. That thought precipitated a panic and heralded depression, so I fired up the engine and headed out to collect the kids from school.

As I strolled from the car I spotted a shop which had a lottery machine, and decided to play my numbers in the next draw. I jotted down 1, 4, 5, 6, 11, and 19, and also allowed the computer to choose a random quickpick for me. If you're not in, you can't win.

Eighteen

Jimmy Nolan sat in his car wearing shades and trying to look like a regular human being. I expected Mick to make some comment about what a gobshite his eldest son was, but he was strangely silent. I realised that he hadn't said anything at all for quite some time. Strange. I saluted Jimmy as I entered the school yard, and he pretended not to notice me. But rather than let him think that he had done a subtle thing, I returned and rapped on his window until he paid me attention and rolled it down.

'What?' he wanted to know.

'Just wondered how the case was going?'

'For starters, you're ruining it. That do you?'

I shrugged. ''Spose,' I said.

He relented then. 'If you really want to know what's going on, you could do worse than talk to your two buddies. They lead very interesting lives, after hours, if you know what I mean.' He rolled his window back up. Actually, I didn't know what he meant, but I nodded sagely at him and went to join Lisa and Colette. They began to look angry as I approached, which worried me.

233

Then I saw that they were looking beyond and behind me, as were a lot of other parents. Carmel Lally, I guessed, correctly. But this time Carmel did not skulk in, she took centre stage and began to shout.

'I have had enough of you lot giving me a hard time! You have no idea what I'm going through, and if you did you still wouldn't understand the pain and pressure that I put up with every day. I don't know which of you is responsible for the harassment I'm experiencing, but when I find out, you'll be sorry you ever started with me. Leave me and my family and our home alone, do you hear?' Her voice had begun to crack with emotion. 'Leave us alone.' She rushed into the crêche, away from the crowd. I looked at Colette and Lisa and saw that they were smiling, slyly.

'What's going on there?' I asked, lightly.

Lisa replied, 'Oh, a spot of bother with her car, I heard, and her garden was dug up a bit, I think.'

'And someone daubed paint on her garage door,' Colette added.

Suddenly they didn't look like the people I had grown up with. There was a cruelty in their faces which frightened me, and I didn't want to be involved in their schemes. I made my excuses and put some distance between us. Were they responsible for the attacks on Carmel Lally's property? Did Jimmy know the score? I made a note to look into the matter later that evening, when I had some time to myself.

Mary showed me a beautifully illustrated book she'd made that day. It was called *The Queen Was Sick* and

went along the single line of 'One day the queen was
sick, because she ate too much'. It was a simple parable,
with colourful graphics, not least the sick. Dominick
was no less wise as he told me that 'water will always
find a way'. I had no reason to doubt him. They both
liked the new colour of my car, and wanted to know
exactly why I had changed it. Then I remembered
where I had met the woman who had thrown the pint
over Michael O'Donoghue at Bridgecross. In fact, we
had promised to keep in touch. I even had her name
and address on a screwed up piece of paper in my
handbag. But first things first.

My delivery of the children was swift and efficient. I
was anxious to get to the office to deal with Tara
O'Donoghue and whatever baggage she brought with
her. The needles of potential began to click together in
search of the correct tension and the right pattern.
Would the result be a complex Fair Isle, or an Aran-
style slipover? Might it be a plain but functional scarf, or
a pair of gloves destined to end their day stuffed down
an ancient toilet bowl?

I rang a sleepy Ciara, and reeled her in with the
promise of a one-on-one with an O'Donoghue. She
promised to hang by as soon as she was compos mentis
and fit for human consumption, or whichever came
first. And before I left Angela's, I got a general idea of
where Carmel Lally lived. I could nail the address down
easier if I had a notion of where to look. I had not
thought about Andy or Barry in an hour and a half and
that felt good. Keep busy, fill the day.

The Indigent Sweeps' Society was the very model of
spick and span, and Kevin Mack was singing as he
worked. My glove was still hanging on the main notice
board like a little red badge of shame, and I felt guilty as
I walked by, denying it. No. 4 gave it a glance, but was
far more interested in getting off his lead and racing up
the stairs. I figured this was good exercise, so I let him.
It was not lost on me that the glove was the same colour
as the dress I had committed my 'adultery' in. Or, to be
more exact, the garment I had shed beforehand.

My office was ordered, gleaming and fragrant. I put
on a pot of coffee to percolate and found myself
humming. With any luck Mrs Mack would join a closed
order of nuns while on her pilgrimage, or be kidnapped
by an obscure religious cult and never returned. Then
the rest of the world could live in perfect harmony
without her. Kevin would eventually recover from the
shock, losing himself in his work until then, and taking
solace in it after his acceptance that she was gone. I was
happily indulging in these thoughts and a good scratch
of my head when Angela phoned to tell me that the
kids had brought home another letter, this time telling
all parents that the school was infested with nits.

'What're they?' I asked, like a big gobdaw.

'Headlice and their eggs,' she explained.

I stood bolt upright. 'LICE!'

'Yes, but don't worry, you can get rid of them easily
enough, you just have to be diligent.'

I was totally freaked out by the news. My head now
felt like it was on fire. Angela talked me through getting

a nit comb in the local pharmacy, along with tea tree oil shampoo and conditioner. And she broke the news that it would take at least three weeks to deal with the outbreak. I was diseased, unclean. And I might have passed them on to anyone I had made head-to-head contact with over the last few days. I could now officially kiss goodbye to any notion I'd had of forging a romance with Andy Raynor; who would want to sleep with a woman who'd given them headlice? My day began to crumble and fall apart.

'What do they look like?' I wailed.

'You'll know when you see them,' Angela replied, then hung up.

I sat back down in my chair and sneezed a bit, blew my nose and rubbed it vigorously; my nostrils were decidedly tender. I could feel my eyes tear up with irritation, and my sinuses began to ache. My head was host to the armies of insect hell. All I needed now was thrush to complete the package. Were these the wages of sin?

I was nursing strong caffeine and murderous thoughts when Ciara landed. I couldn't taste the steaming liquid because I was now totally bunged up and feeling very sorry for myself.

'Germ City, Arizona,' she said. 'You don't take proper care of yourself.' She was the picture of health, of course, just to rub it in. 'Did you get the ride at least?'

'Ciara, what kind of question is that to ask your boss?'

'A good, sensible one. Looking at you now, even

though you're a fright with that lurgy, I'd say you did. You're sitting differently, that's always a sign.'

'Ciara, we're here to discuss business, not my love life.'

'Aha! *Love life.* You did get laid. Brilliant! You needed it. And he's a big gorge, for an aul' fella. What's his name?'

'Andy,' I replied, without thinking. Then I corrected her. 'He's not old, and he's just a friend. You've got the wrong end of the stick.'

She just grinned at me. I let it go.

'These are the photographs you wanted,' she said, throwing a large envelope on to the desk. I sifted through the black and whites.

'Oh wait,' Ciara said. 'They seem to be mine, but that can't be. I only just gave the guy my film.' She frowned at the riddle.

'No, these are ones that I took,' I confirmed.

'Odd,' she said. 'Because that's Maria Flood.' Ciara pointed to a portrait of Michael O'Donoghue's colleague with the Egyptian bob hairstyle.

'That's the woman he gave a lift to while I was following him.'

'It's the woman he went to see very late the night before last,' she added. 'Daughter of another woman he's been known to call on in the wee small hours.'

'Do you think he's up to some pervy, shag all the family, thing?' I mused.

'Could be. It's up to us to find out.'

I put the photographs down and filled her in on the

pint-throwing at the Bridgecross function.

'He did look a bit sodden when he left,' she remarked. 'I had to keep myself from screaming with frustration when he got home because he just stayed there like a lump. The wife arrived back an hour or so later, all the lights went out, and when there wasn't a move out of either of them within the next hour, I decided to grab some shut eye myself in my own bed. I'm getting really fed up of that car.'

'That's the glamour of the job.'

'Shite. I'll probably end up with varicose veins and all,' she moaned.

I knew what she was talking about. If you spend enough time sitting in the confined space of your driver's seat, you end up going numb from the waist down. But only after your body isolates each area in a ring of muscle, ligament and bone ache, before robbing it of all sensation. In this way, I am well aware of where my coccyx is, for instance, but not where it goes to, my lovely, when the paralysis sets in. I spend a lot of time flexing my legs and toes to silly songs and rhymes in my head, just to encourage the blood to keep flowing in my veins.

We both turned to the door after a few small taps alerted us to our visitor. No. 4 had given up all pretence of guard-dog duty, and was snoring in a box under the desk. The intruder was carrying neither axe nor gun, so he didn't get fired on the spot. I would issue a warning presently; for now he would be let lie, as sleeping dogs should.

Tara O'Donoghue was in the throes of teenage acne and puppy fat. As a result she saw more of the ground than her surroundings as she shyly hid her adolescent horror. She hulked awkwardly into the room, unsure of where to place herself. A brief 'hello' was marked by the sibilance that comes of brace-wearing, in her case a version nothing short of a crown of thorns nailed into her mouth. It's hard to lisp on a word without an 's' but she was cursed even on that. I welcomed her and indicated the armchair, where she sat self-consciously hugging a leather school bag to her chest. Her knuckles were white. She refused coffee, nodded at Ciara as I introduced her, then glued her eyes to the floor. I picked up the baton and ran with it.

'You seemed anxious to talk to me about something,' I began.

This didn't have much effect.

'What was it that you wanted to tell me, Tara?' Her knee twitched. 'Did you have something to show me?'

She raised her eyes to meet mine. They had something of her mother in them, but were a warmer colour and looked troubled. When she spoke, she was the voice of upper-middle-class south county Dublin, a version of Valley Speak, Irish-style.

'I need to speak to Mr Street. Like, he's the one I'm here to see.'

Ah.

'Em, Tara, there's been a bit of a mix up, I think. You see, *I'm* Leo Street. And, eh, I'm not a man, as you can see.' At least I hoped she could make that out.

'Cool,' she said. 'So you'd be, like, Miss Marple or someone?'

'When she grows up,' Ciara interjected, mischievously.

Tara smiled at this.

'So now that you've found me, what did you have to tell me?' I asked, steering us back to our original point, and shooting the slightest of daggers at my lovely young assistant.

Tara looked from one to the other of us, and decided that we weren't the worst in the world. Then she took a deep breath and began.

'My dad has been, like, getting these letters, you know? I don't know how many, 'cos I'm away during the week, but I've, like, seen maybe three.'

'Could you tell me what they say, generally?' I prodded.

'Well, they're, like, all "you're gonna die" and "you're scum", you know?'

'Yes. And what do they look like, Tara? Could you describe them to me?'

'Oh, better than that,' she said, loosening her grip on the bag and beginning to undo the straps. Her nails were bitten to the quick, and the exposed skin showed red, raw and too young to be protecting anything. I marvelled at how she could get a grip on such thin slivers with the width of the hardware she had on her teeth. Jagged shavings of dead skin were still attached to the areas around the tips of her fingers, indicating that the gnawing continued long after the nail had succumbed. She ceased her rummaging and produced her

241

booty. 'I've got one here,' she said, raising the item to show us. Good girl, Tara.

I suppose we all watch too much television these days. But there are times when you could run over to the set and give it a big, wet smacker on the screen. This was one of those times. Not only did Tara O'Donoghue have a threatening letter in her possession, she had wrapped it, and the envelope it came in, in clear plastic. I made a sound which expressed praise, and she rewarded me with a glimpse of a thousand pounds' worth of dental hardware.

'I wore latex gloves when I handled them,' she added. 'We've got lots of that shit around, what with Dad being a doctor and all, like.'

I could have kissed her.

The letter was all colour and malice. A plain white sheet of paper held various magazine and newspaper letters glued to it. The message was straightforward: 'You will die for your aberrations. You are the lowest of the low. You will burn in hell.' The culprit had neglected to sign a name or codeword. The envelope simply said 'Michael O'Donoghue', no address and no postage stamp. Hand delivered, then.

All three heads pored over the cellophaned evidence, then I remembered my 'condition' and jerked back. The others hardly noticed, busy as they were collecting impressions. A quick scan of their locks revealed nothing in the way of wildlife.

'What makes you think you know who did this?' I asked Tara.

She gave me a distrustful look. Oh, no, now was not the time for her to go all Marcel Marceau.

'You did mention that you thought you knew who was responsible,' I added, as if she owed me.

Tears began to edge from the corners of her eyes. I reached for a tissue. 'There, there,' I cooed. What in hell is that supposed to mean or accomplish – there bloody there? There *what*? *There* where?

She blew her nose, and reached for the bag a second time. This next offering was a selection of magazines, also carefully wrapped. Some were up-market glossies of the sort that advise on how many orgasms you should be having per day, and what to read while you're waiting for them. And some were fashion rags full of designer labels and stick-thin women and men who probably didn't even exist but were digitally manufactured.

'I'm assuming that these have letters missing?' I said.

Tara sniffled and nodded.

'And where did you get them?'

'I found them in my mum's wastepaper basket,' she wailed.

This was strange. Even if Tara's mother were responsible, why was her daughter suspicious enough in the first place to be rooting around in her rubbish?

'Bummer,' Ciara was saying to her. 'I hate it when they get involved in this sorta shit.'

They both nodded wearily. A vista was opening up here that I probably wasn't ready for.

'Let's go through life at home for the last while, shall we?' I said quickly.

Two sets of young eyes turned to me. 'Tara,' I clarified.

'Well, I'm not there, like, all the time, you know? But they row a lot, I know that. And they don't really bother to hide that from me and Ben any more. It kinda all came to a head with Mum's new car recently. She really wanted a new one, even though her old one wasn't that old or anything. And it just had to be a certain kind of grey. Just *had* to be, like.'

Both Ciara and I concentrated very hard on the desk top during this piece of information.

'Anything else?' I asked, casually.

'I've only heard bits of the arguments. Mum says she doesn't approve of Dad's work any more. She's gone all holy on it, like. You know, kinda religious and stuff, quoting the Bible, or at least it sounds kinda biblical. And I wouldn't mind but she doesn't even go to Mass, like. I'm hoping to work in genetic research too when I've done college and all that. It's the way of the future, you know?'

'Does your mother know you have this letter or the magazines?'

'No way. I'd be, like, really dead meat. I mean, I'd probably get grounded and all.'

'Right. Tara, I think you should leave these here with us, and I'll go see your mum about all of this. Okay?'

She nodded.

'And you have my number if you need to talk to me or if you come across anything else you think might be relevant.'

'Hang in there,' Ciara said. 'You know parents, it's

probably just a phase they're going through.'

'Tell me about it,' said a worldly Tara O'Donoghue, hoisting herself to her feet. Then she stopped dead in her tracks.

'Oh my God, you know about *her*,' she gasped, indicating the photograph of Maria Flood on the desk with a pudgy, gnawed finger. She was now visibly unsettled and her breath quickened, while Ciara and I held ours. As if sensing that the game was somehow up, Tara sank back into the chair and gave a pained sigh.

'Dad came to visit me during the week at St Columba's about a month ago. Sometimes he does that, you know, if he wants to talk, like. But this time he had *her* with him. Maria, that's her name. He was being all vague and mysterious about 'news' that he'd have for the family soon, and I think he thought I'd be all chummy, like, but no way. I didn't want anything to do with her. He kept saying that he knew me and her would be great friends in the fullness of time, or some other stupid grown-up phrase, like. I haven't seen her since, but I bet that's another reason why my parents are at each other's throats.'

'Thank you, Tara, for being so frank with us,' I said. 'We'll try to get to the bottom of things from here. There is just one thing that I'm still wondering about, and that's how you decided to come to me with this? How did you know to contact me?'

She gave a watery smile and said, 'Good detective work.' Then she shuffled off, leaving an imprint of her unhappiness behind.

'Jeez, that Mrs O'D must be properly pissed off at her hubby for seeing other women,' Ciara ventured.

'Yes. But does she even know about Maria? And don't forget that she doesn't seem to share any zeal for his researches either. Would she actually act on her threat, I wonder, or is this just meant to scare him? And why insist on a grey car? Is she aware that Bernadette Flood drives one too? *They* know one another from ages back, remember, though how friendly they are now, we don't know. And which car is on your tail and consequently his?'

'We're close to something, aren't we?' Ciara said.

'Yep,' I acknowledged. 'But I'm not sure what it is. You know, I think it mightn't be a bad thing to give old Miranda a bell.'

I reached for the phone and dialled the O'Donoghue number, putting the call on the speakers in the office so that Ciara could hear. As always, it was answered on the third ring. I did the preliminaries then got to the reason we were speaking. 'Miranda, some very interesting evidence has come into my possession and I think we should discuss it.'

'Oh, really?' was the disinterested reply.

Sod this for a game of cowboys, I thought. I crossed my eyes to Ciara, in a thoroughly adult and professional manner, immediately regretting it, as I didn't want her picking up my bad habits.

'Yes, really,' I said, getting briskly back on track. 'I have in my hand one of the death threats issued to your husband. And I know where it came from. When should we meet?'

Her pause was well-nigh imperceptible. 'Today is no good,' she told me. 'I'll call you when I've established a convenient time. I must say though, Miss Street, that I really don't see what this might have to do with my husband and his affair. I do hope you're not wasting my time and money on an unrelated goose chase.' And then she simply hung up on me. I disconnected from my end to stop the repetitive tone of an electronic 'fuck you'.

'And that is the woman who hired us,' I told Ciara.

'Niiice.'

'Now what has she got to hide?' I wondered aloud.

'And why did she tell you about the threats in the beginning? Was she trying to throw you off her scent?'

'She couldn't have known that I'd get my hands on one of them, that's for sure. What *is* she up to?'

Ciara and I sat thinking for a few moments, but the sound was not unlike two empty cans clattering along the road. I glanced at my watch and made a decision. 'I'm off. I've got to go see a woman about a car.' I caught her expression. 'No, not that woman and not that car. They might be related, though. I'll tell you after I've dug about a bit. You're in charge. Be careful and keep in touch. Things may hot up considerably now, and I want to know where you are and who you're with at all times. Savvy?'

She saluted, hand to head. 'Aye, aye, Captain.'

I left.

Then I went back.

'Forgot the dog.'

'He knows,' she said. 'I wouldn't like to be in your shoes.'

I thought mothers could lay on a guilt trip, but none that I've seen in action could hold a candle to No. 4. I had to carry him down the stairs. Kevin Mack met us at the foot and said, 'Ah, the poor wee thing, is he not well?'

'He's fine,' I said, a mite tersely. 'Just feeling massively sorry for himself.'

Mr Mack rubbed the dog's white and black and tan head, and gave him a piece of chocolate which he produced from his pocket. No. 4 brightened enough to wolf this down, then slumped back into my arms like a dead weight.

'He'll be better again before he's twice married,' Kevin said. I think this was meant to be a comfort to me. Imagine being lumbered with the cost of two weddings, which I would have to bankroll as a lone parent. Much as my own dad would love to see me live as an 'honest' woman, he knows he'll have to foot the bill for the accompanying revels, so he's not as eager as my mother to bring the subject up. He's really never been in any danger of paying out for his only daughter's honour, more's the pity.

'Give it a rest,' I said to the dog. 'The long face won't work with me.'

I still ended up carrying him to the car.

'Garlic, and plenty of it,' was Molly's advice for my cold, as he hoiked some more phlegm on to the gravel from the endless supply within his frail body.

'Thanks,' I said. 'I'll remember that. And it'll ward off vampires too.'

He bobbed his ancient head up and down. 'The cross is a handy tool as well, for getting rid of those lads.' I looked hard, but there was no trace of irony. More reasons to be afraid of the dark.

'The little fella needs a bit of sunshine,' was his verdict on the dog. Now it looked like I'd have to shell out for a Mediterranean holiday as well as two weddings. This was one expensive mutt.

He cheered up once he got into the car. As usual he took up position with front paws on the dash, back legs on the passenger seat; Iggy Pop, eat your heart out. I flicked on the heaters, and when we'd built up a head of speed, I could see the warm air blow over his face, flapping his ears back. His long pink tongue lolled out of the side of his mouth. All he was missing was a pair of goggles.

We stopped by a pharmacy to get an arsenal of supplies for my various ailments. I sprayed my head liberally with a leave-in tea tree oil conditioner, in a make-do measure till I could deal with the problem properly. All it did was drive the vile creatures mad and more active than ever. I gave myself a good, vigorous scratching, and with my scalp raw, headed out on my next mission. The song is correct: sometimes it's hard to be a woman . . .

Nineteen

Kate Mulligan lived in a terraced house on a quiet street adjacent to the canal and town. I imagined it was the sort of area which had unofficial hanging basket competitions in the summer. In the cold April air, it seemed scoured and deserted. Her familiar red car looked forlorn on the road with its crumpled front bumper. In all likelihood there were flecks of my old paintwork still embedded in it. I parked a few doors away and dialled the number she'd given me. She answered on the eighth ring and I invited myself over for a little chat. I left No. 4 in the car because he couldn't be trusted, the mood he was in; this was a dog who'd been barred from at least one pub that I knew of, for activities I knew nothing of. Better to be safely clichéd than sorry.

Kate looked awful. No, worse than that. I reckoned she was normally a dress size twelve; now her clothes were hanging from her skeletal frame and I thought an eight would do. Her breath had the sweet, rank smell characteristic of hunger. Dark circles indicated her eyes, which were bloodshot from crying and lack of sleep. I didn't think she'd washed that day. She was in that

bizarre mixture of agitation and torpor which epito-
mises severe depression. I felt it best to leave out any
beating around bushes.

'I saw you in Bridgecross last night,' I began.

She gave a hollow gurgle, which I took to be a laugh.
'If I'd had a gun I would have killed him there and
then,' she said.

'Were you following Michael O'Donoghue the night
you ran into me?'

'Of course.'

'Why?'

'You know, I really don't know that. I suppose I was
waiting for some plan to occur to me along the way. I've
not been too rational this last while.' She twisted her
cardigan as she spoke, moving on when one section was
tightly bound up; it left a hedgehog pattern on one side.

'No,' I said. 'Why were you following him at all?'

'Ah. You might want to sit down. I'll make us some
tea.'

I looked around the room, which had seen better times.
The once cheery orange ragrolled walls now looked
smeared with grime. Rings from long-forgotten cuppas
and glasses of red wine were evident on all surfaces.
Dust and despair lay heavy over the house, and didn't
show much sign of lifting. I was afraid to drink what
was eventually put in front of me. The mug had seen
many other brews in its day. Brown circles marked the
interior and dark dribbles of various lengths decorated
the exterior. I thanked Kate, and nursed the mug in my

hands; at least it kept them warm. I had begun to shiver from the chill, but she seemed oblivious. I thought she might at least have noticed the steam from her breath each time she spoke, but apparently she did not.

'Michael O'Donoghue has ruined my life,' she said. 'Death is too good for him. But before he goes, I need some answers.'

She began to rock gently, and salt tears wet her cheeks. After a time she resumed. 'This used to be a very happy house. Are you married, Leo?'

'No. I live with a guy.'

'Well, you'll have some idea then.'

Only if I was in a fulfilling relationship, I thought, but didn't interrupt her with this observation.

'My husband Mark and me were mad to have children. After a year and a half of trying, with no success, we thought it might be good to get everything checked out. Nothing to panic about, just a look at all of our respective bits to make sure that we were both working properly, or what have you. It turned out that I needed a little hormonal prodding on egg manufacture and Mark had a slightly low sperm count, but nothing to be concerned about. It's a mucky old business, but we were both up for it and we took all of our tablets and temperatures and so on. Still there was no sign of a baby. And that's when Michael O'Donoghue suggested we try some of the newer products available.

'He explained that some of them were still a little unconventional, but we didn't care. We weren't desperate at this stage, we just wanted to have a baby and be done with the whole process. I did get pregnant and we were delighted, of course. By then Michael O'Donoghue was practically a god in our eyes.'

There was that word again. It made me feel distinctly uncomfortable.

Kate had begun to cry again, softly. 'I lost the baby at four months. We were devastated, both of us. And there were complications, which meant it was going to be even more difficult to conceive again. But we regrouped ourselves and went on an *in vitro* programme. It was tough for Mark too. It's not the easiest thing to be sent into a room alone with a magazine to try to produce some sperm while an army of medics is waiting outside. Anyway, to cut a long story short, we ran out of money. It's a really, really expensive procedure. And the pressure was unbearable. We'd started to fight, and throw recriminations around. It was awful. Then Michael O'Donoghue suggested that we join a test project he was in charge of. It was highly experimental, he said, but he had high hopes for success.

'At that stage I would have done almost anything. I was a crazy woman. Mark went along with it because he loved me, but I knew he had his doubts. After eight more months of agony, and pain too – there were some surgeries involved – Michael O'Donoghue told us it was hopeless, and he just shed us. Just threw us off the programme, said we were of no more use to him. He was so cruel, so heartless. We were in bits. And there was nothing we could do about it. He'd made his mind up and that was that.'

I left my mug on the kitchen table, it had gone completely cold by now. I was glad of my leather jacket and woolly jumper, lumpy or not.

'Then something happened,' Kate said. She began to have difficulty getting full sentences out. She was struggling for control of her emotions. In bursts of two or three words, interspersed with laboured breathing, she told me, 'I went back to the clinic one day, to ask for my charts, and I met someone. She said she'd help me, that what was going on wasn't right. She told me some terrible things.' Now Kate was sobbing loudly. I didn't know whether to comfort her or to let her finish her story. Whatever she knew had broken part of her, and it was doubtful it could ever be fixed. Her speech was disjointed with weeping.

'She said that Michael O'Donoghue had kept bits of my baby, for tissue samples. And that he had samples from me and Mark. He had stolen bits of us, of our very selves, for his FUCKING EXPERIMENTS. How *could* he? How *dare* he? Who does he think he is? GOD?'

She was gasping for air now, struggling to keep herself conscious. Her panic and sorrow were palpable, pressing down on the house and everything in it. I knew, without being told, that Mark had left, and she was alone in her crusade for justice. I went to her and put my arms around her. When she was calm again, I said, 'That was you on the radio this morning, wasn't it?' She nodded. 'So what now?'

'We expose the bastard, and all of his evil.'

'Can you tell me who your source is?'

'No.' She shook her head slowly and blew her nose. 'No.' She held my eyes in a gaze of pure hurt and said, 'Do you know what the worst thing is? I have no idea what that bastard has done to me. He experimented with me, and I have no idea what he did. And I will kill him, given half a chance.' She looked away into a middle distance that only she could go to.

I left, shaking. What sort of person would prey on the desperation of a young couple and leave them torn apart and ruined? Their lives were rent asunder, their dreams betrayed and destroyed. I got into the car and hugged No. 4. In all of my visit, Kate Mulligan had not once mentioned our cars. She hadn't even wondered why I was asking those questions.

We spend most of our adult lives avoiding pregnancy; this is the thrust of birth-control education. No one tells us what to do when the opposite is the case: how to deal with not being able to conceive. Then the label of 'barren' is thrown about, an ancient stigma courtesy of the fruitful and ignorant. I felt anger rise in me for Kate and Mark and all those couples like them whose lives are used and ruined by unscrupulous bio-pirates and immoral scientists just out to make their mark in the cut-throat world of scientific competition. I waited a moment for Mick Nolan to put the boot in about excessive 'mawkishness' on my part. He didn't. Odd, that.

Lots of detectives that I know would have established all of this by telephone. They could make a visual at any time, and follow up with a call. All nice and neat and sterile. That's not my way. I believe in the one to one encounter, but it has its disadvantages. This was a prime example. I had got close, too close, and it can burn a body out. I was touched by the raw emotion of this woman's plight and that made things personal.

I dragged myself home for some sort of comfort, all the while saying a silent prayer that Barry would be out. He was. I boiled a kettle and made a hot lemon drink fortified by two extra Aspirin. Then I washed my hair and ran the nit comb through it. Angela was right, I did know the creepies when I saw them, and their vile grey eggs. I felt terrible, and for the first time in months, I crawled into bed at tea-time and fell into a deep and sweaty sleep. I really didn't care if I never woke up again.

I did, of course, life being inexorable. It was dark as pitch in the room, and I was totally disorientated and groggy. My nasal passages had solidified and my mouth, having done all of the breathing work, was the Gobi of oral areas. That didn't last long. When my brain let my sinuses know that I had rejoined the world, the water-works started again. I stuffed two lumps of cotton wool up my nostrils, which were flaking and tender from the friction of too many tissues. I tried to move, but was trapped in a deep mattress crater; the power of gravity and pain held me prostrate. My muscles and bones ached, begging me to stay in the warm safe bed, but I had places to go, and people to see. By the time I had heaved my racked body downstairs, I was a little more alert, and rested, in an exhausted sort of way. I did not fall apart under the hot shower spray, which was a surprise of the pleasant variety. I bundled myself into several layers of clothing, told No. 4 that he would have to guard the castle and the cats, fed the lot of them and took to the night.

It's not often that business mixes with pleasure for me, so I was chuffed to be able to start the evening with a visit to the Chinese takeaway featured on Maeve's list. I ran through the usual dire warnings of a swoop by the cops if the nuisance calls did not stop. Then I treated myself to some spring rolls and chicken with cashew nuts and fried rice. Feed a cold, I told myself. The car was fragrant with the oils and spices of the east (Dublin) and I stopped just short of having the same again. A glance at my watch told me that it was eleven o'clock, which I felt was as good a time as any to wheel by Carmel Lally's in search of paint daubers and garden diggers.

The house was a detached dormer bungalow set off a tree-lined road which was itself off the main coastal road in Clontarf, townside. Not cheap by any means. I drove up and down a few times, assessing where best to leave my car, and settling for an unobtrusive space a few doors along from Casa Lally. I scanned the area, my eye lighting on a familiar vehicle close by, within full view of the Lally drive. Inside, I saw the sleeping form of Jack Nolan. I couldn't even muster mild amazement. After all, we're dealing with a man here who once ordered a buffalo mozzarella sandwich and asked where the meat was when it arrived. I left him to his dreams. Again, I was surprised that Mick was schtum. Where had he got to?

I crossed the road to the Lally pad and began a surreptitious survey of the property. The generous driveway held a station wagon, essential for family transport as I now knew from the school runs. It was parked in front of a closed garage to the side of the house, newly painted to cover whatever graffiti had been added without the Lallys' consent. The front garden was about a hundred feet in length and thirty feet wide, and it also showed signs of recent attention, no doubt to repair the damage done by the unwanted visitor. A narrow pathway led to the back garden which was a considerable size, if neglected. In the broad moonlight, it looked like a jungle adventure waiting to happen. Kids' bikes and toys were strewn throughout, and I could make out a sand pit close to the kitchen door.

I went to the front again, and stood back for an overview. Something was puzzling me. Through the thin membrane of the curtains I could see the flickering of a fire. Nothing unusual here, it was a chilly night and lots of homes throughout the town were showing similar jolly lights. It was just that these seemed too jolly. Without warning I was attacked by a fit of sneezing, and when it subsided and I had blown my nose for the umpteenth time, I found that I could breathe freely again. Which meant I could also smell. And what I could smell was fire. Not domestic fire, a house *on* fire.

I banged loudly on the front door as I reached for my mobile to call the fire brigade. I barked the address to the 999 number and continued to call at the door for Carmel and her family. The commotion attracted a few neighbours, one of whom was a chunky man who obviously worked out. He began to throw himself at the door to break it down while I ran around the back of the house again. I tried the kitchen door. It was unlocked. As soon as I opened it, a huge fug of smoke enveloped me and drove me back. My eyes stung, wickedly. I put my jumper over my nose and mouth and tried to figure out the geography of the room, but the smoke was too dense. I could feel it burn my lungs and invade my hair and clothes. I called out to Carmel as loudly as I could, but the fumes were reducing any sound I could make. I heard sirens in the distance, and prayed that the fire department would get here in time to save whoever was trapped. If the back door was left undone, then it was reasonable to assume that someone was home.

The noise and flashing lights of the fire engines brought other neighbours out on to the street. It's hard to resist the fascination of a potential tragedy on your doorstep. For all that, there was a silence about this gathering, and the squawking of walkie-talkies and the hum of the fire truck were really the only distinguishable sounds in the air. Firemen surrounded the house and invaded it through both doors. The fire was concentrated to the front and they quickly doused it. I envied them their metal breathing apparatus; my biological equivalent was also manmade but my innards were clogged and painful to use. They emerged with two small bundles and a larger one. Tears stung my eyes and rolled down my cheeks, creating rivulets through the soot. I rushed to the ambulance with the men and their human treasure. 'Are they alive?' I asked. 'I'm the one who made the call.'

'Yes, they're alive. But they need attention. We'll send them to the nearest hospital, you can follow on if you want.'

I walked back to the front door and told the man in charge who I was, more or less. I asked about the fire.

'Don't quote me, but it looks as if someone put something like a lit firelighter in through the letter box. That fell on to the carpet and it went from there. It's a good thing you came along when you did. Any later and it would have taken a greater hold and they might all have died. As it is they'll be pretty sick with smoke inhalation for the next while. Whoever did this should be locked up.'

I agreed.

I joined the neighbour who had helped me at the start. If he was anything to go by, I must have looked a right sight.

'That poor woman,' he said. 'She has nothing but trouble.'

'Where is her husband?' I asked. 'We should probably call him.'

'She chucked him out a fortnight ago, and I don't know where he went to. He's been back a few times to see the children, but I don't know where he's staying. He has a bit of a drink problem, and one night it got out of hand and he hit Carmel and she kicked him out. Can't blame her. It's not something anyone should have to put up with.'

I recalled the suggestion of a bruise on Carmel's face the first day I saw her. 'Was this regular, the beating?'

'Oh, no, I don't think so. He'd normally settle for breaking things and making a lot of noise. She called the Guards on him a few times and that always calmed him down for a while. He'd go on the wagon, and I have to say there was no nicer man you'd meet in a day's walk when he was off the sauce. Then he'd go back to his old ways and be a real Mr Hyde.'

A horrible thought was forming in my head. I let it out. 'Do you think there's any chance he did this?'

'Oh, God, no. Oh, no, I wouldn't think so at all. No. He's bad with the drink all right, but he'd never do anything to harm those kids. He's plain crazy about them. Oh, no, no, I can't see that at all.'

'You know someone's been messing up the garden and that?' I said. 'Have you seen anything suspicious?'

'Oh, that, yeah. Carmel seemed to think it was to do with her insurance claim. She slipped at the crêche, I think, and she's been in a neck collar thing. Mmn, no, I haven't seen anything odd, but then again I'm out at work most of the day. My mother thought she saw a blonde woman lurking around the place, but there are a lot of couples with kids coming and going all the time, and the Mammy isn't as alert as she used to be. Could be nothing.'

Or could be something, I thought. 'Do you think we should ask her if she saw anything tonight?' I asked. I hoped he realised that I meant this as a rhetorical question.

'No, no,' he said. 'She's in the hospice now. I can't do anything more for her at home.' He looked away, so that I wouldn't see him cry.

You drive along street after street, road after road every day, and you look in at the houses where people are living their lives. And you just don't know the half of what goes on behind those doors. The daily living and dying of a nation. Behind one façade joy, behind another sorrow, with no distinguishing marks to help you know the human minutiae or magnitudes of this world.

I gave my details and a brief statement to a cop who'd just arrived, and agreed to come down to the station for a fuller report at a time convenient to the Force and myself.

'I believe you've been here before,' I said.

He looked at me through suspicious eyes. 'This house is known to us,' was all he would part with.

Jack Nolan was stirring as I walked by his car. If his father wouldn't say it, I would: 'Gobshite!' I turned around and called the policeman. 'Officer,' I said. 'This man was here for the evening, perhaps he saw something.' Yeah, and I'm winning gold in the unicycle marathon at the next Olympics, I could have added. Jack was infamous for sleeping on the job, his excuse being that he had a demanding wife and hyperactive kids. My own opinion was that he was the laziest man alive, and the public should be warned before parting with money for his services.

It took me a while to get motoring again. I was knocked for six by the gritty vapours in my lungs, mixing as they were with gallons of sticky mucus. I'd heard of smoking out wasps' nests, and wondered if the same was true of the nits from my thatch. It was an extreme measure, and not as fragrant as the antiseptic smell of tea tree oil. I would stick with the conventional approach from now on, I decided.

I was not certain that Carmel Lally's husband was innocent of any involvement in the night's events, but even so, I had an idea who two of the other prime suspects were in this scenario and the thought did little to cheer me. It was time to visit my old school chums. What did I expect when I confronted them? A full and frank confession, complete with a statement to the police? Hardly. But I wanted to know if they were involved, even if it tarnished some childhood memories. Most of all I wanted to clear them of suspicion. But I'll admit that I wasn't expecting a good result. I tried not to assume that I knew anything of what was going on, but it was hard not to jump to a few conclusions. With a heavy heart, and heavier lungs, I pointed the car in the direction of Lisa's house. I needed some answers, though I wasn't sure yet what the questions were.

My breathing had settled into a worrying wheeze, as I tried to regain a regular pattern for delivery of oxygen to my body. It was true then, and is still true now, that if you don't breathe you die, and I was acutely aware of that. I coughed once or twice in the hope that this would loosen the blockage in my lungs.

I thought about Lisa Farrelly. To be truthful, we had never been the best of mates at school, but as is the way of these things, we saw a lot of one another. I remembered the day she had punctured every bicycle in the school yard with her compass because she hadn't got one for Christmas. It wasn't funny, even at the time. And a more uncomfortable thought was that she wouldn't have thought too hard about sticking that compass into a human being, though to my knowledge she never did. Would she be vicious in protecting her children's right to daycare? To be a mother was to protect, after all. But where might the line be drawn?

Call me suspicious, but the first thing I did was to feel the bonnet of the car parked in the driveway. It was warm. Someone had made a journey earlier that evening. I rang the bell, which did a Big Ben thing, and a few moments later I was looking at the lady of the house.

'Phew,' she said. 'Have you gone all crusty and started living the good life outdoors?'

'No.' A short answer, which probably wouldn't get us very far. 'I just saved Carmel Lally and her family from a fire. Another few minutes and they'd've been killed.'

Did she redden slightly, or was that my wishful thinking?

'Why call to tell me?' she asked.

'I just thought you might know something about the

incident.' I was grasping at straws and added, 'A blonde woman was seen leaving the scene shortly before I arrived.'

We both let that sink in briefly.

'I've been here all night,' she said. 'The kids can vouch for me.'

'I'll bet,' I countered. 'Why is your car engine still warm then?'

She let the silence last just a touch too long before coming back with the information that her husband had gone out to the shop because they'd run out of milk and bread for the morning. A little too much detail, I thought, and why hadn't she mentioned that her husband as well as the children could vouch for her whereabouts that evening?

'Tell it to the cops when they call,' I said, bluffing still. Then I upped the ante a little by remarking that the neighbour who had seen the blonde woman acting suspiciously was hopeful of an identification.

I could tell she was rattled, but to be fair anyone would have been in the same circumstances, whether they were innocent or not. I let her stew.

Colette's house wasn't very far from Lisa's. I knew it was outrageously late to be calling, but hadn't my brother Peter seen her out and about late at night? I made a deal with myself that if the main lights of the house were on, I would knock, if they were not I would go home and return in the morning at a more suitable time. Luck was a lady that night and the lights were shining. I thank you.

'Jesus, you look like you've been dragged backwards through a very mucky place.' Colette stood in her doorway holding a glass of white wine. 'Come in and I'll make you a hot whiskey. I can practically smell the germs off you.'

I followed her into the house listening to a non-stop volley of words. 'Ray did Santa Claus one year in town and he had every walking infection in Dublin sit on his knee. We didn't know what to give him for all the diseases he caught. I think he was glad of the cold, though, because it stuffed him up and he couldn't smell the children's breath when they were talking to him. A mixture of cheese and onion crisps and chocolate and Coke is just awful, he says. We got a collection of soothers too . . . the state of some of them! Worn down to the nub. It was a great way for parents to get the kids to give them up. Jesus, what a year that was! I suppose you got the letter about the nits? They're a curse, and a bitch to get rid of. I hope you have your special comb and so on?'

By now, I was sitting in an armchair by the fire with a steaming hot toddy in my hands and an overwhelming desire to doze off.

'What brings you here at this hour?' she asked.

With a heart-weary sigh, I told her the story of Carmel Lally's fire.

'And you thought I might have something to do with that?' Colette looked visibly upset at the notion.

'Everyone has a lot to lose if the crèche closes down.'

'That's no reason to go around trying to kill people.'

'True.' I sipped my whiskey. We both studied the fire for a bit. Then I said, 'You've been seen out a lot at night-time recently. That might look suspicious.'

Colette smiled. 'I have a job with those sort of hours,' she said, and sized me up before continuing. 'Actually, I can't present an alibi for earlier, though I was working. What I do is technically outside the law, and the people I deal with would be reticent about coming forward to say the least.' Then she let off a laugh. 'Your face is an absolute picture, Leo! And it's not just the soot. Close your mouth at least.'

'I can't,' I said. 'I'm using it to breathe through.'

Colette wore a mischievous smile. She was toying with me, I could tell, in the way that used to drive our teachers nuts in the old days. Whatever went through her head, she decided to come clean.

'I'm a call girl,' she said. 'That's how I make my money. I work as a whore.'

My chin hit my chest.

Twenty

Like I've said, you can't always guess what goes on in the privacy of a life. My job takes me into the specifics sometimes, but as far as people in general are concerned, I know as little as the next person. I looked around Colette's comfortable home and I saw that it all made sense. Ray was more unemployed than not, and wouldn't have been much help financially with the regular upkeep of a house and family. His wife now had a cash-based income, which was enviably tax-free, I assumed.

'Ray doesn't know, in case you're wondering,' Colette said. 'So I'd appreciate some discretion.'

'Of course,' I spluttered. 'What do you tell him, if you don't mind my asking?'

'Not at all. He thinks I do shift work in one of the hotels in town.' She snorted and added, 'Of course, in a way I suppose I do.'

I began to laugh. Huge guffaws seized the muscles in my torso with that special ache somewhere between pleasure and pain that mankind will never be able to identify or isolate. 'Colette, you are unbelievable,' I said, with genuine awe. 'The things you get up to. You'll have to write a book about your adventures.'

'Oh, the things I could tell you about this country,' she said, letting the remark hang to tantalise me.

'Is it not dangerous?' I asked. I've seen the bleaker end of the sex industry in my excursions through the underworld. It's not a place I would voluntarily choose to be.

'Leo, I know this will seem hard to believe, but I'm lucky to be doing what I am. I don't have a habit to support – barring Ray and the kids,' she chortled. 'I work decent enough hours, I get well paid, and I'm not out on the streets desperate for a score. It doesn't knock a spot off me. I couldn't care less about the actual act itself. And the clients I see most of often look after that end of things themselves, whacking off and whatnot. Sometimes they just want to talk to someone who won't argue back, or they might want to be chastised – I'm very good at that, thanks to living in this house. And other times I might just have to walk around a hotel room with or without my clothes on.'

I must have had some sort of 'oh, sure' expression on my face because she said, 'Really, Leo, it's a lot less hard work than serving in a bar or cleaning up after people. I have my own safety procedures in place, and I rarely take on an unknown quantity.'

'I think I saw you going into a hotel the night before last, early in the evening.'

She thought a moment. 'Ah, yes. I had to dress as a businesswoman. That was for a little Japanese man who

270

visits three or four times a year. He likes to watch me lie about in a variety of submissive poses. It makes him feel powerful. Then I admire his penis, and he refuses me sex when I beg for it. I leave him the panties I've been wearing that day and he pays me generously. He never lays a finger on me. He doesn't want to: that would undermine his dominance.'

'What would the nuns make of it all?' I asked, as I finished the last of my hot whiskey and got up to leave.

'Well, you know, Mary Magdalene was no saint, but Jesus thought she was okay.'

'Yeah. She isn't a saint yet either, is she? I haven't been keeping up with the march of the martyrs over the last while.'

'Em, not as far as I know. I'd have asked Mel normally, but she's off schmoozing with all that lot now and not returning calls.'

'Isn't it weird that no one we know who's died has given any sign that there is something after we shuffle off the mortal coil?'

'Maybe it would be cheating if they did.'

'Yeah, I guess none of us would make any class of an effort then, just a bit of genuine repentance on the death bed and you're in.'

'I'm going to try that anyway, just in case.'

'How is Ray?' I asked.

'He's fine, fine. He's the one writing a book.' Her eyes met mine. We both smiled.

'Good old Ray.'

'Yeah. I know a lot of people think he's useless, but

he's one of the best men I've ever met. And funny and sexy on top of that.'

'Hard combination to beat,' I acknowledged.

'So how *is* Andy Raynor these days?'

'The same.'

'Wow.'

'Yeah.'

We had reached the door. I turned to Colette and asked the question I'd been reluctant to put since I'd arrived. 'Do you think Lisa might have done something stupid tonight at Carmel Lally's?'

'Maybe,' she said, hedging. 'But even if she did, I don't think she would have meant to harm anyone. Just warn Carmel off, perhaps? You know yourself that she was never any good at thinking through consequences.'

I could only reply 'Mmm' to that.

'Leo, I know it's hard for you to understand this, but when a mother feels that someone is threatening her children or her life with them, there isn't much she wouldn't do to protect them or their way of living.'

'You're right, that *is* difficult for me to believe.'

We said our goodbyes and I headed out into the cold, hurrying to the car before it caught hold of me and froze my already aching bones. I sat in and honked up my blocked nose into a paper hanky. The contents of the handkerchief were an upsetting molten black. Why had I looked?

The early hours of that Dublin morning saw me battle to keep my eyes open. I drove with the care of a learner, window down to blast my face with icy wind. I yearned for my warm bed, with its flannelette sheets and all-encompassing duvet. I would have some Aspirin, climb into a pair of pyjamas and hide under the covers for as long as sleep would let me. I could practically taste the sensation. It would be a different night from my last, but that was a madness best forgotten. Or was it? Was it a sign that I could or should change life to accommodate another situation? Was this the time to make a big change? I found that with each block I passed I was wider and wider awake as I thought about Andy and the world he might offer. Of course, the fact was that he had offered nothing. He had shown me a good time, but promises had not featured. What it did underline was the staleness of my arrangement with Barry. If we were now, as we seemed to be, friends who loved one another but rarely made love to celebrate this, then surely we should have a different living arrangement?

At what stage in our lives do we take our courage in hand and change everything we are comfortable with and used to? Surely it shouldn't take a crisis to precipitate this. It often does, but from time to time can we not act according to our hopes and aspirations rather than a momentous incident? Steely resolve was gaining a hold on me.

I parked by my familiar curb for which there was, as yet, no municipal charge. Some day soon the inner city would reach out this far and claim taxes, but for now we were safe. There were lights alight, and I expected a few live specimens of the human animal to be dotted around the downstairs living area. What I found was a more furred variety. The lack of a distinctly human presence was a comfort: I am a total coward when it comes to confrontation, I've decided.

The apparition in my bathroom mirror was enough to frighten two continents. My face was a grey mixture of soot and sweat, with red areas of demarcation for my eyes and nostrils. I sniffed my clothes, to no avail; my nose was not functioning in the traditional manner. I reached for the luminous pink toilet roll which had been a birthday present from my family and pulled off half a mile. Then I blew my hooter so hard my ears popped. The paper roll filled again with a glutinous gack reminiscent of green and black Playdo mixed in a bizarre marbled effect. I hurried under the shower and sluiced away the night.

There was a pain in my face where my sinuses should have been, and my head was threatening to burst so I dissolved some medication and downed it in one gulp. Eight eyes were watching my every move, so I lined up three bowls at one end of the kitchen and one at the other and began to fill them from the requisite tins. The hairy ones approved, and fighting was kept to a minimum. I could barely keep my eyes open as I slowly climbed the stairs, into my peejays and under bed clothes warmed by Barry Agnew. So much for resolve. Oh, what the hell. There was no point in waking half the neighbourhood with a row-stroke-discussion that could wait until my head stopped throbbing with a cold and nit bites, and I had enough sleep in me to bear the agony that it would generate.

It was a very dark 3.30 a.m. when my phone rang and Ciara said, 'Come get me. I'm in Donnybrook cop shop. Michael O'Donoghue is dead.'

Parking around Donnybrook Garda Station is a bugger at any time of the day or night. I wedged the car into a tight spot in a nearby laneway, where I thought it wouldn't block the path of too many ambulances. I crossed the deserted main road, led by the shining blue light above the door. Ciara was in reception, looking cold and lonely, and very young.

'Thank God for that,' she said. 'If I have another cup of the rat poison they call tea here, I might as well book a coffin for myself.'

The Desk Sergeant smiled. 'She's a character,' he said.

Ciara was done giving her report on events, so I bundled her off to the coffee dock of Jury's Hotel in nearby Ballsbridge. She didn't offer to drive there herself, and I didn't press her. She was drawn and shaken. We walked past the main desk where a young couple were drunkenly booking in for the night. They were fighting over whose credit card they should use. At the rate they were going they would be fit for nothing but sleep by the time they got to their room, I thought. Illicit sex takes energy, as I had come to know so recently myself, and I didn't fancy their chances that night. Life is gone in an instant, grab it while you can. I knew then that I was going to see Andy again as soon as possible. We had things to sort out, I hoped.

Ciara was very quiet. When we were settled in front of two mugs of frothing steam, I asked her what had happened.

'I've never seen anyone die before,' she said, studying her spoon intently. 'He must have died while I was looking. He's dead. He just . . . expired. He's dead.'

'Put some sugar in your coffee,' I told her. She didn't respond, so I heaped in two large ones and stirred.

She took a gulp, then gagged. 'Fuck, I've burned my tongue. Ah, shite, this is going from bad to worse.' But at least she was back with me in a slightly less distracted state. She panted like No. 4 for a few minutes then proceeded with her story.

Michael O'Donoghue had a humdrum day of private practice patients, then rounds at the Fledgling, where the only excitement appeared to be a slight argument with one of his staff.

'How do you know that?' I asked.

'I went in for a while. I was going stir crazy in the car so I sat in a waiting area near his office reading magazines. I was getting nicely stuck into an article about female circumcision when I heard raised voices, not loud, but enough. It didn't amount to much, just him asking where some files were, and saying that the system was a disgrace. I didn't get a good look at the woman involved, though she was probably young enough because she shifted down the corridor at a fair pace.'

He lunched with a male colleague in a sandwich bar

on the edge of Merrion Square, where, according to Ciara, he went mad and had butter *and* mayonnaise on his ham salad ciabatta. 'He didn't need to worry about a heart attack,' she commented. A few journalists had doorstepped him that evening as he left the clinic, but they didn't seem interested in following him further than the corner. 'Lazy bunch of gits,' Ciara said. He drove to Sandymount Strand and sat watching the sea from his car before making some calls on his mobile, during which he was clearly agitated. Afterwards he walked along the beach, kicking up the sand, then sat behind his steering wheel for a while more. When he had bought as much time alone as he probably could, he returned to the family home. Ciara could see no evidence of his wife's grey car, either following her or in the driveway.

'Then there was nothing for hours. I thought I'd go mad.' She drained the last of her coffee. 'Little did I know he'd make up for it so spectacularly.'

I ordered us another shot of caffeine each; we were both so wired now, it would not make that much difference to our systems.

'We were headed along the coast road when it happened. He was taking it at quite a lick, and on a corner he lost control. Odd, though, he didn't slow down at all, just ploughed into a skip full of odds and ends outside a house with a Sold sign attached to it. Nice housewarming present for someone.'

'I wonder what happens now,' I said aloud.

'Yeah, hardly much need to follow him any more.

He's unlikely to be making too many more journeys.'

'Ciara, I'm really sorry you had to go through this. It can't be easy for you.'

'It's different, I'll give it that,' she said. 'I guess we'll be needing another job, a.s.a.p.'

'Down but not out, eh?'

'Company policy, boss.'

It was about then that it dawned on me why Mick Nolan was no longer around. I had to sort things out with him, and soon. I owed him an apology.

'You should go home and get a good night's sleep,' I told Ciara.

'Yes, Mum.'

'Tomorrow we'll type up our report, such as it is, and calculate any money owed. Jesus, I hate grubbing around for that at a time like this. We'll play it by ear.'

I told Ciara about my own investigations that night, including an instructive story about Jack Nolan to lighten our mood.

'He was complaining about hangovers once upon a time,' I began, 'so I advised him to put three Rubex in a pint glass of water and leave it by his bed to drink during the night whenever he might waken. That way, he'd be getting re-hydrated by a tasty orange drink with some vitamins included in the bargain. He arrived to work the following day a pale shade of emerald. He swore he'd tried the cure but it didn't work. When I quizzed him, I discovered that he'd put three spoonfuls of *Radox* in the water and drunk it. I'm sure it made for a very fragrant vomit.'

Ciara smiled for the first time in ages. 'Relax with a Radox barf,' she said.

When I told her about my visit to Kate Mulligan she looked pensive again, mulling over some thoughts in her head before giving verbal shape to them. 'You know, Maria Flood works at the Fledgling, and obviously both she and her mother were involved with Michael O'Donoghue. What if she's the source who was going to help Kate?'

'But if she was having an affair with him, that would be an odd thing to do. It would be a massive betrayal.'

'True.'

'Might it have been her he was rowing with at the clinic earlier?'

'Could have been, I suppose. And of course he saw her later in the evening . . .'

'We should speak to her so.'

'Even though we're no longer needed on the case, with our main interest currently negotiating at the Pearly Gates?'

'I hate loose ends,' I said, fidgeting in my seat. 'Maybe just one last teeny-weeny dig about. I mean, what harm is there in a chat?'

'Easier said than done, I'm afraid. She's unconscious in the hospital.'

'Back up there a bit, Ciara. What happened?'

'Oh, didn't I mention it? Maria Flood was in the car with Michael O'Donoghue when it crashed.'

Twenty-One

I am not overly fond of hospitals; I rarely go into one for a good reason. Mostly I'm there to check on broken people, or damaged ones. And occasionally I have to get fixed up myself, so the sight of one can trigger memories of pain that I would normally rather forget. I had not been in Dublin for Rose's birth some weeks earlier because of a case down the country so I missed the one happy event which might have put hospitals on a temporary reprieve list for me.

I pulled up outside Saint Benedict's and parked the car in the vast area designated for such things. Traffic was brisk, given the late hour, or early, whichever way you wanted to look at it. Then again, I don't suppose illness and death follow a timetable convenient to regular office hours. Benedict's was built in the sixties, in the days when hospitals still got saints' names in good old Catholic Ireland. It was a boxy, pre-cast concrete structure that had not weathered well, and now sported tentacles of modernity that neither matched the main building nor attempted to. It didn't inspire confidence at first glance, but I was looking at it from the luxurious standpoint of good health. No doubt if I was rushed in by ambulance, Benny's would be the Grace Kelly of hospitals.

I passed the nurses' home, from which chatty young women and men poured forth to do a red-eye shift for far too little money. It's known as the 'Virgin Megastore' to the drinkers who sup in the cavernous pub across the road. My caffeine hit had begun to wane, and I wondered if I should have left this bit of business until the morning. Ciara had been despatched for some R 'n' R, after a spirited dog fight. I was feeling distinctly weary myself, but couldn't resist a quick shufti at the Flood situation. If things were too tense, I could come back another time.

My nose had begun to dribble again. I popped two tablets which I thought might be Aspirin; the label was too worn and old to read. Even if they were Smarties, I was willing to give them a try. Placebos are fine in my book.

I entered the building through the swing doors of the Accident and Emergency Department, past some smokers, pacing up and down furtively in the cold and an eerie backwash of second-hand light. Good for future business, I surmised. Inside was all disinfectant and mild panic. Fluorescent bulbs shone down, cruelly removing any trace of personality from worried faces. Apprehension bounced off every wall, endlessly revived and renewed with each admission.

Nurses and doctors moved swiftly from one area to another, all studiously avoiding a pool of blood on the floor. I followed suit. Crying, choking and groaning supplied a soundtrack in the curiously hushed air. Was this what's referred to as ambient music? I continued along the antiseptic blue corridor leading to the main reception desk where I found a middle-aged man in a uniform reading a pile of yesterday's tabloids. He didn't seem too interested in my presence but I persisted and was finally rewarded with the information that Maria Flood was in Intensive Care. As a relative (ahem) I was allowed to look through the large windows into her room, where she was hooked up to more technology than the main Microsoft computer system.

Maria looked even tinier in this environment. She lay silently on her back, arms resting on a crisp white sheet which seemed to pin her to the bed. Bandages swathed her head, letting only the merest wisp of dark hair escape. There were tubes in her nose and mouth and a drip fed liquid into a vein in the back of her alabaster hand. Monitors regulated life in a gentle ebb and flow, softly, fearful of disturbing their patient, yet hopeful that she would awaken. She was motionless, but for the gentle movements of her chest as a ventilator helped it bring oxygen into and throughout her body. I had the impression that if she moved she might somehow break. Her stark form shone against the dim background of her transparent cube. She looked safe.

I found her mother watching paint peel in another dingy corner of the medical sprawl. She looked as worn as the hospital itself, hunched into an almost foetal position in her chair. I had never been this close, but I could see that Bernadette Flood was taller than I had expected, perhaps 5′ 7″ or 8″. Her hair was shoulder-length and dragged back into a loose plait, with strands of silver appearing at the sides. She brushed an invisible stray wisp away several times, unsure what to do with herself or her hands. She had a pale complexion, rendered even more ghostly by her present situation. And in all of this, two soft brown eyes struggled to make sense of her predicament. I kept my introduction short and to the point. She was distracted, obviously, but she was listening and that was a start.

'How is Maria doing?' I asked.

'She's stable, but we're not sure about the extent of her injuries. It's weird, I can't sit and watch her even though I spent years as a nurse. It's different when it's one of your own.'

I made a soothing noise.

'She's only young, you know. She's got her whole life ahead of her.' Her gaze had returned to the wall.

'Bernadette,' I said, recalling her. 'Would you mind if I asked a few questions? I'll understand if you're not up to it, but I'd really appreciate it if you could answer me. I just need to figure a few things out, and you're the only one who can help me.'

She shrugged, as if to suggest that it couldn't hurt. In fact, it might, but a window of opportunity was creaking open and I pushed it just a little wider.

'Bernadette, I need to know what your connection was with Michael O'Donoghue.'

'Right, all the easy ones first, then,' she said, drawing

her lips into a smile that never reached her eyes. Nowhere near. 'It's odd to think of it as "was" now.' Her voice dropped. 'But not unpleasant.' She ran both hands along her thighs awhile before continuing. The action seemed both to calm and galvanise her. The navy gabardine of her trousers purred and fell back perfectly into place each time; quality is always worth paying for. When she spoke again, I saw that she was struggling to keep an even tone, but it was impossible not to hear venom somewhere beneath the surface. She kept her gaze on the floor, nervously raising her eyes from time to time to punctuate her story. Or was she just checking me out, analysing my reaction – or shaping it?

'I met Michael when I was just twenty. I was nursing at the Rotunda and he joined the staff hot out of medical school and determined to make his mark as an interim. That meant off the field as well as on, if you get my meaning. He was terribly charismatic then. Yes . . . that's the word . . . terribly . . . terrible. It was attractive in a handsome young blood. We all hoped to be chosen. Of course, he was horribly arrogant too. But again, this was put down to youthful exuberance. He was good at his job, very good, so there were never any complaints about that. He managed to catch the eye of the Master and of the money types around. In time he secured a small grant for some studies he wanted to make into DNA and what have you. He was clearly a man going places. Eventually, he got around to dating me. Looking back on it now, I see that it was most likely some kind of rota he had in his head; just knocking us down like bowling pins.

'He was as fierce when it came to romance as he was with his work. I really don't know where he got his energy from. He was able to survive on about three hours' sleep a night, which of course is handy for any doctor. Inevitably, rumours went about that he was taking drugs to stay awake. If he was, I never saw any evidence of it. He just had one of those metabolisms. I think he enjoyed going out with me because I'm a good listener. He took this for adoration, and maybe it was a bit of that too. Whatever the case, it suited him. I suited him. And it was handy that we worked in the same hospital, easier to see one another and so on. All part of the manipulation of circumstance and people that suited Michael. I didn't see it like that at the time, but that's what it was. I was useful for getting him the odd interesting sample as well. He didn't like to be seen to do too much grubby stuff; that wouldn't have looked good in a golden boy.'

An orderly came by with a refreshment trolley. 'Ah, Bernie, there you are. I'd say you could do with a cup of tea right now.'

'Thanks, Stan, that would be lovely.'

'And yourself?' he asked, turning to me.

'Tea would be great.'

'Tea for two and two for tea. I had a look in at Maria. No change. But at least she's comfortable. You're not to worry now,' he said, handing over the scalding disposable cups. 'She's in the best place. Amn't I right?'

I passed mine from one hand to the other in rapid

succession, waving the empty one each time. I cannot get over the fact that thin plastic doesn't melt at these temperatures. I'd hate to think what that says about the manufacturing process. It's not natural.

We sat in our regulation chairs, juggling, listening to the rumble of Stan's cart as it faded into the distance, accompanied by the squeak of his crêpe soles on the polished hospital floor. All that was left in the air was the sound of women blowing on tea to cool it. Bernadette Flood looked over at me. 'It's ridiculous, isn't it? Here we are, removing the prints from our fingers with the heat, and when it's right to drink we'll have all of seven seconds to get it down before it goes completely cold.'

'How involved were you with Michael O'Donoghue's researches?' I gently prodded her back to her recollections.

'Oh, hardly at all. I was a nurse, not a scientist. I really couldn't follow a lot of what he talked about, let alone did. As long as he wasn't sewing body parts together and electrocuting them, it seemed fine to me. He was very involved with his test tubes while I was a bed pan woman.'

'I take it there was a parting of the ways at some stage?'

'Yes. He met a laboratory technician who was on the up and up, so he dumped me. I was devastated. Lost weight, couldn't stop crying. Eventually, I got a job in another hospital, and that was the saving of me. I met the most wonderful man and married him. People say there's a rebound time, and maybe there is. But when the right person comes along you just know, rebound or not. And that's what happened to me.'

Something about that last statement echoed deep inside of me, and it had nothing to do with this case.

'And Michael? Did you keep in contact?'

'No, no. Next thing I knew, he was getting married too, to the lab woman, Miranda. He's still married to her. Sorry, was.' She sipped her tea. 'Quick,' she said, 'it's just right now.'

We drained our cups and tossed them in a brown bin in the corner. Bernadette went to check on Maria. I made good my opportunity to visit the Ladies. All those diuretics flowing through my system had to exit sometime. It's disconcerting when urine smells similar to the last meal you had or the last round of drinks. Tonight, I was treated to the coffees and teas of the Orient, mixed so as to be pungent yet indistinguishable. It made me wonder about people who drink their own first thing each morning. I mean, what about that Tikka Masala you had the night before; could you face it again for breakfast in liquid form? My stomach growled with hunger at the prospect, which was worrisome. I looked at my watch and the bad news that it was now 5 a.m. I took up my place in the waiting area once more. A yawn welled up, but I refused to let it out; next thing I'd be hosting a festival.

Bernadette had not been so lucky. When she returned she was in the midst of a spree.

'I won't keep you up much longer,' I promised. 'You obviously need a nap.'

'Don't worry about me,' she said. 'This is what I grew up on, really. And I don't want to miss Maria waking up . . .' Her last statement trailed off, because no one was certain that Maria Flood would ever do that.

'Why were you seeing Michael O'Donoghue again?'

'Oh, that,' she said, disgusted. 'He could never leave things be. Especially if he wasn't the centre of attention.' She paced the worn linoleum. 'Maria started work at the Fledgling eight months ago. Of course, when he figured out who she was, he took a special interest. Took her under his wing, you might say. Then all I heard was "Michael this" and "Michael that". I didn't interfere, because she seemed to be enjoying the work, and it was a wonderful opportunity for her. Then things took a turn. She came to her Sunday dinner very upset one week, and when I eventually got through to her, she told me that she knew all about me and him. Well, what was there to know? A short-lived romance with no love lost. But I had underestimated that bastard. Do you know what he'd done?' Bernadette was struggling now, searching for ways to explain. She waved her hands in every direction, seeking the right words and attitude. 'He'd told her that he was her father, and that he had stopped me from having an abortion when I was pregnant with her.' She shook her head violently. 'Jesus! Imagine that. How twisted can a man get?'

'I take it he was not Maria's dad?'

'NO. For one thing I would have had to have been pregnant for a year and a half if he was. I don't know what he thought he was up to with that particular yarn, or what he intended to achieve, but it backfired on him, I'm happy to say.' She allowed herself a pained smile. 'Whether he knew it or not, *that* was when his troubles really started.'

She looked around for something to do with herself as she spoke. 'Times like this, I'm sorry I gave up smoking.'

I worried that she had broken her concentration and would stop talking about Michael and Maria. She caught my eye and read my mind.

'Where was I?' She looked back to some middle distance in her mind, then continued.

'I've never seen Maria so angry. She felt betrayed and manipulated. Of course, those were Michael's specialities. Yet he still thought he could get her back on side. He started to visit her at home, then me. Wouldn't leave us alone. Do you know, I think he almost came to believe that somehow she *was* his daughter. I never understood what he thought he'd achieve with the charade. Perhaps he calculated that she'd be even more loyal to him if she believed they were related. Maybe he wanted her help with his illicit experiments. It doesn't make sense to me; he was so rational and ordered about everything else in his life, a control freak. He seemed a little unhinged in these last weeks. But Maria was adamant that she would expose him, so she started to delve into files from before her time. I don't think it made for pretty reading. From what she told me it seems he was making babies to his own design, if you like. Experimenting on early fertilised cells, then chucking them when he was done. Often he wouldn't tell the couples involved whether they'd actually succeeded in conceiving, which to me was the cruellest thing of all. He was a completely immoral man, Miss Street. He deserved to die.'

Somewhere in the sterile distance, a patient cried out in his sleep. It could have been the sound of Michael O'Donoghue reaching the portals of Hell. It seemed to spook Bernadette and she got up to go and check on her daughter. I followed and we both stood watching the machines by the bed draw their electronic chart of life in peaks and dips, the steady beeps beating out a reassurance.

'Why were you following him?' I asked her.

'Who?'

'Michael O'Donoghue.'

'What makes you think that I was?'

'A silver-grey saloon was seen tailing him over the last week.'

'That's a common enough colour and you know it.'

Interesting that she didn't deny the proposition. But she was clearly exhausted now and wanted shut of me. I could see her lips pressing closed into silence. I gave her one last push.

'Why do you think Maria was with him tonight?'

'They were on their way to my house,' Bernadette said. 'We were all going to sit down and have this out. She rang to tell me they were leaving. When the next call came, and they still hadn't arrived, I knew something was wrong.' She raised a hand to her mouth to stifle her anguish.

'It must have been a terrible shock to you,' I said, probably about the blandest words ever uttered.

'Yes. And no one was to know that Maria would be in the car . . . Why didn't she take her own? Why did she travel with him?'

'It was an awful accident,' I conceded, still trying to gauge her last sentences. Bernadette gave off a sound which could have been classified as nervous laughter.

'The Guards were here earlier,' she said. 'They don't seem to think that it *was* an accident. They think there was foul play involved.'

'You mean, Michael O'Donoghue might have been murdered?' I was mistress of the obvious that night, but there are times when only that will do.

Bernadette turned to me and twisted her mouth into a parody of a smile. In the subdued light, her small, white teeth looked like fangs. 'Imagine that,' she said.

I don't know how I got myself out of the hospital, I just remember feeling that it was imperative that I left. I'm not sure if I said 'goodbye' or simply lurched away. The world was buzzing angrily about me and an unpleasant feeling of foreboding flexed its icy fingers around my heart. I sucked in the cold night air as I staggered back through the car park. A mist was trying to settle before dawn, but nature was playing hardball and negotiations were ongoing.

My head was thumping and my chest struggled against cement-like congestion. I had lights flickering in my peripheral vision, like an Aurora Borealis of pain and disorientation. I was torn between a desire to pass out or to vomit, both manifestations of exhaustion and a shattered mind. I laid my forehead on the steering wheel while I waited for the car to heat up. My skull was full of voices, all of them wishing Michael O'Donoghue harm. I had so much to do, but I would be useless until sleep had soothed me. In slow motion, I started the engine, put the car in gear and carefully headed for home. I don't remember much of the journey or of letting myself in and getting undressed. Just the wonderful sinking, sinking, sinking into oblivion.

I jerked back to consciousness at seven minutes past noon when the telephone finally got my brain's attention. With a groan, I lifted the receiver to my head and croaked a response.

'You sound like I feel,' Maeve said.

'Welcome to Hell,' I returned.

Twenty-Two

I chewed on some charcoaled toast, dreading the moment I swallowed when it would scrape my throat like a cheese grater. I looked at the line of pills which were to make up the rest of my brunch. Beside a steaming hot lemon drink, laced with Paracetamol, stood a line of vitamins, decongestants, Aspirin and a nasal spray. It was certainly a cure that could kill, and I was beyond caring which outcome prevailed. Then came the nit comb and tea-tree oil conditioner. Lovely. A perfect marriage of insult with injury.

Barry had left a note on the kitchen table telling me that his Chelsea socks were AWOL. I couldn't find a sympathetic fibre in my body with which to share his loss. I don't think I would have given even a half-shrug of regret if the house had burned down around me right at that moment. It might have warmed me up. The heating was roaring at full blast, but I still shivered. I was also jittery about life, work and everything, in roughly that order, and in a way I usually associate with hangovers; that sort of unreasonable panic is impossible to deal with and I detest it. This morning, above many others, I had full reason to be anxious.

I hauled myself to my feet when I had ingested as much of my burned breakfast and medication as I could. The room did a few revolutions, and when it stopped my head took over on the spinning. This was not auguring the finest day of my life. I desperately wanted to return to bed, and sleep until I was fixed again.

Angela called to check on how many ailments I had picked up from the kids. 'I'd say it was them who gave you pretty well all of those,' she said. 'They're walking around like the living dead themselves, and I nearly didn't have the heart to send them to school today.'

'Believe me, Angela, I think I may have deserved punishment anyway because I am a very bad person and payola time comes to all who sin.'

'Get down off that soapbox, would you? The bush telegraph is buzzing with news of your heroics last night. So you can't be that awful.'

'Don't bet on it,' I said, as I tried to expunge an image of my infidelity from my mind's eye. 'If I die, and that is my preferred choice right now, tell the world I did my best, even if it wasn't good enough.'

'Will do. Actually, I called to say that you don't have to collect the children today if you don't want to. I'd say you're wrecked from your adventures.'

'If it's all the same to you, Angela, I will. I'd like to follow up on the Carmel Lally incident.'

'The choice is yours. Good luck out there, it's a dangerous place.'

'Now you tell me.'

'By the way, the husky voice is great. Very sexy. You might want to keep that.'

'Sex causes nothing but trouble,' I growled, vowing to remember that for ever. It did nothing to quell my longing for Andy. I was going to have to confront that issue sooner rather than later. My back burner of 'things to do' was becoming dangerously overcrowded, but I walked away from it nonetheless. 'Later,' I muttered to myself, 'later.'

I busied myself with a call to the hospital where the Lallys had been brought the previous night. After a few off-white lies about my position on the family tree, I was told that the three patients were comfortable and would probably be released the following day. This was positive and good, so I vowed that the rest of my day would match it, at least in intention. It was a tough call, though, and my body still turned towards the bedroom every time I held my breath. To put it technically, I felt like shit.

No. 4 chased the cats around, with much squawling and yapping. Then they ganged up on him and the positions were reversed. At least they were getting some exercise and amusing themselves at the same time. I decided to leave them to their own devices for the day, as I didn't think I'd be very good company for the dog if he was to come with me in the car. I dragged my sorry self upstairs and threw on the biggest, bulkiest clothes I could find. I was the spitting image of the Michelin Man as I made to leave on my errands. It was not a day I was looking forward to.

I had just loaded up the last of the unnecessary items I tote around in my bag when the landline rang and Barry's voice said, 'Yo, Coleman, any special requests?'

'Sorry to rain on your parade, Baz, but it's Leo here'

'Jeez, you're late going out. And you sound all croaky.'

'That's because I feel like shite and I'm mean as a taxman to go with it.'

'Oh, right.' I could tell he wanted to go away now, but I wasn't done with him.

'What made you think that Coleman, who didn't live in this house the last I heard, would be here? The answer's in the question, Barry.'

'Er, yeah. Well, we just thought we'd chill for the day, you know.'

'Oh, yes indeed I know. Now, one last question: does Coleman now have a key to my house?'

'Not as such. I gave him the spare, just for today.'

'Barry, I haven't the energy to tell you exactly what to do with yourself, but use your imagination and I think you'll end up in the territory I have in mind, doing what I think you're fit for. Gottit?'

'Yep. Sorry about that.'

'Don't say sorry when you're clearly not. You're just sore that I've caught you out. Now, I'm going to give you a top tip here, so listen very carefully. Sort out the key situation, or pack up and fuck off. Do I make myself clear?'

'Crystal.'

'Lovely. I really like it when we communicate.'

I could hear sounds in the background which registered somewhere in my gummed-up subconscious.

'Barry, where are you right now?'

'I'm in the video place, picking up a few movies.'

'Of *course*.'

'Ah, God, Leo, what's the harm in renting a few films?'

'No, no, it's not that. I just figured something out. And don't worry, it has nothing whatsoever to do with you.'

'Praise be for that.'

'Okay, you're dismissed.'

'Get well soon.'

'Sure.'

I met the cheddary Coleman coming through my front door.

'The very man,' I said. 'I've misplaced my key, so I'll take that back now.' I swear I thought he'd burst into tears relinquishing his ill-gotten pass to Funsville. 'Have a nice day,' I instructed.

My first stop had been chosen for me by the phone call. The sounds in the background of Maeve's nuisance calls were obviously from her local video rental store. Earlier, she'd reported the latest of them so if I was in luck the perpetrator would still be there. He or she was in for one hell of a roasting. In fact, anyone who crossed me today would know all about it. I liked this meaner Leo Street. Enough of the doormat, I wanted to be an ace shit kicker. My time had come.

Dublin was bathed in a wet, dreary mist, and looked as

unattractive as any other city would under the circumstances. It didn't help that my vision was distorted by
rock-solid sinuses pressuring my eyeballs. The journey
took me to a small shopping centre, immortalised in
radio advertisements with one of the worst jingles ever
recorded. It was also insufferably catchy and impossible
to forget. Whoever had 'invented' it could congratulate
themselves on a job done all too well, and the resultant
cack-ophony was a triumph of commercialism over art. I
found myself humming the awful ditty and gave in to the
fact that it would be with me for the next few hours, or
until it was taken over in some drivelly cover by the
newest teen pop sensation. I made a resolution to read
the entire works of Balzac to make up for the failings of
modern culture. My head hurt something rotten now.

'Flix' was typical of its kind, a large, overlit emporium
filled with a thousand good nights in. Or days, as in the
case of Barry and Coleman who would pass these off as
research. I approached the counter where a sign told me
that the management was hiring staff. I glanced at the
television screen above the desk to see a close up of
remarkably pert breasts (two, female) and a slavering
mouth (male). A ginger-topped employee drooled up at
the image. He turned to me when I gestured to the sign
in front of him, and I saw that his eyebrows were in
danger of meeting any day now. They would then be a
hairy orange boa above his hazel eyes. A pug nose
pointed to the ceiling; under it a sparse moustache was
trying hard to gain follicle hold. His mouth was full and
effeminate.

'What're the hours like?' I asked.

'Grand, you know. Your basic eight-hour shift, but plenty of overtime at the moment 'cos of shortages.'

'So what time would you have started today?'

'About ten. Not too bad. Bit borin' in the mornins, but it livens up during the day.'

'And is it just you then, until the next shift?'

'Yep.'

'Right. Let me bring you up to date on a little situation I'm investigating.' I leaned my elbows on the counter, to show just how in charge I was. 'Someone from this store has been making unwelcome sick little phone calls to a customer. Not only is this a pain in the ass for that customer, it is also against the law. You with me so far, sonny?'

He indicated that he was, nervously looking beyond me to the entrance.

'The latest of these calls was just after noon today, from this number. And seeing as you were the only one here, it doesn't take a rocket scientist to figure out that you made it. Does it now?'

He swallowed air, glancing back at the door again.

'Of course, just to prove this, we could get a record of the hours you've worked in the last few months and match them up with the calls to my client, which we have been logging, you'll be comforted to hear. But you know, I don't think there'll be any need for that because these calls will never happen again. Sure they won't.'

He shook his head miserably, then lowered it.

'Good. Because, you see, if they were to continue, I'd

have to bring the cops with me the next time I visit. And then we'd have to go through interrogating you, and charging you, and all have to spend a long time in court roasting your sorry arse. Still with me?'

He gave a jerk of the head which I took to be an affirmative.

'And there's probably no need for me to mention this, but I will, just in case you're thicker than I already take you for – if anyone else has this sort of trouble from you, I'll be back then too. We have very sophisticated methods of monitoring, get it? Good.'

No doubt about it, I could bullshit for Ireland. One down.

Then it was up again. I was about to swan out when I realised that the youngster was sobbing. Ah, shit, now I was going to feel bad, even though I had been on the high ground only twenty seconds earlier. I am a complete softie when it comes to tears.

'What the hell is all this about?' I asked him.

'I told a lie,' he whispered.

'Yeah?'

'I'm only minding the shop for a quarter of an hour, while Fidelma is on her break.'

'And Fidelma would be?'

'She's the boss. *She's* the one who's been on all morning.'

So why would she have a thing against Maeve Kelly? I wondered.

'Okay. Let's calm everything down here, shall we? Now, what's your name?'

'Pat.'

'Right, Pat. Fidelma is in a lot of trouble, as I'm sure you appreciate.' I was at a loss as to what to say or do next when my eye lit on the shop computer. 'Does that have a customer database?' I asked.

He gave an uncertain 'yes', more to do with not liking where this was going rather than being unsure of what the machine contained. I had no time to hang about.

'Here's what we'll do. I want you to call up the details of a Maeve Kelly.'

He hesitated, so I let out a loud 'NOW' and he jumped to.

Maeve's record as a customer was exemplary, in that she paid up on time and never incurred fines for non-rewinding of tapes. Her address and home phone number were listed. And then an intriguing detail, the note 'See also Rolands, Mark'. I felt close to pay dirt. We moved on to the second set of details, and Maeve's address and phone number were there too. But that was all. Just bare facts. My antennae were twitching now.

'Does Fidelma have a computer?'

'Yeah, it's in the office out back.'

'I'd better have a look at that so,' I announced, biting back my excitement.

Pat was sweating, and I could smell it. I ducked under the counter and made for an open door in the back wall, between a poster for *Alien* and one for *Hackers*, appropriately enough. Pat tried to follow me, but was distracted by a customer. I was sweating a bit myself now, keen to be finished before Fidelma returned or her assistant summoned up the courage to halt me in my tracks.

I sat before the screen and was delighted to find that Fidelma had logged on and all features were available to me. I punched in Maeve's name, and was rewarded with her standard details and a note telling me to look under 'Mission', which I did. The file here was very different from the ones for public consumption. Fidelma had downloaded articles about Mark Rolands, and any pictures she had located. These were almost lovingly rendered in sequence. This adoration was followed by information on Maeve, accompanied by on-line photographs and listings, but these had somehow been selected to seem less flattering. Then came the campaign of invective against my friend. All calls were triumphantly recorded, as were the preparations involved. There was a plan for the next few weeks which made the blood jitter in my veins. I sat in the synthetic light, mesmerised by the utter obsession of this woman, and her painstaking attention to detail. Yet nowhere was there any suggestion that she knew Mark Rolands in more than a casual way. Funnily enough, I thought it better to phone Mark on that one, rather than wait to enquire of Fidelma. I couldn't understand what she hoped to achieve, because clearly he could never be hers. Perhaps it was enough for her to know that she was unhinging the woman he wanted to be with.

I glanced at my watch and discovered that I had spent four and a half minutes zipping through the files. This meant two things: one, that I had no time for ill-informed psychoanalysis, and two, Fidelma was due back. Even if she was a sick individual, and ultimately in a lot more hot water than me, I was still trespassing and didn't want to have to talk my way around that. I printed the relevant pages then saved the details on to a disk to verify my findings and sped back out through the shop, telling Pat that he needn't mention my visit just yet to his boss because that would get him into as much trouble as she was in. This last effort was a gamble. I wanted to buy time, and to guard against Fidelma wiping off her precious files before I had decided what course of action to take. Poor old Pat looked distraught; he had had a very bad morning indeed. I might have self-righteously told him not to tell lies in the future, but even I am not that much of a hypocrite.

I raced down the street, putting a good distance between myself and 'Flix'. Then I flipped open my mobile and rang Maeve to bring her up to date on events.

'I think it's time to let Mark loose on this,' she said. 'And I'll ask him about the Fidelma woman, but I can't say that I remember him ever remarking on her before.'

'People get obsessed for lots of different reasons. He may be just that perfect, unattainable stranger for a disturbed woman, the Mr Wrong who came around the right corner at the right time, depending on whose point of view you're looking from.'

'Do you know, I almost feel sorry for her.'

'Don't, Maeve. Remember, she was making your life hell.'

'I suppose you're right,' she sighed. 'Anyway, many, many thanks, and please send me a bill. I mean it.'

'I know you do. We'll see.'

As I hung up, I realised that not only was I buzzing with adrenaline, I was also famished. A reward was in order and no mistake so I loaded up on goodies in the delicatessen and returned to the heavenly dining room that doubles as my car. I had a quick Scotch egg behind the wheel before revving the engine and heading to the Model School to collect the children. I was hyper after my success so it seemed sensible to use that on Carmel Lally's behalf. The car stank of fart from my snack, but the fact that I could smell it at all indicated that my cold was lifting. I popped some more of the Aspirin-like sweeties from the glove compartment and crossed my fingers.

For all my lectures to Ciara about planning and facts, I operate a lot on instinct. Just then, I wasn't too sure of what I would do once I got to the school, but I was prepared to hoist a flag even if it ended up on my own petard. The yard was full of the usual specimens, with a Nolan brother bringing up the rear. No time like the present, I thought, unwilling to let my courage falter now. There was a lot of whispering and pointing as I made my way to the crêche door, where I took a deep, rasping breath and clapped my hands a few times for attention.

'Some of you will know that Carmel Lally and her

children were evacuated from their burning home last night, and are lucky to be alive. It was the culmination of a horrible campaign of intimidation against her. Now, I know you all feel strongly about her claim for compensation but this is no way to go about things. Time and the law will settle all of that. The police take what happened last night very seriously indeed and if any of you knows anything about it, you'd be well advised to come forward. In the meantime, let me assure you that you have no idea of the complexity of Carmel's situation. Leave her alone.'

No one met my eyes now. It was as if the group as a whole was culpable. As it probably was. But I couldn't feel pleased with myself. In fact, I felt like a prig.

The bell rang for the end of classes, and I gathered up the small people and delivered them to their mother. They told me that the earth was round, according to their teachers, but that they felt certain that we'd all fall off the edge if we went too close: from the mouths of babes.

Back at the Indigent Sweeps' gaff, things were going my way. I travelled by elevator, no less, in great form that I didn't have to climb the stairs. The new proactive me was growing more bullish by the minute. I banged out of the cage and barrelled through the office door to tell Mick Nolan my exploits and findings to date. Then, I remembered that we had some unfinished business, which began with an apology from me to him.

I stood in front of the portrait photograph, not knowing where to start. That winded me. I looked into his eyes and said, 'I'm sorry. I didn't realise that it was me who was holding you. It's been me who couldn't let you go all this time. I thought you wanted me to hang around, but I realise now that I prevented you from going.' Tears welled up, but as always I was careful not to show them to him. 'The truth is that I was lonely without you. And I couldn't bear the missing of you, so I kept you here. I didn't know it till Ciara came on board and I let you have the rest you deserve. I'm going to put you by the filing cabinet now, seeing as how that's where you liked to perch in your own office and it always did throw the dynamics of the room off kilter and make people uneasy. You'll still have a role to play whenever you want. But you don't have to.'

I gently removed the photograph from the wall, and tugged out the self-contained leg of the frame to render it free-standing. I kissed the glass lightly and propped the picture on the metal chest.

'Thanks for everything. Don't be a stranger. Hope you haven't missed too many games of golf because of me.'

And we were done. For the time being at least. I knew he'd let me know if I'd missed anything important. We were still a two-way arrangement, and always would be, really.

I was stuffing my face with stodge in a most unlady-like way when Kevin Mack appeared with an enormous bunch of blood red roses.

'These came for you when you were out yesterday, Miss Street, so I kept them in the tea room. Someone is very pleased with you, eh?'

The flowers were exquisite in shape, colour and presentation, and they had a scent too which meant the bouquet had cost the annual turnover of a small African nation. The accompanying card simply read 'Call'. I may be cynical, but I didn't think they'd come from Barry and as I trawled through the extensive Rolodex of my suitors, the name I came up with was Andy Raynor. I sat down quickly, before my knees gave way.

'You've a bit of mayonnaise on your chin,' Kevin said. 'And just a little tomato on the side of your cheek. Eh, both of them.'

I had to do a Scarlett O'Hara on it, because I was busy, but boy, was I looking forward to tomorrow. First thing, I would go and see Andy, and if he gave me so much as half an inkling that he was interested in seeing me on a regular basis, say twice a year to begin with, then I was driving straight back to the northside to evict Barry and tell him we could still be friends. That was the crudely fashioned plan at any rate, and it was something to go on, I thought.

I couriered my booty from 'Flix' to Mark Rolands's office, then I dialled a friend in the Force to gently quiz her on the Michael O'Donoghue case. Sergeant Róisín Duffy snorted when she heard what I wanted.

'Leo, (a) that's another station, and (b) you know it's classified.'

'Does that mean you can't tell me anything?' I wheedled.

'You know it does.'

'Tell you what, Róisín, why don't we do the thing

where I ask questions and you just answer yes, no or maybe?'

'Maybe.'

'Great. Are the police treating this death as suspicious?'

'Yes.'

'Is a post-mortem taking place?'

'Yes.'

'Is there another line of enquiry if toxicology comes up negative?'

'Yes.'

'Would this involve the nature of the accident?'

'Yes.'

'Might that be to do with the car?'

'Yes.'

'Any lead suspect so far?'

'No.'

'A lot of people wanted him dead.'

'That's not a question, but maybe.'

'Can I call you again on this matter?'

'Maybe.'

'I love you too, Róisín. Thanks.'

'Yes.'

I didn't see much point in calling ahead to Miranda O'Donoghue. With warning, she might try to divert me, and I wanted to be face to face with her. With that in mind, I typed up an interim report which loosely skirted the many facets of the case. I sorted out the bill, because I'm a practical person with a mortgage and a slew of dependants, and packed the lot into a large brown envelope addressed to the relict of the late Michael O'Donoghue. I grabbed the package containing the death threat, so kindly supplied by Tara, placed my roses in full view of the door and left. There are many who would say that this was not the perfect moment to be doing business with a grieving widow, but I wanted the props with me in case I needed more reason to call than to offer my condolences. 'Prepared,' I growled, to myself.

Second thoughts are the perfect partners to a false exit. I returned to phone Ciara. Her mother answered in a whisper and I explained that my assistant was to take the day off. We would review our situation the following day. I looked to Mick for approval and his silence gave it. Leo Street was properly '& Co.' now.

Twenty-Three

Low-scale dread filled me during the drive southwards. By the time I turned into the cul-de-sac in which the O'Donoghues' house stood I had residual panic ringing in my ears. I was not looking forward to the rest of the day, steeped as it was in uncertainty and gloom. But a yearning for closure and my own cussed stubbornness forced me on, even if a more natural inclination might have been to run home and bury my head in a pillow.

I was worried about a confrontation with Miranda simply because I knew that I would start my conversation with this woman from a position of inferiority. Always. I wasn't quite pinned down on the purpose of my visit, other than an amorphous hunch that I should check what was going on in the household. Right back to nosy me, then, complete with contents dripping out at intervals. I needn't have worried so much. The house was deserted and I spent an hour sitting in my car, with my buttocks going numb, then painfully coming back to life in a spritz of pins and needles. I flexed my feet, twisting the ankles in a circle, clockwise than anti. A sluggish circulation is often better than none at all. I shifted from cheek to cheek in the bucket of the seat, looking for all the world as if I needed a pee. And eventually I did. I got out of the car and paced the street to return a blood supply to my vitals and to take my mind off the loo. It almost worked, and staved off the inevitable for a short time. A reconnoitre of the neighbours' leafy properties revealed several promising spots for any unfortunate emergency. What bothered me here was the notion that security cameras would also record such an event. That was enough to force a positive regression of my waste fluids; in fact, my bladder shrivelled at the thought.

The estate was select and well-heeled. Each home was similar to the next in size, which was at least five bedrooms and all the rest, but the layouts had changed over the years, with some residents opting for carbuncular conservatories to the side and back, variously. High walls protected large gardens, which ranged from finest Gertrude Jekyll to minimalist Japanese. One individualist had installed Tudor windows and attached a strange black and white Elizabethan wood feature to the façade of his, or her, house; it was nothing less than the cladding of the upper-middle-class.

I had ample time to study the driveway of the O'Donoghue house, along with a car port to the side, big enough to hold two vehicles. Unsurprisingly, it was empty. All ground surfaces were blemish free. If someone had cut the brake cables on Michael O'Donoghue's car, and I considered this a possible cause of the crash, it had not been here because there was no brake fluid to be seen.

I was leaning against my new blue bonnet when a sleek grey saloon purred around the corner, containing the lady of the house, Tara and a lad I assumed to be Tara's brother, Ben. My assumption proved correct, which was gratifying.

'Come to scavenge?' Miranda asked, and I was right back to square one. This woman knew a thing or two about power.

She was dressed to fit the grieving widow bill, with a hint of style guru and a pinch of image consultant. All her own doing too, I suspected. She swept up her driveway, with her children trailing miserably after her. The youngsters' eyes were hollow and red, their steps leaden with grief. Tara avoided eye contact with me, and I kept my distance. Ben hadn't noticed that I was there.

The interior of 14 Sea Point, Blackrock, was as I'd expected: tasteful and immaculate. I was familiar with the exterior and it held few secrets any more. We shuffled down the hallway to a large kitchen which managed to suggest space as well as exhibiting every gadget and domestic fol-de-rol known to the late-twentieth century. I took a surreptitious look back along the cream carpet we had trodden to check that I hadn't brought any unwanted stains into the house with me; dog shit was number one on my list of worries. I seemed to have passed through without incident. Miranda flicked the switch on the kettle with a perfectly manicured hand.

She posed by the sideboard and I had time to admire her expert hair cut and colour job. I did so in silence. When this had stretched to the required length, she announced that I would have a coffee while she fixed herself a gin and tonic.

'What a day,' she commented, which was as unnecessary as calling Mr De Beer a 'diamond geezer', I felt.

Tara stifled a sob and excused herself from the room, in a broken-hearted splutter of sorrow and dental steel. I hoped that some of her mother's mettle was embedded deep in her DNA as an underlay of resolve to help her through this awful time. Come to think of it, her father seemed to have had his fair share of strength too, even if he did use it to the detriment of others. Ben had disappeared silently, unobserved by the household. How would he deal with the decimation of his family? I would probably never know, even though I had crossed his path at this intimate time. The degrees of separation between us two ran deep and parallel to our lives; they mocked any notion of friendship or camaraderie, and underscored the evanescence of the casual encounter, the fragility of human relationships.

'I wonder if I might use your bathroom,' I said, realising that I wouldn't last too much longer. There is nothing worse than pissing yourself in public. Miranda waved me off to a small cubicle under the stairs. There, I perched on the seat trying to aim for the sides of the bowl in order to minimise the noise. A soft tinkling filled the tiny room, and I hoped that it was not travelling too much further. This was unlikely as I could clearly hear the sound of ice hitting glass in the kitchen next door, along with the liquid sounds of gin and the sloshing fizz of tonic. As I washed my hands, I noticed a plastic bag on the floor, full of men's accoutrements. Apparently, all signs of Michael O'Donoghue were due for quick obliteration.

'We'll go into the study and deal with your business,' Miranda said on my return. She made it clear that this was an unsavoury prospect, best dispensed with quickly. At that moment she was still paying, so I let her away with it. She was in no hurry to move and arranged herself like a frieze again, as cool as an Elgin marble and no less beautiful. Eventually she began to glide to a small room on the first return of the stairs. It had clearly been her husband's until a few hours before. A pen he had used was lying casually on a blotter, as if on 'pause' while he took a short break from his business. It looked lonely. Miranda sat in a swivel chair behind the desk and fixed me with her cool stare.

'How much?' she asked. 'What price have you decided on? What is the going rate for chasing up betrayal?' She was smiling now. I had no idea where to go with this, but I opened my mouth and hoped for inspiration to kick in. It did not, but words emerged and for this I gave thanks.

'I know this may not seem the ideal time for this, but I thought you might take some comfort from what I found out.'

'For instance?'

'Your husband was not having an affair.'

She gave a bored shrug. 'Zippideedoodah. Yes, that's a tremendous relief, I'm sure.'

If rudeness was a manifestation of her grief, she was very upset indeed. I didn't think so, though, and I was damned if I was going to let her use me as a punch bag to boost her own ego.

'There are some fascinating elements of this investigation that I think you may be able to shine some light on,' I said.

At least she had the decency to raise one well-plucked eyebrow at that.

'Such as?'

'I'd like to know why you were following your husband in your car?'

'Nice try,' she laughed. 'But I'm sure I don't know what you mean.'

Her fingers had drifted to the scar on her face. She saw that I had noticed.

'Michael gave me this, in a way, you know. I was so angry with him one night that I gouged my own cheek with a ring he had given me. It hurt like hell, and of course I regretted it almost immediately. But it scared the pants off him, which was what he deserved, and not just on that occasion either.'

She diverted her attention to the bureau and began to open and close various drawers. Finally she found what she was looking for, a packet of cigarettes and a gold lighter which she placed on the blotter. 'A filthy habit.' She grinned. 'But at this stage, who gives a fuck?' The unexpected coarseness echoed like a bullet from a gun;

a small, modern and lethal weapon. She lit a cigarette with practised ease and inhaled with palpable relish. 'That's better.' She threw the lighter on to the desk without caring where it landed. Leaning back in the chair, she blew a long satisfied stream of smoke into the air.

I wanted to scream at her to continue talking. I willed her on, with as much brain power as I could muster in my disease-ridden skull. She did, and this probably counted as a third-class miracle, if such a thing can be quantified.

'He was a very vain man, you know.' A pot and kettle situation, then. 'And not half as clever or innovative as he would have had himself and everyone else believe. He was nothing without me.' Now she spat. 'Nothing.'

She looked around for an ashtray, seeming vulnerable for a moment as she balanced the long ash in mid-air. Then she was back to her power position as she tipped the waste contemptuously on to the desktop. In a measure of status, I would have to call this woman a red ten. She took up where she had left off with what seemed like enjoyment.

'Michael O'Donoghue was an amateur playing around with his Petri dishes. He had no idea of the potential he was sitting on. Every supposed breakthrough he made was known to anyone who uses the Internet properly. And he was negative in his approach, narrow-minded. He had no vision. But *I* do. I continually fed him information, brought him up to speed. But, of course, information is only useful if you know how to apply it. And he saw to it that I could not do that, that I was kept away from my rightful place. How dare he? Who the hell did he think he was to do that to me, of all people? I *made* the bastard, and he would have done better to remember that. Well, I suppose, he's finally realised it now, wherever he's frying.'

It was interesting to me that at no time did Miranda mention any religious objection to Michael's work. Tara had heard biblical quotations about fire and brimstone being hurled about when her parents had argued, but perhaps they had merely been Miranda's smokescreen. It made sense that she would be interested in her husband's research; she had worked with him on his projects when they'd met.

I didn't really know what to say so I put the envelope containing my report on the desk as another gambit. She barely acknowledged it.

'Where's the bill?'

I passed it to her. She gave the note a cursory once over before signing a cheque for the amount specified. It was from a joint account and had already been co-signed by her late husband. 'Handy, eh?' she crowed. As she ripped along the serrated edge, Miranda flashed me another of her frozen smiles. Her eyes were pale enough to take on the shades of her surroundings, like a lizard changing colour. Right now, they conspired to look brown, and almost warm.

'Thank you so much, Miss Street,' she said. 'You have been most useful.'

I shivered involuntarily. Why did I suddenly feel that

I too had played a part in the death of Michael O'Donoghue?

'Was there anything else?' she asked, in a tone clearly intended to end our meeting.

'Yes. I'd like to ask you about the threatening notes your husband had been receiving. As I mentioned to you on the phone yesterday, I've come into possession of one of them. I have it here, actually. Police forensics will, of course, be testing it for DNA evidence and so on, but could you tell me if you recognise it?' I held the plastic folder well away from her grasp and let her read the note.

She reddened slightly, then barked a short laugh. 'They all looked the same to me. That might be one, but I doubt it.'

'What makes you say that?'

'We . . . he . . . Michael destroyed them all.'

'Not this one.'

She sat in contemplation for a moment, then narrowed her eyes. 'Of course. Tara gave you that, didn't she?' She waited for a response, but didn't get one. I clenched my toes in an effort to stay as still as I possibly could. This made both my feet cramp, and it took all my strength not to jump up and dance around the room in agony.

'Let me tell you something, Miss Street, my daughter idolised her father with childish tunnel vision and Michael was a big fan of such simple, uncomplicated adoration. I sometimes think he took what she said to him about his work to be true, ridiculous as that was, because that was what he wanted to hear. He could not rely on me to be so deluded, or to give praise where it clearly was not due. I don't know what she thinks she has achieved by meddling in this way, but you'd be better off ignoring her and any so-called information she may have given you. She is just a hysterical little girl. All you have there is a worthless piece of paper – rubbish.'

'Hard to believe she could be so devious as to conjure this up.'

'Miss Street, I'm not sure what this cheap trick is supposed to achieve, but I would remind you that my husband was killed only hours ago and I should be allowed to grieve. I would thank you to leave now.'

'I'm interested to hear you say "killed" rather than "died", Mrs O'Donoghue.'

'Get out now, before I call the police.'

'Oh, I think you can expect to see them soon,' I said, as I rose to leave. 'And don't think you can threaten me,' I added. 'I know what you're up to, and I intend to do everything I can to aid the investigation surrounding your husband's death. Please stay where you are, I can see myself out.'

I think the last remark annoyed her more than anything else because of course she'd had no intention of going to the door with me. She was temporarily struck dumb as she searched for a retort.

At the top of the stairs, I turned. 'Your husband was said to have a God Complex,' I told her. 'It seems to me that you shared it.' That got her moving. I had reached the front door when she swept after me and roughly thrust forward her hand to grasp the folder containing the death threat. 'If that is as pertinent to my husband's death as you seem to think, I should pass it along to the relevant authorities,' she hissed.

'No need,' I said, wrenching it back from her. She lifted her hand to hit me, just as a tortured wail rang through the air. For a moment I wondered if I had made the sound.

'Randy, Randy,' cried a woman's voice. 'I came as soon as I heard. How *are* you?'

A screeching dervish in black weeds from top to toe bore down the driveway and into the accidentally open arms of 'Randy' O'Donoghue, who never managed to land that punch on me. Our visitor had the glazed eyes of one too many early-afternoon cocktails. Miranda's were filled with hatred and frustration, which she quickly veiled with more acceptable sorrow.

'Margaret,' she said, 'how sweet of you to call.'

'How will you manage? What's to become of you?' Margaret wanted to know.

'Oh, I shouldn't think she'll let a little thing like this hold her back for long,' I muttered as I hastened my exit. It took rather longer to remove the daggers from my back.

I was shaking badly by the time I got to my car. I reached beneath my voluminous jumper and removed the tape recorder nestled within. I rewound the tape a little, then pressed 'play'. I heard myself say, 'I'm interested to hear you say "killed" rather than "died", Mrs O'Donoghue.' 'Get out now, before I call the police,' came Miranda's voice. I rewound the tape completely, then packed it into its carton, with the date, time, and location on the label. I placed the cassette and the death threat in an envelope with a full report on my company's investigations and headed for the police station. I wasn't all that sure that I had anything of import to share with the authorities, but there was a stink about this case that needed pointing up, so the time had come to hand my information over to the Boys in Blue.

Twenty-Four

My night was sleepless and not without incident. I presented my 'evidence' to the relevant Garda station, then quizzed Sergeant Róisín Duffy, by way of the telephone, for more information. Through our elaborate game of 'yes, no or maybe' I learned that, yes, the O'Donoghue vehicle had been tampered with, and yes, the brake lines had been cut, with a very sharp instrument. ('Perhaps a scalpel?' 'That is absolute conjecture, but maybe.') Yes, Miranda O'Donoghue was a suspect, but not the only one. ('Our nearest and dearest are often the deadliest?' I got a complete set of 'yes, no and maybe' for that). Yes, my help was cautiously welcomed, and no, she would not confirm any of the above.

I was attempting to breathe in the vapours of a menthol-based honey and lemon drink when I noticed the edge of a t-shirt sticking out from under the legs of the couch. I reached down to pull it free, and discovered that it was snagged on a loose spring on the underside of the seat. I placed the piping hot toddy at a safe distance because I am a prudent woman who hates being scalded. In general, pain and suffering are best avoided; something of which I constantly have to remind myself. I got down on all fours and reached into the murky depths. Amongst the old magazines and biros, I met with resistance and serious disapproval from No. 4. I tipped the sofa on to its back legs for easier access and surveyed the undercarriage.

Someone, or some creature, had been very busy. Through the torn webbing I could discern a cache of stolen goodies. They ranged from Barry's lucky underwear to a tea towel and a rawhide chew. I turned to my favourite choice as culprit and said, 'Is this where you hid the tie of my dressing gown then?' He had the grace to bark in the affirmative. I dithered over what course of action to take. It was clear that the little dog had been through a hard time, what with the death of his previous guardian and taking up residence in this unfamiliar house, so I suggested a compromise. 'How about I leave you the food, and I return Barry's stuff? And if anything goes missing again, we'll all know where to find it?' This was acceptable.

I took him on to my knee and cuddled him. 'I know you're probably worried about losing everything again, but don't be. You live here now, with me. And I love you,' I whispered. He licked me full on the face. Oh, yummy. What a way to celebrate acknowledgement of our feelings for one another. While I was vaguely ahead, I thought I'd chance a query. 'Did you have anything to do with my red glove ending up in the office loo?' He buried his snout in my armpit, without giving a definitive answer.

Barry fell in the door with the actor currently known as Coleman Pearse. Even though they doled me a beer, I was not a feature of their evening. I felt fury begin somewhere deep in a place I had been ignoring for a long time now. They were taken up with the subject of piles, which led me to believe that one of them was afflicted. Barry dubbed them 'the devil's grapes', while Coleman preferred the notion of piles as 'the arse's answer to gravity'. As they continued their rant, I told Barry, 'I found your missing clothes, I'm going to throw you out of the house, and your fly is open.' Although all of these things were true at the time, he didn't hear, and most of all, he didn't care. I ran a bath, swiped another lager and soaked my aches away. I wanted to be clean for tomorrow as I had a lot to do. Tomorrow was Sorting Out Day, and I was excited and appalled at the prospect.

I am not a brave woman, I thought. And I'm not decisive enough. Or am I? I teased myself. But I had come to realise how precious life was over the last few days. And fleeting. And fragile. I didn't want to wake up at forty, trapped and feeling bitter. My destiny was firmly in my own hands. No one was to blame but me if I did not act to change my circumstances. I was sorely aware that I was hinging some key elements on the possibility that Andy Raynor would be available and interested in playing a part in my life, but I had to start somewhere. If he was the catalyst to all of this, so be it. I lay in bed later, staring at the ceiling and its Australia-shaped damp patch, and told myself that this time I was in the driving seat and things were looking up. Also, Australia's progress would have to be halted.

I came over all shy after my coffee the following 6.30 a.m. But fortune favours the foolhardy and all that, so I had a bracing shower and wondered at how squeaky I was from all the washing I'd done in the last while. I dosed up on drugs for my ailment, and ran a nit comb at length through my tresses. The results were satisfying. I very nearly passed for human. Lots of bits were up for swaps, of course; my nostrils probably won that particular bout, red and flaking as they were from days of rubbing. I tried a dab of foundation, but it clung stubbornly to the flakes, rather than smoothing away the blemishes. I cleaned it off with, according to the label, the kindest, gentlest, least perfumed remover on the market. It stung me like nobody's business; whatever that phrase means is beyond me, as I feel most things are, at the very least, *my* business, but it's acceptable parlance, and so it goes.

It was a ridiculously early hour to be leaving the house, but I was set on a course of action and knew that even the slightest prevarication on my part would result in going back to bed with a man I was about to ditch, and the avoidance of 'action'. So, I promised the cats extra long cuddles later in the day when I got back, then called No. 4 and together we bravely faced our destiny. The dog took up his regular stance in the Streetmobile; today, he was the canine Isadora Duncan. Minus the scarf, I'm happy to report. We headed into a darkness that was trying its best to suggest dawn and I took this to be a metaphor for our new life.

We were still inordinately early for a breakfast visit anywhere but a Trappist monastery so I brought us for a walk on the strand at Sandymount. As light encroached on the horizon, the wind whipped us mercilessly. Still, I threw driftwood and No. 4 chased it, like in the best television movies (I'm not sure what the musical accompaniment would have been, but I would have been happy with anything but the execrable 'Stranger On the Shore'). I stared at the curved patterns in the sand and made myself dizzy. No. 4 caked himself in muck. When I looked romantically into the middle distance, involuntary tears ran down my cheeks. It was me against the elements, among them the biting, chill air. Michael O'Donoghue had come here only hours before his death, and I wondered if he had been trying to sort out the big issues in his own life. If so, I'll venture he didn't get the result he was hoping for.

The time came when it was decent for me to release myself back into the community. We sheltered briefly by the Martello Tower while I tried to formulate a strategy, or at the very least a few plausible words. My brain was frozen in my head and my face was set in the rictus of a smile, not unlike an astronaut headed for the moon. I finally gave in to the inevitable, loaded up the dog and drove to Andy's house. I told No. 4 that this might take a while, but hopefully it would be worth the wait. He was too busy grooming the ends of his extremities to pay much heed. Without giving myself the option of any more time to reflect, I rang the bell on the Raynor gate, and walked through when the buzzer sounded. The climb to the front door was long, but eventually I was there and knocking on the door and feeling the stirrings of an excitement that was hard to fathom. I turned to look at Andy's garden, and when I heard the lock click open I turned back, smiling, to face a tall specimen of the female persuasion. She was drop dead you-know-what, and I found myself wishing that she would give in to fate and fall lifeless on the step. This was a setback and no doubt about it.

'Oh, hi,' I managed, cheerily. 'I was just passing by and thought I'd call in. I'm an old friend of Andy's.'

She squeezed out a far from happy grin; more an ill-disguised sneer. 'It's very early, you know. We might have been . . . well, busy.' I noticed she was not wearing any shoes; feeling at home, so. 'Take a seat and I'll fix you a coffee, you look like you could use one.' Great, I looked every bit the bag of shite I felt. And worse, my heart had started a downward journey within my chest that was beginning to hurt.

The beauty didn't even have the grace merely to glide through the house, she clearly belonged there while I was a tub of whale waste that had accidentally been delivered to the wrong address. Before I could RUN AWAY QUICKLY, Andy appeared, in a towelling robe, looking sleepy and sheepish.

'God Almighty, Leo. Em, I wasn't expecting you.'

I bit back the 'clearly' that was on the tip of my venomous, disappointed tongue, and gave an energetic, 'Oh, I was just passing as I told, eh . . .'

'Ah yes, eh.' He looked from one to the other of us, then did the necessaries. 'Leo, this is Heather. Heather, Leo.'

I had reached some sort of limit. A light buzzing started up in my ears and white spots danced before my eyeballs. The room reeled and I put my hand out to steady myself. Instead of reaching a shelf or the back of a chair, I found that I was leaning on Andy's arm. I recoiled with all the elegance of a dancing pot-bellied pig.

'Is she all right?' Fern, or Frond, or Spore wanted to know, her delicate pink lips pursing into a classic moue of distaste. Scratch that, it was a clichéd pout.

'Are you, Leo?' Andy asked, almost passing for concerned.

OF COURSE I'M NOT ALL RIGHT, YOU STUPID PHILANDERING BASTARD, I CAME HERE TO THROW MYSELF AT YOU AND NOW LOOK WHAT'S HAPPENED.

'Yes, yes, I've just had this awful cold, and it makes me unsteady. I think it's all settled in my ears and affected my balance.'

I'm sure I heard Mould or Compost Heap or Decomposition mutter 'too much information', but I wasn't confident enough to make something of it. To be honest, I think that the cold had got into my aurals somehow, and I wasn't sure of much in the way of sound, or smell for that matter. Unfortunately, there was no problem at all with my sight, and what I was seeing was far from ideal. I decided against starting a Bitch Fight, even though some bad angel inside me was saying that I could take her. But I was hanging on to my dignity by an extremely flimsy thread just then and I let reason win out.

I found myself staring into Andy Raynor's fabulous eyes and wanting to cry. I couldn't believe the depth of the pain inside of me, and the fact that it didn't seem apparent to the others in the room. Instead, I said, 'The dog's in the car. I've promised him a walk so I'd better keep my end of things up. You said to call, so I have. See you soon, I guess.'

By the time I had finished this speech, I was well into the process of fleeing as quickly as is allowed in polite society back to my point of entry, with my gracious host hot on my tail, in exactly the way I had not anticipated or wished for.

'Leo, there's no need to rush off.'

YES, THERE BLOODY WELL IS.

'Stay and have a coffee.'

OVER MY DEAD, GERM-FILLED BODY.

I had my hand on the door knob, on the cusp of freedom, when he grabbed my arm and swung me around. We stood there without speaking, listening to our own heaving breaths. Finally, he said, 'I'm delighted to see you, really I am. And this is not what it looks like.' He waved a hand back towards the kitchen. By now, I had a milligrip on my emotions and was determined to salvage something from this disaster.

'Andy, relax. It doesn't matter to me who you play Happy Families with. You're a big boy with a reputation

to keep up. What you do in your own house is your
business. I was just popping in to say hello, that's all.
And now that I have, I'd better go. I have a very busy
day ahead. I'll see you around.'

And with that I just ran out of the door and sped
down the steps as fast as my fat little legs would take
me. I was gulping back tears as I got into the car, fired it
up and squealed away from the kerb. I drove for three
or so streets then pulled over and sobbed till my body
hurt. The sky was red that morning; I should have paid
it more attention.

A good cry is a wonderful purge, not least because it
leaves you too weak to think, or feel any more misery. I
pulled a compact from my bag and checked the damage
to my face. I would be lying if I said it could have been
worse. My eyes were puffy and any soul that I could
discern inside was bruised with humiliation, rejection
and my own stupidity. My lungs were sore from smoke
inhalation, the common cold and weeping, and my
sinews, bones and senses were permeated with a good
measure of the selfs – pity and doubt were playing
blinders, with loathing on the street corner kicking an
empty milk carton around. All present and correct.

There were two directions I could go now: up or
down. One of them wouldn't do at all, so I picked
myself up, tried to dust myself off, with the added
difficulty of a small, worried dog on my lap, and vowed
to start all over again. Above all, I needed some sleep. A
drizzle of rain helped a blob of grey and white birdshit

to travel across my windscreen. It changed shape and size with each wipe of the blades, but never really disappeared. I limped us through the morning traffic jam of glum workers travelling into town.

When we reached Merrion Square I gave in to a whim and drove into the underground car park of the Fledgling. I snagged a space on the lowest level and walked back up to an area sealed off with official tape and burly policemen. A plate on the wall booked this section for Michael O'Donoghue. I looked high up from right to left to remind myself of the position of the security cameras when I'd first cased the joint. One pointed away from the taped off area and I calculated from its angle that the O'Donoghue space would have been its blind spot. But the other pointed directly at it and had a brilliant vantage point from which to record any activity in that parking bay. In a normal world, that is. Before someone had taken a hammer to it and rendered it useless.

The forensics team was dusting surfaces and collecting fibres and microbes and what have you. Smack bang in the middle of the fun was a dark greasy stain. I put my money on that turning out to be brake fluid. Before I could place my bet I was moved on by the cops.

I stepped out into the Dublin morning again. While I was here I might as well check out another hunch I was lugging around with me. I popped across to the florists opposite the hospital and bought a middle-of-the range bouquet of sedate flowers. Armed with these I was ready to blend in at the Fledgling, should the need arise.

Instead, I approached the receptionist.

'I'm looking for my friend Miranda O'Donoghue,' I told her. 'I heard the terrible news an hour ago and I rushed over to her house but she wasn't there. No one was. So I assumed she would have come here. You know, a home away from home.' I sniffled and produced a handkerchief.

'She's not here,' I was told in return. The woman was sympathetic. 'We're all very upset too. We'll miss him. He was a great doctor.'

I gulped back my sorrow. 'I'll try a few of our friends. I just had this idea that she'd come to where she could be closest to him, to his work, his vision.'

'It's understandable,' the woman said. 'There are times when I have to remind myself that Miranda doesn't work here. She seems so much like a member of staff.'

'Yes. Some of his patients will miss her too, for that shoulder to cry on.'

'They will. She was an asset to Mr O'Donoghue's programme.'

So, Miranda had access to the hospital and the patients. Could *she* have been Kate Mulligan's mole in the organisation?

I left with my flowers and my information and rejoined No. 4 in the car. We took up our place again in the plugged up traffic lanes and seven days later Molly was looking critically at me, saying 'I think you're over the worst of it now.'

'I hope so,' I told him. We were more than certainly speaking at cross purposes.

My glove was looking jollier on the notice board, so I put it in my pocket, and resolved to give it a new life far away from here. The post delivered at least one decent item; a cheque from a lawyer I work for from time to time. I let No. 4 race up the stairs, barking all the way to let everyone know that he'd arrived, while I sailed up in style in the elevator. As I approached the office, I heard a happy fugue of women giggling.

Ciara was sitting, legs a-dangle, on the edge of the desk and enthroned in the huge armchair opposite was the diminutive form of a returned Mrs Mack. Her husband was mopping the floor around them, and beaming like a man who'd won a million pounds. Perhaps he had, and he was one of those people who vow that it won't change their lives. It would sure change mine, I can tell you.

'Leo, fantastic. You're just in time to join us for the Lourdes Holy Water,' Ciara told me. She gestured to a child-sized statue of the Blessed Virgin held in Mrs Mack's arms. It was of white opaque plastic with a blue screwtop crown.

'After what I've just been through, it could do no harm,' I said.

'That's the spirit,' Ciara remarked, and Mrs Mack began to laugh.

What had brought about this rather unholy Entente Cordiale, and was it cause for concern?

'Who are the gorgeous flowers from?' Ciara asked, indicating the roses.

'Oh, just a thank you for a favour, nothing special,' I remarked, ultra-casually. For all I knew that was the truth; it was not Andy's fault that I had expected too much, was it?

'This is for our returned traveller,' I said, as I handed over the Fledgling bouquet. I had no other option, the look she was giving me.

Ciara put mugs on the desk and Mrs Mack undid Our Lady's crown and began to pour the contents of the statue into them. Then they were dispensed amongst us and we raised them in a toast, without knowing what the appropriate words were for such a blessed round. I knocked mine back, and it in turn knocked me into the nearest seat, Mrs Mack was beside herself with delight, and Ciara's eyes glittered with mirth. Only Kevin rushed to my aid, clapping me vigorously on the back, and doing quite a bit of internal damage to my already battered person. Eventually I persuaded him to stop and – painfully – caught my breath. When I was confident that I would live, I said, 'Holy God, it's pure vodka, Mrs Mack. Have you smuggled that into the country from your pilgrimage?'

She nodded through the cackles. 'Amn't I a terror altogether?'

'You are that,' I confirmed.

When we had squeezed enough enjoyment out of the morning's ruse, the Macks left and Ciara and I got up to speed on events. She looked refreshed and rested, and seemed none the worse for her adventures.

'I bounce back,' she admitted. 'And I'm a cold-hearted cow, don't forget.'

'I won't,' I assured her.

'What's your best shot on who did what?' she asked.

'If I was pushed I'd pump Kate Mulligan for the name of her informant. I'm not altogether convinced that it was Maria Flood. It could so easily have been Miranda. As far as the crash goes she had every reason for wanting her husband dead. She hated what he'd done to her aspirations of medical advancement. And maybe she did think he was having an affair with Maria. I'd wager a tasty sum that he was well insured too. It's all academic now because the cops will take it from here.'

'That can't be right,' Ciara said. 'How can we just let this go?'

'We have to. This is the real world. It's in the public domain now, and our job is to help the police enquiry. We're off the case. It's one of the most frustrating elements of being a PI. I don't think I'll ever get used to it.'

'Not wanted on journey.'

'Precisely. Besides, the cops are all over the evidence, we'd never get near enough to figure any more out. Sometimes, though, you'll be delighted to pass the burden of proof on to the State. Unless you want to go legit and join the Force?'

'No way. There's far more anarchy on this end of things; that's more my bag.'

Ciara reached and handed me some Post-its. Two were orders for bread from ladies with posh addresses, and one said that Con had called and was due for his transfer to a Dublin inner city parish in five to six weeks. At least they raised a tired smile from me.

'That poor young fella in "Flix",' Ciara remarked. 'He'll never give himself airs and graces. You've probably put him off wanting to go into management. Stunted him.' She grinned as she shook her head from side to side.

'Stop, Ciara, I feel terrible as it is.'

'At least he'll think twice about fiddling with telephones, if he was ever to feel inclined in that direction.'

'I still don't feel like Social Worker of the Month.'

'No, and you shouldn't.'

We sat awhile in a comfortable uncertainty, gently sipping the last of Mrs Mack's treat.

'I hate being taken hostage to fortune on the O'Donoghue thing,' Ciara moaned.

'Yep. When I first started that used to burn me up. But there are times now when I feel an almost guilty relief that I don't have to go any further into some of the messes I've been introduced to. It's kind of "be careful what you wish for", I suppose.'

We let the silence return.

'So what now?' she asked eventually, giving voice to the question on both our minds.

'What indeed? I suppose we need to find more work for you to do.'

I had said the right thing. 'I've been thinking about that, and I have a few leads I'm going to follow up. So, if it's all right with you, I'm off out to drum up some business. You know, you're lucky I came along.'

'Tell you what, why don't you prove that to me?'

'I will.'

'I don't doubt it. I might have known you were up to something when I saw you dressed as one of the common people still.'

She snorted. 'And some advice now, okay?'

'Yeees,' I said, unconvinced.

'Get some sleep. You look wrecked.'

'Thanks, I think. I am, and I will.'

After she left, I put the roses behind my chair, because they were mocking me. I could have thrown the bouquet out, but where's the point in wasting beauty, even if it is the present of a total dickhead? I tucked No. 4 up in his box, but couldn't get settled myself. I had a way around this. If there's anything that sends me off, it's trying to do my accounts. Accordingly I started up the computer and by the time I had given my password and got to the spread sheets I was yawning and nodding. The warmth of the holy vodka was tingling through my veins, and my muscles were finally relaxing from the unwelcome spasms of early morning. My mobile rang, and I recognised the number flashing as Andy's, so I switched it off without answering. I refused to let my brain indulge in thoughts of what might have been. That was then, this would have to be now, and I was the only one who

could look after me. As I drifted into the realm of
crazed imaginings that heralds sleep, the computer
system's Tip Of The Day repeated itself over and over:
'If you run with scissors,' it told me, 'prepare to be
cut.'

Epilogue

The Fledgling saga wound its way through the pages of the newspapers, moving steadily backwards in vanishing column inches, stopping short of the classifieds and the puzzle page before disappearing altogether. An internal enquiry hedged its bets, praised the late Michael O'Donoghue, and effectively dropped his area of research, at least from the public eye. A file concerning the death of the obstetrician was sent to the Director of Public Prosecutions but no one was ever charged in connection with it.

Maria Flood never regained consciousness. Her mother, Bernadette, made the decision to turn off her life support after six months of waiting and hoping for a recovery. I have pictures of both of them in my files.

A body washed ashore on Dollymount Strand two weeks after the doctor's funeral. It was discovered by a family out walking their golden retriever. The woman was identified as Kate Mulligan, née O'Brien, only daughter of Mary and Felim O'Brien, survived by her loving husband, Mark. Her clothes were found three miles along the coast, neatly folded and containing a note which simply said, 'I'm sorry'. As Ciara read the newspaper report over my shoulder, she pointed to the picture of Kate's abandoned car and said, 'She was following Michael O'Donoghue on the night he died. I remember that dent in the front bumper.' I don't really know what to make of that detail, and the only woman who could help me with it has taken her story to the grave. I think of Kate every time I look at the new paint job on my car, which is often, and I never fail to be stirred with regret at the waste of it all. She was thirty-two years old.

Mark Rolands sent the mother of all legal letters to the proprietress of 'Flix', a woman he had only ever met while renting out a movie, and Maeve's frightening ordeal came to an end. He has not moved back to his own apartment so I wonder if I should start shopping for a hat. They are both members of the 'Groovy Movie' video store now.

No one ever admitted to the intimidation of Carmel Lally and her family, but it did stop after the fire at their home. Her compensation case against the crèche is ongoing. I occasionally collect the children from school, and when I do, I keep my distance from my old pals. But sometimes I see Colette in town, at night, and we share a few words or a wave. Her Japanese man is still a regular, and has applied for government grants to set up an off-shoot of his factory in Dublin. Colette reckons this makes her a candidate for Irish Entrepreneur of the Year.

My own lucky numbers netted zilch on the lottery draw, but I won twenty quid on the computer's random selection. What can I tell you? You lose some, you win some.

Now you can buy any of these other bestselling
Headline books from your bookshop or
direct from the publisher.

FREE P&P AND UK DELIVERY
(Overseas and Ireland £3.50 per book)

Backpack	Emily Barr	£5.99
Icebox	Mark Bastable	£5.99
Killing Helen	Sarah Challis	£6.99
Broken	Martina Cole	£6.99
Redemption Blues	Tim Griggs	£5.99
Relative Strangers	Val Hopkirk	£5.99
Homegrown	Gareth Joseph	£5.99
Everything is not Enough	Bernardine Kennedy	£5.99
High on a Cliff	Colin Shindler	£5.99
Winning Through	Marcia Willett	£5.99

TO ORDER SIMPLY CALL THIS NUMBER

01235 400 414

or e-mail <u>orders@bookpoint.co.uk</u>

Prices and availability subject to change without notice.